Top: "The Twelve-Pound Look," by James M. Barrie; l to r: *Kate* (Susan Tiffany), *Butler* (James Goffard), *Lady Sims* (Gwyneth Hovick)
Center: "A Village Wooing," by George Bernard Shaw; l to r: *A, the Man* (Richard Boynton) and *Z, the Young Woman* (Gwyneth Hovick)
Bottom: "The Boor," by Anton Chekhov; l to r: Smirnov (Jeff Hudelson) and Widow Popova (Barbara Shuler)
One-act productions directed by Marcia Gambrell Hovick for the Staff Players Repertory Company
of the Children's Experimental Theatre, Carmel-by-the-Sea, California 93932.

1/2/3/4
For the Show

A Guide to Small-Cast One-Act Plays

by
Lewis W. Heniford

The Scarecrow Press, Inc.
Lanham, Md., and London

SCARECROW PRESS, INC.

Published in the United States of America
by Scarecrow Press, Inc.
4720 Boston Way
Lanham, Maryland 20706

4 Pleydell Gardens, Folkestone
Kent CT20 2DN, England

British Cataloguing-in-Publication Information Available

Library of Congress Cataloging-in-Publication Data

Heniford, Lewis W., 1928-
1/2/3/4 for the show: a guide to small-cast one-act plays /
by Lewis W. Heniford
p. cm.
Includes bibliographical references and index.
1. One-act plays--Indexes. I. Title II. Title: One/two/three/four
for the show. III. Titles: Guide to small-cast one-act plays.
Z5781.H46 1995 [PN6120.05] 016.80882'41--dc20 94-42180

ISBN 0-8108-2985-1 (cloth : alk. paper)

♾™ The paper used in this publication meets the minimum requirements of
American National Standard for Information Sciences—Permanence of
Paper for Printed Library Materials, ANSI Z39.48–1964.
Manufactured in the United States of America.

To Beth Woody,

who, in 1947, knocked on my door
and invited me into the world of theatre.

CONTENTS

ACKNOWLEDGMENTS

Field testing of *1/2/3/4 for the Show* occurred in 1993 in California at several high schools, two colleges, and a community theatre. For that, credit goes to Mary Gale, librarian, at Salinas High School, Salinas; Delia Ybarra, librarian, at Alisal High School, Salinas; Joyce Lowry, dramaturg, at Hartnell College, Salinas; Peter DeBono, drama chairman, at Monterey Peninsula College, Monterey; and Dan Gotch, dramaturg, at Grovemont Theatre, Monterey (subsequently, Pacific Repertory Theatre, Carmel-by-the-Sea).

Staff members of three California libraries assisted research—at Clark Library, San Jose State University; at Harrison Memorial Library, Carmel-by-the-Sea; and at North Salinas High School Library, Salinas.

Joyce Gay, Library Technician at North Salinas High School Library, Salinas, merits special mention as being endlessly helpful.

Dr. Stephanie Jones, formerly in the Division of Library and Information Science, San Jose State University, San Jose, from the first mention of this guide saw its potential. She facilitated its development as a thesis project in library and information science and foresaw the project's evolution into the present publication.

Rory Coster, Emmy Holtzclaw, and Marsha Miller assisted distinctively in their several ways.

Marcia Gambrell Hovick, founder and director of Children's Experimental Theatre, Inc., Carmel-by-the-Sea, generously supplied photographs of her one-act productions.

Catherine H. Lewis, my sister, not only has always inspired me but also scanned every page of the manuscript with a scholarly eye.

Kathleen Maire Dwyer, my wife, with love and forbearance engendered proper perspective through these years.

Tina Louise, my pit bulldog companion, watched me write, took me on walks, and gave me support and affection until April 3, 1993.

I thank them and the many others who helped.

FOREWORD

Anyone eager to find the "right" play, whether it be for study, production, reading or enriching the curriculum of other disciplines, will be grateful to the author for this guide. Unlike the typical play catalog, the guide is organized to provide the reader instant access to a rich range of information necessary for an in-depth, though brief, understanding of worthwhile, selected short plays.

The guide is organized in a logical order with great attention paid to the dramaturgical terminology; appropriate sections, such as the "author index" and "title index," are conveniently arranged in alphabetical order. The author presents the reader with several unique sections. He has identified twenty-five theme programs; that is, he suggests a series of plays which focus on a central idea or theme which one could develop into a viable program for study or presentation. In another section the author offers eighty clear play analyses, which include important data about the play followed by perceptive, critical comments. Attention is paid to the works of ethnic writers. The carefully selected plays are multi-cultural in scope, including contemporary as well as classic titles.

Dr. Heniford's unusual and prodigious experience in the production of short plays and his expertise in research, as well as in educational and theatrical fields, are melded together to provide the reader with a valuable, easily accessible research tool. The overburdened librarian or classroom teacher will find this guide an indispensable sourcebook.

I wish this guide had been available some forty years ago when I embarked on my teaching career, which included experiences in secondary education and university settings. Today, I would urge college professors to place this guide in the hands of cadet student teachers, who would benefit from it in numerous ways. Application of its principles will light up the classroom and make learning a truly rewarding time of life.

—Samuel Elkind, Ph.D.
Professor of Theatre Arts, Emeritus
San Francisco State University
Past President, California Educational Theatre Association
Coauthor, Drama/Theatre Framework for California Public Schools

PREFACE

Purpose, Perspective, Scope, Discoveries and Possibilities,
and Origin of This Guide

Purpose

This guide should help anyone seeking a small-cast one-act play. It focuses on that particular format.

Small-cast here means four or fewer roles in a script. *One-act* means staging the play without an internal intermission (and probably as a part of a theatrical bill).

First use of this guide can prove its value. The user, perhaps a producer, dramaturg, actor, librarian, teacher, or reader seeking a specific cast size, can go to the Title Index and find appropriate classic and modern plays in a variety of genres. Or, armed with the name of the playwright, the user can go to the Author Index and find which playwright offers what in the small-cast one-act format.

Producers of one-act programs can find suggested theme-related plays with analyses in the Playbills section.

Dramaturgs (individuals responsible for locating scripts for theatre-group study and/or production) can find thousands of play possibilities.

Actors can find a lifetime of scripts.

Librarians not specializing in dramatic literature have here a unique bibliographical resource to complement play indexes with which they might be familiar.

Teachers of German, Spanish, ethnic studies, speech, or dance should be able to locate resources, also.

Readers who savor the literature and entertainment of the printed playscript have access here to endless hours of pleasure.

The goal is to offer a source or a substantial lead to find any play cited. Where possible, a pairing for production of a given play with another or others is noted.

This guide augments Firkin's *Index to Plays* (1927) and its *Supplement* (1935), the *Play Index* series (1949 through 1992), and *McGraw-Hill Encyclopedia of World Drama* (1972).

Perspective

The continuum and much of the fun of scholarship rest on transference of information, knowledge, and wisdom from past generations to future generations. Of course, humankind's evolving significant mental capacity, developing opposing thumbs and fingers, long-term nurturing of offspring, building communities, walking upright, and communicating first with speech and ultimately with writing and technology all underpin this ability to learn from the past generations for the present generation's advantage. And, of course, with that advantage goes responsibility. Scholars look beyond past and present to the future.

Guides like *1/2/3/4/ for the Show* bring accumulated information to present attention. But the user's recourse to this guide almost always has the motivation of future activity. Some future scholar might add this guide to information derived elsewhere and present it anew in the continuum of scholarship.

Hence, the accuracy of data in this or any guide is fundamental. Here, although Scarecrow Press, Inc., and the author cannot be held legally liable for errors which may have occurred, the extreme precautions taken in research and multiple proofreadings have produced, it is hoped, trustworthy accuracy. I bear the academic responsibility and ask forbearance of any mistakes. I invite the user to communicate to me corrections for a future edition.

Because locating scripts is so important yet often so difficult, the present guide carefully, when possible, supplies source(s) valid as of July, 1994; in some instances, the contact cited may prove to be but a lead to the ultimate source. Only persistence and sufficient time for research may reach the ultimate source.

Guides to dramatic literature frequently do not satisfy the searcher. The dramaturg may not even know guides exist; equally often, the librarian does not know how the contents of the guides can best help the dramaturg.

An interesting analysis of this dilemma appears in the Winter, 1989, issue of *RQ*. Beginning on page 248 (of volume 29) is L. A. Hitchcock's "The Play's the Thing . . . If You Can Find It! An Assessment of Play Indexes." This intensive analysis of various play indexes argues that ready reference on this subject is an uncertain venture; guides have such serious gaps that the researcher must proceed with caution.

Scope

The scope of this guide focuses tightly on small-cast one-act plays, drawing broadly from history and geography. It includes plays for children and adults, plays published alone or in collections, and plays for stage, broadcast, and puppetry. When reliable sources could be established, it includes unpublished manuscripts.

Inclusion is neither selective nor judgmental. It merely reflects what has come to attention during research. Of course, there remains a vast, unrevealed body of one-act plays for future research.

Short performed narratives—one might call them one-act plays—hark back to the origins of theatre and possess a noble history. At first they, in effect, were the literature of theatre: all plays were short. The professional stage in the twentieth century infrequently and erratically has used one-act plays. Cinema in the 1930s tried short narrative movies as fillers to precede feature attractions but failed to establish a surviving art form. By the 1940s, television thrived on scripts suited to its nearly-half-hour or nearly-hour time segments. Television consumed scripts almost faster than the supply allowed; program managers had to forage far and wide to fill the maw. In what some broadcast media historians deem television's Golden Age, the 1950s, the new medium established and honored the under-one-hour teleplay, even gave much of it literary value. Although professional theatre since the mid-1800s has ventured one-acts as curtain raisers, entr'actes, and artistic experiments, it has not quite known what to do with the form. Yet, for a variety of reasons, established playwrights as well as novices persist in writing short plays. Presentation festivals do occur here and there, on the off-, off-off-, and off-off-off-Broadway fringes of professional theatre districts and in regional theatre. Educational theatre in the United States, however, has given one-acts a home.

Internationally, small-cast one-act plays abound but not in a single reference. This guide includes a measure of those resources. It cites translations into English as well as non-English-language scripts, addressing multicultural and transborder needs.

Present Discoveries and Future Possibilities

A look at the past and present begs a look at the future. The one-act play persists, despite the ignorance of many and the biases of others. Those who do not know the scope and quality of its vast literature can hardly be blamed for overlooking its present usefulness and its potential.

The process of compiling this guide has stimulated insights. So, first follow (A) disjointed thoughts marked by bullets; then follow (B) a few coherent considerations.

A. Discoveries

• For the scholar and producer, a serious problem is that playscripts, particularly one-acts, can go out of print fairly fast. Only a smattering survive, these chiefly in anthologies. The few publishers of theatrical scripts, usually specialty houses (see Source Directory for Scripts, pp. 259-63), rarely keep them in print beyond initial demand. Some lesser companies with small catalogs do keep scripts in print for a long time, but these scripts too frequently lack literary quality. Often, the dramaturg or librarian must cast a wide net to locate a worthwhile play.

• Unfortunately, *Books in Print*, the standard reference regarding whether a book is in print or out of print, offers limited guidance on playscripts and anthologies of playscripts. One is reminded of Shakespeare's era, when plays were not generally regarded as literature worth saving (Ben Jonson's opinions of his own work to the contrary). Almost by chance have dramatic masterpieces of that period survived to the present. *Books in Print*, good now, would be even more useful if it encouraged play publication houses to list their wares with it. Certainly, that would be a major service to the academic and theatre communities.

One wonders about the demographics of play readers, playgoers, or play producers. Present research has encountered no concise source of such statistics. Logically, each constituency has its own priorities; they collectively still have common ground: finding the right script at the right time for the right need. If only more of them knew of one-act guides!

• The Title Index and Author Index of this guide have the apparent distinction of being the most complete listing of one-act scripts.

• Typographical errors in the best catalogs are few. Considering the vast data in these catalogs, the rarity of errors argues that the proofreaders deserve considerable credit. The present writer has taken extreme precautions to present correct data, too.

• One may have difficulty finding the current agent for a play, especially for those not offered by the best-known play-publishing houses. A decided inconvenience is that not all books containing published scripts reveal sources of performance rights.

• One may have trouble obtaining a script. The sad truth that scripts often go out of print quickly can pose access problems. Even a script labeled with a publishing house may have gone out of print there; nonetheless, inquiries directed to publishing houses may lead the inquirer to the current copyright holder or to a clarification that the script is in public domain. Also, book-finding companies might be helpful.

• Sometimes, multiple publishers simultaneously offer a script. Most noteworthy is Baker's Plays' use of Samuel French, Inc., as its Western and Canadian representative.

Small houses sometimes follow the same practice. Of course, if the script is in public domain, any publisher may offer it.

• The most useful play publishers are Baker's Plays (BP), Dramatists Publishing Company (DPC), Dramatists Play Service, Inc. (DPS), and Samuel French, Inc. (SF). They have the largest catalogs and offer convenient terms. In effect, they control the market.

• Available play indexes are of highly variable worth for locating and evaluating short, small-cast shows. The seeker would do well to consult several indexes to accumulate sufficient information on which to base a choice.

• Authors or their agents contract rights to publishers and vendors. These rights can move from one or more companies to one or more other companies whenever a given contract expires or whenever the companies mutually consent. At any time, checking a current catalog or telephoning the source office might be necessary to obtain a copy of the script. The user of the present guide must consider that although the publisher/vendor information might come from an actual copy, that copy cannot clarify any subsequent switch of controlling agencies.

• Vendors rarely send playscripts on approval or allow exchanges. Conveniently for the client in a rush, they do offer overnight delivery—but at premium rates.

• Agencies holding production rights jealously guard their control of scripts. Moreover, they can withdraw any title at any time, especially from amateurs. Any producer scheduling for a geographic area can enjoin through the agency other presentations of that title in that area during or close to the run. Standard practice is that professional rights immediately void amateur rights. Significantly, that voiding could close an amateur company's successful run of a show.

• The trove of small-cast, less-than-half-hour television plays is unfortunately unindexed. Until someone organizes accessibility of the thousands upon thousands of teleplays, this resource remains a black hole from which nothing can escape and be seen again.

• Not enough dramaturgs, drama teachers, directors, students, or librarians know the quantity, quality, and variety of one-act plays. One problem is that they regard the short form as being unimportant, or at least less important than the full-length form. Another problem is the difficulty in accessing scripts, which guides like this can help to alleviate. By the thousands, scripts exist, awaiting study and/or production.

B. Possibilities

The future is bright.

Electronic access will solve most of the problems Hitchcock in his aforementioned interesting analysis found about print access. UseNet, currently the most popular Internet service, serves millions of users daily. The term *UseNet* describes a mechanism supporting discussion groups (newsgroups), several of which focus on theatre. Of the newsgroups that form, many fade, but some persist as valuable fora. Anyone with access can pose a thought or question and receive pertinent responses. Frequently, users seek script evaluations and sources. The exchange is exciting, and electronic access promises to become a major theatre resource. E-mail inquiries about this newest aid will receive prompt attention through *heniford@ix.netcom.com*.

Moreover, full-text access to a growing number of published and unpublished scripts is available through file transfer protocol (FTP) on the Internet. As with questions about theatre newsgroups, e-mail inquiries about FTP will receive prompt attention through *heniford@ix.netcom.com*.

Accuracy of existing guides probably is at the norm for other reference books. Limitations of the guides, though, include scope, depth of item coverage, identification of genre, currency, language provincialism, as well as information about sources for scripts and production rights (especially international sources).

The motion picture and television industries have belatedly established foundations to preserve significant parts of their history, such as scripts. Scattered theatre librarians have established valuable collections, but their attention to the one-act form is incidental. A foundation dedicated to that form would be a pioneering venture.

This guide focuses on scripts in print. One must look, also, to media other than print. The advent of inexpensive high-quality videotaping has created a library of one-act productions, a resource almost totally overlooked. Probably, few people have given much thought to secondary school and college or university drama departments all across America routinely recording their shows. What local use is made of these tapes thereafter is problematical, and wide distribution is rare. Somehow, this resource should be catalogued in a guide. Then, for whatever purposes, everyone interested could consider these one-act productions, scattered though they probably will remain, tantamount to a special library. Furthermore, technology for on-line access to recorded images already exists. A dedicated scholar could devise a guide to taped productions of these one-acts and spur interest in placing on a network these resources.

Paralleling the publishing industry's trend toward giantism (that is, larger companies getting larger and smaller companies struggling to hold on), the field of one-act publishing has its few large houses dominating, even getting better, with sundry outland small presses somehow managing. Desktop publishing has the potential to reshape this niche of the publishing industry if distribution and publicity problems can be surmounted.

One-act guides can educate a public that wants relatively short plays about how to access them. As the *Readers' Guide to Periodical Literature* and similar publications have led their users to access information in periodicals, so guides in the one-act play field lead their users to discover the vast international existence of scripts and lead them to access the scripts they want.

Also, as companies now offer electronic access to periodical literature on-line and on CD-ROM and having found the new formats serviceable and lucrative, so can companies offer guides to one-act plays in electronic-access formats.

Meanwhile, one hopes the user can profit from the present guide's eighty descriptions of scripts and from the Title Index and Author Index in *1/2/3/4 for the Show*. The goal, of course, is to find the right script at the right time for the right need.

Origin of This Guide

In 1947, students under my direction acted in a two-character one-act production during a festival sponsored by the University of North Carolina Playmakers, in Chapel Hill. That production, begun as an extracurricular lark, earned surprising recognition and initiated not only the actors but also their director into serious theatre. I thereby discovered the educational potential in producing one-act plays. The guide draws upon forty-seven years of theatre experience and study by this writer.

Subsequently educated in the graduate program in theatre of the Carolina Playmakers, University of North Carolina/Chapel Hill, I have taught drama and directed plays in North Carolina, Montana, and California; in Germany and Mexico; and in high schools, community colleges, universities, and community theatres. I possess a bachelor of arts degree in English from UNC/Chapel Hill, a master's degree in library and information science from San Jose State University, and a doctorate in speech and drama from Stanford University; this background affords library and theatre skills bearing upon this guide.

In the 1980s, to help directors needing small-cast one-act plays for production, I developed a card index of over two thousand citations. Those original citations have been greatly amplified and appear here as the Title Index and its permutation, the Author Index.

The specialized collection of theatre materials within the general holdings of the library of North Salinas High School, Salinas, California, has increased since I succeeded Grete Flores there in 1985 as librarian. My personal collection of several hundred theatre books, with an emphasis on small-cast one-act plays, now belongs to the North Salinas High School library. This special collection, exceeding four thousand items in 1995, contains copies of the eighty scripts analyzed in Part 4, Playbills with Script Analyses, as well as

copies of numerous additional scripts suggested for consideration in Part 1, Title Index, or Part 2, Author Index. The public may access this collection upon request to the librarian; the address is in Part 5, Source Directory for Scripts.

Tools

Writing this guide lasted from February, 1992, to July, 1995. Formatting employed PageMaker 5.0 for Microsoft Windows 3.1, a page-layout computer program. Writing and formatting used a USM Mach 486DX33 computer. Printing photoready page masters employed a Hewlett-Packard LaserJet 4.

Lewis W. Heniford, M.L.S., Ph.D.
Carmel-by-the-Sea, California 93921-0299
Telephone (408) 624-6960; fax (408) 624-1164

July 1, 1995

INTRODUCTION

How to Use This Guide

> Use of this guide is straightforward. First, consult the Contents (see page v or Contents box below) to see which section directly addresses the question at hand. Then, check this Introduction for a sample citation and its interpretation.

Definitions

The term *small-cast* herein means four or fewer actors. It ignores supernumeraries, that is, extras or chorus necessary or unnecessary for production.

The term *one-act* alludes to the published/unpublished, produced/unproduced text of a dramatic performance entity short enough to stand alone but generally given as part of a larger bill onstage or in other media. It sometimes also alludes to the image record of such an entity for any transmission or playback medium (which opens the field of half-hour TV dramas). Its relationship to the full-length play is analogous to the short story-novel relationship.

A few other definitions may help the reader. Throughout this guide, *one-act*, *play*, *playscript*, and *script* are synonyms, to alleviate repetition. Abbreviations for cast size and gender are joined into one term, such as *1m* (one male), *1f* (one female), *1m3f* (one male and three females), and so on.; offstage voices and extras are usually noted but not counted in cast size. The Glossary of Genres helps to explain theatrical jargon. Annotations in the Source Directory for Scripts and the Bibliography frequently include subjective comments intended to help the user.

Contents

Sample Entries

The **Title Index** lists one-act plays alphabetically by title, with author, cast size and gender, and source(s). Here are two samples with interpretations:

Title Index Sample A

"All Strange Away," a drama by Samuel Beckett, 1m, (published with and can pair with "Ohio Impromptu," "A Piece of Monologue," or "Rockaby") in *Rockaby and Other Short Pieces*, SF 18643, NSHS 27753

Interpretation—The title is "All Strange Away." The genre is drama. The author is Samuel Beckett. The cast size is one. The gender of the role is male. The play comes from *Rockaby and Other Short Pieces,* in which appear three other small-cast one-act plays that suit a bill on which this play might appear. The vendor is Samuel French, Inc., which tags it by the number 18643. The script is in the special theatre collection at North Salinas High School, where it is available for reading (see page 259); the accession number there is 27753. No International Standard Book Number is available.

Title Index Sample B

"Eat Cake," a drama by Jean-Claude Van Itallie, 1m1f, (published with and can pair with "The Girl and the Soldier," "Harold," "Photographs: Mary and Howard," "Rosary," or "Thoughts on the Instant of Greeting a Friend on the Street") in *Seven Short and Very Short Plays,* DPS 4726, NSHS pb65

Interpretation—The title is "Eat Cake." The genre is drama. The author is Jean-Claude Van Itallie. The cast size/gender is one male and one female. The play comes from *Seven Short and Very Short Plays,* in which are five other small-cast one-act plays that suit a bill on which this play might appear. The vendor is Dramatists Play Service, Inc., which tags it by the number 4726. The script is in the special theatre collection at North Salinas High School, where it is available for reading (see page 259); the accession number there is pb65. Neither International Standard Book Number nor Library of Congress number is available.

Library of Congress numbers appear in this guide only when no identifying International Standard Book Number is available and when the Library of Congress number is available.

The **Author Index** lists one-act plays alphabetically by author, with title, cast size and gender, and source(s). Here are two samples with interpretations:

Author Index Sample A

Miles, Keith, "Dostoevsky," a drama, 1m1f, (published with and can pair with "Chekhov") in *Russian Masters,* SF 20092, NSHS p2511, ISBN 0-573-60049-X

Interpretation—The author is Keith Miles. The title is "Dostoevsky." The genre is drama. The cast size/gender is one male and one female. The source is *Russian Masters,* in which volume appears one other small-cast one-act play that suits a bill on which "Dostoevsky" might appear. The vendor is Samuel French, Inc. That company tags the play by the number 20092. The script is in the special theatre collection at North Salinas High School (in Salinas, California), where it is available to the public for reading (see page 259); the accession number there is p2511. The International Standard Book Number is 0-573-60049-X.

Author Index Sample B

Foote, Horton, "The Prisoner's Song," a drama, 2m2f, in *The Tears of My Sister/The Prisoner's Song/The One-Armed Man/The Land of the Astronauts*, DPS 2022

Interpretation—The author is Horton Foote. The title is "The Prisoner's Song." The genre is drama. The cast size/gender is two males and two females. The source is *The Tears of My Sister/The Prisoner's Song/The One-Armed Man/The Land of the Astronauts.* The vendor is Dramatists Play Service, Inc. That company normally does not cite International Standard Book Numbers, and here tags the play by the number 2022. The International Standard Book Number is not available.

The **Glossary of Genres** section presents a small dictionary of dramaturgical terms by which playwrights and cataloguers describe types of plays.

Glossary Sample A

bizarre comedy: a play strikingly out of the ordinary treating trivial material superficially or amusingly or showing serious and profound material in a light, familiar, or satirical manner. Example: "The Lover," a bizarre comedy by Harold Pinter, 2m1f.

Interpretation—The genre term is *bizarre comedy.* Definition of the term is next. A specific example from the Title Index follows the definition.

Glossary Sample B

black comedy: a play essentially a comedy but emphasizing outrageous, serious elements. Example: "Play for Germs," a black comedy by Israel Horovitz, 2m.

Interpretation—The genre term is *black comedy.* Definition of the term is next. A specific example from the Title Index follows the definition.

The **Playbills with Script Analyses** section presents a menu of twenty-seven suggested theme programs, followed by eighty one-page script analyses. Sample A proposes a program of four one-act plays on the theme of ambition.

Playbills Sample A

Ambition
"Comanche Cafe," new revised version of a drama by William Hauptman, 2f, ISBN 0-573-62131-4, in *Domino Courts/Comanche Cafe,* SF 5686, NSHS pb91
"Queens of France," a satiric comedy by Thornton Wilder, 1m3f, SF 886, NSHS pb7963

"Lip Service," a drama by Howard Korder, 2m, in *"The Middle Kingdom," and "Lip Service'': Two Short Plays,* SF 14166, NSHS 27513

"Twelve-Pound Look, The," a comedy by J. M. Barrie, 2m2f, BP, SF 1095, NSHS 19878, NSHS 19883

Interpretation—These four plays form a viable bill united by the theme of ambition. They may be presented to good effect in the order given. The program would run under two hours with a single intermission between the second and third   plays.

Playbills Sample B

Death

"Death of the Hired Man, The," a drama by Jay Reid Gould from Robert Frost, 2m2f, DPC D13, HDS, NSHS 6071

"Other Player, The," a drama by Owen G. Arno, 3m or 3f, DPS 3550, NSHS pb7344

"Phoenix Too Frequent, A," a comedy by Christopher Fry, 1m2f, DPS, HDS

Interpretation—These three plays form a viable bill united by the theme of death. They may be presented to good effect in the order given. The program would run under two hours with a single intermission between the second and third plays. (The key to source abbreviations begins on p. 259.)

Analyses

Analyses of eighty one-act plays follow. For each analysis, headers handily display cast size and gender and specifies genre. The cast list (dramatis personae) clarifies gender and age. Sometimes, one must infer these important details; that accounts for the use of *about* in some designations of age or for the omission of a precise age. Statements of place(s) and time(s) of the action follow. (Authors sometimes do not clarify place and time, choosing to leave specificity to the director.) Bibliographical data identifies the given play.

The primacy of having appropriate talent for any role should be self-evident; a director would never attempt the play *Hamlet* without having an actor capable of playing Hamlet. On the other hand, actors need to stretch in order to grow, and a caring director will cast an actor who is nearly ready, who can grow into a role by the time the play opens. Each of the eighty plays has a plot synopsis and evaluation to assist casting and production. The synopsis captures the step-by-step forward motion of the story. The evaluations variously consider the Aristotelian elements of plot (plausibility and effectiveness), character (credibility and progression), thought

(themes), diction (language), music (aural poetry), and spectacle (visual esthetics). Also, they consider production challenges.

The **Source Directory for Scripts** lists sources for all plays cited and even lists other sources that might supply plays not cited in this guide.

The **Bibliography** documents origins of data used in this guide. Annotations expand information about a source, giving helpful supplementary knowledge and evaluations. The Bibliography has two sections: (a) primary citations, which are non-playscript annotated sources; and (b) secondary citations, which are non-playscript unannotated sources recommended for related research.

Choice of a Script

Although one may have too little time to find the right script, such an important choice, really an artistic marriage, requires care.

Bennett Cerf, in *At Random* (1977), tells of an unprepared commitment by America's foremost playwright. Eugene O'Neill's drinking often led to blackouts; in fact, in 1909 his first marriage had resulted from one. He woke up in some flophouse with a girl in bed next to him, and he said, "Who the hell are you?" and she said, "You married me last night."[1]

An artistic commitment, as does marriage, severely commits time and energies. May this guide help the user find the most appropriate script to enjoy a felicitous commitment or, maybe, even to live happily ever after.

---

[1]Donald Hall, ed., *The Oxford Book of American Literary Anecdotes.* New York: Oxford University Press, 1981, p. 230.

Part 1 — TITLE INDEX

One-Act Plays, Arranged Alphabetically by Title,
With Author, Genre, Cast Size and Gender,
and Source(s)

> Part 1 groups titles by cast size and gender. Within that, individual titles occur alphabetically.
>
> Each citation includes title, genre, author, cast size and gender, and source(s). The cast size and gender appears in each citation to keep the reader on track. Additionally, many citations suggest plays with which this play could pair on a bill, often ones published with it, thereby reducing the cost of scripts and simplifying production rights.
>
> When some element or elements of important information are unavailable or questionable, yet the presented information might provide a vital lead, a question mark in parentheses alerts the reader. Regarding abbreviations or acronyms, see Part 5, p. 259.

One-Male Plays

A

"Act Without Words (1)," a mime by Samuel Beckett, 1m, (see next item) in *Krapp's Last Tape and Other Dramatic Pieces*, SF 203

"Act Without Words I," a mime by Samuel Beckett, 1m, (see above item) (published with and can pair with "Act Without Words II," "Breath," "Cascando," "Catastrophe," "Come and Go," "Eh Joe" "Embers," "Footfalls," "Ghost Trio," "Krapp's Last Tape," "Not I," "Ohio Impromptu," "A Piece of Monologue," "Play," "Quad," "Rockaby," "Rough for Radio I," "Rough for Radio II," "Rough for Theatre I," "Rough for Theatre II," "That Time," or "Words and Music," in *Collected Shorter Plays*, ISBN 0-394-53850-1, ISBN 0-394-62098-4

"Advice to a New Actor," a brief monologue by Lavonne Mueller, 1m or 1f, (published with and can pair with "The American Way," "The Affidavit," "Anniversary," Auld Lang Syne, or I'll Bet You Think This Play Is About You," "Bug Swatter," "Checkers," "Coming for a Visit," "Dalmation," "Dog Eat Dog," "Drowned Out," "Fireworks," "Interview," "Jumping," "Money," "One Beer Too Many" "Phonecall from Sunkist," "Potato Girl," "Property of the Dallas Cowboys," "The Split Decision," "Valley Forgery," "Watermelon Boats," or "Widows") in *One-Act Plays for Acting Students*, MPL, ISBN 0-916260-47-X

"All Strange Away," a drama by Samuel Beckett, 1m, (published with and can pair with "Rockaby," "Ohio Impromptu," or "A Piece of Monologue") in *Rockaby and Other Short Pieces*, SF 18643, NSHS 27753

"American Welcome," a ten-minute play (genre?) by Brian Friel, 1m, SF

"Animal Salvation," a bare-stage dramatic monologue by Don Nigro, 1m, in *Genesis and Other Plays*, SF 3704

"Après moi, le déluge" ["**After Me, the Deluge**"], a drama by Charles Busch and Kenneth Elliott, 1m, in *Tough Acts to Follow: One-Act Plays on the Gay/Lesbian Experience*, edited by Noreen C. Barnes and Nicholas Deutsch (San Francisco: Alamo Square Press, 1992), ISBN 0-9624751-6-5

B

"Back-to-School Blues," a puppet play for children in five scenes by Denise Anton Wright, 1 puppeteer presenting 4 characters, (published with and can pair with "The Boy Who Cried Wolf," "The Case of the Disappearing Books," "Dragon Draws a Picture," "The Easter Egg Hunt," "Easter Rabbit's Basket," "Elephant's Sneeze," "Fox Learns a Lesson," "The Halloween Costume," "The Leprechaun's Gold," "The Lion and the Mouse," "Little Red Riding Hood," "The Monkey and the Crocodile," "The Mysterious Egg," "The Pumpkin Thief," "Santa Cures a Cold," "Take Me to Your Library," "The Three Billy Goats Gruff," "The Town Mouse and the Country Mouse," "Turkey's Thanksgiving Adventure," "Witch Gets Ready," "Witch's Valentine," or "Witch's Winter Kitchen") in Denise Anton Wright's *One-Person Puppet Plays*, illustrated by John Wright (Teacher Ideas Press, 1990), ISBN 0-87287-742-6, TIP

"Big Black Box, The," a comedy by Cleve Haubold, 1m, SF 270

"Billy and Me," a radio drama by Peter Barnes, 1m, (published with and can pair with "Houdini's Heir," "Losing Myself," "Madame Zenobia," "The Road to Strome," "Slaughterman," "The Spirit of Man: A Hand Witch of the Second Stage," "The Spirit of Man: From Sleep and Shadow," "The Spirit of Man: The Night of the Simhat Torah," or "A True-Born Englishman") in Peter Barnes' *The Spirit of Man and More Barnes' People* (New York and London: Methuen & Company, 1990), ISBN 0-413-63130-3

"Boneyard," a bare-stage comedic monologue by Don Nigro, 1m, in *Genesis and Other Plays*, SF 4210

"Border Minstrelsy," a bare-stage comedic monologue by Don Nigro, 1m, in *Winchelsea Dround and Other Plays: Nine Monologue Plays* (New York: Samuel French, Inc., 1992), ISBN 0-573-62598-0, SF 4220

"Box Office" (see p. 188), a comedy by Elinor Jones, 1m, (published with and can pair with "What Would Jeanne Moreau Do"), SF 4670, NSHS pb7960

"Boy Who Cried Wolf, The," a puppet play for children by Denise Anton Wright, 1 puppeteer presenting 4 characters, (published with and can pair with "The Back-to-School Blues," "The Case of the Disappearing Books," "Dragon Draws a Picture," "The Easter Egg Hunt," "Easter Rabbit's Basket," "Elephant's Sneeze," "Fox Learns a Lesson," "The Halloween Costume," "The Leprechaun's Gold," "The Lion and the Mouse," "Little Red Riding Hood," "The Monkey and the Crocodile,"

"The Mysterious Egg," "The Pumpkin Thief," "Santa Cures a Cold," "Take Me to Your Library," "The Three Billy Goats Gruff," "The Town Mouse and the Country Mouse," "Turkey's Thanksgiving Adventure," "Witch Gets Ready," "Witch's Valentine," or "Witch's Winter Kitchen") in Denise Anton Wright's *One-Person Puppet Plays*, illustrated by John Wright (Teacher Ideas Press, 1990), ISBN 0-87287-742-6, TIP

"Breath," a short audio and visual piece for the stage by Samuel Beckett, 1m, or 1f recorded voice, (see next item) in *First Love and Other Stories*, SF 4679

"Breath," a short audio and visual piece for the stage by Samuel Beckett, 1m, or 1f recorded voice, ([see above item] published with and can pair with "Act Without Words I," "Act Without Words II," "Cascando," "Catastrophe," "Come and Go," "Eh Joe," "Embers," "Footfalls," "Ghost Trio," "Krapp's Last Tape," "Not I," "Ohio Impromptu," "A Piece of Monologue," "Play," "Quad," "Rockaby," "Rough for Radio I," "Rough for Radio II," "Rough for Theatre I," "Rough for Theatre II," "That Time," or "Words and Music") in *Collected Shorter Plays,* ISBN 0-394-53850-1, ISBN 0-394-62098-4

C

"Case of the Disappearing Books, The," a puppet play in 2 scenes for children by Denise Anton Wright, 1 puppeteer presenting 3 characters, (published with and can pair with "The Back-to-School Blues," "The Boy Who Cried Wolf," "Dragon Draws a Picture," "The Easter Egg Hunt," "Easter Rabbit's Basket," "Elephant's Sneeze," "Fox Learns a Lesson," "The Halloween Costume," "The Leprechaun's Gold," "The Lion and the Mouse," "Little Red Riding Hood," "The Monkey and the Crocodile," "The Mysterious Egg," "The Pumpkin Thief," "Santa Cures a Cold," "Take Me to Your Library," "The Three Billy Goats Gruff," "The Town Mouse and the Country Mouse," "Turkey's Thanksgiving Adventure," "Witch Gets Ready," "Witch's Valentine," or "Witch's Winter Kitchen") in Denise Anton Wright's *One-Person Puppet Plays*, illustrated by John Wright (Teacher Ideas Press, 1990), ISBN 0-87287-742-6, TIP

"Cemetery Man," a dramatic monologue by Ken Jenkins, 1m, (published with and can pair with "Chug," "An Educated Lady," or "Rupert's Birthday") in *"Rupert's Birthday," and Other Monologues*, DPS 3912

"Chip in the Sugar, A," a half-hour monologue by Alan Bennett, 1m, SF

"Chucky's Hunch," a comedy-drama by Rochelle Owens, 1m, SF

"**Chug,**" a comedic monologue by Ken Jenkins, 1m, (published with and can pair with "An Educated Lady," "Rupert's Birthday," or "Cemetery Man") in *"Rupert's Birthday," and Other Monologues*, DPS 3912

D

"**Dark, The,**" a bare-stage dramatic monologue by Don Nigro, 1m, in *Genesis and Other Plays*, SF 5938

"**Dark Glasses,**" a monodrama by Tom Powers, 1m, SF, NSHS 6066

"**Days Ahead,**" a play (genre?) by Lanford Wilson, 1m, DPS, NSHS 29301

"**Devil and Billy Markham, The**" a bare-stage comedy by Shel Silverstein, 1m, (published with and can pair with "Bobby Gould in Hell," by David Mamet) in *Oh, Hell! Two One-Act Plays* (New York: Samuel French), ISBN 0-573-69254-8, SF 6728, NSHS pb8115

"**Diogenes the Dog,**" a bare-stage comedic monologue by Don Nigro, 1m, in *Genesis and Other Plays*, SF 6737

"**Doctor Galley,**" a drama by Conrad Bromberg, 1m, (published with and can pair with "The Rooming House" or "Transfers") in *Transfers: Three One-Acts Plays*, DPS 4610, NSHS pb7923

"**Dragon Draws a Picture,**" a puppet play for children by Denise Anton Wright, 1 puppeteer presenting 2 characters, (published with and can pair with "The Back-to-School Blues," "The Boy Who Cried Wolf," "The Case of the Disappearing Books," "The Easter Egg Hunt," "Easter Rabbit's Basket," "Elephant's Sneeze," "Fox Learns a Lesson," "The Halloween Costume," "The Leprechaun's Gold," "The Lion and the Mouse," "Little Red Riding Hood," "The Monkey and the Crocodile," "The Mysterious Egg," "The Pumpkin Thief," "Santa Cures a Cold," "Take Me to Your Library," "The Three Billy Goats Gruff," "The Town Mouse and the Country Mouse," "Turkey's Thanksgiving Adventure," "Witch Gets Ready," "Witch's Valentine," or "Witch's Winter Kitchen") in Denise Anton Wright's *One-Person Puppet Plays*, illustrated by John Wright (Teacher Ideas Press, 1990), ISBN 0-87287-742-6, TIP

"**Drinking in America,**" a black comedy by Eric Bogosian, 1m (+ extra), (can pair with "Sex, Drugs, Rock & Roll"), SF

"**Drug Peddler, The,**" a comedy by O T'ae-sok, 1m, PIR

"**Drummer, The**" (see p. 199), a ten-minute comedy by Athol Fugard, 1m, (nonspeaking), (published with and can pair with "Americansaint," "Après Opéra," "'The Asshole Murder Case,'" "Bread," "Cold Water" "Cover," "Downtown," "The Duck Pond," "Eating Out," "Electric Roses,"

"The Field," "4 A.M. (open all night)," "Marred Bliss," "Looking Good," "Love and Peace, Mary Jo," "Loyalties," "Perfect," "Spades," or "Watermelon Boats") in *25 10-Minute Plays from Actors Theatre of Louisville*, SF 22260, NSHS pb2977, ISBN 0-573-62558-1

"**Duet,**" a drama-comedy by David Scott Milton, 1m, SF

E

"**Easter Egg Hunt, The,**" a puppet play in 3 scenes for children by Denise Anton Wright, 1 puppeteer presenting 4 characters, (published with and can pair with "The Back-to-School Blues," "The Boy Who Cried Wolf," "The Case of the Disappearing Books," "Dragon Draws a Picture," "Easter Rabbit's Basket," "Elephant's Sneeze," "Fox Learns a Lesson," "The Halloween Costume," "The Leprechaun's Gold," "The Lion and the Mouse," "Little Red Riding Hood," "The Monkey and the Crocodile," "The Mysterious Egg," "The Pumpkin Thief," "Santa Cures a Cold," "Take Me to Your Library," "The Three Billy Goats Gruff," "The Town Mouse and the Country Mouse," "Turkey's Thanksgiving Adventure," "Witch Gets Ready," "Witch's Valentine," or "Witch's Winter Kitchen") in Denise Anton Wright's *One-Person Puppet Plays*, illustrated by John Wright (Teacher Ideas Press, 1990), ISBN 0-87287-742-6, TIP

"**Easter Rabbit's Basket,**" a puppet play in 3 scenes for children by Denise Anton Wright, 1 puppeteer presenting 3 characters, (published with and can pair with "The Back-to-School Blues," "The Boy Who Cried Wolf," "The Case of the Disappearing Books," "Dragon Draws a Picture," "The Easter Egg Hunt," "Elephant's Sneeze," "Fox Learns a Lesson," "The Halloween Costume," "The Leprechaun's Gold," "The Lion and the Mouse," "Little Red Riding Hood," "The Monkey and the Crocodile," "The Mysterious Egg," "The Pumpkin Thief," "Santa Cures a Cold," "Take Me to Your Library," "The Three Billy Goats Gruff," "The Town Mouse and the Country Mouse," "Turkey's Thanksgiving Adventure," "Witch Gets Ready," "Witch's Valentine," or "Witch's Winter Kitchen") in Denise Anton Wright's *One-Person Puppet Plays*, illustrated by John Wright (Teacher Ideas Press, 1990), ISBN 0-87287-742-6, TIP

"**Emergency, Stand By,**" a drama by Tom Powers, 1m, SF (probably out of print), NSHS 2189

"**Epilogue,**" a sketch by David Mamet, 1m, (part of "The Blue Hour: City Sketches") in *Short Plays and Monologues*, DPS 3025

"**Evils of Tobacco, The**" [under various titles] (see p. 204),

One-Male Plays, continued

a satirical lecture by Anton Chekhov, 1m, in Anton Chekhov's *Plays,* translated by Michael Frayn (London: Methuen & Company, Ltd., 1988), ISBN 0-413-19160-X (see also "Smoking Is Bad for You," translated by Ronald Hingley)

F

"Fever, The," a drama by Wallace Shawn, 1m, in Wallace Shawn's *The Fever* (New York: Noonday Press, 1991), ISBN 0-374-52270-7; also in *The Fever* (New York: Dramatists Play Service, 1992), DPS

"Fox Learns a Lesson," a puppet play for children by Denise Anton Wright, 1 puppeteer presenting 3 characters, (published with and can pair with "The Back-to-School Blues," "The Boy Who Cried Wolf," "The Case of the Disappearing Books," "Dragon Draws a Picture," "The Easter Egg Hunt," "Easter Rabbit's Basket," "Elephant's Sneeze," "The Halloween Costume," "The Leprechaun's Gold," "The Lion and the Mouse," "Little Red Riding Hood," "The Monkey and the Crocodile," "The Mysterious Egg," "The Pumpkin Thief," "Santa Cures a Cold," "Take Me to Your Library," "The Three Billy Goats Gruff," "The Town Mouse and the Country Mouse," "Turkey's Thanksgiving Adventure," "Witch Gets Ready," "Witch's Valentine," or "Witch's Winter Kitchen") in Denise Anton Wright's *One-Person Puppet Plays,* illustrated by John Wright (Teacher Ideas Press, 1990), ISBN 0-87287-742-6, TIP

"From a Madman's Diary," a drama by Eric Bentley from Nikolai Gogol, 1m, SF 8652

"From an Abandoned Work," a dramatic monologue by Samuel Beckett, 1m, (published with and can pair with "Act Without Words I," "Act Without Words II," or "Come and Go") in *Breath and Other Shorts* (London: Faber, 1971), NSHS

G

"George L. Smith," a bare-stage comedy by Cliff Harville, 1m, (published with and can pair with "Hand Me My Afghan," "Sara Hubbard" or "A Silent Catastrophe") in *Sunsets* (New York: Samuel French, Inc., 1989), ISBN 0-573-62522-0, SF 21387

"Ghost Trio," a television drama by Samuel Beckett, 1m, (+ female voice and boy extra, with music), (published with and can pair with "Act Without Words I," "Act Without Words II," "Breath," "Cascando," "Catastrophe," "Come and Go," "Eh Joe," "Embers," "Footfalls," "Krapp's Last

Tape," "Not I," "Ohio Impromptu," "A Piece of Monologue," "Play," "Quad," "Rockaby," "Rough for Radio I," "Rough for Radio II," "Rough for Theatre I," "Rough for Theatre II," "That Time," or "Words and Music") in *Collected Shorter Plays,* ISBN 0-394-53850-1, ISBN 0-394-62098-4

"Gold and Silver Waltz," a comedy by Romulus Linney, 1m, DPS 3684, NSHS pb7913

"Golgotha," a bare-stage dramatic monologue by Don Nigro, 1m, in *Winchelsea Dround and Other Plays: Nine Monologue Plays* (New York: Samuel French, Inc., 1992), ISBN 0-573-62598-0, SF 9942

H

"Halloween Costume, The," a puppet play in 4 scenes for children by Denise Anton Wright, 1 puppeteer presenting 4 characters, (published with and can pair with "The Back-to-School Blues," "The Boy Who Cried Wolf," "The Case of the Disappearing Books," "Dragon Draws a Picture," "The Easter Egg Hunt," "Easter Rabbit's Basket," "Elephant's Sneeze," "Fox Learns a Lesson," "The Leprechaun's Gold," "The Lion and the Mouse," "Little Red Riding Hood," "The Monkey and the Crocodile," "The Mysterious Egg," "The Pumpkin Thief," "Santa Cures a Cold," "Take Me to Your Library," "The Three Billy Goats Gruff," "The Town Mouse and the Country Mouse," "Turkey's Thanksgiving Adventure," "Witch Gets Ready," "Witch's Valentine," or "Witch's Winter Kitchen") in Denise Anton Wright's *One-Person Puppet Plays,* illustrated by John Wright (Teacher Ideas Press, 1990), ISBN 0-87287-742-6, TIP

"Harmfulness of Tobacco, The," [sometimes listed as "The Evils of Tobacco," "On the Harmfulness of Tobacco," or "Smoking Is Bad for You"] a farce monologue by Anton Chekhov, 1m, SF; also in Anton Chekhov's *Plays* (London: Methuen, 1988), ISBN 0-413-19160-X

"Help, I Am," a monologue (drama) by Robert Patrick, 1m, in *Robert Patrick's Cheep Theatricks,* SF 10629

"Herringbone," a drama by Tom Cone, Skip Kennon, and Ellen Fitzhugh, 1m (+1 extra), in *Twenty Years at Play: A New Play Centre Anthology,* edited by Jerry Wasserman (Cordova, Vancouver, British Columbia, Canada: Talonbooks, Ltd., 1990), ISBN 0-88922-275-4, TL

"Highway," a drama by Len Jenkin, 1m, (published with and can pair with "Intermezzo," and "Hotel") in *Limbo Tales,* DPS 2870

"Horse Farce," a bare-stage comedic monologue by Don Nigro, 1m, in *Genesis and Other Plays,* SF 10704

"Hotel," a drama by Len Jenkin, 1m, (published with and can pair with "Intermezzo," and "Highway") in *Limbo Tales*, DPS 2870

"Houdini's Heir," a radio drama by Peter Barnes, 1m, (published with and can pair with "Billy and Me," "Losing Myself," "Madame Zenobia," "The Road to Strome," "Slaughterman," "The Spirit of Man: A Hand Witch of the Second Stage," "The Spirit of Man: From Sleep and Shadow," "The Spirit of Man: The Night of the Simhat Torah," or "A True-Born Englishman") in Peter Barnes' *The Spirit of Man and More Barnes' People* (New York and London: Methuen & Company, 1990), ISBN 0-413-63130-3

I

"I Speak Again of the Sea" ["*Volver a decir el mar*"] (see p. 258), a drama in Spanish by Sergio Peregrina, 1m, OEN, NSHS pb8189

"Ice Chimney, The," a drama by Barry Collins, 1m, in *One Step in the Clouds: An Omnibus of Mountaineering Novels and Short Stories*, compiled by Audrey Salkeld and Rosie Smith (San Francisco: Sierra Club Books, 1991), ISBN 0-87156-638-9

"Intermezzo," a comedy by Len Jenkin, 1m, (published with and can pair with "Highway," and "Hotel") in *Limbo Tales*, DPS 2870

K

"Kaspar," a drama by Peter Handke, 1m, LLA, NSHS

"Killer's Head," a drama by Sam Shepard, 1m, (published with and can play with "Cowboys #2," "4-H Club," "Red Cross," or "The Rock Garden") in *The Unseen Hand & Other Plays*, SF 13610, NSHS pb7928, ISBN 0-553-34263-0

"Krapp's Last Tape," a comedy by Samuel Beckett, 1m, [see next item] in *Krapp's Last Tape and Other Dramatic Pieces*, BP; and in *A Theatre Anthology: Plays and Documents*, edited by David Willinger and Charles Gattnig (Lanham, Maryland: University Press of America, 1990), ISBN 0-8191-7730-X, ISBN 0-8191-7731-8

"Krapp's Last Tape," a drama by Samuel Beckett, 1m, (+ own recorded voice), ([see above item] published with and can pair with "Act Without Words I," "Act Without Words II," "Breath," "Cascando," "Catastrophe," "Come and Go," "Eh Joe," "Embers," "Footfalls," "Ghost Trio," "Not I," "Ohio Impromptu," "A Piece of Monologue,"

"Play," "Quad," "Rockaby," "Rough for Radio I," "Rough for Radio II," "Rough for Theatre I," "Rough for Theatre II," "That Time," or "Words and Music") in *Collected Shorter Plays*, ISBN 0-394-53850-1, ISBN 0-394-62098-4; also in *A Theatre Anthology: Plays and Documents*, edited by David Willinger and Charles Gattnig (Boston: University Press of America, 1990), ISBN 0-8191-7730-X, ISBN 0-8191-7731-8

L

"Last Days of Mankind" (see p. 210), an excerpt (Act V, Scene 54) by Karl Kraus, translated by Max Spalter from the original German, 1m, KV, NSHS 29408

"Laws, The," a comic sketch by Howard Korder, 1m, in *The Pope's Nose: Short Plays and Sketches* (New York: Dramatists Play Service, 1991), DPS 3677

"Leprechaun's Gold, The," a puppet play for children by Denise Anton Wright, 1 puppeteer presenting 2 characters, (published with and can pair with "The Back-to-School Blues," "The Boy Who Cried Wolf," "The Case of the Disappearing Books," "Dragon Draws a Picture," "The Easter Egg Hunt," "Easter Rabbit's Basket," "Elephant's Sneeze," "Fox Learns a Lesson," "The Halloween Costume," "The Lion and the Mouse," "Little Red Riding Hood," "The Monkey and the Crocodile," "The Mysterious Egg," "The Pumpkin Thief," "Santa Cures a Cold," "Take Me to Your Library," "The Three Billy Goats Gruff," "The Town Mouse and the Country Mouse," "Turkey's Thanksgiving Adventure," "Witch Gets Ready," "Witch's Valentine," or "Witch's Winter Kitchen") in Denise Anton Wright's *One-Person Puppet Plays*, illustrated by John Wright (Teacher Ideas Press, 1990), ISBN 0-87287-742-6, TIP

"Lion and the Mouse, The," a puppet play for children by Denise Anton Wright, 1 puppeteer presenting 2 characters, (published with and can pair with "The Back-to-School Blues," "The Boy Who Cried Wolf," "The Case of the Disappearing Books," "Dragon Draws a Picture," "The Easter Egg Hunt," "Easter Rabbit's Basket," "Elephant's Sneeze," "Fox Learns a Lesson," "The Halloween Costume," "The Leprechaun's Gold," "Little Red Riding Hood," "The Monkey and the Crocodile," "The Mysterious Egg," "The Pumpkin Thief," "Santa Cures a Cold," "Take Me to Your Library," "The Three Billy Goats Gruff," "The Town Mouse and the Country Mouse," "Turkey's Thanksgiving Adventure," "Witch Gets Ready," "Witch's Valentine," or "Witch's Winter Kitchen") in Denise Anton Wright's *One-Person Pup-*

pet Plays, illustrated by John Wright (Teacher Ideas Press, 1990), ISBN 0-87287-742-6, TIP

"Litko: A Dramatic Monologue," a sketch by David Mamet, 1m, (part of "The Blue Hour: City Sketches") in *Short Plays and Monologues*, DPS 3025

"Little Red Riding Hood," a puppet play in 2 scenes for children by Denise Anton Wright, 1 puppeteer presenting 3 characters, (published with and can pair with "The Back-to-School Blues," "The Boy Who Cried Wolf," "The Case of the Disappearing Books," "Dragon Draws a Picture," "The Easter Egg Hunt," "Easter Rabbit's Basket," "Elephant's Sneeze," "Fox Learns a Lesson," "The Halloween Costume," "The Leprechaun's Gold," "The Lion and the Mouse," "The Monkey and the Crocodile," "The Mysterious Egg," "The Pumpkin Thief," "Santa Cures a Cold," "Take Me to Your Library," "The Three Billy Goats Gruff," "The Town Mouse and the Country Mouse," "Turkey's Thanksgiving Adventure," "Witch Gets Ready," "Witch's Valentine," or "Witch's Winter Kitchen") in Denise Anton Wright's *One-Person Puppet Plays*, illustrated by John Wright (Teacher Ideas Press, 1990), ISBN 0-87287-742-6, TIP

"Longing for Worldly Pleasures" (see p. 214), a Chinese traditional K'unshan play by Ssu Fan, 1m or 1f, in Adolphe C. Scott's translation of *Traditional Chinese Plays*, Volume 2 (Madison, Wisconsin: The University of Wisconsin Press, 1969), ISBN 0-299-05370-9, ISBN 0-299-05734-1

"Losing Myself," a radio drama by Peter Barnes, 1m, (published with and can pair with "Billy and Me," "Houdini's Heir," "Madame Zenobia," "The Road to Strome," "The Spirit of Man: A Hand Witch of the Second Stage," "Slaughterman," "The Spirit of Man: From Sleep and Shadow," "The Spirit of Man: The Night of the Simhat Torah," or "A True-Born Englishman") in Peter Barnes' *The Spirit of Man and More Barnes' People* (New York and London: Methuen & Company, 1990), ISBN 0-413-63130-3

M

"Mink Ties," a bare-stage comedic monologue by Don Nigro, 1m, in *Winchelsea Dround and Other Plays: Nine Monologue Plays* (New York: Samuel French, Inc., 1992), ISBN 0-573-62598-0, SF 15600

"Monkey and the Crocodile, The," a puppet play for children by Denise Anton Wright, 1 puppeteer presenting 2 characters, (published with and can pair with "The Back-to-School Blues," "The Boy Who Cried Wolf," "The

Case of the Disappearing Books," "Dragon Draws a Picture," "The Easter Egg Hunt," "Easter Rabbit's Basket," "Elephant's Sneeze," "Fox Learns a Lesson," "The Halloween Costume," "The Leprechaun's Gold," "The Lion and the Mouse," "Little Red Riding Hood," "The Mysterious Egg," "The Pumpkin Thief," "Santa Cures a Cold," "Take Me to Your Library," "The Three Billy Goats Gruff," "The Town Mouse and the Country Mouse," "Turkey's Thanksgiving Adventure," "Witch Gets Ready," "Witch's Valentine," or "Witch's Winter Kitchen") in Denise Anton Wright's *One-Person Puppet Plays*, illustrated by John Wright (Teacher Ideas Press, 1990), ISBN 0-87287-742-6, TIP

"Mr. Happiness," a curtain-raiser comedy by David Mamet, 1m, (published with "The Water Engine," with which it can pair), SF 725

"Mysterious Egg, The," a puppet play in 5 scenes for children by Denise Anton Wright, 1 puppeteer presenting 4 characters, (published with and can pair with "The Back-to-School Blues," "The Boy Who Cried Wolf," "The Case of the Disappearing Books," "Dragon Draws a Picture," "The Easter Egg Hunt," "Easter Rabbit's Basket," "Elephant's Sneeze," "Fox Learns a Lesson," "The Halloween Costume," "The Leprechaun's Gold," "The Lion and the Mouse," "Little Red Riding Hood," "The Monkey and the Crocodile," "The Pumpkin Thief," "Santa Cures a Cold," "Take Me to Your Library," "The Three Billy Goats Gruff," "The Town Mouse and the Country Mouse," "Turkey's Thanksgiving Adventure," "Witch Gets Ready," "Witch's Valentine," or "Witch's Winter Kitchen") in Denise Anton Wright's *One-Person Puppet Plays*, illustrated by John Wright (Teacher Ideas Press, 1990), ISBN 0-87287-742-6, TIP

N

"Nice," a satire by Mustapha Matura, 1m, in Mustapha Matura's *Six Plays*, introduced by author (London: Methuen, 1992), ISBN 0-413-66070-2

"Nightmare with Clocks," a dramatic monologue by Don Nigro, 1m, in *Cincinnati and Other Plays*, SF 16647

"No Answer," a drama by William Hanley, 1m, possibly available through DPS, which offers other scripts by Hanley

"No Cure for Cancer," a satire by Denis Leary, 1m, (New York: Anchor Books, 1992) ISBN 0-385-45581-3

O

"Old Jew, The" (see p. 222), a drama by Murray Schisgal,

1m, (published with and can pair with "Memorial Day," "The Basement," or "Fragments") in *Five One Act Plays*, DPS 3975, NSHS pb6057

"Once Upon an Island," a radio play (genre?) by Richardo Keens-Douglas, 1m, in *Take Five: The Morningside Dramas*, edited by D. Carley (Winnipeg, Manitoba, Canada: Blizzard Publishing, 1991), ISBN 0-921368-21-6

"One Beer Too Many," a brief dramatic monologue by Billy Houck, 1m, (published with and can pair with "Advice to a New Actor" "The Affidavit," "The American Way," "Anniversary," "Auld Lang Syne, or I'll Bet You Think This Play Is About You," "Bug Swatter," "Checkers," "Coming for a Visit," "Dalmation," "Dog Eat Dog," "Drowned Out," "Fireworks," "Interview," "Jumping," "Money," "Phonecall from Sunkist," "Potato Girl," "Property of the Dallas Cowboys," "The Split Decision," "Valley Forgery," "Watermelon Boats," or "Widows") in *One-Act Plays for Acting Students* MPL, ISBN 0-916260-47-X

"One Person," a bare-stage monodrama by Robert Patrick, 1m, in *Robert Patrick's Cheep Theatricks*, SF 17602

P

"Passport" (see p. 227), a drama by James Elward, 1m, (published with and can pair with "Mary Agnes Is Thirty-Five") in *Friday Night*, DPS 2045, NSHS 29204

"Picasso," a bare-stage comedic monologue by Don Nigro, 1m, in *Winchelsea Dround and Other Plays*, SF 18956

"Piece of Monologue, A," a drama by Samuel Beckett, 1m, or 1f, ([see next item] published with and can pair with "All Strange Away," "Ohio Impromptu," or "Rockaby") in *Rockaby and Other Short Pieces*, SF 18643, NSHS 27753

"Piece of Monologue, A," a drama by Samuel Beckett, 1m, or 1f, ([see above item] also published with and can pair with "Act Without Words I," "Act Without Words II," "Breath," "Cascando," "Catastrophe," "Come and Go," "Eh Joe," "Embers," "Footfalls," "Ghost Trio," "Krapp's Last Tape," "Not I," "Ohio Impromptu," "Play," "Quad," "Rockaby," "Rough for Radio I," "Rough for Radio II," "Rough for Theatre I," "Rough for Theatre II," "That Time," or "Words and Music") in *Collected Shorter Plays,* ISBN 0-394-53850-1, ISBN 0-394-62098-4

"Ping" (see p. 299), an abstraction by Samuel Beckett, 1m or 1f, possibly DPS (?), NSHS

"Placebo," a drama by Andrew Vachss, 1m, in *Antæus: Plays in One Act*, no. 66 (spring, 1991), Antæus [Ecco Press], ISBN 0-88001-268-4

"Poster of the Cosmos, A," a drama by Lanford Wilson,

1m, (about AIDS, can pair with Harvey Fierstein's "Safe Sex," Alan Bowne's "Beirut," Patricia Loughrey's "The Inner Circle," or Robert Patrick's "Pouf Positive") (published with and can pair with "The Moonshot Tape"); also in *The Best Short Plays* (New York: Applause, 1989) and in *The Way We Live Now: American Plays & the AIDS Crisis*, edited by M. Elizabeth Osborn (New York: Theatre Communications Group, 1990), ISBN 1-55936-006-2, ISBN 1-55936-005-4, DPS 3696

"Pouf Positive," a drama by Robert Patrick, 1m, (about AIDS, can pair with Harvey Fierstein's "Safe Sex," Alan Bowne's "Beirut," Patricia Loughrey's "The Inner Circle," or Lanford Wilson's "A Poster of the Cosmos") (published with and can pair with "Bill Batchelor Road," "Fairy Tale," "Fog," "One of Those People," "Odd Number," or "The River Jordan") in Robert Patrick's *Untold Decades* (New York: St. Martin's Press, Inc., 1988), ISBN 0-312-02307-3

"Prologue," a sketch by David Mamet, 1m, (part of "The Blue Hour: City Sketches") in *Short Plays and Monologues*, DPS 3025

"Pumpkin Thief, The," a puppet play for children by Denise Anton Wright, 1 puppeteer presenting 2 characters, (published with and can pair with "The Back-to-School Blues," "The Boy Who Cried Wolf," "The Case of the Disappearing Books," "Dragon Draws a Picture," "The Easter Egg Hunt," "Easter Rabbit's Basket," "Elephant's Sneeze," "Fox Learns a Lesson," "The Halloween Costume," "The Leprechaun's Gold," "The Lion and the Mouse," "Little Red Riding Hood," "The Monkey and the Crocodile," "The Mysterious Egg," "Santa Cures a Cold," "Take Me to Your Library," "The Three Billy Goats Gruff," "The Town Mouse and the Country Mouse," "Turkey's Thanksgiving Adventure," "Witch Gets Ready," "Witch's Valentine," or "Witch's Winter Kitchen") in Denise Anton Wright's *One-Person Puppet Plays*, illustrated by John Wright (Teacher Ideas Press, 1990), ISBN 0-87287-742-6, TIP

"Puppy Love, the Play," an audience-participation play (genre?), by Bruce Keller, 1m, The Currency Press Pty., Ltd., ISBN 0-86819-288-0

R

"Reticence of Lady Anne, The," a comedy by Jules Tasca adapted from the short story by Saki (H. H. Munro), 1m, in Jules Tasca's *Tales by Saki: Adapted for Stage by Jules Tasca* (New York: Samuel French, Inc., 1989), ISBN 0-573-62560-3

"Road to Strome, The," a radio drama by Peter Barnes, 1m,

One-Male Plays, *continued*

(published with and can pair with "Billy and Me," "Houdini's Heir," "Losing Myself," "Madame Zenobia," "Slaughterman," "The Spirit of Man: A Hand Witch of the Second Stage," "The Spirit of Man: From Sleep and Shadow," "The Spirit of Man: The Night of the Simhat Torah," or "A True-Born Englishman") in Peter Barnes' *The Spirit of Man and More Barnes' People* (New York and London: Methuen & Company, 1990), ISBN 0-413-63130-3

S

"Samuel Hoopes Reading from His Own Works," a play (genre?) by Jan Hartman, 1m, DPS manuscript

"Santa Cures a Cold," a puppet play in 3 scenes for children by Denise Anton Wright, 1 puppeteer presenting 4 characters, (published with and can pair with "The Back-to-School Blues," "The Boy Who Cried Wolf," "The Case of the Disappearing Books," "Dragon Draws a Picture," "The Easter Egg Hunt," "Easter Rabbit's Basket," "Elephant's Sneeze," "Fox Learns a Lesson," "The Halloween Costume," "The Leprechaun's Gold," "The Lion and the Mouse," "Little Red Riding Hood," "The Monkey and the Crocodile," "The Mysterious Egg," "The Pumpkin Thief," "Take Me to Your Library," "The Three Billy Goats Gruff," "The Town Mouse and the Country Mouse," "Turkey's Thanksgiving Adventure," "Witch Gets Ready," "Witch's Valentine," or "Witch's Winter Kitchen") in Denise Anton Wright's *One-Person Puppet Plays*, illustrated by John Wright (Teacher Ideas Press, 1990), ISBN 0-87287-742-6, TIP

"Savage/Love," a monodrama, a bill of theatre poems by Sam Shepard and Joseph Chaikin, 1m, in *Sam Shepard: Seven Plays*, SF 21637

"See Bob Run," a drama by Daniel MacIvor, 1m, (published with and can pair with "Wild Abandon: The Study of Steve") in Daniel MacIvor's *See Bob Run & Wild Abandon* (Toronto, Ontario, Canada: Playwrights Canada Press, 1990), ISBN 0-88754-486-X

"Sermon," a drama by Ellen Violett from James Purdy, 1m, cited in *The Best Plays of 1963-1964*, edited by Henry Hewes (New York, Dodd, Mead & Company, Inc., 1964)

"Sermon, A," a sketch by David Mamet, 1m, (part of "The Blue Hour: City Sketches") in *Short Plays and Monologues*, DPS 3025

"Sex, Drugs, Rock & Roll," a black comedy by Eric Bogosian, 1m, (can pair with "Drinking in America"; trim from full-length version), SF 21629

"Slaughterman," a radio drama by Peter Barnes, 1m, (pub-

lished with and can pair with "Billy and Me," "Houdini's Heir," "Losing Myself," "Madame Zenobia," "The Road to Strome," "The Spirit of Man: A Hand Witch of the Second Stage," "The Spirit of Man: From Sleep and Shadow," "The Spirit of Man: The Night of the Simhat Torah," or "A True-Born Englishman") in Peter Barnes' *The Spirit of Man and More Barnes' People* (New York and London: Methuen & Company, 1990), ISBN 0-413-63130-3

"Smoking Is Bad for You" [under various titles] (see p. 204), a satirical lecture by Anton Chekhov translated by Ronald Hingley, 1m, in Anton Chekhov's *Twelve Plays,* translated by Ronald Hingley (London: Oxford University Press, 1992), ISBN 0-19-282813-4 (See also "The Evils of Tobacco," translated by Michael Frayn.)

See analysis and comments in Part 4, Playbills with Script Analyses, p. 204.

"Spared" (see p. 245), a bare-stage drama by Israel Horovitz, 1m (recorded voices), (published with and can pair with "Stage Directions"; also can pair with "Hopscotch" or "The 75th") in *The Quannapowitt Quartet*, DPS 4235, SF 990, NSHS pb6068

"Struck Dumb," a drama by Jean-Claude Van Itallie and Joseph Chaikin, in *The Best American Short Plays*, 1990/1991-1992, 2 vols., edited by Howard Stein and Glenn Young, Applause, International Standard Serial Number 1062-7561

"Sun," a drama by Adrienne Kennedy, 1m, (can play with "She Talks to Beethoven") in Adrienne Kennedy's *Adrienne Kennedy in One Act* (Minneapolis, Minnesota: University of Minnesota Press, 1988), ISBN 0-8166-1691-4, ISBN 0-8166-1692-2

"Survivalist, The," a drama by Robert Schenkkan, 1m, in *Four One-Act Plays by Robert Schenkkan: "Conversations with the Spanish Lady," "Lunch Break," "Intermission," and "The Survivalist,"* DPS 3972, NSHS pb8022

T

"Take Me to Your Library," a puppet play for children by Denise Anton Wright, 1 puppeteer presenting 2 characters, (published with and can pair with "The Back-to-School Blues," "The Boy Who Cried Wolf," "The Case of the Disappearing Books," "Dragon Draws a Picture," "The Easter Egg Hunt," "Easter Rabbit's Basket," "Elephant's Sneeze," "Fox Learns a Lesson," "The Halloween Costume," "The Leprechaun's Gold," "The Lion and the Mouse," "Little Red Riding Hood," "The Monkey and the Crocodile," "The Mysterious Egg," "The Pumpkin Thief," "Santa Cures a Cold," "The Three Billy Goats Gruff," "The Town Mouse and the Country Mouse," "Turkey's Thanksgiving Adventure," "Witch Gets Ready," "Witch's Valentine," or "Witch's Winter Kitchen") in Denise Anton Wright's *One-Person Puppet Plays*, illustrated by John Wright (Teacher Ideas Press, 1990), ISBN 0-87287-742-6, TIP

"Testimonies," a series of four monologues by August Wilson, 1m, in *Antæus: Plays in One Act*, no. 66 (spring, 1991), Antæus [Ecco Press], ISBN 0-88001-268-4

"Thank You, Miss Victoria," a dramatic monologue by W. M. Hoffman, 1m, (voice), HW

"Three Billy Goats Gruff, The," a puppet play for children by Denise Anton Wright, 1 puppeteer presenting 4 characters, (published with and can pair with "The Back-to-School Blues," "The Boy Who Cried Wolf," "The Case of the Disappearing Books," "Dragon Draws a Picture," "The Easter Egg Hunt," "Easter Rabbit's Basket," "Elephant's Sneeze," "Fox Learns a Lesson," "The Halloween Costume," "The Leprechaun's Gold," "The Lion and the Mouse," "Little Red Riding Hood," "The Monkey and the Crocodile," "The Mysterious Egg," "The Pumpkin Thief," "Santa Cures a Cold," "Take Me to Your Library," "The Town Mouse and the Country Mouse," "Turkey's Thanksgiving Adventure," "Witch Gets Ready," "Witch's Valentine," or "Witch's Winter Kitchen") in Denise Anton Wright's *One-Person Puppet Plays*, illustrated by John Wright (Teacher Ideas Press, 1990), ISBN 0-87287-742-6, TIP

"Tongues," (see p. 253), a monodrama, a piece for voice and percussion by Sam Shepard and Joseph Chaikin, 1m, in *Sam Shepard: Seven Plays*, SF 22733, NSHS 28227

"Town Mouse and the Country Mouse, The," a puppet play in 2 scenes for children by Denise Anton Wright, 1 puppeteer presenting 4 characters, (published with and can pair with "The Back-to-School Blues," "The Boy Who Cried Wolf," "The Case of the Disappearing Books," "Dragon Draws a Picture," "The Easter Egg Hunt," "Easter Rabbit's Basket," "Elephant's Sneeze," "Fox Learns a Lesson," "The Halloween Costume," "The Leprechaun's Gold," "The Lion and the Mouse," "Little Red Riding Hood," "The Monkey and the Crocodile," "The Mysterious Egg," "The Pumpkin Thief," "Santa Cures a Cold," "Take Me to Your Library," "The Three Billy Goats Gruff," "Turkey's Thanksgiving Adventure," "Witch Gets Ready," "Witch's Valentine," or "Witch's Winter Kitchen") in Denise Anton Wright's *One-Person Puppet Plays*, illustrated by John Wright (Teacher

Ideas Press, 1990), ISBN 0-87287-742-6, TIP

"Tradition 1A," a dramatic monologue by Howard Rice, 1m, in *Off-Off Broadway Festival Plays, 14th Series* (New York: Samuel French, Inc., 1989), ISBN 0-573-62363-5, SF 22753

"Travellin' Show," a bare-stage drama by Jane Martin, 1m or 1f, in *What Mama Don't Know*, SF 22752

"True-Born Englishman, A," a radio play (genre?) by Peter Barnes, 1m, (published with and can pair with "Billy and Me," "Houdini's Heir," "Losing Myself," "Madame Zenobia," "The Road to Strome," "Slaughterman," "The Spirit of Man: A Hand Witch of the Second Stage," "The Spirit of Man: From Sleep and Shadow," or "The Spirit of Man: The Night of the Simhat Torah") in Peter Barnes' *The Spirit of Man and More Barnes' People* (New York and London: Methuen & Company, 1990), ISBN 0-413-63130-3

"Turkey's Thanksgiving Adventure," a puppet play for children by Denise Anton Wright, 1 puppeteer presenting 2 characters, (published with and can pair with "The Back-to-School Blues," "The Boy Who Cried Wolf," "The Case of the Disappearing Books," "Dragon Draws a Picture," "The Easter Egg Hunt," "Easter Rabbit's Basket," "Elephant's Sneeze," "Fox Learns a Lesson," "The Halloween Costume," "The Leprechaun's Gold," "The Lion and the Mouse," "Little Red Riding Hood," "The Monkey and the Crocodile," "The Mysterious Egg," "The Pumpkin Thief," "Santa Cures a Cold," "Take Me to Your Library," "The Three Billy Goats Gruff," "The Town Mouse and the Country Mouse," "Witch Gets Ready," "Witch's Valentine," or "Witch's Winter Kitchen") in Denise Anton Wright's *One-Person Puppet Plays*, illustrated by John Wright (Teacher Ideas Press, 1990), ISBN 0-87287-742-6, TIP

"21 A," a lengthy one-act comedy by Kevin Kling, 1m, SF 22237

U

"Uncle Zepp," a drama by Joseph Pintauro, 1m, (published with and can pair with "Charlie and Vito" or "Flywheel and Anna") in *Cacciatore*, DPS 1210

V

"*Volver a decir el mar*" ["I Speak Again of the Sea"] (see p. 258), a drama in Spanish by Sergio Peregrina, 1m, OEN, NSHS pb8189

W

"Wet Paint," a comedy by Frank X. Hogan, 1m, AR

"What She Found There," a ten-minute play (genre?), by John Glore, 1m, SF

"Wild Abandon: The Study of Steve," a drama by Daniel MacIvor, 1m, (published with and can pair with "See Bob Run") in Daniel MacIvor's *See Bob Run & Wild Abandon* (Toronto, Ontario, Canada: Playwrights Canada Press, 1990), ISBN 0-88754-486-X

"Witch Gets Ready," a puppet play for children by Denise Anton Wright, 1 puppeteer presenting 4 characters, (published with and can pair with "The Back-to-School Blues," "The Boy Who Cried Wolf," "The Case of the Disappearing Books," "Dragon Draws a Picture," "The Easter Egg Hunt," "Easter Rabbit's Basket," "Elephant's Sneeze," "Fox Learns a Lesson," "The Halloween Costume," "The Leprechaun's Gold," "The Lion and the Mouse," "Little Red Riding Hood," "The Monkey and the Crocodile," "The Mysterious Egg," "The Pumpkin Thief," "Santa Cures a Cold," "Take Me to Your Library," "The Three Billy Goats Gruff," "The Town Mouse and the Country Mouse," "Turkey's Thanksgiving Adventure," "Witch's Valentine," or "Witch's Winter Kitchen") in Denise Anton Wright's *One-Person Puppet Plays*, illustrated by John Wright (Teacher Ideas Press, 1990), ISBN 0-87287-742-6, TIP

"Witch's Valentine," a puppet play in 2 scenes for children by Denise Anton Wright, 1 puppeteer presenting 4 characters, (published with and can pair with "The Back-to-School Blues," "The Boy Who Cried Wolf," "The Case of the Disappearing Books," "Dragon Draws a Picture," "The Easter Egg Hunt," "Easter Rabbit's Basket," "Elephant's Sneeze," "Fox Learns a Lesson," "The Halloween Costume," "The Leprechaun's Gold," "The Lion and the Mouse," "Little Red Riding Hood," "The Monkey and the Crocodile," "The Mysterious Egg," "The Pumpkin Thief," "Santa Cures a Cold," "Take Me to Your Library," "The Three Billy Goats Gruff," "The Town Mouse and the Country Mouse," "Turkey's Thanksgiving Adventure," "Witch Gets Ready," or "Witch's Winter Kitchen") in Denise Anton Wright's *One-Person Puppet Plays*, illustrated by John Wright (Teacher Ideas Press, 1990), ISBN 0-87287-742-6, TIP

"Witch's Winter Kitchen," a puppet play for children by Denise Anton Wright, 1 puppeteer presenting 2 characters, (published with and can pair with "The Back-to-School Blues," "The Boy Who Cried Wolf," "The Case of the Disappearing Books," "Dragon Draws a Picture," "The Easter Egg Hunt," "Easter Rabbit's Basket,"

"Elephant's Sneeze," "Fox Learns a Lesson," "The Halloween Costume," "The Leprechaun's Gold," "The Lion and the Mouse," "Little Red Riding Hood," "The Monkey and the Crocodile," "The Mysterious Egg," "The Pumpkin Thief," "Santa Cures a Cold," "Take Me to Your Library," "The Three Billy Goats Gruff," "The Town Mouse and the Country Mouse," "Turkey's Thanksgiving Adventure," "Witch Gets Ready," or "Witch's Valentine,") in Denise Anton Wright's *One-Person Puppet Plays*, illustrated by John Wright (Teacher Ideas Press, 1990), ISBN 0-87287-742-6, TIP

Z

"Zimmer," a drama by Donald Margulies, 1m, in *"Pitching to the Star," and Other Short Plays*, DPS 3662

One-Female Plays

A

"Advice to a New Actor," a brief monologue by Lavonne Mueller, 1f or 1m, in *One-Act Plays for Acting Students*, MPL, ISBN 0-916260-47-X

"Alice in Wonderless Land," a monologue by Franca Rame and Dario Fo, 1f, (published with and can pair with "An Arab Woman Speaks," "The Bawd—the Christian Democrat Party in Chile," "Bless Me Father for I Have Sinned," "Coming Home," "The Dancing Mistress: On the Assembly Line," "The Eel-Woman," "Fascism 1922," "I'm Ulrike—Screaming," "It Happened Tomorrow," "Mamma Togni," "Medea," "Michele Lu Lanzone," "A Mother," "Nada Pasini," "The Rape," "Rise and Shine," "The Same Old Story," "The Whore in the Madhouse," or "A Woman Alone") in Franca Rame and Dario Fo's *A Woman Alone & Other Plays* (London: Methuen, 1991), ISBN 0-413-64030-2

"Amelia Lives," (see p. 180) a drama by Laura Annawyn Shamas, 1f, DPC, NSHS pb141

"American Ancestor Worship," (see p. 181), a pick-and-choose bill of satirical skits by Cornelia Otis Skinner, 1f, DPC, NSHS

"Animal," (see p. 182) a bare-stage comedy by Oliver Hailey, 1f, (published with and can pair with "Picture" or "Crisscross") in *Picture Animal Crisscross: Three Short Plays* DPS 3655, NSHS pb7922

"Autumn Leaves," a bare-stage dramatic monologue by Don Nigro, 1f, in *Winchelsea Dround and Other Plays: Nine Monologue Plays* (New York: Samuel French, Inc., 1992), ISBN 0-573-62598-0, SF 25226

"Axis Sally" ["**The Girlhood of Shakespeare's Heroines: Axis Sally**"], a comedic monologue by Don Nigro, 1f, (published with and can pair with "Dead Men's Fingers," "Full Fathom Five," "How Many Children Had Lady Macbeth?" or "Notes from the Moated Grange") in *Cincinnati and Other Plays: Monologues for the Theatre* (New York: Samuel French, 1989), ISBN 0-573-62105-5, SF 3686

B

"Back-to-School Blues," a puppet play for children in five scenes by Denise Anton Wright, 1 puppeteer presenting 4 characters, (published with and can pair with "The Boy Who Cried Wolf," "The Case of the Disappearing Books," "Dragon Draws a Picture," "The Easter Egg Hunt," "Easter Rabbit's Basket," "Elephant's Sneeze,"

"Fox Learns a Lesson," "The Halloween Costume," "The Leprechaun's Gold," "The Lion and the Mouse," "Little Red Riding Hood," "The Monkey and the Crocodile," "The Mysterious Egg," "The Pumpkin Thief," "Santa Cures a Cold," "Take Me to Your Library," "The Three Billy Goats Gruff," "The Town Mouse and the Country Mouse," "Turkey's Thanksgiving Adventure," "Witch Gets Ready," "Witch's Valentine," or "Witch's Winter Kitchen") in Denise Anton Wright's *One-Person Puppet Plays*, illustrated by John Wright (Teacher Idea Press, 1990), ISBN 0-87287-742-6, TIP

"Bag Lady," a drama by Jean-Claude Van Itallie, 1f, (published with and can pair with "Sunset Freeway" or "Final Orders") in *Early Warnings* DPS 1767, (or published alone) DPS 905

"Bawd—the Christian Democrat Party in Chile, The," a monologue by Franca Rame and Dario Fo, 1f, (published with and can pair with "Alice in Wonderless Land," "An Arab Woman Speaks," "Bless Me Father for I Have Sinned," "Coming Home," "The Dancing Mistress: On the Assembly Line," "The Eel-Woman," "Fascism 1922," "I'm Ulrike—Screaming," "It Happened Tomorrow," "Mamma Togni," "Medea," "Michele Lu Lanzone," "A Mother," "Nada Pasini," "The Rape," "Rise and Shine," "The Same Old Story," "The Whore in the Madhouse," or "A Woman Alone") in Franca Rame and Dario Fo's *A Woman Alone & Other Plays* (London: Methuen, 1991), ISBN 0-413-64030-2

"Bed Among the Lentils," a half-hour monologue by Alan Bennett, 1f, SF

"Before Breakfast," (see p. 185) a drama by Eugene O'Neill, 1f, DPS 405, (published with and can pair with "The Dreamy Kid," "Fog," "Shell Shock," "Thirst," or "A Wife for a Life") in Eugene O'Neill's *Complete Plays 1913-1920*, edited by Travis Bogard (New York: Random House, Inc., 1988), ISBN 0-940450-48-8, NSHS pb8121

"Beyond," a drama by Alice Gerstenberg, 1f, perhaps SF (?), which controls "Overtones"

"Bindle Stiff," a comedy by Amlin Gray, 1f, DPS 3132

"Black Woman Speaks, A," a drama by Beah Richards, 1f, NAL

"Blank Pages," a drama by Frank Marcus, 1f, perhaps SF (?), which controls *The Killing of Sister George*

"Bless Me Father for I Have Sinned," a monologue by Franca Rame and Dario Fo, 1f, (published with and can pair with "Alice in Wonderless Land," "An Arab Woman Speaks," "The Bawd—the Christian Democrat Party in

Chile," "Coming Home," "The Dancing Mistress: On the Assembly Line," "The Eel-Woman," "Fascism 1922," "I'm Ulrike—Screaming," "It Happened Tomorrow," "Mamma Togni," "Medea," "Michele Lu Lanzone," "A Mother," "Nada Pasini," "The Rape," "Rise and Shine," "The Same Old Story," "The Whore in the Madhouse," or "A Woman Alone") in Franca Rame and Dario Fo's *A Woman Alone & Other Plays* (London: Methuen, 1991), ISBN 0-413-64030-2

"Box," an abstraction by Edward Albee, 1f, in Edward Albee's *The Plays,* vol. 1 (New York: Macmillan, 1991), ISBN 0-02-501761-6, DPS, NSHS pb7805

"Boy Who Cried Wolf, The," a puppet play for children by Denise Anton Wright, 1 puppeteer presenting 4 characters, (published with and can pair with "The Back-to-School Blues," "The Case of the Disappearing Books," "Dragon Draws a Picture," "The Easter Egg Hunt," "Easter Rabbit's Basket," "Elephant's Sneeze," "Fox Learns a Lesson," "The Halloween Costume," "The Leprechaun's Gold," "The Lion and the Mouse," "Little Red Riding Hood," "The Monkey and the Crocodile," "The Mysterious Egg," "The Pumpkin Thief," "Santa Cures a Cold," "Take Me to Your Library," "The Three Billy Goats Gruff," "The Town Mouse and the Country Mouse," "Turkey's Thanksgiving Adventure," "Witch Gets Ready," "Witch's Valentine," or "Witch's Winter Kitchen") in Denise Anton Wright's *One-Person Puppet Plays,* illustrated by John Wright (Teacher Idea Press, 1990), ISBN 0-87287-742-6, TIP

"Breath," a short audio and visual piece for the stage by Samuel Beckett, 1f or 1m recorded voice, (see next item) in *First Love and Other Stories* SF 4679

"Breath," a short audio and visual piece for the stage by Samuel Beckett, 1f or 1m recorded voice, ([see above item] published with and can pair with "Act Without Words I," "Act Without Words II," "Cascando," "Catastrophe," "Come and Go," "Eh Joe," "Embers," "Footfalls," "Ghost Trio," "Krapp's Last Tape," "Not I," "Ohio Impromptu," "A Piece of Monologue," "Play," "Quad," "Rockaby," "Rough for Radio I," "Rough for Radio II," "Rough for Theatre I," "Rough for Theatre II," "That Time," or "Words and Music") in *Collected Shorter Plays,* ISBN 0-394-53850-1, ISBN 0-394-62098-4

C

"Captain Cook," a dramatic monologue by Don Nigro, 1f, (published with and can pair with "Dead Men's Fingers," "Full Fathom Five," "How Many Children Had Lady Macbeth?" or "Axis Sally") in Don Nigro's *Cincinnati*

and Other Plays (New York: Samuel French, 1989), ISBN 0-573-62105-5, SF 5772

"Case of the Disappearing Books, The," a puppet play in 2 scenes for children by Denise Anton Wright, 1 puppeteer presenting 3 characters, (published with and can pair with "The Back-to-School Blues," "The Boy Who Cried Wolf," "Dragon Draws a Picture," "The Easter Egg Hunt," "Easter Rabbit's Basket," "Elephant's Sneeze," "Fox Learns a Lesson," "The Halloween Costume," "The Leprechaun's Gold," "The Lion and the Mouse," "Little Red Riding Hood," "The Monkey and the Crocodile," "The Mysterious Egg," "The Pumpkin Thief," "Santa Cures a Cold," "Take Me to Your Library," "The Three Billy Goats Gruff," "The Town Mouse and the Country Mouse," "Turkey's Thanksgiving Adventure," "Witch Gets Ready," "Witch's Valentine," or "Witch's Winter Kitchen") in Denise Anton Wright's *One-Person Puppet Plays,* illustrated by John Wright (Teacher Idea Press, 1990), ISBN 0-87287-742-6, TIP

"Chicks," (see p. 192) a comedy by Grace McKeaney, 1f, in *Antæus: Plays in One Act,* edited by Daniel Halpern, no. 66, (spring, 1991), ISBN 0-88001-268-4; also in *Chicks and Other Short Plays* SF 5747, NSHS pb7949, NSHS pb8091

"Cincinnati," a lengthy dramatic monologue by Don Nigro, 1f, (published with and can pair with "Axis Sally," "Captain Cook," "Dead Men's Fingers," "Full Fathom Five," or "How Many Children Had Lady Macbeth?") in *Cincinnati and Other Plays* (New York: Samuel French, 1989), ISBN 0-573-62105-5, SF 5773

"Coming Home," a monologue by Franca Rame and Dario Fo, 1f, (published with and can pair with "Alice in Wonderless Land," "An Arab Woman Speaks," "The Bawd—the Christian Democrat Party in Chile," "Bless Me Father for I Have Sinned," "The Dancing Mistress: On the Assembly Line," "The Eel-Woman," "Fascism 1922," "I'm Ulrike—Screaming," "It Happened Tomorrow," "Mamma Togni," "Medea," "Michele Lu Lanzone," "A Mother," "Nada Pasini," "The Rape," "Rise and Shine," "The Same Old Story," "The Whore in the Madhouse," or "A Woman Alone") in Franca Rame and Dario Fo's *A Woman Alone & Other Plays* (London: Methuen, 1991), ISBN 0-413-64030-2

"Cream Cracker Under the Settee, A," a half-hour monologue by Alan Bennett, 1f, SF

"Cul-de-Sac," a drama by Jane Martin, 1f, in *What Mama Don't Know,* SF 5769

D

"Dancing Mistress: On the Assembly Line, The," a mono-

One-Female Plays, continued

logue by Franca Rame and Dario Fo, 1f, (published with and can pair with "Alice in Wonderless Land," "An Arab Woman Speaks," "The Bawd—the Christian Democrat Party in Chile," "Bless Me Father for I Have Sinned," "Coming Home," "The Eel-Woman," "Fascism 1922," "I'm Ulrike—Screaming," "It Happened Tomorrow," "Mamma Togni," "Medea," "Michele Lu Lanzone," "A Mother," "Nada Pasini," "The Rape," "Rise and Shine," "The Same Old Story," "The Whore in the Madhouse," or "A Woman Alone") in Franca Rame and Dario Fo's *A Woman Alone & Other Plays* (London: Methuen, 1991), ISBN 0-413-64030-2

"Dead Men's Fingers" ["The Girlhood of Shakespeare's Heroines: Dead Men's Fingers"], a monologue by Don Nigro, 1f, (published with and can pair with "Axis Sally," "Full Fathom Five," "How Many Children Had Lady Macbeth?" or "Notes from the Moated Grange") in *Cincinnati and Other Plays: Monologues for the Theatre* (New York: Samuel French, 1989), ISBN 0-573-62105-5, SF 6722

"Desmond," a drama by John Mortimer, 1f, perhaps SF (?), which controls several plays by this author

"Dragon Draws a Picture," a puppet play for children by Denise Anton Wright, 1 puppeteer presenting 2 characters, (published with and can pair with "The Back-to-School Blues," "The Boy Who Cried Wolf," "The Case of the Disappearing Books," "The Easter Egg Hunt," "Easter Rabbit's Basket," "Elephant's Sneeze," "Fox Learns a Lesson," "The Halloween Costume," "The Leprechaun's Gold," "The Lion and the Mouse," "Little Red Riding Hood," "The Monkey and the Crocodile," "The Mysterious Egg," "The Pumpkin Thief," "Santa Cures a Cold," "Take Me to Your Library," "The Three Billy Goats Gruff," "The Town Mouse and the Country Mouse," "Turkey's Thanksgiving Adventure," "Witch Gets Ready," "Witch's Valentine," or "Witch's Winter Kitchen") in Denise Anton Wright's *One-Person Puppet Plays*, illustrated by John Wright (Teacher Idea Press, 1990), ISBN 0-87287-742-6, TIP

"Drowned Out," a brief comedic monologue by Robert Patrick, 1f or 1f (+1 silent male), (published with and can pair with "Advice to a New Actor," "The Affidavit," "The American Way," "Anniversary," "Auld Lang Syne, or I'll Bet You Think This Play Is About You," "Bug Swatter," "Checkers," "Coming for a Visit," "Dalmation," "Dog Eat Dog," "Fireworks," "Interview," "Jumping," "Money," "One Beer Too Many," "Phonecall from Sunkist," "Potato Girl," "Property of the Dallas Cowboys," "The Split Decision," "Valley Forgery," "Watermelon Boats," or "Widows") in *One-Act Plays for Acting Students* MPL, ISBN 0-916260-47-X

E

"Easter Egg Hunt, The," a puppet play in 3 scenes for children by Denise Anton Wright, 1 puppeteer presenting 4 characters, (published with and can pair with "The Back-to-School Blues," "The Boy Who Cried Wolf," "The Case of the Disappearing Books," "Dragon Draws a Picture," "Easter Rabbit's Basket," "Elephant's Sneeze," "Fox Learns a Lesson," "The Halloween Costume," "The Leprechaun's Gold," "The Lion and the Mouse," "Little Red Riding Hood," "The Monkey and the Crocodile," "The Mysterious Egg," "The Pumpkin Thief," "Santa Cures a Cold," "Take Me to Your Library," "The Three Billy Goats Gruff," "The Town Mouse and the Country Mouse," "Turkey's Thanksgiving Adventure," "Witch Gets Ready," "Witch's Valentine," or "Witch's Winter Kitchen") in Denise Anton Wright's *One-Person Puppet Plays*, illustrated by John Wright (Teacher Idea Press, 1990), ISBN 0-87287-742-6, TIP

"Easter Rabbit's Basket," a puppet play in 3 scenes for children by Denise Anton Wright, 1 puppeteer presenting 3 characters, (published with and can pair with "The Back-to-School Blues," "The Boy Who Cried Wolf," "The Case of the Disappearing Books," "Dragon Draws a Picture," "The Easter Egg Hunt," "Elephant's Sneeze," "Fox Learns a Lesson," "The Halloween Costume," "The Leprechaun's Gold," "The Lion and the Mouse," "Little Red Riding Hood," "The Monkey and the Crocodile," "The Mysterious Egg," "The Pumpkin Thief," "Santa Cures a Cold," "Take Me to Your Library," "The Three Billy Goats Gruff," "The Town Mouse and the Country Mouse," "Turkey's Thanksgiving Adventure," "Witch Gets Ready," "Witch's Valentine," or "Witch's Winter Kitchen") in Denise Anton Wright's *One-Person Puppet Plays*, illustrated by John Wright (Teacher Idea Press, 1990), ISBN 0-87287-742-6, TIP

"Educated Lady, An," a dramatic monologue by Ken Jenkins, 1f, (published with and can pair with "Cemetery Man," "Chug," or "Rupert's Birthday") in *"Rupert's Birthday" and Other Monologues* DPS 3912

"Eel-Woman, The," a monologue by Franca Rame and Dario Fo, 1f, (published with and can pair with "Alice in Wonderless Land," "An Arab Woman Speaks," "The Bawd—the Christian Democrat Party in Chile," "Bless Me Father for I Have Sinned," "Coming Home," "The Dancing Mistress: On the Assembly Line," "Fascism 1922," "I'm Ulrike—Screaming," "It Happened Tomorrow," "Mamma Togni," "Medea," "Michele Lu Lanzone," "A Mother," "Nada Pasini," "The Rape," "Rise and Shine," "The Same Old Story," "The Whore in the Madhouse," or "A Woman Alone") in Franca

Rame and Dario Fo's *A Woman Alone & Other Plays* (London: Methuen, 1991), ISBN 0-413-64030-2

"El ultimo instante," a drama (in Spanish) by Franklin Dominguez (of Dominican Republic), 1f, FCE, NSHS 29520

"Elephant's Sneeze," a puppet play in 3 scenes for children by Denise Anton Wright, 1 puppeteer presenting 3 characters, (published with and can pair with "The Back-to-School Blues," "The Boy Who Cried Wolf," "The Case of the Disappearing Books," "Dragon Draws a Picture," "The Easter Egg Hunt," "Easter Rabbit's Basket," "Fox Learns a Lesson," "The Halloween Costume," "The Leprechaun's Gold," "The Lion and the Mouse," "Little Red Riding Hood," "The Monkey and the Crocodile," "The Mysterious Egg," "The Pumpkin Thief," "Santa Cures a Cold," "Take Me to Your Library," "The Three Billy Goats Gruff," "The Town Mouse and the Country Mouse," "Turkey's Thanksgiving Adventure," "Witch Gets Ready," "Witch's Valentine," or "Witch's Winter Kitchen") in Denise Anton Wright's *One-Person Puppet Plays,* illustrated by John Wright (Teacher Idea Press, 1990), ISBN 0-87287-742-6, TIP

F

"Fascism 1922," a monologue by Franca Rame and Dario Fo, 1f, (published with and can pair with "Alice in Wonderless Land," "An Arab Woman Speaks," "The Bawd—the Christian Democrat Party in Chile," "Bless Me Father for I Have Sinned," "Coming Home," "The Dancing Mistress: On the Assembly Line," "The Eel-Woman," "I'm Ulrike—Screaming," "It Happened To-morrow," "Mamma Togni," "Medea," "Michele Lu Lanzone," "A Mother," "Nada Pasini," "The Rape," "Rise and Shine," "The Same Old Story," "The Whore in the Madhouse," or "A Woman Alone") in Franca Rame and Dario Fo's *A Woman Alone & Other Plays* (London: Methuen, 1991), ISBN 0-413-64030-2

"Fish Story, A," a comedy by Alida E. Young, 1f, in *The Big Book of Comedies: 25 One-Act Plays, Skits, Curtain Raisers, and Adaptations for Young Actors,* edited by Sylvia E. Kamerman (Boston: Plays, Inc., 1989), ISBN 0-8238-0289-2, PI

"Footfalls," a drama by Samuel Beckett, 1f (+1 f voice), (see next item) in *Ends and Odds,* SF 8635

"Footfalls," a drama by Samuel Beckett, 1f (+1 f voice), ([see above item] published with and can pair with "Act Without Words I," "Act Without Words II," "Breath," "Cascando," "Catastrophe," "Come and Go," "Eh Joe," "Embers," "Ghost Trio," "Krapp's Last Tape," "Not I," "Ohio Impromptu," "A Piece of Monologue," "Play,"

"Quad," "Rockaby," "Rough for Radio I," "Rough for Radio II," "Rough for Theatre I," "Rough for Theatre II," "That Time," or "Words and Music") in *Collected Shorter Plays,* ISBN 0-394-53850-1, ISBN 0-394-62098-4

"Fox Learns a Lesson," a puppet play for children by Denise Anton Wright, 1 puppeteer presenting 3 characters, (published with and can pair with "The Back-to-School Blues," "The Boy Who Cried Wolf," "The Case of the Disappearing Books," "Dragon Draws a Picture," "The Easter Egg Hunt," "Easter Rabbit's Basket," "Elephant's Sneeze," "The Halloween Costume," "The Leprechaun's Gold," "The Lion and the Mouse," "Little Red Riding Hood," "The Monkey and the Crocodile," "The Mysterious Egg," "The Pumpkin Thief," "Santa Cures a Cold," "Take Me to Your Library," "The Three Billy Goats Gruff," "The Town Mouse and the Country Mouse," "Turkey's Thanksgiving Adventure," "Witch Gets Ready," "Witch's Valentine," or "Witch's Winter Kitchen") in Denise Anton Wright's *One-Person Puppet Plays,* illustrated by John Wright (Teacher Idea Press, 1990), ISBN 0-87287-742-6, TIP

"Frankenstein," a bare-stage monologue by Don Nigro, 1f, in *Genesis and Other Plays,* SF 8936

"French Gray," by Josef Bush, 1f, source unestablished

"Full Fathom Five" ["The Girlhood of Shakespeare's Heroines: Full Fathom Five"], a comedic monologue by Don Nigro, 1f, (published with and can pair with "Axis Sally," "Dead Men's Fingers," "How Many Children Had Lady Macbeth?" or "Notes from the Moated Grange") in *Cincinnati and Other Plays: Monologues for the Theatre* (New York: Samuel French, 1989), ISBN 0-573-62105-5, SF 9696

G

"Genesis," a bare-stage comedic monologue by Don Nigro, 1f, in *Genesis and Other Plays,* SF 9910

"Gift, The," a drama by Karen Patitucci, 1f, in Karen Patitucci's *Three-Minute Dramas for Worship* (San Jose, California: Resource Publications, Inc., 1989), ISBN 0-89390-143-1

"Gift, The," a drama (suitable to Christmas with line changes) by Virginia de Wyze, 1f (or more, up to five), DPS

"Girlhood of Shakespeare's Heroines: Axis Sally, The," a monologue by Don Nigro, 1f, (published with and can pair with "Dead Men's Fingers," "Full Fathom Five," "How Many Children Had Lady Macbeth?" or "Notes from the Moated Grange") in *Cincinnati and Other Plays: Monologues for the Theatre* (New York: Samuel French, 1989), ISBN 0-573-62105-5, SF 3686

One-Female Plays, continued

"Girlhood of Shakespeare's Heroines: Dead Men's Fingers, The," a monologue by Don Nigro, 1f, (published with and can pair with "Axis Sally," "Full Fathom Five," "How Many Children Had Lady Macbeth?" or "Notes from the Moated Grange") in *Cincinnati and Other Plays: Monologues for the Theatre* (New York: Samuel French, 1989), ISBN 0-573-62105-5, SF 6722

"Girlhood of Shakespeare's Heroines: Full Fathom Five, The," a monologue by Don Nigro, (published with and can pair with "Axis Sally," "Dead Men's Fingers," "How Many Children Had Lady Macbeth?" or "Notes from the Moated Grange") 1f, in *Cincinnati and Other Plays: Monologues for the Theatre* (New York: Samuel French, 1989), ISBN 0-573-62105-5, SF 9696

"Girlhood of Shakespeare's Heroines: How Many Children Had Lady Macbeth? The," a monologue by Don Nigro, 1f, (published with and can pair with "Axis Sally," "Dead Men's Fingers," "Full Fathom Five," or "Notes from the Moated Grange") in *Cincinnati and Other Plays: Monologues for the Theatre* (New York: Samuel French, 1989), ISBN 0-573-62105-5, SF 10647

"Girlhood of Shakespeare's Heroines: Notes from the Moated Grange, The," a monologue by Don Nigro, 1f, (published with and can pair with "Axis Sally," "Dead Men's Fingers," "Full Fathom Five," or "How Many Children Had Lady Macbeth?") in *Cincinnati and Other Plays: Monologues for the Theatre* (New York: Samuel French, 1989), ISBN 0-573-62105-5, SF 16646

H

"Halloween Costume, The," a puppet play in 4 scenes for children by Denise Anton Wright, 1 puppeteer presenting 4 characters, (published with and can pair with "The Back-to-School Blues," "The Boy Who Cried Wolf," "The Case of the Disappearing Books," "Dragon Draws a Picture," "The Easter Egg Hunt," "Easter Rabbit's Basket," "Elephant's Sneeze," "Fox Learns a Lesson," "The Leprechaun's Gold," "The Lion and the Mouse," "Little Red Riding Hood," "The Monkey and the Crocodile," "The Mysterious Egg," "The Pumpkin Thief," "Santa Cures a Cold," "Take Me to Your Library," "The Three Billy Goats Gruff," "The Town Mouse and the Country Mouse," "Turkey's Thanksgiving Adventure," "Witch Gets Ready," "Witch's Valentine," or "Witch's Winter Kitchen") in Denise Anton Wright's *One-Person Puppet Plays*, illustrated by John Wright (Teacher Idea Press, 1990), ISBN 0-87287-742-6, TIP

"Haunted," a bare-stage dramatic monologue by Don Nigro, 1f, in *Genesis and Other Plays,* SF 10593

"Her Big Chance," a half-hour monologue by Alan Bennett, 1f, SF

"Homebound," a drama by Lyndall Callan, 1f, in *Off-Off Broadway Festival Plays, 17 Series,* SF 551

"How Many Children Had Lady Macbeth?" [**"The Girlhood of Shakespeare's Heroines: How Many Children Had Lady Macbeth?"**] a monologue by Don Nigro, 1f, (published with and can pair with "Axis Sally," "Dead Men's Fingers," "Full Fathom Five," or "Notes from the Moated Grange") in *Cincinnati and Other Plays: Monologues for the Theatre* (New York: Samuel French, 1989), ISBN 0-573-62105-5, SF 10647

"Human Voice, The" [*"La Voix humaine"*], a drama by Jean Cocteau, 1f, in Jean Cocteau's *The Human Voice* (London: Samuel French, Inc., 1992), ISBN 0-57303381-1, SF

I

"I'm Ulrike—Screaming," a monologue by Franca Rame and Dario Fo, 1f, (published with and can pair with "Alice in Wonderless Land," "An Arab Woman Speaks," "The Bawd—the Christian Democrat Party in Chile," "Bless Me Father for I Have Sinned," "Coming Home," "The Dancing Mistress: On the Assembly Line," "The Eel-Woman," "Fascism 1922," "It Happened Tomorrow," "Mamma Togni," "Medea," "Michele Lu Lanzone," "A Mother," "Nada Pasini," "The Rape," "Rise and Shine," "The Same Old Story," "The Whore in the Madhouse," or "A Woman Alone") in Franca Rame and Dario Fo's *A Woman Alone & Other Plays* (London: Methuen, 1991), ISBN 0-413-64030-2

"It Happened Tomorrow," a monologue by Franca Rame and Dario Fo, 1f, (published with and can pair with "Alice in Wonderless Land," "An Arab Woman Speaks," "The Bawd—the Christian Democrat Party in Chile," "Bless Me Father for I Have Sinned," "Coming Home," "The Dancing Mistress: On the Assembly Line," "The Eel-Woman," "Fascism 1922," "I'm Ulrike—Screaming," "Mamma Togni," "Medea," "Michele Lu Lanzone," "A Mother," "Nada Pasini," "The Rape," "Rise and Shine," "The Same Old Story," "The Whore in the Madhouse," or "A Woman Alone") in Franca Rame and Dario Fo's *A Woman Alone & Other Plays* (London: Methuen, 1991), ISBN 0-413-64030-2

K

"King of the Cats, The," a bare-stage comedic monologue by Don Nigro, 1f, in *Winchelsea Dround and Other Plays: Nine Monologue Plays* (New York: Samuel French, Inc., 1992), ISBN 0-573-62598-0, SF 13037

L

"Lady of Letters, A," a half-hour monologue by Alan Bennett, 1f, SF

"Laughs, Etc.," (see p. 211) a comedy by James Leo Herlihy, 1f, (published with and can pair with "Bad Bad Jo-Jo" or "Terrible Jim Fitch") in *Stop, You're Killing Me,* DPS 4290, NSHS pb7924

"Le Bel indifférent" [**"Sound of Silence, The"**], a drama by Jean Cocteau, translated by Anthony Wood, 1f (+ silent male), in Jean Cocteau's *The Sound of Silence* (London: Samuel French, Inc., 1992), ISBN 0-573-12266-0, SF

"Leprechaun's Gold, The," a puppet play for children by Denise Anton Wright, 1 puppeteer presenting 2 characters, (published with and can pair with "The Back-to-School Blues," "The Boy Who Cried Wolf," "The Case of the Disappearing Books," "Dragon Draws a Picture," "The Easter Egg Hunt," "Easter Rabbit's Basket," "Elephant's Sneeze," "Fox Learns a Lesson," "The Halloween Costume," "The Lion and the Mouse," "Little Red Riding Hood," "The Monkey and the Crocodile," "The Mysterious Egg," "The Pumpkin Thief," "Santa Cures a Cold," "Take Me to Your Library," "The Three Billy Goats Gruff," "The Town Mouse and the Country Mouse," "Turkey's Thanksgiving Adventure," "Witch Gets Ready," "Witch's Valentine," or "Witch's Winter Kitchen") in Denise Anton Wright's *One-Person Puppet Plays,* illustrated by John Wright (Teacher Idea Press, 1990), ISBN 0-87287-742-6, TIP

"Lion and the Mouse, The," a puppet play for children by Denise Anton Wright, 1 puppeteer presenting 2 characters, (published with and can pair with "The Back-to-School Blues," "The Boy Who Cried Wolf," "The Case of the Disappearing Books," "Dragon Draws a Picture," "The Easter Egg Hunt," "Easter Rabbit's Basket," "Elephant's Sneeze," "Fox Learns a Lesson," "The Halloween Costume," "The Leprechaun's Gold," "Little Red Riding Hood," "The Monkey and the Crocodile," "The Mysterious Egg," "The Pumpkin Thief," "Santa Cures a Cold," "Take Me to Your Library," "The Three Billy Goats Gruff," "The Town Mouse and the Country Mouse," "Turkey's Thanksgiving Adventure," "Witch Gets Ready," "Witch's Valentine," or "Witch's Winter Kitchen") in Denise Anton Wright's *One-Person Puppet Plays,* illustrated by John Wright (Teacher Idea Press, 1990), ISBN 0-87287-742-6, TIP

"Little Red Riding Hood," a puppet play in 2 scenes for children by Denise Anton Wright, 1 puppeteer presenting 3 characters, (published with and can pair with "The Back-to-School Blues," "The Boy Who Cried Wolf,"

"The Case of the Disappearing Books," "Dragon Draws a Picture," "The Easter Egg Hunt," "Easter Rabbit's Basket," "Elephant's Sneeze," "Fox Learns a Lesson," "The Halloween Costume," "The Leprechaun's Gold," "The Lion and the Mouse," "The Monkey and the Crocodile," "The Mysterious Egg," "The Pumpkin Thief," "Santa Cures a Cold," "Take Me to Your Library," "The Three Billy Goats Gruff," "The Town Mouse and the Country Mouse," "Turkey's Thanksgiving Adventure," "Witch Gets Ready," "Witch's Valentine," or "Witch's Winter Kitchen") in Denise Anton Wright's *One-Person Puppet Plays,* illustrated by John Wright (Teacher Idea Press, 1990), ISBN 0-87287-742-6, TIP

"Longing for Worldly Pleasures," (see p. 214) a traditional *K'unshan* play by Ssu Fan, 1f, UWP

M

"Madeline Nude in the Rain Perhaps," a bare-stage comedic monologue by Don Nigro, 1f, in *Winchelsea Dround and Other Plays: Nine Monologue Plays* (New York: Samuel French, Inc., 1992), ISBN 0-573-62598-0, SF 14942

"Madrigals," a bare-stage comedic monologue by Don Nigro, 1f, in *Genesis and Other Plays,* SF 14943

"Mamma Togni," a monologue by Franca Rame and Dario Fo, 1f, (published with and can pair with "Alice in Wonderless Land," "An Arab Woman Speaks," "The Bawd—the Christian Democrat Party in Chile," "Bless Me Father for I Have Sinned," "Coming Home," "The Dancing Mistress: On the Assembly Line," "The Eel-Woman," "Fascism 1922," "I'm Ulrike—Screaming," "It Happened Tomorrow," "Medea," "Michele Lu Lanzone," "A Mother," "Nada Pasini," "The Rape," "Rise and Shine," "The Same Old Story," "The Whore in the Madhouse," or "A Woman Alone") in Franca Rame and Dario Fo's *A Woman Alone & Other Plays* (London: Methuen, 1991), ISBN 0-413-64030-2

"Medea," a monologue by Franca Rame and Dario Fo, 1f, (published with and can pair with "Alice in Wonderless Land," "An Arab Woman Speaks," "The Bawd—the Christian Democrat Party in Chile," "Bless Me Father for I Have Sinned," "Coming Home," "The Dancing Mistress: On the Assembly Line," "The Eel-Woman," "Fascism 1922," "I'm Ulrike—Screaming," "It Happened Tomorrow," "Mamma Togni," "Michele Lu Lanzone," "A Mother," "Nada Pasini," "The Rape," "Rise and Shine," "The Same Old Story," "The Whore in the Madhouse," or "A Woman Alone") in Franca Rame and Dario Fo's *A Woman Alone & Other Plays* (London: Methuen,

1991), ISBN 0-413-64030-2

"Michele Lu Lanzone," a monologue by Franca Rame and Dario Fo, 1f, (published with and can pair with "Alice in Wonderless Land," "An Arab Woman Speaks," "The Bawd—the Christian Democrat Party in Chile," "Bless Me Father for I Have Sinned," "Coming Home," "The Dancing Mistress: On the Assembly Line," "The Eel-Woman," "Fascism 1922," "I'm Ulrike—Screaming," "It Happened Tomorrow," "Mamma Togni," "Medea," "A Mother," "Nada Pasini," "The Rape," "Rise and Shine," "The Same Old Story," "The Whore in the Madhouse," or "A Woman Alone") in Franca Rame and Dario Fo's *A Woman Alone & Other Plays* (London: Methuen, 1991), ISBN 0-413-64030-2

"Monkey and the Crocodile, The," a puppet play for children by Denise Anton Wright, 1 puppeteer presenting 2 characters, (published with and can pair with "The Back-to-School Blues," "The Boy Who Cried Wolf," "The Case of the Disappearing Books," "Dragon Draws a Picture," "The Easter Egg Hunt," "Easter Rabbit's Basket," "Elephant's Sneeze," "Fox Learns a Lesson," "The Hal-loween Costume," "The Leprechaun's Gold," "The Lion and the Mouse," "Little Red Riding Hood," "The Mys-terious Egg," "The Pumpkin Thief," "Santa Cures a Cold," "Take Me to Your Library," "The Three Billy Goats Gruff," "The Town Mouse and the Country Mouse," "Turkey's Thanksgiving Adventure," "Witch Gets Ready," "Witch's Valentine," or "Witch's Winter Kitchen") in Denise Anton Wright's *One-Person Pup-pet Plays,* illustrated by John Wright (Teacher Idea Press, 1990), ISBN 0-87287-742-6, TIP

"Moonshot Tape, The," a drama by Lanford Wilson, 1f, pub-lished with and can pair with "A Poster of the Cosmos"), in *Antæus: Plays in One Act,* no. 66 (spring, 1991), Antæus [Ecco Press], ISBN 0-88001-26, DPS 3696

"Mother, A," a monologue by Franca Rame and Dario Fo, 1f, (published with and can pair with "Alice in Wonderless Land," "An Arab Woman Speaks," "The Bawd—the Christian Democrat Party in Chile," "Bless Me Father for I Have Sinned," "Coming Home," "The Dancing Mistress: On the Assembly Line," "The Eel-Woman," "Fascism 1922," "I'm Ulrike—Screaming," "It Happened Tomorrow," "Mamma Togni," "Medea," "Michele Lu Lanzone," "Nada Pasini," "The Rape," "Rise and Shine," "The Same Old Story," "The Whore in the Madhouse," or "A Woman Alone") in Franca Rame and Dario Fo's *A Woman Alone & Other Plays* (London: Methuen, 1991), ISBN 0-413-64030-2

"Movie Mother," (see p. 205) a comedy by Colin Clements and Florence Ryerson, 1f, SF, NSHS 6066

"Mysterious Egg, The," a puppet play in 5 scenes for chil-dren by Denise Anton Wright, 1 puppeteer presenting 4 characters, (published with and can pair with "The Back-to-School Blues," "The Boy Who Cried Wolf," "The Case of the Disappearing Books," "Dragon Draws a Picture," "The Easter Egg Hunt," "Easter Rabbit's Basket," "Elephant's Sneeze," "Fox Learns a Lesson," "The Hal-loween Costume," "The Leprechaun's Gold," "The Lion and the Mouse," "Little Red Riding Hood," "The Mon-key and the Crocodile," "The Pumpkin Thief," "Santa Cures a Cold," "Take Me to Your Library," "The Three Billy Goats Gruff," "The Town Mouse and the Country Mouse," "Turkey's Thanksgiving Adventure," "Witch Gets Ready," "Witch's Valentine," or "Witch's Winter Kitchen") in Denise Anton Wright's *One-Person Pup-pet Plays,* illustrated by John Wright (Teacher Idea Press, 1990), ISBN 0-87287-742-6, TIP

N

"Nada Pasini," a monologue by Franca Rame and Dario Fo, 1f, (published with and can pair with "Alice in Wonderless Land," "An Arab Woman Speaks," "The Bawd—the Christian Democrat Party in Chile," "Bless Me Father for I Have Sinned," "Coming Home," "The Dancing Mistress: On the Assembly Line," "The Eel-Woman," "Fascism 1922," "I'm Ulrike—Screaming," "It Happened Tomorrow," "Mamma Togni," "Medea," "Michele Lu Lanzone," "A Mother," "The Rape," "Rise and Shine," "The Same Old Story," "The Whore in the Madhouse," or "A Woman Alone") in Franca Rame and Dario Fo's *A Woman Alone & Other Plays* (London: Methuen, 1991), ISBN 0-413-64030-2

"Not I," a drama by Samuel Beckett, 1f (+ extra), (published with and can pair with "Act Without Words I," "Act With-out Words II," "Breath," "Cascando," "Catastrophe," "Come and Go," "Eh Joe," "Embers," "Footfalls," "Ghost Trio," "Krapp's Last Tape," "Ohio Impromptu," "A Piece of Monologue," "Play," "Quad," "Rockaby," "Rough for Radio I," "Rough for Radio II," "Rough for Theatre I," "Rough for Theatre II," "That Time," or "Words and Music") in *Collected Shorter Plays,* ISBN 0-394-53850-1, ISBN 0-394-62098-4

"Notes from the Moated Grange" [**"The Girlhood of Shakespeare's Heroines: Notes from the Moated Grange"**], a monologue by Don Nigro, 1f, (published with and can pair with "Axis Sally," "Dead Men's Fin-gers," "Full Fathom Five," or "How Many Children Had Lady Macbeth?") in *Cincinnati and Other Plays: Mono-*

logues for the Theatre (New York: Samuel French, 1989), ISBN 0-573-62105-5, SF 16646

O

"Only a Countess May Dance When She's Crazy," a comedy by H. M. Koutoukas, 1f, (published with and can pair with "Awful People Are Coming Over So We Must Be Pretending to Be Hard at Work and Hope That They Will Go Away") in H. M. Koutoukas' *When Lightning Strikes Twice* (New York: Samuel French, Inc., 1991) ISBN 0-573-62574-3, SF 17939

"Opening Night," a comedy by Roland Fernand from Cornelia Otis Skinner, 1f, DPC

P

"Piece of Monologue, A," a drama by Samuel Beckett, 1f or 1m (published with and can pair with "All Strange Away," "Ohio Impromptu," or "Rockaby") in *Rockaby and Other Short Pieces,* SF 18643, NSHS 27753

"Ping," an abstraction by Samuel Beckett, 1f or 1m, perhaps DPS (?), NSHS

"Pumpkin Thief, The," a puppet play for children by Denise Anton Wright, 1 puppeteer presenting 2 characters, (published with and can pair with "The Back-to-School Blues," "The Boy Who Cried Wolf," "The Case of the Disappearing Books," "Dragon Draws a Picture," "The Easter Egg Hunt," "Easter Rabbit's Basket," "Elephant's Sneeze," "Fox Learns a Lesson," "The Halloween Costume," "The Leprechaun's Gold," "The Lion and the Mouse," "Little Red Riding Hood," "The Monkey and the Crocodile," "The Mysterious Egg," "Santa Cures a Cold," "Take Me to Your Library," "The Three Billy Goats Gruff," "The Town Mouse and the Country Mouse," "Turkey's Thanksgiving Adventure," "Witch Gets Ready," "Witch's Valentine," or "Witch's Winter Kitchen") in Denise Anton Wright's *One-Person Puppet Plays*, illustrated by John Wright (Teacher Idea Press, 1990), ISBN 0-87287-742-6, TIP

R

"Rape, The," a monologue by Franca Rame and Dario Fo, 1f, (published with and can pair with "Alice in Wonderless Land," "An Arab Woman Speaks," "The Bawd—the Christian Democrat Party in Chile," "Bless Me Father for I Have Sinned," "Coming Home," "The

Dancing Mistress: On the Assembly Line," "The Eel-Woman," "Fascism 1922," "I'm Ulrike—Screaming," "It Happened Tomorrow," "Mamma Togni," "Medea," "Michele Lu Lanzone," "A Mother," "Nada Pasini," "Rise and Shine," "The Same Old Story," "The Whore in the Madhouse," or "A Woman Alone") in Franca Rame and Dario Fo's *A Woman Alone & Other Plays* (London: Methuen, 1991), ISBN 0-413-64030-2

"Reginka's Lesson," a drama in ten scenes by Linda Aronson, 1f, in Linda Aronson's *Reginka's Lesson* (Paddington, New South Wales, Australia: The Currency Press Pty., Ltd., 1989), ISBN 0-86819-254-6, CPP

"Rise and Shine," a monologue by Franca Rame and Dario Fo, 1f, (published with and can pair with "Alice in Wonderless Land," "An Arab Woman Speaks," "The Bawd—the Christian Democrat Party in Chile," "Bless Me Father for I Have Sinned," "Coming Home," "The Dancing Mistress: On the Assembly Line," "The Eel-Woman," "Fascism 1922," "I'm Ulrike—Screaming," "It Happened Tomorrow," "Mamma Togni," "Medea," "Michele Lu Lanzone," "A Mother," "Nada Pasini," "The Rape," "The Same Old Story," "The Whore in the Madhouse," or "A Woman Alone") in Franca Rame and Dario Fo's *A Woman Alone & Other Plays* (London: Methuen, 1991), ISBN 0-413-64030-2

"Rockaby," a drama by Samuel Beckett, 1f (+ own recorded voice), ([see next item] published with and can pair with "Act Without Words I," "Act Without Words II," "Breath," "Cascando," "Catastrophe," "Come and Go," "Eh Joe," "Embers," "Footfalls," "Ghost Trio," "Krapp's Last Tape," "Not I," "Ohio Impromptu," "A Piece of Monologue," "Play," "Quad," "Rough for Radio I," "Rough for Radio II," "Rough for Theatre I," "Rough for Theatre II," "That Time," or "Words and Music") in *Collected Shorter Plays*, ISBN 0-394-53850-1, ISBN 0-394-62098-4

"Rockaby," a drama by Samuel Beckett, 1f (+ own recorded voice), ([see previous item] *also* published with and can pair with "All Strange Away," "Ohio Impromptu," or "A Piece of Monologue") in *Rockaby and Other Short Pieces* SF 20627, NSHS 27753

"Rosary," (see p. 237) a comedy by Jean-Claude Van Itallie, 1f, (published with and can pair with "Eat Cake," "Girl and the Soldier," "Harold," "Photographs: Mary and Howard," or "Thoughts on the Instant of Greeting a Friend on the Street") in *Seven Short and Very Short Plays* DPS 4726, NSHS pb65

"Rupert's Birthday," a dramatic monologue by Ken Jenkins, 1f, (published with and can pair with "Cemetery Man," "Chug," or "An Educated Lady") in *"Rupert's Birthday" and Other Monologues* DPS 3912

One-Female Plays, continued

S

"Santa Cures a Cold," a puppet play in 3 scenes for children by Denise Anton Wright, 1 puppeteer presenting 4 characters, (published with and can pair with "The Back-to-School Blues," "The Boy Who Cried Wolf," "The Case of the Disappearing Books," "Dragon Draws a Picture," "The Easter Egg Hunt," "Easter Rabbit's Basket," "Elephant's Sneeze," "Fox Learns a Lesson," "The Halloween Costume," "The Leprechaun's Gold," "The Lion and the Mouse," "Little Red Riding Hood," "The Monkey and the Crocodile," "The Mysterious Egg," "The Pumpkin Thief," "Take Me to Your Library," "The Three Billy Goats Gruff," "The Town Mouse and the Country Mouse," "Turkey's Thanksgiving Adventure," "Witch Gets Ready," "Witch's Valentine," or "Witch's Winter Kitchen") in Denise Anton Wright's *One-Person Puppet Plays*, illustrated by John Wright (Teacher Idea Press, 1990), ISBN 0-87287-742-6, TIP

"Same Old Story, The," a monologue by Franca Rame and Dario Fo, 1f, (published with and can pair with "Alice in Wonderless Land," "An Arab Woman Speaks," "The Bawd the Christian Democrat Party in Chile," "Bless Me Father for I Have Sinned," "Coming Home," "The Dancing Mistress: On the Assembly Line," "The Eel-Woman," "Fascism 1922," "I'm Ulrike—Screaming," "It Happened Tomorrow," "Mamma Togni," "Medea," "Michele Lu Lanzone," "A Mother," "Nada Pasini," "The Rape," "Rise and Shine," "The Whore in the Madhouse," or "A Woman Alone") in Franca Rame and Dario Fo's *A Woman Alone & Other Plays* (London: Methuen, 1991), ISBN 0-413-64030-2

"Sara Hubbard," a comedy by Cliff Harville, 1f, (published with and can pair with "George L. Smith," "Hand Me My Afghan," or "A Silent Catastrophe") in Cliff Harville's *Sunsets*, (New York: Samuel French, Inc., 1989), ISBN 0-573-62522-0, SF 21387

"See Bob Run," a drama by Daniel MacIvor, 1f, (published with and can pair with "Wild Abandon: The Study of Steve") in Daniel MacIvor's *See Bob Run & Wild Abandon* (Toronto, Ontario, Canada: Playwrights Canada Press, 1990), ISBN 0-88754-486-X

"Saturday at the Commodore," a Scottish drama by Rona Munro, 1f, (published with and can pair with "The Letter-Box") in *Scot-Free: New Scottish Plays*, edited by A. Cameron (London: Nick Hern Books, 1990), ISBN 1-85459-017-0

"Shasta Rue," a bare-stage drama by Jane Martin, 1f (black), in *What Mama Don't Know,* SF 21675

"She Does Her Christmas Shopping Early," a comic monologue by M. A. Chaffee, 1f, BP

"Sister Son/ji," a drama by Sonia Sanchez, 1f, in *Wines in the Wilderness: Plays by African American Women from the Harlem Renaissance to the Present*, edited and compiled by Elizabeth Brown-Guillory (Westport, Connecticut: Praeger Publishers, 1990), ISBN 0-275-93567-1

"Soldiering On," a half-hour monologue by Alan Bennett, 1f, SF

"Sound of Silence, The" [*"Le Bel indifférent"*], a drama by Jean Cocteau, translated by Anthony Wood, 1f (+ silent male), in Jean Cocteau's *The Sound of Silence* (London: Samuel French, Inc., 1992), ISBN 0-573-12266-0, SF

"Sudden Acceleration," a bare-stage dramatic monologue by Don Nigro, 1f, in *Winchelsea Dround and Other Plays: Nine Monologue Plays* (New York: Samuel French, Inc., 1992), ISBN 0-573-62598-0, SF 21414

"Sunset Freeway," a comedy by Jean-Claude Van Itallie, 1f, (published with and can pair with "Final Orders," or "Bag Lady") in *Early Warnings,* DPS 1767

T

"Take Me to Your Library," a puppet play for children by Denise Anton Wright, 1 puppeteer presenting 2 characters, (published with and can pair with "The Back-to-School Blues," "The Boy Who Cried Wolf," "The Case of the Disappearing Books," "Dragon Draws a Picture," "The Easter Egg Hunt," "Easter Rabbit's Basket," "Elephant's Sneeze," "Fox Learns a Lesson," "The Halloween Costume," "The Leprechaun's Gold," "The Lion and the Mouse," "Little Red Riding Hood," "The Monkey and the Crocodile," "The Mysterious Egg," "The Pumpkin Thief," "Santa Cures a Cold," "The Three Billy Goats Gruff," "The Town Mouse and the Country Mouse," "Turkey's Thanksgiving Adventure," "Witch Gets Ready," "Witch's Valentine," or "Witch's Winter Kitchen") in Denise Anton Wright's *One-Person Puppet Plays*, illustrated by John Wright (Teacher Idea Press, 1990), ISBN 0-87287-742-6, TIP

"Three Billy Goats Gruff, The," a puppet play for children by Denise Anton Wright, 1 puppeteer presenting 4 characters, (published with and can pair with "The Back-to-School Blues," "The Boy Who Cried Wolf," "The Case of the Disappearing Books," "Dragon Draws a Picture," "The Easter Egg Hunt," "Easter Rabbit's Basket," "Elephant's Sneeze," "Fox Learns a Lesson," "The Halloween Costume," "The Leprechaun's Gold," "The Lion and the Mouse," "Little Red Riding Hood," "The Monkey and the Crocodile," "The Mysterious Egg," "The Pumpkin Thief," "Santa Cures a Cold," "Take Me to Your Library," "The Town Mouse and the Country Mouse," "Turkey's Thanksgiving Adventure," "Witch Gets

Ready," "Witch's Valentine," or "Witch's Winter Kitchen") in Denise Anton Wright's *One-Person Puppet Plays*, illustrated by John Wright (Teacher Idea Press, 1990), ISBN 0-87287-742-6, TIP

"Thursday Is My Day for Cleaning," (see p. 251) a comedy by Jordan Crittenden, 1f, SF 22692, NSHS

"Tophat," an expressionistic satire by Paul Carter Harrison, 1f (+ extras), in *New Plays for the Black Theatre*, edited by Woodie King, Jr. (Chicago: Third World Press, 1989), ISBN 0-88378-124-7

"Town Mouse and the Country Mouse, The," a puppet play in 2 scenes for children by Denise Anton Wright, 1 puppeteer presenting 4 characters, (published with and can pair with "The Back-to-School Blues," "The Boy Who Cried Wolf," "The Case of the Disappearing Books," "Dragon Draws a Picture," "The Easter Egg Hunt," "Easter Rabbit's Basket," "Elephant's Sneeze," "Fox Learns a Lesson," "The Halloween Costume," "The Leprechaun's Gold," "The Lion and the Mouse," "Little Red Riding Hood," "The Monkey and the Crocodile," "The Mysterious Egg," "The Pumpkin Thief," "Santa Cures a Cold," "Take Me to Your Library," "The Three Billy Goats Gruff," "Turkey's Thanksgiving Adventure," "Witch Gets Ready," "Witch's Valentine," or "Witch's Winter Kitchen") in Denise Anton Wright's *One-Person Puppet Plays*, illustrated by John Wright (Teacher Idea Press, 1990), ISBN 0-87287-742-6, TIP

"Travellin' Show," a drama by Jane Martin, 1m or 1f, SF 22752

"Turkey's Thanksgiving Adventure," a puppet play for children by Denise Anton Wright, 1 puppeteer presenting 2 characters, (published with and can pair with "The Back-to-School Blues," "The Boy Who Cried Wolf," "The Case of the Disappearing Books," "Dragon Draws a Picture," "The Easter Egg Hunt," "Easter Rabbit's Basket," "Elephant's Sneeze," "Fox Learns a Lesson," "The Halloween Costume," "The Leprechaun's Gold," "The Lion and the Mouse," "Little Red Riding Hood," "The Monkey and the Crocodile," "The Mysterious Egg," "The Pumpkin Thief," "Santa Cures a Cold," "Take Me to Your Library," "The Three Billy Goats Gruff," "The Town Mouse and the Country Mouse," "Witch Gets Ready," "Witch's Valentine," or "Witch's Winter Kitchen") in Denise Anton Wright's *One-Person Puppet Plays*, illustrated by John Wright (Teacher Idea Press, 1990), ISBN 0-87287-742-6, TIP

U

"Under Observation," a comedy by Howard Korder, 1f, in

The Pope's Nose, DPS 3677

V

"*Voix humaine, La* " ["**The Human Voice**"], a drama by Jean Cocteau, 1f, in Jean Cocteau's *The Human Voice* (London: Samuel French, Inc., 1992), ISBN 0-573-03381-1, SF

W

"Whom Do I Have the Honour of Addressing?" a radio drama by Peter Shaffer, 1f, (London: Andre Deutsch, Ltd., 1990) ISBN 0-233-98615-4

"Whore in the Madhouse, The," a monologue by Franca Rame and Dario Fo, 1f, (published with and can pair with "Alice in Wonderless Land," "An Arab Woman Speaks," "The Bawd—the Christian Democrat Party in Chile," "Bless Me Father for I Have Sinned," "Coming Home," "The Dancing Mistress: On the Assembly Line," "The Eel-Woman," "Fascism 1922," "I'm Ulrike—Screaming," "It Happened Tomorrow," "Mamma Togni," "Medea," "Michele Lu Lanzone," "A Mother," "Nada Pasini," "The Rape," "Rise and Shine," "The Same Old Story," or "A Woman Alone") in Franca Rame and Dario Fo's *A Woman Alone & Other Plays* (London: Methuen, 1991), ISBN 0-413-64030-2

"Winchelsea Dround," a bare-stage dramatic monologue by Don Nigro, 1f, in Don Nigro's *Winchelsea Dround and Other Plays: Nine Monologue Plays* (New York: Samuel French, Inc., 1992), ISBN 0-573-62598-0, SF 25226

"Witch Gets Ready," a puppet play for children by Denise Anton Wright, 1 puppeteer presenting 4 characters, in Denise Anton Wright's *One-Person Puppet Plays*, illustrated by John Wright (Teacher Idea Press, 1990), ISBN 0-87287-742-6, TIP

"Witch's Valentine," a puppet play in 2 scenes for children by Denise Anton Wright, 1 puppeteer presenting 4 characters, in Denise Anton Wright's *One-Person Puppet Plays*, illustrated by John Wright (Teacher Idea Press, 1990), ISBN 0-87287-742-6, TIP

"Witch's Winter Kitchen," a puppet play for children by Denise Anton Wright, 1 puppeteer presenting 2 characters, in Denise Anton Wright's *One-Person Puppet Plays*, illustrated by John Wright (Teacher Idea Press, 1990), ISBN 0-87287-742-6, TIP

"Woman Alone, A," a monologue by Franca Rame and Dario Fo, 1f, in Franca Rame and Dario Fo's *A Woman Alone & Other Plays* (London: Methuen, 1991), ISBN 0-413-64030-2

One-Male-One-Female Plays

A

"Abortive," a drama by Caryl Churchill, 1m1f, (published with and can pair with "Not Not Not Not Not Enough Oxygen," "Schreber's Nervous Illness," "Seagulls," or "Three More Sleepless Nights") in *Churchill: Shorts [Short Plays by Caryl Churchill]* SF 3887, NSHS, ISBN 1-85459-085-5

"Acrobats," a comedy by Israel Horovitz, 1m1f, DPS 615

"Act Without Words II," a mime by Samuel Beckett, 1m1f or 2m or 2f, (published with and can pair with "Act Without Words I," "Breath," "Cascando," "Catastrophe," "Come and Go," "Eh Joe," "Embers," "Footfalls," "Ghost Trio," "Krapp's Last Tape," "Not I," "Ohio Impromptu," "A Piece of Monologue," "Play," "Quad," "Rockaby," "Rough for Radio I," "Rough for Radio II," "Rough for Theatre I," "Rough for Theatre II," "That Time," or "Words and Music") in *Collected Shorter Plays,* ISBN 0-394-53850-1, ISBN 0-394-62098-4

"Adjustment, The," a farce by Albert Bermel, 1m1f, in *Six One-Act Farces,* SF 3615

"Admit One," a comedy by Elyse Nass, 1m1f, (published with and can pair with "The Cat Connection" or "Second Chance") in Elyse Nass' *Three One-Act Plays About the Elderly* (New York: Samuel French, Inc., 1990) ISBN 0-573-69205-X, SF 3697, NSHS pb8161

"Affidavit, The," a brief drama by Janet S. Tiger, 1m1f, (published with and can pair with "Advice to a New Actor," "The American Way," "Anniversary," "Auld Lang Syne, or I'll Bet You Think This Play Is About You," "Bug Swatter," "Checkers," "Coming for a Visit," "Dalmation," "Dog Eat Dog," "Drowned Out," "Fireworks," "Interview," "Jumping," "Money," "One Beer Too Many," "Phonecall from Sunkist," "Potato Girl," "Property of the Dallas Cowboys," "The Split Decision," "Valley Forgery," "Watermelon Boats," or "Widows") in *One-Act Plays for Acting Students,* MPL, ISBN 0-916260-47-X

"Afraid to Fight," a comedy by Courteline translated by Albert Bermel, 1m1f, in *The Plays of Courteline,* SF 3607

"After a Thousand Victories," a farce by Arnold Powell, 1m1f, AR, NSHS

"After the Applebox," a drama by Pat Schneider, 1m1f, in *From Valley Playwrights Theatre*, vol. 2, edited by Susan Vick, introduction by Richard Trousdale (Amherst, Massachusetts: Playwrights Press, 1989), ISBN 0-9617282-3

"After the Fact," (see p. 179), a comedy-drama by Jeffrey Sweet, 1m1f, ISBN 0-573-62028-8, SF 3608, NSHS 27521, PSP

"After You," a ten-minute play (genre?) by Steven Dietz, 1m1f, SF

"Agreement, The," a drama by Douglas Taylor, 1m1f, DPS 640, NSHS pb7788

"All My Pretty Little Ones," a play (genre?) by John Donovan 1m1f, cited in *The Best Plays of 1963-1964*, edited by Henry Hewes (New York City: Dodd, Mead & Company, 1964)

"American Modern," a drama by Joanna M. Glass, 1m1f, (published with and can pair with "Canadian Gothic") DPS 1230, NSHS pb8144

"Amicable Parting," a fifteen-minute sketch by George S. Kaufman and Leueen MacGrath, 1m1f (+dog), DPS 755

"Angel on the Train," a comedy by Jules Tasca, 1m1f, in *The God's Honest, An Evening of Lies,* SF 3074

"Anniversary," a brief comedy by Conrad Bishop, 1m1f, (published with and can pair with "Advice to a New Actor," "The Affidavit," "The American Way," "Auld Lang Syne, or I'll Bet You Think This Play Is About You," "Bug Swatter," "Checkers," "Coming for a Visit," "Dalmation," "Dog Eat Dog," "Drowned Out," "Fireworks," "Interview," "Jumping," "Money," "One Beer Too Many," "Phonecall from Sunkist," "Potato Girl," "Property of the Dallas Cowboys," "The Split Decision," "Valley Forgery," "Watermelon Boats," or "Widows") in *One-Act Plays for Acting Students,* MPL, ISBN 0-916260-47-X

"Applicant," a revue sketch by Harold Pinter, 1m1f, (published with and can pair with "The Black and White," "Interview ," "Last to Go," "That's All," "That's Your Trouble," or "Trouble in the Works") in *Revue Sketches*, DPS 1765, NSHS 27487

"Asleep on the Wind," a comedy by Ellen Byron, 1m1f, (published with and can pair with "Graceland") DPS 2188

"At a Beetle's Pace," a drama by Louis E. Catron, 1m1f, HDS, NSHS pb7729

"At Home," a comedy by Conrad Bromberg, 1m1f, (published with and can pair with "Actors") DPS 625, NSHS pb104, NSHS pb116, NSHS pb117

"At Home," first act of a comedy by Michael Weller, 1m1f, in *Split,* SF 3668

"At the Sign of the Cleft Heart," a fantasy by Theodosia Garrison, 1m1f, NSHS 19988

"Auld Lang Syne, or I'll Bet You Think This Play Is About

You," a brief comedy by Beverly Creasey, 1m1f, (published with and can pair with "Advice to a New Actor," "The Affidavit," "The American Way," "Anniversary," "Bug Swatter," "Checkers," "Coming for a Visit," "Dalmation," "Dog Eat Dog," "Drowned Out," "Fireworks," "Interview," "Jumping," "Money," "One Beer Too Many," "Phonecall from Sunkist," "Potato Girl," "Property of the Dallas Cowboys," "The Split Decision," "Valley Forgery," "Watermelon Boats," or "Widows") in *One-Act Plays for Acting Students,* MPL, ISBN 0-916260-47-X

"Autumn Drive," a bare-stage short drama by Roger Cornish, 1m1f, (published with and can play with "The Close-Down Set-Up of Emma," "Frosting" "Meals on Wheels," "Mrs. Lazar's Caller," or "Running Away from Home,") in *Short Plays for the Long Living,* BP, SF 3664, NSHS pb6043, NSHS pb7838

"Awful People Are Coming Over So We Must Be Pretending to Be Hard at Work and Hope That They Will Go Away," a comedy by H. M. Koutoukas, 1m1f, (published with and can pair with "Only a Countess May Dance When She's Crazy") in H. M. Koutoukas' *When Lightning Strikes Twice* (New York: Samuel French, Inc., 1991), ISBN 0-573-62574-3, SF 3151

B

"Babies, The," a drama by Anna Lippman, 1m1f, DPC B10, NSHS pb179, NSHS pb6076, NSHS pb6088

"Baggage, The," a comedy by Bertha Moore, 1m1f, BP, NSHS 19988

"Bank Street Breakfast," a bare-stage drama by Robert Patrick, 1m1f, in *One Man, One Woman,* SF 4608

"Bar and Ger," a drama by Geraldine Aron, 1m1f, SF 4609, HDS

"Battling Brinkmires, The," a comedy by Daniel Meltzer, 1m1f, in *The Square Root of Love,* SF 21314

"Bel indifférent, Le" ["The Sound of Silence"], a drama by Jean Cocteau, translated by Anthony Wood, 1m1f, in Jean Cocteau's *The Sound of Silence* (London: Samuel French, Inc., 1992), ISBN 0-573-12266-0, SF

"Betrothal, A," a comedy by Lanford Wilson, 1m1f, DPS 992

"Birdbath," a drama by Leonard Melfi, 1m1f, (published with and can play with "Lunchtime," "Halloween," "Ferryboat," or "The Shirt") in *Encounters: Six One-Act Plays,* SF 271, NSHS 29331, NSHS 16674

"Birth of Jesus, The," a craft cycle drama from "N. towne Plays," 1m1f, HMC, NSHS 29216

"Black and Silver," a comic sketch by Michael Frayn, 1m1f, in *The Two of Us,* SF 4643

"Blonds," a ten-minute play (genre?) by Jon Jory, 1m1f, DPC, NSHS pb149

"Bold Decision," a comedy by Clay Franklin, 1m1f, (published with and can pair with "The Daffy World of Daphne de Witt," "No Sweet Revenge," "Small Victory," "Suddenly Last Friday," or "Western Lament") in *Two for a Happening: A Dramatic Duo in Three Acts, Six One-Act Plays,* SF, NSHS pb8199, NSHS 29203

"Bondage," a drama by David Henry Hwang, 1m1f, DPS 1067

"Bottled-Up Man, The," a drama by John O'Brien, 1m1f, ISBN 0-573-62063-6, SF, NSHS 29205

"Boy Who Ate the Moon, The," a drama by Jane Martin, 1m1f, in *What Mama Don't Know,* SF 4701

"Bread," a ten-minute drama by Andy Backer, 1m1f, (published with and can pair with "Americansaint," "Après Opéra," "'The Asshole Murder Case,'" "Cold Water" "Cover," "Downtown," "The Drummer," "The Duck Pond," "Eating Out," "Electric Roses," "The Field," "4 A.M. (open all night)," "Looking Good," "Love and Peace, Mary Jo," "Loyalties," "Marred Bliss," "Perfect," "The Road to Ruin," "Spades," or "Watermelon Boats") in *25 10-Minute Plays from Actors Theatre of Louisville,* SF 4658, NSHS pb29777, ISBN 0-573-62558-1

"Brief Period of Time, A," a comedy by Don Rifkin, 1m1f, (published with and can pair with "Two Eggs Scrambled Soft") DPS 1127

"Budding Lovers," a comedy by Georges Feydeau, translated by Barnett Shaw, 1m1f, SF, NSHS

"Bug Swatter," a brief comedy by Joel Selmeier, 1m1f, (published with and can pair with "Advice to a New Actor," "The Affidavit," "The American Way," "Anniversary," "Auld Lang Syne, or I'll Bet You Think This Play Is About You," "Checkers," "Coming for a Visit," "Dalmation," "Dog Eat Dog," "Drowned Out," "Fireworks," "Interview," "Jumping," "Money," "One Beer Too Many," "Phonecall from Sunkist," "Potato Girl," "Property of the Dallas Cowboys," "The Split Decision," "Valley Forgery," "Watermelon Boats," or "Widows") in *One-Act Plays for Acting Students,* MPL, ISBN 0-916260-47-X

C

"Cabbie from Calcutta, The," a drama for youth by Robert Mauro, 1m1f, (published with and can pair with "The Audition," "The Day Mother Left Home," "A Death in the Family," "Going Down!" "The Golden Door," "Joan," "My Baby," "My Friend Never Said Goodbye," "The Man in the Box," "The No-Fault Driving School," "The Park Bench," "The Proposal," "Sherlock Holmes:

10 Minutes to Doom," or "Uptown/Downtown") in Robert Mauro's *Two-Character Plays for Student Actors: A Collection of 15 One-Act Plays* (Colorado Springs, Colorado: Meriwether Publishing, Ltd., 1988), ISBN 0-916260-4, MPL

"Camera Obscura," a science-fiction play (genre?) by Robert Patrick, 1m1f, in *Robert Patrick's Cheep Theatricks,* SF 302

"Cascando," a radio play (genre?) by Samuel Beckett, 1m1f or 2m or 2f (+ music), (published with and can pair with "Act Without Words I," "Act Without Words II," "Breath," "Catastrophe," "Come and Go," "Eh Joe," "Embers," "Footfalls," "Ghost Trio," "Krapp's Last Tape," "Not I," "Ohio Impromptu," "A Piece of Monologue," "Play," "Quad," "Rockaby," "Rough for Radio I," "Rough for Radio II," "Rough for Theatre I," "Rough for Theatre II," "That Time," or "Words and Music") in *Collected Shorter Plays,* ISBN 0-394-53850-1, ISBN 0-394-62098-4

"Checkers," a brief comedy by Dale Doerman, 1m1f, (published with and can pair with "Advice to a New Actor," "The Affidavit," "The American Way," "Anniversary," "Auld Lang Syne, or I'll Bet You Think This Play Is About You," "Bug Swatter," "Coming for a Visit," "Dalmation," "Dog Eat Dog," "Drowned Out," "Fireworks," "Interview," "Jumping," "Money," "One Beer Too Many," "Phonecall from Sunkist," "Potato Girl," "Property of the Dallas Cowboys," "The Split Decision," "Valley Forgery," "Watermelon Boats," or "Widows") in *One-Act Plays for Acting Students,* MPL, ISBN 0-916260-47-X

"Chekhov," (see p. 191) a drama by Keith Miles, 1m1f, ISBN 0-573-60049-X, (published with "Dostoevsky") in *Russian Masters,* SF 20091, NSHS pb2511

"Cheesecake," a bare-stage drama by Robert Patrick, 1m1f, in *One Man, One Woman,* SF 5625

"Children of the Southern Pacific," a drama by Eller Martin, 1m1f, DPC C68, NSHS pb169

"Chinamen," a farce by Michael Frayn, 1m1f, in *The Two of Us,* SF 5632

"Chocolate Cake," a children's comedy by Ruth Young, 1m1f (that is, one boy, one girl), (published with and can pair with "Lemonade" or "Peanut Butter and Jelly") in Ruth Young's *Starring Francine & Dave: Three One-Act Plays* (New York: Orchard Books, 1988), ISBN 0-531-05781-X, ISBN 0-531-08381-0, OB

"Civilization and Its Malcontents," a comedy by Stanley Taikeff, 1m1f, in *Off-Off Broadway Festival Plays, 14th Series,* SF 5776

"Clair de Lune," a comedy by Romulus Linney, 1m1f, (published with and can pair with "Can Can," "Gold And

Silver Waltz," or "Yankee Doodle") in *Pops,* DPS 3684, NSHS pb7913

"Clara and the Gambler," a comedy by Jason Milligan, 1m1f, in *Cross Country: Seven More One-Act Plays,"* SF 5582

"Class of '77," a drama by Jason Milligan, 1m1f, in *Cross Country: Seven More One-Act Plays,"* SF 5265

"Cleaning House," a bare-stage drama by Robert Patrick, 1m1f, in *One Man, One Woman,* SF 5664

"Close-Down Set-Up of Emma, The," a bare-stage drama by John Orlock, 1m1f, (published with and can play with "Autumn Drive," "Frosting," "Meals on Wheels," "Mrs. Lazar's Caller," or "Running Away from Home") in *Short Plays for the Long Living* BP, SF 5672, NSHS pb6043, NSHS pb7838

"Colette in Love," a playlet by Lavonne Mueller, 1m1f, SF

"Come Next Tuesday," a drama by Frank D. Gilroy, 1m1f, (published with and can play with "Present Tense," "So Please Be Kind," or "'Twas Brillig") in Frank D. Gilroy's *Present Tense* (New York: Samuel French, Inc., 1973), SF 5693, NSHS pb5486, NSHS pb6048, NSHS pb6050, NSHS pb8169

"Coming for a Visit," a brief drama by Ben Josephson, 1m1f, published with and can pair with "Advice to a New Actor," "The Affidavit," "The American Way," "Anniversary," "Auld Lang Syne, or I'll Bet You Think This Play Is About You," "Bug Swatter," "Checkers," "Dalmation," "Dog Eat Dog," "Drowned Out," "Fireworks," "Interview," "Jumping," "Money," "One Beer Too Many," "Phonecall from Sunkist," "Potato Girl," "Property of the Dallas Cowboys," "The Split Decision," "Valley Forgery," "Watermelon Boats," or "Widows" in *One-Act Plays for Acting Students,* MPL, ISBN 0-916260-47-X

"Comings and Goings," a bare-stage nonliteral exercise by Megan Terry, 1m1f, SF 5698

"Companions of the Fire," a comedy by Ali Wadud, 1m1f, DPS 1410

"Confessions," a comedy by A. Conan Doyle, 1m1f, BP, NSHS 19988

"Consequences of Goosing, The," a comedy by Murray Schisgal, 1m1f, (published with and can pair with "How We Reached an Impasse on Nuclear Energy" or "74 Georgia Avenue") in *Man Dangling,* DPS 3032

"Conversations with the Spanish Lady," a fantasy-drama by Robert Schenkkan, 1m1f, in *Four One-Act Plays by Robert Schenkkan: Conversations with the Spanish Lady/ Lunch Break/Intermission/The Survivalist,* DPS 3972, NSHS pb8022

"Cornered," a bare-stage comedy by Robert Patrick, 1m1f, in *Robert Patrick's Cheep Theatricks,* SF 5713

"**Counting the Ways,**" a vaudeville (series of blackout sketches) by Edward Albee, 1m1f, (published with "Listening") DPS 1440

D

"**Daddy's Home,**" a drama by Ivan Menchell, 1m1f, in *Off-Off Broadway Festival Plays, 11th Series*, SF 6705, NSHS pb7494, 27508

"**Daffy World of Daphne de Witt, The,**" a comedy by Clay Franklin, 1m1f, (published with and can pair with "Bold Decision," "No Sweet Revenge," "Small Victory," "Suddenly Last Friday," or "Western Lament") in *Two for a Happening: A Dramatic Duo in Three Acts, Six One-Act Plays*, SF, NSHS pb8199, NSHS 29203

"**Damn You, Scarlett O'Hara,**" a comedy by John Donovan, 1m1f, cited in *The Best Plays of 1963-1964*, edited by Henry Hewes

"**Dark, The**" ["**Romance Ranch: The Dark**"], a comedy by Jules Tasca, 1m1f, (published with "Data Entry," "The Fantasy Bond," "Finding the Love of Your Life," "Inflatable You," "The Man in Blue," "Penance," or "Snocky,") in Jules Tasca's *Romance Ranch* (New York: Samuel French, Inc., 1991), ISBN 0-573-62434-8, SF 5944

"**Dark Corners,**" a drama by Stanley Koven, 1m1f, DPS, cited in *The Best Plays of 1963-1964*, edited by Henry Hewes

"**Dark Pony,**" a bare-stage drama by David Mamet, 1m1f, in *Reunion: Three Plays by David Mamet*, SF 20029

"**Data Entry**" ["**Romance Ranch: Data Entry**"], a comedy by Jules Tasca, 1m1f, (published with "The Dark," "Data Entry," "The Fantasy Bond," "Finding the Love of Your Life," "Inflatable You," "The Man in Blue," "Penance," or "Snocky,") in Jules Tasca's *Romance Ranch* (New York: Samuel French, Inc., 1991), ISBN 0-573-62434-8, SF 5942

"**David and Nancy,**" a comedy by Renée Taylor and Joseph Bologna, 1m1f, in *Bedrooms*, SF 244

"**Day for Surprises, A,**" a comedy by John Guare, 1m1f, (published with and can pair with "Kissing Sweet") DPS 1555, NSHS pb7793

"**Day in the Night of Rose Arden, A,**" a drama by Jules Tasca, 1m1f, (published with and can pair with [Athens:] "Passion" [Engleberg:] "Swiss Miss," [Munich:] "A Side Trip to Dachau," [Paris:] "Escape," [Rome:] "Going to the Catacombs," [Venice:] "The Best Souvenirs," or [Vienna:] "The Stop at the Palace") in Jules Tasca's *Tour di Europa* (New York: Samuel French, Inc.), ISBN 0-573-69222-X, SF 6729, NSHS pb8105

"**Death of Von Horvath, The,**" a drama by Don Nigro, 1m1f, SF 6585

"**Diaries of Adam and Eve, The,**" a royalty-free readers theatre comedy adapted from Mark Twain by Leslie Irene Coger, 1m1f, SFC, NSHS 16373

"**Diary,**" a bare-stage suspense drama by Marcia Ann Shenk, 1m1f, BP, SF 6646, NSHS 29142

"**Diary of Adam and Eve, The,**" a comedy by Marc Bucci from Mark Twain, 1m1f (+ extras), HDS, DPC D15, NSHS pb7755

"**Disneyland on Parade,**" a comedy by Roy London, 1m1f, DPS

"**Do Over,**" a comedy by Frederick Stroppel, 1m1f, in *Off-Off Broadway Festival Plays, 14th Series*, SF 6724

"**Doctor,**" a sketch by David Mamet, 1m1f, (part of "The Blue Hour: City Sketches") in *Short Plays and Monologues*, DPS 3025

"**Domestic Violence,**" a drama by Frederick Stroppel, 1m1f, (published and can pair with "The Mamet Women," "Morning Coffee," "Package Deal," or "Single and Proud") in Frederick Stroppel's *Single and Proud and Other Plays* (New York: Samuel French, Inc.), ISBN 0-573-69411-7, SF 6934, NSHS pb8090

"**Don't Call Me by My Right Name,**" a drama by Ellen Violett from James Purdy, 1m1f, cited in *The Best Plays of 1963-1964*, edited by Henry Hewes

"**Door to Door,**" a drama by Claudia Barnett, 1m1f, in *Dramatics*, 64, no. 7 (March 1993): 24-29. Inquiries regarding performance rights and royalties should be directed to the playwright at 1505 West 3rd Avenue, Apartment 18, Columbus, OH 43212.

"**Dostoevsky,**" a drama by Keith Miles, 1m1f, ISBN 0-573-60049-X, (published with "Chekhov") in *Russian Masters*, SF 20092, NSHS p2511

"**Doublers, The,**" a comedy by Betzie Parker White, 1m1f, SF 6669

"**Dutch Treat,**" a comedy by Peg Lynch, 1m1f, (published with and can pair with "Fishing Hat," "Just a Little Something for Christmas," "To Open, Pry Cover," or "What's That Tune?") in *Ethel and Albert Comedies*, SF 6693 (single play), SF 7645 (anthology), NSHS pb7825 (anthology)

"**Dutchman,**" a drama by LeRoi Jones, 1m1f, SLA, NSHS 15366, NSHS 16374, NSHS 16370

E

"**Eat Cake,**" a drama by Jean-Claude Van Itallie, 1m1f, (published with and can pair with "The Girl and the Soldier," "Harold," "Photographs: Mary and Howard," "Rosary," or "Thoughts on the Instant of Greeting a Friend on the Street") in *Seven Short and Very Short Plays*, DPS 4726, NSHS pb65

"Eh Joe," a television drama by Samuel Beckett, 1m1f, (published with and can pair with "Act Without Words I," "Act Without Words II," "Breath," "Cascando," "Catastrophe," "Come and Go," "Embers," "Footfalls," "Ghost Trio," "Krapp's Last Tape," "Not I," "Ohio Impromptu," "A Piece of Monologue," "Play," "Quad," "Rockaby," "Rough for Radio I," "Rough for Radio II," "Rough for Theatre I," "Rough for Theatre II," "That Time," or "Words and Music") in *Collected Shorter Plays,* ISBN 0-394-53850-1, ISBN 0-394-62098-4

"Elegy for a Lady," a drama by Arthur Miller, 1m1f, (can pair with "Some Kind of a Love Story") DPS 1800

"Empty Space, An," (see p. 200) a drama by Ron Villane, 1m1f, (published with and can pair with "Open Admissions" or "Nothing Immediate") in Double Image Theatre's *Off-Off Broadway Festival Plays, Fourth Series* (New York: Samuel French, Inc., 1983), SF 7613, NSHS 27533, ISBN 0-573-60044-9

"Enchanted Mesa, The," a comic drama by George Maguire, 1m1f, in *Off-Off Broadway Festival Plays, Series 9*, SF 7615, NSHS pb27532

"Encounter," a drama by Ruth Jacobson, 1m1f, DPC E23, NSHS pb187

"End of the Picnic, The," a drama by David Campton, 1m1f, DPC, NSHS pb6082

"Epiphany," a drama by Lewis John Carlino, 1m1f, (published with and can pair with "Snowangel") DPS 1215

"Essentials," a comedy by Pat Rahmann, 1m1f, BP, SF 7644

"Evening Primrose in Ohio," a comedy-drama by Robin Rice Lichtig, 1m1f, BP

"Every Goodbye Ain't Gone," a drama with singing by Bill Harris, 1m1f, (published with and can pair with "Mary Goldstein and the Author") in *New Plays for the Black Theatre*, edited by Woodie King, Jr. (Chicago: Third World Press, 1989), ISBN 0-88378-124-7

"Exeunt O'Brien and Krasnov," a comedy by Hindi Brooks, 1m1f, (published with and can pair with "Jennifer's First Christmas," "Lamentable Affair of the Vicar's Wife," or "A Portrait of Portia") in *An Evening with Eve*, IEC 316-0

"Exit, an Illusion," a symbolic drama by Marita Bonner, 1m1f (+ extras), in *Black Female Playwrights: An Anthology of Plays before 1950*, edited by Kathy A. Perkins (Bloomington, Indiana: Indiana University Press, 1989), ISBN 0-253-34358-5; and in Marita Bonner's *Frye Street & Environs: The Collected Works of Marita Bonner*, edited and introduced by Joyce Flynn and Joyce Occomy Stricklin (Boston: Beacon Press, 1987), ISBN 0-8070-6300-2

F

"Fantasy Bond, The" ["**Romance Ranch: The Fantasy Bond**"], a drama by Jules Tasca, 1m1f, (published with "The Dark," "Data Entry," "Finding the Love of Your Life," "Inflatable You," "The Man in Blue," "Penance," or "Snocky") in Jules Tasca's *Romance Ranch* (New York: Samuel French, Inc., 1991), ISBN 0-573-62434-8, SF 8162

"Father and Son," a drama by Jules Tasca from Guy de Maupassant, 1m1f, (published with and can pair with "The Devil," "Forbidden Fruit," or "The Necklace") in *The Necklace and Other Stories*, SF 15990, NSHS 27500, NSHS pb7917, NSHS pb7919

"Ferryboat," a drama by Anna Marie Barlow, 1m1f, (can pair with "A Limb of Snow" or "The Meeting") DPS 1970

"Ferryboat," a drama by Leonard Melfi, 1m1f, (published with and can play with "Birdbath," "Halloween," "Lunchtime," or "The Shirt") in *Encounters: Six One-Act Plays*, SF 8611, NSHS 29331

"Few Last Words, A," a revue sketch by David Lloyd Crowder, 1m1f, SF, NSHS pb6051

"Fire," a drama by Mario Fratti, 1m1f, in *Races*, SF, NSHS pb8060

"Fireworks," a brief comedy by Megan Terry, 1m1f, (published with and can pair with "Advice to a New Actor," "The Affidavit," "The American Way," "Anniversary," "Auld Lang Syne, or I'll Bet You Think This Play Is About You," "Bug Swatter," "Checkers," "Coming for a Visit," "Dalmation," "Dog Eat Dog," "Drowned Out," "Interview," "Jumping," "Money," "One Beer Too Many," "Phonecall from Sunkist," "Potato Girl," "Property of the Dallas Cowboys," "The Split Decision," "Valley Forgery," "Watermelon Boats," or "Widows") in *One-Act Plays for Acting Students*, MPL, ISBN 0-916260-47-X

"Fisherman and the Flounder, The," a Kabuki and puppet drama for children by Richard Slocum based on a Japanese version of a classic fairy tale, 1m1f (+ extras), (published with and can pair with "The Gemshield Sleeper" or "The Love Song of A. Nellie Goodrock"), in Richard Slocum's *The Gemshield Sleeper and Other Plays for Children* (New York: Samuel French, Inc., 1988), ISBN 0-573-65223-6, SF

"Fishing Hat," a comedy by Peg Lynch, 1m1f, (published with and can pair with "Dutch Treat," "Just a Little Something for Christmas," "To Open, Pry Cover," or "What's That Tune?") in *Ethel and Albert Comedies*, SF 7645 (anthology), SF 8626 (single play), NSHS pb7825

"Flywheel and Anna," a drama by Joseph Pintauro, 1m1f,

(published with and can pair with "Charlie and Vito" or "Uncle Zepp") in *Cacciatore*, DPS 1210

"For Anne," a comedy by Peter Gruen, 1m1f, in *Off-Off Broadway Festival Plays, 15th Series*, SF 8934, NSHS pb8079

"Forbidden Fruit," a comedy by Jules Tasca from Guy de Maupassant, 1m1f, in *Off-Off Broadway Festival Plays, Series 9*, SF 15990, NSHS 27500

"Fortress," a drama by Michael Scanlan, 1m1f (+ extras), in Michael Scanlan's *Fortress* (Boston: Bakers Plays, 1988), BP

"From Okra to Greens: A Different Kinda Love Story," a choreopoem (for Black groups) by, Ntozake Shange, 1m1f (+ dancers), ISBN 0-573-62173-X, SF 4666, NSHS 27531

"Frosting," a bare-stage drama by Roger Cornish, 1m1f, in *Short Plays for the Long Living*, BP, SF 8653, NSHS pb6043, NSHS pb7838

"Frustrations," a comedy by John Patrick, 1m1f, SF

G

"Galway Girl, A," a drama by Geraldine Aron, 1m1f, SF 9605

"Gettin' It Together," a comedy-drama by Richard Wesley, 1m1f, (published with "The Past Is Past") DPS 3595

"Ghost Trio," a bare-stage television play (genre?) by Samuel Beckett, 1m1f (silent male + female voice), in *Ends and Odds*, SF 9634

"Gift of the Magi, The," a Christmas drama by Mindy Starns Clark from O. Henry, 1m1f, ELD

"Gift of the Magi, The," a Christmas musical by Peter Ekstrom from O. Henry, 1m1f (+pianist), SF 9642, NSHS 27516, ISBN 0-553-68132-5

"Gift of the Magi, The," a Christmas drama by Thomas Hischak from O. Henry, 1m1f, DPS

"Gigolo of Jerome Avenue, The," a drama by Richard Morton, 1m1f, DPC, NSHS pb154

"Giles in Love," a comedy by Potocki, translated by Daniel Gerould, 1m1f, (published with and can pair with "The Blind One-Armed Deaf-Mute," "Cassander Supports the Revolution," "Cassander, Man of Letters," "Cassander's Trip to the Indies," "The Shit Merchant," or "The Two Doubles") in *Gallant and Libertine, Divertissements and Parades of 18th Century France*, SF 9693, NSHS pb7927, ISBN 0-933826-49-4

"Girl and the Soldier, The," a drama by Jean-Claude Van Itallie, 1m1f, (published with and can pair with "Eat Cake," "Harold," "Photographs: Mary and Howard," "Rosary," or "Thoughts on the Instant of Greeting a Friend on the Street") in *Seven Short and Very Short Plays*, DPS 4726, NSHS pb65

"Girl Who Loved the Beatles, The," a comedy by D. B. Gilles, 1m1f, DPS 2130

"Going Down!" a drama for youth by Robert Mauro, 1m1f, (published with and can pair with "The Audition," "The Cabbie from Calcutta," "The Day Mother Left Home," "A Death in the Family," "The Golden Door," "Joan," "The Man in the Box," "My Baby," "My Friend Never Said Goodbye," "The No-Fault Driving School," "The Park Bench," "The Proposal," "Sherlock Holmes: 10 Minutes to Doom," or "Uptown/Downtown") in Robert Mauro's *Two-Character Plays for Student Actors: A Collection of 15 One-Act Plays* (Colorado Springs, Colorado: Meriwether Publishing, Ltd., 1988), ISBN 0-916260-4, MPL

"Goldberg Street," a drama by David Mamet, 1m1f, in *Three Jewish Plays* and in *A Collection of Dramatic Sketches and Monologues*, SF 9141

"Golden Fleece, The," a bare-stage comedy by A. R. Gurney, Jr., 1m1f, SF 488, NSHS pb4241

"Good Time, A," a comedy by Ernest Thompson, 1m1f, (published with and can pair with "The Constituent" or "Twinkle, Twinkle") in *Answers*, DPS 810

"Good Time for a Change, A," a comedy by Daniel Meltzer, 1m1f, in *The Square Root of Love*, SF 21314

"Grave Encounter, A," a comedy by Gene Ruffini, 1m1f, in *Off-Off Broadway Festival Plays, 13th Series*, SF 9616, NSHS pb8083

"Guernica," a drama by Fernando Arrabal, 1m1f, in *Guernica and Other Plays by Arrabal*, SF 9679

H

"Halloween," a drama by Leonard Melfi, 1m1f, (published with and can play with "Ferryboat," "Halloween," "Lunchtime," or "The Shirt") in *Encounters: Six One-Act Plays*, SF 10602, NSHS 29331

"Happy Birthday, Girl," a comedy by Molly Ann Mullin, 1m1f, BP, SF

"Harold," a drama by Jean-Claude Van Itallie, 1m1f, (published with and can pair with "Eat Cake," "The Girl and the Soldier," "Photographs: Mary and Howard," "Rosary," or "Thoughts on the Instant of Greeting a Friend on the Street") in *Seven Short and Very Short Plays*, DPS 4726, NSHS pb65

"Heatstroke," a drama by James Purdy, 1m1f, in *Antæus: Plays in One Act*, edited by Daniel Halpern, No. 66 (Spring 1991), ISBN 0-88001-268-4, ANT

"Her Voice," a drama by Mario Fratti, 1m1f, (published with "The Piggy Bank") SF 10077, NSHS

"Here We Are," (see p. 206) a comedy by Dorothy Parker, 1m1f, variously published in Modern Library, possibly SF (?), which controls Dorothy Parker's *Ladies of the Corridor*, NSHS pb4019, NSHS 14824, NSHS 20483, NSHS 21389, NSHS 21514, NSHS 21776

"Hero, The," a comic mime by Arthur Kopit, 1m1f, (published with and can pair with "The Conquest of Everest," "The Questioning of Nick," or "Sing to Me Through Open Windows") in *The Day the Whores Came Out to Play Tennis and Other Plays*, SF 10636, NSHS pb7930, ISBN 0-374-52233-2

"High Hopes," a comedy by Susan C. Hunter, 1m1f, AR

"Home Free," a drama by Lanford Wilson, 1m1f, DPS 205, NSHS

"Hopscotch," a drama by Israel Horovitz, 1m1f, (published with and can pair with "The 75th"; also can pair with "Spared" or "Stage Directions") in *The Quannapowitt Quartet*, DPS 2400, SF 990, NSHS pb6068

"How We Reached an Impasse on Nuclear Energy," a comedy by Murray Schisgal, 1m1f, (published with and can pair with "The Consequences of Goosing" or "74 Georgia Avenue") in *Man Dangling*, DPS 3032

"Hunter and the Bird, The," a bare-stage absurdist comic fantasy by Jean-Claude van Itallie, 1m1f, (published with and can pair with "I'm Really Here" or "War") in *Five Short Plays*, DPS 4725, NSHS pb7878

I

"I Bring You Flowers," a drama by William Lang, 1m1f, BP, NSHS 29144

"I Can't Imagine Tomorrow," a drama by Tennessee Williams, 1m1f, DPS 290

"I Can't Remember Anything," a drama by Arthur Miller, 1m1f, (published with and can pair with "Clara") in *Danger: Memory!: Two Plays* (New York: Dramatists Play Service, Inc., 1987), DPS 1526, NSHS pb7869

"I'm Herbert," a comedy by Robert Anderson, 1m1f, DPS, NSHS 29201, NSHS 28438, NSHS 16671

"I'm Really Here," comedy by Jean-Claude van Itallie, 1m1f, (published with and can pair with "The Hunter and the Bird" or "War") in *Five Short Plays*, DPS 4725, NSHS pb7878

"If You Were My Wife I'd Shoot Myself," a comedy by Elinor Jones, 1m1f, in *6:15 on the 104/If You Were My Wife I'd Shoot Myself/Under Control,* DPS 4121, NSHS pb7892

"Ijapa, the Tortoise: The Bush Spirits," a children's comedy by Barbara Winther based on a Nigerian folktale, 1m1f or 2m or 2f, (published with and can play with "Anansi, the African Spider: How Anansi Brought the Stories Down," "Anansi, the African Spider: Tall-Tale Man," or "Two Dilemma Tales: The Snore or the Song") in Barbara Winther's *Plays from African Tales: One-Act, Royalty-Free Dramatizations for Young People, from Stories and Folktales of Africa* (Boston: Plays, Inc., 1992), ISBN 0-8238-0296-5, PI

"Ikke, Ikke, Nye, Nye, Nye," a farce by Lanford Wilson, 1m1f, (published with and can pair with "The Great Nebula in Orion") DPS 1905

"Imagine," a comedy by Kevin Corrigan, 1m1f, in *Sparks in the Park, and Other Prize-Winning Plays: From the 1987 and 1988 Young Playwrights Festivals: Produced by The Foundation of the Dramatists Guild*, edited by Wendy Lamb (New York: Dell Publishing Company, Inc., 1989), ISBN 0-440-20415-1

"Implausible Clause, An," a comedy by Nikki Harmon, 1m1f, DPC I47

"In Old Vermont," a sketch by David Mamet, 1m1f, (part of "The Blue Hour: City Sketches") in *Short Plays and Monologues*, DPS 3025

"Interrogation, The," a ten-minute play (genre?) by Murphy Guyer, 1m1f, SF

"Interview," a brief comedy by Conrad Bishop, 1m1f, (published with and can pair with "Advice to a New Actor," "The Affidavit," "The American Way," "Anniversary," "Auld Lang Syne, or I'll Bet You Think This Play Is About You," "Bug Swatter," "Checkers," "Coming for a Visit," "Dalmation," "Dog Eat Dog," "Drowned Out," "Fireworks," "Jumping," "Money," "One Beer Too Many," "Phonecall from Sunkist," "Potato Girl," "Property of the Dallas Cowboys," "The Split Decision," "Valley Forgery," "Watermelon Boats," or "Widows") in *One-Act Plays for Acting Students*, MPL, ISBN 0-916260-47-X

"Interview," a brief dramatic sketch by Joanna A. Kraus and Greer Woodward, 1m1f, in *One-Act Plays for Acting Students*, MPL, ISBN 0-916260-47-X

"Interview with the Sphinx, An," a drama by Jack Matthews, 1m1f, DPC I48

"It Sometimes Happens," a comedy by an anonymous author, 1m1f, BP, NSHS 19988

"It's a Sin to Tell a Lie," a comedy by Jason Miller, 1m1f, (published with and can pair with "Lou Gehrig Did Not Die of Cancer") DPS 3162

"It's a Small World," a comedy by Roy London, 1m1f, (published with and can pair with "Meet Me in Disneyland" or "Disneyland on Parade") in *Disneyland on Parade*, DPS 1672

"It's Called the Sugar Plum," a satire by Israel Horovitz, 1m1f, (can pair with "The Indian Wants the Bronx") DPS 2585

J

"Jennifer's First Christmas," a comedy-drama by Ev Miller, 1m1f, (published with and can pair with "Exeunt O'Brien and Krasnov," "Lamentable Affair of the Vicar's Wife," or "A Portrait of Portia") in *An Evening with Eve,* IEC 316-0

"Jewish Wife, The," (see p. 209) a drama by Bertolt Brecht translated into English by Eric Bentley, 1m1f, BP, in *The Jewish Wife and Other Short Plays,* SF 604, NSHS 29533

"Joan," a drama for youth by Robert Mauro, 1m1f, (published with and can pair with "The Audition," "The Cabbie from Calcutta," "The Day Mother Left Home," "A Death in the Family," "Going Down!" "The Golden Door," "The Man in the Box," "My Baby," "My Friend Never Said Goodbye," "The No-Fault Driving School," "The Park Bench," "The Proposal," "Sherlock Holmes: 10 Minutes to Doom," or "Uptown/Downtown") in Robert Mauro's *Two-Character Plays for Student Actors: A Collection of 15 One-Act Plays* (Colorado Springs, Colorado: Meriwether Publishing, Ltd., 1988), ISBN 0-916260-4, MPL

"Jumping," a brief comedy by William Borden, 1m1f, (published with and can pair with "Advice to a New Actor," "The Affidavit," "The American Way," "Anniversary," "Auld Lang Syne, or I'll Bet You Think This Play Is About You," "Bug Swatter," "Checkers," "Coming for a Visit," "Dalmation," "Dog Eat Dog," "Drowned Out," "Fireworks," "Interview," "Money," "One Beer Too Many," "Phonecall from Sunkist," "Potato Girl," "Property of the Dallas Cowboys," "The Split Decision," "Valley Forgery," "Watermelon Boats," or "Widows") in *One-Act Plays for Acting Students,* MPL, ISBN 0-916260-47-X

L

"L. A.," a drama by Donald Margulies, 1m1f, in *"Pitching to the Star" and Other Short Plays,* DPS 3662

"Labor Pains," a comedy by Michele Palermo, 1m1f, (published with and can pair with "A New York Minute") in Michele Palermo's *The Other Half* (New York: Samuel French, Inc., 1992), ISBN 0-573-62268-X, SF 13866

"Lady of Fadima, The," a drama by Edward Allan Baker, 1m1f, DPS

"Landscape," a comedy by Harold Pinter, 1m1f, SF, NSHS 27487

"Landscape with Waitress," a comedy by Robert Pine, 1m1f, SF 14619

"Last Laugh, The," a drama by Beverly Mills, 1m1f, IEC, NSHS pb96

"Last Word, The," a comedy by James Broughton, 1m1f, BP, SF, NSHS pb5484

"Leapyear," a comedy by Allan Curtis, 1m1f, (published with and can pair with "A Very Black Comedy Indeed") in *Comedy Tonight: Three Award Winning One Acters* (Ashgrove, Queensland, Australia: Playlab Press, 1989), ISBN 0-908156-37-5

"Lemonade," a children's comedy by Ruth Young, 1m1f (that is, one boy, one girl), (published with and can pair with "Chocolate Cake" or "Peanut Butter and Jelly") in Ruth Young's *Starring Francine & Dave: Three One-Act Plays* (New York: Orchard Books, 1988), ISBN 0-531-08381-0, OB

"Lemonade Stand, The," a drama by Brian Harnetiaux, 1m1f, DPC L60, NSHS pb153

"Lena and Louie," a drama by Leonard Malfi, 1m1f (+1m1f voices), (published with and can play with "Mr. Tucker's Taxi," "Rusty and Rico" "The Teaser's Taxi," "Toddy's Taxi," or "Tripper's Taxi") in Leonard Melfi's *Later Encounters: Seven One-Act Plays* (New York: Samuel French, Inc., 1980), SF 14628, ISBN 0-573-60050-3, NSHS

"Let Us Go out into the Starry Night," a drama by John Patrick Shanley, 1m1f, DPS

"Life with No Joy in It, A," a drama by David Mamet, 1m1f, in *Antæus: Plays in One Act,* edited by Daniel Halpern, No. 66 (Spring 1991), ISBN 0-88001-268-4

"Limb of Snow, A," a drama by Anna Marie Barlow, 1m1f, (published with "The Meeting"; can pair with "Ferryboat" or "The Meeting") DPS 2865

"Little Something for the Ducks, A," a bare-stage comedy-drama by Jean Lenox Toddie, 1m1f, ISBN 0-573-60059-7, (published with "A Scent of Honeysuckle") SF 14911, NSHS 27492

"Long Walk to Forever," a drama by Bryan P. Harnetiaux from Kurt Vonnegut, Jr., 1m1f, DPC L61

"Looking Backwards," a comedy by Pamela McManus, 1m1f, in Pamela McManus' *Comedy in Flight: Three One Act Plays,* introduction by Jack Hollingsworth (Ashgrove, Queensland, Australia: Playlab Press, 1991), ISBN 0-908156-39-1, PPR

"Lost and Found," a comedy by Peter Maloney, 1m1f, SF 14649

"Love and Peace, Mary Jo," a ten-minute play (genre?) by James Nicholson, 1m1f, (published with and can pair with "Americansaint," "Après Opéra," "'The Asshole Murder Case,'" "Bread," "Cold Water," "Cover," "Downtown," "The Drummer," "The Duck Pond," "Eating Out," "Electric Roses," "The Field," "4 A.M. (open all night)," "Looking Good," or "Loyalties," "Marred Bliss," "Perfect," "The Road to Ruin," "Spades," or "Watermelon

Boats") in *25 10-Minute Plays from Actors Theatre of Louisville,* SF 22260, NSHS pb29777, ISBN 0-573-62558-1

"Love Lace," a bare-stage drama by Robert Patrick, 1m1f, in *One Man, One Woman,* SF 14601

"Loveliest Afternoon of the Year, The," a bare-stage absurd comedy by John Guare, 1m1f, DPS 2975

"Love's Light Wings," a drama by Lewis W. Heniford, 2m2f (can pair with "An Odious Damnéd Lie" or "Shrew You: or, Who Hath Need of Men? As Goode Accounte As Anye Knowne Describing How Sweet Shagsper Shuffles Off His Mortal Coil"), WO, NSHS

"Lunchtime," a drama by Leonard Melfi, 1m1f, (published with and can play with "Birdbath," "Ferryboat," "Halloween," or "The Shirt") in *Encounters: Six One-Act Plays,* SF 14606, NSHS 29331

"Lurker," a bare-stage drama by Don Nigro, 1m1f, in *Something in the Basement and Other Plays,"* SF 14679

M

"M Word, The," a comedy by Alan Ball, 1m1f, in *Five One Act Plays by Alan Ball,* DPS 0911, NSHS pb8021

"Madame President," a comedy by Wallace Acton, 1m1f, SF 15903 (no royalty)

"Made for a Woman," a comedy by Alan Ball, 1m1f, in *Five One Act Plays by Alan Ball,* DPS 0911, NSHS pb8021

"Make Like a Dog," a comic drama by Jerome Kass, 1m1f, (published with and can pair with "Suburban Tragedy" or "Young Marrieds at Play) DPS 2662, NSHS pb8055

"Make-Up Artist, The," a drama by David Henry Wilson, 1m1f (+voice), DPC M13, NSHS pb135

"Making Contact," a drama by Patricia Bosworth, 1m1f, in *The Best American Short Plays 1991-1992,* edited by Howard Stein and Glenn Young (New York: Applause Theatre Book Publishers, 1992), ISSN 1062-7561, ATB

"Man in Blue, The" ["**Romance Ranch: The Man in Blue**"], a comedy by Jules Tasca, 1m1f, (published with "The Dark," "Data Entry," "The Fantasy Bond," "Finding the Love of Your Life," "Inflatable You," "Penance," or "Snocky") in Jules Tasca's *Romance Ranch* (New York: Samuel French, Inc., 1991), ISBN 0-573-62434-8, SF 14962

"Man in the Box, The," a drama for youth by Robert Mauro, 1m1f, (published with and can pair with "The Audition," "The Cabbie from Calcutta," "The Day Mother Left Home," "A Death in the Family," "Going Down!" "The Golden Door," "Joan," "My Baby," "My Friend Never Said Goodbye," "The No-Fault Driving School," "The Park Bench," "The Proposal," "Sherlock Holmes: 10 Minutes to Doom," or "Uptown/Downtown") in Robert Mauro's *Two-Character Plays for Student Actors: A Collection of 15 One-Act Plays* (Colorado Springs, Colorado: Meriwether Publishing, Ltd., 1988), ISBN 0-916260-4, MPL

"Man on the Ledge," a comic skit by Randy Galvin, 1m1f, IEC

"Man Who Wouldn't Dance, The," a ten-minute play (genre?) by Jason Katims, 1m1f, SF

"Many Happy Returns," a comedy by Willie Reale, 1m1f, (published with "Fast Women") DPS 3052

"Margaret's Bed," a drama by William Inge, 1m1f, in *The Disposal and Margaret's Bed,* DPS

"Maria," a drama-comedy by Jules Tasca, 1m1f (or 4m2f), in *Spirit of Hispania,* SF 14939

"Mary Agnes Is Thirty-five," a drama by James Elward, 1m1f, (published with and can pair with "Passport") in *Friday Night,* DPS 2045, NSHS 29204

"Mary Goldstein and the Author," a drama by Oyamo, 1m1f, (published with and can pair with "Every Goodbye Ain't Gone") in *New Plays for the Black Theatre,* edited by Woodie King, Jr. (Chicago: Third World Press, 1989), ISBN 0-88378-124-7

"Masks," a fantasy by Perry Boyer Corneau, 1m1f, CC, NSHS 28572

"May Day," a drama by Carrie Luft, 1m1f, in *Cool Guys Don't Go out with Smart Girls and Other Revelations,* BP

"MD 20/20," a comedy by Matt Williams, 1m1f, ISBN 0-573-60061-9, in *Off-Off Broadway Festival Plays, Vol. 7,* SF 15080, NSHS 27530

"Meals on Wheels," a bare-stage short comedy by Roger Cornish, 1m1f, (published with and can play with "Autumn Drive," "The Close-Down Set-Up of Emma," "Frosting" "Mrs. Lazar's Caller," or "Running Away from Home,") in *Short Plays for the Long Living,* BP, SF 15604, NSHS pb6043, NSHS pb7838

"Meet Me in Disneyland," a comedy by Roy London, 1m1f, (published with and can pair with "Disneyland on Parade" or "It's a Small World") in *Disneyland on Parade,* DPS 1672

"Memorial Day," a drama by Murray Schisgal, 1m1f, (published with and can pair with "The Basement," "Fragments," or "The Old Jew") in *Five One Act Plays,* DPS 3975, NSHS pb6057

"Mental Reservations," a ten-minute play (genre?) by Roger Cormish, 1m1f, SF

"Middle Kingdom, The," a comic drama by Howard Korder, 1m1f, (published with "Lip Service") in *The Middle Kingdom and Lip Service: Two Short Plays,* SF 15189, NSHS 27513

"Minstrel Boy, The," a drama by Philip Hayes Dean, 1m1f, (can pair with "This Bird of Dawning Singeth All Night Long") in *American Night Cry*, DPS 735

"Mirage," a bare-stage drama by Robert Patrick, 1m1f, in *One Man, One Woman*, SF 15601

"Miss Dally Has a Lover," a drama by William Hanley, 1m1f, (published with and can pair with "Whisper into My Good Ear") DPS 4855

"Modest Proposal, A," a comedy by Selma Thompson, 1m1f, SF 15687

"Mojo," a drama by Alice Childress, 1m1f, DPS 3195, NSHS pb7738

"Molly and James," a drama about Molly Bloom and James Joyce by Sheila Walsh, 1m1f, (published with and can pair with "Dispatches from Hell," "Senior Prom," or "12:21 P.M.") in Double Image Theatre's *Off-Off Broadway Festival Plays, Tenth Series* (New York: Samuel French, Inc., 1985), SF 15187, NSHS 27488, ISBN 0-573-68904-0

"Moments: A Love Story," a drama by Howard W. Miller, 1m1f, BP

"Mongolian Idiot," a comedy by Fredric Sirasky, 1m1f, in *High School Plays: A Collection of Three One-Act Plays*, edited by Samuel French, Inc. (New York: Samuel French, Inc., 1989), ISBN 0-573-62229-9, SF 15946

"Moony's Kid Don't Cry," a drama by Tennessee Williams, 1m1f (+ baby), in *American Blues*, DPS 710, NSHS pb6064

"Morning Coffee," a drama by Frederick Stroppel, 1m1f, (published and can pair with "Domestic Violence," "The Mamet Women," Package Deal," or "Single and Proud") in Frederick Stroppel's *Single and Proud and Other Plays* (New York: Samuel French, Inc.), ISBN 0-573-69411-7, SF 15262, NSHS pb8090

"Mr. Foot," a comic sketch by Michael Frayn, 1m1f, in *The Two of Us*, SF 15703

"Mr. Lewis and Mrs. Wexel," a comedy by Renée Taylor and Joseph Bologna, 1m1f, in *Bedrooms*, SF 244

"Mrs. Cage," a drama by Nancy Barr, 1m1f, DPS 3244

"Mrs. Lazer's Caller," a bare-stage short comedy by Roger Cornish, 1m1f, (published with and can play with "Autumn Drive," "The Close-Down Set-Up of Emma," "Frosting," "Meals on Wheels," or "Running Away from Home") in *Short Plays for the Long Living*, BP, SF 15607, NSHS pb6043, NSHS pb7838

"My Friend Never Said Goodbye," a drama for youth by Robert Mauro, 1m1f, (published with and can pair with "The Audition," "The Cabbie from Calcutta," "The Day Mother Left Home," "A Death in the Family," "Going Down!" "The Golden Door," "Joan," "The Man in the Box," "My Baby," "The No-Fault Driving School," "The

Park Bench," "The Proposal," "Sherlock Holmes: 10 Minutes to Doom," or "Uptown/Downtown") in Robert Mauro's *Two-Character Plays for Student Actors: A Collection of 15 One-Act Plays* (Colorado Springs, Colorado: Meriwether Publishing, Ltd., 1988), ISBN 0-916260-4, MPL

N

"Need for Brussels Sprouts, A," a comedy by Murray Schisgal, 1m1f, in *Twice Around the Park*, SF 22788

"Need for Less Expertise, A," a comedy by Murray Schisgal, 1m1f, in *Twice Around the Park*, SF 22788

"New Quixote, The," a romantic comedy by Michael Frayn, 1m1f, in *The Two of Us*, SF 16615

"New York Minute, A," a comic drama by Michele Palermo, 1m1f, (published with and can pair with "Labor Pains") in Michele Palermo's *The Other Half* (New York: Samuel French, Inc., 1992), ISBN 0-573-62268-X, SF 15972

"Next," [revised version] a comedy by Terrence McNally, 1m1f (published with and can play with "Botticelli" or "Tour") in Terrence McNally's *Apple Pie* (New York: Dramatists Play Service, Inc., 1969), DPS 825, NSHS pb8164

"Next Tuesday," a comedy by Jason Milligan, 1m1f, in *New York Stories: Five Plays About Life in New York*, SF 15984

"Nicky and the Theatre for a New World," a comic drama by Ernest Joselovitz, 1m1f, (published with and can pair with "Romance" or "There Is No John Garfield") in Ernest Joselovitz' *Four One-Act Plays* (New York: Samuel French, Inc., 1991), SF 16648

"Night," a brief sketch by Harold Pinter, 1m1f, in *Complete Works; Three*, SF 16652, NSHS 27487

"Nightstream," a drama by Jon Jory, 1m1f, in *Dramatics*, 63, no. 7 (March 1992): 35-37, DPC

"No-Fault Driving School, The," a drama for youth by Robert Mauro, 1m1f, (published with and can pair with "The Audition," "The Cabbie from Calcutta," "The Day Mother Left Home," "A Death in the Family," "Going Down!" "The Golden Door," "Joan," "The Man in the Box," "My Baby," "My Friend Never Said Goodbye," "The Park Bench," "The Proposal," "Sherlock Holmes: 10 Minutes to Doom," or "Uptown/Downtown") in Robert Mauro's *Two-Character Plays for Student Actors: A Collection of 15 One-Act Plays* (Colorado Springs, Colorado: Meriwether Publishing, Ltd., 1988), ISBN 0-916260-4, MPL

"No Sweet Revenge," a comedy by Clay Franklin, 1m1f, (published with and can pair with "Bold Decision," "The Daffy World of Daphne de Witt," "Small Victory," "Suddenly Last Friday," or "Western Lament") in *Two for a Happening: A Dramatic Duo in Three Acts, Six One-Act Plays*, SF, NSHS pb8199, NSHS 29203

"North of Providence," a drama by Edward Allan Baker, 1m1f, (published with and can pair with "Lady of Fadima" and "North of Providence") in Edward Allan Baker's *North of Providence; Dolores; Lady of Fadima* (New York: Dramatists Play Service, Inc., 1991), DPS

"Not I," a drama by Samuel Beckett, 1m1f, SF, DPS 385

O

"Odious, Damnéd Lie, An," a dramatic comedy by Lewis W. Heniford, 1m1f, (can pair with "Love's Light Wings" or "Shrew You: or, Who Hath Need of Men? As Goode Accounte As Anye Knowne Describing How Sweet Shagsper Shuffles Off His Mortal Coil") WO, NSHS

"Of Poems, Youth, and Spring," a comedy by John Logan, 1m1f (+3 voices, chorus), BP

"Omega's Ninth," a drama by Ramon Delgado, 1m1f (+ cat—real or stuffed or human), IEC 146-X, NSHS pb109

"On Sundays," a symbolic drama in six scenes by Lynne Alvarez, 1m1f, in *Antæus: Plays in One Act*, edited by Daniel Halpern, No. 66 (Spring 1991), ISBN 0-88001-268-4

"On the Way Home," a comedy by Esther E. Olson, 1m1f, BP, NSHS 19988

"Once Upon a Summertime," a comedy by Mary W. Schaller, 1m1f, DPC O40

"One Naked Woman and a Fully-Clothed Man," a comedy by Diana Amsterdam, 1m1f, in *Sex and Death: Four One-Act Plays*, SF 17666

"Open Admissions," (see p. 224) new revised edition of a one-act version of a full-length drama by Shirley Lauro, 1m1f, (published with and can play with "An Empty Space" or "Nothing Immediate") in Double Image Theatre's *Off-Off Broadway Festival Plays, Fourth Series* (New York: Samuel French, Inc., 1983), SF 17640, NSHS 27533, ISBN 0-573-60044-9 [Note: An excellent nationally televised version starred Jane Alexander.]

"Open Couple, The," a farce by Dario Fo and Franca Rame translated by Stuart Hood, Ron Jenkins, and Joan Jolden, 1m1f, SF 17947

"Orison," a bare-stage satiric drama by Fernando Arrabal translated into English by Barbara Wright, 1m1f, in *Arrabal: Plays*, vol. 1, SF 17643

"Our Man in Madras," a satire by Gert Hofmann, 1m1f, in *Antæus: Plays in One Act*, edited by Daniel Halpern, No. 66 (Spring 1991), ISBN 0-88001-268-4, SF 857

"Out of Hours," a play (genre?) by Richard C. Reyland, 1m1f, in *Triad 71*, NPN

"Out the Window," a ten-minute play (genre?) by Neal Bell, 1m1f, SF

"Outwitted," a comedy by Harry L. Newton, 1m1f, BP, NSHS 19988

P

"Painting Distant Men," a drama by Richard Greene, 1m1f, ISBN 0-573-62423-2, SF 18009, NSHS 7719

"Pair of Lunatics, A," a sketch by W. R. Walkes, 1m1f, ISBN 0-573-62915-3, BP (no royalty with purchase of two copies), DPC, HDS (no royalty with purchase of two copies), SF 18930 (no royalty), NSHS pb6090, NSHS pb6084, NSHS pb7747

"Parade, The," a comedy by Warren Giarraputo, 1m1f, SF 18611

"Park Bench, The," a drama for youth by Robert Mauro, 1m1f, (published with and can pair with "The Audition," "The Cabbie from Calcutta," "The Day Mother Left Home," "A Death in the Family," "Going Down!" "The Golden Door," "Joan," "The Man in the Box," "My Baby," "My Friend Never Said Goodbye," "The No-Fault Driving School," "The Proposal," "Sherlock Holmes: 10 Minutes to Doom," or "Uptown/Downtown") in Robert Mauro's *Two-Character Plays for Student Actors: A Collection of 15 One-Act Plays* (Colorado Springs, Colorado: Meriwether Publishing, Ltd., 1988), ISBN 0-916260-4, MPL

"Passing Fancy," a comedy by Claris Nelson, 1m1f, ISBN 0-573-60061-9, in *Off-Off Broadway Festival Plays, Series 7*, SF 18622, NSHS 27530

"Passion Comedy," a drama by Jules Tasca [set in Athens], 1m1f, (published with and can pair with [Engelberg:] "Swiss Miss," [London:] "A Day in the Night of Rose Arden," [Munich:] "A Side Trip to Dachau," [Paris:] "Escape," [Rome:] "Going to the Catacombs," [Venice:] "The Best Souvenirs," or [Vienna:] "The Stop at the Palace") in Jules Tasca's *Tour di Europa* [*Tour of Europe*] (New York: Samuel French, Inc.), ISBN 0-573-69222-X, SF 18949, NSHS pb8105

"Pastoral," a comedy by Peter Maloney, 1m1f, (published with "Last Chance Texaco") SF 17995, NSHS pb7893

"Peanut Butter and Jelly," a children's comedy by Ruth Young, 1m1f (that is, one boy, one girl), (published with and can pair with "Chocolate Cake" or "Lemonade") in Ruth Young's *Starring Francine & Dave: Three One-Act Plays* (New York: Orchard Books, 1988), ISBN 0-531-05781-X, ISBN 0-531-08381-0, OB

"Penguin Blues," a comic drama by Ethan Phillips, 1m1f, in Ethan Phillips' *Penguin Blues* (New York: Samuel French, Inc., 1988), ISBN 0-573-62391-0, SF 18934

"Pepper and Sand," a duologue by Emlyn Williams, 1m1f, BP, NSHS pb7753

"Perfect Match, A," a comedy by Joan Forster, 1m1f, in Joan Forster's *A Perfect Match* (New York: Samuel French, Inc., 1988), ISBN 0-573-62397-X, SF 18933

"Photographs: Mary and Howard," a drama by Jean-Claude Van Itallie, 1m1f, (published with and can pair with "Eat Cake," "The Girl and the Soldier," "Harold," "Rosary," or "Thoughts on the Instant of Greeting a Friend on the Street") in *Seven Short and Very Short Plays*, DPS 4726, NSHS pb65

"Picking up the Pieces," a play (genre?) by Edward Salmon, 1m1f, in *Triad 71*, NPN

"Piece for an Audition," a bare-stage monologue by Steven Tenney, 1m1f (silent male +speaking female), in *Off-Off Broadway Festival Plays, Series 9*, SF 18919, NSHS 27532

"Please Call Me Sol," a comedy by Rena and Stanley Waxman, 1m1f, SF, NSHS pb6046

"Plumber's Apprentice, The," a comedy drama by Mark Stein, 1m1f, (published with and can pair with "The Groves of Academe") DPS 2245

"Pokey, The," a drama by Stephen Black, 1m1f, DPS, NSHS pb7750

"Popcorn," a comedy by John O'Brien, 1m1f, DPC P55

"Poppa Dio!" a drama by Reinaldo Povod, 1m1f, in *La Puta Vida*, SF 14673

"Portfolio," a comedy by Tom Donaghy, 1m1f (1 voice), SF 18952

"Postcards," a comedy by James Prideaux, 1m1f, DPS 3685, NSHS pb106, NSHS pb111

"Present-Day Courtship," a wordy duologue comedy by Roland Bottomley, 1m1f, SF, NSHS pb7754

"Present Tense," a drama by Frank D. Gilroy, 1m1f, (published with and can play with "Come Next Tuesday," "So Please Be Kind," or "'Twas Brillig") in Frank D. Gilroy's *Present Tense* (New York: Samuel French, Inc., 1973), SF 18664, NSHS pb5486, NSHS pb6048, NSHS pb6050, NSHS pb8169

"Prettiest Girl in Lafayette County, The," a comedy by Jason Milligan, 1m1f, in *Off-Off Broadway Festival Plays, 12th Series*, SF 18167

"Problem, The," a comedy by A. R. Gurney, Jr., 1m1f, (can pair with "Another Antigone," "The Love Course," or "The Open Meeting") in *Antaeus: Plays in One Act*, edited by Daniel Halpern, No. 66 (Spring 1991), ISBN 0-88001-268-4, SF 857

"Proposal, The," a drama for youth by Robert Mauro, 1m1f, (published with and can pair with "The Audition," "The Cabbie from Calcutta," "The Day Mother Left Home," "A Death in the Family," "Going Down!" "The Golden

Door," "Joan," "The Man in the Box," "My Baby," "My Friend Never Said Goodbye," "The No-Fault Driving School," "The Park Bench," "Sherlock Holmes: 10 Minutes to Doom," or "Uptown/Downtown") in Robert Mauro's *Two-Character Plays for Student Actors: A Collection of 15 One-Act Plays* (Colorado Springs, Colorado: Meriwether Publishing, Ltd., 1988), ISBN 0-916260-4, MPL

Q

"Quadrangle, The," a ten-minute play (genre?) by Jon Jory, 1m1f, DPC, NSHS pb149

R

"Radio I," a play (genre?) by Samuel Beckett, 1m1f, in *Ends and Odds*, SF 20604

"Ragnarok," a bare-stage drama by Don Nigro, 1m1f, in *The Gypsy Woman and Other Plays*, SF 19986

"Rain of Terror, The," a drama by Frank Manley, 1m1f, ISBN 0-573-62559-X, (published with "Errand of Mercy") in *Two Masters*, SF 20089, NSHS 27510

"Rape of Emma Bunche, The," a comedy by Jules Tasca, 1m1f, (published with and can play with "Angel on the Train," "Between the Lines," "Brothers," "Hardstuff," "Opening Act," or "The Twin Mendaccios") in *The God's Honest, An Evening of Lies*, SF 20653, NSHS pb8020

"Real Life," a revue sketch by David Lloyd Crowder, 1m1f, SF, NSHS pb6051

"Real to Reel," a comedy by Frank D. Gilroy, 1m1f, in *A Way with Words*, SF 19977

"Recensio," a light and dark show, a drama by Eddie de Santis, 1m1f, in *Off-Off Broadway Festival Plays, 11th Series*, SF 20649, NSHS pb7494, 27508

"Red Coat, The," a drama by John Patrick Shanley, 1m1f, (published with and can pair with "Down and Out," "Let Us Go out into the Starry Night," or "A Lonely Impulse of Delight") in *Welcome to the Moon and Other Plays*, DPS 4807

"Refusal, The," a drama by Mario Fratti, 1m1f, in *Races*, SF, NSHS pb8060

"Reservations for Two," a comedy by Lori Goodman, 1m1f, in *Off-Off Broadway Festival Plays, 13th Series*, SF 8672, NSHS pb8083

"Reticence of Lady Anne, The," a dark comedy adapted for stage by Jules Tasca from the short story by Saki (H. H. Munro), 1m1f, (published with and can play with "The Background," "Blind Spot," "Dusk," "The Hen," "Secret Sin," "The Unrest Cure," or "The Tiger") in Jules

Tasca's *Tales by Saki* (New York: Samuel French, Inc.), ISBN 0-573-62560-3, SF 22133, NSHS pb7798, NSHS pb8113

"Reunion," a bare-stage drama by David Mamet, 1m1f, in *Reunion: Three Plays by David Mamet,* SF 20029

"Ringrose the Pirate," a dark comedy by Don Nigro, 1m1f, in *the Gypsy Woman and Other Plays*, SF 20911

"Romance Ranch: The Dark" **["The Dark"]**, a comedy by Jules Tasca, 1m1f, (published with "Data Entry," "The Fantasy Bond," "Finding the Love of Your Life," "Inflatable You," "The Man in Blue," "Penance," and "Snocky") in Jules Tasca's *Romance Ranch* (New York: Samuel French, Inc., 1991), ISBN 0-573-62434-8, SF 5944

"Romance Ranch: Data Entry" **["Data Entry"]**, a comedy by Jules Tasca, 1m1f, (published with "The Dark," "The Fantasy Bond," "Finding the Love of Your Life," "Inflatable You," "The Man in Blue," "Penance," and "Snocky") in Jules Tasca's *Romance Ranch* (New York: Samuel French, Inc., 1991), ISBN 0-573-62434-8, SF 5944

"Romance Ranch: The Fantasy Bond" **["The Fantasy Bond"]**, a drama by Jules Tasca, 1m1f, (published with "The Dark," "Data Entry," "Finding the Love of Your Life," "Inflatable You," "The Man in Blue," "Penance," and "Snocky") in Jules Tasca's *Romance Ranch* (New York: Samuel French, Inc., 1991), ISBN 0-573-62434-8, SF 5944

"Romance Ranch: The Man in Blue" **["The Man in Blue"]**, a comedy by Jules Tasca, 1m1f, (published with "The Dark," "Data Entry," "The Fantasy Bond," "Finding the Love of Your Life," "Inflatable You," "Penance," and "Snocky") in Jules Tasca's *Romance Ranch* (New York: Samuel French, Inc., 1991), ISBN 0-573-62434-8, SF 5944

"Romance Ranch: Snocky" **["Snocky"]**, a comedy by Jules Tasca, 1m1f, (published with "The Dark," "Data Entry," "The Fantasy Bond," "Finding the Love of Your Life," "Inflatable You," "The Man in Blue," "Penance") in Jules Tasca's *Romance Ranch* (New York: Samuel French, Inc., 1991), ISBN 0-573-62434-8, SF 5944

"Rough for Radio I," (same as "Radio I") an experimental radio drama by Samuel Beckett, 1m1f, (published with and can pair with "Act Without Words I," "Act Without Words II," "Breath," "Cascando," "Catastrophe," "Come and Go," "Eh Joe," "Embers," "Footfalls," "Ghost Trio," "Krapp's Last Tape," "Not I," "Ohio Impromptu," "A Piece of Monologue," "Play," "Quad," "Rockaby," "Rough for Radio II," "Rough for Theatre I," "Rough for Theatre II," "That Time," or "Words and Music") in *Collected Shorter Plays,* ISBN 0-394-53850-1, ISBN 0-

394-62098-4

"Running Away from Home," a bare-stage short drama by Roger Cornish, 1m1f, (published with and can play with "Autumn Drive," "The Close-Down Set-Up of Emma," "Frosting," "Meals on Wheels," or "Mrs. Lazar's Caller") in *Short Plays for the Long Living*, BP, SF 20603, NSHS pb6043, NSHS pb7838

"Rusty and Rico," a drama by Leonard Malfi, 1m1f, (published with and can play with "Lena and Louie," "Mr. Tucker's Taxi," "The Teaser's Taxi," "Toddy's Taxi," or "Tripper's Taxi") in Leonard Melfi's *Later Encounters: Seven One-Act Plays* (New York: Samuel French, Inc., 1980), SF 20640, ISBN 0-573-60050-3, NSHS

S

"Sailing," a drama by Michael Shurtleff, 1m1f, SF 21604

"Sanctity of Marriage, The," a bare-stage drama by David Mamet, 1m1f, in *Reunion: Three Plays by David Mamet*, SF 20029

"Sanibel and Captiva," a radio drama by Megan Terry, 1m1f, SF

"Sara Hubbard," a comedy by Cliff Harville, 1f, (published with and can pair with "George L. Smith," "Hand Me My Afghan," or "A Silent Catastrophe") in Cliff Harville's *Sunsets*, (New York: Samuel French, Inc., 1989), ISBN 0-573-62522-0, SF 21387

"Sarah and the Sax," a drama by Lewis John Carlino, 1m1f, (can pair with "The Dirty Old Man") DPS 2355, NSHS

"Scars & Stripes," a drama by Thomas Cadwaleder Jones, 1m1f, in *Dramatics*, 66. no.9 (May, 1995):28-41; address inquires regarding rights and royalties to Encore Performance Publishing, P. O. Box 692, Orem UT 84059, telephone (801) 225-0605

"Sea Waves Inn," a comedy-drama by Joseph Lizardi, 1m1f, in Joseph Lizardi's *Sea Waves Inn* (New York: Samuel French, Inc., 1989), ISBN 0-573-62525-5, SF 21658

"Seduction Duet," a comedy by H. Appleman, 1m1f, in *Off-Off Broadway Festival Plays, Series 6*, SF 21066

"Self-Accusation," a *Sprechstuck* by Peter Handke, 1m1f, LLA, NSHS

"Senior Prom" (see p. 240), a comedy by Robert Mearns, 1m1f, (published with and can pair with "Dispatches from Hell," "Molly and James," or "12:21 P.M.") in Double Image Theatre's *Off-Off Broadway Festival Plays, Tenth Series* (New York: Samuel French, Inc., 1985), SF 21652, NSHS 27488, ISBN 0-573-68904-0

"75th, The," a sentimental comedy by Israel Horovitz, 1m1f, (published with and can pair with "Hopscotch"; also can pair with "Spared" or "Stage Directions") in *The Quannapowitt Quartet*, DPS 2400, SF 990, NSHS

One-Male-One-Female Plays, continued

pb6068

"She Talks to Beethoven," a symbolic drama by Adrienne Kennedy, 1m1f (+ extras), (can play with "Sun") in Adrienne Kennedy's *The Alexander Plays* (Minneapolis, Minnesota: University of Minnesota Press, 1991), ISBN 0-8166-2077-6; also in *Antæus: Plays in One Act,* edited by Daniel Halpern, No. 66 (Spring 1991), ISBN 0-88001-268-4, ANT

"Silent Catastrophe, A," a comedy by Cliff Harville, 1m1f, published with and can pair with "George L. Smith," "Hand Me My Afghan," or "Sara Hubbard") in Cliff Harville's *Sunsets* (New York: Samuel French, Inc., 1989), ISBN 0-573-62522-0, SF 21387

"Slam the Door Softly," a drama by Clare Booth Luce from Ibsen, 1m1f, DPS 4125

"Slick Harry (The Welfare Pimp)," a drama by Sy Richardson, 1m1f, AR, NSHS pb5723

"Slivovitz," a drama by Roderick B. Nash, 1m1f, in *Off-Off Broadway Festival Plays, 12th Series,* SF 21219

"Slot, The," an adult comedy by Tom Gillespie, 1m1f, AR, NSHS pb5720

"Slow Brick on a Still Day, A," a drama by Richard Kalinoski, 1m1f, in *Dramatics,* 63, no. 8 (April 1992): 22-26. Inquiries regarding performance rights and royalties should be directed to the playwright at 139 West Chestnut Street, East Rochester, NY 14445.

"Small Victory," a comedy by Clay Franklin, 1m1f, (published with and can pair with "Bold Decision," "The Daffy World of Daphne de Witt," "No Sweet Revenge," "Suddenly Last Friday," or "Western Lament") in *Two for a Happening: A Dramatic Duo in Three Acts, Six One-Act Plays,* SF, NSHS pb8199

"Smoking Pistols," a tragicomedy by Donald Kvares, 1m1f, ISBN 0-573-62127-3, SF, NSHS pb83, NSHS pb7765, NSHS pb7834

"Snocky" ["Romance Ranch: Snocky"], a comedy by Jules Tasca, 1m1f, (published with "The Dark," "Data Entry," "The Fantasy Bond," "Finding the Love of Your Life," "Inflatable You," "The Man in Blue," or "Penance") in Jules Tasca's *Romance Ranch* (New York: Samuel French, Inc., 1991), ISBN 0-573-62434-8, SF 21229

"Snowangel," a drama by Lewis John Carlino, 1m1f, (published with and can pair with "Epiphany") DPS 1215

"Some Kind of a Love Story," a drama by Arthur Miller, 1m1f, (can pair with "Elegy for a Lady") DPS 4178

"Something Else," a bare-stage drama by Robert Patrick, 1m1f, in *One Man, One Woman,* SF 21602

"Something in the Basement," a comedy-drama by Don Nigro, 1m1f, in *Something in the Basement and Other Plays,* SF 21620

"Something to Eat," a comedy by Norman L. Rhodes, 1m1f,

in *Off-Off Broadway Festival Plays, Series 9,* SF 21738, NSHS 27532

"Sound of a Voice, The," a drama by David Henry Hwang, 1m1f, (can pair with "The House of Sleeping Beauties"), DPS 4205

"Sound of Silence, The" [*"Le Bel indifférent"*], a monologue drama by Jean Cocteau, translated by Anthony Wood, 1m1f (male silent), in Jean Cocteau's *The Sound of Silence* (London: Samuel French, Inc., 1992), ISBN 0-573-12266-0, SF

"Specter," a bare-stage dark comedy by Don Nigro, 1m1f, (published with and can play with "The Daughters of Edward D. Boit" or "The Woodman and the Goblin") in *Green Man and Other Plays,* SF 21765, NSHS pb7916, ISBN 0-573-62207-8

"Split Decision, The," a brief drama by William Moseley, 1m1f, (published with and can pair with "Advice to a New Actor," "The Affidavit," "The American Way," "Anniversary," "Auld Lang Syne, or I'll Bet You Think This Play Is About You," "Bug Swatter," "Checkers," "Coming for a Visit," "Dalmation," "Dog Eat Dog," "Drowned Out," "Fireworks," "Interview," "Jumping," "Money," "One Beer Too Many," "Phonecall from Sunkist," "Potato Girl," "Property of the Dallas Cowboys," "Valley Forgery," "Watermelon Boats," or "Widows") in *One-Act Plays for Acting Students,* MPL, ISBN 0-916260-47-X

"Square Root of Love, The," a comedy by Daniel Meltzer, 1m1f, in *The Square Root of Love,* SF 21314

"Steinway Grand," a drama by Ferenc Karinthy, 1m1f, SF 21774

"Still-Love," a romance by Robert Patrick, 1m1f, in *Robert Patrick's Cheep Theatricks,* SF 21612

"Stonewater Rapture, The," a drama by Doug Wright, 1m1f, also in *The Best Short Plays of 1987,* DPS 4283

"Storm Is Breaking, A," a comedy by Jim Damico, 1m1f (adult male, boy + female offstage), HDS, SF 21779

"Suburban Tragedy," (see p. 248) a drama by Jerome Kass, 1m1f, (published with and can pair with "Make Like a Dog" or "Young Marrieds at Play") DPS 2662, NSHS pb8055

"Suddenly Last Friday," a comedy by Clay Franklin, 1m1f, (published with and can pair with "Bold Decision," "The Daffy World of Daphne de Witt," "No Sweet Revenge," "Small Victory," or "Western Lament") in *Two for a Happening: A Dramatic Duo in Three Acts, Six One-Act Plays,* SF, NSHS pb8199

"Sugar-Mouth Sam Don't Dance No More," a drama by Don Evans, 1m1f, (published with and can pair with "Orrin") in *The Prodigals,* DPS 3725, NSHS pb8035

"Sure Thing," a comedy by David Ives, 1m1f, (published

One-Male-One-Female Plays, continued

with and can pair with "Mere Mortals" or "Words, Words, Words") in *Four Short Comedies* (New York: Dramatists Play Service, Inc., 1989), DPS 2593

"**Sweet Eros,**" a drama by Terrence McNally, 1m1f, (published with and can pair with "Witness") DPS 4385, NSHS pb8043

"**Swiss Miss,**" a comedy by Jules Tasca, 1m1f, (published with and can pair with [Athens:] "Passion," [London:] "A Day in the Night of Rose Arden," [Munich:] "A Side Trip to Dachau," [Paris:] "Escape," [Rome:] "Going to the Catacombs," [Venice:] "The Best Souvenirs," or [Vienna:] "The Stop at the Palace") in Jules Tasca's *Tour di Europa* [*Tour of Europe*] (New York: Samuel French, Inc.), ISBN 0-573-69222-X, SF 21825, NSHS pb8105

T

"**Table for Two,**" a comedy by Rena and Stanley Waxman, 1m1f (+2 optional extras), SF, NSHS pb6046

"**Talk to Me like the Rain and Let Me Listen,**" a drama by Tennessee Williams, 1m1f (+voices and guitar), in *27 Wagons Full of Cotton*, DPS 485

"**Tantalizing, A,**" a drama by William Mastrosimone, 1m1f, ISBN 0-573-62521-2, SF 22021, NSHS 27520

"**Tape,**" a drama by José Rivera, 1m1f or 2m or 2f, in *Dramatics*, 65 (May 1994): 24-26, ICM

"**Tape Recorder, The,**" a drama by Pat Flower, 1m1f (male is recorded voice), CBC, NSHS pb4241

"**Ten Worst Things About a Man, The,**" a readers theatre comedy adapted by Leslie Irene Coger from Jean Kerr, 1m1f, DC, NSHS 16373

"**Tender Offer,**" a drama by Wendy Wasserstein, 1m1f, in *Antæus: Plays in One Act*, edited by Daniel Halpern, No. 66 (Spring 1991), ISBN 0-88001-268-4

"**Terrible Jim Fitch,**" a drama by James Leo Herlihy, 1m1f, (published with and can pair with "Bad Bad Jo-Jo" or "Laughs, Etc.") in *Stop, You're Killing Me*, DPS 4290, NSHS pb7924

"**Then . . . ,**" a drama by David Campton, 1m1f, (published with and can pair with "A Smell of Burning") DPS 4155, NSHS pb7810

"'**There Is No John Garfield,**'" a comic drama by Ernest A. Joselovitz, 1m1f, (published with and can pair with "Nicky and the Theatre for a New World" or "Romance") in Ernest Joselovitz' *Four One-Act Plays* (New York: Samuel French, Inc., 1991), ISBN 0-573-62170-5, SF 22634

"**This Property Is Condemned,**" a dramatic dialogue by Tennessee Williams, 1m1f, in *27 Wagons Full of Cotton*, DPS 485

"**Thoughts on the Instant of Greeting a Friend on the**

Street,**" a drama by Jean-Claude Van Itallie, 1m1f, (published with and can pair with "Eat Cake," "The Girl and the Soldier," "Harold," "Photographs: Mary and Howard," or "Rosary") in *Seven Short and Very Short Plays*, DPS 4726, NSHS pb65

"**Tiger, The,**" a drama by Murray Schisgal, 1m1f, (published with and can pair with "The Typists") DPS 4545

"**Tira Tells Everything There Is to Know About Herself,**" a black comedy by Michael Weller, 1m1f, (published with and can pair with "The Bodybuilders") DPS 1065, NSHS pb8046

"**Toneclusters,**" a bare-stage drama by Joyce Carol Oates, 1m1f, in *In Darkest America*, SF 22727, NSHS pb8092

"**Touch the Bluebird's Song,**" a drama by Louis E. Catron, 1m1f, BP, HDS, SF 1087, NSHS 29206, NSHS pb5482

"**Traveler's Rest,**" a drama by William Wise, 1m1f, IEC 194-X

"**Twin Mendaccios, The,**" a farce by Jules Tasca, 1m1f, in *The God's Honest, An Evening of Lies*, SF 22243

"**Twist of the Script,**" a drama by Richard Burwell, AR, NSHS pb6842

"**Twister,**" a comedy by Jack Heifner, 1m1f, (published with and can pair with "Tropical Depression") in *Natural Disasters*, DPS 3332

"**Two and Twenty,**" a bare-stage comic-drama by Paul Parente, 1m1f, in *Off-Off Broadway Festival Plays, 12th Series*, SF 22244

"**Two Doubles or the Surprising Surprise, The,**" a comedy by Gueullette, translated by Daniel Gerould, 1m1f, (published with and can pair with "The Blind One-Armed Deaf-Mute," "Cassander Supports the Revolution," "Cassander, Man of Letters," "Cassander's Trip to the Indies," "Giles in Love," "The Shit Merchant," or "The Two Doubles") in *Gallant and Libertine, Divertissements and Parades of 18th Century France*, SF 22252, NSHS 7927

"**Two Part Harmony,**" a drama by Katharine Long, 1m1f, SF 22775

"**Two's a Crowd,**" a comedy by Willard Simms, 1m1f, DPS 4670

"**Typists, The,**" a drama by Murray Schisgal, 1m1f, (published with and can pair with "The Tiger") DPS 4545

U

"**Unbeatable Harold,**" a comedy by Randy Noojin, 1m1f, DPC U19, NSHS pb171

"**Uncle Lumpy Comes to Visit,**" a comedy by Laurence Klavan, 1m1f, DPS 4678

"**Undefeated Rhumba Champ, The,**" a comedy by Charles Leipart, 1m1f, DPS 4695

One-Male-One-Female Plays, *continued*

"Unexpurgated Memoirs of Bernard Mergendeiler, The," a sketch by Jules Feiffer, 1m1f, DPS, NSHS

"Unpublished Letters," a comic drama by Jonathan C. Levine, 1m1f, (published with and can pair with "The End of the Shifty") in Jonathan C. Levine's *Two One-Act Plays* (New York: Samuel French, Inc., 1992), ISBN 0-573-69328-5, SF 23033

"Uptown/Downtown," a drama for youth by Robert Mauro, 1m1f, (published with and can pair with "The Audition," "The Cabbie from Calcutta," "The Day Mother Left Home," "A Death in the Family," "Going Down!" "The Golden Door," "Joan," "The Man in the Box," "My Baby," "My Friend Never Said Goodbye," "The No-Fault Driving School," "The Park Bench," "The Proposal," "Sherlock Holmes: 10 Minutes to Doom") in Robert Mauro's *Two-Character Plays for Student Actors: A Collection of 15 One-Act Plays* (Colorado Springs, Colorado: Meriwether Publishing, Ltd., 1988), ISBN 0-916260-4, MPL

"Uranium," a comedy by Pamela Hunt, 1m1f, in *Off-Off Broadway Festival Plays, XVI Series*, SF 23620

V

"Valentines and Killer Chili," a drama by Kent R. Brown, 1m1f, DPC V21, NSHS pb128

"Village Wooing," a comedy by [George] Bernard Shaw, 1m1f, (published with and can pair with "Annajanska, the Bolshevik Empress," "Augustus Does His Bit," "The Dark Lady of the Sonnets," "The Glimpse of Reality," "How He Lied to Her Husband," "The Music-Cure," "O'Flaherty V.C.," or "Overruled") in [George] Bernard Shaw's *Selected Short Plays,* definitive text under the editorial supervision of Dan H. Laurence (London: Penguin Books, Ltd., 1988), ISBN 0-14-045031-9, SF 24604

"Violets, Gladiolas and Arthur's Breakfast," a drama by Jack Morse, 1m1f, DPC, NSHS pb6085

"Visit, The," a ten-minute play (genre?) by Lyudmila Petrushevskaya, translated by Steve Jones, 1m1f, SF

W

"Waiting for to Go," a comedy by Daniel Meltzer, 1m1f, in *The Square Root of Love*, SF 21314

"Walter," a comedy by Murray Schisgal, 1m1f, (published with and can pair with "The Flatulist," "Little Johnny," or "The Pushcart Peddlers") in *The Pushcart Peddler, The Flatulist and Other Plays*, DPS 3740

"Warm and Tender Love," a comedy by Ralph Pape, 1m1f, (published with and can pair with "Girls We Have Known," or "Soap Opera") in *Girls We Have Known and Other One Act Plays*, DPS 2137

"Wealth and Wisdom," a comedy by Oliphant Down, 1m1f, in *One Act Plays for Stage and Study: A Collection of Twenty-five Plays by Well-Known Dramatists, American, English and Irish*, First Series, preface by Augustus Thomas (New York: Samuel French, Inc., 1925), SF, NSHS

"Welcome Home," a comedy by Rena and Stanley Waxman, 1m1f, SF, NSHS pb6046

"Western Lament," a comedy by Clay Franklin, 1m1f, (published with and can pair with "Bold Decision," "The Daffy World of Daphne de Witt" "No Sweet Revenge," "Small Victory," or "Suddenly Last Friday") in *Two for a Happening: A Dramatic Duo in Three Acts, Six One-Act Plays*, SF, NSHS pb8199, NSHS 29203

"What Did You Say *What* For?" a bare-stage absurd comedy by James Paul Dey, 1m1f, BP, SF 1187, NSHS pb5443

"What Is Making Gilda So Gray," a comedy by Tom Eyen, 1m1f (+ voices), in *Tom Eyen: Ten Plays*, SF 25601, NSHS 29246

"When the Cat Goes Away," a drama by Erica Christ, 1m1f, DPC W60, NSHS pb130

"Whence," a drama by Leo Smith, 1m1f, SF 25661

"Where Are You Going, Hollis Jay?" a comedy by Benjamin Bradford, 1m1f, SF 25080

"Where Have All the Lightning Bugs Gone?" a drama by Louis E. Catron, 1m1f, BP, HDS, SF 1190, NSHS pb7758

"Whole Truth and the Honest Man, The," a comedy by Cleve Haubold, 1m1f or 2m or 2f, available only in manuscript, SF 25678, NSHS pb5440

"Wisp in the Wind," a drama by Jack Cunningham, 1m1f, SF, NSHS pb6053, NSHS pb7736

"Wooden Pear, The," a drama by Gillian Plowman, 1m1f, DPC W71

"Wooed and Viewed," a comedy by Georges Feydeau, 1m1f, SF

"Words and Music," a radio drama by Samuel Beckett, 1m1f or 2m or 2f (+ music), in *Collected Shorter Plays,* ISBN 0-394-53850-1, ISBN 0-394-62098-4

"Workout!" a drama by Sandy Asher, 1m1f, in *Center Stage: One-Act Plays for Teenage Readers and Actors*, edited by Donald R. Gallo (New York: Harper & Row, 1990), ISBN 0-06-022170-4, ISBN 0-06-022171-2

"Workout, The," a farce by Albert Bermel, 1m1f, in *Six One-Act Farces*, SF 25737

Y

"You Can't Trust the Male," a comedy by Randy Noojin, 1m1f, DPC Y18

"Your Mother's Butt," a comedy by Alan Ball, 1m1f, in *Five One Act Plays by Alan Ball*, DPS 0911, NSHS pb8021

Two-Male Plays

A

"*A* Is for All," a drama by Marian Winters, 2m, in *All Saints' Day*, DPS 600

"A.I.D.S.," a drama by Mario Fratti, 2m (+1 female optional), SF 3877

"Absolutely Free," a revue sketch by David Lloyd Crowder, 2m (+2 voices), SF, NSHS pb6051

"Act Without Words (2)," a mime by Samuel Beckett, 2m, (see next item), SF 203

"Act Without Words II," a mime by Samuel Beckett, 2m or 1m1f or 2f, ([see above item] published with and can pair with "Act Without Words I," "Breath," "Cascando," "Catastrophe," "Come and Go," "Eh Joe," "Embers," "Footfalls," "Ghost Trio," "Krapp's Last Tape," "Not I," "Ohio Impromptu," "A Piece of Monologue," "Play," "Quad," "Rockaby," "Rough for Radio I," "Rough for Radio II," "Rough for Theatre I," "Rough for Theatre II," "That Time," or "Words and Music") in *Collected Shorter Plays,* ISBN 0-394-53850-1, ISBN 0-394-62098-4

"All Saint's Day," a drama by Marian Winters, 2m, DPS, NSHS 29200

"Angela," a revue sketch by David Lloyd Crowder, 2m (+ voice), SF, NSHS pb6051

"Animal," a comedy by Oliver Hailey, 2m (see p. 182), DPS

"Audition, The," a drama for youth by Robert Mauro, 2m, (published with and can pair with "The Cabbie from Calcutta," "The Day Mother Left Home," "A Death in the Family," "Going Down!" "The Golden Door," "Joan," "The Man in the Box," "My Baby," "My Friend Never Said Goodbye," "The No-Fault Driving School," "The Park Bench," "The Proposal," "Sherlock Holmes: 10 Minutes to Doom," or "Uptown/Downtown") in Robert Mauro's *Two-Character Plays for Student Actors: A Collection of 15 One-Act Plays* (Colorado Springs, Colorado: Meriwether Publishing, Ltd., 1988), ISBN 0-916260-47-X, MPL

B

"Babel Rap," a comedy by John Lazarus, 2m, in *Six Canadian Plays* (Toronto, Ontario, Canada: Playwrights Canada Press, 1992), ISBN 0-88754-469-X, PCP

"Backbone of America," a comedy by Mark D. Kaufmann, 2m (that is, 1 man and 1 boy), JAT, DPC B73

"Beggar or the Dead Dog, The," an allegory by Bertolt Brecht translated from the original German into English by Michael Hamburger, 2m, in *A Respectable Wedding and Other One-Act Plays*, SF 4175

"Bench at the Edge, A," a comedy by Luigi Jannuzzi, 2m, in *Off-Off Broadway Festival Plays, Series 6*, SF 4617

"Big Al," a comedy-drama by Bryan Goluboff, 2m, in *Big Al and My Side of the Story*, DPS 0998

"Birth of a Blues!" a satire by Ben Caldwell, 2m (+ extras), in *New Plays for the Black Theatre*, edited by Woodie King, Jr. (Chicago: Third World Press, 1989), ISBN 0-88378-124-7

"Boaz," a drama by Randy Noojin, 2m, DPC B57, NSHS pb184

"Botticelli," a drama by Terrence McNally, 2m (+1m bit), (published with and can play with "Next" or "Tour" [revised version]) in Terrence McNally's *Apple Pie* (New York: Dramatists Play Service, Inc., 1969), DPS 825, NSHS pb8164

"Breakdown," a comedy-drama by Bill Bozzone, 2m, (published with and can play with "Buck Fever" or "Good Honest Food") in *Buck Fever and Other Plays*, SF 4674, NSHS pb8017

"Breaking of Bread, The," a drama by William Watson, 2m, BP (no royalty with purchase of three copies)

"Businessmen," a sketch by David Mamet, 2m, (part of "The Blue Hour: City Sketches") in *Short Plays and Monologues*, DPS 3025

C

"Call, The," (see p. 190) a drama by William Inge, 2m, DPS manuscript, NSHS pb86

"Cascando," a radio play (genre?) by Samuel Beckett, 2m or 1m1f or 2f (+ music), (published with and can pair with "Act Without Words I," "Act Without Words II," "Breath," "Catastrophe," "Come and Go," "Eh Joe," "Embers," "Footfalls," "Ghost Trio," "Krapp's Last Tape," "Not I," "Ohio Impromptu," "A Piece of Monologue," "Play," "Quad," "Rockaby," "Rough for Radio I," "Rough for Radio II," "Rough for Theatre I," "Rough for Theatre II," "That Time," or "Words and Music") in *Collected Shorter Plays,* ISBN 0-394-53850-1, ISBN 0-394-62098-4

"Chalky White Substance, The," a drama by Tennessee Williams, 2m, in *Antæus: Plays in One Act,* edited by Daniel Halpern, no. 66 (Spring 1991), ISBN 0-88001-268-4, ANT

"Change from Routine, A," a drama by Ross M. Levine, 2m, in *Off-Off Broadway Festival Plays, 8th Series*, SF 5679

"Charlie and Vito," a drama by Joseph Pintauro, 2m, (published with and can pair with "Flywheel and Anna" or "Uncle Zepp") in *Cacciatore*, DPS 1210

"Chateau René," a drama by Sam Ingraffia, 2m, in *Off-Off Broadway Festival Plays, 15th Series*, SF, NSHS pb8079

"City, The," a drama by J. P. Allen, 2m, (published with and can pair with "Tornado Ultra") in J. P. Allen's *Cities: Five Plays* (San Francisco: Ventana Publications, 1990)

"Closet Madness," a comedy by Murray Schisgal, 2m, in *Closet Madness & Other Plays*, SF 5678, NSHS 27490

"Cold," a sketch by David Mamet, 2m, DPS

"Constituent, The," a comedy by Ernest Thompson, 2m, (published with and can pair with "A Good Time" or "Twinkle, Twinkle") in *Answers*, DPS 810

"Conversation at Night with a Despised Character: A Curriculum for Our Times," (see p. 194) a drama by Friedrich Dürrenmatt translated by Robert David Macdonald from the original German, 2m, **analyzed on p. 194**, DPC C32, NSHS pb177

"Correct Address," a drama by Judd Silverman, 2m, in *Off-Off Broadway Festival Plays, 17th Series*, SF 342

"Crisscross," a bare-stage five-minute passion play by Oliver Hailey, 2m, (published with and can pair with "Picture") in *Picture Animal Crisscross: Three Short Plays*, DPS 3655, NSHS pb7922

D

"Dance and the Railroad, The," (see p. 195) a drama by David Henry Hwang, 2m, in David Henry Hwang's *FOB and Other Plays* (New York: New American Library, 1990), ISBN 0-452-26323-9; also in *The Dance and the Railroad and Family Devotions*, DPS 1523, NSHS pb7918

"Dansen," an allegory by Bertolt Brecht, translated from the German by Rose and Martin Kastner, 2m, SF

"A Death in the Family," a drama for youth by Robert Mauro, 2m, (published with and can pair with "The Audition," "The Cabbie from Calcutta," "The Day Mother Left Home," "Going Down!" "The Golden Door," "Joan," "The Man in the Box," "My Baby," "My Friend Never Said Goodbye," "The No-Fault Driving School," "The Park Bench," "The Proposal," "Sherlock Holmes: 10 Minutes to Doom," or "Uptown/Downtown") in Robert Mauro's *Two-Character Plays for Student Actors: A Collection of 15 One-Act Plays* (Colorado Springs, Colorado: Meriwether Publishing, Ltd., 1988), ISBN 0-

916260-47-X, MPL

"Death Knocks," a comedy by Woody Allen, 2m, in *Getting Even*, SF 6046

"Dialogue the Content of Which Is an Argument between the Romans and a Small Band of Christians Pertaining to Extreme Stinginess and Other Public Vices, A" [*"Ein Dialog, dessen Inhalt ein Argument der Römer gegen das christliche Häuflein, Geitz und andere öffentliche Laster betreffend, diskutiert" / "Ein Dialogus des inhalt ein argumennt der Römischen wider das Christlich heüflein den Geytz auch ander offenlich laster etc. betreffend"*], a *fastnachtsspiel* by Hans Sachs, 2m, in Hans Sach's *Die Wittenbergisch Nachtigall: Spruchgedicht, Vier Reformationsdialoge und das Meisterlied das Walt Got*, compiled by Gerald H. Seufert (Stuttgart: Philipp Reclam jun., 1974), Universal-Bibliothek Nr. 9737/38/38a, ISBN 3-15-009737-1, NSHS

"Dicks, The," a comedy by Jules Feiler, 2m, in *Off-Off Broadway Festival Plays, Series 9*, SF 6663, NS 7532

"Disappearance of the Jews, The," a drama by David Mamet, 2m, in *Three Jewish Plays*, SF 6711

"Do," a bare-stage drama by Gary Apple, 2m, in *Plays for an Undressed Stage*, SF 6653

"Do Not Pass Go," a drama by Charles M. Nolte, 2m, UM

"Dock Brief, The," (see p. 198) a comedy by John Mortimer, 2m, (can pair with "What Shall We Tell Caroline?"), SF 6649, NSHS

"Dreams of Flight," a tragicomedy by Brian Richard Mori, 2m, DPS 1721

"Duck Variations, The," a bare-stage comedy by David Mamet, 2m, BP, (published with and can pair with the full-length 2m2f "Sexual Perversity in Chicago"), SF 6694

"Dumb Waiter, The," a drama by Harold Pinter, 2m, (can pair with "The Collection") in *The Pinter Plays*, DPS 270

E

"Ein Dialog, dessen Inhalt ein Argument der Römer gegen das christliche Häuflein, Geitz und andere öffentliche Laster betreffend, diskutiert" / "Ein Dialogus des inhalt ein argumennt der Römischen wider das Christlich heüflein den Geytz auch ander offenlich laster etc. betreffend" ["A Dialogue the Content of Which Is an Argument between the Romans and a Small Band of Christians Pertaining to Extreme Stinginess and Other Public Vices"], a *fastnachtsspiel* by Hans Sachs, 2m, in Hans Sach's *Die Wittenbergisch Nachtigall:*

Two-Male Plays, *continued*

Spruchgedicht, Vier Reformationsdialoge und das Meisterlied das Walt Got, compiled by Gerald H. Seufert (Stuttgart: Philipp Reclam jun., 1974), Universal-Bibliothek Nr. 9737/38/38a, ISBN 3-15-009737-1, NSHS

"Enemies," a drama by Arkady Leokum, 2m, in *Friends and Enemies*, SF 7621

"Eukiah," a ten-minute drama by Lanford Wilson, 2m, in *Dramatics*, 63, no. 3 (November 1991): 16-19, SF

"Everything Under the Sun," a drama by Ellen Violett from James Purdy, 2m, cited in *The Best Plays of 1963-1964*, edited by Henry Hewes

"Exhibition, The; Scenes from the Life of John Merrick," a drama by Thomas Gibbons, 2m, DPS 1875

F

"Fairy Tale," a drama by Robert Patrick, 2m (+ extras), (published with and can pair with "Bill Batchelor Road," "Fog," "Odd Number," "One of Those People," "Pouf Positive," or "The River Jordan") in Robert Patrick's *Untold Decades* (New York: St. Martin's Press, Inc., 1988), ISBN 0-312-02307-3

"Fam and Yam," a satire by Edward Albee, 2m, (can pair with Edward Albee's "The Zoo Story" or Peter Tolan's "Pillow Talk") DPS 725

"Field, The," a ten-minute play (genre?) by Robert Spera, 2m, (published with and can pair with "Americansaint," "Après Opéra," "'The Asshole Murder Case,'" "Bread," "Cold Water," "Cover," "Downtown," "The Drummer," "The Duck Pond," "Eating Out," "Electric Roses," "4 A.M. (open all night)," "Looking Good," or "Love and Peace, Mary Jo," "Loyalties," "Marred Bliss," "Perfect," "The Road to Ruin," "Spades," or "Watermelon Boats") in *25 10-Minute Plays from Actors Theatre of Louisville*, SF 22260, NSHS pb2977, ISBN 0-573-62558-1

"Final Orders," a satire by Jean-Claude van Itallie, 2m, (published with and can pair with "Bag Lady" or "Sunset Freeway") in *Early Warnings*, DPS 1767

"Flatulist, The," a black comedy by Murray Schisgal, 2m, (published with and can pair with "Little Johnny," "The Pushcart Peddlers," or "Walter") in *The Pushcart Peddlers, The Flatulist and Other Plays*, DPS 3740

"Fog," a drama by Robert Patrick, 2m (+ extras), (published with and can pair with "Bill Batchelor Road," "Fairy Tale," "Odd Number," "One of Those People," "Pouf Positive," or "The River Jordan") in Robert Patrick's *Untold Decades* (New York: St. Martin's Press, Inc., 1988), ISBN 0-312-02307-3

"Foghorn," a drama by Ray Bradbury, 2m, HMC, NSHS 21382

"Former One-on-One Basketball Champion, The," a bare-stage drama by Israel Horovitz, 2m, (published with "The Great Labor Day Classic"), DPS 2225

"Frosting," a bare-stage short drama by Roger Cornish, 2m, (published with and can play with "Autumn Drive," "The Close-Down Set-Up of Emma," "Meals on Wheels," "Mrs. Lazar's Caller," or "Running Away from Home") in *Short Plays for the Long Living* BP, SF 3664, NSHS pb6043, NSHS pb7838

G

"Girls We Have Known," a comedy by Ralph Pape, 2m, (published with and can pair with "Soap Opera" or "Warm and Tender Love") in *"Girls We Have Known," and Other One Act Plays*, DPS 2137

"Goods," a drama by Isidore Ilias, 2m, in *Off-Off Broadway Festival Plays, XVI Series*, SF 9940

"Groves of Academe, The," a comedy drama by Mark Stein, 2m, (published with and can pair with "The Plumber's Apprentice"), DPS 2245

H

"Habitual Acceptance of the Near Enough," a comedy-drama by Kent Broadhurst, 2m, DPS 2253

"Hardstuff," a drama by Jules Tasca, 2m, in *The God's Honest, An Evening of Lies*, SF 10608

"Homework for Men," a drama by John Lazarus, 2m, in *Homework & Curtains* (Toronto, Ontario, Canada: Playwrights Canada Press, 1992), ISBN 0-88754-500-9, PCP

"Hot Air," a drama by Ferenc Karinthy, translated into English by Jo Ann Burbank, 2m, SF 10668

"Hughie," a drama by Eugene O'Neill, 2m, (can pair with "Before Breakfast," "The Dreamy Kid," "Fog," "Shell Shock," "Thirst," or "A Wife for a Life") in Eugene O'Neill's *Complete Plays, 1932-1943* (New York: Library of America, 1988), ISBN 0-940450-48-8, DPS, NSHS 11910, NSHS 28438, NSHS 27069

I

"Ijapa, the Tortoise: The Bush Spirits," a children's comedy by Barbara Winther based on a Nigerian folktale, 2m or 1m1f or 2f, (published with and can play with "Anansi, the African Spider: How Anansi Brought the Stories Down," "Anansi, the African Spider: Tall-Tale Man," or "Two Dilemma Tales: The Snore or the Song") in Barbara Winther's *Plays from African Tales: One-Act,*

Royalty-Free Dramatizations for Young People, from Stories and Folktales of Africa (Boston: Plays, Inc., 1992), ISBN 0-8238-0296-5, PI

"Imagining 'America,'" a comedy by Howard Korder, 2m, in *The Pope's Nose*, DPS 3677

"In a Music Shop," a comedy adapted by Joseph Buloff and Luba Kadison from a story by Chekhov, 2m, in *The Chekhov Sketchbook*, SF 11673

"In the Way," a drama by Stephen Gutwillig, 2m, FDG, NSHS

"Inflatable You" ["**Romance Ranch: Inflatable You**"], a comedy by Jules Tasca, 2m, (published with "The Dark," "Data Entry," "The Fantasy Bond," "Finding the Love of Your Life," "The Man in Blue" "Penance," or "Snocky,") in Jules Tasca's *Romance Ranch* (New York: Samuel French, Inc., 1991), ISBN 0-573-62434-8, SF 11112

"Instincts," a drama by Jason Milligan, 2m, in *Southern Exposures: Five Plays About Life in the South*, SF 11656

"Interview," a revue sketch by Harold Pinter, 2m, (published with and can pair with "Applicant," "The Black and White," "Last to Go," "That's All," "That's Your Trouble," or "Trouble in the Works") in *Revue Sketches*, DPS 1765, NSHS 27487

"Interview, The," a drama by Peter Swet, 2m, DPS 2560

"It Should Happen to a Dog," a comedy by Wolf Mankowitz, 2m, SF (out of print)

K

"King of the Pekinese Yellowtail," a comedy by Sarah Brown, 2m, in *Off-Off Broadway Festival Plays, XVI Series*, SF 13039

L

"Last Straw, The," a comedy by Charles Dizenzo, 2m, (published with and can pair with "Sociability"), DPS 2775, NSHS 29202

"Last to Go," a drama by Harold Pinter, 2m, (published with and can pair with "The Black and White," "The Collection," "The Dwarfs," "The Lover," "Special Offer," or "Trouble in the Works") in Harold Pinter's *Plays: Two* (London and Boston: Faber & Faber, 1991), ISBN 0-571-16075-1; and (published with and can pair with "Applicant," "The Black and White," "Interview," "That's All," "That's Your Trouble," or "Trouble in the Works") in *Revue Sketches*, DPS 1765, NSHS pb7737, NSHS pb8102, NSHS 27487

"Last Yankee, The," a drama by Arthur Miller, 2m, DPS 2783

"Leavin' Cheyenne," a comedy by Percy Granger, 2m, in *Three Plays by Percy Granger*, SF 14629

"Lip Service," (see p. 213) a drama by Howard Korder, 2m, in *The Middle Kingdom and Lip Service: Two Short Plays*, SF 14166, NSHS 27513

"Lonely Impulse of Delight, A," a comedy by John Patrick Shanley, 2m, DPS

"Looking Good," a ten-minute play (genre?) by John W. Williams, 2m, (published with and can pair with "Americansaint," "Après Opéra," "'The Asshole Murder Case,'" "Bread," "Cold Water" "Cover," "Downtown," "Electric Roses," "The Duck Pond," "The Drummer," "Eating Out," "The Field," "4 A.M. (open all night)," "Love and Peace, Mary Jo," "Loyalties," "Marred Bliss," "Perfect," "Spades," "The Road to Ruin," or "Watermelon Boats") in *25 10-Minute Plays from Actors Theatre of Louisville*, SF 22260, NSHS pb2977, ISBN 0-573-62558-1

"Lost Saint, The," an Irish folk-drama by Douglas Hyde, 2m, (published with and can pair with "The Marriage" or "The Tinker and the Sheeog") in Douglas Hyde's *Selected Plays of Douglas Hyde,* chosen by Gareth W. Dunleavy and Janet Egleson Dunleavy, with translations by Lady Augusta Gregory, with parallel texts in Irish and English (Boston: University Press of America, 1991), ISBN 0-86140-095-X, ISBN 0-86140-096-8

"Luftmensch, The," a drama by David Mamet, 2m, in *Three Jewish Plays*, SF 14672

"Lunch Break," a drama by Robert Schenkkan, 2m, in *Four One-Act Plays by Robert Schenkkan: Conversations with the Spanish Lady/Lunch Break/Intermission/The Survivalist*, DPS 3972, NSHS pb8022

M

"Manny and Jake," a drama by Harvey Fierstein, 2m, (published with and can pair with "On Tidy Endings" or "Safe Sex") in Harvey Fierstein's *Safe Sex* (New York: Samuel French, Inc.), ISBN 0-573-64233-8, SF 14964, NSHS pb8112

"Money," a brief comedy by Matthew Calhoun, 2m, (published with and can pair with "Advice to a New Actor" "The Affidavit," "The American Way," "Anniversary," "Auld Lang Syne, or I'll Bet You Think This Play Is About You," "Bug Swatter," "Checkers," "Coming for a Visit," "Dalmation," "Dog Eat Dog," "Drowned Out," "Fireworks," "Interview," "Jumping," "One Beer Too

Two-Male Plays, *continued*

Many," "Phonecall from Sunkist," "Potato Girl," "Property of the Dallas Cowboys," "The Split Decision," "Valley Forgery," "Watermelon Boats," or "Widows") in *One-Act Plays for Acting Students*, MPL, ISBN 0-916260-47-X

"Moonshine," a drama by Arthur Hopkins, 2m, in *One Act Plays for Stage and Study: A Collection of Twenty-five Plays by Well-Known Dramatists, American, English and Irish*, First Series, preface by Augustus Thomas (New York: Samuel French, Inc., 1925), SF, NSHS

"Movie of the Month," a comedy by Daniel Meltzer, 2m, SF 17621

"My Side of the Story," a comedy-drama by Bryan Goluboff, 2m, in *Big Al and My Side of the Story*, DPS 0998

N

"Nightpiece," an absurdity by Wolfgang Hildesheimer, translated by the author from the German *Nachtsstück*, 2m, (published with and can pair with "Freedom for Clemens/*Freiheit für Clemens*" or "Let's Eat Hair!/*Essen Wir Haare!*") in *Postwar German Theatre*, GB, NSHS pb7857

"Nights in Hohokus," a comedy by Jason Milligan, 2m, in *New York Stories: Five Plays About Life in New York*, SF 16649

"Nijinsky Choked His Chicken," a drama by Reinaldo Povod, 2m (adult male + 12-year-old boy), in *La Puta Vida*, SF 14673

"Now Departing," a comedy by Robert Mearns, 2m, in *Off-Off Broadway Festival Plays, Series 9*, SF 16059, NSHS 27532

O

"Ohio Impromptu," a dramatic abstraction by Samuel Beckett, 2m or 2f, ([see next item] published with and can pair with "All Strange Away," "A Piece of Monologue," or "Rockaby") in *Rockaby and Other Short Pieces*, SF 17656 or SF 18643, NSHS 27753

"Ohio Impromptu," a drama by Samuel Beckett, 2m or 2f, ([see above item] published with and can pair with "Act Without Words I," "Act Without Words II," "Breath," "Cascando," "Catastrophe," "Come and Go," "Eh Joe," "Embers," "Footfalls," "Ghost Trio," "Krapp's Last Tape," "Not I," "A Piece of Monologue," "Play," "Quad," "Rockaby," "Rough for Radio I," "Rough for Radio II," "Rough for Theatre I," "Rough for Theatre II," "That Time," or "Words and Music") in *Collected Shorter*

Plays, ISBN 0-394-53850-1, ISBN 0-394-62098-4

"One of Those People," a drama by Robert Patrick, 2m, (published with and can pair with "Bill Batchelor Road," "Fairy Tale," "Fog," "Odd Number," "Pouf Positive," or "The River Jordan") in Robert Patrick's *Untold Decades* (New York: St. Martin's Press, Inc., 1988), ISBN 0-312-02307-3

"Out of the Frying Pan," a bare-stage absurdity by David Campton, 2m, (published with and can pair with "Little Brother: Little Sister"), DPS 2875

P

"Passage," a drama by David S. Raine, 2m, DPC P65, NSHS pb172

"Past Is the Past, The," a drama by Richard Wesley with background music, 2m, (published with "Gettin' It Together") in *New Plays for the Black Theatre*, edited by Woodie King, Jr. (Chicago: Third World Press, 1989), ISBN 0-88378-124-7, DPS 3595

"Pedestrian, The," a melodrama by Ray Bradbury, 2m, (can pair with "The Day It Rained Forever") SF 838

"Penance," a drama by Jules Tasca, 2m, in *Romance Ranch*, SF 17974

"Pillow Talk," a comedy by Peter Tolan, 2m, (published with and can play with "Best Half Foot Forward") in *Stay Carl Stay, Best Half Foot Forward, and Pillow Talk; Three One-Act Plays* (New York: Dramatists Play Service, Inc., 1991) DPS 4266, NSHS pb7887

"Play for Germs," a black comedy by Israel Horovitz, 2m, (published with and can pair with "Shooting Gallery"), DPS 4075, NSHS pb93

"Playing Hardball," a drama by Don Kukla, 2m, BP

"Porch," a drama by Jack Heifner, 2f, (published with and can pair with "Patio") in *Texas Plays*, edited by William B. Martin (Dallas, Texas: Southern Methodist University Press, 1990); also in *Patio/Porch*, DPS 3600

"Preggin and Liss," a tragicomedy by Robert Patrick, 2m, in *Robert Patrick's Cheep Theatricks*, SF 18605

"Protest," a drama by Václav Havel, translated by Vera Blackwell, 2m, in *Antæus: Plays in One Act,* edited by Daniel Halpern, no. 66 (Spring 1991), ISBN 0-88001-268-4

R

"Rabbi and the Toyota Dealer, The," a comedy by Murray Schisgal, 2m, in *Closet Madness & Other Plays*, SF 19990, NSHS 27490

"Righting," a drama by Ernest A. Joselovitz, 2m, SF, DPS 3825

"Romance Ranch: Inflatable You" ["Inflatable You"], a comedy by Jules Tasca, 2m, (published with "The Dark," "Data Entry," "The Fantasy Bond," "Finding the Love of Your Life," "The Man in Blue," "Penance," and "Snocky") in Jules Tasca's *Romance Ranch* (New York: Samuel French, Inc., 1991), ISBN 0-573-62434-8, SF 11112

"Rough for Theatre I," (see "Theatre I") a drama by Samuel Beckett, 2m, (published with and can pair with "Act Without Words I," "Act Without Words II," "Breath," "Cascando," "Catastrophe," "Come and Go," "Eh Joe," "Embers," "Footfalls," "Ghost Trio," "Krapp's Last Tape," "Not I," "Ohio Impromptu," "A Piece of Monologue," "Play," "Quad," "Rockaby," "Rough for Radio I," "Rough for Radio II," "Rough for Theatre II," "That Time," or "Words and Music") in *Collected Shorter Plays*, ISBN 0-394-53850-1, ISBN 0-394-62098-4

"Rough for Theatre II," (see "Theatre II") a drama by Samuel Beckett, 2m, (published with and can pair with "Act Without Words I," "Act Without Words II," "Breath," "Cascando," "Catastrophe," "Come and Go," "Eh Joe," "Embers," "Footfalls," "Ghost Trio," "Krapp's Last Tape," "Not I," "Ohio Impromptu," "A Piece of Monologue," "Play," "Quad," "Rockaby," "Rough for Radio I," "Rough for Radio II," "Rough for Theatre I," "That Time," or "Words and Music") in *Collected Shorter Plays*, ISBN 0-394-53850-1, ISBN 0-394-62098-4

S

"Safe Sex," a comic drama by Harvey Fierstein, 2m, (about AIDS, can pair with Alan Bowne's "Beirut," Patricia Loughrey's "The Inner Circle," Robert Patrick's "Pouf Positive," or Lanford Wilson's "A Poster of the Cosmos"; published with and can pair with "Manny and Jake" or "On Tidy Endings") in Harvey Fierstein's *Safe Sex* (New York: Samuel French, Inc.), ISBN 0-573-64233-8, SF 20992, NSHS pb8112

"Sammi," a drama by Ernest A. Joselovitz, 2m, SF, DPS 3925

"Scooter Thomas Makes It to the Top of the World," a drama by Peter Parnell, 2m, HDS, DPS 3982

"74 Georgia Avenue," a drama by Murray Schisgal, 2m, (published with and can pair with "The Consequences of Goosing" or "How We Reached an Impasse on Nuclear Energy") in *Man Dangling*, DPS 3032

"Sherlock Holmes: 10 Minutes to Doom," a drama for youth

by Robert Mauro, 2m, (published with and can pair with "The Audition," "The Cabbie from Calcutta," "The Day Mother Left Home," "A Death in the Family," "Going Down!" "The Golden Door," "Joan," "The Man in the Box," "My Baby," "My Friend Never Said Goodbye," "The No-Fault Driving School," "The Park Bench," "The Proposal," or "Uptown/Downtown") in Robert Mauro's *Two-Character Plays for Student Actors: A Collection of 15 One-Act Plays* (Colorado Springs, Colorado: Meriwether Publishing, Ltd., 1988), ISBN 0-916260-47-X, MPL

"Shiny Red Ball, The," a comedy by Cleve Haubold, 2m, SF 976

"Slam!" a comedy-drama by Jane Willis, 2m, (published with and can pair with "Men Without Dates"), DPS 3117

"Space," a drama by Donald Margulies, 2m, in *Pitching to the Star and Other Short Plays*, DPS 3662

"Spittin' Image," (see p. 246) a drama by Stephen Metcalfe, 2m, (published with and can play with "Sorrows and Sons") in *Sorrows and Sons*, SF 21742, NSHS pb7896

"Striptease," a drama by Slawomir Mrozek, 2m, SF, NSHS 29300

"Swan Song," a drama by Anton Chekhov, 2m, in Anton Chekhov's *Plays,* translated by Michael Frayn (London: Methuen & Company, Ltd., 1988), ISBN 0-413-19160-X

T

"Tape," a drama by José Rivera, 2m or 1m1f or 2f, in *Dramatics*, 65 (May 1944): 24-26, ICM

"Tattoo," a comedy by Cleve Haubold, 2m, SF 22613

"Terminal," a comedy by Corinne Jacker, 2m, (published with and can pair with "Night Thoughts"), DPS 3400, NSHS pb49, NSHS pb50

"That's Your Trouble," a revue sketch by Harold Pinter, 2m, (published with and can pair with "Applicant," "The Black and White," "Interview," "Last to Go," "That's All" or "Trouble in the Works") in *Revue Sketches*, DPS 1765, NSHS 27487

"Theatre I," (see "Rough for Theatre I") a drama by Samuel Beckett, 2m, (can pair with "Act Without Words I," "Act Without Words II," "Breath," "Cascando," "Catastrophe," "Come and Go," "Eh Joe," "Embers," "Footfalls," "Ghost Trio," "Krapp's Last Tape," "Not I," "Ohio Impromptu," "A Piece of Monologue," "Play," "Quad," "Rockaby," "Rough for Radio I," "Rough for Radio II," "Rough for Theatre II," "That Time," "Theatre II," or "Words and Music") in *Ends and Odds*, SF 22604

"Theatre II," (see "Rough for Theatre II") a drama by Sam-

Two-Male Plays, continued

uel Beckett, 2m, (can pair with "Act Without Words I," "Act Without Words II," "Breath," "Cascando," "Catastrophe," "Come and Go," "Eh Joe," "Embers," "Footfalls," "Ghost Trio," "Krapp's Last Tape," "Not I," "Ohio Impromptu," "A Piece of Monologue," "Play," "Quad," "Rockaby," "Rough for Radio I," "Rough for Radio II," "Rough for Theatre II," "That Time," "Theatre I," or "Words and Music") in *Collected Shorter Plays*, ISBN 0-394-53850-1, ISBN 0-394-62098-4

"Tragic Role, A," a farce by Anton Chekhov, adapted by Ronald Hingley, 2m, in Anton Chekhov's *Twelve Plays*, translated by Ronald Hingley (London: Oxford University Press, 1992), ISBN 0-19-282813-4

"Trouble in the Works," a revue sketch by Harold Pinter, 2m, (published with and can pair with "The Black and White," "The Collection," "The Dwarfs," "The Lover," or "Special Offer") in Harold Pinter's *Plays: Two* (London and Boston: Faber & Faber, 1991), ISBN 0-571-16075-1, and (published with and can pair with "Applicant," "Interview," "Last To Go," "That's All," or "That's Your Trouble") in *Revue Sketches*, DPS 1765, NSHS 27487, NSHS pb7737, NSHS pb8102

"Two Beers and a Hook Shot," a drama by Kent R. Brown, 2m, DPC T76, NSHS pb133

V

"Very Black Comedy Indeed, A," a black comedy by Stephen Davis, 2m, (published with and can pair with "Leapyear") in *Comedy Tonight: Three Award Winning One Acters* (Ashgrove, Queensland, Australia: Playlab Press, 1989), ISBN 0-908156-37-5

"Victoria Station," a comedy by Harold Pinter, 2m, (published with and can pair with "Family Voices," "A Kind of Alaska," or "One for the Road") in *Other Places*, DPS 3548, NSHS pb8041

W

"Wall, The," an Easter drama by Richard Lauchman, 2m, PDS

"Whisper into My Good Ear," a drama by William Hanley, 2m, (published with and can pair with "Miss Dally Has a Lover"), DPS 4855

"Who's on First?" a comedy by Harry Gilles, 2m or 2f, BP

"Whole Truth and the Honest Man, The," a comedy by Cleve Haubold, 2m or 2f or 1m1f, manuscript, SF 25678, NSHS pb5440 NSHS pb5440

"Women and Shoes," a sketch by Nina Shengold, 2m, JAT

"Words and Music," a radio drama by Samuel Beckett, 2m or 1m1f or 2f (+ music), (published with and can pair with "Act Without Words I," "Act Without Words II," "Breath," "Cascando," "Catastrophe," "Come and Go," "Eh Joe," "Embers," "Footfalls," "Ghost Trio," "Krapp's Last Tape," "Not I," "Ohio Impromptu," "A Piece of Monologue," "Play," "Quad," "Rockaby," "Rough for Radio I," "Rough for Radio II," "Rough for Theatre I," "Rough for Theatre II," or "That Time") in *Collected Shorter Plays*, ISBN 0-394-53850-1, ISBN 0-394-62098-4

Z

"Zoo Story, The," a drama by Edward Albee, 2m, (can pair with Edward Albee's "Fam and Yam" or Peter Tolan's "Pillow Talk") DPS 5045, HDS, NSHS 29313, NSHS 16382

Two-Female Plays

A

"Act Without Words II," a mime by Samuel Beckett, 2f or
1m1f or 2m, (published with and can pair with "Act With-
out Words I," "Breath," "Cascando," "Catastrophe,"
"Come and Go," "Eh Joe," "Embers," "Footfalls," "Ghost
Trio," "Krapp's Last Tape," "Not I," "Ohio Impromptu,"
"A Piece of Monologue," "Play," "Quad," "Rockaby,"
"Rough for Radio I," "Rough for Radio II," "Rough for
Theatre I," "Rough for Theatre II," "That Time," or
"Words and Music") in *Collected Shorter Plays*, ISBN
0-394-53850-1, ISBN 0-394-62098-4

"Autumn Leaves," a drama by Julianne Bernstein, 2f, in *Off-
Off Broadway Festival Plays, XVI Series*, SF 3180

"Avenue of Dream," a drama by Elyse Nass, 2f, DPS 875

B

"Batbrains," a comedy by Barbara Daniel, 2f, in *Off-Off
Broadway Festival Plays, Vol. 5*, SF 4610, NSHS 27534

"Binnorie," a drama by Don Nigro, 2f, in *The Gypsy Woman
and Other Plays*, SF 4201

"Black and White, The," a revue sketch by Harold Pinter,
2f, (published with and can pair with "The Collection,"
"The Dwarfs," "The Lover," "Special Offer," or
"Trouble in the Works") in Harold Pinter's *Plays: Two*
(London and Boston: Faber & Faber, 1991), ISBN 0-
571-16075-1; and (published with and can pair with "Ap-
plicant," "Interview," "Last to Go," "That's All," "That's
Your Trouble," or "Trouble in the Works") in *Revue
Sketches*, DPS 1765, NSHS 27487, NSHS pb7737, NSHS
pb8102

C

"Cascando," a radio play (genre?) by Samuel Beckett, 2f or
2m or 1m1f (+ music), (published with and can pair with
"Act Without Words I," "Act Without Words II,"
"Breath," "Catastrophe," "Come and Go," "Eh Joe,"
"Embers," "Footfalls," "Ghost Trio," "Krapp's Last
Tape," "Not I," "Ohio Impromptu," "A Piece of Mono-
logue," "Play," "Quad," "Rockaby," "Rough for Radio
I," "Rough for Radio II," "Rough for Theatre I," "Rough
for Theatre II," "That Time," or "Words and Music") in
Collected Shorter Plays, ISBN 0-394-53850-1, ISBN 0-
394-62098-4

"Cat Connection, The," a comedy by Elyse Nass, 2f, (pub-

lished with and can pair with "Admit One" or "Second
Chance") in Elyse Nass' *Three One-Act Plays About the
Elderly* (New York: Samuel French, Inc., 1990), ISBN
0-573-69205-X, SF 5785, NSHS pb8161

"Chocolate Cake," a comedy by Mary Gallagher and Ara
Watson, 2f, (published with and can pair with "Final
Placement" or "Little Miss Fresno") in *Win/Lose/Draw*,
DPS 4923, NSHS pb8145

"College Letters," a comedy-drama by Dailyn Rodriguez,
2f, in *Throwing Off the Covers: A Collection of Four
One Act Plays*, BP

"Comanche Cafe," (see p. 193) new revised version of a
drama by William Hauptman, 2f, ISBN 0-573-62131-4,
in *Domino Courts/Comanche Cafe*, SF 5686, NSHS pb91

"Coser y Cantar" **["To Be Very Easy"]**, a drama in English
and Spanish by Dolores Prida, 2f, in Dolores Prida's
Beautiful Señoritas & Other Plays, edited and introduced
by Judith Weiss (Arte Público Press, 1991), ISBN 1-
55885-026-0, APP

D

"Dalmation," a brief drama by Conrad Bishop, 2f, (published
with and can pair with "Advice to a New Actor," "The
Affidavit," "The American Way," "Anniversary," "Auld
Lang Syne, or I'll Bet You Think This Play Is About
You," "Bug Swatter," "Checkers," "Coming for a Visit,"
"Dog Eat Dog," "Drowned Out," "Fireworks," "Inter-
view," "Money," "Jumping," "One Beer Too Many,"
"Phonecall from Sunkist," "Potato Girl," "Property of
the Dallas Cowboys," "The Split Decision," "Valley
Forgery," "Watermelon Boats," or "Widows") in *One-
Act Plays for Acting Students*, MPL, ISBN 0-916260-
47-X

"Day Mother Left Home, The," a drama by Robert Mauro,
2f, (published with and can pair with "The Audition,"
"The Cabbie from Calcutta," "A Death in the Family,"
"Going Down!" "The Golden Door," "Joan," "The Man
in the Box," "My Baby," "My Friend Never Said
Goodbye," "The No-Fault Driving School," "The Park
Bench," "The Proposal," "Sherlock Holmes: 10 Minutes
to Doom," or "Uptown/Downtown") in Robert Mauro's
*Two-Character Plays for Student Actors: A Collection
of 15 One-Act Plays* (Colorado Springs, Colorado:
Meriwether Publishing, Ltd., 1988), ISBN 0-916260-4,
MPL

"Dear Mrs. Martin," a comedy by Kate Aspengren, 2f, (published with and can pair with "Mother's Day") in Kate Aspengren's *Dear Mrs. Martin & Mother's Day: Two One-Act Plays* (New York: Samuel French, Inc.), SF 6919, NSHS 8114

"Dolores," a drama by Edward Allan Baker, 2f, (published with and can pair with "Lady of Fadima" and "North of Providence") in Edward Allan Baker's *North of Providence; Dolores; Lady of Fadima* (New York: Dramatists Play Service, Inc., 1991); also in *The Best Short Plays, 1988-1989,* edited by Ramon Delgado (New York: Applause Theatre Book Publishers, 1989), DPS, ATB

"Dormant Heritage, The," a comedy by Reby Edmond, 2f, (published with and can pair with "Enterprising Oswald," "Girls Will Be Girls," "Grandma Fought the Indians," "Make-Up," "Paris Sets the Styles," "'Rosemary—That's for Remembrance,'" "She Goes the Rounds," or "Truant Husbands") in *Two by Two,* BP, NSHS pb6044, NSHS 29326

"Drapes Come, The," a comic drama by Charles Dizenzo, 2f, DPS 1705

"Duel," a drama by Carol Holtzman, 2f, AR, NSHS pb5723

E

"Enterprising Oswald," a Christmas play (genre?) by Reby Edmond, 2f, (published with and can pair with "The Dormant Heritage," "Girls Will Be Girls," "Grandma Fought the Indians," "Make-Up," "Paris Sets the Styles," "'Rosemary—That's for Remembrance,'" "Truant Husbands," or "She Goes the Rounds") in *Two by Two,* BP, NSHS pb6044, NSHS 29326

F

"Final Placement," a drama by Mary Gallagher and Ara Watson, 2f, (published with and can pair with "Chocolate Cake" or "Little Miss Fresno") in *Win/Lose/Draw,* DPS 4923, NSHS pb8145

"Fine Line," a comedy by Janice Van Horne, 2f, SF 8130

"Flounder Complex, The," a thriller by Anthony Damato, 2f, DPS 2015

"Freeze Tag," a comedy by Jacquelyn Reingold, 2f, SF 8678

G

"Girls Will Be Girls," a comedy by Edna Zola Wayne, 2f, (published with and can pair with "The Dormant Heritage," "Enterprising Oswald," "Grandma Fought the Indians," "Make-Up," "Paris Sets the Styles," "'Rose-

mary—That's for Remembrance,'" "She Goes the Rounds," or "Truant Husbands") in *Two by Two,* BP, NSHS pb6044, NSHS 29326

"Golden Door, The," a drama for youth by Robert Mauro, 2f, (published with and can pair with "The Audition," "The Cabbie from Calcutta," "The Day Mother Left Home," "A Death in the Family," "Going Down!" "Joan," "The Man in the Box," "My Baby," "My Friend Never Said Goodbye," "The No-Fault Driving School," "The Park Bench," "The Proposal," "Sherlock Holmes: 10 Minutes to Doom," or "Uptown/Downtown") in Robert Mauro's *Two-Character Plays for Student Actors: A Collection of 15 One-Act Plays* (Colorado Springs, Colorado: Meriwether Publishing, Ltd., 1988), ISBN 0-916260-4, MPL

"Graceland," a comedy-drama by Ellen Byron, 2f, (published with and can pair with "Asleep on the Wind") DPS 2188

"Grandma Fought the Indians," a comedy by Marion Holbrook, 2f, (published with and can pair with "The Dormant Heritage," "Enterprising Oswald," "Girls Will Be Girls," "Make-Up," "Paris Sets the Styles," "'Rosemary—That's for Remembrance,'" "She Goes the Rounds," or "Truant Husbands") in *Two by Two,* BP, NSHS pb6044, NSHS 29326

"Great Nebula in Orion, The," a drama by Lanford Wilson, 2f, (published with and can pair with "Ikke, Ikke, Nye, Nye, Nye") DPS 1905

H

"Hat, The," a sketch by David Mamet, 2f, (part of "The Blue Hour: City Sketches") in *Short Plays and Monologues,* DPS 3025

"Hello, Ma!" (see p. 205) a comedy by Trude Stone, 2f, in *Off-Off Broadway Festival Plays, Vol. 5,* SF 10630, NSHS 27534

"Hospice," a drama by Pearl Cleage, 2f, in *New Plays for the Black Theatre,* edited by Woodie King, Jr. (Chicago: Third World Press, 1989), ISBN 0-88378-124-7, TWP

I

"Ijapa, the Tortoise: The Bush Spirits," a children's comedy by Barbara Winther based on a Nigerian folktale, 2f or 2m or 1m1f, (published with and can play with "Anansi, the African Spider: How Anansi Brought the Stories Down," "Anansi, the African Spider: Tall-Tale Man," or "Two Dilemma Tales: The Snore or the Song") in Barbara Winther's *Plays from African Tales: One-Act, Royalty-Free Dramatizations for Young People, from Stories and Folktales of Africa* (Boston: Plays, Inc., 1992), ISBN 0-8238-0296-5, PI

L

"Ladies' Man" [*"Notre futur"*], a comedy by Georges Feydeau, translated into English from the French by Norman R. Shapiro, 2f, (published with and can pair with "The Boor Hug" [*"Les Pavés de l'ours"*], "Romance in A Flat" [*"Amour et piano"*], or "Wooed and Viewed" [*"Par la fenêtre"*] in Georges Feydeau's *Feydeau, First to Last*, translated by Norman R. Shapiro (Ithaca, New York, and London: Cornell University Press), SF 14016, NSHS

"Lamentable Affair of the Vicar's Wife," a comedy by Guida M. Jackson, 2f, (published with and can pair with "Exeunt O'Brien and Krasnov," "Jennifer's First Christmas," or "A Portrait of Portia") in *An Evening with Eve*, IEC 316-0

"Last to Go," a drama by Harold Pinter, 2f or 2m, (published with and can pair with "The Black and White," "The Collection," "The Dwarfs," "The Lover," "Special Offer," or "Trouble in the Works") in Harold Pinter's *Plays: Two* (London and Boston: Faber & Faber, 1991), ISBN 0-571-16075-1; and (published with and can pair with "Applicant," "Interview," "That's All," "That's Your Trouble," or "Trouble in the Works") in *Revue Sketches*, DPS 1765, NSHS 27487, NSHS pb7737, NSHS pb8102

"Lemonade," a bare-stage comedy-drama by James Prideaux, 2f, (published with and can pair with "The Autograph Hound") DPS 865

"Lifestyles," a drama by Sylvia Vaughan, 2f, (can pair with "Bella, Bella") in Sylvia Vaughan's *Lifestyles* (Burton Joyce, Nottingham, England: Playwrights Publishing Company, 1991), ISBN 0-873130-03-1

"Little Miss Fresno," a comedy by Mary Gallagher and Ara Watson, 2f, (published with and can pair with "Chocolate Cake" or "Final Placement") in *Win/Lose/Draw*, DPS 4923, NSHS pb8145

"Lookin' for a Better Berry Bush," a comic drama by Jean Lenox Toddie, 2f, (can pair with "A Bag of Green Apples") in Jean Lenox Toddie's "Lookin' for a Better Berry Bush," (New York, Samuel French, Inc., 1991), ISBN 0-573-63301-0, SF 14927

"Ludlow Fair," a drama by Lanford Wilson, 2f, DPS 205, NSHS pb7789

"Lullaby," a drama by Jason Milligan, 2f, in *Southern Exposures: Five Plays About Life in the South*, SF 14681

"Lunch or Something," a bare-stage drama by Elizabeth Gray, 2f, SF 14664

M

"Make-Up," a comedy by George Savage, 2f, (published with and can pair with "The Dormant Heritage," "Enterprising Oswald," "Girls Will Be Girls," "Grandma Fought the Indians," "Paris Sets the Styles," "'Rosemary—That's for Remembrance,'" "She Goes the Rounds," or "Truant Husbands") in *Two by Two* BP, NSHS pb6044, NSHS 29326

"Mamet Women," a comedy by Frederick Stroppel, 2f, (published and can pair with "Domestic Violence," "Morning Coffee" "Package Deal," or "Single and Proud" in Frederick Stroppel's *Single and Proud and Other Plays* (New York: Samuel French, Inc.), ISBN 0-573-69411-7, SF 15585, NSHS pb8090

"My Baby," a drama for youth by Robert Mauro, 2f, (published with and can pair with "The Audition," "The Cabbie from Calcutta," "The Day Mother Left Home," "A Death in the Family," "Going Down!" "The Golden Door," "Joan," "The Man in the Box," "My Friend Never Said Goodbye," "The No-Fault Driving School," "The Park Bench," "The Proposal," "Sherlock Holmes: 10 Minutes to Doom," or "Uptown/Downtown") in Robert Mauro's *Two-Character Plays for Student Actors: A Collection of 15 One-Act Plays* (Colorado Springs, Colorado: Meriwether Publishing, Ltd., 1988), ISBN 0-916260-4, MPL

"My Cup Ranneth Over," a comedy by Robert Patrick, 2f, DPS 3300

N

"New Girl, The," a comedy by Vaughn McBride, 2f, SF 16047, NSHS 27502

"Next Tuesday," a comedy by Jason Milligan, 2f, SF

"Night Thoughts," an absurd comedy by Corinne Jacker, 2f, (published with and can pair with "Terminal") DPS 3400, NSHS pb49, NSHS pb50

"Nothing Immediate," a drama by Shirley Mezvinsky Lauro, 2f, (published with and can play with "An Empty Space" or "Open Admissions") in Double Image Theatre's *Off-Off Broadway Festival Plays, Fourth Series* (New York: Samuel French, Inc., 1983), SF 16637, NSHS 27533, ISBN 0-573-60044-9

"Notre futur" ["**Ladies' Man**"], a comedy by Georges Feydeau, translated into English from the French by Norman R. Shapiro, 2f, (published with and can pair with "The Boor Hug" [*"Les Pavés de l'ours"*], "Romance in A Flat" [*"Amour et piano"*], or "Wooed and Viewed" [*"Par la fenêtre"*]) in Georges Feydeau's *Feydeau, First to Last*, translated by Norman R. Shapiro (Ithaca, New York, and London: Cornell University Press), SF 14016, NSHS

O

"**Ohio Impromptu,**" a dramatic abstraction by Samuel Beckett, 2f or 2m, ([see next item] published with and can pair with "All Strange Away," "A Piece of Monologue," or "Rockaby") in *Rockaby and Other Short Pieces*, SF 17656 or SF 18643, NSHS 27753

"**Ohio Impromptu,**" a drama by Samuel Beckett, 2f or 2m, ([see above item] published with and can pair with "Act Without Words I," "Act Without Words II," "Breath," "Cascando," "Catastrophe," "Come and Go," "Eh Joe," "Embers," "Footfalls," "Ghost Trio," "Krapp's Last Tape," "Not I," "A Piece of Monologue," "Play," "Quad," "Rockaby," "Rough for Radio I," "Rough for Radio II," "Rough for Theatre I," "Rough for Theatre II," "That Time," or "Words and Music") in *Collected Shorter Plays*, ISBN 0-394-53850-1, ISBN 0-394-62098-4

P

"**Package Deal,**" a comedy by Frank Stroppel, 2f, (published and can pair with "Domestic Violence," "The Mamet Women," "Morning Coffee," or "Single and Proud") in Frederick Stroppel's *Single and Proud and Other Plays* (New York: Samuel French, Inc.), ISBN 0-573-69411-7, SF 17955, NSHS pb8090

"**Papa Never Done Nothing . . . Much,**" a comedy by E. P. Conkle, 2f, SF 18610, NSHS pb7748

"**Paris Sets the Styles,**" a farce by William Ellis Jones, 2f, (published with and can pair with "The Dormant Heritage," "Enterprising Oswald," "Girls Will Be Girls," "Grandma Fought the Indians," "Make-Up," "'Rosemary—That's for Remembrance,'" "She Goes the Rounds," or "Truant Husbands") in *Two by Two* BP, NSHS pb6044, NSHS 29326

"**Patio,**" a drama by Jack Heifner, 2f, (published with and can pair with "Porch") in *Texas Plays*, edited by William B. Martin (Dallas, Texas: Southern Methodist University Press, 1990); also in *Patio/Porch*, DPS 3600

"**Perfect Match, A,**" a comedy by Joan Forster, 2f, SF

"**Pioneer, The,**" a drama by Megan Terry, 2f or 2m, IEC

"**Pledge, The,**" a drama by Victoria Norman, 2f, in *Off-Off Broadway Festival Plays, 15th Series*, SF 18953, NSHS pb8079

"**Porch,**" a comedy-drama by Jack Heifner, 2f, (published with and can pair with "Patio") in *Patio/Porch*, DPS 3600

"**Post Mortems,**" a drama by Jill Hyem, 2f, in *Triad 79*, NPN

"**Prisoners,**" a drama by Mike Wells, 2f, in Mike Wells' *Prisoners* (Macclesfield, Cheshire, England: New Playwrights Network, 1991), ISBN 0-86319-262-9, NPN

"**Procedure,**" a ten-minute play (genre?) by Joyce Carol Oates, 2f, SF

"**Purpose of the Moon,**" a drama by Carrie Luft, 2f, BP

R

"**Recluse, The,**" a drama by Paul Foster, 2f, in "Balls & Other Plays," SF 20609

"**Recognition Scene from *Anastasia*, The,**" a dramatic second-act scene adapted by Guy Bolton from Marcelle Maurette, 2f, BP, SF 131

"**Request Stop,**" a revue sketch by Harold Pinter, 2f, DPS, NSHS pb7737

"**Roommates,**" a bare-stage comedy by Mary Orr, 2f, in Mary Orr's *Roommates* (New York: Dramatists Play Service, Inc., 1989), DPS 3871

"'**Rosemary—That's for Remembrance,**'" a comedy by Marjorie Seligman, 2f, (published with and can pair with "The Dormant Heritage," "Enterprising Oswald," "Girls Will Be Girls," "Grandma Fought the Indians," "Make-Up," "Paris Sets the Styles," "She Goes the Rounds," or "Truant Husbands") in *Two by Two* BP, NSHS pb6044, NSHS 29326

"**Rouge Atomique,**" a fantasy-drama by N. Richard Nash, 2f, DPS 3895

S

"**Save Me a Place at Forest Lawn,**" (see p. 238) a comedy-drama by Lorees Yerby, 2f, HDS, DPS 3955, NSHS pb7914

"**Second Chance,**" a comedy by Elyse Nass, 2f, (published with and can pair with "Admit One" or "The Cat Connection") in Elyse Nass' *Three One-Act Plays About the Elderly* (New York: Samuel French, Inc., 1990), ISBN 0-573-69205-X, SF 21661, NSHS pb8161

"**Serving-Girl and the Lady: or Just Us and the Medium, The,**" a drama by Myrna Lamb, 2f, SF

"She Goes the Rounds," a comedy by Tom Taggart, 2f, (published with and can pair with "The Dormant Heritage," "Enterprising Oswald," "Girls Will Be Girls," "Grandma Fought the Indians," "Make-Up," "Paris Sets the Styles," "'Rosemary—That's for Remembrance,'" or "Truant Husbands") in *Two by Two*, BP, NSHS pb6044, NSHS 29326

"Snow Leopards [Act One]," a lengthy comedy-drama by Martin Jones, 2f, SF 21245

"Something Unspoken," (see p. 243) a drama by Tennessee Williams, 2f, in *27 Wagons Full of Cotton*, DPS 485

"Square Pegs," a rhymed fantasy by Clifford Bax, 2f, BP, NSHS 19988

"Stronger, The," (see p. 247) a drama by August Strindberg, translated by Michael Meyer, 2f (+extra), (can pair with "Miss Julie") in *Plays by August Strindberg*, DPS 252, NSHS 29262

T

"Tape," a drama by José Rivera, 2f or 1m1f or 2m, in *Dramatics*, 65 (May 1944): 24-26, ICM

"Tell Me Another Story, Sing Me Another Song," a bare-stage drama by Jean Lenox Toddie, 2f, SF 22033, NSHS 27504, NSHS 27504

"That's All," (see p. 250) a revue sketch by Harold Pinter, 2f, (published with and can pair with "Applicant," "The Black and White," "Interview," "Last to Go," "That's Your Trouble," or "Trouble in the Works") in *Revue Sketches*, DPS 1765, NSHS 27487

"Third and Oak: The Laundromat," a comedy by Marsha Norman, 2f, (can pair with "Third and Oak: The Pool Hall") DPS 4485

"This Bird of Dawning Singeth All Night Long," a drama by Philip Hayes Dean, 2f, (can pair with "The Minstrel Boy") in *American Night Cry*, DPS 735

"Thistle Blossoms," a drama by Roseanna Beth Whitlow, 2f, PDS

"Tiger, The," a comedy adapted for stage by Jules Tasca from the short story by Saki (H. H. Munro), 2f, (published with and can pair with "The Background," "Blind Spot," "Dusk," "The Hen," "The Reticence of Lady Anne," "Secret Sin," or "The Unrest Cure") in Jules Tasca's *Tales by Saki* (New York: Samuel French, Inc.), ISBN 0-573-62560-3, SF 22133, NSHS pb7798, NSHS pb8113

"To Be Very Easy" [*"Coser y Cantar"*] a drama in English and Spanish by Dolores Prida, 2f, in Dolores Prida's *Beautiful Señoritas & Other Plays*, edited and introduced by Judith Weiss (Arte Público Press, 1991), ISBN 1-

55885-026-0, APP

"Tropical Depression," a comedy by Jack Heifner, 2f, (published with and can pair with "Twister") in *Natural Disasters* DPS 3332

"Truant Husbands," a skit by Wilmer Baffle, 2f, (published with and can pair with "The Dormant Heritage," "Enterprising Oswald," "Girls Will Be Girls," "Grandma Fought the Indians," "Make-Up," "Paris Sets the Styles," "'Rosemary—That's for Remembrance,'" or "She Goes the Rounds") in *Two by Two* BP, NSHS pb6044, NSHS 29326

U

"Umbrella Duologue, The," a sketch by E. Dora Battiscombe, 2f, BP, NSHS 19988

W

"Watermelon Boats," a ten-minute drama by Wendy MacLaughlin, 2f, (published with and can pair with "Americansaint," "Après Opéra," "'The Asshole Murder Case,'" "Bread," "Cold Water," "Cover," "Downtown," "The Drummer," "The Duck Pond," "Eating Out," "Electric Roses," "The Field," "4 A.M. (open all night)," "Looking Good," "Love and Peace, Mary Jo," "Loyalties," "Marred Bliss," "Perfect," "The Road to Ruin," or "Spades") in *25 10-Minute Plays from Actors Theatre of Louisville*, SF 22260, NSHS pb29777, ISBN 0-573-62558-1; also (published with and can pair with "Advice to a New Actor," "The Affidavit," "The American Way," "Anniversary," "Auld Lang Syne, or I'll Bet You Think This Play Is About You," "Bug Swatter," "Checkers," "Coming for a Visit," "Dalmation," "Dog Eat Dog," "Drowned Out," "Fireworks," "Interview," "Jumping," "Money," "One Beer Too Many," "Phonecall from Sunkist," "Potato Girl," "Property of the Dallas Cowboys," "The Split Decision," "Valley Forgery," or "Widows") in *One-Act Plays for Acting Students*, MPL, ISBN 0-916260-47-X

"White Whore and the Bit Player, The," a comedy-tragedy by Tom Eyen, 2f, in *Tom Eyen: Ten Plays*, SF 25602, NSHS 29246

"Who's on First?" a comedy by Harry Gilles, 2f or 2m, BP

"Whole Truth, The," a comedy by Viki Boyle, 2f, in *Off-Off Broadway Festival Plays, XVI Series*, SF 25682

"Whole Truth and the Honest Man, The," a comedy by Cleve Haubold, 2m or 2f or 1m1f, available only in manuscript, SF 25678, NSHS pb5440, NSHS pb5440

"Widows," a brief comedy by Stephen Grecco, 2f, (published

with and can pair with "Advice to a New Actor," "The
Affidavit," "The American Way," "Anniversary," "Auld
Lang Syne, or I'll Bet You Think This Play Is About
You," "Bug Swatter," "Checkers," "Coming for a Visit,"
"Dalmation," "Dog Eat Dog," "Drowned Out," "Fire-
works," "Interview," "Jumping," "Money," "One Beer
Too Many," "Phonecall from Sunkist," "Potato Girl,"
"Property of the Dallas Cowboys," "The Split Decision,"
"Valley Forgery," or "Watermelon Boats") in *One-Act
Plays for Acting Students*, MPL, ISBN 0-916260-47-X
"Winning Number, The," a comedy by Sarah Brown, 2f, in
Off-Off Broadway Festival Plays, XVI Series, SF 25703
"Women in Motion," a drama by Donald Margulies, 2f, in
"Pitching to the Star" and Other Short Plays, DPS 3662
"Words and Music," a radio drama by Samuel Beckett, 2f
or 1m1f or 2m (+ music), (published with and can pair
with "Act Without Words I," "Act Without Words II,"
"Breath," "Cascando," "Catastrophe," "Come and Go,"
"Eh Joe," "Embers," "Footfalls," "Ghost Trio," "Krapp's
Last Tape," "Not I," "Ohio Impromptu," "A Piece of
Monologue," "Play," "Quad," "Rockaby," "Rough for
Radio I," "Rough for Radio II," "Rough for Theatre I,"
"Rough for Theatre II," or "That Time") in *Collected
Shorter Plays*, ISBN 0-394-53850-1, ISBN 0-394-62098-4

A

"**Agnes,**" a dramatic chamber opera by Michael John LaChiusa, 1m2f, (published with and can pair with these other musicals: "Break," "Eulogy for Mister Hamm," or "Lucky Nurse") in *Lucky Nurse and Other Short Musicals*, DPS 2986, NSHS pb8120

"**Alan, Betty and Riva,**" a comedy by Renée Taylor and Joseph Bologna, 1m2f, in *Bedrooms*, SF 244

"**American Sunset, An,**" a comedy by James Prideaux, 1m2f, (published with and can pair with "Stuffings") DPS 750

"**American Tropical,**" a drama by Richard Ford, 1m2f, in *Antæus: Plays in One-Act*, edited by Daniel Halpern, no. 66 (spring, 1991), ISBN 0-88145-056-4

"**American Way, The,**" a brief comedy by Lavonne Mueller, 1m2f, (published with and can pair with "Advice to a New Actor" "The Affidavit," "Anniversary," "Auld Lang Syne, or I'll Bet You Think This Play Is About You," "Bug Swatte," "Coming for a Visit," "Dog Eat Dog," "Drowned Out," "Fireworks," "Interview," "Jumping," "Money," "One Beer Too Many," "Phonecall from Sunkist," "Potato Girl," "Property of the Dallas Cowboys," "The Split Decision," "Valley Forgery," "Watermelon Boats," or "Widows") in *One-Act Plays for Acting Students*, MPL, ISBN 0-916260-47-X

"**Angels Don't Marry,**" a comedy by Florence Ryerson and Colin Clements, 1m2f, SF

"**Arizona Anniversaries,**" a ten-minute play (genre?) by John Bishop, 1m2f, in *More Ten-Minute Plays from Actors Theatre of Louisville*, SF 3705

"**Autograph Hound, The,**" a comedy by James Prideaux, 1m2f, (published with and can pair with "Lemonade") DPS 865

B

"**Betrothed, The,**" a drama by Jerome McDonough, 1m2f, ISBN 0-573-62040-3, SF 265, NSHS 7510

"**Between the Lines,**" a comedy by Jules Tasca, 1m2f, in *The God's Honest, An Evening of Lies,* SF 3983, NSHS

"**Bible,**" a bare-stage dark comedy by Don Nigro, 1m2f, (can pair with "God's Spies") in *Something in the Basement and Other Plays*, SF 4699, NSHS

"**Birthday Present, The,**" (see p. 187) a drama by Peter Brook, 1m2f, DPC B21, NSHS pb6070

"**Bite the Hand,**" a comedy by Ara Watson, 1m2f, (published with and can pair with "Mooncastle") DPS 1033

"**Blind Date with Mary, A,**" a comedy by Sura Shachnovitz, 1m2f, in *Off-Off Broadway Festival Plays, 14th Series*, SF 4703

"**Boogeyman, The**" ["**The Boogeyman: The Boogeyman**"], a comedy-drama by Edward Clinton, 1m2f, (published with and can play with "First of the Month" or "Small Claims") in *The Boogeyman: Three Related One Acts* (New York: Samuel French, Inc., 1992), ISBN 0-573-69388-9, SF 4720, NSHS pb8106

"**Breakfast, Lunch, and Dinner,**" a drama by Corinne Jacker, 1m2f, DPS 1035

"**Brontosaurus,**" a comedy-drama by Lanford Wilson, 1m2f, (can pair with "Cabin 12") DPS 1150

"**Brujerías,**" a comedy by Rodrigo Duarte-Clark, 1m2f, in *Nuevos Pasos: Chicano and Puerto Rican Dramas*, edited by Nicolás Kanellos and Jorge A. Huerta (Arte Público Press, 1989), ISBN 0-934770-98-0, APP

C

"**Cameo, The,**" a drama by Ray Fry, 1m2f, DPS 1223

"**Catherine Parr, or Alexander's Horse,**" a comedy by Maurice Baring, 1m2f, BP, NSHS 19988

"**Chinese Restaurant Syndrome, The,**" a comedy by Corinne Jacker, 1m2f, (published with "In Place") DPS 2507

"**Christmas Tea,**" a Christmas fantasy by Robert Neil Porter, 1m2f (+voice), DPS

"**Christmas Tree, The,**" a Christmas drama by Laurence Housman, 1m2f, ISA, NSHS 27000

"**Coleman, S. D.,**" a drama by Anne Pierson Wiese, 1m2f, FDG, NSHS

"**Come and Gone,**" a drama by James Edward Luczak, 1m2f, DPC C86

"**Conspiracy of Angels, A,**" a comedy by Charles Ferruza, 1m2f, NSHS 29210

"**Contribution,**" a comedy by Ted Shine, 1m2f, DPS 1425

"**Crossing the Bar,**" a comedy by Don Nigro, 1m2f, ISBN 0-573-60050-3, (published with "God's Spies") SF 5935, NSHS 27501

"**Crossings,**" a drama by Barbara Schneider, 1m2f, (published with and can pair with "Flight Lines") DPS 2012

"**Crosspatch,**" a comedy by Larry Randolph from Anton Chekhov, 1m2f, HDS, DPC C36

"**Curtains for a Crazy Old Lady,**" a play with music by John Lazarus, 1m2f, in *Homework & Curtains* (Toronto, Ontario, Canada: Playwrights Canada Press, 1991), ISBN

0-88754-500-9, PCP

"Cut in the Rates, A," a television thriller by Alan Ayckbourn, 1m2f, in Alan Ayckbourn's *A Cut in the Rates* (London: Samuel French, Ltd., 1991), ISBN 0-573-12084-6, SF 5798

D

"Dark Room, The," a drama by Tennessee Williams, 1m2f, in *American Blues*, DPS 710, NSHS pb6064

"Das heiss Eysen" ["**The Hot Iron**"], a farce by Hans Sachs, 1m2f, (published with and can pair with *"Der Farendt Schuler im Paradeis"* ["The Wandering Scholar in Paradise"] or *"Der doctor mit der grosen nasen"* ["The Doctor with the Big Nose"]) in Hans Sachs' *Meistergesänge Fastnachtsspiele Schwänke*, compiled by Eugen Geiger (Stuttgart: Phillip Reclam jun., 1981), ISBN 3-15-007627-7, NSHS

"Daughter of a Traveling Lady," a comedy-drama by Peter Dee, 1m2f, SF 6606

"Dearie, Ye're a Dreamer," a comedy by Francis Michael Casey, 1m2f, originally produced at the University of North Carolina/Chapel Hill around 1950, once handled by Samuel French but no longer listed there; hilarious portrayal of Irish sisters and their angel of death; well worth the search

"Deceivers," a comedy by William C. De Mille, 1m2f, in *One Act Plays for Stage and Study: A Collection of Twenty-five Plays by Well-Known Dramatists, American, English and Irish*, First Series, preface by Augustus Thomas (New York: Samuel French, Inc., 1925), SF, NSHS

"Devil, The," a comedy by Don Nigro, 1m2f, in *Something in the Basement and Other Plays*, SF 6721

"Does This Woman Have a Name?" a comedy by Theresa Rebeck, 1m2f, in *Off-Off Broadway Festival Plays, 15th Series,* SF 6732, NSHS pb8079

"Doubting Saint, The," a religious drama by Warren Keliewer, 1m2f or 2m1f, SF, NSHS

"Duck Pond, The," a drama by Ara Watson, 1m2f, (published with and can pair with "Americansaint," "Après Opéra," "'The Asshole Murder Case,'" "Bread," "Cold Water," "Cover," "Downtown," "The Drummer," "The Duck Pond," "Eating Out," "Electric Roses," "The Field," "4 A.M. (open all night)," "Looking Good," "Love and Peace, Mary Jo," "Loyalties," "Marred Bliss," "The Road to Ruin," "Spades," or "Watermelon Boats") in *25 10-Minute Plays from Actors Theatre of Louisville*, SF 22260, NSHS pb29777, ISBN 0-573-62558-1

E

"Eddie Lee, Eddie Lee," a comedy by Joe Sears, 1m2f, SF 6991

"Election Year," a comedy by Ellen Byron, 1m2f, (published with and can pair with "So When You Get Married . . . (The *Quando Si Sposa* Fund)," in *Election Year and So When You Get Married . . . (The Quando Si Sposa Fund): Two Short Plays*, DPS 1791, NSHS pb7912

"Erasure," a drama by Carrie Luft, 1m2f, in *Cool Guys Don't Go out with Smart Girls and Other Revelations*, BP

"Errand of Mercy," a drama by Frank Manley, 1m2f, (paired and published with "The Rain of Terror") in "Two Masters," SF 7068

"Estoy enamorado de tu hermana" ["**I Am in Love with Your Sister**"] (see p. 201), a *farsa* by Jesús Assaf, 1m2f, OEN, NSHS pb8189

F

"Fan and Two Candlesticks, A," a verse comedy by Mary MacMillan, 1m2f, SKC, NSHS 27002

"Fifteenth Candle, The," a tragedy by Rachel Field, 1m2f, SF, NSHS 8266

"Finders-Keepers," a play (genre?) by George Kelly, 1m2f, SF 437

"First of the Month" ["**The Boogeyman: First of the Month**"], a comedy-drama by Edward Clinton, 1m2f, (published with and can play with "First of the Month" or "Small Claims") in *The Boogeyman: Three Related One Acts* (New York: Samuel French, Inc., 1992), ISBN 0-573-69388-9, SF 8187, NSHS pb8106

"Flight Lines," a drama by Barbara Schneider, 1m2f, (published with and can pair with "Crossings") DPS 2012

"Fragile Unions," a drama by Nancy Pahl Gilsenan, 1m2f, DPC F34

"Frau Wahrheit will niemand beherbergen" [**Mrs. Truth Will Not Take In Anybody Overnight**"] a *fastnachtsspiel* by Hans Sachs, 1m2f, HDB, NSHS

"Free the Frogs," a drama by Carrie Luft, 1m2f, in *Cool Guys Don't Go out with Smart Girls and Other Revelations*, BP

"Freshman Orientation," a ten-minute play (genre?) by Jon Jory, 1m2f, DPC, NSHS pb149

G

"Girls' Talk," a comedy by Howard Korder, 1m2f, in *The Pope's Nose*, DPS 3677

"Goblins Plot to Murder God, The," a ten-minute play (genre?) by Mark O'Donnel, 1m2f or 3f or 3m or 2m1f or 4m or 4f or 1m3f or 2m2f or 3m1f, SF

"God's Spies," a comedy by Don Nigro, 1m2f, ISBN 0-573-60050-3, (published with "Crossing the Bar") SF 9643, NSHS 27501

"Good Night, Sweet Mother," a drama by William Groves, 1m2f, IEC 385-3

"Gotta Dance," a comedy by Maura Swanson, 1m2f, in *Dramatics*, 64, no. 9 (May 1992): 22-25. Inquiries regarding performance rights and royalties should be directed to the playwright at 339 Skyline Drive, Cold Spring, Kentucky 41076.

"Graduation Suite: Shifting Gears," a drama by Thomas P. Millar, 1m2f, (published with and can pair with "Graduation Suite: The Contract") in Thomas P. Millar's *Graduation Suite* (West Vancouver, British Columbia, Canada: Palmer Press, 1987), ISBN 0-9693271-0-2, PAL

"Great Career, A," an absurd comedy by Charles Dizenzo, 1m2f, DPS 2220

"Gretna Green," a verse drama by Constance D'Arcy Mackay, 1m2f, BP, NSHS 19990

"Guest for Breakfast," a comedy by C. B. Gilford, 1m2f, TPH, NSHS 29199, NSHS pb5456, NSHS

H

"Half Hour, The," a drama by Don Helland, 1m2f, ACP, HPC

"Hitting Town," a play (genre?) by Stephen Poliakoff, 1m2f, SF 10648, NSHS pb7806

"Hot Iron, The" ["**Das heiss Eysen**"], a farce by Hans Sachs, 1m2f, (published with and can pair with *"Der Farendt Schuler im Paradeis"* ["The Wandering Scholar in Paradise"] or *"Der doctor mit der grosen nasen"* ["The Doctor with the Big Nose"]) in Hans Sachs' *Meistergesänge Fastnachtsspiele Schwänke*, compiled by Eugen Geiger (Stuttgart: Phillip Reclam jun., 1981), ISBN 3-15-007627-7, NSHS

I

"I Am in Love with Your Sister" [*"Estoy enamorado de tu hermana"*] (see p. 201), *una farsa*/farce *en español*/in Spanish by Jesús Assaf, 1m2f, OEN, NSHS pb8189

"I Hate Mothers," a comedy by James Rayfield, 1m2f, BP

"I Rise in Flame, Cried the Phoenix," a drama by Tennessee Williams about D. H. Lawrence, 1m2f, DPS 2475

"I'll Be Home for Christmas," a comedy by Robert Ander-

son, 1m2f, DPS, NSHS 29201, NSHS 28438, NSHS 16671

"In Place," a comedy by Corinne Jacker, 1m2f, (published with "The Chinese Restaurant Syndrome") DPS 2507

"In the Suds," a medieval French farce translated into English verse by Barnard and Rose Hewitt, 1m2f, BP, SF, NSHS pb5458

"Incident at the Standish Arms, An," a drama by William Inge, 1m2f, (published with and can pair with "The Boy in the Basement," "Memory of Summer," "The Rainy Afternoon," "A Social Event," or "The Tiny Closet") DPS 2535, NSHS pb6069

J

"Judgment Morning," a drama by Robert Brome, 1m2f, DPC, NSHS

"Just One Day," a drama by Eddie Kennedy, 1m2f, DPC J17, NSHS pb173

K

"Kentucky Marriage Proposal, The," a comedy by Alice H. Houstle from Anton Chekhov, 1m2f, DPS 2665

"Kind of Alaska, A," a drama by Harold Pinter, 1m2f, (published with and can pair with "Family Voices," "One for the Road," or "Victoria Station") in Harold Pinter's *Other Places: Four Plays*, DPS, NSHS pb8041 [Note: The catalog says, "If produced separately, 'A Kind of Alaska' may be presented only with another play written by Harold Pinter or with a companion piece approved by Mr. Pinter. In the latter instance all requests must be approved in writing by the Play Service."]

L

"Lady of Fadima," a drama by Edward Allan Baker, 1m2f, (published with and can pair with "Dolores" and "North of Providence") in Edward Allan Baker's *North of Providence; Dolores; Lady of Fadima* (New York: Dramatists Play Service, Inc., 1991), DPS

"Lady of Larkspur Lotion, The," a dramatic sketch by Tennessee Williams, 1m2f, in *27 Wagons Full of Cotton*, DPS 485

"Lesson, The," a comedy by Eugene Ionesco translated by Donald M. Allen, 1m2f, in *Four Plays by Eugene Ionesco*, BP, in *Four Plays by Eugene Ionesco*, SF 647, NSHS

"Letter-Box, The," a drama by Ann Mare Di Mambro, 1m2f,

(published with and can pair with "Saturday at the Commodore") in *Scot-Free: New Scottish Plays,* edited by Alasdair Cameron (London: Nick Hern Books, 1990), ISBN 1-85459-017-0

"**Lingerie,**" a comedy by Diana Amsterdam, 1m2f, in *Sex and Death: Four One-Act Plays,* SF 14682

"**Listening,**" a chamber play developed from a radio play (genre?) by Edward Albee, 1m2f, (published with "Counting the Ways"), in *Edward Albee's The Plays,* vol. 2 (New York: Macmillan Publishing Company, 1991), ISBN 0-02-501762-4, MAC, DPS 1440

"**Long Stay Cut Short, The, or The Unsatisfactory Supper,**" a drama by Tennessee Williams, 1m2f, in *American Blues,* DPS 710, NSHS pb6064

"**Lou Gehrig Did Not Die of Cancer,**" a comedy by Jason Miller, 1m2f, (published with and can pair with "It's a Sin to Tell a Lie") DPS 3162

"**Luck of the Draw, The,**" a play (genre?) by Susan Quinn, 1m2f, in *Triad 75,* NPN

"**Lunch Hour,**" a drama by John Mortimer, 1m2f, SF 14662

M

"**Match Point,**" a comedy by Frank D. Gilroy, 1m2f, in *A Way with Words,* SF 15590

"**Matter of Gender, A,**" a comedy by Sloane Drayson-Knigge, 1m2f, BP

"**Matter of Like Life and Death, A,**" a comedy by John Cromwell, 1m2f, cited in *The Best Plays of 1963-1964,* edited by Henry Hewes

"**Memory of Summer,**" a drama by William Inge, 1m2f, (published with and can pair with "The Boy in the Basement," "A Social Event," "The Tiny Closet," "The Rainy Afternoon," or "An Incident at the Standish Arms") DPS 2535, NSHS pb6069

"**Mickey's Teeth,**" a comedy by Amlin Gray, 1m2f, DPS 3132

"**Miss Julie,**" a drama by August Strindberg, translated by Elizabeth Sprigge, 1m2f (+extras), (can pair with "The Stronger") in *Eight Plays for Theatre,* edited by Robert Cohen (Mountain View, California: Mayfield Publishing Company, 1988), SF 15116; (translated by E. M. Sprinchorn), SF 15674; (translated by Harry G. Carlson), DPS 273; (translated by Michael Meyer) WKW, CPC, NSHS 29262, NSHS 19878, NSHS 19883, NSHS 29323, NSHS 29252, NSHS 5211, NSHS 27003, NSHS 16361, NSHS 20545

"**Mrs. Truth Will Not Take In Anybody Overnight**" ["*Frau Wahrheit will niemand beherbergen*"] a *fastnachtsspiel* by Hans Sachs, 1m2f, HDB, NSHS

N

"**Nanny,**" a comedy by Henri Duvernois, adapted by Percival Wilde from the original French, 1m2f, BP, NSHS 19987

"**Necklace, The,**" (see p. 219) a drama by Jules Tasca from Guy de Maupassant, 1m2f, SF 15990, DPC N10, NSHS 27500, NSHS pb7919

"**No Problem,**" a comedy by Catherine Butterfield, 1m2f, in *Off-Off Broadway Festival Plays, 13th Series,* SF 16651, NSHS pb8083

"**Not Enough Rope,**" (see p. 221) a farce by Elaine May, 1m2f, BP, SF 85, NSHS pb5466, NSHS pb7751

O

"**Omega's Ninth,**" a comedy by Ramon Delgado, 1m2f (that is, 1f is cat), IEC -146-X, NSHS pb109

"**One Day in the Life of Ivy Dennison,**" a bare-stage comedy by Stewart H. Benedict, 1m2f, SF 17627

"**Opening Night,**" a play (genre?) by John Cromwell, 1m2f, cited in *The Best Plays of 1963-1964,* edited by Henry Hewes

"**Optimism,**" a comedy by John Patrick, 1m2f, in *That's Not My Mother,* SF 17954

"**Ordinary Day, An,**" a comedy by Dario Fo and Franca Rame translated by Joe Farrell, 1m2f (voices), (published with "The Open Couple") SF 17940

"**Other One, The,**" a play (genre?) by Mario Fratti, 1m2f, in *Races,* SF, NSHS pb8060

"**Owl Killer, The,**" a drama by Philip Hayes Dean, 1m2f, DPS 3560

P

"**Perfect,**" a ten-minute play (genre?) by Mary Gallagher, 1m2f, (published with and can pair with "Americansaint," "Après Opéra," "'The Asshole Murder Case,'" "Bread," "Cold Water," "Cover," "Downtown," "The Drummer," "The Duck Pond," "Eating Out," "Electric Roses," "The Field," "4 A.M. (open all night)," "Looking Good," "Love and Peace, Mary Jo," "Loyalties," "Marred Bliss," "The Road to Ruin," "Spades," or "Watermelon Boats") in *25 10-Minute Plays from Actors Theatre of Louisville,* SF 22260, NSHS pb29777, ISBN 0-573-62558-1

"**Perfect Match, A,**" a romantic comedy for youth by Ron Charles, 1m2f, in Sylvia E. Kamerman's *The Big Book of Comedies* (Boston: Plays, Inc., 1989), ISBN 0-8238-0289-2

"**Person I Once Was, The,**" a drama by Cindy Lou Johnson, 1m2f, DPS 3632

"Phoenix Too Frequent, A," (see p. 228) a comedy by Christopher Fry, 1m2f, DPS, HDS

"Play," a bare-stage drama by Samuel Beckett, 1m2f, [see next item] in *Cascando and Other Short Pieces,* SF 849

"Play," a bare-stage drama by Samuel Beckett, 1m2f, ([see above item] published with and can pair with "Act Without Words I," "Act Without Words II," "Breath," "Cascando," "Catastrophe," "Come and Go," "Eh Joe," "Embers," "Footfalls," "Ghost Trio," "Krapp's Last Tape," "Not I," "Ohio Impromptu," "A Piece of Monologue," "Quad," "Rockaby," "Rough for Radio I," "Rough for Radio II," "Rough for Theatre I," "Rough for Theatre II," "That Time," or "Words and Music") in *Collected Shorter Plays,* ISBN 0-394-53850-1, ISBN 0-394-62098-4

"Please Hang Up," a comedy by Arthur S. Rosenblatt, 1m2f, DPC P58, NSHS

"Portrait of Portia, A," a drama by S. V. Gersovitz, 1m2f, (published with and can pair with "Exeunt O'Brien and Krasnov," "Jennifer's First Christmas," or "Lamentable Affair of the Vicar's Wife") in *An Evening with Eve,* IEC 316-0

"Postponing the Heat Death of the Universe," a comedy by Stephen Gregg, 1m2f, DPC P61

"Post-Script, The," a comedy by Émile Augier, 1m2f, in Émile Augier's *Four Plays,* translated by Barrett H. Clark (New York: Howard Fertig, Inc., Publisher, 1989), ISBN 0-86527-367-7

"Potato Girl," a brief drama by Christine Rusch, 1m2f, (published with and can pair with "Advice to a New Actor" "The Affidavit," "The American Way," "Anniversary," "Auld Lang Syne, or I'll Bet You Think This Play Is About You," "Bug Swatte," "Coming for a Visit," "Dog Eat Dog," "Drowned Out," "Fireworks," "Interview," "Jumping," "Money," "One Beer Too Many," "Phonecall from Sunkist," "Property of the Dallas Cowboys," "The Split Decision," "Valley Forgery," "Watermelon Boats," or "Widows") in *One-Act Plays for Acting Students,* MPL, ISBN 0-916260-47-X

"Primrose Path, The," a comedy by Gillian Plowman, 1m2f, in *Triad 73,* NPN, DPC P70

"Prince of Court Painters," a verse drama by Constance D'Arcy Mackay, 1m2f, BP, NSHS 19990

"Prisonbreak," a drama by Louis Lippa, 1m2f, DPC, NSHS pb155

"Property of the Dallas Cowboys," a brief comedy by Sam Smiley, 1m2f, (published with and can pair with "Advice to a New Actor" "The Affidavit," "The American Way," "Anniversary," "Auld Lang Syne, or I'll Bet You Think This Play Is About You," "Bug Swatte," "Com-

ing for a Visit," "Dog Eat Dog," "Drowned Out," "Fireworks," "Interview," "Jumping," "Money," "One Beer Too Many," "Phonecall from Sunkist," "Potato Girl," "The Split Decision," "Valley Forgery," "Watermelon Boats," or "Widows") in *One-Act Plays for Acting Students,* MPL, ISBN 0-916260-47-X

"Proposin'," a comedy western by Richard Slocum from Anton Chekhov, 1m2f, BP

Q

"Quo Vadis, Tinker Bell?" a comedy by Cleve Haubold, 1m2f, SF 19607

R

"Rainy Afternoon, The," a drama by William Inge, 1m2f, (published with and can pair with "The Boy in the Basement," "An Incident at the Standish Arms," "Memory of Summer," "A Social Event," or "The Tiny Closet,") DPS 2535, NSHS pb6069

"Rape of Bunny Stuntz, The," a comedy by A. R. Gurney, Jr., 1m2f, SF 20606

"Red Cross," a drama by Sam Shepard, 1m2f, in "Chicago and Other Plays," and (published with and can play with "Cowboys #2," "4-H Club," "Killer's Head," or "The Rock Garden") in *The Unseen Hand & Other Plays,* SF 20611, NSHS pb7928, ISBN 0-553-34263-0

"Red Key, The," a drama by Charles Emery, 1m2f, SF 911, HDS

"Resounding Tinkle, A," a comedy by N. F. Simpson, 1m2f, ISBN 0-573-02229-1, SF 20, NSHS pb5477

"Revival, The," a comedy by Edward Murch, 1m2f, BP

"Roman Fever," a drama by Hugh Leonard, 1m2f, in *Pizzazz,* SF 20919

S

"Say De Kooning," a play (genre?) by Lanford Wilson, 1m2f, DPS manuscript

"Scarecrow," a bare-stage drama by Don Nigro, 1m2f, in *Something in the Basement and Other Plays,* SF 21619

"Seagulls," a bare-stage drama by Caryl Churchill, 1m2f, (published with and can pair with "Abortive," "Not Not Not Not Not Enough Oxygen," "Schreber's Nervous Illness," or "Three More Sleepless Nights") in *Churchill: Shorts [Short Plays by Caryl Churchill],* SF 21634, NSHS, ISBN 1-85459-085-5

One-Male-Two-Female Plays, continued

"Seniority," a play (genre?) by Eric Ziegenhagen, 1m2f, in *Sparks in the Park, and Other Prize-Winning Plays: From the 1987 and 1988 Young Playwrights Festivals: Produced by the Foundation of the Dramatists Guild,* edited by Wendy Lamb (New York: Dell Publishing Company, 1989), ISBN 0-440-20415-1

"Sex Lives of Superheroes," a comedy by Stephen Gregg, 1m2f (+ 3 extras), in Stephen Gregg's "Sex Lives of Superheroes," (Woodstock, Illinois: The Dramatic Publishing Company, 1990), DPC S92

"She Was Lost, and Is Found," a drama by Richard Hensley, 1m2f, SF 1024

"Short Walk After Dinner, A," a drama by Cleve Haubold, 1m2f, SF 21691, NSHS pb5472

"Sisters McIntosh, The," a comedy by Richard Corson, 1m2f, SF 983

"Sittin'," a comedy by Cris Ceraso, 1m2f, SF 1028

"Soap Opera," a comedy by Ralph Pape, 1m2f, (published with and can pair with "Girls We Have Known" or "Warm and Tender Love") in *Girls We Have Known and Other One Act Plays,* DPS 2137

"Social Event, A," a drama by William Inge, 1m2f, (published with and can pair with "The Boy in the Basement," "An Incident at the Standish Arms," "Memory of Summer," "The Rainy Afternoon," or "The Tiny Closet") DPS 2535, NSHS pb6069

"Softly, and Consider the Nearness," a play (genre?) by Rosalyn Drexler, 1m2f, cited in *The Best Plays of 1963-1964,* edited by Henry Hewes

"Solemn Communion, The," a drama by Fernando Arrabal, 1m2f, in *Arrabal: Plays: Volume 3,* SF 21732

"Song of Louise in the Morning, The," a drama by Patricia Joudry, 1m2f, DPS 4190

"Springtime," a drama by Mari Irene Fornes, 1m2f, in *Antæus: Plays in One-Act,* edited by Daniel Halpern, no. 66 (spring, 1991), ISBN 0-88145-056-4

"Stage Directions," a comedy-drama by Israel Horovitz, 1m2f, (published with and can pair with "Spared"; also, can pair with "Hopscotch" or "The 75th") in *The Quannapowitt Quartet,* DPS 4235, SF 990, NSHS pb6068

"Stomach-Ache," a musical for children translated and adapted by Anita Page and Lisa Tate from Ninnie Olsson, 1m2f, BP

"Stop at the Palace, The," a drama by Jules Tasca [set in Vienna], 1m2f, (published with and can pair with [Athens:] "Passion Comedy," [Engelberg:] "Swiss Miss," [London:] "A Day in the Night of Rose Arden," [Munich:] "A Side Trip to Dachau," [Paris:] "Escape," [Rome:] "Going to the Catacombs," or [Venice:] "The Best Souvenirs") in Jules Tasca's *Tour di Europa [Tour of Europe]* (New York: Samuel French, Inc.), ISBN 0-573-69222-X, SF 21806, NSHS pb8105

"Strife Faces Jan," a revue sketch by David Lloyd Crowder, 1m2f, SF, NSHS pb6051

"Stud," a comedy by Alex Gottliev, 1m2f, CBC, NSHS pb4241

"Success," a black comedy by Arthur Kopit, 1m2f, in *Antæus: Plays in One-Act,* edited by Daniel Halpern, no. 66 (spring, 1991), ISBN 0-88145-056-4; also in *The Best American Short Plays, 1991-1992,* edited by Howard Stein and Glenn Young (New York: Applause Theatre Book Publishers, 1992), ISSN 1062-7561

"Suicide, The," a drama by Mario Fratti, 1m2f, (published with and can pair with "The Return") in *Four by Fratti,* ISBN 0-573-69034-0, SF 21613, NSHS 16646, NSHS pb8107

"Summer Morning Visitor," a comedy-drama by Bernard Sabath about Mark Twain, 1m2f, (published with and can pair with "A Barbarian in Love," "The Loneliest Wayfarer," or "The Trouble Begins at 8") in Bernard Sabath's *Twain Plus Twain* (New York: Dramatists Play Service, Inc., 1984), DPS 4635, NSHS pb8024

"Suppressed Desires," (see p. 249) a comedy by Susan Glaspell, 1m2f, BP, HDS, NSHS pb5483. NSHS 19878, NSHS 19883

T

"Telephone, The," a parody by Paul Coates, 1m2f, in Paul Coates' *The Telephone* (Nottingham, England: Playwrights Publishing Company, 1991), ISBN 1-873130-02-3

"Then Again, Maybe I Will," a comedy by Greg Loselle, 1m2f, DPC T58

"Thymus Vulgaris," a comedy drama by Lanford Wilson, 1m2f, DPS 4535

"Ties That Bind, The," a drama by Matthew Witten, 1m2f, in *Off-Off Broadway Festival Plays, 11th Series,"* SF 22679, NSHS 27508, NSHS pb749

"Tomato on Tuesday," a comedy by Larry Randolph, 1m2f, DPC, NSHS pb6100

"Toussaint," a drama about Toussaint-Louverture (circa 1743-1803, originally François-Dominique Toussaint, Haitian general and liberator) by Lorraine Hansberry, 1m2f, in *9 Plays by Black Women,* SF 22173

"Two Eggs Scrambled Soft," a comedy by Don Rifkin, 1m2f, (published with and can pair with "A Brief Period of Time"), in Don Rifkin's *A Brief Period of Time and Two Eggs Scrambled Soft: Two One-Act Plays* (New York: Dramatists Play Service, Inc., 1989), DPS 1127

U

"Under Control," a comedy by Elinor Jones, 1m2f, in *6:15 on the 104/If You Were My Wife I'd Shoot Myself/Under Control,"* DPS 4121, NSHS pb7892

W

"Wall Hanging, The," a drama by Barbara Milne, 1m2f, DPC W52, NSHS pb181

"Wanted . . . Dead or Alive," a comedy by Mark R. Edwards, 1m2f (+male voice), SF 25614

"Wax Museum, The," a drama by John Hawkes, 1m2f, in *Plays for a New Theater: Playbook 2*, HOA, NSHS 29328

"Weak Spot, The," a comedy by George Kelly, 1m2f, SF 25631

"What's a Girl to Do?!" a comedy by Jim Hansen, 1m2f, in *Off-Off Broadway Festival Plays, 13th Series*, SF 25657, NSHS pb8083

Y

"Yes Dear," a comedy by Warren C. Graves, 1m2f, SF 27602

"You Reach for Your Hat," a drama by Ellen Violett from James Purdy, 1m2f, cited in *The Best Plays of 1963-1964*, edited by Henry Hewes

Two-Male-One-Female Plays

A

"A-Killin'," a drama by Patricia Ramsey, 2m1f, DPC K22

"Abstraction," a 14th or 15th century Japanese comedy of anonymous origin, 2m1f, DP, NSHS 16631

"Actors," a bare-stage comedy-drama by Conrad Bromberg, 2m1f, (published with and can pair with "At Home") DPS 625, NSHS pb104, NSHS pb116, NSHS pb117

"Adam and Eve Driven from Eden," a 14th century English mystery play with music, drawn from the Book of Genesis by the Armourers, 2m1f, in *York Plays* based on the manuscript in the library of Lord Ashburnham, edited with introduction and glossary by Lucy Toulmin Smith (New York: Russell & Russell, 1963)

"Ah, Eurydice!" a lyrical fantasy by Stanley Taikeff, 2m1f, DPS 645

"All for Art," a comedy by Roy Friedman, 2m1f, SF 3703

"All Men Are Whores: An Inquiry," a sketch by David Mamet, 2m1f, (part of "The Blue Hour: City Sketches") in *Short Plays and Monologues*, DPS 3025

"Ambiguity," a comedy by John Patrick, 2m1f, in *Sex on the Sixth Floor*, SF 3630

"American Century, The," a comedy by Murphy Guyer, 2m1f, DPS 712

"American Roulette," a drama by Tom McCormack, 2m1f, DPS 745, NSHS pb7800

"Amour et piano" ["**Romance in a Flat**"], a comedy by Georges Feydeau translated into English from the original French by Norman R. Shapiro, 2m1f, (published with and can pair with "The Boor Hug" [*"Les Pavés de l'ours"*], "Ladies' Man" [*"Notre futur"*], or "Wooed and Viewed" [*"Par la fenêtre"*] in Georges Feydeau's *Feydeau, First to Last*, translated by Norman R. Shapiro (Ithaca, New York, and London: Cornell University Press), SF 20629, NSHS

"And Jack Fell Down," a drama by Richard Weaver, 2m1f, IEC 023-4

"Annajanska, the Bolshevik Empress," a comedy by [George] Bernard Shaw, 1m1f, (published with and can pair with "Augustus Does His Bit," "The Dark Lady of the Sonnets," "The Glimpse of Reality," "How He Lied to Her Husband," "The Music-Cure," "O'Flaherty V.C.," "Overruled" or "Village Wooing") in [George] Bernard Shaw's *Selected Short Plays*, definitive text under the editorial supervision of Dan H. Laurence (London: Penguin Books, Ltd., 1988), ISBN 0-14-045031-9, SF 24604

"Answers from the Center of the Universe About Things Unknown," a drama by Kent R. Brown, 2m1f, DPC A49

"Anton Chekhov's The Proposal," a farce by Anton Chekhov, adapted by Alfred Emmet, 2m1f, in Alfred Emmet's *Anton Chekhov's The Proposal* (London: Samuel French, Inc., 1989), ISBN 0-573-12213-X [See also versions by Michael Frayn, Michael Henry Heim, and Ronald Hingley.]

"Aptitude," a comedy by John Patrick, 2m1f, in *People!* SF 18041

"Augustus Does His Bit," a farce by George Bernard Shaw, 2m1f, (published with and can pair with "Annajanska, the Bolshevik Empress," "The Dark Lady of the Sonnets," "The Glimpse of Reality," "How He Lied to Her Husband," "The Music-Cure," "O'Flaherty V.C.," "Overruled" or "Village Wooing") in [George] Bernard Shaw's *Selected Short Plays*, definitive text under the editorial supervision of Dan H. Laurence (London: Penguin Books, Ltd., 1988), ISBN 0-14-045031-9, SF 3666

"Author's Voice, The," a comedy by Richard Greenberg, 2m1f, DPS 857

"Auto-Erotic Misadventure," a drama by F. J. Hartland, 2m1f, in *Off-Off Broadway Festival Plays, 8th Series*, SF 3898

B

"Balcony Scene, The," a romantic comedy by Wil Calhoun, 2m1f, in Wil Calhoun's *The Balcony Scene* (New York: Samuel French, Inc., 1992), ISBN 0-573-69308-0

"Barbarian in Love, A," a comedy by Bernard Sabath about Mark Twain, 2m1f, (published with and can pair with "The Loneliest Wayfarer," "Summer Morning Visitor," or "The Trouble Begins at 8") in *Twain Plus Twain* (New York: Dramatists Play Service, Inc., 1984), DPS 4635, NSHS pb8024

"Basement, The," a drama by Murray Schisgal, 2m1f, (published with and can pair with "Fragments," "Memorial Day," or "The Old Jew") in *Five One Act Plays*, DPS 3975, NSHS pb6057

"Basement, The," a drama by Harold Pinter, 2m1f, DPS 935, NSHS pb7967

"Bear with a Sore Head, A," a romantic comedy by Brian J. Burton adapted from Anton Chekhov's one-act farce "The Bear," 2m1f, in Brian J. Burton's *A Bear with a Sore Head* (Droitwich, Worcestershire, England: Hanbury Plays, 1989), ISBN 1-85205-077-2

"Bear, The," [variant titles] a farce by Anton Chekhov, 2m1f, (can pair with "The Anniversary," "The Proposal," "Swan Song," or "A Tragic Role") in Anton Chekhov's *Plays,* translated by Michael Frayn (London: Methuen & Company, Ltd., 1988), ISBN 0-413-19160-X; also in Anton Chekhov's *Twelve Plays,* translated by Ronald Hingley (London: Oxford University Press, 1992), ISBN 0-19-282813-4 [See also "A Bear with a Sore Head," an adaptation by Brian J. Burton, and "A Wild Boor," an adaptation by Joseph Wallace.]

"Beast of a Different Burden," a comedy by Faith Whithill, 2m1f, SF 4620

"Beau of Bath, The," a verse drama by Constance D'Arcy Mackay, 2m1f, BP, NSHS 19990

"Beirut," a drama by Alan Bowne, 2m1f, (about AIDS, can pair with Harvey Fierstein's "Safe Sex," Patricia Loughrey's "The Inner Circle," Robert Patrick's "Pouf Positive," or Lanford Wilson's "A Poster of the Cosmos") in Alan Bowne's *Beirut* (New York: Broadway Play Publishing, Inc., 1988), ISBN 0-88145-057-X BPP

"Best Souvenirs, The," a comedy by Jules Tasca [set in Venice], 2m1f, (published with and can pair with [Athens:] "Passion Comedy," [Engelberg:] "Swiss Miss," [London:] "A Day in the Night of Rose Arden," [Munich:] "A Side Trip to Dachau," [Paris:] "Escape," or [Rome:] "Going to the Catacombs," or [Vienna:] "The Stop at the Palace") in Jules Tasca's *Tour di Europa* [*Tour of Europe*] (New York: Samuel French, Inc.), ISBN 0-573-69222-X, SF 4708, NSHS pb8105

"Bleeders," a drama by Bryan Patrick Harnetiaux, 2m1f, DPC B59, NSHS pb152

"Boor, The," a farce by Anton Chekhov, 2m1f (+ extras), BP (no royalty with purchase of four copies), SF 4111 (no royalty), HDS, GCB, NSHS 19878, NSHS 19883, NSHS 8266, NSHS 5345

"Boredom," a comedy by John Patrick, 2m1f, in *People!* SF 18041

"Box and Cox," (see p. 189) an English farce by John Maddison Morton, 2m1f, BP (no royalty with purchase of three copies), SF 4672 (no royalty), HDS, GCB, NSHS 5345

"Break," a chamber opera by Michael John LaChiusa, 2m1f, DPS

"Brute, The," a comedy by Eric Bentley from the Russian of Anton Chekhov, 2m1f, SF 4688

"Brute, The," a comedy by Anton Chekhov, 2m1f, BP (no royalty with purchase of three copies)

"But Not for Me," a comedy by Tom Topor, 2m1f, (published with "Here to Stay") in *Romance,* SF 20085

"But What Have You Done for Me Lately?" a drama by Myrna Lamb, 2m1f, SF

C

"Cafe Fledermaus," a symbolic musical revue by Robyn Archer, 2m1f (+ extras), in Robyn Archer's *Cafe Fledermaus* (Paddington, New South Wales, Australia: The Currency Press Pty., Ltd., 1990), ISBN 0-86819-266-X, CPP

"Catastrophe," an experimental play-within-a-play (genre?) by Samuel Beckett, 2m1f, (published with and can pair with "Act Without Words I," "Act Without Words II," "Breath," "Cascando," "Come and Go," "Eh Joe," "Embers," "Footfalls," "Ghost Trio," "Krapp's Last Tape," "Not I," "Ohio Impromptu," "A Piece of Monologue," "Play," "Quad," "Rockaby," "Rough for Radio I," "Rough for Radio II," "Rough for Theatre I," "Rough for Theatre II," "That Time," or "Words and Music") in *Collected Shorter Plays,* ISBN 0-394-53850-1, ISBN 0-394-62098-4; also in *Three Plays: Ohio Impromptu, Catastrophe, What Where,* ISBN 0-394-53851-X, ISBN 0-394-62061-5

"Cecè" ["Chee Chee," 1920], a drama by Luigi Pirandello, 2m1f, (published with and can pair with "At the Exit," "I'm Dreaming, But Am I?" "The Man with the Flower in His Mouth," or "The Vise") in *Pirandello's One-Act Plays,* translated into English from the original Italian by William Murray (New York: Samuel French, Inc., 1970), SF 5630, NSHS

"Chairs, The," a tragic farce by Eugene Ionesco, 2m1f, in "Four Plays by Eugene Ionesco," BP, in *Four Plays by Eugene Ionesco,* SF 308, NSHS 2212, NSHS 16382, NSHS 16612

"Chance Meeting, A," a comedy by Frederick Stroppel, 2m1f, in *Off-Off Broadway Festival Plays, 15th Series,* SF 5787, NSHS pb8079

"Chee Chee" [*"Cecè,"* 1920], a drama by Luigi Pirandello, 2m1f, (published with and can pair with "The Vise," "At the Exit," "The Man with the Flower in His Mouth," or "I'm Dreaming, But Am I?") in *Pirandello's One-Act Plays,* translated into English from the original Italian by William Murray (New York: Samuel French, Inc., 1970), SF 5630, NSHS

"Christmas Spirit," a comedy by John Patrick, 2m1f, in *People!* SF 18041

"Christmas: 1933," a Christmas play (genre?) by Larry King, 2m1f, SF 5207, HDS

"Clean," a drama by Michael Bigelow Dixon and Valerie

Two-Male-One-Female Plays, continued

Smith, 2m1f, (published with and can pair with "Blind Alleys," "Clean," or "The Pick-Up") in *Big Trouble: Six 10-Minute Plays from Actors Theatre of Louisville*, IEC 324-1

"**Co-Incidence,**" a comedy by John Patrick, 2m1f, in *It's a Dog's Life*, SF 11087

"**Cold Water,**" a ten-minute play (genre?) by Lee Blessing, 2m1f, (published with and can pair with "Americansaint," "Après Opéra," "'The Asshole Murder Case,'" "Bread," "Cover," "Downtown," "The Drummer," "The Duck Pond," "Electric Roses," "Eating Out," "The Field," "4 A.M. (open all night)," "Looking Good," "Love and Peace, Mary Jo," "Loyalties," "Marred Bliss," "Perfect," "The Road to Ruin," "Spades," or "Watermelon Boats"), in *25 10-Minute Plays from Actors Theatre of Louisville* SF 22260, NSHS pb2977, ISBN 0-573-62558-1

"**Compulsion,**" a comedy by John Patrick, 2m1f, (published with and can pair with "Integrity," or "Habit") in *Divorce—Anyone?* DPS 1675

"**Confession,**" a comedy by John Patrick, 2m1f, (published with and can pair with "Loyalty," or "Empathy") in *Suicide—Anyone?* DPS 4340

"**Confession,**" a ten-minute play (genre?) by Conrad Bishop and Elizabeth Fuller, 2m1f, SF

"**Confluence,**" a drama by John Bishop, 2m1f, (published with and can pair with "The Skirmishers") DPS 1415

"**Conquest of Everest, The,**" a comedy by Arthur Kopit, 2m1f, (published with and can pair with "The Hero," "The Questioning of Nick," or "Sing to Me Through Open Windows") in *The Day the Whores Came out to Play Tennis and Other Plays*, SF 5705, NSHS pb7930, ISBN 0-374-52233-2

"**Counsel Retained,**" a verse comedy by Constance D'Arcy Mackay, 2m1f, BP, NSHS 19990

"**Courting of Kevin and Roxanne, The,**" a drama by Claude McNeal, 2m1f, SF 5717

"**Cover,**" a ten-minute play (genre?) by Jeffrey Sweet with Stephen Johnson and Sandra Hastie, 2m1f, (published with and can pair with "Americansaint," "Après Opéra," "'The Asshole Murder Case,'" "Bread," "Cold Water," "Downtown," "The Drummer," "The Duck Pond," "Electric Roses," "Eating Out," "The Field," "4 A.M. (open all night)," "Looking Good," "Love and Peace, Mary Jo," "Loyalties," "Marred Bliss," "Perfect," "The Road to Ruin," "Spades," or "Watermelon Boats"), in *25 10-Minute Plays from Actors Theatre of Louisville* SF 22260, NSHS pb2977, ISBN 0-573-62558-1

"**Cowboy Mouth,**" a lengthy one-act drama by Sam Shepard, 2m1f, in *Fool for Love & Other Plays*, SF 5158, NSHS pb8099

"**Cowboys, Indians and Waitresses,**" a comic-drama by Raymond King Shurtz, 2m1f, in *Off-Off Broadway Festival Plays, 17 Series*, SF 349

"**Criminal Minds,**" a comic drama by Robin Swicord, 2m1f, SF, NSHS pb7512

"**Curtains,**" a comedy by Gloria Gonzalez, 2m1f, DPS 1520, NSHS pb101, NSHS pb7635

D

"*Das Kalberbruten*/**The Brooding of the Calf,**" a German-language "*fastnachtsspiel*," by Hans Sachs, 2m1f, HDB, NSHS

"**Decisions,**" a comedy by John Patrick, 2m1f, in *Love Nest for Three*, SF 6635

"**Der farendt Schuler im Paradeiss**" ["**The Wandering Scholar from Paradise**"], a farce by Hans Sachs, 2m1f, (published with and can pair with *"Dass heiss Eysen"* ["The Hot Iron"] or *"Der doctor mit der grosen nasen"* ["The Doctor with the Big Nose"]) in Hans Sachs' *Meistergesänge Fastnachtsspiele Schwänke*, compiled by Eugen Geiger (Stuttgart: Phillip Reclam jun., 1981), ISBN 3-15-007627-7, NSHS

"*Der fahrende Schuler im Paradies,*" a German-language "*fastnachtsspiel*," by Hans Sachs, 2m1f, HDB, NSHS pb7746

"*Der ins Paradies fahrende Schuler,*" a German-language farce by Hans Sachs, 2m1f, HDB

"**Desperadoes,**" a drama by Keith Reddin, 2m1f, in *"Desperadoes": "Throwing Smoke": "Keyhole Lover,"* DPS 1622

"**Dialog for Three,**" a revue sketch by Harold Pinter, 2m1f, SF, NSHS 27487

"**Dirty Old Man, The,**" a drama by Lewis John Carlino, 2m1f (1m is boy), (can pair with "Sarah and the Sax") DPS 1665, NSHS pb7808

"**Dispatches from Hell,**" a drama by Melvin I. Cooperman, 2m1f, (published with and can pair with "Molly and James," "Senior Prom," or "12:21 P.M.") in Double Image Theatre's *Off-Off Broadway Festival Plays, Tenth Series* (New York: Samuel French, Inc., 1985), SF 6688, NSHS 27488, ISBN 0-573-68904-0

"**Divorce, The,**" a comedy by John Patrick, 2m1f, in *It's a Dog's Life*, SF 11087

"**Doing a Good One for the Red Man,**" a farce by Mark Medoff, 2m1f, (published with and can pair with "The Froegle Dictum" or "The Ultimate Grammar of Life") in Mark Medoff's *Four Short Plays* (New York: Dramatists Play Service, Inc., 1974), DPS 3107, NSHS pb8211, NSHS 26932

"Dolly's Little Bills," a comedy by Henry Arthur Jones, 2m1f, in *One Act Plays for Stage and Study: A Collection of Twenty-five Plays by Well-Known Dramatists, American, English and Irish,* First Series, preface by Augustus Thomas (New York: Samuel French, Inc., 1925), SF, NSHS

"Doubting Saint, The," a religious drama by Warren Keliewer, 2m1f or 1m2f, SF, NSHS

"Down and Out," a fantasy by John Patrick Shanley, 2m1f, (published with and can pair with "Let Us Go out into the Starry Night," "A Lonely Impulse of Delight," or "The Red Coat") in *Welcome to the Moon and Other Plays,* DPS 4807

"Downtown," a ten-minute play (genre?) by Jeffrey Hatcher, 2m1f, *25 10-Minute Plays from Actors Theatre of Louisville, edited* by Actors Theatre of Louisville (New York: Samuel French, Inc., 1989), ISBN 0-573-62558-1, SF

"Duck Pond, The," a ten-minute play (genre?) by Ara Watson, 2m1f, (published with and can pair with "Americansaint," "Après Opéra," "'The Asshole Murder Case,'" "Bread," "Cold Water," "Cover," "Downtown," "The Drummer," "Electric Roses," "Eating Out," "The Field," "4 A.M. (open all night)," "Looking Good," "Love and Peace, Mary Jo," "Loyalties," "Marred Bliss," "Perfect," "The Road to Ruin," "Spades," or "Watermelon Boats"), in *25 10-Minute Plays from Actors Theatre of Louisville* SF 22260, NSHS pb2977, ISBN 0-573-62558-1

"Dumping Ground," a comedy drama by Elizabeth Diggs, 2m1f, DPS 1745

E

"*El hacha,*" a *farsa* by José Luna, 2m1f, OEN, NSHS pb8189

"Electric Roses," a ten-minute play (genre?) by David Howard, 2m1f, (published with and can pair with "Americansaint," "Après Opéra," "'The Asshole Murder Case,'" "Bread," "Cold Water," "Cover," "Downtown," "The Drummer," "The Duck Pond," "Eating Out," "The Field," "4 A.M. (open all night)," "Looking Good," "Love and Peace, Mary Jo," "Loyalties," "Marred Bliss," "Perfect," "The Road to Ruin," "Spades," or "Watermelon Boats"), in *25 10-Minute Plays from Actors Theatre of Louisville* SF 22260, NSHS pb2977, ISBN 0-573-62558-1

"Empathy," a comedy by John Patrick, 2m1f, (published with and can pair with "Confession" or "Loyalty") in

Suicide—Anyone? DPS 4340

"Encore," a drama by Ellen Violett from James Purdy, 2m1f, cited in *The Best Plays of 1963-1964,* edited by Henry Hewes (New York: Dodd, Mead & Company, 1964)

"End of I, The," a drama by Diana Amsterdam, 2m1f, in *Sex and Death: Four One-Act Plays,* SF 7630

"End of the Beginning, The," a comedy by Sean O'Casey, 2m1f, LD, NSHS 28268

"End of the Trail, The," a drama by Ernest Howard Culbertson, 2m1f, IPC, NSHS 6066

"Extracurriculars," a comedy by Joseph Fedorko, 2m1f, BP

"Eye to Eye," a ten-minute play (genre?) by Chris Graybill, 2m1f, SF

F

"Family Voices," a drama by Harold Pinter, 2m1f, (published with and can pair with "A Kind of Alaska," "One for the Road," or "Victoria Station") in Harold Pinter's *Other Places,* DPS 3548, NSHS pb8041

"Fast Women," a comedy by Willie Reale, 2m1f, (published with "Many Happy Returns") DPS 3052

"Fettucine," a comedy by John Patrick, 2m1f, in *That's Not My Father!* SF 8166

"Finding the Love of Your Life" [**"Romance Ranch: Finding the Love of Your Life"**], a drama by Jules Tasca, 2m1f, (published with "The Dark," "The Fantasy Bond," "Inflatable You," "The Man in Blue," "Penance," or "Snocky") in Jules Tasca's *Romance Ranch* (New York: Samuel French, Inc., 1991), ISBN 0-573-62434-8, SF 7997

"Finger of God, The," a drama by Percival Wilde, 2m1f, BP, NSHS pb5489, NSHS 27108

"Florentine Tragedy, A," a drama by Oscar Wilde, 2m1f, in *24 Favorite One-Act Plays,* edited by Bennett Cerf and Van H. Cartmell (New York: Doubleday & Company, Inc., 1958), NSHS pb4019 NSHS 14824, NSHS 20483, NSHS 21389, NSHS 21514, NSHS 21776

"Fog," a drama by Eugene O'Neill, 2m1f, in *Eugene O'Neill, Complete Plays, Vol. 1,* SF 8671

"Fore," a comedy by Frank D. Gilroy, 2m1f, in *A Way with Words,* SF 8938

"Fortunata Writes a Letter," a drama by Theodore Apstein, 2m1f, MM, NSHS 2401

"Freedom for Clemens," a dark comedy by Tankred Dorst, translated by George E. Wellwarth from the German *Freiheit für Clemens,* 2m1f, (published with and can pair with "Let's Eat Hair!/*Essen Wir Haare*" "or "Nightpiece/

Nachtsstück") in *Postwar German Theatre*, GB, NSHS pb7857

"From Here to the Library," a drama by Jimmie Chinn, 2m1f, SF 8928, NSHS 27523

"Frustration," a comedy by John Patrick, 2m1f, in *Sex on the Sixth Floor*, SF 8077

"Frying Pan, The," a drama by Paul Avila Mayer, 2m1f, in *Three Hand Reel*, DPS 4510

G

"Ghost Story, A," a drama by John Pielmeier, 2m1f, (published with and can pair with "A Gothic Tale" or "A Witch's Brew") in *Haunted Lives*, DPS 2297

"Gift, The," a comedy by John Patrick, 2m1f, in *It's a Dog's Life*, SF 11087

"Give the Bishop My Faint Regards," a comedy by Frank D. Gilroy, 2m1f, in *A Way with Words*, SF 9169

"Goblins Plot to Murder God, The," a ten-minute play (genre?) by Mark O'Donnel, 2m1f or 1m2f or 3m or 3f or 4m or 4f or 1m3f or 2m2f, or 3m1f, SF

"Golden Accord, The," a ten-minute play (genre?) by Wole Soyinka, 2m1f, SF

"Good Day," a drama by Emanuel Peluso, 2m1f (1m silent), DPS 2170

"Goodbye, The," a drama by Paul Green, 2m1f, SF, NSHS 16609

"Gothic Tale, A," a drama by John Pielmeier, 2m1f, (published with and can pair with "A Ghost Story" or "A Witch's Brew") in *Haunted Lives*, DPS 2297

"Green-Eyed Monster Comic Strip, The," a drama by Alec Taylor, 2m1f, (can pair with "Candy-Floss Man") in Alec Taylor's *Candy-Floss Man* (Macclesfield, Cheshire, England: New Playwrights Network, 1991), ISBN 0-86319-273-4, NPN

H

"Habit," a comedy by John Patrick, 2m1f, (published with and can pair with "Compulsion" or "Integrity") in *Divorce—Anyone?* DPS 1675

"Half Fare," a drama by Shoshana Marchand, 2m1f, FDG, NSHS

"Hand Me My Afghan," a comedy by Cliff Harville, 2m1f, (published with and can pair with "George L. Smith," "Sara Hubbard," or "A Silent Catastrophe") in Cliff Harville's *Sunsets*, (New York: Samuel French, Inc., 1989), ISBN 0-573-62522-0, SF 21387

"Harold," a satire by Jean-Claude van Itallie, 2m1f, (pub-

lished with and can pair with "Eat Cake," "The Girl and the Soldier," "Photographs: Mary and Howard," "Rosary," or "Thoughts on the Instant of Greeting a Friend on the Street") in *Seven Short and Very Short Plays*, DPS 4726, NSHS pb65

"Heat Lighting," a comedy by Robert F. Carroll, 2m1f, SF 10625, HDS

"Heaven Sent," a fantasy-comedy by Craig C. Bailey, 2m1f, in Craig C. Bailey's *Heaven Sent* (Franklin, Ohio: Eldridge Publishing Company, 1988), EPC

"Here to Stay," a comedy by Tom Topor, 2m1f, (published with "But Not for Me") in *Romance*, SF 20084

"How He Lied to Her Husband," (see p. 207) a farce by George Bernard Shaw, 2m1f, (published with and can pair with "Annajanska, the Bolshevik Empress," "Augustus Does His Bit," "The Dark Lady of the Sonnets," "The Glimpse of Reality," "The Music-Cure," "O'Flaherty V.C.," "Overruled," or "Village Wooing,") in *Selected Short Plays*, definitive text under editorial supervision of Dan H. Laurence (London: Penguin Books, Ltd., 1988), ISBN 0-14-045031-9, ISBN 0-14-045024-6, SF 10670, NSHS

"Hurricane of the Eye," a drama by Emanuel Peluso, 2m1f, DPS 2450, NSHS pb7724

I

"I Saw Your Picture in the Paper and I Had to Call," a drama by Roger Cornish, 2m1f, AR, NSHS pb6124

"I'm Dreaming, but Am I?" ["Sogno (ma forse no)," 1931] a drama by Luigi Pirandello, 2m1f, (published with and can pair with "At the Exit," "Chee-Chee," "The Man with the Flower in His Mouth" or "The Vise") in *Pirandello's One-Act Plays*, translated into English from the original Italian by William Murray (New York: Samuel French, Inc., 1970), SF 11601, NSHS, ISBN 0-573-60039-2

"In the Beginning Was Eve," a comedy by Warren Kliewer, 2m1f, SF, NSHS pb7834, ISBN 0-573-62127-6

"Integrity," a comedy by John Patrick, 2m1f, (published with and can pair with "Compulsion" or "Habit") in *Divorce—Anyone?* DPS 1675

"Interview—Job, The," a comedy by Jerry DiCairano, 2m1f, PBC, NSHS pb97

J

"Jealousy," a comedy by Murray Schisgal, 2m1f, (can pair with "The Pushcart Peddlers"; published with and can pair with "There Are No Sacher Tortes in Our Society") DPS 2598

"Just One Day," a drama by Eddie Kennedy, 2m1f, DPC

"Just a Little Something for Christmas," a Christmas comedy by Charles Emery, 2m1f, (published with and can pair with "Dutch Treat," "Fishing Hat," "To Open, Pry Cover," or "What's That Tune") in *Ethel and Albert Comedies*, SF 7645 (anthology), SF 12622 (single play), NSHS pb7825 (anthology)

K

"Keyhole Lover," a drama by Keith Reddin, 2m1f, in *"Desperadoes": "Throwing Smoke": "Keyhole Lover,"* DPS 1622

L

"L'uomo dal fiore in bocca" ["The Man with the Flower in His Mouth," 1923], a drama by Luigi Pirandello, 2m1f, (published with and can pair with "At the Exit," "Chee-Chee," "I'm Dreaming, But Am I?" or "The Vise") in *Pirandello's One-Act Plays*, translated into English from the original Italian by William Murray (New York: Samuel French, Inc., 1970), SF 15602 (state translator when ordering), NSHS, ISBN 0-573-60039-2

"La tercera ley de Newton" ["The Third Law of Newton"], a Spanish-language *farsa* by Leticia Tellez, 2m1f, OEN, NSHS pb8189

"Last Act Is a Solo, The," a drama by Robert Anderson, 2m1f, SF 13850

"Last Day of Camp," a ten-minute play (genre?) by Jeffrey Sweet, 2m1f, SF 13852

"Let's Eat Hair!" an absurdity by Carl Laszlo, translated by George E. Wellwarth from the German *Essen Wir Haare!* 2m1f, (published with and can pair with "Freedom for Clemens/*Freiheit für Clemens*" or "Nightpiece/*Nachtsstück*") in *Postwar German Theatre*, GB, NSHS pb7857

"Life Is Only Seven Points," a drama by David Rush, 2m1f, DPC L53, NSHS pb158

"Little Brother: Little Sister," a drama by David Campton, 2m1f, (published with and can pair with "Out of the Frying Pan") DPS 2875

"Little Johnny," a drama by Murray Schisgal, 2m1f, (published with and can pair with "The Flatulist," "The Pushcart Peddlers," or "Walter") in *The Pushcart Peddlers, The Flatulist and Other Plays*, DPS 3740

"Loneliest Wayfarer, The," a comedy by Bernard Sabath about Mark Twain, 2m1f, (published with and can pair with "A Barbarian in Love," "Summer Morning Visi-

tor," or "The Trouble Begins at 8") in Bernard Sabath's *Twain Plus Twain* (New York: Dramatists Play Service, Inc., 1984), DPS 4635, NSHS pb8024

"Lovely Afternoon," a comedy by Howard Delman, 2m1f, BP, HDS, SF 14660

"Lover, The," a bizarre comedy revue sketch by Harold Pinter, 2m1f, (published with and can pair with "The Black and White," "The Collection," "The Dwarfs," "Special Offer," or "Trouble in the Works") in Harold Pinter's *Plays: Two* (London and Boston: Faber & Faber, 1991), NSHS pb8102, ISBN 0-571-16075-1; and (published with and can pair with "Applicant," "Interview," "Last to Go," "That's All," or "That's Your Trouble") in *Revue Sketches*, HDS DPS 1765, DPS 2980, NSHS 27487, NSHS pb7737

"Loyalty," a comedy by John Patrick, 2m1f, (published with and can pair with "Confession" or "Empathy") in *Suicide—Anyone?* DPS 4340

"Lynette at 3:00 A. M.," a ten-minute play (genre?) by Jane Anderson, 2m1f, SF

M

"Madness of Lady Bright, The," a drama by Lanford Wilson, 2m1f, DPS 355, NSHS 29301, NSHS pb7760

"Maggie and the Bird Go Fishing," a comedy by Dudley W. Sanders, 2m1f, BP

"Maid to Marry," a farce by Eugene Ionesco, 2m1f, SF

"Maker of Dreams, The," a fantasy by Oliphant Down, 2m1f, ISBN GB-573-02152-X, SF, NSHS pb4019, NSHS pb5421, NSHS 5471, NSHS 14824, NSHS 20483, NSHS 21389, NSHS 21514, NSHS 21776, NSHS 27039

"Man Who Died at Twelve o'clock, The," a farce by Paul Green, 2m1f, in *Fifteen American One-Act Plays*, SF 15628, NSHS 16609

"Man with the Flower in His Mouth, The" ["L'uomo dal fiore in bocca," 1923], (see p. 216) a drama by Luigi Pirandello, 2m1f, (published with and can pair with "At the Exit," "Chee-Chee," "I'm Dreaming, But Am I?" or "The Vise,") in *Pirandello's One-Act Plays*, translated into English from the original Italian by William Murray (New York: Samuel French, Inc., 1970), SF 15602 (state translator when ordering), NSHS, ISBN 0-573-60039-2

"Marriage, The," an Irish folk-drama by Douglas Hyde, 2m1f, (published with and can pair with "The Lost Saint" or "The Tinker and the Sheeog") in Douglas Hyde's *Selected Plays of Douglas Hyde*, chosen by Gareth W. Dunleavy and Janet Egleson Dunleavy, with translations by Lady Augusta Gregory, with parallel texts in Irish and English (Boston: University Press of America, 1991), ISBN 0-86140-095-X, ISBN 0-86140-096-8

"Marriage Proposal, A," a farce by Anton Chekoff, 2m1f, (no royalty with purchase of three copies) BP, NSHS pb4019, NSHS 14824, NSHS 20483, NSHS 21389, NSHS 21514, NSHS 21776, NSHS 16020, NSHS 21405

"Marriage Proposal, The," a farce by Anton Chekhov, adapted by Hilmar Baukhage and Barrett H. Clark, 2m1f, SF 15935 (no royalty), NSHS 27039

"Masquerade," a comedy by John Patrick, 2m1f, in *That's Not My Father!* SF 15583

"Me Too, Then!" (see p. 217) a comedy by Tom Dudzick and Steven Smith, 2m1f, in *Off-Off Broadway Festival Plays, Vol. 5*, SF 15651, NSHS 27534

"Meeting, The," a drama by Anna Marie Barlow, 2m1f, (published with "A Limb of Snow"; can pair with "Ferryboat" or "A Limb of Snow") DPS 2865

"Mery Play betwene Johan Johan the Husbande, Tyb his Wyfe, and Syr Johan the Preest, A," a medieval farce probably by John Heywood, 2m1f, HMC, NSHS 29216

"Minuet, A," a drama by Louis N. Parker, 2m1f, in *One Act Plays for Stage and Study: A Collection of Twenty-five Plays by Well-Known Dramatists, American, English and Irish*, First Series, preface by Augustus Thomas (New York: Samuel French, Inc., 1925), SF 15675, NSHS pb5469

"Money Talks," a comedy by Jason Milligan, 2m1f, in *Cross Country: Seven More One-Act Plays*," SF 15265

"Mooncastle," a comedy by Ara Watson, 2m1f, (published with and can pair with "Bite the Hand") DPS 1033

"Motor Show, The," a farce by Eugene Ionesco, 2m1f, SF

"Mrs. McWilliams and the Lighting," a comedy by Jules Tasca from Mark Twain, 2m1f, in *Five One-Act Plays by Mark Twain*, SF 15613

"Murder, A," a black comedy by William Inge, 2m1f, available only in manuscript from DPS, NSHS pb86

"Music-Cure, The," a comedy by George Bernard Shaw, 2m1f, (published with and can pair with "Annajanska, the Bolshevik Empress," "Augustus Does His Bit," "The Dark Lady of the Sonnets," "The Glimpse of Reality," "How He Lied to Her Husband," "O'Flaherty V.C.," "Overruled," or "Village Wooing") in *Selected Short Plays*, definitive text under editorial supervision of Dan H. Laurence (London: Penguin Books, Ltd., 1988), ISBN 0-14-045031-9, ISBN 0-14-045024-6, SF 15711, NSHS

N

"Needs," a drama by Steven M. Jacobson, 2m1f (female silent), DPS 3340

"Next Contestant, The," a drama by Frank D. Gilroy (first published in *The Best Short Plays*), 2m1f, SF 16618

"Nick and Wendy," a comedy by Renée Taylor and Joseph Bologna, 2m1f, in *Bedrooms*, SF 244

"No Snakes in the Grass," a drama by James Magnuson, 2m1f, SF 771

"Noble Lord, The," a comedy by Percival Wilde, 2m1f, BP, NSHS pb5468

"Not Not Not Not Not Enough Oxygen," a drama by Caryl Churchill, 2m1f, (published with and can pair with "Abortive," "Schreber's Nervous Illness," "Seagulls," or "Three More Sleepless Nights") in *Churchill: Shorts [Short Plays by Caryl Churchill]*, SF 16083, SF 3887, NSHS, ISBN 1-85459-085-5

O

"Ofay Watcher, The," a drama in three scenes by Frank Cucci, 2m1f, DPS, NSHS pb7791

"Old One-Two, The," a drama by A. R. Gurney, Jr., 2m1f, SF 17616

"Ole George Comes to Tea," a comedy by St. John G. Ervine, 2m1f, NSHS pb5465

"Omega's Ninth," a comedy by Ramon Delgado, 2m1f (that is, 1m is cat), IEC -146-X, NSHS pb109

"One Egg," a farce by Babette Hughes, 2m1f, SF 17628

"Open Meeting, The," a comedy by A. R. Gurney, Jr., 2m1f, (can pair with "Another Antigone," "The Love Course," or "The Problem") in A. R. Gurney, Jr.'s *Public Affairs* (New York: Samuel French, Inc., 1992), ISBN 0-573-69318-8, SF 17636

"Opening Act," a comedy by Jules Tasca, 2m1f, in *The God's Honest, An Evening of Lies*, SF 17663

"Overlaid," a comedy by Robertson Davies, 2m1f, in Robertson Davies' *At My Heart's Core & Overlaid* (Toronto, Ontario, Canada: Simon & Pierre Publishing Company, Ltd., 1991), ISBN 0-88924-225-9; also in *10 Canadian Short Plays*, SF 17601

"Owl," a comedy by Cleve Haubold, 2m1f, SF 17654

P

"Painted Rain," a drama by Janet Allard, 2m1f, in *Hey Little Walter, and Other Prize-Winning Plays,* edited by Wendy Lamb (New York: Dell, 1991), ISBN 0-440-21025-9

"Pas de Deux," (Act I from *Slow Dance on the Killing Ground*), a drama by William Hanley, 2m1f, DPS, NSHS 28438 [Note: Act can stop just prior to entrance of female character.]

"Path of the Ancient Chinaman, The," a drama by William Severson, 2m1f, AR

"People in the Glass Paperweight, The," a tragicomedy by Gene McKinney, 2m1f, BP, SF 18627, NSHS pb5461

"Period," a farce by Richard McBrien, 2m1f, in *Off-Off Broadway Festival Plays, Series 6, SF* 18139

"Phamtom's Dance," a drama by Edward Kinchley Evans, 2m1f, AR, NSHS pb7522

"Phipps," a comedy by Stanley Houghton, 2m1f, in *One Act Plays for Stage and Study: A Collection of Twenty-five Plays by Well-Known Dramatists, American, English and Irish,* First Series, preface by Augustus Thomas (New York: Samuel French, Inc., 1925), SF, NSHS

"Physician, The," a comedy by John Patrick, 2m1f, (published with and can pair with "The Chiropodist," "The Gynecologist," or "The Psychiatrist") in John Patrick's *The Doctor Will See You Now* (New York: Dramatists Play Service, 1991), DPS

"Piggy Bank, The," a comedy by Mario Fratti, 2m1f, (published with "Her Voice") SF 18155, NSHS

"Private Ear, The," a comedy by Peter Shaffer, 2m1f, BP, HDS, (can pair with "The Public Eye") SF 855, NSHS pb5485, NSHS 29198

"Progress," a drama by St. John G. Ervine, 2m1f, GAU, NSHS pb5473 GAU?

"Progression," a comedy by John Patrick, 2m1f, in *Love Nest for Three,* SF 18602

"Proposal, The," a farce by Anton Chekhov, translated by Michael Frayn, 2m1f, in Anton Chekhov's *Plays* (London: Methuen & Company, Ltd., 1988), ISBN 0-413-19160-X [See also the versions by Alfred Emmet ("Anton Chekhov's The Proposal"), Michael Henry Heim, and Ronald Hingley.]

"Proposal, The," a farce by Anton Chekhov, translated by Ronald Hingley, 2m1f (+ extras), in Anton Chekhov's *Twelve Plays,* translated by Ronald Hingley (London: Oxford University Press, 1992), ISBN 0-19-282813-4 [See also the versions by Alfred Emmet ("Anton Chekhov's The Proposal"), Michael Frayn, and Michael Henry Heim.]

"Psychiatrist, The," a comedy by John Patrick, 2m1f, (published with and can pair with "The Chiropodist," "The Gynecologist," or "The Physician") in John Patrick's *The Doctor Will See You Now* (New York: Dramatists Play Service, 1991, DPS 1677

"Psychoneurotic Phantasies," a comedy by Gilbert David Feke, 2m1f, BP

"Public Eye, The," a comedy by Peter Shaffer, 2m1f, BP, (can pair with "The Private Ear") SF 856, NSHS pb5474,

NSHS pb8168

"Puppet Master, The," a bare-stage fantasy by Dennis Noble, 2m1f, BP

"Pushcart Peddlers, The," a comedy by Murray Schisgal, 2m1f, (published with and can pair with "The Flatulist," "Little Johnny," or "Walter") in *The Pushcart Peddler, The Flatulist and Other Plays,* DPS 3740

R

"Raconteur," a comedy by John Patrick, 2m1f, in *That's Not My Father!* SF 19974

"Radio II," (same as "Rough for Radio II") an experimental radio drama by Samuel Beckett, 2m1f, (published with and can pair with "Act Without Words I," "Act Without Words II," "Breath," "Cascando," "Catastrophe," "Come and Go," "Eh Joe," "Embers," "Footfalls," "Ghost Trio," "Krapp's Last Tape," "Not I," "Ohio Impromptu," "A Piece of Monologue," "Play," "Quad," "Rockaby," "Rough for Radio I," "Rough for Theatre I," "Rough for Theatre II," "That Time," or "Words and Music") in *Collected Shorter Plays,* ISBN 0-394-53850-1, ISBN 0-394-62098-4

"Rapes," (see p. 234) a drama by Mario Fratti, 2m1f, in *Races,* SF, NSHS pb8060

"Recovery, The," a farce by Albert Bermel, 2m1f, in *Six One-Act Farces,* SF 20639

"Red Carnations," a comedy by Glenn Hughes, 2m1f, BP, SF 20610, HDS

"Redemption," a comedy by John Patrick, 2m1f, in *That's Not My Mother!* SF 20924

"Return to Dust," a radio drama by George Bamber, 2m1f, CSS, NSHS 20719

"Road to Nineveh, The," a Christmas comedy by Le Wilhelm, 2m1f, in *Off-Off Broadway Festival Plays, 17 Series,* SF 19979

"Road Trip," a drama by Jason Milligan, 2m1f, in *Cross Country: Seven More One-Act Plays,"* SF 20136

"Rock Garden, The," a drama by Sam Shepard, 2m1f, (published with and can play with "Cowboys #2," "4-H Club," "Killer's Head," or "Red Cross") in *The Unseen Hand & Other Plays,* SF 20625, NSHS pb7928, ISBN 0-553-34263-0

"Roll Over . . . Play Dead," a comedy by T. Sharpe, 2m1f, in *Triad 72,* NPN

"Romance," a drama by Ernest Joselovitz, 2m1f, (published with and can pair with "Nicky and the Theatre for a New World" or "There Is No John Garfield") in Ernest Joselovitz' *Four One-Act Plays* (New York: Samuel

French, Inc., 1991), ISBN 0-573-62170-5, SF 20662

"Romance in a Flat" [*"Amour et piano"*], a comedy by Georges Feydeau translated.into English from the original French by Norman R. Shapiro, 2m1f, (published with and can pair with "The Boor Hug" [*"Les Pavés de l'ours"*], "Ladies' Man" [*"Notre futur"*], or "Wooed and Viewed" [*"Par la fenêtre"*] in Georges Feydeau's *Feydeau, First to Last*, translated by Norman R. Shapiro (Ithaca, New York, and London: Cornell University Press), SF 20629, NSHS

"Romance Ranch: Finding the Love of Your Life" ["Finding the Love of Your Life"], a drama by Jules Tasca, 2m1f, (published with "The Dark," "The Fantasy Bond," "Inflatable You," "The Man in Blue," "Penance," or "Snocky") in Jules Tasca's *Romance Ranch* (New York: Samuel French, Inc., 1991), ISBN 0-573-62434-8, SF 7997

"Rooming House, The," a drama by Conrad Bromberg, 2m1f, (published with and can pair with "Doctor Galley" or "Transfers") in *Transfers: Three One-Acts Plays*, DPS 4610, NSHS pb7923

"Rough for Radio II" (same as **"Radio II"**), an experimental radio drama by Samuel Beckett, 2m1f, (published with and can pair with "Act Without Words I," "Act Without Words II," "Breath," "Cascando," "Catastrophe," "Come and Go," "Eh Joe," "Embers," "Footfalls," "Ghost Trio," "Krapp's Last Tape," "Not I," "Ohio Impromptu," "A Piece of Monologue," "Play," "Quad," "Rockaby," "Rough for Radio I," "Rough for Theatre I," "Rough for Theatre II," "That Time," or "Words and Music") in *Collected Shorter Plays,* ISBN 0-394-53850-1, ISBN 0-394-62098-4

"Ruffian on the Stair, The," a drama by Joe Orton, 2m1f, in *The Complete Plays of Joe Orton*, SF 20638

S

"Sankes," a drama by Edwin R. Gilwelt, 2m1f, DPC

"Scrimmages," a comedy by Joseph Fedorko, 2m1f, in *Extracurriculars*, BP

"Second Vows," a comedy by Jules Tasca, 2m1f, in *The God's Honest, An Evening of Lies*, SF 21653

"Secret Sin," a comedy adapted for the stage by Jules Tasca from the short story by Saki (H. H. Munro), 2m1f, (published with and can pair with "The Background," "Blind Spot," "Dusk" "The Hen," "The Unrest Cure," "The Reticence of Lady Anne," or "The Tiger") in Jules Tasca's *Tales by Saki* (New York: Samuel French, Inc.) ISBN 0-573-62560-3, SF 22133, NSHS pb7798, NSHS pb8113

"Seniority," a comedy by John Patrick, 2m1f, in *That's Not My Mother*, SF 20970

"Shadow of a Sovereign," a drama by Gloria Gonzalez, 2m1f, PPC, NSHS pb7749

"Shawl, The," a drama by David Mamet, 2m1f, SF 21697

"Shirkers, The," a thriller by C. M. S. McLellan, 2m1f, SF 21690

"Shirt, The," a drama by Leonard Melfi, 2m1f, (published with and can play with "Birdbath," "Ferryboat," "Halloween," or "Lunchtime,") in *Encounters: Six One-Act Plays*, SF 21608

"Shoemaker's Wife, The," a farce by David Thompson from Hans Sach's *"Der Todte Mann,"* 2m1f, (no royalty with purchase of three copies) BP 4663, NSHS 19998, NSHS pb7799

"Shooting Gallery," a bare-stage comedy by Israel Horovitz, 2m1f, (published with and can pair with "Play for Germs") DPS 4075, NSHS pb93

"Side Trip to Dachau, A," a drama by Jules Tasca, 2m1f, (published with and can pair with [Athens:] "Passion Comedy" [Engelberg:] "Swiss Miss," [London:] "A Day in the Night of Rose Arden," [Paris:] "Escape," [Rome:] "Going to the Catacombs," [Venice:] "The Best Souvenirs," or [Vienna:] "The Stop at the Palace") in Jules Tasca's *Tour di Europa* [*Tour of Europe*] (New York: Samuel French, Inc.), ISBN 0-573-69222-X, SF 21667, NSHS pb8105

"Sightings," a comedy by Brad Slaight, 2m1f, (can pair with "Senior Prom") in *High Tide*, BP

"Silence," a comedy by Harold Pinter, 2m1f, SF, NSHS 27487

"Silver Lining, The," a verse comedy by Constance D'Arcy Mackay, 2m1f, BP, NSHS 19990

"Silver Linings," bare-stage revue sketches by Ted Tally, 2m1f, DPS 4088

"Sire de Maletroit's Door, The," a drama by Jules Tasca from Robert Louis Stevenson, 2m1f, DPC S75, NSHS pb161

"Skirmishers, The," a comedy drama by John Bishop, 2m1f, (published with and can pair with "Confluence") DPS 1415

"Slight Ache, A," a drama by Harold Pinter, 2m1f (1m silent), DPS 375

"Smell of Burning, A," a comedy by David Campton, 2m1f (+voice), (published with and can pair with "Then . . .") DPS 4155, NSHS pb7810

"So Please Be Kind," a drama by Frank D. Gilroy, 2m1f, (published with and can play with "Come Next Tuesday," "Present Tense," or "'Twas Brillig") in Frank D. Gilroy's *Present Tense* (New York: Samuel French, Inc.,

1973), SF 21722, NSHS pb5486, NSHS pb6048, NSHS pb6050, NSHS pb8169

"Sogno (ma forse no)" ["**I'm Dreaming, but Am I?**" 1931], a drama by Luigi Pirandello, 2m1f, (published with and can pair with "At the Exit," "Chee-Chee," "The Man with the Flower in His Mouth," or "The Vise") in *Pirandello's One-Act Plays*, translated into English from the original Italian by William Murray (New York: Samuel French, Inc., 1970), SF 11601, NSHS, ISBN 0-573-60039-2

"**Sometime Thing, A,**" a drama by James Lineberger, 2m1f, SF 989

"**Son Who Hunted Tigers in Jakarta, The,**" a drama by Ronald Ribman, 2m1f, (published with and can pair with "The Burial of Esposito" or "Sun-Stroke") in *Passing Through from Exotic Places*, DPS 3585

"**Sponge Room, The,**" a play (genre?) by Keith Waterhouse, 2m1f, cited in *The Best Plays of 1963-1964*, edited by Henry Hewes (New York: Dodd, Mead & Company, 1964)

"**Squat Betty,**" a play (genre?) by Keith Waterhouse, 2m1f, cited in *The Best Plays of 1963-1964*, edited by Henry Hewes (New York: Dodd, Mead & Company, 1964)

"**Squirrel,**" a play (genre?) by Jack Dunphy, 2m1f, available only in manuscript from DPS

"**Squirrels,**" a comedy by David Mamet, 2m1f, SF 21763

"**Sticks and Stones,**" a comedy by Don Kukla, 2m1f, BP

"**Strategy,**" a comedy by John Patrick, 2m1f, in *Love Nest for Three*, SF 21603

"**Strawberry Envy,**" a comedy by Kitty Johnson, 2m1f, in *Triplet: Three One-Act Plays* (New York: Samuel French, Inc., 1991), ISBN 0-573-69290-4, SF 21939

"**Stray Cats,**" a comedy by John Rustan and Frank Semerano, 2m1f, AR, NSHS pb6842

"**Stuffings,**" a comedy by James Prideaux, 2m1f, (published with and can pair with "An American Sunset") DPS 750

"**Such a Nice Little Kitty,**" a comedy by Pat Cook, 2m1f, DPC S66, NSHS pb196

T

"**Take a Deep Breath,**" by Jean-Claude Van Itallie, 2m1f, DPS, NSHS pb65

"**Tenacity,**" a comedy by John Patrick, 2m1f, in *Sex on the Sixth Floor*, SF 22602

"**Terrible Meek, The,**" an Easter drama by Charles Rann Kennedy, 2m1f, SF 22645 (no royalty), GCB, NSHS 5345

"**There Are No Sacher Tortes in Our Society,**" a comedy by Murray Schisgal, 2m1f, (can pair with "The Pushcart Peddlers"; published with and can pair with "Jealousy") DPS 2598

"**Third and Oak: The Pool Hall,**" a comedy-drama by Marsha Norman, 2m1f, (can pair with "Third and Oak: The Laundromat") DPS 4486

"**Third Law of Newton, The**" ["*La tercera ley de Newton*"], a *farsa* in Spanish by Leticia Tellez, 2m1f, OEN, NSHS pb8189

"**Thirst,**" a drama by Eugene O'Neill, 2m1f, Eugene O'Neill's *Complete Plays, 1913-1920*, vol. 1," SF 22627; also (published with and can pair with "Before Breakfast," "The Dreamy Kid," "Fog," "Shell Shock," or "A Wife for a Life") in Eugene O'Neill's *Complete Plays 1913-1920*, ed. by Travis Bogard (New York: Random House, Inc., 1988), ISBN 0-940450-48-8, NSHS pb8121

"**This Isn't Scarsdale, Gus,**" a comedy by Richard Urdahl, 2m1f, in *Don't Listen to Us Lord We're Only Praying*, BP

"**This Night Shall Pass,**" a religious drama by Dorothy Clarke Wilson, 2m1f, BP, NSHS pb5442

"**To Open, Pry Cover,**" a comedy by Peg Lynch, 2m1f, (published with and can pair with "Dutch Treat," "Fishing Hat," "Just a Little Something for Christmas," or "What's That Tune") in *Ethel and Albert Comedies*, SF 7645 (anthology), SF 22718 (single play), NSHS pb7825 (anthology)

"**Today a Little Extra,**" a comedy by Michael Kassin, 2m1f, BP

"**Treats,**" a comedy in nine scenes by Christopher Hampton, 2m1f, in Christopher Hampton's *The Philanthropist with Total Eclipse and Treats* (New York and London: Faber & Faber, Ltd., 1991), ISBN 0-571-16218-5

"**Triumph of the Egg,**" a comedy by Sherwood Anderson, 2m1f (+ extras), MM, GCB, NSHS 5345

"**Try! Try!**" a verse comedy by Frank O'Hara, 2m1f, GP, NSHS 16607

"**12:21 P.M.,**" (see p. 256) a comedy by F. J. Hartland, 2m1f, (published with and can pair with "Dispatches from Hell," "Molly and James," or "Senior Prom") in Double Image Theatre's *Off-Off Broadway Festival Plays, Tenth Series* (New York: Samuel French, Inc., 1985), SF 22772, NSHS 27488, ISBN 0-573-68904-0

"**27 Wagons Full of Cotton,**" a drama by Tennessee Williams in *27 Wagons Full of Cotton*, DPS 485, NSHS pb4019 NSHS 14824, NSHS 20483, NSHS 21389, NSHS 21514, NSHS 21776, NSHS 2401

"**Twinkle, Twinkle,**" a comedy by Ernest Thompson, 2m1f, (published with and can pair with "The Constituent" or "A Good Time") in *Answers*, DPS 810

U

"**Ultimate Grammar of Life,**" a black comedy by Mark Medoff, 2m1f, (published with and can pair with "Doing a Good One for the Red Man" or "The Froegle Dictum") in Mark Medoff's *Four Short Plays* (New York: Dramatists Play Service, Inc., 1974), DPS 3107, NSHS pb8211, NSHS 26932

"**Uncertain Samaritan, The,**" a comedy by Jack Morse, 2m1f, DPC, NSHS pb192

"**Unprogrammed,**" a play (genre?) by Carol K. Mack, 2m1f, in *The Best American Short Plays, 1990,* edited by Howard Stein and Glenn Young (New York: Applause Theatre Book Publishers, 1992), ISSN 1062-7561

"**Unrest Cure, The,**" a comedy adapted for the stage by Jules Tasca from the short story by Saki (H. H. Munro), 2m1f, (published with and can pair with "The Background," "Blind Spot," "Dusk" "The Hen," "The Reticence of Lady Anne," "Secret Sin," or "The Tiger") in Jules Tasca's *Tales by Saki* (New York: Samuel French, Inc.), ISBN 0-573-62560-3, SF 22133, NSHS pb7798, NSHS pb8113

V

"**Variations on the Death of Trotsky,**" a comedy by David Ives, 2m1f, (published with and can pair with "Philip Glass Buys a Loaf of Bread") in *Variations on the Death of Trotsky and Other Short Comedies* (New York: Dramatists Play Service,Inc., 1992), DPS 4729, NSHS pb8089

"**View from the Obelisk, A,**" a play (genre?) by Hugh Leonard, 2m1f, in *Pizzazz*, SF 24053

"**Visiting Dan,**" a ten-minute play (genre?) by Judith Fein, 2m1f, SF

"**Vivien,**" a comic drama by Percy Granger, 2m1f, SF 24615

W

"**Wandering,**" a bare-stage turn by Lanford Wilson, 2m1f, (published with and can pair with "Stoop") DPS 3930, NSHS 29301, NSHS pb7760

"**Wandering Scholar from Paradise, The**" [*"Der farendt Schuler im Paradeiss"*], a farce by Hans Sachs, 2m1f, (published with and can pair with *"Dass heiss Eysen"* ["The Hot Iron"] or *"Der doctor mit der grosen nasen"* ["The Doctor with the Big Nose"]) in Hans Sachs' *Meistergesänge Fastnachtsspiele Schwänke*, compiled by Eugen Geiger (Stuttgart: Phillip Reclam jun., 1981), ISBN 3-15-007627-7, NSHS

"**Waning Crescent Moon,**" a drama by Stephen Serpas, 2m1f, BP

"**War,**" a drama by Jean-Claude van Itallie, 2m1f, (published with and can pair with "The Hunter and the Bird" or "I'm Really Here") in *Five Short Plays*, DPS 4725, NSHS pb7878

"**Way with Words, A,**" a comedy by Frank D. Gilroy, 2m1f, in *A Way with Words*, SF 25031

"**Web, The,**" a drama by Eugene O'Neill, 2m1f," in *Eugene O'Neill, Complete Plays, Vol. I,* SF 25613

"**What Would Jeanne Moreau Do?**" a comedy by Elinor Jones, 2m1f, (published with "Box Office") SF 25660, NSHS pb7960

"**What's That Tune,**" a comedy by Peg Lynch, 2m1f, (published with and can pair with "Dutch Treat," "Fishing Hat," "Just a Little Something for Christmas," or "To Open, Pry Cover") in *Ethel and Albert Comedies*, SF 7645 (anthology), SF 25659 (single play), NSHS pb7825 (anthology)

"**When God Comes for Breakfast, You Don't Burn the Toast,**" a comedy by Gary Apple, 2m1f, BP, SF 25669, NSHS 27514

"**White Liars,**" a comedy by Peter Shaffer, 2m1f, BP, HDS, (published with "Black Comedy") SF 1192, NSHS 16674

"**Wife for a Life, A,**" a drama by Eugene O'Neill, 2m1f, *Eugene O'Neill, Complete Plays, Vol. I*, SF 25615

"**Witch, The,**" a farce adapted by Joseph Buloff and Luba Kadison Buloff from Anton Chekhov, 2m1f, in *The Chekhov Sketchbook*, SF 25162

"**Witch's Brew, A,**" a drama by John Pielmeier, 2m1f, (published with and can pair with "A Ghost Story" or "A Gothic Tale") in *Haunted Lives*, DPS 2297

"**Words, Words, Words,**" a comedy by David Ives, 2m1f, (published with and can pair with "Mere Mortals" or "Sure Thing") in *Four Short Comedies* (New York: Dramatists Play Service, Inc., 1989), DPS 2593

"**Workhouse Ward, The,**" a farce by Lady Gregory, 2m1f, ISBN 0-573-02301-8, SF 25736, NSHS pb82, NSHS pb 5449, NSHS pb5444, NSHS 2212

Y

"**Yancey,**" a drama by Romulus Linney, 2m1f, (published with and can pair with "Juliet") in Romulus Linney's *Juliet, Yancey, April Snow: Three Plays* (New York: Dramatists Play Service, Inc., 1989), LC 90-103850, DPS 831, NSHS pb8032

"**Yankee Doodle,**" a comedy by Romulus Linney, 2m1f, (published and can pair with "Can Can," "Clair de Lune," or "Gold and Silver Waltz") in *Pops*, DPS 3684, NSHS pb7913

Three-Male Plays

A

"Answers," (see p. 183) a drama by Tom Topor, 3m, DPS 811, NSHS 29209, NSHS pb8208

B

"Bachelor Holiday," a comedy by Alan Ball, 3m, in *Five One Act Plays by Alan Ball*, DPS 0911, NSHS pb8021

"Bad Bad Jo-Jo," a drama by James Leo Herlihy, 3m, (published with and can pair with "Laughs, Etc." or "Terrible Jim Fitch") in *Stop, You're Killing Me*, DPS 4290, NSHS pb7924

"Badin the Bold," a comedy by Courteline, 3m, *The Plays of Courteline*, SF 4611

"Barbarians Are Coming, The," a satirical comedy by Luigi Jannuzzi, 3m, SF 3972, NSHS pb7902

"Beauty's Duty," a comedy by George Bernard Shaw, 3m, SF

"Best Warm Beer in Brooklyn, The," a comedy by Jason Milligan, 3m, in *New York Stories: Five Plays About Life in New York*, SF 3953

"Bill Batchelor Road," a drama by Robert Patrick, 3m, (published with and can pair with "Fairy Tale," "Fog," "Odd Number," "One of Those People," "Pouf Positive," or "The River Jordan") in Robert Patrick's *Untold Decades* (New York: St. Martin's Press, Inc., 1988), ISBN 0-312-02307-3

"Blind One-Armed Deaf-Mute, The," a comedy by Gueullette, 3m, (published with and can pair with "Cassander, Man of Letters," "Cassander Supports the Revolution," "Cassander's Trip to the Indies," "Giles in Love," "The Shit Merchant," or "The Two Doubles") in *Gallant and Libertine, Divertissements and Parades of 18th Century France*, SF 3989, NSHS pb7927, ISBN 0-933826-49-4

"Blind Spot," a comedy by Jules Tasca from Saki (H. H. Munro), 3m, (published with and can play with "The Background," "Dusk," "The Hen," "The Reticence of Lady Anne," "Secret Sin," "The Tiger," or "The Unrest Cure") in *Tales by Saki*, SF 22133, NSHS pb7798

"Botticelli," a drama by Terrence McNally, 3m (1m is a bit), (published with and can play with "Next" or "Tour" [revised version]) in Terrence McNally's *Apple Pie* (New York: Dramatists Play Service, Inc., 1969) DPS 825, NSHS pb8164

"Box for One," a drama by Peter Brook, 3m (+ optional extras), DPC B28, NSHS 6072, pb6089

"Bridge, The," a play (genre?) by Mario Fratti, 3m, in *Races*, SF

C

"Chastening, The," a drama by Richard Weaver, 3m, IEC 023-4

"A Conversation about Pretended Good Deeds of the Clergy" [*"Ein Gespräch von den Scheinwerken der Geistlichen"* / *"Ein Gespräch von den Scheinwerken der Gaystlichen vun jren gelübdten damit sy zuuerlesterung des bluts Christi vermaynen selig zu werden"*], a *fastnachtsspiel* by Hans Sachs, 3m, in Hans Sach's *Die Wittenbergisch Nachtigall: Spruchgedicht, Vier Reformationsdialoge und das Meisterlied das Walt Got*, compiled by Gerald H. Seufert (Stuttgart: Philipp Reclam jun., 1974), Universal-Bibliothek Nr. 9737/38/38a, ISBN 3-15-009737-1, NSHS

"A Conversation of an Evangelistic Christian with a Lutheran in Which the Angry Charge of Those Who Call Themselves Lutheran Is Pointed out and Is Being Stressed in Brotherly Fashion" [*"Ein Gespräch eines evangelischen Christen mit einem Lutherischen . . ."* / *"Ein Gespräch von den Scheinwerken der Gaystlichen vun jren gelübdten damit sy zuuerlesterung des bluts Christi vermaynen selig zu werden"*], a *fastnachtsspiel* by Hans Sachs, 3m, in Hans Sach's *Die Wittenbergisch Nachtigall: Spruchgedicht, Vier Reformationsdialoge und das Meisterlied das Walt Got*, compiled by Gerald H. Seufert (Stuttgart: Philipp Reclam jun., 1974), Universal-Bibliothek Nr. 9737/38/38a, ISBN 3-15-009737-1, NSHS

"Curve, The," a drama by Tankred Dorst, tr. James L. Rosenberg, 3m, NTK, 16622

D

"Dawn Will Come," a morality play by David Weinstock, 3m, SF 6608, NSHS pb7900

"Deserter, The," a drama by Norman Beim, 3m, SF 6644, NSHS pb7903

"Device out of Time, A," a drama by Ray Bradbury, 3m, DPC D44, NSHS pb170

"Dog Eat Dog," a brief drama by Tim Kelly, 3m, in *One-Act Plays for Acting Students*, SF 6715, MPL, ISBN 0-916260-47-X

"Dusk," a comedy by Jules Tasca from Saki (H. H. Munro), 3m, (published with and can play with "The Background," "Blind Spot," "The Hen," "The Reticence of Lady Anne," "Secret Sin," "The Tiger," or "The Unrest Cure") in *Tales by Saki*, SF 22133, NSHS pb7798

E

"Ein Gespräch von den Scheinwerken der Geistlichen" / "Ein Gespräch von den Scheinwerken der Gaystlichen vun jren gelübdten damit sy zuuerlesterung des bluts Christi vermaynen selig zu werden" ["A Conversation about Pretended Good Deeds of the Clergy"], a *fastnachtsspiel* by Hans Sachs, 3m, in Hans Sach's *Die Wittenbergisch Nachtigall: Spruchgedicht, Vier Reformationsdialoge und das Meisterlied das Walt Got*, compiled by Gerald H. Seufert (Stuttgart: Philipp Reclam jun., 1974), Universal-Bibliothek Nr. 9737/38/38a, ISBN 3-15-009737-1, NSHS

"Ein Gespräch eines evangelischen Christen mit einem Lutherischen . . ." / "Ein Gespräch von den Scheinwerken der Gaystlichen vun jren gelübdten damit sy zuuerlesterung des bluts Christi vermaynen selig zu werden" ["A Conversation of an Evangelistic Christian with a Lutheran in Which the Angry Charge of Those Who Call Themselves Lutheran Is Pointed out and Is Being Stressed in Brotherly Fashion"], a *fastnachtsspiel* by Hans Sachs, 3m, in Hans Sach's *Die Wittenbergisch Nachtigall: Spruchgedicht, Vier Reformationsdialoge und das Meisterlied das Walt Got*, compiled by Gerald H. Seufert (Stuttgart: Philipp Reclam jun., 1974), Universal-Bibliothek Nr. 9737/38/38a, ISBN 3-15-009737-1, NSHS

"End of the Shifty, The," a drama by Jonathan C. Levine, 3m, (published with and can pair with "Unpublished Letters") in Jonathan C. Levine's *Two One-Act Plays* (New York: Samuel French, Inc., 1992), ISBN 0-573-69328-5, SF 7634

"Eye of the Beholder, The," a comedy by Kent Broadhurst, 3m or 3f, DPS 1880, NSHS pb7919

F

"Final Performance [or, The Curtain Falls]," a drama by Charles George, 3m, DPS 1515

"Final Play," a drama by William Lang, 3m, DPC F16, HDS, NSHS pb140

"Flying Machine, The," a drama by Ray Bradbury, 3m or 3f, DPC F36, NSHS pb188

"Fool and His Money, A: A Wayside Comedy," a comedy by Laurence Housman, 3m, ISA, NSHS 27000

"Forget Him," a drama by Harvey Fierstein, 3m, (can pair with "Andre's Mother," "Bill Batchelor Road," "Fairy Tale," "Fog," "Odd Number," "One of Those People," "Pouf Positive," "The River Jordan," or "Safe Sex") in *Out Front: Contemporary Gay and Lesbian Plays*, edited by D. Shewey (New York: Grove Press, Inc., 1988), ISBN 0-8021-1041, ISBN 0-8021-3025-9

"4-H Club, The," a drama by Sam Shepard, 3m, (published with and can play with "Cowboys #2," "4-H Club," "Killer's Head," or "Red Cross") in *The Unseen Hand and Other Plays*, SF 8641, NSHS pb7928, ISBN 0-553-34263-0

"Four Men and a Monster," a drama by Maryat Lee, 3m, SF 8642, NSHS pb7898

"Friends," a comedy by Arkady Leokum, 3m, in *Friends and Enemies*, SF 8648

G

"Girl, The," a drama by Edward Peple, 3m, in *One Act Plays for Stage and Study: A Collection of Twenty-five Plays by Well-Known Dramatists, American, English and Irish*, First Series, preface by Augustus Thomas (New York: Samuel French, Inc., 1925), SF, NSHS

"Goblins Plot to Murder God, The," a ten-minute play (genre?) by Mark O'Donnel, 3m or 3f or 1m2f or 2m1f or 4m or 4f or 1m3f or 2m2f or 3m1f, SF

H

"Hills Send Off Echoes, The," a drama by Ernest C. Ferlita, 3m, TPH

"In the Cemetery," a comic drama by Michael Hardstark, 3m, (published with "The Cure") in *The Last Laugh*, SF 11109

I

"Indian Wants the Bronx, The," a bare-stage drama by Israel Horovitz, 3m, (can pair with "It's Called the Sugar Plum") DPS 2530, HDS, NSHS pb4241

"Interview with God," a comedy drama by Madolin Shorey Cervantes, 3m, SF 11603

J

"Juvie," a drama by Jerome McDonough, 3m or 4m, HDS

K

"Keep, The," a drama by Michael Firth, 3m or 3f, IEC

"Keep Tightly Closed in a Cool Dry Place," a drama by Megan Terry 3m, SF 13605, NSHS pb7899

"Killing of Abel, The," a craft cycle drama from "N. towne Plays," 3m, HMC, NSHS 29216

L

"Las Dos Caras del Patroncito" [**"The Two Faces of the Dear Boss"**], (see p. 215) an agitprop (political satire) by Luis Valdez, 3m, (published with and can pair with "The Militants") in Luis Valdez' *Luis Valdez—Early Works: Bernabé and Pensamiento Serpentino* (Houston, Texas: Arte Público Press, 1990), ISBN 1-55885-003-1, APP, NSHS

"Last of My Solid Gold Watches, The," a drama by Tennessee Williams, 3m, in *27 Wagons Full of Cotton*, DPS 485

"Last to Go," a drama, 2m or 3m, (published with and can pair with "The Black and White," "The Collection," "The Dwarfs," "The Lover," "Special Offer," or "Trouble in the Works") in Harold Pinter's *Plays: Two* (London and Boston: Faber & Faber, 1991), ISBN 0-571-16075-1; and (published with and can pair with "Applicant," "The Black and White," "Interview," "That's All," "That's Your Trouble" or "Trouble in the Works") in *Revue Sketches*; DPS 1765, NSHS pb7737, NSHS pb8102, NSHS 27487

"Ledge, Ledger, and the Legend," (see p. 212) a farce by Paul Elliott, 3m or 3f, DPC L15, HDS, NSHS pb142, NSHS pb7941

"Lone Star," a comedy by James McLure, 3m, (can pair with "Laundry and Bourbon") in *Texas Plays*, edited by William B. Martin (Dallas, Texas: Southern Methodist University Press, 1990), ISBN 0-87074-300-7, ISBN 0-87074-301-5, DPS 2910, NSHS pb7920

M

"Medal of Honor Rag," a drama by Tom Cole, 3m, ISBN 0-573-64018-1, SF, NSHS pb7756

"Meeting, The," a drama by Jeff Stetson, 3m, DPS 3108

"Men Without Dates," a comedy by Jane Willis, 3m, (published with and can pair with "Slam!") DPS 3117

"Mere Mortals," a comedy by David Ives, 3m, (published with and can pair with "Sure Thing" or "Words, Words, Words") in *Four Short Comedies* (New York: Drama-

tists Play Service, Inc., 1989), DPS 2593

"Militants, The," an agitprop (political satire) by Luis Valdez, 3m, (published with and can pair with *"Las Dos Caras del Patroncito"* ["The Two Faces of the Dear Boss"]) in Luis Valdez' *Luis Valdez—Early Works: Bernabé and Pensamiento Serpentino* (Houston, Texas: Arte Público Press, 1990), ISBN 1-55885-003-1, APP, NSHS

"Monica," a drama by Pauline Macaulay, 3m, SF, NSHS 16674

"Motel," a masque for three dolls from "America Hurrah," by Jean-Claude Van Itallie, 3m or 3f, (in doll masks and bodies + offstage voice), in *America Hurrah*, DPS 705

N

"Napoleon's Dinner," a comedy by Samuel Shem, 3m, (published with and can play with "Room for One Woman") in *Napoleon's Dinner and Room for One Woman*, SF 16602, NSHS pb7921, ISBN 0-573-60052-1

"*Narrenschneiden*, The: or, The Fool-Ectomy," a *fastnachtsspiel* by Hans Sachs, translated by I. E. Clark, 3m or 3f, IEC, NSHS pb94

"Near Thing, A," a comedy by Joe Corrie, 3m, BP, NSHS 19987

"New World Order, The," a sketch by Harold Pinter, 3m, DPS 3368

"Noodle Doodle Box," a comedy for children by Paul Maar translated from the German by Anita and Alex Page, 3m or 3f, BP

O

"Odd Number," a drama by Robert Patrick, 3m, (published with and can pair with "Bill Batchelor Road," "Fairy Tale," "Fog," "One of Those People," "Pouf Positive," or "The River Jordan") in Robert Patrick's *Untold Decades* (New York: St. Martin's Press, Inc., 1988), ISBN 0-312-02307-3

"Old Grad, The," a comedy by Robert Finch, 3m, TSD, NSHS 10922

"One-Armed Man, The," a drama by Horton Foote, 3m, (published with and can pair with "The Prisoner's Song") in *"The Tears of My Sister," "The Prisoner's Song," "The One-Armed Man," and "The Land of the Astronauts,"* DPS 2022; also in Horton Foote's *Selected One-Act Plays of Horton Foote*, edited by Gerald C. Wood (Dallas, Texas: Southern Methodist University Press, 1989), ISBN 0-87074-274-4, ISBN 0-87074-275-2

"Other Player, The," (see p. 225) a drama by Owen G. Arno, 3m or 3f, DPS 3550, NSHS pb7344

P

"The Perfect Tribute," a drama by Glenhall Taylor, 3m (+ extras), in *The Big Book of Holiday Plays: 21 Modern and Traditional One-Act Plays for the Celebration of Christmas,* edited by Sylvia E. Kamerman (Boston: Plays, Inc., 1988), ISBN 0-8238-0288-4

"Phonecall from Sunkist," a brief drama by Norman A. Bert, 3m, (published with and can pair with "Advice to a New Actor" "The Affidavit," "The American Way," "Anniversary," "Auld Lang Syne, or I'll Bet You Think This Play Is About You," "Bug Swatter," "Checkers," "Coming for a Visit," "Dalmation," "Money," "Dog Eat Dog," "Drowned Out," "Fireworks," "Interview," "Jumping," "One Beer Too Many," or "Potato Girl," "Property of the Dallas Cowboys," "The Split Decision," "Valley Forgery," "Watermelon Boats," or "Widows") in *One-Act Plays for Acting Students,* MPL, ISBN 0-916260-47-X

"Picture," a bare-stage drama by Oliver Haily, 3m, (published with and can pair with "Animal" or "Crisscross") in *Picture Animal Crisscross: Three Short Plays,* DPS 3655, NSHS pb7922

"Prodigal Son," a comic parody by Garrison Keillor based on the Biblical parable, 3m (+ extras), in *Antaeus: Plays in One Act,* No. 66, edited by Daniel Halpern (Spring 1991), ISBN 0-88001-268-4, ANT

"Pvt. Wars," a comedy by James McLure, 3m, (can pair with "Lone Star") DPS 3745

Q

"Questioning of Nick, The," a drama by Arthur Kopit, 3m, (published with and can pair with "The Conquest of Everest," "The Hero," or "Sing to Me Through Open Windows") in *The Day the Whores Came out to Play Tennis and Other Plays,* SF 19601, NSHS pb7930, ISBN 0-374-52233-2

R

"Rats," a bare-stage comedy-drama by Israel Horovitz, 3m, DPS 3765

S

"Schreber's Nervous Illness," a bare-stage drama by Caryl Churchill, 3m (+ various recorded voices), (published with and can pair with "Abortive," "Not Not Not Not Not Enough Oxygen," "Seagulls," or "Three More Sleepless Nights") in *Churchill: Shorts [Short Plays by Caryl Churchill],* SF 16083, SF 3887, NSHS, ISBN 1-85459-085-5

"Shell Shock," a drama by Eugene O'Neill, 3m (+ extra), (published with and can pair with "Before Breakfast," "The Dreamy Kid," "Fog," "Thirst," or "A Wife for a Life") in Eugene O'Neill's *Complete Plays, 1913-1920,* vol. 1, ed. by Travis Bogard (New York: Random House, 1988), ISBN 0-940450-48-8, NSHS pb8121

"Shoes," a drama by Jason Milligan, 3m, in *New York Stories: Five Plays About Life in New York,* SF 21135

"Sing to Me Through Open Windows," (see p. 242) a drama by Arthur Kopit, 3m, (published with and can pair with "The Questioning of Nick") in *The Day the Whores Came Out to Play Tennis and Other Plays,* SF 21705, NSHS pb7930, ISBN 0-374-52233-2

"Sorrows and Sons," a drama by Stephen Metcalfe, 3m, (published with and can play with "Spittin' Image") in *Sorrows and Sons,* SF 21741, NSHS pb7896

"South of Tomorrow," a drama by Reinaldo Povod, 3m, in *La Puta Vida,* SF 14673

"Spades," a ten-minute play (genre?) by Jim Beaver, 3m, (published with and can pair with "Americansaint," "Après Opéra," "'The Asshole Murder Case,'" "Bread," "Cold Water," "Cover," "Downtown," "The Drummer," "The Duck Pond," "Eating Out," "Electric Roses," "The Field," "4 A.M. (open all night)," "Looking Good," "Love and Peace, Mary Jo," "Loyalties," "Marred Bliss," "Perfect," "The Road to Ruin," or "Watermelon Boats") in *25 10-Minute Plays from Actors Theatre of Louisville,* SF 22260, NSHS pb29777, ISBN 0-57-62558-1

"Special Offer," a drama by Harold Pinter, 3m, (published with and can pair with "The Black and White," "The Collection," "The Dwarfs," "Last to Go," "The Lover," or "Trouble in the Works") in Harold Pinter's *Plays: Two* (London and Boston: Faber & Faber, 1991), ISBN 0-571-16075-1; and in *Revue Sketches;* DPS 1765, NSHS pb7737, NSHS pb8102

"Support Your Local Police," a satire by Jules Tasca from Mark Twain, 3m, in *Five One-Act Plays by Mark Twain,* SF 21606

T

"That Time," a bare-stage drama by Samuel Beckett, 3m, in *Ends and Odds,* SF 22603

"Theatre II," a drama by Samuel Beckett, 3m, in *Ends and Odds,* SF 22605

"Third Street," a drama for youth by Richard Colman, 3m, in *Ten out of Ten: Ten Winning Plays Selected from the Young Playwrights Festival, 1982-1991: Produced by the Foundation of the Dramatists Guild*, edited by Wendy Lamb, preface by Wendy Wasserstein, introduction by Nancy Quinn (New York: Delacorte Press, 1992), ISBN 0-385-30811-6

"Torch of Time, The: A Study in Revolution," a drama by Laurence Housman, 3m, ISA, NSHS 27000

"Toronto at Dreamer's Rock," a Canadian Indian drama by Drew Hayden Taylor, 3m, in Drew Hayden Taylor's *Toronto at Dreamer's Rock and Education Is Our Right: Two One-Act Plays* (Saskatoon, Saskatchewan, Canada: Fifth House, 1990), ISBN 0-920079-64-4, FH

"Transfers," a drama by Conrad Bromberg, 3m, (published with and can pair with "Doctor Galley" or "The Rooming House") in *Transfers: Three One-Acts Plays*, DPS 4610, NSHS pb7923

"Traveler, The," a comedy by Marc Connelly, 3m, DPS, NSHS 27039, NSHS pb4019, NSHS 14824, NSHS 20483, NSHS 21389, NSHS 21514, NSHS 21776

"Tridget of Greva, The," a comedy by Ring Lardner, 3m, SF, NSHS 27039, NSHS pb4019, NSHS 14824, NSHS 20483, NSHS 21389, NSHS 21514, NSHS 21776

"The Two Faces of the Dear Boss" ["**Las Dos Caras del Patroncito**"], an agitprop (political satire) by Luis Valdez, 3m, (published with and can pair with "The Militants") in Luis Valdez' *Luis Valdez—Early Works: Bernabé and Pensamiento Serpentino* (Houston, Texas: Arte Público Press, 1990), ISBN 1-55885-003-1, APP, NSHS

U

"Unseen Friends," a comedy by Katharine Long, 3m, SF 23013, NSHS pb7901

V

"Vagabond, The," a comedy adapted by Joseph Buloff and Luba Kadison Buloff from Anton Chekhov, 3m, in *The Chekhov Sketchbook*, SF 24607

"Villainous Company," an abridgment/adaptation by Amlin Gray of Shakespeare's *Henry IV, Parts I and II*, 3m, DPS 4745

W

"Window, The," a drama by Frank Marcus, 3m, MR, NSHS 16674

Y

"York Play of the Crucifixion, The," a medieval mystery play by unknown author, 3m, manuscript in British Museum, London

Three-Female Plays

A

"Admissions," a drama by Colleen Neuman, 3f, PDS

"a.k.a. Marleen," a comedy by Carol K. Mack, 3f, (published with and can play with "Postcards") in *Postcards and Other Short Plays*, SF 3912, NSHS pb7905

"Approaching Lavendar," a comic drama by Julie Beckett Crutcher, 3f, SF 3649, NSHS pb7897

B

"Blind Date," a comedy by Ruth Putnam Kimball, 3f, ISBN 0-573-62130-6, BP, NSHS pb7727, NSHS 29211

C

"Calm Down Mother," a bare-stage drama by Megan Terry, 3f, SF 301, NSHS pb7961

"Camping," a ten-minute play (genre?) by Jon Jory, 3f, DPC, NSHS pb149

"Can't Buy Me Love," a comedy by Jason Milligan 3f, in *Southern Exposures: Five Plays About Life in the South*, SF 5779

"Cecily," a drama by Gillian Plowman, 3f, DPC C83

"Chimera," a drama by Alec Baron, 3f, SF 5752

"Come and Go," a drama by Samuel Beckett, 3f, (published with and can pair with "Act Without Words I," "Act Without Words II," "Breath," "Cascando," "Catastrophe," "Eh Joe," "Embers," "Footfalls," "Ghost Trio," "Krapp's Last Tape," "Not I," "Ohio Impromptu," "A Piece of Monologue," "Play," "Quad," "Rockaby," "Rough for Radio I," "Rough for Radio II," "Rough for Theatre I," "Rough for Theatre II," "That Time," or "Words and Music") in *Collected Shorter Plays,* ISBN 0-394-53850-1, ISBN 0-394-62098-4

"Cotton Girls," a comedy by Scott Tobin, 3f, BP

D

"Dear Mrs. Martin," a comedy by Kate Aspengren, 3f, (published with and can pair with "Mother's Day") in Kate Aspengren's *Dear Mrs. Martin & Mother's Day* (New York: Samuel French, Inc., 1992), SF, ISBN 0-573-60144-5

"Donahue Sisters, The," a drama by Geraldine Aron, 3f, in Geraldine Aron's *The Donahue Sisters* (New York: Samuel French, Inc., 1991), ISBN 0-573-13234-8, SF 6738

E

"Eating Out," a ten-minute play (genre?) by Marcia Dixcy, 3f, (published with and can pair with "Americansaint," "Après Opéra," "'The Asshole Murder Case,'" "Bread," "Cold Water," "Cover," "Downtown," "Electric Roses," "The Drummer," "The Duck Pond," "The Field," "4 A.M. (open all night)," "Looking Good," "Love and Peace, Mary Jo," "Loyalties," "Marred Bliss," "Perfect," "The Road to Ruin," "Spades," or "Watermelon Boats") in *25 10-Minute Plays from Actors Theatre of Louisville*, SF 22260, NSHS pb2977, ISBN 0-573-62558-1

"Ex-Miss Copper Queen on a Set of Pills," a drama by Megan Terry 3f, (published with "People vs. Ranchman") SF 7650, NSHS pb7895

"Eye of the Beholder, The," a comedy by Kent Broadhurst, 3f or 3m, DPS 1880, NSHS pb7919

F

"Flying Machine, The," a drama by Ray Bradbury, 3f or 3m, DPC, NSHS pb188

G

"Ghost Stories," a drama by Annie Evans, 3f, in *Off-Off Broadway Festival Plays, 11th Series*, SF 9629, NSHS pb7494, 27508

"Goblins Plot to Murder God, The," a ten-minute play (genre?) by Mark O'Donnel, 3f or 3m or 1m2f or 2m1f or 4m or 4f or 1m3f or 2m2f or 3m1f, SF

"Going to the Catacombs," a drama by Jules Tasca [set in Rome], 3f, (published with and can pair with [Athens:] "Passion Comedy," [Engelberg:] "Swiss Miss," [London:] "A Day in the Night of Rose Arden," [Munich:] "A Side Trip to Dachau," [Paris:] "Escape," [Venice:] "The Best Souvenirs," or [Vienna:] "The Stop at the Palace") in Jules Tasca's *Tour di Europa* [*Tour of Europe*] (New York: Samuel French, Inc.), ISBN 0-573-69222-X, SF 9701, NSHS pb8105

H

"Haiku," a drama by Katherine Snodgrass, 3f, in *The Best Short Plays, 1988-1989*, edited by Ramon Delgado (New York: Applause Theatre Book Publishers, 1989); also in Katherine Snodgrass' *Haiku* (New York: Samuel French, Inc., 1989), ISBN 0-573-63254-5, SF 10650

"Heads," a ten-minute play (genre?) by Jon Jory, 3f, DPC, NSHS pb149

"House-Fairy, The," a comedy by Laurence Housman, 3f, ISA, NSHS 27000

I

"I Don't Know Where You're Coming from at All," a drama by Shirley Lauro, 3f, SF 11606, NSHS pb7904

J

"John's Ring," a comedy by Jason Milligan, 3f, in *New York Stories: Five Plays About Life in New York*, SF 12635

K

"Keep, The," a drama by Michael Firth, 3f or 3m, IEC

L

"Ladies Alone," a comedy by Florence Ryerson and Colin Clements, 3f, SF 14608, NSHS pb7906

"Lantern in the Wind," a drama by Tim Kelly, 3f, IEC 106-0

"Last Chance Texaco," a drama by Peter Maloney, 3f, (published with "Pastoral") SF 13887, NSHS pb7893

"Laundry and Bourbon," a comedy by James McLure, 3f, (can pair with "Lone Star"), in *Texas Plays*, edited by William B. Martin (Dallas, Texas: Southern Methodist University Press, 1990), ISBN 0-87074-300-7, ISBN 0-87074-301-5, DPS 2790, NSHS pb7920

"Ledge, Ledger, and the Legend," a comedy by Paul Elliott, 3f or 3m, DPC, HDS, NSHS pb142, NSHS pb7941

"Luther's Birthday," a comedy by Paul Gater, 3f, (can pair with "Over the Edge") in Paul Gater's *Luther's Birthday* (Droitwich, Worcestershire, England: Hanbury Plays, 1989), ISBN 1-85205-063-2, HP

M

"Maids, The," a lengthy one-act drama by Jean Genet, 3f, in Jean Genet's *The Maids and Deathwatch: Two Plays*, translated from the original French into English by Bernard Frechtman (New York: Grove Weidenfeld, 1982), SF 15036

"Martha's Mourning," a drama by Phoebe Hoffman, 3f, *Drama Magazine* 1918, NSHS

"Medusa of Forty-seventh Street," a drama by Nancy Henderson, 3f, SF 15653, NSHS pb7907

"Mirror, Mirror," a drama by Kitty Johnson, 3f, in *Triplet: Three One-Act Plays* (New York: Samuel French, Inc., 1991), ISBN 0-573-69290-4, SF 15698

"Motel," a masque for three dolls from "America Hurrah," by Jean-Claude Van Itallie, 3f or 3m, (in doll masks and bodies + offstage voice), in *America Hurrah*, DPS 705

N

"*Narrenschneiden*, The," a *fastnachtsspiel* by Hans Sachs, 3f or 3m, IEC 134-6

"Noodle Doodle Box," a comedy for children by Paul Maar translated from the German by Anita and Alex Page, 3f or 3m, BP

"Not My Cup of Tea," a comedy by Albert Groff, 3f, PDS

O

"Other Player, The," (see p. 225) a drama by Owen G. Arno, 3f or 3m, DPS 3550, NSHS pb7344

"Out of Our Father's House," a play (genre?) with music by Paula Wagner, Jack Hofsiss and Eve Merriam based on Eve Merriam's *Growing up Female in America*, 3f (in six roles), SF 811, BP

P

"Postcards," a comedy by Carol K. Mack, 3f, (published with and can play with "a.k.a. Marleen") in *Postcards and Other Short Plays*, SF 18939, NSHS pb7905

"Purple Door Knob, The," (see p. 232) a comedy by Walter Prichard Eaton, 3f, SF 863, NSHS pb7959

R

"Rats," a ten-minute drama by James Edward Luczak, 3f, DPC R52

"Return, The," a drama by Robert Finch, 3f, GCB, NSHS 5345

"Room for One Woman," a drama by Samuel Shem, 3f, (published with and can play with "Napoleon's Dinner") in *Napoleon's Dinner and Room for One Woman*, SF 20636, NSHS pb7921, ISBN 0-573-60052-1

S

"Scent of Honeysuckle, A," (see p. 239) a bare-stage comedy-drama by Jean Lenox Toddie, 3f, ISBN 0-573-60059-7, (published with "A Little Something for the Ducks") SF 21041, NSHS 27492

"Still Life with Violets," a drama by Ian Austin, 3f, (published with and can pair with "Private Worlds" and "Remains to Be Seen") in Ian Austin's *For Ladies Only: Five One-Act Plays with All Women Casts*, foreword by Babette Stephens (Ashgrove, Queensland, Australia: Playlab Press, 1988), ISBN 0-908156-31-6

"Stoop," a bare-stage turn by Lanford Wilson, 3f, (published with and can pair with "Wandering") DPS 3930, NSHS 29301, NSHS pb7732

T

"Temp, The," a comedy by Roy Friedman, 3f, (New York: Samuel French, Inc., 1992) ISBN 0-573-62599-9, SF 22167

"Tired Feet and Dancing Shoes," a drama by Susan Hunter, 3f, AR, NSHS pb6124

"Triplet," a comedy by Kitty Johnson, 3f, in *Triplet: Three One-Act Plays* (New York: Samuel French, Inc., 1991), ISBN 0-573-69290-4, SF 22217

U

"Unforeseen Consequences of a Patriotic Act, The," a Biblical drama by Howard Barker, 3f, in Howard Barker's *The Unforeseen Consequences of a Patriotic Act* (New York: Riverrun Press, 1988), ISBN 0-7145-4135-4, RP

V

"Valley Forgery," a brief satire by Patricia Montley, 3f, (published with and can pair with "Advice to a New Actor" "The Affidavit," "The American Way," "Anniversary," "Auld Lang Syne, or I'll Bet You Think This Play Is About You," "Bug Swatter," "Checkers," "Coming for a Visit," "Dalmation," "Dog Eat Dog," "Drowned Out," "Fireworks," "Interview," "Jumping," "Money," "One Beer Too Many," or "Phonecall from Sunkist," "Potato Girl," "Property of the Dallas Cowboys," "The Split Decision," "Watermelon Boats," or "Widows") in Norman A. Bert's *One-Act Plays for Acting Students* (Colorado Springs, Colorado: Meriwether Publishing Ltd, 1987), MPL, ISBN 0-916260-47-X

Vanities, **Act I,** (see p. 257) the first act of a comedy by Jack Heifner, 3f, in, *Vanities,* SF 120, NSHS PB92

W

"Welfare Lady, The," a drama by Louis Lippa, 3f, DPC

W31, NSHS pb162

"Womantalk," a comedy-drama by Sloane Drayson-Knigge, 3f (in multiple roles), BP

"Wrong Numbers," a comedy by Essex Dane, 3f, BP, NSHS 19988

One-Male-Three-Female Plays

A

"Anansi, the African Spider: How Anansi Brought the Stories Down," a children's comedy by Barbara Winther, 1m3f or 4m or 3m1f or 4f or 2m2f (+ extras), (published with and can play with "Anansi, the African Spider: Tall-Tale Man," "Ijapa, the Tortoise: The Bush Spirits," or "Two Dilemma Tales: The Snore or the Song"), in Barbara Winther's *Plays from African Tales: One-Act, Royalty-Free Dramatizations for Young People, from Stories and Folktales of Africa* (Boston: Plays, Inc., 1992), ISBN 0-8238-0296-5, PI

"Anansi, the African Spider: Tall-Tale Man," a children's comedy by Barbara Winther, 1m3f or 4m or 3m1f or 4f or 2m2f (+ extras), (published with and can play with "Anansi, the African Spider: How Anansi Brought the Stories Down," "Ijapa, the Tortoise: The Bush Spirits," or "Two Dilemma Tales: The Snore or the Song"), in Barbara Winther's *Plays from African Tales: One-Act, Royalty-Free Dramatizations for Young People, from Stories and Folktales of Africa* (Boston: Plays, Inc., 1992), ISBN 0-8238-0296-5, PI

"Answers on a Postcard," a play (genre?) by Andrew Rock, 1m3f, in *Triad 75*, NPN

"At Her Age," a drama by Eve Merriam, 1m3f, SF 3674

"*Auto-da-fe,*" a drama by Tennessee Williams, 1m3f, in *27 Wagons Full of Cotton*, DPS 485

B

"Bag of Green Apples, A," a drama by Jean Lennox Toddie, 1m3f (male child, 2 females, female child), (can pair with "Lookin' for a Better Berry Bush") in Jean Lennox Toddie's *A Bag of Green Apples* (New York: Samuel French, Inc., 1990), ISBN 0-573-62032-6, SF 4705, NSHS pb8109

"Bauble for Baby, A," a comedy by E. P. Conkle, 1m3f, SF 4607, NSHS pb7909

"Blue Blood," a comedy by Georgia Douglas Johnson, 1m3f, (published with and can pair with "Blue-Eyed Black Boy") in *Black Female Playwrights: An Anthology of Plays before 1950*, edited by Kathy A. Perkins (Bloomington, Indiana: Indiana University Press, 1989), ISBN 0-253-34358-5

"Blue-Eyed Black Boy," a comedy by Georgia Douglas Johnson, 1m3f, (published with and can pair with "Blue Blood") in *Black Female Playwrights: An Anthology of*

Plays before 1950, edited by Kathy A. Perkins (Bloomington, Indiana: Indiana University Press, 1989), ISBN 0-253-34358-5

C

"Can Can," a comedy-drama by Romulus Linney, 1m3f, in *Antaeus: Plays in One Act*, No. 66, edited by Daniel Halpern (Spring 1991), ISBN 0-88001-268-4, ANT; (published with and can pair with "Clair de Lune," "Gold and Silver Waltz," or "Yankee Doodle") also in *Pops*, DPS 3684, NSHS pb7913

"Christmas Stranger, The," a Christmas play (genre?) by Charles Emery, 1m3f, SF 5644

"Cola Wars, The," a comedy by B. Burgess Clark, 1m3f, in *Dramatics*, 65, no. 1 (September 1993): 22-29. Inquiries regarding performance rights and royalties should be directed to Francis Del Duca, Fifi Oscard Associates, 24 West 40th Street, Suite 1700, New York, NY 10018.

"Coming of Mr. Pine, The," a comedy by Grace McKeaney, 1m3f, in *Chicks and Other Short Plays*, SF 5210, NSHS pb7949, NSHS pb8091, NSHS pb7949

"Cradle Camp," a drama by Craig Sodaro, 1m3f, ACP

"*¡Cuba Sí!*" ["Yes, Cuba"], a fantasy by Terrence McNally, 1m3f, DPS 1490, NSHS pb8036

D

"Date," a comedy by Sam Smiley, 1m3f, SF 6605, NSHS pb7727

"Don't Blame It on the Boots," a comedy by N. J. Warburton, 1m3f, SF 6713, NSHS pb7910

"Dreamy Kid, The," a drama by Eugene O'Neill, 1m3f, DPS 405 (published with and can pair with "Before Breakfast," "The Dreamy Kid," "Fog," "Thirst," "Shell Shock," "The Sniper," or "A Wife for a Life") in Eugene O'Neill's *Complete Plays 1913-1920*, ed. by Travis Bogard (New York: Random House, Inc., 1988), ISBN 0-940450-48-8, NSHS pb8121

"Drunken Sisters, The," a comedy by Thornton Wilder, 1m3f, published with *The Alcestiad*, SF 6682, NSHS pb7942

E

"Eclipse, The," a drama by Joyce Carol Oates, 1m3f, (published with "Toneclusters") in *In Darkest America*, SF 7633, NSHS pb8092

One-Male-Three-Female Plays, *continued*

F

"**F.M.,**" a comedy by Romulus Linney, 1m3f, in *Laughing Stock*, DPS 2788, NSHS pb8150

"**Florence,**" a drama by Alice Childress, 1m3f, in *Wines in the Wilderness: Plays by African American Women from the Harlem Renaissance to the Present*, edited and compiled by Elizabeth Brown-Guillory (Westport, Connecticut: Praeger Publishers, 1990), ISBN 0-275-93567-1

"**Flower of Yeddo, A,**" a comedy by Victor Mapes, 1m3f, in *One Act Plays for Stage and Study: A Collection of Twenty-five Plays by Well-Known Dramatists, American, English and Irish, First Series*, preface by Augustus Thomas (New York: Samuel French, Inc., 1925), SF, NSHS

"**Fumed Oak,**" (see p. 203) a comedy by Noel Coward, one of the *Tonight at 8:30* series, 1m3f, BP, SF 450, HDS, NSHS 19878, NSHS 19883, NSHS pb8201

G

"**Going Nowhere Apace,**" a ten-minute play (genre?) by Glen Merzer, 1m3f, SF

"**Golden Slippers,**" a drama by Jean Mizer, 1m3f, HPC

"**Good Help Is Hard to Find,**" a comedy by Arthur Kopit, 1m3f, ISBN 0-573-62205-1, SF 9081, NSHS 7515, NSHS 27498

"**Graduation Suite: The Contract,**" a comedy by Thomas P. Millar, 1m3f, (published with and can pair with "Graduation Suite: The Contract") in Thomas P. Millar's *Graduation Suite* (West Vancouver, British Columbia, Canada: Palmer Press, 1987), ISBN 0-9693271-0-2, PAL

"**Grandma and Mistletoe,**" a Christmas comedy by Marguerite Kreger Phillips, 1m3f, TSD, NSHS 10922

H

"**Hanging and Wiving,**" a comedy by J. Hartley Manners, 1m3f, in *One Act Plays for Stage and Study: A Collection of Twenty-five Plays by Well-Known Dramatists, American, English and Irish, First Series*, preface by Augustus Thomas (New York: Samuel French, Inc., 1925), SF, NSHS

"**Hey Neighbor!**" a comedy by Peter Walker, 1m3f, BP

I

"**Interior Designs,**" a bare-stage comedy by Jimmie Chinn, 1m3f, SF 11652

L

"**Linda Her,**" an absurd comedy by Harry Kondoleon, 1m3f, (can pair with "Self Torture and Strenuous Exercise") in *Antaeus: Plays in One Act*, No. 66, edited by Daniel Halpern (Spring 1991), ISBN 0-88001-268-4, ANT; also in *Linda Her and The Fairy Garden*, DPS 2872, NSHS pb7925

"**Lord Byron's Love Letter,**" a drama by Tennessee Williams, 1m3f, in *27 Wagons Full of Cotton*, DPS 485

"**Love Talker, The,**" a drama by Deborah Pryor, 1m3f, DPS 2977, NSHS pb7962, NSHS pb8023, NSHS pb7962

N

"**Necklace, The,**" a drama by Jules Tasca from Guy de Maupassant, 1m3f, (published with and can pair with "The Devil," "Father and Son," or "Forbidden Fruit") in *The Necklace and Other Stories*, SF 15990, DPC N10, NSHS 27500, NSHS pb7919

"**Nightingale, A**" ["**The Roads to Home: A Nightingale**"], (see p. 220) a drama by Horton Foote, 1m3f, (published with and can pair with "The Roads to Home: The Dearest of Friends" or "The Roads to Home: Spring Dance"); in Horton Foote's *Selected One-Act Plays of Horton Foote*, edited by Gerald C. Wood (Dallas, Texas: Southern Methodist University Press, 1989), ISBN 0-87074-274-4, ISBN 0-87074-275-2; also in *The Roads to Home*, DPS 3845, NSHS pb8033

O

"**Open Window, The,**" a comedy by James Fuller from H. H. (Saki) Munro, 1m3f (+ extras), DPC O17, HDS, NSHS

P

"**Party, The,**" a comedy by Robert J. Flaherty, 1m3f, in Robert J. Flaherty's *The Party* (New York: Samuel French, Inc., 1990), ISBN 0-573-62393-9, SF 18941, NSHS pb7948, NSHS pb7950, NSHS pb7948

"**Pink and Patches,**" a comedy by Margaret Bland, 1m3f, SF 18641, NSHS pb8097, NSHS pb8093

"**Poor Aubrey,**" a comedy by George Kelly later developed into the full-length *The Show-Off*, 1m3f, BP, SF 18654, NSHS pb7908

"**Pro Game,**" a drama by Megan Terry, 1m3f or 3m1f, EIC 217-2

"**Protest,**" by Norman Williams, 1m3f, publisher unknown (?), NSHS

Q

"Quad," a television experiment by Samuel Beckett, 1m3f or 4m or 4f or 2m2f or 3m1f, (published with and can pair with "Act Without Words I," "Act Without Words II," "Breath," "Cascando," "Catastrophe," "Come and Go," "Eh Joe," "Embers," "Footfalls," "Ghost Trio," "Krapp's Last Tape," "Not I," "Ohio Impromptu," "A Piece of Monologue," "Play," "Rockaby," "Rough for Radio I," "Rough for Radio II," "Rough for Theatre I," "Rough for Theatre II," "That Time," or "Words and Music") in *Collected Shorter Plays,* ISBN 0-394-53850-1, ISBN 0-394-62098-4

"Queens of France," (see p. 233) a satiric comedy by Thornton Wilder, 1m3f, SF 886, NSHS pb7963

"Quem-Quaeritis Trope, The," a trope belonging to the Introit of the Mass at Easter from the St. Gall MS. 484, of the ninth century, 1m3f, HMC, NSHS 29216

R

"Reduced for Quick Sale," a comedy by Kent R. Brown, 1m3f, DPC R41, NSHS pb129

"Richest Girl in the World Finds Happiness, The," a bare-stage farce by Robert Patrick, 1m3f, in *Robert Patrick's Cheep Theatricks*, SF 20602

"Riders to the Sea," (see p. 235) a drama by John Millington Synge, 1m3f, BP, HDS, SF 920, NSHS 2212, NSHS 7095, NSHS 8162, NSHS 16020, NSHS 16370, NSHS 16374, NSHS 19878, NSHS 19883, NSHS 21405, NSHS 26428, NSHS 29310

"Roads to Home: A Nightingale, The" ["A Nightingale"], a drama by Horton Foote, 1m3f, (published with and can pair with "The Roads to Home: The Dearest of Friends" or "The Roads to Home: Spring Dance"); in Horton Foote's *Selected One-Act Plays of Horton Foote*, edited by Gerald C. Wood (Dallas, Texas: Southern Methodist University Press, 1989), ISBN 0-87074-274-4, ISBN 0-87074-275-2; also in *The Roads to Home*, DPS 3845, NSHS pb8033

"Rough Draft," a comedy by Cliff Harville, Jr., 1m3f, manuscript, SF 20635

S

"Silk Shirt, The," a drama by Tim Kelly, 1m3f, SF 21699, NSHS pb7945, NSHS pb8108

"Single and Proud," a comedy by Frederick Stroppel, 1m3f, (published and can pair with "Domestic Violence," "The Mamet Women," "Morning Coffee," or "Package Deal") in Frederick Stroppel's *Single and Proud and Other Plays* (New York: Samuel French, Inc.), ISBN 0-573-69411-7, SF 21158, NSHS pb8090

"Slipcovered King, The," a comedy in four scenes by Kristine Kurian, 1m3f, in Kristine Kurian's *The Slipcovered King* (Franklin, Ohio: Eldridge Publishing Company, 1991), EPC

"Slow Memories," a bare-stage drama by Barry Litvack, 1m3f, DPS 4140, NSHS pb7964, NSHS pb8143

"So When You Get Married . . . (The *Quando Si Sposa* Fund)," a comedy by Ellen Byron, 1m3f, (published with and can pair with "Election Year") in *Election Year and So When You Get Married . . . (The Quando Si Sposa Fund): Two Short Plays*, DPS 1791, NSHS pb7912

"Someone from Assisi," a symbolical play (genre?) by Thornton Wilder, 1m3f, SF 21735

"Sparkin'," a comedy by E. P. Conkle, 1m3f, BP, SF, NSHS 8266

"Strange Road," a drama by John M. Houston, 1m3f, BP, SF 21355

"Summer Romance," a comedy by Murray Schisgal, 1m3f, in *Closet Madness & Other Plays*, SF 221397, NSHS 27490

T

"Tiny Closet, The," a drama by William Inge, 1m3f, (published with and can pair with "The Boy in the Basement," "An Incident at the Standish Arms," "Memory of Summer," "A Social Event," or "The Rainy Afternoon") DPS 2535, NSHS pb6069

"Trap Is a Small Place, A," (see p. 254) a drama by Marjean Perry, 1m3f, MMP, NSHS 2401

"Two Fools Who Gained a Measure of Wisdom," a comedy by Tim Kelly from Anton Chekhov, 1m3f, DPS 4660, NSHS pb8025

W

"Waterworks," a comic-drama by E. J. Safirstein, 1m3f (+ 1m voice), in *Award-Winning Plays: Waterworks/E. J. Safirstein/When Esther Saw the Light/Michael Sargent* (New York: Samuel French, Inc., 1989), ISBN 0-573-62613-8, SF 25616, NSHS pb7947, NSHS pb8014

"Woodman and the Goblins, The," a bare-stage dark comedy by Don Nigro, 1m3f, (published with and can play with "Specter" or "The Daughters of Edward D. Boit") in *Green Man and Other Plays*, SF 25731, NSHS 7916

One-Male-Three-Female Plays, <small>continued</small>

"World Affairs," a drama by Susan Beth Pfeffer, 1m3f, in
*Center Stage: One-Act Plays for Teenage Readers and
Actors*, edited by Donald R. Gallo (New York: Harper &
Row, 1990), ISBN 0-06-122170-4, ISBN 0-06-022171-2, HR

A

"Action," a comedy by Robert Patrick, 2m2f, part of the comedy suite "Lights, Camera, Action," in *Robert Patrick's Cheep Theatricks*, SF 3008

"Action," a drama by Sam Shepard, 2m2f, in *Fool for Love & Other Plays*, SF 3603, NSHS pb8099

"Adventure Faces," a play (genre?) for children by Brian Way, 2m2f, BP

"Adventure of the Clouded Crystal, The," a comedy-drama by Tim Kelly, 2m2f, SF 3606, NSHS pb8068

"Adventures of Captain Neato-Man, The," a farce by Timothy Harris, 2m2f, in *Off-Off Broadway Short Play Festival Plays, 15th Series,* SF 3698, NSHS pb8079

"Anansi, the African Spider: How Anansi Brought the Stories Down," a children's comedy by Barbara Winther, 2m2f or 4m or 3m1f or 4f or 1m3f (+ extras), (published with and can play with "Anansi, the African Spider: How Anansi Brought the Stories Down," "Anansi, the African Spider: Tall-Tale Man," "Ijapa, the Tortoise: The Bush Spirits," or "Two Dilemma Tales: The Snore or the Song"), in Barbara Winther's *Plays from African Tales: One-Act, Royalty-Free Dramatizations for Young People, from Stories and Folktales of Africa* (Boston: Plays, Inc., 1992), ISBN 0-8238-0296-5, PI

"Anansi, the African Spider: Tall-Tale Man," a children's comedy by Barbara Winther, 2m2f or 4m or 3m1f or 4f or 1m3f (+ extras), (published with and can play with "Anansi, the African Spider: How Anansi Brought the Stories Down," "Ijapa, the Tortoise: The Bush Spirits," or "Two Dilemma Tales: The Snore or the Song"), in Barbara Winther's *Plays from African Tales: One-Act, Royalty-Free Dramatizations for Young People, from Stories and Folktales of Africa* (Boston: Plays, Inc., 1992), ISBN 0-8238-0296-5, PI

And the Air Didn't Answer," a drama for youth by R. Kerr, 2m2f, in *Sparks in the Park, and Other Prize-Winning Plays: From the 1987 and 1988 Young Playwrights Festivals: Produced by The Foundation of the Dramatists Guild*, edited by Wendy Lamb (New York: Dell Publishing Company, Inc., 1989), ISBN 0-440-20415-1

"Anniversary, The," a farce by Anton Chekhov, translated by Ronald Hingley, 2m2f (+ extras), in Anton Chekhov's *Twelve Plays*, translated by Ronald Hingley (London: Oxford University Press, 1992), ISBN 0-19-282813-4

"Another Antigone," a drama by A. R. Gurney, Jr., 2m2f, (can pair with "The Love Course," "The Opening Meeting," or "The Problem") in A. R. Gurney, Jr.'s *Another Antigone* (New York: Dramatists Play Service, Inc., 1988), DPS

"Anyone for Tennis?" a farce by Gwyn Clark, 2m2f, SF 3643, NSHS pb8073

"Après Opéra," a ten-minute play (genre?) by Michael Bigelow Dixon and Valerie Smith, 2m2f, (published with and can pair with "Americansaint," "'The Asshole Murder Case,'" "Bread," "Cold Water," "Cover," "Downtown," "The Drummer," "The Duck Pond," "Eating Out," "Electric Roses," "The Field," "4 A.M. (open all night)," "Looking Good," "Love and Peace, Mary Jo," "Loyalties," "Marred Bliss," "Perfect," "The Road to Ruin," "Spades," or "Watermelon Boats") in *25 10-Minute Plays from Actors Theatre of Louisville*, SF 22260, NSHS pb2977, ISBN 0-573-62558-1

B

"Balloon Faces," a play (genre?) for children by Brian Way, 2m2f, BP

"Banker's Dilemma, The," a farce melodrama by Cleve Haubold, 2m2f, SF 253, BP, HDS

"Bartok as a Dog," a drama by Patrick Tovatt, 2m2f, DPS 932, NSHS pb7966, NSHS pb8034, NSHS pb7966

"Bay at Nice, The," a drama by David Hare, 2m2f, in *Antaeus: Plays in One Act*, edited by Daniel Halpern, No. 66 (Spring 1991), ANT

"Bell, The," a play (genre?) for children by Brian Way, 2m2f, BP

"Bermondsey," a drama by John Mortimer, 2m2f, in *Come as You Are*, SF 4626, NSHS pb8037

"Big Mother," a play (genre?) by Charles Dizenzo, 2m2f, DPS manuscript

"Blake's Design," a drama by Kenneth H. Brown, 2m2f, BNA, NSHS pb4241

"Blind Alleys," a ten-minute drama by Michael Bigelow Dixon and Valerie Smith, 2m2f, (published with and can pair with "Clean" or "The Pick-Up") in *Big Trouble: Six 10-Minute Plays from Actors Theatre of Louisville*, IEC 324-1

"Blind Date," a comedy by Horton Foote, 2m2f, DPS 1043, NSHS pb8104

"Bloodline; or, Hanged in Their Own Family Tree," a sing-along musical mellerdrammer by Richard S. Dunlop, 2m2f, SF 4092, NSHS pb8048

"Bon Bons and Other Passions," a comedy by Nancy

Two-Males-Two-Female Plays, continued

Gilsenan, 2m2f, DPC, NSHS 159

"Boor Hug, The [*"Les Pavés de l'ours"*], a farce by Georges Feydeau, translated from the original French into English by Norman R. Shapiro, 2m2f, (published with and can pair with "Ladies' Man" [*"Notre futur"*], "Romance in A Flat" [*"Amour et piano"*], or "Wooed and Viewed" [*"Par la fenêtre"*], in Georges Feydeau's *Feydeau, First to Last,* translated by Norman R. Shapiro (Ithaca, New York, and London: Cornell University Press), SF 4667, NSHS

"Boy Upstairs, The," a comedy by Lucile Vaughan Payne, 2m2f, SF 4663, NSHS pb8072

"Bread," a ten-minute play (genre?) by Andy Backer, 2m2f, (published with and can pair with "Americansaint," "Après Opéra," "'The Asshole Murder Case,'" "Cold Water," "Cover," "Downtown," "The Drummer," "The Duck Pond," "Eating Out," "Electric Roses," "The Field," "4 A.M. (open all night)," "Looking Good," "Love and Peace, Mary Jo," "Loyalties," "Marred Bliss," "Perfect," "The Road to Ruin," "Spades," or "Watermelon Boats") in *25 10-Minute Plays from Actors Theatre of Louisville,* SF 22260, NSHS pb2977, ISBN 0-573-62558-1

"Broken Band, The," a Scottish drama by Alan Richardson, 2m2f (+ extra), (can pair with "Perfect Partners" or "Telltale") in Alan Richardson's *The Broken Band* (Glasgow, Scotland: Brown, Son & Ferguson, Ltd., 1990), ISBN 0-85174-588-1

"Brotherhood," a black comedy by Douglas Turner Ward, 2m2f, DPS 1155, NSHS pb7965, NSHS pb8151

"Buster Keaton's Promenade" ["El paseo de Buster Keaton," 1926?], 2m2f (a cock and an owl), a comedy by Federico Garcia Lorca (Spanish playwright, 1898-1936), [1] translated by Tim Reynolds, *Accent,* XVII, no. 3, Urbana, Illinois, 1957, agent unknown; [2] "Buster Keaton's Constitutional," translated by William I. Oliver, microfilm of manuscript, New York City, Columbia University Library, 1957, agent unknown

"But Listen!" a comedy by Susan C. Cottrell, 2m2f, DPC B35, NSHS pb156

C

"Camera," a comedy by Robert Patrick, 2m2f, part of the comedy suite "Lights, Camera, Action," in *Robert Patrick's Cheep Theatricks,* SF 302

"Camouflage," a Scottish play (genre?) by Nancy McPherson, 2m2f, in *Triad 73,* NPN

"Canadian Gothic," a drama by Joanna M. Glass, 2m2f, (published with and can pair with "American Modern"),

DPS 1230, NSHS pb8144

"Candy-Floss Man," a drama by Alec Taylor, 2m2f, (can pair with "The Green-Eyed Monster Comic Strip") in Alec Taylor's *Candy-Floss Man* (Macclesfield, Cheshire, England: New Playwrights Network, 1991), ISBN 0-86319-274-2, NPN

"Case of the Crushed Petunias, The," a lyrical fantasy by Tennessee Williams, 2m2f, in *American Blues,* DPS 710, NSHS pb6064

"Chance of a Lifetime, The," a comedy by H. Michael Krawitz, 2m2f, IEC 021-8

"Chimera" [*"Quimera,"* 1928], a play (genre?) by Federico García Lorca (Spanish playwright, 1898-1936), 2m2f, [1] translated by Tim Reynolds, in *Accent,* XVII, no.3, Urbana, Illinois, 1957, agent unknown; [2] translated by Edwin Honig, *New Directions, no. 8,* Norfolk, Connecticut, 1944, agent unknown; [3] translated by William I. Oliver, microfilm of manuscript, New York City, Columbia University Library, 1957, agent unknown

"Chiropodist, The," a comedy by John Patrick, 2m2f, (published with and can pair with "The Psychiatrist," "The Gynecologist," or "The Physician") in John Patrick's *The Doctor Will See You Now* (New York: Dramatists Play Service, 1991, DPS 1677

"Clown, The," a play (genre?) for children by Brian Way, 2m2f, BP

"Come in to the Garden Maud," a comedy by Noël Coward, 2m2f, in *Noël Coward in Two Keys,* SF 5692, NSHS 16674

"Cracks," a drama by James Purdy, 2m2f, cited in *The Best Plays of 1963-1964,* edited by Henry Hewes (New York: Dodd & Company, Inc., 1964)

D

"Dark Lady of the Sonnets, The," a comedy by George Bernard Shaw, 2m2f, (published with and can pair with "Annajanska, the Bolshevik Empress," "Augustus Does His Bit," "How He Lied to Her Husband," "O'Flaherty V.C.," "Overruled," "The Glimpse of Reality," "The Music-Cure," or "Village Wooing,") in [George] Bernard Shaw's *Selected Short Plays,* definitive text under the editorial supervision of Dan H. Laurence (London: Penguin Books, Ltd., 1988), ISBN 0-14-045031-9, SF 351

"Dearest of Friends, The," a drama by Horton Foote, 2m2f, (published with and can pair with "The Roads to Home: A Nightingale" or "The Roads to Home: Spring Dance"); in Horton Foote's *Selected One-Act Plays of Horton Foote,* edited by Gerald C. Wood (Dallas, Texas: South-

Two-Males-Two-Female Plays, continued

ern Methodist University Press, 1989), ISBN 0-87074-274-4, ISBN 0-87074-275-2 ; also in *The Roads to Home,* DPS 3845, NSHS pb8033

"Death of King Philip, The," a drama by Romulus Linney, 2m2f, DPS 1607, NSHS pb8042

"Death of the Hired Man, The," (see p. 197) a drama by Jay Reid Gould from Robert Frost, 2m2f, DPC D13, HDS, NSHS 6071

"Decision, The," a play for children by Brian Way, 2m2f, BP

"Devil, The," a farce by Jules Tasca from Guy de Maupassant, 2m2f, (published with and can pair with "The Necklace," "Father and Son," or "Forbidden Fruit") in *The Necklace and Other Stories,* SF 15990, NSHS 27500, NSHS pb7919

"Doctor Is In, The," a comedy by J. Michael Shirley, 2m2f (6 flexible roles), ELD

"Doing Poetry with Helen, Veronica, Sonny, and Poor Dead Charlie," a drama by Peter Dee, 2m2f, BP

"Domino Courts," new revised version of a drama by William Hauptman, 2m2f, ISBN 0-573-62131-4, in *Domino Courts/Comanche Cafe,* SF 6089, NSHS pb91

"Don't Wake Henry," a drama by Phyllis Vernick, 2m2f, PPC, NSHS pb7796

"Dr. Fish," a comedy by Murray Schisgal, 2m2f, DPS 1330, NSHS pb8044

"Dreams of Glory," a comedy by Frank D. Gilroy, 2m2f, SF 6678, NSHS pb8094

"Dreamwalk," a drama by Eddie Kennedy, 2m2f, DPC D42, NSHS pb174

"Dropout, The," a drama by Jerry Twedt, 2m2f (+voice), PPC, NSHS pb7726

E

"Echo," a drama by Robert Kasper, 2m2f, DPC E11, NSHS pb132

"El Paseo de Buster Keaton" ["Buster Keaton's Promenade," 1926?], a comedy by Federico García Lorca (Spanish playwright, 1898-1936), 2m2f (a cock and an owl), [1] translated by Tim Reynolds, *Accent,* XVII, no. 3, Urbana, Illinois, 1957, agent unknown; [2] "Buster Keaton's Constitutional," translated by William I. Oliver, microfilm of manuscript, New York City, Columbia University Library, 1957, agent unknown

"Emil's Leap," a comedy by Thomas Terefenko, 2m2f, PPC, NSHS pb54

"Escape," a comedy by Jules Tasca [set in Paris], 2m2f, (published with and can pair with [Athens:] "Passion Comedy," [Engelberg:] "Swiss Miss," [London:] "A Day in

the Night of Rose Arden," [Munich:] "A Side Trip to Dachau," [Venice:] "The Best Souvenirs," [Vienna:] "The Stop at the Palace," or [Rome:] "Going to the Catacombs,") in Jules Tasca's *Tour di Europa* [*Tour of Europe*] (New York: Samuel French, Inc.), ISBN 0-573-69222-X, SF 7635, NSHS pb8105

"Eulogy for Mr. Hamm," a chamber opera by Michael John LaChiusa, 2m2f, DPS 2986

F

"Faith, Hope, and Cyanide," a comedy by D. Roome, 2m2f (+voice), DPC F10, NSHS pb134

"Family-Go-Round," a comedy by Marie Hansen Lewis, 2m2f, PPC, NSHS pb55

"Fascinating Foundling, The," a comedy by George Bernard Shaw, 2m2f, SF

"Filleting Machine, The," a drama by Tom Hadaway, 2m2f, PPC, NSHS pb8163

"First Date," a comedy by J. T. Elias, 2m2f, BP, SF 8621, NSHS pb8062

"First Dress Suit, The," a comedy by Russell Medcraft, 2m2f, SF 8624, NSHS pb8069

"Fits and Starts," a comedy by Grace McKeaney, 2m2f, in *Chicks and Other Short Plays,* SF 8138, NSHS pb7949, NSHS pb8091, NSHS pb7949

"Flame, The," a biblical parable by the National Christian Education Council, 2m2f, in National Christian Education Council's *The Flame* (Redhill, Surrey, England: National Christian Education Council, 1990), ISBN 0-7197-0709-9, NCE

"Footsteps of Doves, The," a comedy by Robert Anderson, 2m2f, DPS, NSHS 29201, NSHS 28438, NSHS 16671

"Form, The," a comedy by N. F. Simpson, 2m2f, SF 8639, NSHS pb8066

"Four Baboons Adoring the Sun," a drama by John Guare, 2m2f, in *Antaeus: Plays in One Act,* edited by Daniel Halpern, No. 66 (Spring 1991), ANT

"Fragments," a drama by Murray Schisgal, 2m2f, (published with and can pair with "The Basement," "Memorial Day," or "The Old Jew") in *Five One Act Plays,* DPS 3975, NSHS pb6057

"Friend from High School," a drama by Conrad Bishop and Elizabeth Fuller, 2m2f, in *Dramatics,* 65, no. 7 (March 1994): 24-32, WW

"Friend Like Artie, A," a drama by Wil Denson, 2m2f, IEC 330-6

"Froegle Dictum, The," an absurdist comedy by Mark Medoff, 2m2f, (published with and can pair with "Doing a Good One for the Red Man" or "The Ultimate Grammar of Life") in Mark Medoff's *Four Short Plays* (New York: Dramatists Play Service, Inc., 1974), DPS 3107, NSHS pb8211, NSHS 26932

"**Frog Prince, The,**" (see p. 202) a comic fantasy by David Mamet, 2m2f, ISBN 0-573-65220-1, SF 472, NSHS 27529

"**Full Moon in March, A,**" a drama by William Butler Yeats, 2m2f, MAC, NSHS 16618

G

"**Gloucester Road,**" a drama by John Mortimer, 2m2f, SF, NSHS pb8037

"**Good Night, Caroline,**" a farce by Conrad Seiler, 2m2f, DPS 2175, NSHS pb8030

"**Gorgo's Mother,**" a comedy by Laurence Klavan, 2m2f, DPS 2181, NSHS pb8146

"**Great-Grandaddy's Skull,**" a drama by Scott Davis, 2m2f, BP

"**Gunshot Love,**" a comedy-drama by Dailyn Rodriguez, 2m2f, in *Throwing Off the Covers: A Collection of Four One Act Plays*, BP

"**Gynecologist, The,**" a comedy by John Patrick, 2m2f, (published with and can pair with "The Chiropodist," "The Physician," or "The Psychiatrist") in John Patrick's *The Doctor Will See You Now* (New York: Dramatists Play Service, 1991), DPS 1677

H

"**Happy Ending,**" a satiric comedy by Douglas Turner Ward, 2m2f, DPS 1560, NSHS 8148

"**Hat, The,**" a play (genre?) for children by Brian Way, 2m2f, BP

"**Haunted Auditorium, The,**" a mystery by Rosemary Owens, 2m2f, DPC H12

"**Heartbreak Tour, The,**" a comedy by Peter Morris, 2m2f, in *Off-Off Broadway Festival Plays, 15th Series*, SF 10687, NSHS pb8079

"**Help Wanted,**" a comedy by Michael Dixon and Valerie Smith, 2m2f, in *Dramatics*, 64, no. 1 (September 1992): 22-25. Inquiries regarding performance rights and royalties should be directed to Michael Dixon at Actors Theatre of Louisville, 316 West Main Street, Louisville, KY 40202.

"**Hen, The,**" a comedy adapted for the stage by Jules Tasca from the short story by Saki (H. H. Munro), 2m2f, (published with and can pair with "The Background," "Blind Spot," "Dusk" "The Reticence of Lady Anne," "Secret Sin," "The Tiger," or "The Unrest Cure,") in Jules Tasca's *Tales by Saki* (New York: Samuel French, Inc.), ISBN 0-573-62560-3, SF 22133, NSHS pb7798, NSHS pb8113

"**Horse Latitudes, The,**" a drama by Stephen Black, 2m2f, DPS, NSHS pb7750

"**Humphrey Pumphrey Had a Great Fall,**" a comedy by Alfred Greenaway, 2m2f, SF 10691, NSHS pb8063

"**Husbandry,**" a drama by Patrick Tovatt, 2m2f, SF, NSHS pb7509

I

"**I Never Saw Another Butterfly,**" a one-act cutting by Celeste Raspanti, 2m2f, DPC I33

"**I Remember You,**" a drama by Alvin Boretz, 2m2f, IEC 383-7

"**If It Don't Hurt It Ain't Love,**" a drama by John R. Carrol, 2m2f, BP

"**Impromptu,**" (see p. 208) a drama by Tad Mosel, 2m2f, DPS 2495, HDS, NSHS 21387

"**In the Desert of My Soul,**" a drama by John Glines, 2m2f, DPS 2515, NSHS pb7723

"**Informer, The,**" a drama by Bertolt Brecht, translated by Eric Russell Bentley, 2m2f, in *The Jewish Wife and Other Short Plays*, SF 11653, NSHS 29533

"**Inner Circle, The,**" a drama by Patricia Loughrey, 2m2f, (about AIDS, can pair with Alan Bowne's "Beirut," Harvey Fierstein's "Safe Sex," Robert Patrick's "Pouf Positive," or Lanford Wilson's "A Poster of the Cosmos") in Patricia Loughrey's *The Inner Circle* (Boston: Bakers Plays, 1989), BP, SF 11632

J

"**Jack Pot Melting: A Commercial,**" a drama by Amiri Baraka, 2m2f, in *Antaeus: Plays in One Act*, edited by Daniel Halpern, No. 66 (Spring 1991), ANT

"**Joggers,**" a play (genre?) by Geraldine Aron, 2m2f, SF 12616, NSHS pb8067

"**Judge Lynch,**" a drama by J. W. Rogers, Jr., 2m2f, in *One Act Plays for Stage and Study: A Collection of Twenty-five Plays by Well-Known Dramatists, American, English and Irish, First Series*, preface by Augustus Thomas (New York: Samuel French, Inc., 1925), SF, NSHS

"**Juliet,**" a drama by drama by Romulus Linney, 2m2f, (published with and can pair with "Yancey") in Romulus Linney's *Juliet, Yancey, April Snow: Three Plays* (New

York: Dramatists Play Service, Inc., 1989), LC 90-103850, DPS 831, NSHS pb8032

"Just What They Wanted," a comedy by Mary Cunningham, 2m2f, HDS

K

"Key, The," a play (genre?) for children by Brian Way, 2m2f, BP

"Kissing Sweet," a comedy by John Guare, 2m2f, (published with and can pair with "A Day for Surprises"), DPS 1555, NSHS pb7793

L

"La Morsa" ["**The Vise,**" 1910], a drama by Luigi Pirandello, 2m2f, (published with and can pair with "At the Exit," "Chee-Chee," "I'm Dreaming, But Am I?" or "The Man with the Flower in His Mouth,") in *Pirandello's One-Act Plays*, translated into English from the original Italian by William Murray (New York: Samuel French, Inc., 1970), SF 24601, NSHS

"Ladder, The," a play (genre?) for children by Brian Way, 2m2f, BP

"Lantern, The," a play (genre?) for children by Brian Way, 2m2f, BP

"Las Aceitunas" ["**Olives, The**"], a *paso* by Lope de Rueda, 2m2f, CML, NSHS 27052

"Last Call for Breakfast," a sketch by Richard Gaunt and Michael Langridge, 2m2f, in *The Coarse Acting Show 2*, SF 5920

"Last Leaf, The," a drama by Thomas Hischak from O. Henry, 2m2f, PDS

"Last of Captain Bedford, The," a drama by Pat Cook, 2m2f, ELD

"Leather Belt, The," a drama by Ev Miller, 2m2f, DPC, NSHS pb163

"Lefgook," a drama by Wade Barnes, 2m2f, IEC 107-9

"Les Pavés de l'ours" ["**The Boor Hug**"]*,* a farce by Georges Feydeau, translated from the original French into English by Norman R. Shapiro, 2m2f, (published with and can pair with "Ladies' Man" [*"Notre futur"*], "Romance in A Flat" [*"Amour et piano"*], or "Wooed and Viewed" [*"Par la fenêtre"*], in Georges Feydeau's *Feydeau, First to Last*, translated by Norman R. Shapiro (Ithaca, New York, and London: Cornell University Press), SF 4667, NSHS

"Lifesaver, The," a drama by Charles Coburn, 2m2f, ELD

"Lights," a comedy by Robert Patrick, 2m2f, part of the comedy suite "Lights, Camera, Action," in *Robert Patrick's*

Cheep Theatricks, SF 14604

"Little Comedy, The," a comedy in prologue and ten scenes (published with and can pair with "Summer Share") by Keith Herrmann, 2m2f, in Keith Herrmann's *Romance/Romance: Two New Musicals,* book and lyrics by Barry Harman (New York: Samuel French, Inc., 1989), ISBN 0-573-68916-6, SF

"Little Fears," an avant-garde comic drama by Emanuel Peluso, 2m2f, DPS 2880, NSHS pb7742, NSHS pb7752

"Little Toy Dog, The," a drama by Ramon Delgado, 2m2f

"Living Doll," a drama by Laura Annawyn Shamas, 2m2f, DPC L67

"Lonesome-Like," a comedy by Harold Brighouse, 2m2f, in *One Act Plays for Stage and Study: A Collection of Twenty-five Plays by Well-Known Dramatists, American, English and Irish, First Series*, preface by Augustus Thomas (New York: Samuel French, Inc., 1925), SF, NSHS

"Long Goodbye, The," a short study, i.e., a drama, by Tennessee Williams, 2m2f, in *27 Wagons Full of Cotton*, DPS 485

"Look Who's Playing God," a comedy by Albert Johnson, 2m2f, BP

"Lost Colony, The," a comedy by Wendy MacLeod, 2m2f, (published with and can play with "The Shallow End") in Wendy MacLeod's *The Shallow End and The Lost Colony* (New York: Dramatists Play Service, Inc., 1993), DPS 4064, NSHS pb8148

"Love and How to Cure It," a comedy by Thornton Wilder, 2m2f, in *The Long Christmas Dinner & Other One-Act Plays*, SF 14657

"Love Course, The," a comedy by A. R. Gurney, Jr., 2m2f, (can pair with "Another Antigone," "The Opening Meeting," or "The Problem") in A. R. Gurney, Jr.'s *Public Affairs* (New York: Samuel French, Inc., 1992), ISBN 0-573-69318-8, BP, SF 659, NSHS 27489

"Love Song of A. Nellie Goodrock, The," a melodrama for children by Richard Slocum, 2m2f (+ extras), (published with and can pair with "The Fisherman and the Flounder" or "The Gemshield Sleeper"), in Richard Slocum's *The Gemshield Sleeper and Other Plays for Children* (New York: Samuel French, Inc., 1988), ISBN 0-573-65223-6, SF

"Love's Light Wings," a drama by Lewis W. Heniford, 2m2f (can pair with "An Odious, Damnéd Lie" or "Shrew You: or, Who Hath Need of Men? As Goode Accounte As Anye Knowne Describing How Sweet Shagsper Shuffles Off His Mortal Coil"), WO, NSHS

"Loyalties," a ten-minute play (genre?) by Murphy Guyer, 2m2f, (published with and can pair with "Americansaint,"

"Après Opéra," "'The Asshole Murder Case,'" "Bread," "Cold Water," "Cover," "Downtown," "The Drummer," "The Duck Pond," "Eating Out," "Electric Roses," "The Field," "4 A.M. (open all night)," "Looking Good," "Love and Peace, Mary Jo," "Marred Bliss," "Perfect," "The Road to Ruin," "Spades," or "Watermelon Boats") in *25 10-Minute Plays from Actors Theatre of Louisville,* SF 22260, NSHS pb2977, ISBN 0-573-62558-1

"**Lucky Nurse,**" a chamber opera by Michael John LaChiusa, 2m2f, (published with and can pair with "Agnes," "Break," or "Eulogy for Mister Hamm") DPS 2986

M

"**Magical Faces,**" a play (genre?) for children by Brian Way, 2m2f, BP

"**Man at the Door, The,**" a comedy by Laura Cunningham, 2m2f, (published with and can pair with "Where She Went, What She Did") in *I Love You, Two,* SF 15943, NSHS pb8016

"*Mañana de sol*" ["**Sunny Morning, A**"], a comedy by Serafín and Joaquín Álvarez Quintero, translated from the Spanish by Lucretia Xavier Floyd, 2m2f, BP, SF 1012, NSHS 2189, NSHS 19878, NSHS 19883

"**Mandy and the Magus,**" a children's musical (singing) in three scenes by Brian Tremblay, 2m2f (one male is boy, one female is girl), in *Class Acts: Six Plays for Children,* edited by Tony Hamill (Toronto, Ontario, Canada: Playwrights Canada Press, 1992), ISBN 0-88754-487-8, PCP

"**Marble Arch,**" a comedy by John Mortimer, 2m2f, SF, NSHS pb8037

"**Marred Bliss,**" a ten-minute play (genre?) by Mark O'Donnell, 2m2f, (published with and can pair with "Americansaint," "Après Opéra," "'The Asshole Murder Case,'" "Bread," "Cold Water," "Cover," "Downtown," "The Drummer," "The Duck Pond," "Eating Out," "Electric Roses," "The Field," "4 A.M. (open all night)," "Looking Good," "Love and Peace, Mary Jo," "Loyalties," "Perfect," "The Road to Ruin," "Spades," or "Watermelon Boats") in *25 10-Minute Plays from Actors Theatre of Louisville,* SF 15957, NSHS pb2977, ISBN 0-573-62558-1

"**Mask, The,**" a drama by Dorothy R. Murphree, 2m2f, DPC M22, HDS, NSHS pb180, NSHS pb7743, NSHS pb7745

"**Matter of Wife and Death, A**" ["*La Lettre Chargée*"], a farce by Eugène Labiche, adapted and translated into English from the original French by Norman R. Shapiro, 2m2f, in *Tour de Farce: A New Series of Farce Through the Ages, A Slap in the Farce & A Matter of Wife and*

Death (New York: Applause Theatre Book Publishers), ISBN 0-936839-82-1, SF 14997, NSHS pb8116

"**Mayor and the Manicure, The,**" a comedy by George Ade, 2m2f, in *One Act Plays for Stage and Study: A Collection of Twenty-five Plays by Well-Known Dramatists, American, English and Irish, First Series,* preface by Augustus Thomas (New York: Samuel French, Inc., 1925), SF, NSHS

"**Mice Have Been Drinking Again, The,**" a comedy by Cleve Haubold, 2m2f, BP, SF 694, NSHS 27528

"**Mill Hill,**" a comedy by John Mortimer, 2m2f, in *Come as You Are,* SF 15665

"**Mirrorman, The,**" a play (genre?) for children by Brian Way, 2m2f, BP

"**Mr. Grump and the Clown,**" a play (genre?) for children by Brian Way, 2m2f, BP

"**Mr. Tucker's Taxi,**" a play (genre?) by Leonard Melfi, 2m2f, (published with and can play with "Lena and Louie," "Rusty and Rico," "The Teaser's Taxi," "Toddy's Taxi," or "Tripper's Taxi") in Leonard Melfi's *Later Encounters: Seven One-Act Plays* (New York: Samuel French, Inc., 1980), SF 15705, ISBN 0-573-60050-3, NSHS

"**Murder Play,**" a thriller by Brian J. Burton, 2m2f, SF 15712, NSHS pb8084

"**My Next Husband Will Be a Beauty,**" a comedy-tragedy by Tom Eyen, 2m2f, in *Tom Eyen: Ten Plays,* SF 15608, NSHS 29246

"**My Son's the One in the Flowered Apron,**" a comedy by Richard Urdahl, 2m2f, BP

N

"**Neighbors,**" a drama by Arkady Leokum, 2m2f, SF, DPS 3345, NSHS pb7888

"**New Sunrise, A,**" a comedy by Herman Coble, 2m2f, BP

"**Night Errant,**" a comedy by Georges Feydeau, "*Feu la Mère de Madame,*" translated from the original French by Michael Pilch, 2m2f, SF 16056, NSHS pb8071

"**Night Out, The,**" a Scottish comedy by John Watson, 2m2f, in John Watson's *The Night Out* (Glasgow, Scotland: Brown, Son & Ferguson, 1992), ISBN 0-85174-612-8

"**Nightingale and Not the Lark, The,**" a drama by Jennifer Johnston, 2m2f, SF 16641, NSHS pb8064

"**No 'Count Boy, The,**" a comedy by Paul Green, 2m2f, SF, NSHS 6066

"**No Exit,**" a lengthy one-act existentialist fantasy-drama, by Jean-Paul Sartre (French philosopher, novelist and playwright, 1905-1980), 2m2f, SF 765

O

"O'Flaherty V.C.," a comedy by George Bernard Shaw, 2m2f, (published with and can pair with "Annajanska, the Bolshevik Empress," "Augustus Does His Bit," "The Dark Lady of the Sonnets," "The Glimpse of Reality," "How He Lied to Her Husband," "The Music-Cure," "Overruled," or "Village Wooing") in *Selected Short Plays*, definitive text under editorial supervision of Dan H. Laurence (London: Penguin Books, Ltd., 1988), ISBN 0-14-045031-9, ISBN 0-14-045024-6, SF 17607, NSHS

"Objective Case," a drama by Lewis John Carlino, 2m2f, in Lewis John Carlino's *Two Short Plays: Mr. Flannery's Ocean, Objective Case* (New York: Dramatists Play Service, Inc., 1961), HDS, DPS 3235, NSHS pb8149

"Of All the Wide Torsos in All the Wild Glen," a comedy by Paul Peditto, 2m2f, DPC O47

"Off the Hook," a drama by Peter Hardy, 2m2f, AR

"Old Adam, The," a Scottish drama by Charles Barron, 2m2f, Brown, Son & Ferguson, ISBN 0-95174-585-7

"Old Oak Encounter, The," a comedy by Jerome McDonough, 2m2f, IEC, NSHS pb108

"Olives, The" [*"Las Aceitunas"*], (see p. 223) a *paso* by Lope de Rueda, 2m2f, CML, NSHS 27052

"On Tiny Endings," a drama by Harvey Fierstein, 2m2f, in *Safe Sex,* SF 17936

"On Trial," a play (genre?) for children by Brian Way, 2m2f, BP

"Other Half, The," a comedy by Elda Cadogan, 2m2f, BP

"Overruled," a comedy by George Bernard Shaw, 2m2f, (published with and can pair with "Annajanska, the Bolshevik Empress," "Augustus Does His Bit," "The Dark Lady of the Sonnets," "The Glimpse of Reality," "How He Lied to Her Husband," "The Music-Cure," "O'Flaherty V.C.," or "Village Wooing") in *Selected Short Plays*, definitive text under editorial supervision of Dan H. Laurence (London: Penguin Books, Ltd., 1988), ISBN 0-14-045031-9, ISBN 0-14-045024-6, SF 17651, NSHS

P

"Painting, The," a farce by Eugene Ionesco, 2m2f, SF

"Pals," a drama by David Perkins, 2m2f, BP

"Pastiche," a romantic farce by Nick Hall, 2m2f, SF 18601, NSHS pb8049

"Perfect Partners," a Scottish drama by Alan Richardson, 2m2f (+ extra), (can pair with "The Broken Band" or "Telltale") in Alan Richardson's *The Broken Band* (Glasgow, Scotland: Brown, Son & Ferguson, Ltd.,

1990), ISBN 0-85174-588-1

"Philip Glass Buys a Loaf of Bread," a comedy by David Ives, 2m2f, (published with and can pair with "Variations on the Death of Trotsky") in *Variations on the Death of Trotsky, and Other Short Comedies* (New York: Dramatists Play Service, Inc., 1992), DPS 4729, NSHS pb8089

"Phone Callers, The," a revue sketch by David Lloyd Crowder, 2m2f, SF, NSHS pb6051

"Pick-Up, The," a comedy by Michael Bigelow Dixon and Valerie Smith, 2m2f (+optional extras), (published with and can pair with "Blind Alleys" or "Clean") in *Big Trouble: Six 10-Minute Plays from Actors Theatre of Louisville*, IEC 324-1

"Pillow Talk," a ten-minute play (genre?) by John Pielmeier, 2m2f, SF

"Pink Lemonade for Tomorrow," a drama by Ruth Angell Purkey, 2m2f (+optional chorus), BP

"Pleasure of Detachment, The," a play (genre?) by Perry Souchuk, 2m2f (+ extras), in *Antaeus: Plays in One Act*, No. 66, edited by Daniel Halpern (Spring 1991), ISBN 0-88001-268-4, ANT

"Potholes," a comedy by Gus Kaikkonen, 2m2f, DPS 3687, NSHS pb8142

"Power Lunch," a comedy by Alan Ball, 2m2f, in *Five One Act Plays by Alan Ball*, DPS 0911, NSHS pb802

"Prisoner's Song, The," a drama by Horton Foote, 2m2f, (published with and can pair with "The One-Armed Man") in *"The Tears of My Sister," "The Prisoner's Song," "The One-Armed Man," and "The Land of the Astronauts,"* DPS 2022; also in Horton Foote's *Selected One-Act Plays of Horton Foote*, edited by Gerald C. Wood (Dallas, Texas: Southern Methodist University Press, 1989), ISBN 0-87074-274-4, ISBN 0-87074-275-2

"Private Lives of Sherlock Holmes, The," a parody by Michael Lambe, 2m2f, in *Triad 65*, NPN

"Private Moment, A," a drama by Stephen Gregg, 2m2f, in *Dramatics*, 65, no. 2 (October 1993): 20-23. Inquiries regarding performance rights and royalties should be directed to the author, 335 South Cochran, No. 201, Los Angeles, CA 90036.

"Private Prop. of Roscoe Pointer, The," a drama by Louis Damelio, 2m2f (+3 offstage voices), SF 18671, NSHS pb7958

"Promise, The," a drama by Joe Robertson, 2m2f, ELD

Q

"Quad," a television experiment by Samuel Beckett, 2m2f

or 4m or 4f or 1m3f or 3m1f, (published with and can pair with "Act Without Words I," "Act Without Words II," "Breath," "Cascando," "Catastrophe," "Come and Go," "Eh Joe," "Embers," "Footfalls," "Ghost Trio," "Krapp's Last Tape," "Not I," "Ohio Impromptu," "A Piece of Monologue," "Play," "Rockaby," "Rough for Radio I," "Rough for Radio II," "Rough for Theatre I," "Rough for Theatre II," "That Time," or "Words and Music") in *Collected Shorter Plays,* ISBN 0-394-53850-1, ISBN 0-394-62098-4

"Quimera" [*"Chimera,"* 1928], a play (genre?) by Federico García Lorca, (Spanish playwright, 1898-1936), 2m2f, [1] translated by Tim Reynolds, in *Accent,* XVII, no. 3, Urbana, Illinois, 1957, agent unknown [2] translated by Edwin Honig, *New Directions, no. 8,* Norfolk, Connecticut, 1944, agent unknown; [3] translated by William I. Oliver, microfilm of manuscript, New York City, Columbia University Library, 1957, agent unknown

"Quotations from Chairman Mao Tse-Tung," a drama by Edward Albee, 2m2f (+ voice), DPS, NSHS pb7805

R

"Rats, The," a mystery melodrama by Agatha Christie, 2m2f, BP, SF 20608, NSHS pb8111

"Recklessness," a drama by Eugene O'Neill, 2m2f, in *Eugene O'Neill, Complete Plays, Vol. 1,* SF 20655

"Return, The," a mystery-drama by Mario Fratti, 2m2f, (published with and can pair with "The Suicide") in *Four by Fratti,* ISBN 0-573-69034-0, SF 20601, NSHS 16646, NSHS pb8107

"Rise and Shine," a comedy by Elda Cadogan, 2m2f, BP

"Roads to Home, The: The Dearest of Friends," a drama by Horton Foote, 2m2f, (published with and can pair with "The Roads to Home: A Nightingale" or "The Roads to Home: Spring Dance") in Horton Foote's *Selected One-Act Plays of Horton Foote,* edited by Gerald C. Wood (Dallas, Texas: Southern Methodist University Press, 1989), ISBN 0-87074-274-4, ISBN 0-87074-275-2 ; also in *The Roads to Home,* DPS 3845, NSHS pb8033

S

"Save My Child! or Trapped by the Bottle," a melodrama by Brian J. Burton, 2m2f, in *Cheers, Tears and Screamers!! Three Short Melodramas for Old-Time Music Hall,* SF 21623, NSHS pb8075

"Search for Christmas, A," by author not named in catalog, 2m2f, HDS

"Seeing Someone," a comedy by Laurence Klavan, 2m2f, (can pair with "Gorgo's Mother") in Laurence Klavan's *The Show Must Go On/Seeing Someone/If Walls Could Talk* (New York, Dramatists Play Service, Inc., 1990), DPS 4082, NSHS pb8047

"Self Torture and Strenuous Exercise," a comedy by Harry Kondoleon, 2m2f, (can pair with "Linda Her") in Harry Kondoleon's *Self Torture and Strenuous Exercise: Selected Plays* (Theatre Communications Group, 1991), ISBN 1-55936-037-2, ISBN 1-55936-036-4, TCG

"Shadows of the Evening," a long one-act comedy by Noël Coward, 2m2f, SF 21106, NSHS pb8074

"She Walks in Beauty," a television sketch appropriate for stage by James Truex, 2m2f, NSHS 8266

"Shrew You: or, Who Hath Need of Men? As Goode Accounte As Anye Knowne Describing How Sweet Shagsper Shuffles Off His Mortal Coil," (see p. 241) a comedy by Lewis W. Heniford, 2m2f, (can pair with "An Odious, Damnéd Lie" or "Love's Light Wings") WO, NSHS

"Sidetracked," a drama by Carl Albert, 2m2f, ACP, HPC

"Small Claims" [**"The Boogeyman: Small Claims"**], a comedy-drama by Edward Clinton, 2m2f, (published with and can play with "First of the Month" or "The Boogeyman") in *The Boogeyman: Three Related One Acts* (New York: Samuel French, Inc., 1992), ISBN 0-573-69388-9, SF 21415

"Sociability," a comedy of manners by Charles Dizenzo, 2m2f (published with and can pair with "The Last Straw") DPS 2775, NSHS 29202

"Sod," a drama by Stuart McK. Hunter, 2m2f, TSD, NSHS 10922

"Son, Come Home, A," a drama by Ed Bullins, 2m2f, BMC, NSHS 16361

"Still Stands the House," a drama by Gwen Pharis Ringwood, 2m2f, SF 21338, NSHS pb8050

"Stops," a drama by Robert Auletta, 2m2f, in *Antaeus: Plays in One Act,* No. 66, edited by Daniel Halpern (Spring 1991), ISBN 0-88001-268-4, ANT

"Summer Share," a comedy in prologue and ten scenes (published with and can pair with "The Little Comedy") by Keith Herrmann, 2m2f, in Keith Herrmann's *Romance/Romance: Two New Musicals,* book and lyrics by Barry Harman (New York: Samuel French, Inc., 1989), ISBN 0-573-68916-6, SF

"Sunny Morning, A" [*"Mañana de sol,"* 1905], a comedy by Serafín and Joaquín Álvarez Quintero, translated from the Spanish by Lucretia Xavier Floyd, 2m2f, BP, SF 1012, NSHS 2189, NSHS 19878, NSHS 19883

T

"T V Special," a revue sketch by David Lloyd Crowder, 2m2f, SF, NSHS pb6051

"Teaser's Taxi, The," a play (genre?) by Leonard Melfi, 2m2f, (published with and can play with "Lena and Louie," "Mr. Tucker's Taxi," "Rusty and Rico," "Toddy's Taxi," or "Tripper's Taxi") in Leonard Melfi's *Later Encounters: Seven One-Act Plays* (New York: Samuel French, Inc., 1980), SF 22620, ISBN 0-573-60050-3, NSHS

"Telltale," a Scottish drama by Alan Richardson, 2m2f (+ extra), (can pair with "The Broken Band" or "Perfect Partners") in Alan Richardson's *The Broken Band* (Glasgow, Scotland: Brown, Son & Ferguson, Ltd., 1990), ISBN 0-85174-588-1

"That Pig, Morin," a drama by Jules Tasca from Guy de Maupassant, 2m2f (+ 2m extras), (published with and can pair with "The Devil," "Father and Son," or "Forbidden Fruit") in *The Necklace and Other Stories*, SF 15990, DPC N10, NSHS 27500, NSHS pb7919

"This Way to Heaven," a fantasy-comedy by Douglas Parkhirst, 2m2f, HDS, SF 1073, NSHS pb8081

"Three More Sleepless Nights," a drama by Caryl Churchill, 2m2f, (published with and can pair with "Abortive," "Not Not Not Not Not Enough Oxygen," "Schreber's Nervous Illness," or "Seagulls") in *Churchill: Shorts [Short Plays by Caryl Churchill]*, SF 22656, NSHS, ISBN 1-85459-085-5

"Three on a Bench," a whimsical comedy by Doris Estrada, 2m2f, BP, HDS, SF 1074, NSHS 19998

"Three Years," a comedy for youth by Paul Coates, 2m2f, in Paul Coates' *Two One-Act Plays* (Nottingham, England: Playwrights Publishing Company, 1991), ISBN 1-873130-05-8, PLP

"Toddy's Taxi," a play (genre?) by Leonard Melfi, 2m2f, (published with and can play with "Lena and Louie," "Mr. Tucker's Taxi," "Rusty and Rico," "The Teaser's Taxi," or "Tripper's Taxi") in Leonard Melfi's *Later Encounters: Seven One-Act Plays* (New York: Samuel French, Inc., 1980), SF 22723, ISBN 0-573-60050-3, NSHS

"Tooth or Shave," a comedy by Josephine (Josefina) Niggli, 2m2f, SF 22730, NSHS pb8088

"Tornado Ultra," a drama by J. P. Allen, 2m2f, (published with and can pair with "The City") in J. P. Allen's *Cities: Five Plays* (San Francisco: Ventana Publications, 1990)

"Totally Cool," a drama by Jan Buttram, 2m2f (2m play 6 roles), SF 22724, NSHS pb8018

"Tripper's Taxi," a drama by Leonard Melfi, 2m2f, (published with and can play with "Lena and Louie," "Rusty and Rico," "The Teaser's Taxi," "Toddy's Taxi," or "Mr. Tucker's Taxi") in Leonard Melfi's *Later Encounters: Seven One-Act Plays* (New York: Samuel French, Inc., 1980), SF 22764, ISBN 0-573-60050-3, NSHS

"'Twas Brillig," a drama by Frank D. Gilroy, 2m2f, (published with and can play with "Come Next Tuesday," "Present Tense," or "So Please Be Kind") in Frank D. Gilroy's *Present Tense* (New York: Samuel French, Inc., 1973), SF 22781, NSHS pb5486, NSHS pb6048, NSHS pb6050, NSHS pb8169

"Twelve Pound Look, The," (see p. 255) a comedy by J. M. Barrie, 2m2f, BP, SF 1095, NSHS 19878, NSHS 19883

"Two Bottles of Relish," a mystery by Edward Darby from Lord Dunsany, 2m2f, HDS, DPC T45, NSHS pb139

V

"Vacant Possession," a play (genre?) by Eileen Clark, 2m2f, in *Triad 64*, NPN

"Vacant Possession," a drama by Don West, 2m2f, SF 24608, NSHS pb8065

"Valley of Echoes, The," a play (genre?) for children by Brian Way, 2m2f, BP

"Vicky," a comedy by Phyllis Vernick from Saki (H. H. Munro), 2m2f, DPC V13

"Vise, The" [*"La Morsa,"* 1910], a drama by Luigi Pirandello, 2m2f, (published with and can pair with "Chee-Chee," "At the Exit," "I'm Dreaming, But Am I?" or "The Man with the Flower in His Mouth") in *Pirandello's One-Act Plays*, translated into English from the original Italian by William Murray (New York: Samuel French, Inc., 1970), SF 24601, NSHS

"Vital Statistics," a comedy by Bryan P. Harnetiaux, 2m2f, BP

W

"Waiting for the Bus," an allegory drama by Ramon Delgado, 2m2f, BP

"We Brents Pay Our Debts," a drama by Helen Mannix, 2m2f, TSD, NSHS 10922

"Wedding Gown," a drama by Francesco Bivona, 2m2f, PPI

"Werewolf," a comedy by William Gleason, 2m2f, DPC W16

"What Shall We Tell Caroline?" a comedy by John Mortimer, 2m2f, (can pair with "The Dock Brief") SF 25658

"Wheat Fire," a drama by Hermine Duthie, 2m2f, TSD, NSHS 10922

"Wheel, The," a play (genre?) for children by Brian Way, 2m2f, BP

"Where Late the Sweet Birds Sang," a drama by Cherith Baldry, 2m2f, in New Playwrights Network's *Triad 74*

"Which Is the Way to Boston?" a drama by Ronald Lorenzen, 2m2f, HDS, NSHS pb166

"White Cat," a play (genre?) by Mario Fratti, 2m2f, SF, NSHS pb8060

"White Tablecloths," a drama by Winifred Bell Fletcher, 2m2f, NSHS 10922

"Why Hanna's Skirt Won't Stay Down, or Admission $.10," one-act version of a tragic-comedy by Tom Eyen, 2m2f, SF 22911, NSHS 29246

"Wild Boor, A," a farce by Joseph Wallace from Anton Chekhov, 2m2f, (Boston: Baker's Plays, 1991) BP. See also "A Bear with a Sore Head," an adaptation by Brian J. Burton and translations of "The Bear" by Michael Frayn and Ronald Hingley.

"Will," a drama by Jules Tasca from Robert Louis Stevenson, 2m2f, BP

"Will Someone Please Tell Me What's Going on Here?" a comedy by Jim Lee, 2m2f, SF, NSHS pb8110, NSHS pb8153

"Will You Join Me for Dinner," a comedy by Ira N. Nottonson, 2m2f, BP, NSHS pb8155

"Winter Sunset," a drama by Robert Brome, 2m2f, TSD, NSHS 10922

"Would You Like a Cup of Tea?" a comedy by Warren Graves, 2m2f, SF 25200, NSHS pb8082

Y

"Young Marrieds at Play," a drama by Jerome Kass, 2m2f, (published with and can pair with "Make Like a Dog" or "Suburban Tragedy") DPS 2662, NSHS pb8055

Three-Male-One-Female Plays

A

"Acting Lesson, The," a drama by Willard Simms, 3m1f, (part of the trilogy *Variations on an Untitled Theme* and can pair with "Miss Farnsworth"*)* DPS 620, NSHS pb8082

"Adaptation," a comedy by Elaine May, 3m1f, DPS 630, NSHS pb8031

"After School Special," a drama by Keith Reddin, 3m1f, Keith Reddin's *Big Time: Scenes from a Service Economy and After School Special* (New York: Broadway Play Publishing, Inc., 1988), ISBN 0-88145-063-4, BPP

"Afterwards," a drama by Geraldine McGaughan, 3m1f, SF 210, NSHS pb8019

"Alternation of Perchings, An," a drama by Bill Anawalt, 3m1f, AR, NSHS pb5724

"All' uscita" ["At the Exit," 1922], a drama by Luigi Pirandello, 3m1f (+ extras), (published with and can pair with "Chee-Chee," "I'm Dreaming, But Am I?" "The Man with the Flower in His Mouth" or "The Vise") in *Pirandello's One-Act Plays,* translated into English from the original Italian by William Murray (New York: Samuel French, Inc., 1970) SF 15602, NSHS, ISBN 0-573-60039-2

"Americansaint," a ten-minute play (genre?) by Adam LeFevre, 3m1f, (published with and can pair with "Après Opéra," "'The Asshole Murder Case,'" "Bread," "Cold Water," "Cover," "Downtown," "The Drummer," "The Duck Pond," "Eating Out," "Electric Roses," "The Field," "4 A.M. (open all night)," "Looking Good," "Love and Peace, Mary Jo," "Loyalties," "Marred Bliss," "Perfect," "The Road to Ruin," "Spades," or "Watermelon Boats") in *25 10-Minute Plays from Actors Theatre of Louisville,* SF 22260, NSHS pb2977, ISBN 0-573-62558-1

"Anansi, the African Spider: How Anansi Brought the Stories Down," a children's comedy by Barbara Winther, 3m1f or 2m2f, or 1m3f or 4m or 4f (+ extras), (published with and can play with "Anansi, the African Spider: Tall-Tale Man," "Ijapa, the Tortoise: The Bush Spirits," or "Two Dilemma Tales: The Snore or the Song"), in Barbara Winther's *Plays from African Tales: One-Act, Royalty-Free Dramatizations for Young People, from Stories and Folktales of Africa* (Boston: Plays, Inc., 1992), ISBN 0-8238-0296-5, PI

"Anansi, the African Spider: Tall-Tale Man," a children's comedy by Barbara Winther, 3m1f or 2m2f, or 1m3f or 4m or 4f (+ extras), (published with and can play with "Anansi, the African Spider: How Anansi Brought the Stories Down," "Ijapa, the Tortoise: The Bush Spirits,"

or "Two Dilemma Tales: The Snore or the Song"), in Barbara Winther's *Plays from African Tales: One-Act, Royalty-Free Dramatizations for Young People, from Stories and Folktales of Africa* (Boston: Plays, Inc., 1992) ISBN 0-8238-0296-5, PI

"And None for the Road," a drama for youth by Sally-Anne Milgrim, 3m1f (+ extras), in Sally-Anne Milgrim's *Plays to Play with Everywhere*, drawings by Anthony Vercesi (New York: Samuel French, Inc., 1991), ISBN 0-573-65225-0

"Andrea's Got Two Boyfriends," a comedy-drama by David Willinger, 3m1f, DPS 787, NSHS pb8122

"archy and mehitabel," (see p. 184) a one-act version of a full-length musical comedy [originally on Broadway as *Shinbone Alley,* 1957] by Joe Darion and Mel Brooks, with music by George Kleinsinger and lyrics by Joe Darion, 3m1f (+ singers/dancers), MTI

"Arnold Bliss Show, The," a farce by Robert Patrick, 3m1f, in *Robert Patrick's Cheep Theatricks,* SF 3655

"'Asshole Murder Case, The,'" a ten-minute play (genre?) by Stuart Hample, 3m1f, (published with and can pair with "Americansaint," "Après Opéra," "Bread," "Cold Water," "Cover," "Downtown," "The Drummer," "The Duck Pond," "Eating Out," "Electric Roses," "The Field," "4 A.M. (open all night)," "Looking Good," "Love and Peace, Mary Jo," "Loyalties," "Marred Bliss," "Perfect," "The Road to Ruin," "Spades," or "Watermelon Boats") in *25 10-Minute Plays from Actors Theatre of Louisville,* SF 22260, NSHS pb2977, ISBN 0-573-62558-1

"At the Exit" [*All' uscita,* 1922], a drama by Luigi Pirandello, 3m1f (+ extras), (published with and can pair with "Chee-Chee," "I'm Dreaming, But Am I?" "The Man with the Flower in His Mouth," or "The Vise") in *Pirandello's One-Act Plays,* translated into English from the original Italian by William Murray (New York: Samuel French, Inc., 1970), SF 15602, NSHS, ISBN 0-573-60039-2

B

"Background, The," a comedy adapted for the stage by Jules Tasca from the short story by Saki (H. H. Munro), 3m1f, (published with and can play with "Blind Spot," "Dusk" "The Hen," "The Reticence of Lady Anne," "Secret Sin," "The Tiger," or "The Unrest Cure") in *Tales by Saki,* ISBN 0-573-62560-3, SF 22133, NSHS pb7798, NSHS pb8113

"Ballad of Love Canal, The," a drama by Joyce Carol Oates, 3m1f, in Joyce Carol Oates' *The Ballad of Love Canal*

(New York: Plume [New American Library], 1991), ISBN 0-452-26701-3, NAL

"Benjamin Goodright's Bedtime Story," a Christmas drama by Ron Betts, 3m1f, ISBN 0-86319-289-0 (1992), NPN

"Blind Spot," a comedy adapted for the stage by Jules Tasca from the short story by Saki (H. H. Munro), 2m2f, (published with and can pair with "The Background," "Dusk," "The Hen, "The Reticence of Lady Anne," "Secret Sin," "The Tiger," or "The Unrest Cure") in Jules Tasca's *Tales by Saki* (New York: Samuel French, Inc.), ISBN 0-573-62560-3, SF 22133, NSHS pb7798, NSHS pb8113

"Bobby Gould in Hell," a comedy by David Mamet, 3m1f, (published with and can pair with "The Devil and Billy Markham," by Shel Silverstein) in *Oh, Hell! Two One-Act Plays* (New York: Samuel French), ISBN 0-573-69254-8, SF 4189, NSHS pb8115

"Bodybuilders, The," a comedy by Michael Weller, 3m1f, (published with and can pair with "Tira Tells Everything There Is to Know about Herself") DPS 1065, NSHS pb8046

"Box, The," a symbolic allegory in seven scenes by Daniel W. Owens, 3m1f (+ extra), in *New Plays for the Black Theatre*, edited by Woodie King, Jr. (Chicago: Third World Press, 1989), ISBN 0-88378-124-7, TWP

"Boy in the Basement, The," a drama by William Inge, 3m1f, (published with and can pair with "An Incident at the Standish Arms," "Memory of Summer," "The Rainy Afternoon," "A Social Event," or "The Tiny Closet") DPS 2535, NSHS pb6069

"Brothers," a drama by Jules Tasca, 3m1f, in *The God's Honest, An Evening of Lies*, SF 4162

"Brothers in Arms," a comedy drama by Merrill Denison, 3m1f, SF 4686, NSHS pb8085

"Buck Fever," a comedy by Bill Bozzone, 3m1f, in *Buck Fever and Other Plays*, SF 4697, NSHS pb8017

"Burial of Esposito, The," a drama by Ronald Ribman, 3m1f, (published with and can pair with "The Son Who Hunted Tigers in Jakarta" or "Sun-Stroke") in *Passing Through from Exotic Places*, DPS 3585

"By the Waters of Babylon," a drama by Brainerd Duffield from Stephen Vincent Benet, 3m1f (variable chorus), DPC B37, HDS, NSHS pb175

C

"Cabin 12," a drama by John Bishop, 3m1f, (can pair with "Brontosaurus") DPS 1205, HDS

"Cassander, Man of Letters," a comedy by Potocki, translated by Daniel Gerould, 3m1f, (published with and can

pair with "The Blind One-Armed Deaf-Mute," "Cassander Supports the Revolution," "Cassander's Trip to the Indies," "Giles in Love," "The Shit Merchant," or "The Two Doubles") in *Gallant and Libertine, Divertissements and Parades of 18th Century France*, SF5756, NSHS pb7927, ISBN 0-933826-49-4

"Cassander Supports the Revolution," a comedy by Potocki, translated by Daniel Gerould, 3m1f, (published with and can pair with "The Blind One-Armed Deaf-Mute," "Cassander, Man of Letters," "Cassander Supports the Revolution," "Cassander's Trip to the Indies," "The Shit Merchant," or "The Two Doubles") in *Gallant and Libertine, Divertissements and Parades of 18th Century France*, SF 5757, NSHS pb7927, ISBN 0-933826-49-4

"Cassander's Trip to the Indies," a comedy by Potocki, translated by Daniel Gerould, 3m1f, (published with and can pair with "The Blind One-Armed Deaf-Mute," "Giles in Love," "Cassander Supports the Revolution," "Cassander, Man of Letters," "The Shit Merchant," or "The Two Doubles") in *Gallant and Libertine, Divertissements and Parades of 18th Century France*, SF 5758, NSHS pb7927, ISBN 0-933826-49-4

"Clara," a drama by Arthur Miller, 3m1f, (published with and can pair with "I Can't Remember Anything") in Arthur Miller's *Danger: Memory!: Two Plays* (New York: Dramatists Play Service, Inc., 1987), DPS 1526, NSHS pb7869

"Clown, The," a play (genre?) for children by C. Robert Jones, 3m1f (extras), BP

"Collection, The," a drama by Harold Pinter, 3m1f, (can pair with "The Dumb Waiter") in *The Pinter Plays* DPS 270; and (published with and can pair with "The Black and White," "The Dwarfs," "Last to Go," "The Lover," "Special Offer," or "Trouble in the Works") in Harold Pinter's *Plays: Two* (London and Boston: Faber & Faber, 1991), NSHS pb8102, ISBN 0-571-16075-1, DPS 2980, NSHS 27487

D

"Daft Danny," a comedy by Luke Stewart, 3m1f (+ voice), SF 6602, NSHS pb7744

"Day It Rained Forever, The," a comedy by Ray Bradbury, 3m1f, DPC, SF 6610, NSHS pb8087

"Day of Atonement," a melodrama by Margaret Wood, 3m1f, SF 6611, NSHS pb8097

"*Der Teufel im Haus*" (or, "*Der fahrende Schuler mit dem Teufelsbannen*") ["**The Devil in the House**"], a *fastnachtsspiel*, by Hans Sachs, adapted by Horst Ulrich Wendler, 3m1f, MVH, NSHS pb95

"Disputation between a Choir Director and a Shoemaker during Which the Word of God and a True Christian Being Was Argued About" [***"Disputation zwischen einem Chorherren und Schuhmacher darin das Wort.. ." / "Disputation zwischen einem Chorherren und Schuchmacher darinn das wort gottes vnd ein recht Christlich wesen verfochten würdt"***], a *fastnachtsspiel* by Hans Sachs, 3m1f, in Hans Sach's *Die Wittenbergisch Nachtigall: Spruchgedicht, Vier Reformationsdialoge und das Meisterlied das Walt Got*, compiled by Gerald H. Seufert (Stuttgart: Philipp Reclam jun., 1974), Universal-Bibliothek Nr. 9737/38/38a, ISBN 3-15-009737-1, NSHS

"Disputation zwischen einem Chorherren und Schuhmacher darin das Wort . . ." / "Disputation zwischen einem Chorherren und Schuchmacher darinn das wort gottes vnd ein recht Christlich wesen verfochten würdt" [***"Disputation between a Choir Director and a Shoemaker during Which the Word of God and a True Christian Being Was Argued About"***], a *fastnachtsspiel* by Hans Sachs, 3m1f, in Hans Sach's *Die Wittenbergisch Nachtigall: Spruchgedicht, Vier Reformationsdialoge und das Meisterlied das Walt Got*, compiled by Gerald H. Seufert (Stuttgart: Philipp Reclam jun., 1974), Universal-Bibliothek Nr. 9737/38/38a, ISBN 3-15-009737-1, NSHS

"Dust of the Road," a Christmas drama by Kenneth Sawyer Goodman, 3m1f, SF 6700

E

"Embers," a radio drama by Samuel Beckett, 3m1f (+ music), (published with and can pair with "Act Without Words I," "Act Without Words II," "Breath," "Cascando," "Catastrophe," "Come and Go," "Eh Joe," "Footfalls," "Ghost Trio," "Krapp's Last Tape," "Not I," "Ohio Impromptu," "A Piece of Monologue," "Play," "Quad," "Rockaby," "Rough for Radio I," "Rough for Radio II," "Rough for Theatre I," "Rough for Theatre II," "That Time," or "Words and Music") in *Collected Shorter Plays*, ISBN 0-394-53850-1, ISBN 0-394-62098-4

"Episode of the Lieutenant Colonel of the Civil Guard" [***"Escena del teniente coronel de la guardia civil,"*** 1922], a play (genre?) by Federico García Lorca (Spanish playwright, 1898-1936), 3m1f, translated by Edwin Honig, in *New Directions, no. 8*, Norfolk, Connecticut, 1944, agent unknown

"Escena del teniente coronel de la guardia civil" ["Episode of the Lieutenant Colonel of the Civil Guard," 1922], a play (genre?) by Federico García Lorca (Spanish playwright, 1898-1936), 3m1f, translated by Edwin Honig, in *New Directions, no. 8*, Norfolk, Connecticut, 1944, agent unknown

F

"Filiation," a drama by Jerome McDonough, 3m1f, IEC, NSHS

"Fog," a drama by Eugene O'Neill, 3m1f, (published with and can pair with "Before Breakfast," "The Dreamy Kid," "Shell Shock," "Thirst," or "A Wife for a Life") in Eugene O'Neill's *Complete Plays, 1913-1920, Vol. 1*, ed. by Travis Bogard (New York: Random House, 1988), ISBN 0-940450-48-8, NSHS pb8121

"Fool for Love," a lengthy one-act drama by Sam Shepard, 3m1f, HDS, NSHS pb8099

"4 A.M. (open all night)," a ten-minute play (genre?) by Bob Krakower, 3m1f, (published with and can pair with "Americansaint," "Après Opéra," "'The Asshole Murder Case,'" "Bread," "Cold Water," "Cover," "Downtown," "The Duck Pond," "The Drummer," "Eating Out," "Electric Roses," "The Field," "Looking Good," "Love and Peace, Mary Jo," "Loyalties," "Marred Bliss," "Perfect," "The Road to Ruin," "Spades," or "Watermelon Boats") in *25 10-Minute Plays from Actors Theatre of Louisville*, SF 22260, NSHS pb2977, ISBN 0-573-62558-1

G

"Gemshield Sleeper, The," a Kabuki and puppet drama for children by Richard Slocum based on a Japanese version of a classic fairy tale, 3m1f, (published with and can pair with "The Love Song of A. Nellie Goodrock" or "The Fisherman and the Flounder"), in Richard Slocum's *The Gemshield Sleeper and Other Plays for Children* (New York: Samuel French, Inc., 1988), ISBN 0-573-65223-6, SF

"Go Back to Your Precious Wife and Son," a comedy by Vaughn McBride from Kurt Vonnegut, Jr., 3m1f (1 male is a boy), DPC G50, NSHS pb7968

"Good Honest Food," a comedy by Bill Bozzone, 3m1f (+ 1m voice), in *Buck Fever and Other Plays*, SF 9688, NSHS pb8017

H

"Harry and Sylvia," a comedy-drama by Richard Strand, 3m1f, AR, NSHS pb5723

"He's Dead All Right," a play (genre?) by John Gainfort, 3m1f, SF 10638, NSHS pb8038

Three-Male-One-Female Plays, continued

"Heroes," a black comedy by Ken Mitchell, 3m1f, (published with and can pair with "Babel Rap") in *Six Canadian Plays* (Toronto, Ontario, Canada: Playwrights Canada Press, 1992), ISBN 0-88754-469-X, PCP

"Holy Ghostly, The," a drama by Sam Shepard, 3m1f, in *The Unseen Hand and Other Plays*, SF 10655

"Hum It Again, Jeremy," a drama for youth by Jean Davies Okimoto, 3m1f, in *Center Stage: One-Act Plays for Teenage Readers and Actors*, edited by Donald R. Gallo (New York: Harper & Row, 1990), ISBN 0-06-022170-4, ISBN 0-06-022171-2, HR

I

"Imbecile, The," a comedy by Luigi Pirandello translated by William Murray, 3m1f, in *Pirandello's One-Act Plays*, SF 11602

"In the Shadow of the Glen," a comedy by John Millington Synge, 3m1f, in *Complete Plays of Synge*, SF 11646, NSHS 27039, NSHS pb4019 NSHS 14824, NSHS 20483, NSHS 21389, NSHS 21514, NSHS 21776

L

"Late Arrival of Incoming Aircraft," a drama by Hugh Leonard, 3m1f, SF 14621, NSHS pb8076

"Leprechaun, The," a fantasy by Ruth Angell Purkey, 3m1f, BP, NSHS 19998

"Letty," a drama by Omar Paxson, 3m1f, AR, NSHS pb5724

"Life After Elvis," a comedy by Jason Milligan, 3m1f, in *Cross Country: Seven More One-Act Plays*, SF 14194

"Lie, The," a drama by Vaughn McBride from Kurt Vonnegut, Jr., 3m1f, DPC L75

M

"Mayhem at the Mill, or Fortune's Fate," 3m1f (+ extras), a melodrama by Brian J. Burton, in *Cheers, Tears and Screamers!! Three Short Melodramas for Old-Time Music Hall*, SF 15969, NSHS pb8075

"Memory," a drama by John O'Brien, 3m1f, DPC M52

"Minor Incident, A," a comedy by Hindi Brooks, 3m1f, IEC 131-1

"Miss Farnsworth," a comedy-drama by Willard Simms, 3m1f, (part of the trilogy *Variations on an Untitled Theme*, can pair with "The Acting Lesson") DPS 620

"Moonlight," a comedy by Mary Hays Weik, 3m1f, MAC, NSHS 15088

N

"New Tenant, The," a farce by Eugene Ionesco translated from the original French by Donald Watson, 3m1f, in Eugene Ionesco's *Three Plays by Ionesco* and in Eugene Ionesco's *Amédée, The New Tenant, Victims of Duty*, translated by Donald Watson (New York: Grove Press, 1958), ISBN 0-8021-3101-8, SF 16617, NSHS pb8118

"Nine to Five," a comedy by Jack Bingham, 3m1f, ISBN 0-86319-211-4 (1990), NPN

"Now [or, Soft Discs Don't Drive Hard Enough]," a comedy by Willard Simms, 3m1f, in *Then and Now*, DPS 4482, NSHS pb8026

O

"Once Around the Block," a comedy by William Saroyan, 3m1f, SF 17622, NSHS pb8039

"One for the Road," a drama by Harold Pinter, 3m1f, (published with and can pair with "Family Voices," "A Kind of Alaska," or "Victoria Station") in *Other Places*, DPS 3548

"Orrin," a drama by Don Evans, 3m1f, (published with and can pair with "Sugar-Mouth Sam Don't Dance No More") in *The Prodigals*, DPS 3725

"Outlanders," a drama by Amlin Gray from August Strindberg, 3m1f, (published with and can pair with "Wormwood") in *Zones of the Spirit*, DPS 5043, NSHS pb7915

"Over the Edge," a comedy by Paul Gater, 3m1f, (can pair with "Luther's Birthday") in *Triad 64*, NPN

P

"Passing of an Actor, The," a comedy-drama by Willard Simms, 3m1f, (part of the trilogy *Variations on an Untitled Theme*) DPS 3575

"Peace Manoeuvres," a drama by Richard Harding Davis, 3m1f, in *One Act Plays for Stage and Study: A Collection of Twenty-five Plays by Well-Known Dramatists, American, English and Irish, First Series*, preface by Augustus Thomas (New York: Samuel French, Inc., 1925), SF, NSHS

"Pie and the Tart, The," a comedy by Margaret Hall, 3m1f, in *The Big Book of Folktale Plays: One-Act Adaptations of Folktales from Around the World, for Stage and Puppet Performance*, edited by Sylvia E. Kamerman (Boston: Plays, Inc., 1991), ISBN 0-8238-0294-9, PI

"Prisoner, The," a drama by Neville A. Husband, 3m1f (+ extras), in Neville A. Husband's *The Prisoner* (Macclesfield, Cheshire, England: New Playwrights Network, 1990), ISBN 0-86319-236-X, NPN

"Pro Game," a drama by Megan Terry, 3m1f or 1m3f, EIC 217-2

"Purgatory," (see p, 231) a melodrama by William Butler Yeats, 3m1f, in *Eleven Plays by W. B. Yeats* and in *The Modern Theatre, Vol. 2,* SF 18674, NSHS 16369

"Pound on Demand, A," a brief sketch by Sean O'Casey, 3m1f, LD, NSHS 28268

Q

"Quad," a television experiment by Samuel Beckett, 3m1f or 4m or 4f or 1m3f or 2m2f, (published with and can pair with "Act Without Words I," "Act Without Words II," "Breath," "Cascando," "Catastrophe," "Come and Go," "Eh Joe," "Embers," "Footfalls," "Ghost Trio," "Krapp's Last Tape," "Not I," "Ohio Impromptu," "A Piece of Monologue," "Play," "Rockaby," "Rough for Radio I," "Rough for Radio II," "Rough for Theatre I," "Rough for Theatre II," "That Time," or "Words and Music") in *Collected Shorter Plays,* ISBN 0-394-53850-1, ISBN 0-394-62098-4

"Quare Medicine," a comedy by Paul Green, 3m1f, SF, NSHS 16609

R

"Radio II," a play (genre?) by Samuel Beckett, 3m1f, in *Ends and Odds,* SF 20605

"Rebuttals," a comedy by Joseph Fedorko, 3m1f, in *Extracurriculars,* BP

"Road to Ruin, The," a ten-minute comedy by Richard Dresser, 3m1f, in *Splitsville: Three One-Act Plays* SF 20654 and (published with and can pair with "Americansaint," "Après Opéra," "'The Asshole Murder Case,'" "Bread," "Cold Water," "Cover," "Downtown," "The Drummer," "The Duck Pond," "Eating Out," "Electric Roses," "The Field," "4 A.M. (open all night)," "Looking Good," "Love and Peace, Mary Jo," "Loyalties," "Marred Bliss," "Perfect," "Spades," or "Watermelon Boat") in *25 10-Minute Plays from Actors Theatre of Louisville,* SF 22260, NSHS pb2977, ISBN 0-573-62558-1

"Roads to Home: Spring Dance, The" ["Spring Dance"], a drama by Horton Foote, 1m3f, (published with and can pair with "The Roads to Home: The Dearest of Friends" or "The Roads to Home: A Nightingale"); in Horton Foote's *Selected One-Act Plays of Horton Foote,* edited by Gerald C. Wood (Dallas, Texas: Southern Methodist University Press, 1989), ISBN 0-87074-274-4, ISBN 0-87074-275-2 ; also in *The Roads to Home,* DPS 3845, NSHS pb8033

"Romancers, The," a comedy by Aurand Harris from Edmond Rostand's first act of *Les Romanesques,* the basis for the musical *The Fantasticks,* 3m1f, BP

S

"Sham," a satire by Frank G. Tompkins, 3m1f, BP

"Shaved Splits," a drama by Sam Shepard, 3m1f, in *The Unseen Hand and Other Plays,* SF 21674

"Shock of Recognition, The," by a comedy by Robert Anderson, 3m1f, DPS, NSHS 29201, NSHS 28438, NSHS 16671

"Shut Up, Martha!" a comedy by Cleve Haubold, 3m1f, SF 21696, NSHS pb8086

"Singer in the White Pajamas, The," a drama by Louis Phillips, 3m1f, DPC S97

"Snakes," a drama by Edwin R. Gilweit, 3m1f, DPC, NSHS pb164

"Some Live, Some Die," a drama by Michael Firth, IEC, NSHS pb110

"Soul Gone Home," (see p. 244) a comedy by Langston Hughes, 3m1f, HOA, NSHS

"Spring Dance" ["The Roads to Home: Spring Dance"], a drama by Horton Foote, 3m1f, (published with and can pair with "The Roads to Home: The Dearest of Friends" or "The Roads to Home: A Nightingale"); in Horton Foote's *Selected One-Act Plays of Horton Foote,* edited by Gerald C. Wood (Dallas, Texas: Southern Methodist University Press, 1989), ISBN 0-87074-274-4, ISBN 0-87074-275-2 ; also in *The Roads to Home,* DPS 3845, NSHS pb8033

"Stallion, The," a drama by William I. Oliver, 3m1f (+ extras), MM, NSHS 2401

"Strangest Kind of Romance, The," a dramatic sketch by Tennessee Williams, 3m1f, in *27 Wagons Full of Cotton,* DPS 485

"Strawberry Preserves," a comedy-drama by Le Wilhelm, 3m1f, in *Off-Off Broadway Festival Plays, 13th Series,* ISBN 0-573-62364-3, SF 21770, NSHS pb8083

"Sun-Stroke," a fantasy by Ronald Ribman, 3m1f, (published with and can pair with "The Burial of Esposito" or "The Son Who Hunted Tigers in Jakarta") in *Passing Through from Exotic Places,* DPS 3585

T

"Then [or, I Love Lucy Who?]," a comedy by Willard Simms, 3m1f, in *Then and Now,* DPS 4482, NSHS pb8026

"**Tinker and the Sheeog, The,**" an Irish folk-drama by Douglas Hyde, 3m1f, in Douglas Hyde's *Selected Plays of Douglas Hyde,* with translations by Lady Augusta Gregory, compiled and introduced by Gareth W. Dunleavy and Janet Egleson Dunleavy, with parallel texts in Irish and English (Washington, D.C.: Catholic University of America Press, 1991), ISBN 0-86140-095-X, ISBN 0-86140-096-8

"**Too Close for Comfort,**" a play (genre?) by Jack Dunphy, 3m1f, DPS manuscript

"**Tour,**" a drama by Terrence McNally, 3m1f (+ 1m bit) [described in DPS catalog as for 2m + 2 bits], (published with and can play with "Next" [revised version] or "Botticelli") in Terrence McNally's *Apple Pie* (New York: Dramatists Play Service, Inc., 1969), DPS 825, NSHS pb8164

"**Treadmill to the Goodtime Star,**" a drama by Stanley Disney, 3m1f (+ voice), AR, NSHS pb5722

"**Trees,**" a bare-stage fantasy by Israel Horovitz, 3m1f (+ extras), in *Trees and Leader: Two Short Plays,* DPS 2800, NSHS pb8103

"**Trouble Begins at 8, The,**" a comedy-drama by Bernard Sabath about Mark Twain, 3m1f, (published with and can pair with "A Barbarian in Love," "The Loneliest Wayfarer," or "Summer Morning Visitor") in Bernard Sabath's *Twain Plus Twain* (New York: Dramatists Play Service, Inc., 1984), DPS 4635, NSHS pb8024

"**Two Dilemma Tales: The Snore of the Song,**" a comedy by Barbara Winther based on a West African tale, 3m1f, in Barbara Winther's *Plays from African Tales: One-Act, Royalty-Free Dramatizations for Young People, from Stories and Folktales of Africa* (Boston: Plays, Inc., 1992), ISBN 0-8238-0296-5, PI

U

"**Used Car for Sale,**" a drama by Lewis John Carlino, 3m1f, DPS 4715, NSHS pb8027

W

"**Where She Went, What She Did,**" a comedy by Laura Cunningham, 3m1f, (published with and can pair with "The Man at the Door") in *I Love You, Two,* SF 25096, NSHS pb8016

"**Why the Chimes Rang,**" a Christmas drama by E. A. McFadden, 3m1f, BPF

"**Witness,**" a black comedy by Terrence McNalley, 3m1f, (published with and can pair with "Sweet Eros") DPS

4385, NSHS pb8043

"**Wormwood,**" a drama by Amlin Gray from August Strindberg, 3m1f, (published with and can pair with "Outlanders") in *Zones of the Spirit,* DPS 5043, NSHS pb7915

Four-Male Plays

A

"Anansi, the African Spider: How Anansi Brought the Stories Down," a children's comedy by Barbara Winther, 4m or 4f (+ extras), (published with and can play with "Anansi, the African Spider: Tall-Tale Man," "Ijapa, the Tortoise: The Bush Spirits," or "Two Dilemma Tales: The Snore or the Song"), in Barbara Winther's *Plays from African Tales: One-Act, Royalty-Free Dramatizations for Young People, from Stories and Folktales of Africa* (Boston: Plays, Inc., 1992), ISBN 0-8238-0296-5, PI

"Anansi, the African Spider: Tall-Tale Man," a children's comedy by Barbara Winther, 4m or 4f (+ extras), (published with and can play with "Anansi, the African Spider: How Anansi Brought the Stories Down," "Ijapa, the Tortoise: The Bush Spirits," or "Two Dilemma Tales: The Snore or the Song"), in Barbara Winther's *Plays from African Tales: One-Act, Royalty-Free Dramatizations for Young People, from Stories and Folktales of Africa* (Boston: Plays, Inc., 1992), ISBN 0-8238-0296-5, PI

"Arthur and the Acetone," a comedy by G. B. Shaw, 4m, SF

"Automatic Santa," a comedy by Randy Galvin, 4m or 4f, IEC

B

"Baker's Neighbor, The," a comedy by Jules Tasca, 4m or 4f, BP

"Bespoke Overcoat, The," (see p. 186) a tragedy by Wolf Mankowitz, 4m, SF 4627, NSHS 19991

"Best Half-Foot Forward," a sexual comedy by Peter Tolan, 4m, (published with and can play with "Pillow Talk") in Peter Tolan's *Stay Carl Stay, Best Half-Foot Forward, and Pillow Talk* (New York: Dramatists Play Service, Inc., 1991), DPS 4266, NSHS pb7887

C

"Charity Case," a drama by Ford Ainsworth, 4m or 4f, IEC 022-6

"Cowboys #2," a drama by Sam Shepard, 4m, (published with and can play with "Cowboys #2," "4-H Club," "Killer's Head," "Red Cross") in *Unseen Hand & Other Plays*, SF 5721, NSHS pb7928, ISBN 0-553-34263-0

"Crucifixion, The," a mystery play by anonymous [the "York Realist"], 4m (+ voice of Jesus), in *Everyman and Medieval Miracle Plays*, edited by A. C. Cawley (New York:

E. P. Dutton & Co., Inc., 1959), SBN [sic] 0-525-47036-0, NSHS pb4354

D

"Deathwatch," a drama by Jean Genet, 4m, (published with and can pair with "The Maids") in Jean Genet's *The Maids and Deathwatch: Two Plays,* translated from the original French into English by Bernard Frechtman (New York: Grove Weidenfeld, 1982), ISBN 0-8021-5056-X, BP, SF 357, SF 15036, NSHS pb8117

"*Der doctor mit der grosen nasen*" ["The Doctor with the Big Nose"], a farce by Hans Sachs, 4m, (published with and can pair with *"Dass heiss Eysen"* ["The Hot Iron"] or *"Der farendt Schuler im Paradeiss"* ["The Wandering Scholar in Paradise"]) in Hans Sachs' *Meistergesänge Fastnachtsspiele Schwänke*, compiled by Eugen Geiger (Stuttgart: Phillip Reclam jun., 1981), ISBN 3-15-007627-7, NSHS

"*Der Rossdieb zu Funsing*" ["The Horsethief at Funsing"], a *fastnachtsspiel* by Hans Sachs, adapted by Horst Ulrich Wendler, 4m, MVH, NSHS pb95

"*Der Rossdieb zu Funsing mit den tollen diebischen Bauern*" ["The Horsethief at Funsing with the Fantastic Thief-like Farmers"], a *fastnachtsspiel* by Hans Sachs, 4m, HDB, NSHS pb7746

"*Der rossdieb zw* [sic] *Fünssing mit den dollen diebischen Pauern*" / "*Der Rossdieb zu Funsing mit den tollen diebischen Bauern*" ["The Horsethief at Funsing with the Fantastic Thief-like Farmers"], a *fastnachtsspiel* by Hans Sachs, 4m, (published with and can pair with *"Dass heiss Eysen"* ["The Hot Iron"], *"Der doctor mit der grosen nasen"* ["The Doctor with the Big Nose"], or *"Der farendt Schuler im Paradeiss"* ["The Wandering Scholar in Paradise"]) in Hans Sachs' *Meistergesänge Fastnachtsspiele Schwänke*, compiled by Eugen Geiger (Stuttgart: Phillip Reclam jun., 1981), ISBN 3-15-007627-7, NSHS

"Doctor with the Big Nose, The" [*"Der doctor mit der grosen nasen"*], a farce by Hans Sachs, 4m, (published with and can pair with *"Dass heiss Eysen"* ["The Hot Iron"], *"Der Rossdieb zu Funsing mit den tollen diebischen Bauern"* ["The Horsethief at Funsing with the Fantastic Thief-like Farmers"], or *"Der farendt Schuler im Paradeiss"* ["The Wandering Scholar in Paradise"]) in Hans Sachs' *Meistergesänge Fastnachtsspiele Schwänke*, compiled by Eugen Geiger (Stuttgart: Phillip Reclam jun., 1981), ISBN 3-15-007627-7, NSHS

E

"El tigre" ["**The Tiger**"], a drama (in Spanish) by Demetrio Aguilera Malta (of Ecuador), 4m, FCE, NSHS 29520

"**Elephant Calf, The,**" a drama by Bertolt Brecht, 4m (+extras), in *Baal, A Man's a Man and The Elephant Calf: Early Plays* by Bertolt Brecht (New York: Grove Weidenfeld, 1964), ISBN 0-8021-3159-X; and in *The Jewish Wife and Other Short Plays,* SF 7640, NSHS pb8100

"**Eris, or The Night People,**" a drama by Lee Falk, 4m, in *Eris and Home at Six,* DPS 1820, NSHS pb7926

F

"**Fall of Lucifer, The,**" a craft cycle drama by an anonymous playwright, from *N. towne Plays,* 4m, HMC, NSHS 29216

"**Final Justice**" [*"Juicio final"*], a drama in Spanish by José de Jesús Martínez (of Panama), 4m, FCE, NSHS 29520

"**From Paradise to Butte,**" a comedy by Robert Finch, 4m, GCB

G

"**Game, A,**" a drama by Dennis Noble, 4m or 4f, SF, IEC 062-5

"**Game of Chess, The,**" a drama by Kenneth Sawyer Goodman, 4m, possibly in public domain, NSHS 19878, NSHS 19883

"**Glimpse of Reality, The,**" a tragedietta by George Bernard Shaw, 4m, (published with and can pair with "Annajanska, the Bolshevik Empress," "Augustus Does His Bit," "The Dark Lady of the Sonnets," "How He Lied to Her Husband," "The Music-Cure," "O'Flaherty V.C.," "Overruled," or "Village Wooing," in [George] Bernard Shaw's *Selected Short Plays,* definitive text under the editorial supervision of Dan H. Laurence (London: Penguin Books, Ltd., 1988), ISBN 0-14-045031-9, SF 351, SF 9647

"**Goblins Plot to Murder God, The,**" a ten-minute play (genre?) by Mark O'Donnel, 4m or 3m or 3f or 1m2f or 2m1f or 4f or 1m3f or 2m2f or 3m1f, SF

"**Great Caesar's Ghost,**" a farce for youth by Lewy Olfson, 4m, in Sylvia E. Kamerman's *The Big Book of Comedies: 25 One-Act Plays, Skits, Curtain Raisers, and Adaptations for Young Actors* (Boston: Plays, Inc., 1989), ISBN 0-8238-0289-2, PI

"**Great Moments in American Oratory,**" a dramatic reading by Val Cheatham, 4 narrators (male or female), ELD

H

"**Hidden in This Picture,**" a satire by Aaron Sorkin that subsequently became the second act of *Making Movies,* 4m, (published with *Making Movies*) also in *The Best American Short Plays, 1990,* edited by Howard Stein and Glenn Young (New York: Applause Theatre Book Publishers, 1991), ISSN 1062-7561, SF 10687

"**Horsethief at Funsing, The**" [*"Der Rossdieb zu Funsing"*], a *fastnachtsspiel* by Hans Sachs, adapted by Horst Ulrich Wendler, 4m, MVH, NSHS pb95

"**Horsethief at Funsing with the Fantastic Thief-like Farmers, The**" [*"Der rossdieb zw* [sic] *Fünssing mit den dollen diebischen Pauern"* / *"Der Rossdieb zu Funsing mit den tollen diebischen Bauern"*], a *fastnachtsspiel* by Hans Sachs, 4m, (published with and can pair with *"Dass heiss Eysen"* ["The Hot Iron"], *"Der doctor mit der grosen nasen"* ["The Doctor with the Big Nose"], or *"Der farendt Schuler im Paradeiss"* ["The Wandering Scholar in Paradise"]) in Hans Sachs' *Meistergesänge Fastnachtsspiele Schwänke,* compiled by Eugen Geiger (Stuttgart: Phillip Reclam jun., 1981), ISBN 3-15-007627-7, NSHS

"**Horsethief at Funsing with the Fantastic Thief-like Farmers, The**" [*"Der Rossdieb zu Funsing mit den tollen diebischen Bauern"*], a *fastnachtsspiel* by Hans Sachs, 4m, HDB, NSHS pb7746

"**Hunting of the Snark, The,**" a musical comedy by R. Eugene Jackson, 4m or 4f, IEC

I

"**If Men Played Cards As Women Do,**" a satire by George S. Kaufman, 4m, BP, HDS, SF 570, NSHS 19878, NSHS 19883

"**Intermission,**" a drama by Robert Schenkkan, 4m, in Robert Schenkkan's *Four One-Act Plays by Robert Schenkkan: Conversations with the Spanish Lady/Lunch Break/Intermission/The Survivalist,* DPS 3972, NSHS pb8022

J

"**Jest of Hahalaba, The,**" a drama by Edward John Moreton Drax Plunkett, Lord Dunsany, 4m, SF, NSHS 2703

"*Juicio final,*" a drama in Spanish by José de Jesús Martínez (of Panama), 4m, FCE, NSHS 29520

"**Juvie,**" a drama by Jerome McDonough, 3m or 4m, HDS

L

"**Laziest Man in the World, The,**" a comedy by Carl Webster Pierce, 4m, SF 14915 (no royalty), HDS, NSHS pb8157

"**Little David,**" a play (genre?) by Marc Connelly, 4m, available only in manuscript from DPS

"**Logical Conclusion,**" a drama by Jon Jory, 4m, in *Dramatics*, 63, no. 7 (March 1992): 34-35, DPC

M

"**Mañana Bandits: A Legend of the Rio Grande,**" a drama by Betty Smith and Chase Webb, 4m, GCB, NSHS 5345

"**Mice That Ate the Money, The,**" a dramatization of a folktale from India by Beatrice S. Smith, 4m, in *The Big Book of Folktale Plays*, edited by Syliva E. Kamerman (Boston: Plays, Inc., 1991), ISBN 0-8238-0294-9

P

"**Personal Thing, A,**" a comedy by Paul G. Wildman, 4m, SF 18634, NSHS pb8040

"**Playe Called the Foure PP, The: A Newe and a Very Mery Enterlude of a Palmer, a Pardoner, a Potycary, and a Pedler,**" (see p. 230) a medieval comedy by John Heywood, 4m, ATB, HMC, NSHS 29216

Q

"**Quad,**" a television experiment by Samuel Beckett, 4m or 4f or 1m3f or 2m2f or 3m1f, (published with and can pair with "Act Without Words I," "Act Without Words II," "Breath," "Cascando," "Catastrophe," "Come and Go," "Eh Joe," "Embers," "Footfalls," "Ghost Trio," "Krapp's Last Tape," "Not I," "Ohio Impromptu," "A Piece of Monologue," "Play," "Rockaby," "Rough for Radio I," "Rough for Radio II," "Rough for Theatre I," "Rough for Theatre II," "That Time," or "Words and Music") in *Collected Shorter Plays,* ISBN 0-394-53850-1, ISBN 0-394-62098-4

"*Quem Quaeritis* **Trope, The**" ["**Whom Seek Ye?**"], an Introit of the Mass at Easter, from MS 484 at St. Gall, Switzerland, ninth century, 4m, HMC, NSHS 29216 [Note: From this, liturgical drama began its evolution into a major element of the Medieval church.]

R

"**Resurrection, The,**" a drama by William Butler Yeats, 4m

(+ 3 musicians), MAC, NSHS 16618

"**Rising of the Moon, The,**" (see p. 236) a comedy by Lady Isabella Augusta Gregory, 4m, SF 20040 (no royalty in U.S.A., royalty in Canada), NSHS 19878, NSHS 19883, NSHS 16020, NSHS 21405, NSHS 26581, NSHS 20718

"**River Jordan, The,**" a drama by Robert Patrick, 4m, (published with and can pair with "Bill Batchelor Road," "Fairy Tale," "Fog" "Odd Number," "One of Those People," or "Pouf Positive") in Robert Patrick's *Untold Decades* (New York: St. Martin's Press, 1988), ISBN 0-312-02307-3

S

"**Sacrifice of Isaac, The,**" a non-craft-cycle drama, 4m (+ extras), HMC, NSHS 29216

"*Sankt Peter vergnugt sich mit seinen Freunden unten auf Erden,*" *a fastnachtsspiel*, by Hans Sachs, translated from the original German into modern German by Heinrich Detjen, 4m, HDB, NSHS pb63

"**Shell Shock,**" a drama by Eugene O'Neill, 4m, in *Eugene O'Neill, Complete Plays, Vol. 1*, SF 21616; also DPS 405, (published with and can pair with "Before Breakfast," "The Dreamy Kid," "Thirst," "The Sniper," or "A Wife for a Life") in Eugene O'Neill's *Complete Plays 1913-1920*, edited by Travis Bogard (New York: Random House, Inc., 1988), ISBN 0-940450-48-8, NSHS

"**Shit Merchant, The,**" a parade by Thomas Simon Gueullette, 4m or 4f, (published with and can pair with "The Blind One-Armed Deaf-Mute," "Cassander Supports the Revolution," "Cassander, Man of Letters," "Cassander's Trip to the Indies," or "The Two Doubles") in *Gallant and Libertine, Divertissements and Parades of 18th Century France*, SF 21134, NSHS pb7927, ISBN 0-933826-49-4

"**Shore Leave,**" a drama by Jason Milligan, 4m, in *Cross Country: Seven More One-Act Plays*, SF 21117

"**Sleep of Prisoners, A,**" a drama by Christopher Fry, 4m, DPS, NSHS pb7944

"**Sniper, The,**" a drama by Eugene O'Neill, 4m (+ 4m extras), probably DPS, in *Eugene O'Neill, Complete Plays, Vol. I*, SF 22627; also (published with and can pair with "Before Breakfast," "The Dreamy Kid," "Shell Shock," "Thirst," or "A Wife for a Life") in Eugene O'Neill's *Complete Plays 1913-1920*, ed. by Travis Bogard (New York: Random House, Inc., 1988), ISBN 0-940450-48-8, NSHS

"**Stopwatch,**" a ten-minute play (genre?) by Jon Jory, 4m, DPC, NSHS pb149

T

"Thinking Heart, The," Act II, an excerpt viable as a one-
act play from a drama by George M. Faulkner, 4m, CSS,
NSHS 26581, NSHS 20718

"Tiger, The" [*"El tigre"*], a drama (in Spanish) by Demetrio
Aguilera Malta (of Ecuador), 4m, FCE, NSHS 29520

W

"Whatever Happened to Chrissie," a fantasy for youth by
Dilys Gater, 4m or 4f (gender unidentified), NPN

"When You're by Yourself, You're Alone," a satirical comedy by Gene McKinney, 4m, SF 25668, NSHS pb8080

Four-Female Plays

A

"**All Risks,**" a drama by Margaret Moffatt, 4f, in *Triad 78*, NPN

"**Anansi, the African Spider: How Anansi Brought the Stories Down,**" a children's comedy by Barbara Winther, 4f or 4m or 3m1f or 2m2f or 1m3f (+ extras), (published with and can play with "Anansi, the African Spider: Tall-Tale Man," "Ijapa, the Tortoise: The Bush Spirits," or "Two Dilemma Tales: The Snore or the Song"), in Barbara Winther's *Plays from African Tales: One-Act, Royalty-Free Dramatizations for Young People, from Stories and Folktales of Africa* (Boston: Plays, Inc., 1992), ISBN 0-8238-0296-5, PI

"**Anansi, the African Spider: Tall-Tale Man,**" a children's comedy by Barbara Winther, 4f or 4m or 3m1f or 2m2f or 1m3f (+ extras), (published with and can play with "Anansi, the African Spider: How Anansi Brought the Stories Down," "Ijapa, the Tortoise: The Bush Spirits," or "Two Dilemma Tales: The Snore or the Song"), in Barbara Winther's *Plays from African Tales: One-Act, Royalty-Free Dramatizations for Young People, from Stories and Folktales of Africa* (Boston: Plays, Inc., 1992), ISBN 0-8238-0296-5, PI

"**Apple Pie,**" a drama by Margaret Kressman, 4f, SF 3642

"**Automatic Santa,**" a comedy by Randy Galvin, 4f or 4m, IEC

B

"**Baby Talk,**" a drama by Eileen Nelson, 4f, in *Triad 69*, NPN

"**Bad Penny, The,**" a drama by Rachel Field, 4f, SF 4603, NSHS pb7891

"**Baker's Neighbor, The,**" a comedy by Jules Tasca, 4f or 4m, BP

"**Bella, Bella,**" a comedy by Sylvia Vaughan, 4f, (can pair with "Lifestyles") in Sylvia Vaughan's *Bella, Bella* (Macclesfield, Cheshire, England: New Playwrights Network, 1989), ISBN 0-86319-221-1

"**Better Halves,**" a play (genre?) by Alan Ogden, 4f, in *Triad 68*, NPN

"**Beyond the Mirror,**" a drama by Patricia Chown, 4f (Macclesfield, Cheshire, England: New Playwrights Network, 1992), NPN

C

"**Candle on the Table, A,**" a comedy-drama by Patricia Clapp, 4f, BP, SF 5610, NSHS pb7728

"**Cards, Cups and Crystal Ball,**" a mystery by David Campton, 4f, DPC C67

"**Charity Case,**" a drama by Ford Ainsworth, 4f or 4m, IEC 022-6

"**Coal Diamond, The,**" a comedy by Shirley Lauro, 4f, DPS 1375, NSHS pb7890

D

"**Daughters of Edward D. Boit, The,**" (see p. 196) a dark comedy by Don Nigro, 4f, (published with and can play with "Specter" or "The Woodman and the Goblins") in *Green Man and Other Plays*, SF, NSHS pb7916, ISBN 0-573-62207-8

"**Distant Thunder,**" a drama by author unnamed in catalog, 4f, HDS

F

"**First Time Club, The,**" a drama by KT Curran, 4f, IEC 392-6

G

"**Game, A,**" a drama by Dennis Noble, 4f or 4m, SF, IEC 062-5

"**Goblins Plot to Murder God, The,**" a ten-minute play (genre?) by Mark O'Donnel, 4f or 3m or 3f or 1m2f or 2m1f or 4m or 1m3f or 2m2f or 3m1f, SF

"**Great Moments in American Oratory,**" a dramatic reading by Val Cheatham, 4 narrators (male or female), EPC

"**Ground Plans,**" a play (genre?) by J. B. Cooper, 4f, in *Triad 68*, NPN

H

"**Hello from Bertha,**" a drama by Tennessee Williams, 4f, (can pair with "The Chalky White Substance" and "The Case of the Crushed Petunias") in *27 Wagons Full of Cotton*, DPS 485

"**Hunting of the Snark, The,**" a musical comedy by R. Eugene Jackson, 4f or 4m, IEC

I

"**I Know This for Sure**," a Christmas drama by Peggy Welch Mershon, 4f, ELD

"**If the Shoe Pinches**," a play (genre?) by Babette Hughes, 4f, DPS manuscript

"**If Women Played Cards as Men Do**," a comedy by Ellen Goodfellow, 4f, BP, SF 11908 (no royalty)

"**If Women Worked as Men Do**," a comedy by Ellen Goodfellow, 4f, HDS, BP, NSHS pb8098

"**Infinite Deal of Nothing, An**," a comedy by Mary Fournier Bill, 4f, BP, SF 576, NSHS pb7911, ISBN 0-553-63269-3

J

"**Joint Owners in Spain**," a comedy by Alice Brown, 4f, HDS, BP, NSHS pb8196

"**Just Us Girls**," a comedy by Gordon Mauermann, 4f, ACP, HPC

L

"**Ladies of the Mop**," a comedy in rhyme and rhythm by Aurand Harris, 4f, BP, HDS, SF 14903 (no royalty), NSHS

"**Lady Fingers**," a comedy by Glenn Hughes, 4f, formerly listed by SF (out of print?), NSHS pb7722

"**Lesson in Revenge, A**," a fantasy drama by Richard Booth, 4f, EPC

"**Lost in the Shuffle**," a comedy by Katherin E. Morrison, 4f, (Franklin, Ohio: Eldridge Publishing Company, 1987) EPC

"**Lovely Sunday for Creve Coeur, A**," a drama by Tennessee Williams, 4f (+ extras), (can pair with "The Chalky White Substance" and "The Case of the Crushed Petunias") in Tennessee Williams' *The Theatre of Tennessee Williams*, vol. 8 (New York: New Directions Publishing Corporation, 1992), ISBN 0-8112-1201-7, NDP

M

"**Moonshine**," a Christmas drama by Laurence Housman, 4f, ISA, NSHS 27000

"**Mother's Day**," a comedy by Kate Aspengren, 4f, (published with and can pair with "Dear Mrs. Martin") in Kate Aspengren's *Dear Mrs. Martin & Mother's Day: Two One-Act Plays* (New York: Samuel French, Inc., 1992), SF 15244, NSHS 8114, ISBN 0-573-60144-5

N

"**Night Is Far Spent, The**," a drama by Cecil Davies, 4f, BP

"**Night Voice**," a suspense drama by Laurie Woodward, 4f, BP

O

"**Overtones**," (see p. 226) a drama by Alice Gerstenberg, 4f, BP, SF 17912, NSHS 19878, NSHS 19883

P

"**Princess**," a drama by Benjamin Bradford, 4f, PPC, NSHS pb8165

"**Private Worlds**," a play (genre?) by Ian Austin, 4f, (published with and can pair with "Remains to Be Seen" and "Still Life with Violets") in Ian Austin's *For Ladies Only: Five One-Act Plays with All Women Casts*, foreword by Babette Stephens (Ashgrove, Queensland, Australia: Playlab Press, 1988), ISBN 0-908156-31-6

Q

"**Quad**," a television experiment by Samuel Beckett, 4f or 4m or 1m3f or 2m2f or 3m1f, (published with and can pair with "Act Without Words I," "Act Without Words II," "Breath," "Cascando," "Catastrophe," "Come and Go," "Eh Joe," "Embers," "Footfalls," "Ghost Trio," "Krapp's Last Tape," "Not I," "Ohio Impromptu," "A Piece of Monologue," "Play," "Rockaby," "Rough for Radio I," "Rough for Radio II," "Rough for Theatre I," "Rough for Theatre II," "That Time," or "Words and Music") in *Collected Shorter Plays*, ISBN 0-394-53850-1, ISBN 0-394-62098-4

R

"**Raincheck**," a drama by Claudia Allen, 4f, in Claudia Allen's *She's Always Liked the Girls Best* (Chicago: Third Side Press, 1992), ISBN 1-879427-11-7, TSP

"**Remains to Be Seen**," a murder mystery by Ian Austin, 4f, (published with and can pair with "Private Worlds" and "Still Life with Violets") in Ian Austin's *"For Ladies Only: Five One-Act Plays with All Women Casts,"* foreword by Babette Stephens (Ashgrove, Queensland, Australia: Playlab Press, 1988), ISBN 0-908156-31-6

"**Running Past**," a drama by Margaret Bower, 4f, in New Playwrights' Network's *Triad 66* NPN

Four-Female Plays, *continued*

S

"Shallow End, The," a comedy by Wendy MacLeod, 4f, (published with and can play with *"The Lost Colony"*) in Wendy MacLeod's *The Shallow End and The Lost Colony* (New York: Dramatists Play Service, Inc., 1993) DPS 4064, NSHS pb8148

"She Writes a Roof," a comedy by Noel Houston, 4f, GCB, NSHS 5345

"6:15 on the 104," a comedy by Elinor Jones, 4f, in *"6:15 on the 104"*; *"If You Were My Wife I'd Shoot Myself"*; *"Under Control,"* DPS 4121, NSHS pb7892

"Strawberry Jam," a comedy by Bruce Fisk, 4f, BP

"Street of Good Friends, The," a comedy by Owen G. Arno, 4f, DPS 3550, NSHS pb7344

"Sunday Go to Meetin'," a ten-minute play (genre?) by Shirley Lauro, 4f, SF

T

"To Burn a Witch," (see p. 252) a drama by James L. Bray, 4f, DPC T32, HDS, NSHS pb160

W

"Weird Is the Night," a comedy by Fred Rogerson, 4f, DPC W14

"Whatever Happened to Chrissie," a fantasy for youth by Dilys Gater, 4f or 4m (gender unidentified), NPN

"When Altars Burn," a drama by Kay Arthur, 4f, SF 25664, NSHS pb7889

One-Act Plays, Arranged Alphabetically by Author,
with Title, Genre, Cast Size and Gender,
and Source(s)

Part 2, Author Index, alphabetically presents authors.

Each citation includes author, title, genre, cast size and gender, and source(s). The cast size and gender appears in each citation to keep the reader on track. Like the Title Index, this index of authors has many citations that suggest plays with which this play could pair on a bill, often ones published with it, thereby reducing the cost of scripts and simplifying production rights.

A

Ade, George, "The Mayor and the Manicure," a comedy, 2m2f, in *One Act Plays for Stage and Study: A Collection of Twenty-five Plays by Well-known* [sic] *Dramatists, American, English and Irish, First Series*, preface by Augustus Thomas (New York: Samuel French, Inc., 1925), SF, NSHS

Aguilera Malta, Demetrio (Ecuadorian playwright and novelist in Spanish, 1905-   ), "The Tiger" [*"El tigre"*], a drama (not to be confused with the play of the same name by Jules Tasca from Saki, a.k.a. H. H. Munro, and, furthermore, not to be confused with the play of the same name by Murray Schisgal), 4m, FCE, NSHS 29520

Ainsworth, Ford, "Charity Case," a drama, 4m or 4f, IEC 022-6

Albee, Edward (1928-   ), "Fam and Yam," a satire, 2m, DPS 725

Albee, Edward (1928-   ), "Listening," a chamber play developed from a radio play (genre?), 1m2f, (published with "Counting the Ways") in Edward Albee's *The Plays*, Vol. 2 (New York: Macmillan Publishing Company, 1991), ISBN 0-02-501762-4, MAC, DPS 1440

Albee, Edward (1928-   ), "Quotations from Chairman Mao Tse-Tung," a drama, 2m2f (+voice), DPS, NSHS pb7805

Albee, Edward (1928-   ), "The Zoo Story," a drama, 2m, DPS 5045, HDS, NSHS 29313, NSHS 16382

Albert, Carl, "Sidetracked," a drama, 2m2f, ACP, HPC

Allard, Janet, "Painted Rain," a drama, 2m1f, in *Hey Little Walter, and Other Prize-Winning Plays*, edited by Wendy Lamb (New York: Dell, 1991), ISBN 0-440-21025-9

Allen, Claudia, "Raincheck," a drama, 4f, in Claudia Allen's *She's Always Liked the Girls Best* (Chicago: Third Side Press, 1992), ISBN 1-879427-11-7, TSP

Allen, Donald M. (translator from French), "The Lesson," a comedy by Eugene Ionesco, 1m2f, in *Four Plays by Eugene Ionesco*, BP, SF 647, NSHS

Allen, J. P., "The City," a drama, 2m, (published with and can pair with "Tornado Ultra") in J. P. Allen's *Cities: Five Plays* (San Francisco: Ventana Publications, 1990)

Allen, J. P., "Tornado Ultra," a drama, 2m2f, (published with and can pair with "The City") in J. P. Allen's *Cities: Five Plays* (San Francisco: Ventana Publications, 1990)

Allen, Woody, "Death Knocks," a comedy, 2m, in *Getting Even*, SF 6046

Álvarez Quintero, Joaquín and Serafín (Spanish playwrights, brothers, Serafín 1871-1938 and Joaquín 1873-1944), "A Sunny Morning" [*"Mañana de sol,"* 1905], a comedy by brothers Serafín and Joaquín Álverez Quintero translated from the Spanish by Lucretia Xavier

Floyd, 2m2f, BP, SF 1012, NSHS 2189, NSHS 19878, NSHS 19883

Álvarez Quintero, Serafín and Joaquín (Spanish playwrights, brothers, Serafín 1871-1938 and Joaquín 1873-1944), "A Sunny Morning" [*"Mañana de sol,"* 1905], a comedy translated from the Spanish by Lucretia Xavier Floyd, 2m2f, BP, SF 1012, NSHS 2189, NSHS 19878, NSHS 19883

Amsterdam, Diana, "The End of I," a drama, 2m1f, in *Sex and Death: Four One-Act Plays*, SF 7630

Amsterdam, Diana, "Lingerie," a comedy, 1m2f, in *Sex and Death: Four One-Act Plays*, SF 14682

Anawalt, Bill, "An Alternation of Perchings," a drama, 3m1f, AR, NSHS pb5724

Anderson, Jane, "Lynette at 3:00 A. M.," a ten-minute play (genre?), 2m1f, SF

Anderson, Robert, "The Footsteps of Doves," a comedy, 2m2f, DPS, NSHS 29201, NSHS 28438, NSHS 16671

Anderson, Robert, "I'll Be Home for Christmas," a comedy, 1m2f, DPS, NSHS 29201, NSHS 28438, NSHS 16671

Anderson, Robert, "The Last Act Is a Solo," a drama, 2m1f, SF 13850

Anderson, Robert, "The Shock of Recognition," a comedy, 3m1f, DPS, NSHS 29201, NSHS 28438, NSHS 16671

Anderson, Sherwood (American playwright, 1876-1941), "Triumph of the Egg," a comedy, 2m1f (+ extras), MM, GCB, NSHS 5345

Anonymous (author unnamed in catalog), "Distant Thunder," a drama, 4f, HDS

Anonymous (source West African folk story tellers), "Two Dilemma Tales: The Snore or the Song," a children's comedy by Barbara Winther based on a West African Story, 3m1f (+ extras), (published with and can pair with "Anansi, the African Spider: How Anansi Brought the Stories Down," "Anansi, the African Spider: Tall-Tale Man," or "Ijapa, the Tortoise: The Bush Spirits") in Barbara Winther's *Plays from African Tales: One-Act, Royalty-Free Dramatizations for Young People, from Stories and Folktales of Africa* (Boston: Plays, Inc., 1992), ISBN 0-8238-0296-5, PI

Anonymous (omitted name), "A Search for Christmas," by author not named in catalog, 2m2f, HDS

Anonymous (English playwright), "The Sacrifice of Isaac," a non-craft-cycle drama, 4m (+ extras), HMC, NSHS 29216

Anonymous (English playwright), *"The Quem Quaeritis Trope"* ["Whom Seek Ye?"], an Introit (trope) of the Mass at Easter, from MS 484 at St. Gall, Switzerland, ninth century, 4m, HMC, NSHS 29216 [Note: From this, liturgical drama began its evolution into a major element of the Medieval church.]

Anonymous (English playwright), "The Killing of Abel," a craft cycle drama from *N. towne Plays*, 3m, HMC, NSHS 29216

Anonymous (Japanese playwright), "Abstraction," a 14th- or 15th-century Japanese comedy, 2m1f, DP, NSHS 16631

Anonymous (English playwright), "The Fall of Lucifer," a craft cycle drama from *N. towne Plays*, 4m, HMC, NSHS 29216

Anonymous (English playwright), "The York Play of the Crucifixion," a medieval mystery play by unknown author, 3m, manuscript in British Museum

Anonymous (source Japanese fairy tale writer), "The Gemshield Sleeper," a Kabuki and puppet drama by Richard Slocum for children based on a Japanese version of a classic fairy tale, 3m1f, (published with and can pair with "The Fisherman and the Flounder" or "The Love Song of A. Nellie Goodrock") in Richard Slocum's *The Gemshield Sleeper and Other Plays for Children* (New York: Samuel French, Inc., 1988), ISBN 0-573-65223-6, SF

Anonymous (English playwright, the "York Realist"), "The Crucifixion," a mystery play, 4m (+ voice of Jesus), in *Everyman and Medieval Miracle Plays*, edited by A. C. Cawley (New York: E. P. Dutton & Co., Inc., 1959), SBN [sic] 0-525-47036-0, NSHS pb4354

Apple, Gary, "Do," a bare-stage drama, 2m, in *Plays for an Undressed Stage*, SF 6653

Apple, Gary, "When God Comes for Breakfast, You Don't Burn the Toast," a comedy, 2m1f, BP, SF 25669, NSHS 27514

Apstein, Theodore, "Fortunata Writes a Letter," a drama, 2m1f, MM, NSHS 2401

Archer, Robyn (Australian playwright), "Cafe Fledermaus," a symbolic musical revue, 2m1f (+ extras), in Robyn Archer's *Cafe Fledermaus* (Paddington, New South Wales, Australia: The Currency Press Pty., Ltd., 1990), ISBN 0-86819-266-X, CPP

Arno, Owen G., "The Other Player," a drama, 3m or 3f, **analyzed in Part 4, p. 225**, DPS 3550, NSHS pb7344

Arno, Owen G., "The Street of Good Friends," a comedy, 4f, DPS 3550, NSHS pb7344

Aron, Geraldine, "The Donahue Sisters," a drama, 3f, in Geraldine Aron's *The Donahue Sisters* (New York: Samuel French, Inc., 1991), ISBN 0-573-13234-8, SF 6738

Aron, Geraldine, "Joggers," a play (genre?), 2m2f, SF 12616, NSHS pb8067

Arrabal, Fernando (born in Spain, resident of France, writing chiefly in French, 1932-   ), "The Solemn Communion," a drama, 1m2f, in *Arrabal: Plays: Volume 3*, SF 21732

Arthur, Kay, "When Altars Burn," a drama, 4f, SF 25664, NSHS pb7889

Asher, Sandy, "Workout!" a drama, 1m1f, in *Center Stage: One-Act Plays for Teenage Readers and Actors*, edited by Donald R. Gallo (New York: Harper & Row, 1990), ISBN 0-06-022170-4, ISBN 0-06-022171-2

Aspengren, Kate, "Dear Mrs. Martin," a comedy, 2f or 3f or

4f, (published with and can pair with "Mother's Day") in *Kate Aspengren's Dear Mrs. Martin & Mother's Day: Two One-Act Plays* (New York: Samuel French, Inc.), SF 6919, NSHS 8114

Assaf, Jesús (Mexican playwright), *"Estoy enamorado de tu hermana"* ["I Am in Love with Your Sister], *una farsa/* farce *en español*/in Spanish, 1m2f, **analyzed on p. 201**, OEN, NSHS pb8189

Augier, Émile (French poet and playwright, 1920- , 1820-1889), "The Post-Script," a comedy, 1m2f, in Émile Augier's *Four Plays*, translated by Barrett H. Clark (New York: Howard Fertig, Inc., Publisher, 1989), ISBN 0-86527-367-7

Auletta, Robert, "Stops," a drama, 2m2f, in *Antaeus: Plays in One Act*, No. 66, edited by Daniel Halpern (Spring 1991), ISBN 0-88001-268-4, ANT

Austin, Ian (Australian playwright), "Private Worlds," a play (genre?), 4f, (published with and can pair with "Remains to Be Seen" and "Still Life with Violets") in Ian Austin's *For Ladies Only: Five One-Act Plays with All Women Casts*, foreword by Babette Stephens (Ashgrove, Queensland, Australia: Playlab Press, 1988), ISBN 0-908156-31-6

Austin, Ian (Australian playwright), "Remains to Be Seen," a murder mystery, 4f, (published with and can pair with "Private Worlds" and "Still Life with Violets") in Ian Austin's *For Ladies Only: Five One-Act Plays with All Women Casts*, foreword by Babette Stephens (Ashgrove, Queensland, Australia: Playlab Press, 1988), ISBN 0-908156-31-6

Austin, Ian (Australian playwright), "Still Life with Violets," a drama, 3f, (published with and can pair with "Private Worlds" and "Remains to Be Seen") in Ian Austin's *For Ladies Only: Five One-Act Plays with All Women Casts*, foreword by Babette Stephens (Ashgrove, Queensland, Australia: Playlab Press, 1988), ISBN 0-908156-31-6

Author unknown, "The Doubting Saint," a drama, 1m2f or 2m1f, SF (possibly out of print), NSHS

Ayckbourn, Alan (English playwright), "A Cut in the Rates," a television thriller, 1m2f, in Alan Ayckbourn's *A Cut in the Rates* (London: Samuel French, Ltd., 1991), ISBN 0-573-12084-6, SF 5798

B

Backer, Andy, "Bread," a ten-minute play (genre?), 2m2f, (published with and can pair with "Americansaint," "Après Opéra," "'The Asshole Murder Case,'" "Cold Water," "Cover," "Downtown," "The Drummer," "The Duck Pond," "Eating Out," "Electric Roses," "The Field," "4 A.M. (open all night)," "Looking Good," or "Love and Peace, Mary Jo," "Loyalties," "Marred Bliss," "Perfect," "The Road to Ruin," "Spades," or "Watermelon Boats") in *25 10-Minute Plays from Actors Theatre of*

Louisville, edited by Actors Theatre of Louisville (New York: Samuel French, Inc., 1989), ISBN 0-573-62558-1, SF 6716

Baffle, Wilmer, "Truant Husbands," a skit, 2f, (published with and can pair with "The Dormant Heritage," "Enterprising Oswald," "Girls Will Be Girls," "Grandma Fought the Indians," "Make-Up," "Paris Sets the Styles," "'Rosemary—That's for Remembrance,'" or "She Goes the Rounds") in *Two by Two*, BP, NSHS pb6044, NSHS 29326

Bailey, Craig C., "Heaven Sent," a fantasy-comedy, 2m1f, in Craig C. Bailey's *Heaven Sent* (Franklin, Ohio: Eldridge Publishing Company, 1988), EPC

Baker, Edward Allan, "Dolores," a drama, 2f, (published with and can pair with "Lady of Fadima" and "North of Providence") in Edward Allan Baker's *North of Providence; Dolores; Lady of Fadima* (New York: Dramatists Play Service, Inc., 1991); also in *The Best Short Plays, 1988-1989*, edited by Ramon Delgado (New York: Applause Theatre Book Publishers, 1989), DPS, ATB

Baker, Edward Allan, "Lady of Fadima," a drama, 1m2f, (published with and can pair with "Dolores" and "North of Providence") in Edward Allan Baker's *North of Providence; Dolores; Lady of Fadima* (New York: Dramatists Play Service, Inc., 1991), DPS

Baldry, Cherith, "Where Late the Sweet Birds Sang," a drama, 2m2f, in New Playwrights Network's *Triad 74*

Ball, Alan, "Bachelor Holiday," a comedy, 3m, (published with and can pair with "Power Lunch" or "Your Mother's Butt") in *Five One Act Plays by Alan Ball*, DPS 0911, NSHS pb8021

Ball, Alan, "Power Lunch," a comedy, 2m2f, (published with and can pair with "Bachelor Holiday" or "Your Mother's Butt") in *Five One Act Plays by Alan Ball*, DPS 0911, NSHS pb802

Ball, Alan, "Your Mother's Butt," a comedy, 1m1f, (published with and can pair with "Bachelor Holiday" or "Power Lunch") in *Five One Act Plays by Alan Ball*, DPS 0911, NSHS pb8021

Bamber, George, "Return to Dust," a radio drama, 2m1f, CSS, NSHS 20719

Baraka, Amiri, "Jack Pot Melting: A Commercial," a drama, 2m2f, in *Antaeus: Plays in One Act*, edited by Daniel Halpern, No. 66 (Spring 1991), ANT

Baring, Maurice, "Catherine Parr, or Alexander's Horse," a comedy, 2m1f, BP, NSHS 19988

Barker, Howard, "The Unforeseen Consequences of a Patriotic Act," a biblical drama, 3f, in Howard Barker's *The Unforeseen Consequences of a Patriotic Act* (New York: Riverrun Press, 1988), ISBN 0-7145-4135-4, RP

Barlow, Anna Marie, "The Meeting," a drama, 2m1f, (published with "A Limb of Snow"; can pair with "Ferryboat" or "A Limb of Snow") DPS 2865

Barnes, Peter (English playwright), "Billy and Me," a radio drama, 1m, (published with and can pair with "Houdini's Heir," "Losing Myself," "Madame Zenobia," "The Road to Strome," "Slaughterman," "The Spirit of Man: A Hand Witch of the Second Stage," "The Spirit of Man: From Sleep and Shadow," "The Spirit of Man: The Night of the Simhat Torah," or "A True-Born Englishman") in Peter Barnes' *The Spirit of Man and More Barnes' People* (New York and London: Methuen & Company, 1990), ISBN 0-413-63130-3

Barnes, Peter (English playwright), "Houdini's Heir," a radio drama, 1m, (published with and can pair with "Billy and Me," "Losing Myself," "Madame Zenobia," "The Road to Strome," "Slaughterman," "The Spirit of Man: A Hand Witch of the Second Stage," "The Spirit of Man: From Sleep and Shadow," "The Spirit of Man: The Night of the Simhat Torah,"or "A True-Born Englishman") in Peter Barnes' *The Spirit of Man and More Barnes' People* (New York and London: Methuen & Company, 1990), ISBN 0-413-63130-3

Barnes, Peter (English playwright), "Losing Myself," a radio drama, 1m, (published with and can pair with "Billy and Me," "Houdini's Heir," "Madame Zenobia," "The Road to Strome," "The Spirit of Man: From Sleep and Shadow," "The Spirit of Man: A Hand Witch of the Second Stage," "The Spirit of Man: The Night of the Simhat Torah," "Slaughterman,"or "A True-Born Englishman") in Peter Barnes' *The Spirit of Man and More Barnes' People* (New York and London: Methuen & Company, 1990), ISBN 0-413-63130-3

Barnes, Peter (English playwright), "The Road to Strome," a radio drama, 1m, (published with and can pair with "Billy and Me," "Houdini's Heir," "Madame Zenobia," "Losing Myself," "The Spirit of Man: A Hand Witch of the Second Stage," "The Spirit of Man: From Sleep and Shadow," "The Spirit of Man: The Night of the Simhat Torah," "Slaughterman,"or "A True-Born Englishman") in Peter Barnes' *The Spirit of Man and More Barnes' People* (New York and London: Methuen & Company, 1990), ISBN 0-413-63130-3

Barnes, Peter (English playwright), "Slaughterman," a radio drama, 1m, (published with and can pair with "Billy and Me," "Houdini's Heir," "Madame Zenobia," "Losing Myself," "The Spirit of Man: From Sleep and Shadow," "The Spirit of Man: A Hand Witch of the Second Stage," "The Spirit of Man: The Night of the Simhat Torah," "The Road to Strome," or "A True-Born Englishman") in Peter Barnes' *The Spirit of Man and More Barnes' People* (New York and London: Methuen & Company, 1990), ISBN 0-413-63130-3

Barnes, Peter (English playwright), "A True-Born Englishman," a radio play (genre?), 1m, (published with and can pair with "Billy and Me," "Houdini's Heir," "Losing Myself," "Madame Zenobia," "Slaughterman," "The Road to Strome," "The Spirit of Man: From Sleep and

Shadow," "The Spirit of Man: A Hand Witch of the Second Stage," or "The Spirit of Man: The Night of the Simhat Torah") in Peter Barnes' *The Spirit of Man and More Barnes' People* (New York and London: Methuen & Company, 1990), ISBN 0-413-63130-3

Barnes, Wade, "Lefgook," a drama, 2m2f, IEC 107-9

Baron, Alec, "Chimera," a drama, 3f, SF 5752

Barrie, James Matthew, Sir (Scottish novelist and playwright, 1920- , 1860-1937), "The Twelve Pound Look," a comedy, 2m2f, **analyzed in Part 4, p. 255**, BP, SF 1095, NSHS 19878, NSHS 19883

Barron, Charles (Scottish playwright), "The Old Adam," a Scottish drama, 2m2f, Brown, Son & Ferguson, ISBN 0-95174-585-7

Battiscombe, E. Dora, "The Umbrella Duologue," a sketch, 2f, BP, NSHS 19988

Baukhage, Hilmar, and Barrett H. Clark (adaptors), "The Marriage Proposal," a farce by Anton Chekhov (source Russian playwright, 1860-1904), 2m1f, SF 15935 (no royalty), NSHS 27039

Bax, Clifford, "Square Pegs," a rhymed fantasy, 2f, BP, NSHS 19988

Beaver, Jim, "Spades," a ten-minute play (genre?), 3m, (published with and can pair with "'The Asshole Murder Case,'" "Americansaint," "Après Opéra," "Bread," "Cold Water" "Cover," "Downtown," "The Drummer," "The Duck Pond," "Eating Out," "Electric Roses," "The Field," "4 A.M. (open all night)," "Looking Good," "Love and Peace, Mary Jo," "Loyalties," "Marred Bliss," "Perfect," "The Road to Ruin," "Watermelon Boats") in *25 10-Minute Plays from Actors Theatre of Louisville,* edited by Actors Theatre of Louisville (New York: Samuel French, Inc., 1989), ISBN 0-573-62558-1, SF 6716

Beckett, Samuel (Irish playwright in France, 1906-1989), "Act Without Words (1)," a mime, 1m, (see next item) in *Krapp's Last Tape and Other Dramatic Pieces*, SF 203

Beckett, Samuel (Irish playwright in France, 1906-1989), "Act Without Words I," a mime, 1m, see above item (published with and can pair with "Act Without Words II," "Breath," "Cascando," "Catastrophe," "Come and Go," "Eh Joe," "Embers," "Footfalls," "Ghost Trio," "Krapp's Last Tape, "Not I," "Ohio Impromptu," "A Piece of Monologue," "Play," "Quad," "Rockaby," "Rough for Radio I," "Rough for Radio II," "Rough for Theatre I," "Rough for Theatre II," "That Time," or "Words and Music") in *Collected Shorter Plays*, ISBN 0-394-53850-1, ISBN 0-394-62098-4

Beckett, Samuel (Irish playwright in France, 1906-1989), "Act Without Words (2)," a mime, 2m, (see next item), SF 203

Beckett, Samuel (Irish playwright in France, 1906-1989), "Act Without Words II," a mime, 2m or 1m1f or 2f, ([see above item] published with and can pair with "Act Without

out Words I," "Act Without Words II," "Breath," "Cascando," "Catastrophe," "Come and Go," "Eh Joe," "Embers," "Footfalls," "Ghost Trio," "Krapp's Last Tape," "Not I," "A Piece of Monologue," "Play," "Quad," "Rockaby," "Rough for Radio I," "Rough for Radio II," "Rough for Theatre I," "Rough for Theatre II," "That Time," or "Words and Music") in *Collected Shorter Plays*, ISBN 0-394-53850-1, ISBN 0-394-62098-4; published with and can pair with "Rockaby," "A Piece of Monologue," or "All Strange Away") in *Rockaby and Other Short Pieces*, SF 17656 or SF 18643, NSHS 27753

Beckett, Samuel (Irish playwright in France, 1906-1989), "A Piece of Monologue," a drama, 1m or 1f, ([see above item] also published with and can pair with "Act Without Words I," "Act Without Words II," "Breath," "Cascando," "Catastrophe," "Come and Go," "Eh Joe," "Embers," "Footfalls," "Ghost Trio," "Krapp's Last Tape," "Not I," "Ohio Impromptu," "Play," "Quad," "Rockaby," "Rough for Radio I," "Rough for Radio II," "Rough for Theatre I," "Rough for Theatre II," "That Time," or "Words and Music") in *Collected Shorter Plays*, ISBN 0-394-53850-1, ISBN 0-394-62098-4; published with and can pair with "Rockaby," "Ohio Impromptu," or "All Strange Away") in *Rockaby and Other Short Pieces*, SF 18643, NSHS 27753

Beckett, Samuel (Irish playwright in France, 1906-1989), "Ping," an abstraction, 1m or 1f, **analyzed in Part 4, p. 229**, possibly DPS (?), NSHS

Beckett, Samuel (Irish playwright in France, 1906-1989), "Play," a bare-stage drama, 1m2f, ([see above item] published with and can pair with "Act Without Words I," "Act Without Words II," "Breath," "Cascando," "Catastrophe," "Come and Go," "Eh Joe," "Embers," "Footfalls," "Ghost Trio," "Krapp's Last Tape," "Not I," "Ohio Impromptu," "A Piece of Monologue," "Quad," "Rockaby," "Rough for Radio I," "Rough for Radio II," "Rough for Theatre I," "Rough for Theatre II," "That Time," or "Words and Music") in *Collected Shorter Plays*, ISBN 0-394-53850-1, ISBN 0-394-62098-4; also in *Cascando and Other Short Pieces* SF 849

Beckett, Samuel (Irish playwright in France, 1906-1989), "Quad," a television experiment, 1m3f or 4m or 4f or 2m2f or 3m1f, (published with and can pair with "Act Without Words I," "Act Without Words II," "Breath," "Cascando," "Catastrophe," "Come and Go," "Eh Joe," "Embers," "Footfalls," "Ghost Trio," "Krapp's Last Tape," "Not I," "Ohio Impromptu," "A Piece of Monologue," "Play," "Rockaby," "Rough for Radio I," "Rough for Radio II," "Rough for Theatre I," "Rough for Theatre II," "That Time," or "Words and Music") in *Collected Shorter Plays*, ISBN 0-394-53850-1, ISBN 0-394-62098-4

Beckett, Samuel (Irish playwright in France, 1906-1989), "Radio II," (same as "Rough for Radio II") an experimental radio drama, 2m1f, (published with and can pair with "Act Without Words I," "Act Without Words II," "Breath," "Cascando," "Catastrophe," "Come and Go," "Eh Joe," "Embers," "Footfalls," "Ghost Trio," "Krapp's Last Tape," "Not I," "Ohio Impromptu," "A Piece of Monologue," "Play," "Quad," "Rockaby," "Rough for Radio I," "Rough for Theatre I," "Rough for Theatre II," "That Time," or "Words and Music") in *Collected Shorter Plays*, ISBN 0-394-53850-1, ISBN 0-394-62098-4; 3m1f, in *Ends and Odds* SF 20605

Beckett, Samuel (Irish playwright in France, 1906-1989), "Rough for Radio II," (same as "Radio II") an experimental radio drama, 2m1f, (published with and can pair with "Act Without Words I," "Act Without Words II," "Breath," "Cascando," "Catastrophe," "Come and Go," "Eh Joe," "Embers," "Footfalls," "Ghost Trio," "Krapp's Last Tape," "Not I," "Ohio Impromptu," "A Piece of Monologue," "Play," "Quad," "Rockaby," "Rough for Radio I," "Rough for Theatre I," "Rough for Theatre II," "That Time," or "Words and Music") in *Collected Shorter Plays*, ISBN 0-394-53850-1, ISBN 0-394-62098-4

Beckett, Samuel (Irish playwright in France, 1906-1989), "Rough for Theatre I," (same as "Theatre I") a drama, 2m, (published with and can pair with "Act Without Words I," "Act Without Words II," "Breath," "Cascando," "Catastrophe," "Come and Go," "Eh Joe," "Embers," "Footfalls," "Ghost Trio," "Krapp's Last Tape," "Not I," "Ohio Impromptu," "A Piece of Monologue," "Play," "Quad," "Rockaby," "Rough for Radio I," "Rough for Radio II," "Rough for Theatre II," "That Time," or "Words and Music") in *Collected Shorter Plays*, ISBN 0-394-53850-1, ISBN 0-394-62098-4

Beckett, Samuel (Irish playwright in France, 1906-1989), "Rough for Theatre II," (same as "Theatre II") a drama, 2m, (published with and can pair with "Act Without Words I," "Act Without Words II," "Breath," "Cascando," "Catastrophe," "Come and Go," "Eh Joe," "Embers," "Footfalls," "Ghost Trio," "Krapp's Last Tape," "Not I," "Ohio Impromptu," "A Piece of Monologue," "Play," "Quad," "Rockaby," "Rough for Radio I," "Rough for Radio II," "Rough for Theatre I," "That Time," or "Words and Music") in *Collected Shorter Plays*, ISBN 0-394-53850-1, ISBN 0-394-62098-4

Beckett, Samuel (Irish playwright in France, 1906-1989), "That Time," a bare-stage drama, 3m, (published with and can pair with "Act Without Words I," "Act Without Words II," "Breath," "Cascando," "Catastrophe," "Come and Go," "Eh Joe," "Embers," "Footfalls," "Ghost Trio," "Krapp's Last Tape," "Not I," "Ohio Impromptu," "A Piece of Monologue," "Play," "Quad," "Rockaby," "Rough for Radio I," "Rough for Radio II," "Rough for Theatre I," "Rough for Theatre II," or "Words and Music") in *Collected Shorter Plays*, ISBN 0-394-53850-1, ISBN 0-394-62098-4; in *Ends and Odds* SF 22603

Beckett, Samuel (Irish playwright in France, 1906-1989), "Theatre I," (see "Rough for Theatre I") a drama, 2m, in *Ends and Odds*, SF 22604

Beckett, Samuel (Irish playwright in France, 1906-1989), "Theatre II," (see "Rough for Theatre II") a drama, 3m, in *Collected Shorter Plays*, ISBN 0-394-53850-1, ISBN 0-394-62098-4, SF 22605

Beckett, Samuel (Irish playwright in France, 1906-1989), "Words and Music," a radio drama, 1m1f or 2m or 2f (+ music), (published with and can pair with "Act Without Words I," "Act Without Words II," "Breath," "Cascando," "Catastrophe," "Come and Go," "Eh Joe," "Embers," "Footfalls," "Ghost Trio," "Krapp's Last Tape," "Not I," "Ohio Impromptu," "A Piece of Monologue," "Play," "Quad," "Rockaby," "Rough for Radio I," "Rough for Radio II," "Rough for Theatre I," "Rough for Theatre II," or "That Time") in *Collected Shorter Plays*, ISBN 0-394-53850-1, ISBN 0-394-62098-4

Beim, Norman, "The Deserter," a drama, 3m, SF 6644, NSHS pb7903

Benedict, Stewart H., "One Day in the Life of Ivy Dennison," a bare-stage comedy, 1m2f, SF 17627

Benét, Stephen Vincent (source American poet, 1898-1943) "By the Waters of Babylon," a drama by Brainerd Duffield from Stephen Vincent Benét, 3m1f (+ variable chorus), DPC B37, HDS, NSHS pb175

Bennett, Alan, "A Chip in the Sugar," a half-hour monologue, 1m, SF

Bentley, Eric (adaptor from Russian), "The Brute," a comedy from Anton Chekhov, 2m1f, SF 4688

Bentley, Eric (adaptor from Russian), "From a Madman's Diary," a drama from Nikolai Gogol, 1m, SF 8652

Bentley, Eric Russell (translator from German), "The Informer," a drama by Bertolt Brecht, translated by Eric Russell Bentley, 2m2f, in *The Jewish Wife and Other Short Plays*, SF 11653, NSHS 29533

Bermel, Albert, "The Recovery," a farce, 2m1f, in *Six One-Act Farces*, SF 20639

Bermel, Albert, "The Workout," a farce, 1m1f, in *Six One-Act Farces*, SF 25737

Bernstein, Julianne, "Autumn Leaves," a drama, 2f, in *Off-Off Broadway Festival Plays, XVI Series*, SF 3180

Bert, Norman A., "Phonecall from Sunkist," a brief drama, 3m, (published with and can pair with "Advice to a New Actor," "The Affidavit," "The American Way," "Anniversary," "Auld Lang Syne, or I'll Bet You Think This Play Is About You," "Bug Swatter," "Checkers," "Coming for a Visit," "Dalmation," "Dog Eat Dog," "Drowned Out," "Fireworks," "Interview," "Jumping," "Money," "One Beer Too Many," "Potato Girl," "Property of the Dallas Cowboys," "The Split Decision," "Valley Forgery," "Watermelon Boats," or "Widows") in Norman A. Bert's *One-Act Plays for Acting Students*, MPL, ISBN 0-916260-47-X, pb7929

Betts, Ron, "Benjamin Goodright's Bedtime Story," a Christmas drama, 3m1f, ISBN 0-86319-289-0 (1992), NPN

Bill, Mary Fournier, "An Infinite Deal of Nothing," a comedy, 4f, BP, SF 576, NSHS pb7911, ISBN 0-553-63269-3

Bingham, Jack, "Nine to Five," a comedy, 3m1f, ISBN 0-86319-211-4 (1990), NPN

Bishop, Conrad, "Dalmation," a brief drama, 2f, (published with and can pair with "Advice to a New Actor," "The Affidavit," "The American Way," "Anniversary," "Auld Lang Syne, or I'll Bet You Think This Play Is About You," "Bug Swatter," "Checkers," "Coming for a Visit," "Dog Eat Dog," "Drowned Out," "Fireworks," "Interview," "Jumping," "Money," "One Beer Too Many," "Phonecall from Sunkist," "Potato Girl," "Property of the Dallas Cowboys," "The Split Decision," "Valley Forgery," "Watermelon Boats," or "Widows") in Norman A. Bert's *One-Act Plays for Acting Students*, MPL, ISBN 0-916260-47-X, pb7929

Bishop, Conrad, and Elizabeth Fuller, "Confession," a ten-minute play (genre?), 2m1f, SF

Bishop, Conrad, and Elizabeth Fuller, "Friend from High School," a drama, 2m2f, in *Dramatics*, 65, no. 7 (March 1994): 24-32, WW

Bishop, John, "Arizona," a ten-minute play (genre?), 1m2f, SF

Bishop, John, "Cabin 12," a drama, 3m1f, (can pair with "Brontosaurus") DPS 1205, HDS

Bishop, John, "Confluence," a drama, 2m1f, (published with and can pair with "The Skirmishers") DPS 1415

Bishop, John, "The Skirmishers," a comedy drama, 2m1f, (published with and can pair with "Confluence") DPS 1415

Bivona, Francesco, "Wedding Gown," a drama, 2m2f, PPI

Black, Stephen, "The Horse Latitudes," a drama, 2m2f (1m is boy, 1f is girl), DPS, NSHS pb7750

Blackwell, Vera (translator from Czech), "Protest," a drama by Václav Havel, 2m, in *Antæus: Plays in One Act*, edited by Daniel Halpern, no. 66 (Spring 1991), ISBN 0-88001-268-4

Bland, Margaret, "Pink and Patches," a comedy, 1m3f, SF 18641, NSHS pb8097, NSHS pb8093

Blessing, Lee "Cold Water," a ten-minute play (genre?), 2m1f, (published with and can pair with "Americansaint," "Après Opéra," "'The Asshole Murder Case,'" "Bread," "Cover," "Downtown," "The Drummer," The Duck Pond," "Eating Out," "Electric Roses," "4 A.M. (open all night)," "Looking Good" "Love and Peace, Mary Jo," "Loyalties," "Marred Bliss," "Perfect," "The Road to Ruin," "Spades," or "Watermelon Boat") in *25 10-Minute Plays from Actors Theatre of Louisville*, edited by Actors Theatre of Louisville (New York: Samuel French, Inc., 1989), ISBN 0-573-62558-1, SF 6716

Bogosian, Eric, *Drinking in America*, a collection of black comedy monologues adaptable to one-act format, 1m (+ extra), (can pair with "Sex, Drugs, Rock & Roll"), SF

Bogosian, Eric, *Sex, Drugs, Rock & Roll*, a collection of black comedy monologues adaptable to one-act format, 1m, (can pair with "Drinking in America"), SF 21629

Bologna, Joseph, and Renée Taylor, "Alan, Betty and Riva," a comedy, 1m2f, in *Bedrooms*, SF 244

Bologna, Joseph, and Renée Taylor, "Nick and Wendy," a comedy, 2m1f, in *Bedrooms*, SF 244

Bolton, Guy (adaptor from French), "The Recognition Scene from *Anastasia*," a dramatic second-act scene adapted by Guy Bolton from Marcelle Maurette, 2f, BP, SF 131

Booth, Richard, "A Lesson in Revenge," a fantasy drama, 4f, EPC

Boretz, Alvin, "I Remember You," a drama, 2m2f, IEC 383-7

Bower, Margaret, "Running Past," a drama, 4f, in New Playwrights Network's *Triad 66*, NPN

Bowne, Alan, "Beirut," a drama, 2m1f, (about AIDS, can pair with Harvey Fierstein's "Safe Sex," Patricia Loughrey's "The Inner Circle," Robert Patrick's "Pouf Positive," or Lanford Wilson's "A Poster of the Cosmos") in Alan Bowne's *Beirut* (New York: Broadway Play Publishing, Inc., 1988), ISBN 0-88145-057-X BPP

Boyle, Viki, "The Whole Truth," a comedy, 2f, in *Off-Off Broadway Festival Plays, XVI Series*, SF 25682

Bozzone, Bill, "Breakdown," a comedy-drama, 2m, (published with and can pair with "Buck Fever" or "Good Honest Food") in *Buck Fever and Other Plays*, SF 4674, NSHS pb8017

Bozzone, Bill, "Buck Fever," a comedy, 3m1f, in *Buck Fever and Other Plays*, SF 4697, NSHS pb8017

Bozzone, Bill, "Good Honest Food," a comedy, 3m1f (+ 1m voice), in *Buck Fever and Other Plays*, SF 9688, NSHS pb8017

Bradbury, Ray (American novelist and playwright, 1920-), "The Day It Rained Forever," a comedy, 3m1f, DPC, SF 6610, NSHS pb8087

Bradbury, Ray (American novelist and playwright, 1920-), "A Device out of Time," a drama, 3m, DPC D44, NSHS pb170

Bradbury, Ray (American novelist and playwright, 1920-), "The Flying Machine," a drama, 3m or 3f, DPC F36, NSHS pb188

Bradbury, Ray (American novelist and playwright, 1920-), "Foghorn," a drama, 2m, HMC, NSHS 21382

Bradbury, Ray (American novelist and playwright, 1920-), "The Pedestrian," a melodrama, 2m, SF 838

Bradford, Benjamin, "Princess," a drama, 4f, PPC, NSHS pb8165

Bradford, Benjamin, "Where Are You Going, Hollis Jay?" a comedy, 1m1f, SF 25080

Bray, James L., "To Burn a Witch," a drama, 4f, **analyzed in Part 4, p. 252**, DPC T32, HDS, NSHS pb160

Brecht, Bertolt (German playwright, 1898-1956), "The Beggar or the Dead Dog," an allegory translated from the original German into English by Michael Hamburger, 2m, in *A Respectable Wedding and Other One-Act Plays*, SF 4175

Brecht, Bertolt (German playwright, 1898-1956), "Dansen," an allegory, translated from the German by Rose and Martin Kastner, 2m, SF

Brecht, Bertolt (German playwright, 1898-1956), "The Elephant Calf," a drama, 4m (+extras), in *Baal, A Man's a Man and The Elephant Calf: Early Plays by Bertolt Brecht* (New York: Grove Weidenfeld, 1964), ISBN 0-8021-3159-X; and in *The Jewish Wife and Other Short Plays*, SF 7640, NSHS pb8100

Brecht, Bertolt (German playwright, 1898-1956), "The Informer," a drama, translated by Eric Russell Bentley, 2m2f, in *The Jewish Wife and Other Short Plays*, SF 11653, NSHS 29533

Brecht, Bertolt (German playwright, 1898-1956), "The Jewish Wife," (see p. 209) a drama by Bertolt Brecht translated into English by Eric Bentley, 1m1f, **analyzed in Part 4, p. 210**, BP, in *The Jewish Wife and Other Short Plays*, SF 604, NSHS 29533

Brighouse, Harold, "Lonesome-Like," a comedy, 2m2f, in *One Act Plays for Stage and Study: A Collection of Twenty-five Plays by Well-known* [sic] *Dramatists, American, English and Irish, First Series*, preface by Augustus Thomas (New York: Samuel French, Inc., 1925), SF, NSHS

Broadhurst, Kent, "The Eye of the Beholder," a comedy, 3m or 3f, DPS 1880, NSHS pb7919

Broadhurst, Kent, "Habitual Acceptance of the Near Enough," a comedy-drama, 2m, DPS 2253

Bromberg, Conrad, "Actors," a bare-stage comedy-drama, 2m1f, (published with and can pair with "At Home") DPS 625, NSHS pb104, NSHS pb116, NSHS pb117

Bromberg, Conrad, "Doctor Galley," a drama, 1m, (published with and can pair with "The Rooming House" or "Transfers") in *Transfers: Three One-Acts Plays*, DPS 4610, NSHS pb7923

Bromberg, Conrad, "The Rooming House," a drama, 2m1f, (published with and can pair with "Doctor Galley" or "Transfers") in *Transfers: Three One-Acts Plays*, DPS 4610, NSHS pb7923

Bromberg, Conrad, "Transfers," a drama, 3m, (published with and can pair with "Doctor Galley" or "The Rooming House") in *Transfers: Three One-Acts Plays*, DPS 4610, NSHS pb7923

Brome, Robert, "Judgment Morning," a drama, 1m2f, DPC, NSHS

Brome, Robert, "Winter Sunset," a drama, 2m2f, TSD, NSHS 10922

Brook, Peter (English playwright), "The Birthday Present," (see p. 187) a drama, 1m2f, DPC B21, NSHS pb6070

C

ley Forgery," "Watermelon Boats," or "Widows") in Norman A. Bert's *One-Act Plays for Acting Students*, MPL, ISBN 0-916260-47-X, pb7929

Calhoun, Wil, "The Balcony Scene," a romantic comedy, 2m1f, in Wil Calhoun's *The Balcony Scene* (New York: Samuel French, Inc., 1992), ISBN 0-573-69308-0

Campton, David, "Cards, Cups and Crystal Ball," a mystery, 4f, DPC C67

Campton, David, "Little Brother: Little Sister," a drama, 2m1f, (published with and can pair with "Out of the Frying Pan") DPS 2875

Campton, David, "Out of the Frying Pan," a bare-stage absurdity, 2m, (published with and can pair with "Little Brother: Little Sister") DPS 2875

Campton, David, "A Smell of Burning," a comedy, 2m1f (+voice), (published with and can pair with "Then . . .") DPS 4155, NSHS pb7810

Carlino, Lewis John, "The Dirty Old Man," a drama, 2m1f (1m is boy), (can pair with "Sarah and the Sax") DPS 1665, NSHS pb7808

Carlino, Lewis John, "Objective Case," a drama, 2m2f, in Lewis John Carlino's *Two Short Plays: Mr. Flannery's Ocean, Objective Case* (New York: Dramatists Play Service, Inc., 1961), HDS, DPS 3235, NSHS pb8149

Carlino, Lewis John, "Used Car for Sale," a drama, 3m1f, DPS 4715, NSHS pb8027

Carlson, Harry G. (translator from Swedish), Strindberg, August, "Miss Julie," a drama, translated by Elizabeth Sprigge, 1m2f (+extras), (can pair with "The Stronger") in *Eight Plays for Theatre*, edited by Robert Cohen (Mountain View, California: Mayfield Publishing Company, 1988), SF 15116; (translated by E. M. Sprinchorn, in *Seeds of Modern Drama*), SF 15674; (translated by Harry G. Carlson, in *Strindberg: Five Plays*), DPS 273; (translated by Michael Meyer) WKW, CPC, NSHS 29262, NSHS 19878, NSHS 19883, NSHS 29323, NSHS 29252, NSHS 5211, NSHS 27003, NSHS 16361, NSHS 20545

Carrol, John R., "If It Don't Hurt It Ain't Love," a drama, 2m2f, BP

Carroll, Robert F., "Heat Lighting," a comedy, 2m1f, SF 10625, HDS

Casey, Francis Michael, "Dearie, Ye're a Dreamer," a comedy, 1m2f, originally produced at the University of North Carolina/Chapel Hill around 1950, once handled by Samuel French but no longer listed there; hilarious portrayal of Irish sisters and their angel of death; well worth the search

Catron, Louis E., "Touch the Bluebird's Song," a drama, 1m1f, BP, HDS, SF 1087, NSHS 29206, NSHS pb5482

Catron, Louis E., "Where Have All the Lightning Bugs Gone?" a drama, 1m1f, BP, HDS, SF 1190, NSHS pb7758

Ceraso, Cris, "Sittin'," a comedy, 1m2f, SF 1028

Cervantes, Madolin Shorey, "Interview with God," a comedy drama, 3m, SF 11603

Chaikin, Joseph, and Jean-Claude van Itallie, "Struck Dumb," a drama, in *The Best American Short Plays, 1990/1991-1992*, 2 vols., edited by Howard Stein and Glenn Young, ATB, ISSN 1062-7561

Chaikin, Joseph, and Sam Shepard, "Savage/Love," a monodrama, a bill of theatre poems, 1m, in *Sam Shepard: Seven Plays*, SF 21637

Chaikin, Joseph, and Sam Shepard, "Tongues," a monodrama, a piece for voice and percussion, 1m, **analyzed in Part 4, p. 253**, in *Sam Shepard: Seven Plays*, SF 22733, NSHS 28227

Charles, Ron, "A Perfect Match," a romantic comedy for youth, 1m2f, in Sylvia E. Kamerman's *The Big Book of Comedies* (Boston: Plays, Inc., 1989), not to be confused with Joan Forster's play by the same name, ISBN 0-8238-0289-2

Cheatham, Val, "Great Moments in American Oratory," a dramatic reading, 4 narrators (male or female), EPC

Chekhov, Anton (Russian playwright, 1860-1904), "The Anniversary," a farce, translated by Ronald Hingley, 2m2f (+ extras), in Anton Chekhov's *Twelve Plays*, translated by Ronald Hingley (London: Oxford University Press, 1992), ISBN 0-19-282813-4

Chekhov, Anton (Russian playwright, 1860-1904), "The Bear," [variant titles] a farce, 2m1f, (can pair with "The Anniversary," "The Proposal," "Swan Song," or "A Tragic Role") in Anton Chekhov's *Plays*, translated by Michael Frayn (London: Methuen & Company, Ltd., 1988), ISBN 0-413-19160-X; also in Anton Chekhov's *Twelve Plays*, translated by Ronald Hingley (London: Oxford University Press, 1992), ISBN 0-19-282813-4 [See also "A Bear with a Sore Head," an adaptation by Brian J. Burton and "A Wild Boar," an adaptation by Joseph Wallace.]

Chekhov, Anton (Russian playwright, 1860-1904), "The Boor," a farce, 2m1f (+ extras), BP (no royalty with purchase of four copies), SF 4111 (no royalty), HDS, GCB, NSHS 19878, NSHS 19883, NSHS 8266, NSHS 5345

Chekhov, Anton (Russian playwright, 1860-1904), "The Brute," a comedy, 2m1f, BP (no royalty with purchase of three copies)

Chekhov, Anton (Russian playwright, 1860-1904), "The Evils of Tobacco" [under various titles] a satirical lecture translated by Michael Frayn, 1m, **analyzed in Part 4, p. 204**, in Anton Chekhov's *Plays*, translated by Michael Frayn (London: Methuen & Company, Ltd., 1988), ISBN 0-413-19160-X [See also "Smoking Is Bad for You," translated by Ronald Hingley.]

Chekhov, Anton (Russian playwright, 1860-1904), "The Harmfulness of Tobacco," [sometimes listed as "The Evils of Tobacco," "On the Harmfulness of Tobacco," or "Smoking Is Bad for You"] a farce monologue, 1m, analyzed in Part 4, p. 204, SF; also in Anton Chekhov's *Plays* (London: Methuen & Company, Ltd., 1988), ISBN 0-413-19160-X

Chekhov, Anton (source Russian playwright, 1860-1904), "The Kentucky Marriage Proposal," a comedy by Alice H. Houstle from Anton Chekhov, 1m2f, DPS 2665

Chekhov, Anton (Russian playwright, 1860-1904), "A Marriage Proposal," a farce, 2m1f, (no royalty with purchase of three copies) BP, NSHS pb4019, NSHS 14824, NSHS 20483, NSHS 21389, NSHS 21514, NSHS 21776, NSHS 16020, NSHS 21405

Chekhov, Anton (source Russian playwright, 1860-1904), "The Marriage Proposal," a farce, adapted by Hilmar Baukhage and Barrett H. Clark, 2m1f, SF 15935 (no royalty), NSHS 27039

Chekhov, Anton (source Russian playwright, 1860-1904), "Anton Chekhov's The Proposal" a farce, adapted by Alfred Emmet, 2m1f, in Alfred Emmet's *Anton Chekhov's The Proposal* (London: Samuel French, Inc., 1989), ISBN 0-573-12213-X [See also versions by Michael Frayn, Michael Henry Heim, and Ronald Hingley.]

Chekhov, Anton (Russian playwright, 1860-1904), "The Proposal," a farce, translated by Michael Frayn, 2m1f, in Anton Chekhov's *Plays* (London: Methuen & Company, Ltd., 1988), ISBN 0-413-19160-X [See also the versions by Alfred Emmet ("Anton Chekhov's The Proposal"), Michael Henry Heim, and Ronald Hingley.]

Chekhov, Anton (Russian playwright, 1860-1904), "Smoking Is Bad for You," [under various titles] a satirical lecture translated by Ronald Hingley, 1m, analyzed in Part 4, p. 204, in Anton Chekhov's *Twelve Plays*, translated by Ronald Hingley (London: Oxford University Press, 1992), ISBN 0-19-282813-4 [See also "The Evils of Tobacco," translated by Michael Frayn.]

Chekhov, Anton (Russian playwright, 1860-1904), "Swan Song," a drama, 2m, in Anton Chekhov's *Plays*, translated by Michael Frayn (London: Methuen & Company, Ltd., 1988), ISBN 0-413-19160-X

Chekhov, Anton (source Russian playwright, 1860-1904), "A Tragic Role," a farce, adapted by Ronald Hingley, 2m, in Anton Chekhov's *Twelve Plays*, translated by Ronald Hingley (London: Oxford University Press, 1992), ISBN 0-19-282813-4

Chekhov, Anton (source Russian playwright, 1860-1904), "Two Fools Who Gained a Measure of Wisdom," a comedy adapted by Tim Kelly, 1m3f, DPS 4660, NSHS pb8025

Chekhov, Anton (source Russian playwright, 1860-1904), "The Vagabond," a comedy adapted by Joseph Buloff and Luba Kadison Buloff from Anton Chekhov, 3m, in *The Chekhov Sketchbook*, SF 24607

Chekhov, Anton (source Russian playwright, 1860-1904), "A Wild Boar," a farce by Joseph Wallace from Anton Chekhov, 2m2f, (Boston: Baker's Plays, 1991) BP. See also "A Bear with a Sore Head," an adaptation by Brian J. Burton and translations of "The Bear" by Michael Frayn and Ronald Hingley.

Chekhov, Anton (source Russian playwright, 1860-1904), "The Witch," a farce adapted by Joseph Buloff and Luba Kadison Buloff from Anton Chekhov, 1m1f, in *The Chekhov Sketchbook*, SF 25162

Childress, Alice, "Florence," a drama, 1m3f, in *Wines in the Wilderness: Plays by African American Women from the Harlem Renaissance to the Present*, edited and compiled by Elizabeth Brown-Guillory (Westport, Connecticut: Praeger Publishers, 1990), ISBN 0-275-93567-1

Chinn, Jimmie, "From Here to the Library," a drama, 2m1f, SF 8928, NSHS 27523

Chinn, Jimmie, "Interior Designs," a bare-stage comedy, 1m3f, SF 11652

Chown, Patricia (English playwright), "Beyond the Mirror," a drama, 4f (Macclesfield, Cheshire, England: New Playwrights Network, 1992), NPN

Christ, Erica, "When the Cat Goes Away," a drama, 1m1f, DPC W60, NSHS pb130

Christie, Agatha, (Dame, *née* Miller, English novelist and playwright, 1890 or 1891-1976), "The Rats," a mystery melodrama, 2m2f, BP, SF 20608, NSHS pb8111

Churchill, Caryl, "Not Not Not Not Not Enough Oxygen," a drama, 2m1f, (published with and can pair with "Abortive," "Schreber's Nervous Illness," "Seagulls," or "Three More Sleepless Nights") in *Churchill: Shorts* [*Short Plays by Caryl Churchill*], SF 16083, SF 3887, NSHS, ISBN 1-85459-085-5

Churchill, Caryl, "Schreber's Nervous Illness," a bare-stage drama, 3m (+ various recorded voices), (published with and can pair with "Abortive," "Not Not Not Not Not Enough Oxygen," "Seagulls," or "Three More Sleepless Nights") in *Churchill: Shorts* [*Short Plays by Caryl Churchill*], SF 16083, SF 3887, NSHS, ISBN 1-85459-085-5

Churchill, Caryl, "Seagulls," a bare-stage drama, 1m2f, (published with and can pair with "Abortive," "Not Not Not Not Not Enough Oxygen," "Schreber's Nervous Illness," or "Three More Sleepless Nights") in *Churchill: Shorts* [*Short Plays by Caryl Churchill*], SF 21634, NSHS, ISBN 1-85459-085-5

Churchill, Caryl, "Three More Sleepless Nights," a drama, 2m2f, (published with and can pair with "Abortive," "Not Not Not Not Not Enough Oxygen," "Schreber's Nervous Illness," or "Seagulls") in *Churchill: Shorts* [*Short Plays by Caryl Churchill*], SF 22656, NSHS, ISBN 1-85459-085-5

Clapp, Patricia, "A Candle on the Table," a comedy-drama, 4f, BP, SF 5610, NSHS pb7728

Clark, B. Burgess, "The Cola Wars," a comedy, 1m3f, in *Dramatics*, 65, no. 1 (September 1993): 22-29. Inquiries regarding performance rights and royalties should be directed to Francis Del Duca, Fifi Oscard Associates, 24 West 40th Street, Suite 1700, New York, NY 10018.

Clark, Barrett H., and Hilmar Baukhage, (adaptors), "The Marriage Proposal," a farce by Anton Chekhov (source Russian playwright, 1860-1904), 2m1f, SF 15935 (no royalty), NSHS 27039

Clark, Barrett H. (translator from French), "The Post-Script," a comedy by Émile Augier, 1m2f, in Émile Augier's *Four Plays*, (New York: Howard Fertig, Inc., Publisher, 1989), ISBN 0-86527-367-7

Clark, Eileen, "Vacant Possession," a play (genre?), 2m2f, in Triad 64, NPN

Clark, Gwyn, "Anyone for Tennis?" a farce, 2m2f, SF 3643, NSHS pb8073

Clark, I. E. (translator from German), "The Narrenschneiden: or, The Fool-Ectomy," a *fastnachtsspiel* by Hans Sachs, translated by I. E. Clark, 3m or 3f, IEC, NSHS pb94

Cleage, Pearl, "Hospice," a drama, 2f, (published with and can pair with "The Box," "Birth of a Blues!" or "The Past Is the Past") in *New Plays for the Black Theatre*, edited by Woodie King, Jr. (Chicago: Third World Press, 1989), ISBN 0-88378-124-7, TWP

Clemens, Samuel Langhorne (subject here, a.k.a. Mark Twain, 1835-1910), "The Loneliest Wayfarer," a comedy by Bernard Sabath about Mark Twain, 2m1f, (published with and can pair with "A Barbarian in Love," "Summer Morning Visitor," or "The Trouble Begins at 8") in Bernard Sabath's *Twain Plus Twain* (New York: Dramatists Play Service, Inc., 1984) DPS 4635, NSHS pb8024

Clemens, Samuel Langhorne (source short story writer), "Mrs. McWilliams and the Lighting," a comedy by Jules Tasca from Mark Twain, 2m1f, in *Five One-Act Plays by Mark Twain*, SF 15613

Clemens, Samuel Langhorne (source short story writer, a.k.a. Mark Twain, 1835-1910), "Summer Morning Visitor," a comedy-drama by Bernard Sabath about Mark Twain, 1m2f, (published with and can pair with "A Barbarian in Love," "The Loneliest Wayfarer" or "The Trouble Begins at 8") in Bernard Sabath's *Twain Plus Twain* (New York: Dramatists Play Service, Inc., 1984) DPS 4635, NSHS pb8024

Clemens, Samuel Langhorne (a.k.a. Mark Twain, source American short story writer, 1935-1910), "Support Your Local Police," a satire by Jules Tasca from Mark Twain (a.k.a. Samuel Langhorne Clemens), 3m, in *Five One-Act Plays by Mark Twain*, SF 21606

Clemens, Samuel Langhorne (source short story writer, a.k.a. Mark Twain, 1835-1910), "The Trouble Begins at 8," a comedy-drama by Bernard Sabath about Mark Twain, 3m1f, (published with and can pair with "A Barbarian in Love," "The Loneliest Wayfarer," or "Summer Morning Visitor") in Bernard Sabath's *Twain Plus Twain* (New

York: Dramatists Play Service, Inc., 1984), DPS 4635, NSHS pb8024

Clements, Colin, and Florence Ryerson, "Movie Mother," a comedy, 1f, **analyzed in Part 4, p. 218**, possibly SF (?), NSHS pb6066

Clinton, Edward, "The Boogeyman: The Boogeyman," a comedy-drama, 1m2f, (published with and can pair with "First of the Month" or "Small Claims") in *The Boogeyman: Three Related One Acts* (New York: Samuel French, Inc., 1992), ISBN 0-573-69388-9, SF 4720, NSHS pb8106

Clinton, Edward, "The Boogeyman: First of the Month," a comedy-drama, 1m2f, (published with and can pair with "First of the Month" or "Small Claims") in *The Boogeyman: Three Related One Acts* (New York: Samuel French, Inc., 1992), ISBN 0-573-69388-9, SF 8187, NSHS pb8106

Clinton, Edward, "The Boogeyman: Small Claims," a comedy-drama, 2m2f, (published with and can pair with "First of the Month" or "The Boogeyman") in *The Boogeyman: Three Related One Acts* (New York: Samuel French, Inc., 1992), ISBN 0-573-69388-9, SF 21415

Coates, Paul, "The Telephone," a parody, 1m2f, in Paul Coates' *The Telephone* (Nottingham, England: Playwrights Publishing Company, 1991), ISBN 1-873130-02-3

Coates, Paul, "Three Years," a comedy for youth, 2m2f, in Paul Coates' *Two One-Act Plays* (Nottingham, England: Playwrights Publishing Company, 1991), ISBN 1-873130-05-8, PLP

Coble, Herman, "A New Sunrise," a comedy, 2m2f, BP

Coburn, Charles, "The Lifesaver," a drama, 2m2f, ELD

Cocteau, Jean (French playwright, 1889-1963), *"La Voix humaine"* ["The Human Voice"], a drama, 1f, in Jean Cocteau's *The Human Voice* (London: Samuel French, Inc., 1992), ISBN 0-573-03381-1, SF

Cole, Tom, "Medal of Honor Rag," a drama, 3m, ISBN 0-573-64018-1, SF, NSHS pb7756

Collins, Barry, "The Ice Chimney," a drama, 1m, in *One Step in the Clouds: An Omnibus of Mountaineering Novels and Short Stories*, compiled by Audrey Salkeld and Rosie Smith (San Francisco: Sierra Club Books, 1991), ISBN 0-87156-638-9

Colman, Richard, "Third Street," a drama for youth, 3m, in *Ten out of Ten: Ten Winning Plays Selected from the Young Playwrights Festival, 1982-1991: Produced by the Foundation of the Dramatists Guild*, edited by Wendy Lamb, preface by Wendy Wasserstein, introduction by Nancy Quinn (New York: Delacorte Press, 1992), ISBN 0-385-30811-6

Cone, Tom, Skip Kennon, and Ellen Fitzhugh, "Herringbone," a drama, 1m (+1 extra), in *Twenty Years at Play: A New Play Centre Anthology*, edited by Jerry Wasserman (Cordova, Vancouver, British Columbia, Canada:

Talonbooks, Ltd., 1990), ISBN 0-88922-275-4, TL

Conkle, E. P., "A Bauble for Baby" a comedy, 1m3f, SF 4607, NSHS pb7909

Conkle, E. P., "Papa Never Done Nothing . . . Much," a comedy, 2f, SF 18610, NSHS pb7748

Conkle, E. P., "Sparkin'," a comedy, 1m3f, BP, SF, NSHS 8266

Connelly, Marc, "Little David," a play (genre?), 4m, DPS manuscript

Connelly, Marc, "The Traveler," a comedy, 3m, DPS, NSHS 27039, NSHS pb4019 NSHS 14824, NSHS 20483, NSHS 21389, NSHS 21514, NSHS 21776

Cook, Pat, "The Last of Captain Bedford," a drama, 2m2f, ELD

Cook, Pat, "Such a Nice Little Kitty," a comedy, 2m1f, DPC S66, NSHS pb196

Cooper, J. B., "Ground Plans," a play (genre?), 4f, in *Triad 68*, NPN

Cooperman, Melvin I., "Dispatches from Hell," a drama, 2m1f, (published with and can pair with "Molly and James," "Senior Prom," or "12:21 P.M.") in *Double Image Theatre's Off-Off Broadway Festival Plays, Tenth Series* (New York: Samuel French, Inc., 1985) SF 6688, NSHS 27488, ISBN 0-573-68904-0

Cornish, Roger, "Frosting," a bare-stage short drama, 2m, (published with and can pair with "Autumn Drive," "The Close-Down Set-Up of Emma," "Meals on Wheels," "Mrs. Lazar's Caller," or "Running Away from Home") in *Short Plays for the Long Living*, BP, SF 3664, NSHS pb6043, NSHS pb7838

Cornish, Roger, "I Saw Your Picture in the Paper and I Had to Call," a drama, 2m1f, AR, NSHS pb6124

Cornish, Roger, "Mental Reservations," a ten-minute play (genre?), 1m1f, SF

Corrie, Joe, "A Near Thing," a comedy, 3m, BP, NSHS 19987

Corson, Richard, "The Sisters McIntosh," a comedy, 1m2f, SF 983

Cottrell, Susan C., "But Listen!" a comedy, 2m2f, DPC B35, NSHS pb156

Courteline, Georges (French playwright, 1861-1929), "Badin the Bold," a comedy, 3m, in *The Plays of Courteline*, SF 4611

Coward, Noël Peirce (Sir, English playwright, composer, and actor, 1899-1973), "Come into the Garden Maud," a comedy, 2m2f, in *Noël Coward in Two Keys*, SF 5692, NSHS 16674

Coward, Noël Peirce (Sir, English playwright, composer, and actor, 1899-1973), "Fumed Oak," a long one-act comedy, one of the *Tonight at 8:30* series, 1m3f, **analyzed in Part 4, p. 203**, BP, SF 450, HDS, NSHS 19878, NSHS 19883, NSHS pb8201

Coward, Noël Peirce (Sir, English playwright, composer, and actor, 1899-1973), "Shadows of the Evening," a long one-

act comedy, 2m2f, SF 21106, NSHS pb8074

Crittenden, Jordan, "Thursday Is My Day for Cleaning," a comedy, 1f, **analyzed in Part 4, p. 251**, SF 22692, NSHS

Cromwell, John, "A Matter of Like Life and Death," a comedy, 1m2f, cited in *The Best Plays of 1963-1964*, edited by Henry Hewes

Cromwell, John, "Opening Night," a play (genre?), 1m2f, cited in *The Best Plays of 1963-1964*, edited by Henry Hewes

Crowder, David Lloyd, "Absolutely Free," a revue sketch, 1m (+2 voices), SF, NSHS pb6051

Crowder, David Lloyd, "Angela," a revue sketch, 2m (+voice), SF, NSHS pb6051

Crowder, David Lloyd, "The Phone Callers," a revue sketch, 2m2f, SF, NSHS pb6051

Crowder, David Lloyd, "Strife Faces Jan," a revue sketch, 1m2f, SF, NSHS pb6051

Crowder, David Lloyd, "T V Special," a revue sketch, 2m2f, SF, NSHS pb6051

Crutcher, Julie Beckett, "Approaching Lavendar," a comic drama, 3f, SF 3649, NSHS pb7897

Cucci, Frank, "The Ofay Watcher," a drama in three scenes, 2m1f, DPS, NSHS pb7791

Culbertson, Ernest Howard, "The End of the Trail," a drama, 2m1f, IPC, NSHS 6066

Cunningham, Jack, "Wisp in the Wind," a drama, 1m1f, SF, NSHS pb6053, NSHS pb7736

Cunningham, Laura, "The Man at the Door," a comedy, 2m2f, (published with and can pair with "Where She Went, What She Did") in *I Love You, Two*, SF 15943, NSHS pb8016

Cunningham, Laura, "Where She Went, What She Did," a comedy, 3m1f, in *I Love You, Two,* (published with and can pair with "The Man at the Door") SF 25096, NSHS pb8016

Cunningham, Mary, "Just What They Wanted," a comedy, 2m2f, HDS

Curran, KT, "The First Time Club," a drama, 4f, IEC 392-6

D

Damato, Anthony, "The Flounder Complex," a thriller, 2f, DPS 2015

Damelio, Louis, "The Private Prop. of Roscoe Pointer," a drama, 2m2f (+3 offstage voices), SF 18671, NSHS pb7958

Dane, Essex, "Wrong Numbers," a comedy, 3f, BP, NSHS 19988

Daniel, Barbara, "Batbrains," a comedy, 2f, in *Off-Off Broadway Festival Plays,* Vol. 5, SF 4610, NSHS 27534

Darby, Edward (adaptor), "Two Bottles of Relish," a mystery from Lord Dunsany, 2m2f, HDS, DPC T45, NSHS pb139

Darion, Joe, and Mel Brooks, "archy and mehitabel," a one-act version of a full-length musical comedy (originally on Broadway as *Shinbone Alley*, 1957), with music by George Kleinsinger and lyrics by Joe Darion, 3m1f (+singers/dancers), **analyzed in Part 4, p. 184**, MTI

Davies, Cecil, "The Night Is Far Spent," a drama, 4f, BP

Davies, Robertson (Canadian playwright), "Overlaid," a comedy, 2m1f, in Robertson Davies' *At My Heart's Core & Overlaid* (Toronto, Ontario, Canada: Simon & Pierre Publishing Company, Ltd., 1991), ISBN 0-88924-225-9; also in *10 Canadian Short Plays*, SF 17601

Davis, Richard Harding, "Peace Manoeuvres," a drama, 3m1f, in *One Act Plays for Stage and Study: A Collection of Twenty-five Plays by Well-known* [sic] *Dramatists, American, English and Irish, First Series*, preface by Augustus Thomas (New York: Samuel French, Inc., 1925), SF, NSHS

Davis, Scott, "Great-Grandaddy's Skull," a drama, 2m2f, BP

Davis, Stephen (Australian playwright), "A Very Black Comedy Indeed," 2m, (published with and can pair with "Leapyear") in *Comedy Tonight: Three Award Winning One Acters* (Ashgrove, Queensland, Australia: Playlab Press, 1989), ISBN 0-908156-37-5

de Maupassant, Guy (Henri-René-Albert-, source French short story writer, 1850-1893), "The Devil," a farce adapted by Jules Tasca from a short story by Guy de Maupassant, 2m2f, (published with and can pair with "Father and Son," "Forbidden Fruit," "The Necklace," or "That Pig, Morin") in *The Necklace and Other Stories*, SF 15990, NSHS 27500, NSHS pb7919

de Maupassant, Guy (Henri-René-Albert-, source French short story writer, 1850-1893), "Father and Son," a drama by Jules Tasca from Guy de Maupassant, 1m1f, (published with and can pair with "The Devil," "Forbidden Fruit," "The Necklace," or "That Pig, Morin") in *The Necklace and Other Stories*, SF 15990, DPC N10, NSHS 27500, NSHS pb7919

de Maupassant, Guy (Henri-René-Albert-, source French short story writer, 1850-1893), "The Necklace," a drama by Jules Tasca from Guy de Maupassant, 1m2f, **analyzed in Part 4, p. 219**, (published with and can pair with "The Devil," "Father and Son," "Forbidden Fruit" or "That Pig, Morin") in *The Necklace and Other Stories*, SF 15990, DPC N10, NSHS 27500, NSHS pb7919

de Maupassant, Guy (Henri-René-Albert-, source French short story writer, 1850-1893), "That Pig, Morin," a drama by Jules Tasca from Guy de Maupassant, 2m2f (+ 2m extras), (published with and can pair with "Father and Son," "The Devil," or "Forbidden Fruit") in *The Necklace and Other Stories*, SF 15990, DPC N10, NSHS 27500, NSHS pb7919

De Mille, William C., "Deceivers," a comedy, 1m2f, in *One Act Plays for Stage and Study: A Collection of Twenty-five Plays by Well-known* [sic] *Dramatists, American, English and Irish, First Series*, preface by Augustus Tho-

mas (New York: Samuel French, Inc., 1925), SF, NSH

de Rueda, Lope (Spanish playwright, *comediógrafo español*, 1510?-1565), "The Olives" [*"Las Aceitunas"*] a paso, 2m2f, **analyzed in Part 4, p. 233**, CML, NSHS 27052

Dean, Philip Hayes, "The Owl Killer," a drama, 1m2f, DPS 3560

Dean, Philip Hayes, "This Bird of Dawning Singeth All Night Long," a drama, 2f, (can pair with "The Minstrel Boy") in *American Night Cry*, DPS 735

Dee, Peter, "Daughter of a Traveling Lady," a comedy-drama, 1m2f, SF 6606

Dee, Peter, "Doing Poetry with Helen, Veronica, Sonny, and Poor Dead Charlie," a drama, 2m2f, BP

Delgado, Ramon, "The Little Toy Dog," a drama, 2m2f

Delgado, Ramon, "Omega's Ninth," a comedy, 1m1f (+m/f human cat), IEC, NSHS pb109

Delgado, Ramon, "Waiting for the Bus," an allegory drama, 2m2f, BP

Delman, Howard, "Lovely Afternoon," a comedy, 2m1f, BP, HDS, SF 14660

Denison, Merrill, "Brothers in Arms," a comedy drama, 3m1f, SF 4686, NSHS pb8085

Denson, Wil, "A Friend Like Artie," a drama, 2m2f, IEC 330-6

Dey, James Paul, "What Did You Say What For?" a bare-stage absurd comedy, 1m1f, BP, SF 1187, NSHS pb5443

Di Mambro, Ann Mare, "The Letter-Box," a drama, 1m2f, (published with and can pair with "Saturday at the Commodore") in *Scot-Free: New Scottish Plays*, edited by Alasdair Cameron (London: Nick Hern Books, 1990), ISBN 1-85459-017-0

DiCairano, Jerry, "The Interview—Job," a comedy, 2m1f, PBC, NSHS pb97

Diggs, Elizabeth, "Dumping Ground," a comedy drama, 2m1f, DPS 1745

Disney, Stanley, "Treadmill to the Goodtime Star," a drama, 3m1f (+voice), AR, NSHS pb5722

Dixcy, Marcia, "Eating Out," a ten-minute play (genre?), 3f, (published with and can pair with "Americansaint," "Après Opéra," "'The Asshole Murder Case,'" "Bread," "Cold Water," "Cover," "Downtown," "The Drummer," "The Duck Pond," "Electric Roses," "The Field," "4 A.M. (open all night)," "Looking Good," "Love and Peace, Mary Jo," "Loyalties," "Marred Bliss," "Perfect," "The Road to Ruin," "Spades," or "Watermelon Boats") in *25 10-Minute Plays from Actors Theatre of Louisville*, edited by Actors Theatre of Louisville (New York: Samuel French, Inc., 1989), ISBN 0-573-62558-1, SF 6716

Dixon, Michael Bigelow, and Valerie Smith, "Après Opéra," a ten-minute play (genre?), 2m2f, (published with and can pair with "Americansaint," "'The Asshole Murder Case,'" "Bread," "Cold Water," "Cover," "Downtown," "The Drummer," "The Duck Pond," "Eating Out," "Electric Roses," "The Field," "4 A.M. (open all night),"

"Looking Good," "Love and Peace, Mary Jo," "Loyalties," "Marred Bliss," "Perfect," "The Road to Ruin," "Spades," or "Watermelon Boats") in *25 10-Minute Plays from Actors Theatre of Louisville,* edited by Actors Theatre of Louisville (New York: Samuel French, Inc., 1989), ISBN 0-573-62558-1, SF 6716

Dixon, Michael Bigelow, and Valerie Smith, "Blind Alleys," a ten-minute drama, 2m2f, (published with and can pair with "Clean" or "The Pick-Up") in *Big Trouble: Six 10-Minute Plays from Actors Theatre of Louisville,* IEC 324-1

Dixon, Michael Bigelow, and Valerie Smith, "Clean," a drama, 2m1f, (published with and can pair with "Blind Alleys," "Clean," or "The Pick-Up") in *Big Trouble: Six 10-Minute Plays from Actors Theatre of Louisville,* IEC 324-1

Dixon, Michael (Bigelow), and Valerie Smith, "Help Wanted," a comedy, 2m2f, in *Dramatics,* 64, no. 1 (September 1992): 22-25. Inquiries regarding performance rights and royalties should be directed to Michael Dixon at Actors Theatre of Louisville, 316 West Main Street, Louisville, KY 40202.

Dixon, Michael Bigelow, and Valerie Smith, "The Pick-Up," a comedy, 2m2f (+optional extras), (published with and can pair with "Blind Alleys" or "Clean") in *Big Trouble: Six 10-Minute Plays from Actors Theatre of Louisville,* IEC 324-1

Dizenzo, Charles, "Big Mother," a play (genre?), 2m2f, DPS manuscript

Dizenzo, Charles, "The Drapes Come," a comic drama, 2f, DPS 1705

Dizenzo, Charles, "A Great Career," an absurd comedy, 1m2f, DPS 2220

Dizenzo, Charles, "The Last Straw," a comedy, 2m, (published with and can pair with "Sociability"), DPS 2775, NSHS 29202

Dizenzo, Charles, "Sociability," a comedy of manners, 2m2f (published with and can pair with "The Last Straw") DPS 2775, NSHS 29202

Dorst, Tankred (Swiss playwright), "The Curve," a drama, translated by James L. Rosenberg, 3m, NTK, 16622

Dorst, Tankred (Swiss playwright, 1925-   ), "Freedom for Clemens," [*Freiheit für Clemens,* 1960] a dark comedy, translated from the German by George E. Wellwarth, 2m1f, (published with and can pair with "Let's Eat Hair!/ *Essen Wir Haare!"* or "Nightpiece/*Nachtsstück*") in *Postwar German Theatre,* GB, NSHS pb7857

Down, Oliphant, "The Maker of Dreams," a fantasy, 2m1f, ISBN GB-573-02152-X, SF, NSHS pb4019, NSHS pb5421, NSHS 5471, NSHS 14824, NSHS 20483, NSHS 21389, NSHS 21514, NSHS 21776, NSHS 27039

Down, Oliphant, "Wealth and Wisdom," a comedy, 1m1f, in *One Act Plays for Stage and Study: A Collection of Twenty-five Plays by Well-known* [sic] *Dramatists, American, English and Irish, First Series,* preface by Augustus

Thomas (New York: Samuel French, Inc., 1925), SF, NSHS

Drayson-Knigge, Sloane, "A Matter of Gender," a comedy, 1m2f, BP

Drayson-Knigge, Sloane, "Womantalk," a comedy-drama, 3f (in multiple roles), BP

Dresser, Richard, "The Road to Ruin," a ten-minute comedy, 3m1f, in *Splitsville: Three One-Act Plays,* SF 20654, and (published with and can pair with "Americansaint," "Après Opéra," "'The Asshole Murder Case,'" "Bread," "Cold Water," "Cover," "Downtown," "The Drummer," "The Duck Pond," "Eating Out," "Electric Roses," "The Field," "4 A.M. (open all night)," "Looking Good," "Love and Peace, Mary Jo," "Loyalties," "Marred Bliss," "Perfect," "Spades," or "Watermelon Boat") in *25 10-Minute Plays from Actors Theatre of Louisville,* edited by Actors Theatre of Louisville (New York: Samuel French, Inc., 1989), ISBN 0-573-62558-1, SF 6716

Drexler, Rosalyn, "Softly, and Consider the Nearness," a play (genre?), 1m2f, cited in *The Best Plays of 1963-1964,* edited by Henry Hewes

Duarte-Clark, Rodrigo, "Brujerías," a comedy, 1m2f, in *Nuevos Pasos: Chicano and Puerto Rican Dramas,* edited by Nicolás Kanellos and Jorge A. Huerta (Arte Público Press, 1989), ISBN 0-934770-98-0, APP

Dudzick, Tom, and Steven Smith, "Me Too, Then!" a comedy, 2m1f, **analyzed in Part 4, p. 217,** in *Off-Off Broadway Festival Plays,* Vol. 5, SF 15651, NSHS 27534

Duffield, Brainerd, "By the Waters of Babylon," a drama from Stephen Vincent Benét, 3m1f (variable chorus), DPC B37, HDS, NSHS pb175

Dunlop, Richard S., "Bloodline, or Hanged in Their Own Family Tree," a sing-along musical mellerdrammer, 2m2f, SF 4092, NSHS pb8048

Dunphy, Jack, "Squirrel," a play (genre?), 2m1f, DPS manuscript

Dunphy, Jack, "Too Close for Comfort," a play (genre?), 3m1f, DPS manuscript

Dunsany (Lord, 18th Baron, a.k.a. Edward John Moreton Drax Plunkett, Irish poet and dramatist, 1878-1957), "The Jest of Hahalaba," a drama, 4m, SF, NSHS 27039

Dunsany (Lord, 18th Baron, a.k.a. Edward John Moreton Drax Plunkett, Irish poet and dramatist, 1878-1957), "Two Bottles of Relish," a mystery by Edward Darby from Lord Dunsany, 2m2f, HDS, DPC T45, NSHS pb139

Dürrenmatt, Friedrich (Swiss playwright in German, 1921-1990), "Conversation at Night with a Despised Character: A Curriculum for Our Times," [*"Nächtliches gespräch mit einem verachteten Menschen,"* 1957], a drama (written first as a radio play, 1952) translated by Robert David Macdonald from the original German, 2m, **analyzed in Part 4, p. 195,** DPC C32, NSHS pb177

Duthie, Hermine, "Wheat Fire," a drama, 2m2f, TSD, NSHS 10922

Duvernois, Henri (source French playwright), "Nanny," a comedy, adapted by Percival Wilde from the original French, 2m1f, BP, NSHS 19987

E

Eaton, Walter Prichard, "The Purple Door Knob," a comedy, 3f, **analyzed in Part 4, p. 232**, SF 863, NSHS pb7959

Edmond, Reby, "The Dormant Heritage," a comedy, 2f, (published with and can pair with "Enterprising Oswald," "Girls Will Be Girls," "Grandma Fought the Indians," "Make-Up," "Paris Sets the Styles," "'Rosemary—That's for Remembrance,'" "She Goes the Rounds," or "Truant Husbands") in *Two by Two*, BP, NSHS pb6044, NSHS 29326

Edmond, Reby, "Enterprising Oswald," a Christmas comedy, 2f, (published with and can pair with "The Dormant Heritage," "Girls Will Be Girls," "Grandma Fought the Indians," "Make-Up," "Paris Sets the Styles," "'Rosemary—That's for Remembrance,'" "She Goes the Rounds," or "Truant Husbands") in *Two by Two*, BP, NSHS pb6044, NSHS 29326

Edward, Clinton, "The Boogeyman" ["The Boogeyman: The Boogeyman"], a comedy-drama, 1m2f, (published with and can pair with "First of the Month" or "Small Claims") in *The Boogeyman: Three Related One Acts* (New York: Samuel French, Inc., 1992), ISBN 0-573-69388-9, SF 4720, NSHS pb8106

Edwards, Mark R., "Wanted . . . Dead or Alive," a comedy, 1m2f (+ male voice), SF 25614

Elias, J. T., "First Date," a comedy, 2m2f, BP, SF 8621, NSHS pb8062

Elliott, Kenneth, and Charles Busch, "Après moi, le déluge," a drama, 1m, in *Tough Acts to Follow: One-Act Plays on the Gay/Lesbian Experience*, edited by Noreen C. Barnes and Nicholas Deutsch (San Francisco: Alamo Square Press, 1992), ISBN 0-9624751-6-5

Elliott, Paul, "Ledge, Ledger, and the Legend," a comedy, 3f or 3m, **analyzed in Part 4, p. 212**, DPC, HDS, NSHS pb142, NSHS pb7941

Elward, James, "Passport," a drama, 1m, **analyzed in Part 4, p. 227**, (published with and can pair with "Mary Agnes Is Thirty-five") in *Friday Night*, DPS 2045, NSHS 29204

Emery, Charles, "The Christmas Stranger," a Christmas play (genre?), 1m3f, SF 5644

Emery, Charles, "Just a Little Something for Christmas," a Christmas comedy, 2m1f, (published with and can pair with "Dutch Treat," "Fishing Hat," "To Open, Pry Cover," or "What's That Tune") in *Ethel and Albert Comedies* SF 7645 (anthology), SF 12622 (single play), NSHS pb7825 (anthology)

Emery, Charles, "The Red Key," a drama, 1m2f, SF 911, HDS

Emmet, Alfred (translator from Russian), "The Proposal," a farce by Anton Chekhov, translated by Michael Frayn, 2m1f, in Anton Chekhov's *Plays* (London: Methuen & Company, Ltd., 1988), ISBN 0-413-19160-X [See also the versions by Alfred Emmet ("Anton Chekhov's The Proposal"), Michael Henry Heim, and Ronald Hingley.]

Ervine, St. John Greer (Irish dramatist and novelist, 1883-1971), "Ole George Comes to Tea," a comedy, 2m1f, NSHS pb5465

Ervine, St. John Greer (Irish dramatist and novelist, 1883-1971), "Progress," a drama, 1m2f, GAU, NSHS pb5473

Estrada, Doris, "Three on a Bench," a whimsical comedy, 2m2f, BP, HDS, SF 1074, NSHS 19998

Evans, Annie, "Ghost Stories," a drama, 3f, in *Off-Off Broadway Festival Plays*, 11th Series," SF 9629, NSHS pb7494, 27508

Evans, Don, "Orrin," a drama, 3m1f, (published with and can pair with "Sugar-Mouth Sam Don't Dance No More") in *The Prodigals*, DPS 3725

Evans, Edward Kinchley, "Phamtom's Dance," a drama, 2m1f, AR, NSHS pb7522

Eyen, Tom, "My Next Husband Will Be a Beauty," a comedy-tragedy, 2m2f, in *Tom Eyen: Ten Plays*, SF 15608, NSHS 29246

Eyen, Tom, "What Is Making Gilda So Gray," a comedy, 1m1f (+ voices), in *Tom Eyen: Ten Plays*, SF 25601, NSHS 29246

Eyen, Tom, "The White Whore and the Bit Player," a comedy-tragedy, 2f, in *Tom Eyen: Ten Plays*, SF 25602, NSHS 29246

Eyen, Tom, "Why Hanna's Skirt Won't Stay Down, or Admission $.10," one-act version of a tragic-comedy, 2m2f, SF 22911, NSHS 29246

F

Falk, Lee, "Eris, or The Night People," a drama, 4m, in *Eris and Home at Six*, DPS 1820, NSHS pb7926

Farrell, Joe (translator from Italian), "An Ordinary Day," a comedy by Dario Fo and Franca Rame, 1m2f (voices), (published with "The Open Couple") SF 17940

Faulkner, George M., *The Thinking Heart*, Act II, an excerpt from a full-length drama, 4m, CSS, NSHS 26581, NSHS 20718

Fedorko, Joseph, "Extracurriculars," a comedy, 2m1f, in *Extracurriculars*, BP

Fedorko, Joseph, "Rebuttals," a comedy, 3m1f, in *Extracurriculars*, BP

Fedorko, Joseph, "Scrimmages," a comedy, 2m1f, in *Extracurriculars*, BP

Feiffer, Jules, "The Unexpurgated Memoirs of Bernard Mergendeiler," a sketch, 1m1f, DPS, NSHS

Feiler, Jules, "The Dicks," a comedy, 2m, in *Off-Off Broadway Festival Plays, Series 9*, SF 6663, NSHS 27532

Fein, Judith, "Visiting Dan," a ten-minute play (genre?),

2m1f, SF

Feke, Gilbert David, "Psychoneurotic Phantasies," a comedy, 2m1f, BP

Ferlita, Ernest C., "The Hills Send Off Echoes," a drama, 3m, TPH

Ferruza, Charles, "A Conspiracy of Angels," a comedy, 1m2f, NSHS 29210

Feydeau, Georges (French playwright), *"Amour et piano"* ["Romance in A Flat"] a comedy translated into English from the original French by Norman R. Shapiro, 2m1f, (published with and can pair with "The Boor Hug" [*"Les Pavés de l'ours"*], "Ladies' Man" [*"Notre futur"*],or "Wooed and Viewed" [*"Par la fenêtre"*], in Georges Feydeau's *Feydeau, First to Last*, translated by Norman R. Shapiro (Ithaca, New York, and London: Cornell University Press), SF 20629, NSHS

Feydeau, Georges (French playwright), *"Feu la Mère de Madame"* ["Night Errant"], a comedy, translated from the original French by Michael Pilch, 2m2f, SF 16056, NSHS pb8071

Feydeau, Georges (French playwright), *"Les Pavés de l'ours"* ["The Boor Hug"], a farce, translated from the original French into English by Norman R. Shapiro, 2m2f, (published with and can pair with "Ladies' Man" [*"Notre futur"*], "Romance in A Flat" [*"Amour et piano"*], or "Wooed and Viewed" [*"Par la fenêtre"*]) in Georges Feydeau's *Feydeau, First to Last*, translated by Norman R. Shapiro (Ithaca, New York, and London: Cornell University Press), SF 4667, NSHS

Feydeau, Georges (French playwright), *"Notre futur"* ["Ladies' Man"], a comedy, translated into English from the French by Norman R. Shapiro, 2f, (published with and can pair with "The Boor Hug" [*"Les Pavés de l'ours"*],"Romance in A Flat" [*"Amour et piano"*], or "Wooed and Viewed" [*"Par la fenêtre"*]) in Georges Feydeau's *Feydeau, First to Last*, translated by Norman R. Shapiro (Ithaca, New York, and London: Cornell University Press) SF 14016, NSHS

Feydeau, Georges (French playwright), "Wooed and Viewed," a comedy, 1m1f, SF

Field, Rachel, "The Bad Penny," a drama, 4f, SF 4603, NSHS pb7891

Field, Rachel, "The Fifteenth Candle," a tragedy, 1m2f, SF, NSHS 8266

Fierstein, Harvey, "Forget Him," a drama, 3m, (can pair with "Andre's Mother," "Bill Batchelor Road," "Fairy Tale," "Fog," "Odd Number," "One of Those People," "Pouf Positive," "The River Jordan," or "Safe Sex") in *Out Front: Contemporary Gay and Lesbian Plays*, edited by D. Shewey (New York: Grove Press, Inc., 1988), ISBN 0-8021-1041, ISBN 0-8021-3025-9

Fierstein, Harvey, "Manny and Jake," a drama, 2m, (published with and can pair with "On Tidy Endings" or "Safe Sex") in Harvey Fierstein's *Safe Sex* (New York: Sam-

uel French, Inc.), ISBN 0-573-64233-8, SF 14964, NSHS pb8112

Fierstein, Harvey, "On Tiny Endings," a drama, 2m2f, in *Safe Sex*, (published with and can pair with "Manny and Jake" or "Safe Sex") in Harvey Fierstein's *Safe Sex* (New York: Samuel French, Inc.), ISBN 0-573-64233-8, NSHS pb8112, SF 17936

Fierstein, Harvey, "Safe Sex," a comic drama, 2m, (about AIDS, can pair with Alan Bowne's "Beirut," Patricia Loughrey's "The Inner Circle," Robert Patrick's "Pouf Positive," or Lanford Wilson's "A Poster of the Cosmos") (published with and can pair with "Manny and Jake" or "On Tidy Endings") in Harvey Fierstein's *Safe Sex* (New York: Samuel French, Inc.), ISBN 0-573-64233-8, SF 20992, NSHS pb8112

Finch, Robert, "From Paradise to Butte," a comedy, 4m, GCB

Finch, Robert, "The Old Grad," a comedy, 3m, TSD, NSHS 10922

Finch, Robert, "The Return," a drama, 3f, not to be confused with the play of the same name by Mario Fratti, GCB, NSHS 5345

Firth, Michael, "The Keep," a drama, 3m or 3f, IEC

Firth, Michael, "Some Live, Some Die," a drama, 3m1f, IEC, NSHS pb110

Fisk, Bruce, "Strawberry Jam," a comedy, 4f, BP

Fitzhugh, Ellen, Tom Cone and Skip Kennon, "Herringbone," a drama, 1m (+1 extra), 1m, in *Twenty Years at Play: A New Play Centre Anthology*, edited by Jerry Wasserman (Cordova, Vancouver, British Columbia, Canada: Talonbooks, Ltd., 1990), ISBN 0-88922-275-4, TL

Flaherty, Robert J., "The Party," a comedy, 1m3f, in Robert J. Flaherty's *The Party* (New York: Samuel French, Inc., 1990), ISBN 0-573-62393-9, SF 18941, NSHS pb7948, NSHS pb7950, NSHS pb7948

Fletcher, Winifred Bell, "White Tablecloths," a drama, 2m2f, NSHS 10922

Floyd, Lucretia Xavier (translator from Spanish), "A Sunny Morning" [*"Mañana de sol,"* 1905], a comedy by brothers Serafín and Joaquín Álverez Quintero translated from the Spanish, 2m2f, BP, SF 1012, NSHS 2189, NSHS 19878, NSHS 19883

Fo, Dario, and Franca Rame (Italian source playwrights), "An Ordinary Day," a comedy translated from the original Italian by Joe Farrell, 1m2f (voices), (published with "The Open Couple") SF 17940

Fo, Dario, and Franca Rame (Italian playwrights), "The Whore in the Madhouse," a monologue, 1f, (published with and can pair with "Alice in Wonderless Land," "An Arab Woman Speaks," "The Bawd—the Christian Democrat Party in Chile," "Bless Me Father for I Have Sinned," "Coming Home," "The Dancing Mistress: On the Assembly Line," "The Eel-Woman," "Fascism 1922," "I'm Ulrike—Screaming," "It Happened Tomorrow,"

"Mamma Togni," "Medea," "Michele Lu Lanzone," "A Mother," "Nada Pasini," "The Rape," "Rise and Shine," "The Same Old Story," or "A Woman Alone") in Franca Rame and Dario Fo's *A Woman Alone & Other Plays* (London: Methuen, 1991), ISBN 0-413-64030-2

Foote, Horton, "Blind Date," a comedy, 2m2f, DPS 1043, NSHS pb8104

Foote, Horton, "The Dearest of Friends" ["The Roads to Home: The Dearest of Friends"], a drama, 2m2f, (published with and can pair with "The Roads to Home: A Nightingale" or "The Roads to Home: Spring Dance"); in Horton Foote's *Selected One-Act Plays of Horton Foote*, edited by Gerald C. Wood (Dallas, Texas: Southern Methodist University Press, 1989), ISBN 0-87074-274-4, ISBN 0-87074-275-2 ; also in *The Roads to Home*, DPS 3845, NSHS pb8033

Foote, Horton, "A Nightingale" ["The Roads to Home: A Nightingale"], a drama, 1m3f, **analyzed in Part 4, p. 220**, (published with and can pair with "The Roads to Home: The Dearest of Friends" or "The Roads to Home: Spring Dance"); in Horton Foote's *Selected One-Act Plays of Horton Foote*, edited by Gerald C. Wood (Dallas, Texas: Southern Methodist University Press, 1989), ISBN 0-87074-274-4, ISBN 0-87074-275-2 ; also in *The Roads to Home*, DPS 3845, NSHS pb8033

Foote, Horton, "The One-Armed Man," a drama, 3m, (published with and can pair with "The Prisoner's Song") in *The Tears of My Sister/The Prisoner's Song/The One-Armed Man/The Land of the Astronauts*, DPS 2022; also in Horton Foote's *Selected One-Act Plays of Horton Foote*, edited by Gerald C. Wood (Dallas, Texas: Southern Methodist University Press, 1989), ISBN 0-87074-274-4, ISBN 0-87074-275-2

Foote, Horton, "The Prisoner's Song," a drama, 2m2f, (published with and can pair with "The One-Armed Man") in *The Tears of My Sister/The Prisoner's Song/The One-Armed Man/The Land of the Astronauts*, DPS 2022; also in Horton Foote's *Selected One-Act Plays of Horton Foote*, edited by Gerald C. Wood (Dallas, Texas: Southern Methodist University Press, 1989), ISBN 0-87074-274-4, ISBN 0-87074-275-2

Foote, Horton, "Spring Dance" ["The Roads to Home: Spring Dance"] a drama, 3m1f, (published with and can pair with "The Roads to Home: The Dearest of Friends" or "The Roads to Home: A Nightingale"); in Horton Foote's *Selected One-Act Plays of Horton Foote*, edited by Gerald C. Wood (Dallas, Texas: Southern Methodist University Press, 1989), ISBN 0-87074-274-4, ISBN 0-87074-275-2 ; also in *The Roads to Home*, DPS 3845, NSHS pb8033

Ford, Richard, "American Tropical," a drama, 1m2f, in *Antæus: Plays in One-Act*, edited by Daniel Halpern, no. 66 (Spring 1991), ISBN 0-88145-056-4

Fornes, Mari Irene, "Springtime," a drama, 1m2f, in *Antæus: Plays in One-Act*, edited by Daniel Halpern, no. 66 (Spring 1991), ISBN 0-88145-056-4

Forster, Joan, "A Perfect Match," a comedy, 2f, not to be confused with Ron Charles' play by the same name, SF

Foster, Paul, "The Recluse," a drama, 2f, in *Balls & Other Plays*, SF 20609

Franklin, Clay, "Western Lament," a comedy, 1m1f, (published with and can pair with "Bold Decision," "The Daffy World of Daphne de Witt," "No Sweet Revenge," "Small Victory," or "Suddenly Last Friday") in *Two for a Happening: A Dramatic Duo in Three Acts; Six One-Act Plays* SF, NSHS pb8199, NSHS 29203

Fratti, Mario, "A.I.D.S.," a drama, 2m (+1 female optional), SF 3877

Fratti, Mario, "The Bridge," a play (genre?), 3m, in *Races*, SF

Fratti, Mario, "The Other One," a play (genre?), 1m2f, in *Races*, SF, NSHS pb8060

Fratti, Mario, "The Piggy Bank," a comedy, 2m1f, (published with "Her Voice") SF 18155, NSHS

Fratti, Mario, "Rapes," a drama, 2m1f, **analyzed in Part 4, p. 234**, in *Races*, SF, NSHS pb8060

Fratti, Mario, "The Return," a mystery-drama, 2m2f, not to be confused with the play of the same name by Robert Finch (published with and can pair with "The Suicide") in *Four by Fratti*, ISBN 0-573-69034-0, SF 20601, NSHS 16646, NSHS pb8107

Fratti, Mario, "The Suicide," a drama, 1m2f, (published with and can pair with "The Return") in *Four by Fratti*, ISBN 0-573-69034-0, SF 21613, NSHS 16646, NSHS pb8107

Fratti, Mario, "White Cat," a play (genre?), 2m2f, SF, NSHS pb8060

Frayn, Michael (translator), "The Evils of Tobacco," [under various titles] a satirical lecture by Anton Chekhov, 1m, in Anton Chekhov's *Plays*, translated by Michael Frayn (London: Methuen & Company, Ltd., 1988), ISBN 0-413-19160-X [See also "Smoking Is Bad for You," translated by Ronald Hingley.]

Frayn, Michael (translator from Russian), "The Proposal," a farce by Anton Chekhov, translated by Michael Frayn, 2m1f, in Anton Chekhov's *Plays* (London: Methuen & Company, Ltd., 1988), ISBN 0-413-19160-X [See also the versions by Alfred Emmet ("Anton Chekhov's The Proposal"), Michael Henry Heim, and Ronald Hingley.]

Frayn, Michael (translator from Russian), "Swan Song," a drama by Anton Chekhov, 2m, in Anton Chekhov's *Plays*, (London: Methuen & Company, Ltd., 1988), ISBN 0-413-19160-X

Frechtman, Bernard (translator from French), "Deathwatch," a drama by Jean Genet (French novelist and playwright, 1910-1986), 4m, (published with and can pair with "The Maids") in Jean Genet's *The Maids and Deathwatch: Two Plays* (New York: Grove Weidenfeld, 1982), ISBN 0-8021-5056-X, BP, SF 357, SF 15036, NSHS pb8117

Frechtman, Bernard (translator from French), "The Maids," a lengthy one-act drama by Jean Genet (French novelist and playwright, 1910-1986), 3f, (published with and can pair with "Deathwatch") in Jean Genet's *The Maids and Deathwatch: Two Plays* (New York: Grove Weidenfeld, 1982), ISBN 0-8021-5056-X, BP, SF 357, SF 15036, NSHS pb8117

Friedman, Roy, "All for Art," a comedy, 2m1f, SF 3703

Friedman, Roy, "The Temp," a comedy, 3f, in Roy Friedman's *The Temp* (New York: Samuel French, Inc., 1992), ISBN 0-573-62599-9, SF 22167

Friel, Brian, "American Welcome," a ten-minute play (genre?), 1m, SF

Frost, Robert (source poet), "The Death of the Hired Man," a drama by Jay Reid Gould from Robert Frost's poem of the same name, 2m2f, **analyzed in Part 4, p. 197**, DPC D13, HDS, NSHS 6071

Fry, Christopher (English playwright, 1907-), "A Phoenix Too Frequent," [1946] a comedy, 1m2f, **analyzed in Part 4, p. 228**, (can pair with "A Sleep of Prisoners") DPS, HDS

Fry, Christopher (English playwright, 1907-), "A Sleep of Prisoners," [1951] a free-verse drama, 4m, (can pair with "A Phoenix Too Frequent") DPS, NSHS pb7944

Fry, Ray, "The Cameo," a drama, 1m2f, DPS 1223

Fugard, Athol (South African playwright), "The Drummer," a ten-minute pantomime comedy, 1m, **analyzed in Part 4, p. 199**, (nonspeaking), (published with and can pair with "Americansaint," "Après Opéra," "'The Asshole Murder Case,'" "Bread," "Cold Water," "Cover," "Downtown," "The Duck Pond," "Eating Out," "Electric Roses," "The Field," "4 A.M. (open all night)," "Marred Bliss," "Looking Good," "Love and Peace, Mary Jo," "Loyalties," "Perfect," "Spades" or "Watermelon Boats") in *25 10-Minute Plays from Actors Theatre of Louisville,* edited by Actors Theatre of Louisville (New York: Samuel French, Inc., 1989), ISBN 0-573-62558-1, SF 6716

Fuller, James (adaptor) , "The Open Window," a comedy from H. H. (Saki) Munro, 1m3f (+ extras), DPC O17, HDS, NSHS

G

Gainfort, John, "He's Dead All Right," a play (genre?), 3m1f, SF 10638, NSHS pb8038

Gallagher, Mary, "Perfect," a ten-minute play (genre?), 1m2f (published with and can pair with "'The Asshole Murder Case,'" "Americansaint," "Après Opéra," "Bread," "Cold Water," "Cover," "Downtown," "The Drummer," "The Duck Pond," "Eating Out," "Electric Roses," "The Field," "4 A.M. (open all night)," "Looking Good," "Love and Peace, Mary Jo," "Loyalties," "Marred Bliss," "Perfect," "The Road to Ruin," "Spades," or "Water-

melon Boats") in *25 10-Minute Plays from Actors Theatre of Louisville,* edited by Actors Theatre of Louisville (New York: Samuel French, Inc., 1989), ISBN 0-573-1, SF 6716

Gallagher, Mary, and Ara Watson, "Chocolate Cake," a comedy, 2f, (published with and can pair with "Final Placement" or "Little Miss Fresno") in *Win/Lose/Draw,* DPS 4923, NSHS pb8145

Gallagher, Mary, and Ara Watson, "Final Placement," a drama, 2f, (published with and can pair with "Chocolate Cake" or "Little Miss Fresno") in *Win/Lose/Draw,* DPS 4923, NSHS pb8145

Gallagher, Mary, and Ara Watson, "Little Miss Fresno," a comedy, 2f, (published with and can pair with "Chocolate Cake" or "Final Placement") in *Win/Lose/Draw,* DPS 4923, NSHS pb8145

Galvin, Randy, "Automatic Santa," a comedy, 4f or 4m, IEC

García Lorca, Federico (Spanish playwright, 1898-1936), "Episode of the Lieutenant Colonel of the Civil Guard" [*"Escena del teniente coronel de la guardia civil,"* 1922], 3m1f, translated by Edwin Honig, in *New Directions, no. 8,* Norfolk, Connecticut, 1944, agent unknown

García Lorca, Federico (Spanish playwright, 1898-1936), "Buster Keaton's Promenade" ["El paseo de Buster Keaton," 1926?], 2m2f (a cock and an owl), [1] translated by Tim Reynolds, *Accent,* XVII, no. 3, Urbana, Illinois, 1957, agent unknown; [2] "Buster Keaton's Constitutional," translated by William I. Oliver, microfilm of manuscript, New York City, Columbia University Library, 1957, agent unknown

García Lorca, Federico (Spanish playwright, 1898-1936), "Chimera," [*"Quimera,"* 1928], 2m2f, [1] translated by Tim Reynolds, in *Accent,* XVII, no.3, Urbana, Illinois, 1957, agent unknown; [2] translated by Edwin Honig, *New Directions, no. 8,* Norfolk, Connecticut, 1944, agent unknown; [3] translated by William I. Oliver, microfilm of manuscript, New York City, Columbia University Library, 1957, agent unknown

Gater, Dilys, "Whatever Happened to Chrissie," a fantasy for youth, 4m or 4f (gender unidentified), NPN

Gater, Paul, "Luther's Birthday," a comedy, 3f, (can pair with "Over the Edge") in Paul Gater's *Luther's Birthday* (Droitwich, Worcestershire, England: Hanbury Plays, 1989), ISBN 1-85205-063-2, HP

Gater, Paul, "Over the Edge," a comedy, 3m1f, (can pair with "Luther's Birthday") in *Triad 64,* NPN

Gaunt, Richard, and Michael Langridge, "Last Call for Breakfast," a sketch, 2m2f, in *The Coarse Acting Show 2,* SF 5920

Genet, Jean (French novelist and playwright, 1910-1986), "Deathwatch," a drama, 4m, (published with and can pair with "The Maids") in Jean Genet's *The Maids and Deathwatch: Two Plays,* translated from the original French into English by Bernard Frechtman (New York: Grove

Weidenfeld, 1982), ISBN 0-8021-5056-X, BP, SF 357, SF 15036, NSHS pb8117

Genet, Jean (French novelist and playwright, 1910-1986), "The Maids," a lengthy one-act drama, 3f, (published with and can pair with "Deathwatch") in Jean Genet's *The Maids and Deathwatch: Two Plays*, translated from the original French into English by Bernard Frechtman (New York: Grove Weidenfeld, 1982), SF 15036

George, Charles, "Final Performance [or, The Curtain Falls]," a drama, 3m, DPS 1515

Gerould, Danie (translator from French), "The Two Doubles, or the Surprising Surprise," a comedy by Thomas Simon Gueullette, 1m1f, (published with and can pair with "The Blind One-Armed Deaf-Mute," "Cassander's Trip to the Indies," "Cassander, Man of Letters," "Cassander Supports the Revolution," "Giles in Love," "The Shit Merchant," or "The Two Doubles") in *Gallant and Libertine, Divertissements and Parades of 18th Century France*, SF 22252, NSHS 7927

Gersovitz, S. V., "A Portrait of Portia," a drama, 1m2f, (published with and can pair with "Exeunt O'Brien and Krasnov," "Jennifer's First Christmas," or "Lamentable Affair of the Vicar's Wife") in *An Evening with Eve*, IEC 316-0

Gerstenberg, Alice, "Overtones," a drama, 4f, **analyzed in Part 4, p. 226**, BP, SF 17912, NSHS 19878, NSHS 19883

Gibbons, Thomas, "The Exhibition: Scenes from the Life of John Merrick," a drama, 2m, DPS 1875

Gilford, C. B., "Guest for Breakfast," a comedy, 1m2f, TPH, NSHS 29199, NSHS pb5456

Gilles, Harry, "Who's on First?" a comedy, 2m or 2f, BP

Gilroy, Frank D., "Dreams of Glory," a comedy, 2m2f, SF 6678, NSHS pb8094

Gilroy, Frank D., "Fore," a comedy, 2m1f, in *A Way with Words*, SF 8938

Gilroy, Frank D., "Give the Bishop My Faint Regards," a comedy, 2m1f, in *A Way with Words*, SF 9169

Gilroy, Frank D., "Match Point," a comedy, 1m2f, in *A Way with Words*, SF 15590

Gilroy, Frank D., "The Next Contestant," a drama (first published in *The Best Short Plays*), 2m1f, SF 16618

Gilroy, Frank D., "So Please Be Kind," a drama, 2m1f, (published with and can pair with "Come Next Tuesday," "Present Tense" or "'Twas Brillig") in Frank D. Gilroy's *Present Tense* (New York: Samuel French, Inc., 1973) SF 21722, NSHS pb5486, NSHS pb6048, NSHS pb6050, NSHS pb8169

Gilroy, Frank D., "'Twas Brillig," a drama, 2m2f, (published with and can pair with "Come Next Tuesday," "Present Tense," or "So Please Be Kind") in Frank D. Gilroy's *Present Tense* (New York: Samuel French, Inc., 1973), SF 22781, NSHS pb5486, NSHS pb6048, NSHS pb6050, NSHS pb8169

Gilroy, Frank D., "A Way with Words," a comedy, 2m1f, in *A Way with Words*, SF 25031

Gilsenan, Nancy, "Bon Bons and Other Passions," a comedy, 2m2f, DPC, NSHS 159

Gilsenan, Nancy Pahl, "Fragile Unions," a drama, 1m2f, DPC F34

Gilweit, Edwin R., "Snakes," a drama, 3m1f, DPC, NSHS pb164

Glaspell, Susan, "Suppressed Desires," a comedy, 1m2f, **analyzed in Part 4, p. 249**, BP, HDS, NSHS pb5483, NSHS 19878, NSHS 19883

Glass, Joanna M., "Canadian Gothic," a drama, 2m2f, (published with and can pair with "American Modern"), DPS 1230, NSHS pb8144

Gleason, William, "Werewolf," a comedy, 2m2f, DPC W16

Glines, John, "In the Desert of My Soul," a drama, 2m2f, DPS 2515, NSHS pb7723

Glore, John, "What She Found There," a ten-minute play (genre?), 1m, SF

Gogol, Nikolai (source novelist), "From a Madman's Diary," a dramatization by Eric Bentley, 1m, SF 8652

Goluboff, Bryan, "Big Al," a comedy-drama, 2m, in *Big Al and My Side of the Story*, DPS 0998

Goluboff, Bryan, "My Side of the Story," a comedy-drama, 2m, in *Big Al and My Side of the Story*, DPS 0998

González, Gloria, "Curtains," a comedy, 2m1f, DPS 1520, NSHS pb101, NSHS pb7635

González, Gloria, "Shadow of a Sovereign," a drama, 2m1f, PPC, NSHS pb7749

Goodfellow, Ellen, "If Women Played Cards as Men Do," a comedy, 4f, BP, SF 11908 (no royalty)

Goodfellow, Ellen, "If Women Worked as Men Do," a comedy, 4f, HDS, BP, NSHS pb8098

Goodman, Kenneth Sawyer, "Dust of the Road," a Christmas drama, 3m1f, SF 6700

Goodman, Kenneth Sawyer, "The Game of Chess," a drama, 4m, possibly in public domain, NSHS 19878, NSHS 19883

Gottliev, Alex, "Stud," a comedy, 1m2f, CBC, NSHS pb4241

Gould, Jay Reid, "The Death of the Hired Man," a drama from a poem of the same name by Robert Frost, 2m2f, DPC D13, HDS, NSHS 6071

Granger, Percy, "Leavin' Cheyenne," a comedy, 2m, in *Three Plays by Percy Granger*, SF 14629

Granger, Percy, "Vivien," a comic drama, 2m1f, SF 24615

Graves, Warren C., "Would You Like a Cup of Tea?" a comedy, 2m2f, SF 25200, NSHS pb8082

Graves, Warren C., "Yes Dear," a comedy, 1m2f, SF 27602

Gray, Amlin, "Mickey's Teeth," a comedy, 1m2f, DPS 3132

Gray, Amlin (adaptor from Swedish), "Outlanders," a drama from August Strindberg, 3m1f, (published with and can pair with "Wormwood") in *Zones of the Spirit*, DPS 5043, NSHS pb7915

Gray, Amlin (adaptor from Shakespeare), "Villainous Company," an abridgment/adaptation of Shakespeare's *Henry*

IV, Parts I and II, 3m, DPS 4745

Gray, Amlin (adaptor from Swedish), "Wormwood," a drama from August Strindberg, 3m1f, (published with and can pair with "Outlanders") in *Zones of the Spirit*, DPS 5043, NSHS pb7915

Gray, Elizabeth, "Lunch or Something," a bare-stage drama, 2f, SF 14664

Graybill, Chris, "Eye to Eye," a ten-minute play (genre?), 2m1f, SF

Grecco, Stephen, "Widows," a brief comedy, 2f, (published with and can pair with "Advice to a New Actor," "The Affidavit," "The American Way," "Anniversary," "Auld Lang Syne, or I'll Bet You Think This Play Is About You," "Bug Swatter," "Checkers," "Coming for a Visit," "Dalmation," "Dog Eat Dog," "Drowned Out," "Fireworks," "Interview," "Jumping," "Money," "One Beer Too Many," "Phonecall from Sunkist," "Potato Girl," "Property of the Dallas Cowboys," "The Split Decision," "Valley Forgery," or "Watermelon Boats") in Norman A. Bert's *One-Act Plays for Acting Students*, MPL, ISBN 0-916260-47-X, pb7929

Green, Paul Eliot (1894-   ), "The Goodbye," a drama, 2m1f, SF, NSHS 16609

Green, Paul Eliot (1894-   ), "The Man Who Died at Twelve o'clock," a farce, 2m1f, in *Fifteen American One-Act Plays*, SF 15628, NSHS 16609

Green, Paul Eliot (1894-   ), "The No 'Count Boy," a drama, 2m2f, SF 16628, NSHS 6066, NSHS 16609

Green, Paul Eliot (1894-   ), "Quare Medicine," a comedy, 3m1f, SF, NSHS 16609

Greenaway, Alfred, "Humphrey Pumphrey Had a Great Fall," a comedy, 2m2f, SF 10691, NSHS pb8063

Greenberg, Richard, "The Author's Voice," a comedy, 2m1f, DPS 857

Gregg, Stephen, "Postponing the Heat Death of the Universe," a comedy, 1m2f, DPC P61

Gregg, Stephen, "A Private Moment," a drama, 2m2f, in *Dramatics*, 65, no. 2 (October 1993): 20-23. Inquiries regarding performance rights and royalties should be directed to the author, 335 South Cochran, No. 201, Los Angeles, CA 90036.

Gregg, Stephen, "Sex Lives of Superheroes," a comedy, 1m2f (+ 3 extras), in Stephen Gregg's *Sex Lives of Superheroes*, (Woodstock, Illinois: The Dramatic Publishing Company, 1990), DPC S92

Gregory, Isabella Augusta (**Lady**, *née* Persse, Irish playwright, 1852-1932, translator from Gaelic), "The Lost Saint," an Irish folk-drama by Douglas Hyde (a.k.a. An Craoibhin Aoibhinn, Irish playwright and president, 1860-1949), 2m, (published with and can pair with "The Marriage" or "The Tinker and the Sheeog") in Douglas Hyde's *Selected Plays of Douglas Hyde*, chosen by Gareth W. Dunleavy and Janet Egleson Dunleavy, with parallel texts in Gaelic and English (Boston: University

Press of America, 1991), ISBN 0-86140-095-X, ISBN 0-86140-096-8

Gregory, Isabella Augusta (Lady, *née* Persse, Irish playwright, 1852-1932, translator from Gaelic), "The Marriage," an Irish folk-drama by Douglas Hyde (a.k.a. An Craoibhin Aoibhinn, Irish playwright and president, 1860-1949), 2m1f, (published with and can pair with "The Lost Saint" or "The Tinker and the Sheeog") in Douglas Hyde's *Selected Plays of Douglas Hyde*, chosen by Gareth W. Dunleavy and Janet Egleson Dunleavy, with parallel texts in Gaelic and English (Boston: University Press of America, 1991), ISBN 0-86140-095-X, ISBN 0-86140-096-8

Gregory, Isabella Augusta (Lady, *née* Persse, Irish playwright, 1852-1932, translator from Gaelic), Hyde, Douglas (a.k.a. An Craoibhin Aoibhinn, Irish playwright and president, 1860-1949), "The Tinker and the Sheeog," an Irish folk-drama by Douglas Hyde (a.k.a. An Craoibhin Aoibhinn, Irish playwright and president, 1860-1949), 3m1f, (published with and can pair with "The Lost Saint" or "The Marriage") in Douglas Hyde's *Selected Plays of Douglas Hyde*, compiled and introduced by Gareth W. Dunleavy and Janet Egleson Dunleavy, with parallel texts in Gaelic and English (Washington, D.C.: Catholic University of America Press, 1991), ISBN 0-86140-095-X, ISBN 0-86140-096-8

Gregory, Isabella Augusta (Lady, *née* Persse, Irish playwright, 1852-1932), "The Rising of the Moon," a comedy, 4m, **analyzed in Part 4, p. 236**, SF 20040 (no royalty in U.S.A., royalty in Canada), NSHS 19878, NSHS 19883, NSHS 16020, NSHS 21405, NSHS 26581, NSHS 20718

Gregory, Isabella Augusta (Lady, *née* Persse, Irish playwright, 1852-1932), "The Workhouse Ward," a farce, 2m1f, ISBN 0-573-02301-8, SF 25736, NSHS pb82, NSHS pb 5449, NSHS pb5444, NSHS 2212

Groff, Albert, "Not My Cup of Tea," a comedy, 3f, PDS

Groves, William, "Good Night, Sweet Mother," a drama, 1m2f, IEC 385-3

Guare, John, "Four Baboons Adoring the Sun," a drama, 2m2f, in *Antaeus: Plays in One Act*, edited by Daniel Halpern, No. 66 (Spring 1991), ANT

Guare, John, "Kissing Sweet," a comedy, 2m2f, (published with and can pair with "A Day for Surprises"), DPS 1555, NSHS pb7793

Gueullette, Thomas Simon (French playwright), "The Blind One-Armed Deaf-Mute," a comedy, 3m, (published with and can pair with "Cassander, Man of Letters," "Cassander Supports the Revolution," "Cassander's Trip to the Indies," "Giles in Love," "The Shit Merchant," or "The Two Doubles") in *Gallant and Libertine, Divertissements and Parades of 18th Century France*, SF 3989, NSHS pb7927, ISBN 0-933826-49-4

Gueullette, Thomas Simon (French playwright), "The Shit Merchant," a parade, 4m or 4f, (published with and can pair with "The Blind One-Armed Deaf-Mute," "Cassander Supports the Revolution," "Cassander, Man of Letters," "Cassander's Trip to the Indies," or "The Two Doubles") in *Gallant and Libertine, Divertissements and Parades of 18th Century France*, SF 21134, NSHS pb7927, ISBN 0-933826-49-4

Gueullette, Thomas Simon (French playwright), "The Two Doubles or the Surprising Surprise," a comedy, translated by Daniel Gerould, 1m1f, (published with and can pair with "The Blind One-Armed Deaf-Mute," "Cassander's Trip to the Indies," "Cassander, Man of Letters," "Cassander Supports the Revolution," "Giles in Love," "The Shit Merchant," or "The Two Doubles") in *Gallant and Libertine, Divertissements and Parades of 18th Century France*, SF 22252, NSHS 7927

Gurney, A. R., Jr., "Another Antigone," a drama, 2m2f, (can pair with "The Love Course," "The Opening Meeting," or "The Problem") in A. R. Gurney, Jr.'s *Another Antigone* (New York: Dramatists Play Service, Inc., 1988), DPS

Gurney, A. R., Jr., "The Love Course," a comedy, 2m2f, (can pair with "Another Antigone," "The Opening Meeting," or "The Problem") in A. R. Gurney, Jr.'s *Public Affairs* (New York: Samuel French, Inc., 1992), ISBN 0-573-69318-8, BP, SF 659, NSHS 27489

Gurney, A. R., Jr., "The Old One-Two," a drama, 2m1f, SF 17616

Gurney, A. R., Jr., "The Open Meeting," a comedy, 2m1f, (can pair with "Another Antigone," "The Love Course," or "The Problem") in A. R. Gurney, Jr.'s *Public Affairs* (New York: Samuel French, Inc., 1992), ISBN 0-573-69318-8, SF 17636

Gurney, A. R., Jr.,"The Rape of Bunny Stuntz," a comedy, 1m2f, SF 20606

Gutwillig, Stephen, "In the Way," a drama, 2m, FDG, NSHS

Guyer, Murphy, "The American Century," a comedy, 2m1f, DPS 712

Guyer, Murphy, "Loyalties," a ten-minute play (genre?), 2m2f, (published with and can pair with "Americansaint," "Après Opéra," "'The Asshole Murder Case,'" "Bread," "Cold Water," "Cover," "Downtown," "The Drummer," "The Duck Pond," "Eating Out," "Electric Roses," "The Field," "4 A.M. (open all night)," "Looking Good," "Love and Peace, Mary Jo," "Marred Bliss," "Perfect," "The Road to Ruin," "Spades," or "Watermelon Boats") in *25 10-Minute Plays from Actors Theatre of Louisville,* edited by Actors Theatre of Louisville (New York: Samuel French, Inc., 1989), ISBN 0-573-62558-1, SF 6716

H

Hadaway, Tom, "The Filleting Machine," a drama, 2m2f, PPC, NSHS pb8163

Hailey, Oliver, "Animal," a bare-stage brief play, **analyzed**

in Part 4, p. 182, 1f, (published with and can pair with "Picture") in *Picture Animal Crisscross: Three Short Plays*, DPS 3655, NSHS pb7922

Hailey, Oliver, "Crisscross," a bare-stage five-minute passion play, 2m, (published with and can pair with "Animal" or "Picture") in *Picture Animal Crisscross: Three Short Plays*, DPS 3655, NSHS pb7922

Haily, Oliver, "Picture," a bare-stage drama, 3m, (published with and can pair with "Animal" or "Crisscross") in *Picture Animal Crisscross: Three Short Plays*, DPS 3655, NSHS pb7922

Hall, Margaret, "The Pie and the Tart," a comedy, 3m1f, in *The Big Book of Folktale Plays: One-Act Adaptations of Folktales from Around the World, for Stage and Puppet Performance*, edited by Sylvia E. Kamerman (Boston: Plays, Inc., 1991), ISBN 0-8238-0294-9, PI

Hall, Nick, "Pastiche," a romantic farce, 2m2f, SF 18601, NSHS pb8049

Hample, Stuart, "'The Asshole Murder Case,'" a ten-minute play (genre?), 3m1f, (published with and can pair with "Americansaint," "Après Opéra," "Bread," "Cold Water," "Cover," "Downtown," "The Drummer," "The Duck Pond," "Eating Out," "Electric Roses," "The Field," "4 A.M. (open all night)," "Looking Good," "Love and Peace, Mary Jo," "Loyalties," "Marred Bliss," "Perfect," "The Road to Ruin," "Spades," or "Watermelon Boats") in *25 10-Minute Plays from Actors Theatre of Louisville,* edited by Actors Theatre of Louisville (New York: Samuel French, Inc., 1989), ISBN 0-573-62558-1, SF 6716

Hampton, Christopher, "Treats," a comedy in nine scenes, 2m1f, in Christopher Hampton's *The Philanthropist with Total Eclipse and Treats* (New York and London: Faber & Faber, Ltd., 1991), ISBN 0-571-16218-5

Handke, Peter (German playwright), "Kaspar," a drama, 1m, LLA, NSHS

Hanley, William, "No Answer," a drama, 1m, possibly available through DPS (?), which offers other scripts by this playwright

Hanley, William, "*Pas de Deux*," (Act I from *Slow Dance on the Killing Ground*), a drama, 2m1f, DPS, NSHS 28438

Hanley, William, "Whisper into My Good Ear," a drama, 2m, (published with and can pair with "Miss Dally Has a Lover"), DPS 4855

Hansberry, Lorraine (1930-), "Toussaint," a drama about Toussaint-Louverture (circa 1743-1803, originally François-Dominique Toussaint, Haitian general and liberator), 1m2f, in *9 Plays by Black Women*, SF 22173

Hansen, Jim, "What's a Girl to Do?!" a comedy, 1m2f, in *Off-Off Broadway Festival Plays, 13th Series*, SF 25657, NSHS pb8083

Hardstark, Michael, "In the Cemetery," a comic drama, 3m, (published with "The Cure") in *The Last Laugh*, SF 11109

Hardy, Peter, "Off the Hook," a drama, 2m2f, AR

Hare, David, "The Bay at Nice," a drama, 2m2f, in *Antaeus:*

Plays in One Act, edited by Daniel Halpern, No. 66 (Spring 1991), ANT

Harnetiaux, Bryan Patrick, "Bleeders," a drama, 2m1f, DPC B59, NSHS pb152

Harnetiaux, Bryan Patrick, "Vital Statistics," a comedy, 2m2f, BP

Harris, Aurand, "Ladies of the Mop," a comedy in rhyme and rhythm, 4f, BP, HDS, SF 14903 (no royalty), NSHS

Harris, Aurand (adaptor from French), "The Romancers," a comedy from Edmond Rostand's first act of *Les Romanesques*, the basis for the musical *The Fantasticks*, 3m1f, BP

Harris, Timothy, "The Adventures of Captain Neato-Man," a farce, 2m2f, in *Off-Off Broadway Short Play Festival Plays, 15th Series*, SF 3698, NSHS pb8079

Hartland, F. J., "Auto-Erotic Misadventure," a drama, 2m1f, in *Off-Off Broadway Festival Plays, 8th Series*, SF 3898

Hartland, F. J.,"12:21 P.M.," a comedy, 2m1f, **analyzed in Part 4, p. 256**, (published with and can pair with "Dispatches from Hell," "Molly and James," or "Senior Prom") in *Double Image Theatre's Off-Off Broadway Festival Plays, Tenth Series* (New York: Samuel French, Inc., 1985), SF 22772, NSHS 27488, ISBN 0-573-68904-0

Hartman, Jan, "Samuel Hoopes Reading from His Own Works," a play (genre?), 1m, available only in manuscript from DPS

Harville, Cliff, "George L. Smith," a bare-stage comedy, 1m, (published with and can pair with "Hand Me My Afghan," "Sara Hubbard," or "A Silent Catastrophe") in *Sunsets* (New York: Samuel French, Inc., 1989), ISBN 0-573-62522-0, SF 21387

Harville, Cliff, "Hand Me My Afghan," a comedy, 2m1f, (published with and can pair with "George L. Smith," "Sara Hubbard," or "A Silent Catastrophe") in Cliff Harville's *Sunsets*, (New York: Samuel French, Inc., 1989), ISBN 0-573-62522-0, SF 21387

Harville, Cliff, Jr., "Rough Draft," a comedy, 1m3f, available only in manuscript from SF 20635

Hastie, Sandra, Jeffrey Sweet, and Stephen Johnson, "Cover," a ten-minute play (genre?), 2m1f, (published with and can pair with "Americansaint," "Après Opéra," "'The Asshole Murder Case,'" "Bread," "Cold Water," "Downtown," "The Drummer," "The Duck Pond," "Eating Out," "Electric Roses," "The Field," "4 A.M. (open all night)," "Looking Good," "Love and Peace, Mary Jo," "Loyalties," "Marred Bliss," "Perfect," "The Road to Ruin," "Spades," or "Watermelon Boats") in *25 10-Minute Plays from Actors Theatre of Louisville,* edited by Actors Theatre of Louisville (New York: Samuel French, Inc., 1989), ISBN 0-573-62558-1, SF 6716

Hatcher, Jeffrey, "Downtown," a ten-minute drama, 2m1f, (published with and can pair with "Americansaint," "Après Opéra," "'The Asshole Murder Case,'" "Bread," "Cold Water," "Cover," "The Drummer," "The Duck

Pond," "Eating Out," "Electric Roses," "The Field," "4 A.M. (open all night)," "Looking Good," "Love and Peace, Mary Jo," "Loyalties," "Marred Bliss," "Perfect," "The Road to Ruin," "Spades," or "Watermelon Boats") in *25 10-Minute Plays from Actors Theatre of Louisville*, edited by Actors Theatre of Louisville (New York: Samuel French, Inc., 1989), ISBN 0-573-1, SF 6716

Haubold, Cleve, "The Banker's Dilemma," a farce melodrama, 2m2f, SF 253, BP, HDS

Haubold, Cleve, "The Big Black Box," a comedy, 1m, SF 270

Haubold, Cleve, "The Mice Have Been Drinking Again," a comedy, 2m2f, BP, SF 694, NSHS 27528

Haubold, Cleve, "Owl," a comedy, 2m1f, SF 17654

Haubold, Cleve, "Quo Vadis, Tinker Bell?" a comedy, 1m2f, SF 19607

Haubold, Cleve, "The Shiny Red Ball," a comedy, 2m, SF 976

Haubold, Cleve, "A Short Walk After Dinner," a drama, 1m2f, SF 21691, NSHS pb5472

Haubold, Cleve, "Shut Up, Martha!" a comedy, 3m1f, SF 21696, NSHS pb8086

Haubold, Cleve, "Tattoo," a comedy, 2m, SF 22613

Haubold, Cleve, "The Whole Truth and the Honest Man," a comedy, 2m or 2f or 1m1f, available only in manuscript from SF 25678, NSHS pb5440

Hauptman, William, "Comanche Cafe," new revised version of drama, 2f, **analyzed in Part 4, p. 193**, ISBN 0-573-62131-4, in *Domino Courts/Comanche Cafe*, SF 5686, NSHS pb91

Hauptman, William, "Domino Courts," new revised version of drama, 2m2f, ISBN 0-573-62131-4, in *Domino Courts/ Comanche Cafe*, SF 6089, NSHS pb91

Havel, Václav (Czech playwright and president), "Protest," a drama, translated by Vera Blackwell, 2m, in *Antæus: Plays in One Act*, edited by Daniel Halpern, no. 66 (Spring 1991), ISBN 0-88001-268-4

Hawkes, John, "The Wax Museum," a drama, 1m2f, in *Plays for a New Theater: Playbook 2*, HOA, NSHS 29328

Heifner, Jack, "Patio," a drama, 2f, (published with and can pair with "Porch") in *Texas Plays*, edited by William B. Martin (Dallas, Texas: Southern Methodist University Press, 1990); also in *Patio/Porch*, DPS 3600

Heifner, Jack, "Porch," a drama, 2f, (published with and can pair with "Patio") in *Texas Plays*, edited by William B. Martin (Dallas, Texas: Southern Methodist University Press, 1990); also in *Patio/Porch*, DPS 3600

Heifner, Jack, "Tropical Depression," a comedy, 2f, (published with and can pair with "Twister") in *Natural Disasters*, DPS 3332

Heifner, Jack, "Twister," a comedy, 1m1f, (published with and can pair with "Tropical Depression") in *Natural Disasters*, DPS 3332

Heifner, Jack, *Vanities, Act I*," the first act of a comedy, 3f, analyzed in Part 4, p. 257, in *Vanities*, SF 120, NSHS pb92

Heim, Michael Henry (translator from Russian), "The Proposal," a farce by Anton Chekhov, translated by Michael Frayn, 2m1f, in Anton Chekhov's *Plays* (London: Methuen & Company, Ltd., 1988), ISBN 0-413-19160-X [See also the versions by Alfred Emmet ("Anton Chekhov's The Proposal"), Michael Henry Heim, and Ronald Hingley.]

Helland, Don, "The Half Hour," a drama, 1m2f, ACP, HPC

Henderson, Nancy, "Medusa of Forty-seventh Street," a drama, 3f, SF 15653, NSHS pb7907

Heniford, Lewis W. (1928-   ), "Love's Light Wings," a drama, 2m2f, (can pair with "An Odious, Damnéd Lie" or "Shrew You: or, Who Hath Need of Men? as Goode Accounte as Anye Knowne Describing How Sweet Shagsper Shuffles Off His Mortal Coil") WO, NSHS

Heniford, Lewis W. (1928-   ), "An Odious, Damnéd Lie," a drama, 1m1f, (can pair with "Love's Light Wings" or "Shrew You: or, Who Hath Need of Men? as Goode Accounte as Anye Knowne Describing How Sweet Shagsper Shuffles Off His Mortal Coil") WO, NSHS

Heniford, Lewis W. (1928-   ), "Shrew You: or, Who Hath Need of Men? as Goode Accounte as Anye Knowne Describing How Sweet Shagsper Shuffles Off His Mortal Coil," a comedy, 2m2f, (can pair with "An Odious, Damnéd Lie" or "Love's Light Wings") analyzed in Part 4, p. 241, WO, NSHS

Henry, O. (William Sydney Porter, source American short story writer, 1862-1910), "The Last Leaf," a drama by Thomas Hischak, 2m2f, PDS

Hensley, Richard, "She Was Lost, and Is Found," a drama, 1m2f, SF 1024

Herlihy, James Leo, "Bad Bad Jo-Jo," a drama, 3m, (published with and can pair with "Laughs, Etc." or "Terrible Jim Fitch") in *Stop, You're Killing Me*, DPS 4290, NSHS pb7924

Herlihy, James Leo, "Laughs, Etc.," a comedy, 1f, **analyzed in Part 4, p. 211**, (published with and can pair with "Bad Bad Jo-Jo" or "Terrible Jim Fitch") in *Stop, You're Killing Me*, DPS 4290, NSHS pb7924

Herrmann, Keith, "The Little Comedy," a comedy in prologue and ten scenes, 2m2f, (published with and can pair with "Summer Share") in Keith Herrmann's *Romance/Romance: Two New Musicals*, book and lyrics by Barry Harman (New York: Samuel French, Inc., 1989), ISBN 0-573-68916-6, SF

Herrmann, Keith, "Summer Share" a comedy in prologue and ten scenes, 2m2f, (published with and can pair with "The Little Comedy") in Keith Herrmann's *Romance/Romance: Two New Musicals*, book and lyrics by Barry Harman (New York: Samuel French, Inc., 1989), ISBN 0-573-68916-6, SF

Hewitt, Barnard and Rose, "In the Suds," a medieval French farce translated into English verse, 1m2f, BP, SF, NSHS pb5458

Heywood, John (English playwright, 1497?-?1580), "A Mery Play betwene Johan Johan the Husbande, Tyb his Wyfe, and Syr Johan the Preest," a medieval farce probably by John Heywood, 2m1f, (can pair with "The Playe Called the Foure PP: A Newe and a Very Mery Enterlude of a Palmer, a Pardoner, a Potycary, and a Pedler") analyzed in Part 4, p. 230, HMC, NSHS 29216

Heywood, John (English playwright, 1497?-?1580), "The Playe Called the Foure PP: A Newe and a Very Mery Enterlude of a Palmer, a Pardoner, a Potycary, and a Pedler," a medieval comedy, 4m, (can pair with "A Mery Play betwene Johan Johan the Husbande, Tyb his Wyfe, and Syr Johan the Preest") ATB, HMC, NSHS 29216

Hildesheimer, Wolfgang (German playwright), "Nightpiece," an absurdity translated by the author from the German *Nachtsstück*, 2m, (published with and can pair with "Freedom for Clemens/*Freiheit für Clemens*" or "Let's Eat Hair!/*Essen Wir Haare!*") in Postwar German Theatre, GB, NSHS pb7857

Hingley, Ronald (translator from Russian), "The Proposal," a farce by Anton Chekhov, translated by Ronald Hingley, 2m2f (+ extras), in Anton Chekhov's *Twelve Plays*, translated by Ronald Hingley (London: Oxford University Press, 1992), ISBN 0-19-282813-4 [See also the versions by Alfred Emmet ("Anton Chekhov's The Proposal"), Michael Frayn, and Michael Henry Heim.]

Hingley, Ronald (translator from Russian), "Smoking Is Bad for You," [under various titles] a satirical lecture by Anton Chekhov translated by Ronald Hingley, 1m, in Anton Chekhov's *Twelve Plays*, translated by Ronald Hingley (London: Oxford University Press, 1992), ISBN 0-19-282813-4 [See also "The Evils of Tobacco," translated by Michael Frayn.]

Hingley, Ronald (translator from Russian and adaptor), "A Tragic Role," a farce by Anton Chekhov, adapted by Ronald Hingley, 2m, in Anton Chekhov's *Twelve Plays*, translated by Ronald Hingley (London: Oxford University Press, 1992), ISBN 0-19-282813-4

Hischak, Thomas (adaptor of American short story), "The Last Leaf," a drama from the story by O. Henry, 2m2f, PDS

Hoffman, Phoebe, "Martha's Mourning," a drama, 3f, *Drama*, issue (?), 1918, NSHS

Hoffman, W. M., "Thank You, Miss Victoria," a dramatic monologue, 1m (+ voice), HW

Hofsiss, Jack, Paula Wagner, and Eve Merriam, "Out of Our Father's House," a play (genre?) with music based on Eve Merriam's *Growing up Female in America*, 3f (in six roles), SF 811, BP

Hogan, Frank X., "Wet Paint," a comedy, 1m, AR

Holbrook, Marion, "Grandma Fought the Indians," a comedy, 2f, (published with and can pair with "The Dormant

Dance and the Railroad and Family Devotions, DPS 1523, NSHS pb7918

Hyde, Douglas (a.k.a. An Craoibhin Aoibhinn, Irish playwright and president, 1860-1949), "The Lost Saint," an Irish folk-drama, 2m, (published with and can pair with "The Marriage" or "The Tinker and the Sheeog") in Douglas Hyde's *Selected Plays of Douglas Hyde*, with translations by Lady Augusta Gregory, compiled and introduced by Gareth W. Dunleavy and Janet Egleson Dunleavy, with parallel texts in Gaelic and English (Washington, D.C.: Catholic University of America Press, 1991), ISBN 0-86140-095-X, ISBN 0-86140-096-8

Hyde, Douglas (a.k.a. An Craoibhin Aoibhinn, Irish playwright and president, 1860-1949), "The Marriage," an Irish folk-drama, 2m1f, (published with and can pair with "The Lost Saint" or "The Tinker and the Sheeog") in Douglas Hyde's *Selected Plays of Douglas Hyde*, with translations by Lady Augusta Gregory, compiled and introduced by Gareth W. Dunleavy and Janet Egleson Dunleavy, with parallel texts in Gaelic and English (Washington, D.C.: Catholic University of America Press, 1991), ISBN 0-86140-095-X, ISBN 0-86140-096-8

Hyde, Douglas (a.k.a. An Craoibhin Aoibhinn, Irish playwright and president, 1860-1949), "The Tinker and the Sheeog," an Irish folk-drama, 3m1f, (published with and can pair with "The Lost Saint" or "The Marriage") in Douglas Hyde's *Selected Plays of Douglas Hyde*, with translations by Lady Augusta Gregory, compiled and introduced by Gareth W. Dunleavy and Janet Egleson Dunleavy, with parallel texts in Gaelic and English (Washington, D.C.: Catholic University of America Press, 1991), ISBN 0-86140-095-X, ISBN 0-86140-096-8

Hyem, Jill, "Post Mortems," a drama, 2f, in *Triad 79*, NPN

I

Ilias, Isidore, "Goods," a drama, 2m, in *Off-Off Broadway Festival Plays, XVI Series*, SF 9940

Inge, William (1913-1973), "The Boy in the Basement," (see p. 190) a drama, 3m1f, (published with and can pair with "An Incident at the Standish Arms," "Memory of Summer," "The Rainy Afternoon," "A Social Event," or "The Tiny Closet") DPS 2535, NSHS pb6069

Inge, William (1913-1973), "The Call," a drama, 2m, available only in manuscript from DPS, NSHS pb86

Inge, William (1913-1973), "An Incident at the Standish Arms," a drama, 1m2f, (published with and can pair with "The Boy in the Basement," "Memory of Summer," "The Rainy Afternoon," "A Social Event," or "The Tiny Closet") DPS 2535, NSHS pb6069

Inge, William (1913-1973), "Memory of Summer," a drama, 1m2f, (published with and can pair with "The Boy in the Basement," "An Incident at the Standish Arms," "The Rainy Afternoon," "A Social Event," or "The Tiny

Closet") DPS 2535, NSHS pb6069

Inge, William (1913-1973), "A Murder," a black comedy, 2m1f, available only in manuscript from DPS, NSHS pb86

Inge, William (1913-1973), "The Rainy Afternoon," a drama, 1m2f, (published with and can pair with "The Boy in the Basement," "An Incident at the Standish Arms," "Memory of Summer," "A Social Event," or "The Tiny Closet") DPS 2535, NSHS pb6069

Inge, William (1913-1973), "A Social Event," a drama, 1m2f, (published with and can pair with "The Boy in the Basement,""An Incident at the Standish Arms," "Memory of Summer," "The Rainy Afternoon," or "The Tiny Closet") DPS 2535, NSHS pb6069

Inge, William (1913-1973), "The Tiny Closet," a drama, 1m3f, (published with and can pair with "The Boy in the Basement," "An Incident at the Standish Arms," "Memory of Summer," "The Rainy Afternoon," or "A Social Event") DPS 2535, NSHS pb6069

Ingraffia, Sam, "Chateau René," a drama, 2m, in *Off-Off Broadway Festival Plays, 15th Series*, SF, NSHS pb8079

Ionesco, Eugene, (Romanian-born French playwright writing in French, 1912-), "The Chairs," a tragic farce, 2m1f, in *Four Plays by Eugene Ionesco*, BP, SF 308, NSHS 2212, NSHS 16382, NSHS 16612

Ionesco, Eugene (Romanian-born French playwright writing in French, 1912-), "The Lesson," a comedy translated by Donald M. Allen, 1m2f, in *Four Plays by Eugene Ionesco*, BP, SF 647, NSHS

Ionesco, Eugene (Romanian-born French playwright writing in French, 1912-), "Maid to Marry," a farce, 2m1f, possibly SF (?)

Ionesco, Eugene (Romanian-born French playwright writing in French, 1912-), "The Motor Show," a farce, 2m1f, possibly SF (?)

Ionesco, Eugene (Romanian-born French playwright writing in French, 1912-), "The New Tenant," a farce translated from the original French by Donald Watson, 3m1f, in Eugene Ionesco's *Three Plays by Ionesco* and *Amédée/ The New Tenant/Victims of Duty*, translated by Donald Watson (New York: Grove Press, 1958), ISBN 0-8021-3101-8, SF 16617, NSHS pb8118

Ionesco, Eugene (Romanian-born French playwright writing in French, 1912-), "The Painting," a farce, 2m2f, SF

Ives, David, "Mere Mortals," a comedy, 3m, (published with and can pair with "Sure Thing" or "Words, Words, Words") in *Four Short Comedies* (New York: Dramatists Play Service, Inc., 1989), DPS 2593

Ives, David, "Philip Glass Buys a Loaf of Bread," a comedy, 2m2f, (published with and can pair with "Variations on the Death of Trotsky") in *Variations on the Death of Trotsky, and Other Short Comedies* (New York: Dramatists Play Service,Inc., 1992), DPS 4729, NSHS pb8089

Ives, David, "Variations on the Death of Trotsky," a comedy, 2m1f, (published with and can pair with "Philip Glass Buys a Loaf of Bread") in *Variations on the Death of Trotsky, and Other Short Comedies* (New York: Dramatists Play Service,Inc., 1992), DPS 4729, NSHS pb8089

Ives, David, "Words, Words, Words," a comedy, 2m1f, (published with and can pair with "Mere Mortals" or "Sure Thing") in *Four Short Comedies* (New York: Dramatists Play Service, Inc., 1989), DPS 2593

J

Jacker, Corinne, "Breakfast, Lunch, and Dinner," a drama, 1m2m, DPS 1035

Jacker, Corinne, "The Chinese Restaurant Syndrome," a comedy, 1m2f, (published with "In Place") DPS 2507

Jacker, Corinne, "In Place," a comedy, 1m2f, (published with "The Chinese Restaurant Syndrome") DPS 2507

Jacker, Corinne, "Night Thoughts," an absurd comedy, 2f, (published with and can pair with "Terminal") DPS 3400, NSHS pb49, NSHS pb50

Jacker, Corinne, "Terminal," a comedy, 2m, (published with and can pair with "Night Thoughts"), DPS 3400, NSHS pb49, NSHS pb50

Jackson, Guida M., "Lamentable Affair of the Vicar's Wife," a comedy, 2f, (published with and can pair with "Exeunt O'Brien and Krasnov," "Jennifcr's First Christmas," or "A Portrait of Portia") in *An Evening with Eve*, IEC 316-0

Jackson, R. Eugene, "The Hunting of the Snark," a musical comedy, 4f or 4m, IEC

Jacobson, Steven M., "Needs," a drama, 2m1f (the female is silent), DPS 3340

Jannuzzi, Luigi, "The Barbarians Are Coming," a satirical comedy, 3m, SF 3972, NSHS pb7902

Jannuzzi, Luigi, "A Bench at the Edge," a comedy, 2m, in *Off-Off Broadway Festival Plays, Series 6*, SF 4617

Jenkin, Len, "Highway," a drama, 1m, (published with and can pair with "Hotel" and "Intermezzo") in *Limbo Tales*, DPS 2870

Jenkin, Len, "Hotel," a drama, 1m, (published with and can pair with "Highway" and "Intermezzo") in *Limbo Tales*, DPS 2870

Jenkin, Len, "Intermezzo," a comedy, 1m, (published with and can pair with "Highway" and "Hotel") in *Limbo Tales*, DPS 2870

Jenkins, Ken, "Cemetery Man," a dramatic monologue, 1m, (published with and can pair with "Chug," "An Educated Lady," or "Rupert's Birthday") in *Rupert's Birthday and Other Monologues*, DPS 3912

Jenkins, Ken, "Chug," a comedic monologue, 1m, (published with and can pair with "Cemetery Man," "An Educated Lady," or "Rupert's Birthday") in *Rupert's Birthday and Other Monologues*, DPS 3912

Johnson, Albert, "Look Who's Playing God," a comedy, 2m2f, BP

Johnson, Cindy Lou, "The Person I Once Was," a drama, 1m2f, DPS 3632

Johnson, Georgia Douglas, "Blue Blood," a comedy, 1m3f, (published with and can pair with "Blue-Eyed Black Boy") in *Black Female Playwrights: An Anthology of Plays before 1950*, edited by Kathy A. Perkins (Bloomington, Indiana: Indiana University Press, 1989), ISBN 0-253-34358-5

Johnson, Georgia Douglas, "Blue-Eyed Black Boy," a comedy, 1m3f, (published with and can pair with "Blue Blood") in *Black Female Playwrights: An Anthology of Plays before 1950*, edited by Kathy A. Perkins (Bloomington, Indiana: Indiana University Press, 1989), ISBN 0-253-34358-5

Johnson, Kitty, "Mirror, Mirror," a drama, 3f, in *Triplet: Three One-Act Plays* (New York: Samuel French, Inc., 1991), ISBN 0-573-69290-4, SF 15698

Johnson, Kitty, "Strawberry Envy," a comedy, 2m1f, in *Triplet: Three One-Act Plays* (New York: Samuel French, Inc., 1991), ISBN 0-573-69290-4, SF 21939

Johnson, Kitty, "Triplet," a comedy, 3f, in *Triplet: Three One-Act Plays* (New York: Samuel French, Inc., 1991), ISBN 0-573-69290-4, SF 22217

Johnson, Stephen, Jeffrey Sweet, and Sandra Hastie, "Cover," a ten-minute play (genre?), 2m1f, (published with and can pair with "Americansaint," "Après Opéra," "'The Asshole Murder Case,'" "Bread," "Cold Water," "Downtown," "The Drummer," "The Duck Pond," "Electric Roses," "Eating Out," "The Field," "4 A.M. (open all night)," "Looking Good," "Love and Peace, Mary Jo," "Loyalties," "Marred Bliss," "Perfect," "The Road to Ruin," "Spades," or "Watermelon Boats") in *25 10-Minute Plays from Actors Theatre of Louisville*, edited by Actors Theatre of Louisville (New York: Samuel French, Inc., 1989), ISBN 0-573-62558-1, SF 6716

Johnston, Jennifer, "The Nightingale and Not the Lark," a drama, 2m2f, SF 16641, NSHS pb8064

Jones, C. Robert, "The Clown," a play (genre?) for children, 3m1f (extras), BP

Jones, Elinor, "Box Office," a comedy, 1m, **analyzed in Part 4, p. 188**, (published with and can pair with "What Would Jeanne Moreau Do?"), SF 4670, NSHS pb7960

Jones, Elinor, "6:15 on the 104," a comedy, 4f, in *6:15 on the 104/If You Were My Wife I'd Shoot Myself/Under Control*, DPS 4121, NSHS pb7892

Jones, Elinor, "Under Control," a comedy, 1m2f, in *6:15 on the 104/If You Were My Wife I'd Shoot Myself/Under Control*, DPS 4121, NSHS pb7892

Jones, Elinor, "What Would Jeanne Moreau Do?" a comedy, 2m1f, (published with "Box Office") SF 25660, NSHS pb7960

Jones, Henry Arthur (English playwright, 1851-1929),

"Dolly's Little Bills," a comedy, 2m1f, in *One Act Plays for Stage and Study: A Collection of Twenty-five Plays by Well-known* [sic] *Dramatists, American, English and Irish, First Series*, preface by Augustus Thomas (New York: Samuel French, Inc., 1925), SF, NSHS

Jones, Martin, "Snow Leopards [Act One]," a lengthy comedy-drama, 2f, SF 21245

Jones, Steve (translator from Russian), "The Visit," a ten-minute play (genre?) by Lyudmila Petrushevskaya, 1m1f, not to be confused with the full-length play of the same name by Friedrich Dürrenmatt, SF

Jones, William Ellis, "Paris Sets the Styles," a farce, 2f, (published with and can pair with "The Dormant Heritage," "Enterprising Oswald," "Girls Will Be Girls," "Grandma Fought the Indians," "Make-Up," "'Rosemary—That's for Remembrance,'" "She Goes the Rounds" or "Truant Husbands") in *Two by Two*, BP, NSHS pb6044, NSHS 29326

Jory, Jon, "Camping," a ten-minute play (genre?), 3f, contact author at (502) 584-1265, NSHS pb149

Jory, Jon, "Freshman Orientation," a ten-minute play (genre?), 1m2f, contact author at (502) 584-1265, NSHS pb149

Jory, Jon, "Heads," a ten-minute play (genre?), 3f, contact author at (502) 584-1265, NSHS pb149

Jory, Jon, "Logical Conclusion," a drama, 4m, in *Dramatics*, 63, no. 7 (March 1992): 34-35, DPC

Jory, Jon, "Stopwatch," a ten-minute play (genre?), 4m, contact author at (502) 584-1265, NSHS pb149

Joselovitz, Ernest A., "Righting," a drama, 2m, SF, DPS 3825

Joselovitz, Ernest A., "Romance," a drama, 2m1f, (published with and can pair with "Nicky and the Theatre for a New World" or "There Is No John Garfield") in Ernest Joselovitz' *Four One-Act Plays* (New York: Samuel French, Inc., 1991), ISBN 0-573-62170-5, SF 20662

Joselovitz, Ernest A., "Sammi," a drama, 2m, SF, DPS 3925

Joudry, Patricia, "The Song of Louise in the Morning," a drama, 1m2f, DPS 4190

K

Kaikkonen, Gus, "Potholes," a comedy, 2m2f, DPS 3687, NSHS pb8142

Kasper, Robert, "Echo," a drama, 2m2f, DPC E11, NSHS pb132

Kass, Jerome, "Suburban Tragedy," a drama, 1m1f, **analyzed in Part 4, p. 248**, (published with and can pair with "Make Like a Dog" or "Young Marrieds at Play) DPS 2662, NSHS pb8055

Kass, Jerome, "Young Marrieds at Play," a drama, 2m2f, (published with and can pair with "Make Like a Dog" or "Suburban Tragedy"), DPS 2662, NSHS pb8055

Kassin, Michael, "Today a Little Extra," a comedy, 2m1f, BP

Kastner, Martin, and Rose Kastner (translators from Ger-

man), *"Dansen,"* an allegory by Bertolt Brecht (German playwright, 1898-1956), translated from the German by Rose and Martin Kastner, 2m, SF

Kastner, Rose, and Martin Kastner (translators from German), *"Dansen,"* an allegory by Bertolt Brecht (German playwright, 1898-1956), translated from the German by Rose and Martin Kastner, 2m, SF

Kaufman, George S[imon] (1889-1961), "If Men Played Cards as Women Do," a satire, 4m, BP, HDS, SF 570, NSHS 19878, NSHS 19883

Kaufmann, Mark D., "Backbone of America," a comedy, 2m (that is, 1 man and 1 boy), JAT, DPC B73

Keens-Douglas, Richardo, "Once upon an Island," a radio play (genre?), 1m, in *Take Five: The Morningside Dramas*, edited by D. Carley (Winnipeg, Manitoba, Canada: Blizzard Publishing, 1991), ISBN 0-921368-21-6

Keillor, Garrison, "Prodigal Son," a comic parody based on the biblical parable, 3m (+ extras), in *Antaeus: Plays in One Act*, No. 66, edited by Daniel Halpern (Spring 1991), ISBN 0-88001-268-4, ANT

Keliewer, Warren, "The Doubting Saint," a religious drama, 2m1f or 1m2f, SF, NSHS

Keller, Bruce (Australian playwright), "Puppy Love, the Play," an audience-participation play (genre?), 1m, The Currency Press Pty., Ltd., ISBN 0-86819-288-0

Kelly, George, "Finders-Keepers," a play (genre?), 1m2f, SF 437

Kelly, George, "Poor Aubrey," a comedy by later developed into the full-length *The Show-Off*, 1m3f, BP, SF 18654, NSHS pb7908

Kelly, George, "The Weak Spot," a comedy, 1m2f, SF 25631

Kelly, Tim, "The Adventure of the Clouded Crystal," a comedy-drama, 2m2f, SF 3606, NSHS pb8068

Kelly, Tim, "Dog Eat Dog," a brief drama, 2m1f or 3m, (published with and can pair with "Advice to a New Actor," "The Affidavit," "The American Way," "Anniversary," "Auld Lang Syne, or I'll Bet You Think This Play Is About You," "Bug Swatter," "Checkers," "Coming for a Visit," "Dalmation," "Drowned Out," "Fireworks," "Interview," "Jumping," "Money," "One Beer Too Many," "Phonecall from Sunkist," "Potato Girl," "Property of the Dallas Cowboys," "The Split Decision," "Valley Forgery," "Watermelon Boats," or "Widows") in Norman A. Bert's *One-Act Plays for Acting Students*, MPL, ISBN 0-916260-47-X, pb7929

Kelly, Tim, "Lantern in the Wind," a drama, 3f, IEC 106-0

Kelly, Tim, "The Silk Shirt," a drama, 1m3f, SF 21699, NSHS pb7945, NSHS pb8108

Kelly, Tim (adaptor from Russian), "Two Fools Who Gained a Measure of Wisdom," a comedy from Anton Chekhov, 1m3f, DPS 4660, NSHS pb8025

Kennedy, Adrienne, "Sun," a drama, 1m, (can play with "She Talks to Beethoven") in Adrienne Kennedy's *Adrienne Kennedy in One Act* (Minneapolis, Minnesota: Univer-

"Perfect," "The Road to Ruin," "Spades," or "Watermelon Boats") in *25 10-Minute Plays from Actors Theatre of Louisville,* edited by Actors Theatre of Louisville (New York: Samuel French, Inc., 1989), ISBN 0-573-62558-1, SF 6716

Kraus, Karl, *Last Days of Mankind,* Act V, Scene 54, a dramatic monologue, translated by Max Spalter from the original German, 1m, KV, " NSHS 29408

Krawitz, H. Michael, "The Chance of a Lifetime," a comedy, 2m2f, IEC 021-8

Kressman, Margaret, "Apple Pie," a drama, 4f, SF 3642

Kukla, Don, "Playing Hardball," a drama, 2m, BP

Kukla, Don, "Sticks and Stones," a comedy, 2m1f, BP

Kurian, Kristine, "The Slipcovered King," a comedy in four scenes, 1m3f, in Kristine Kurian's *The Slipcovered King* (Franklin, Ohio: Eldridge Publishing Company, 1991), EPC

L

Labiche, Eugène (French source playwright, 1815-1888), "A Matter of Wife and Death," [*"La Lettre Chargée"*] a farce, adapted and translated into English from the original French by Norman R. Shapiro, 2m2f, in *Tour de Farce: A New Series of Farce Through the Ages, A Slap in the Farce & A Matter of Wife and Death* (New York: Applause Theatre Book Publishers), ISBN 0-936839-82-1, SF 14997, NSHS pb8116

LaChiusa, Michael John, "Agnes," a dramatic chamber opera, 1m2f, (published with and can pair with these other musicals: "Break," "Eulogy for Mister Hamm," or "Lucky Nurse") in *Lucky Nurse and Other Short Musicals,* DPS 2986, NSHS pb8120

LaChiusa, Michael John, "Break," a chamber opera, 2m1f, (published with and can pair with these other musicals: "Agnes," "Eulogy for Mister Hamm," or "Lucky Nurse") in *Lucky Nurse and Other Short Musicals,* DPS 2986, NSHS pb8120

LaChiusa, Michael John, "Eulogy for Mr. Hamm," a chamber opera, 2m2f, (published with and can pair with these other musicals: "Agnes," "Break," or "Lucky Nurse") in *Lucky Nurse and Other Short Musicals,* DPS 2986, NSHS pb8120

LaChiusa, Michael John, "Lucky Nurse," a chamber opera, 2m2f, (published with and can pair with these other musicals: "Agnes," "Break," or "Eulogy for Mister Hamm") in *Lucky Nurse and Other Short Musicals,* DPS 2986, NSHS pb8120

Lamb, Myrna, "But What Have You Done for Me Lately?" a drama, 2m1f, SF

Lamb, Myrna, "The Serving-Girl and the Lady, or Just Us and the Medium," a drama, 2f, SF

Lang, William, "Final Play," a drama, 3m, DPC F16, HDS, NSHS pb140

Lardner, Ring (a.k.a. Ringgold Wilmer Lardner, American novelist and playwright, 1920- , 1885-1933), "The Tridget of Greva," a comedy, SF, NSHS 27039, NSHS pb4019 NSHS 14824, NSHS 20483, NSHS 21389, NSHS 21514, NSHS 21776

Laszlo, Carl, "Let's Eat Hair!" an absurdity, translated by George E. Wellwarth from the German *"Essen Wir Haare!"* 2m1f, (published with and can pair with "Freedom for Clemens/*Freiheit für Clemens*" or "Nightpiece/*Nachtsstück*") in *Postwar German Theatre,* GB, NSHS pb7857

Lauchman, Richard, "The Wall," an Easter drama, 2m, PDS

Lauro, Shirley, "The Coal Diamond," a comedy, 4f, DPS 1375, NSHS pb7890

Lauro, Shirley, "I Don't Know Where You're Coming from at All," a drama, 3f, SF 11606, NSHS pb7904

Lauro, Shirley Mezvinsky, "Nothing Immediate," a drama, 2f, (published with and can pair with "An Empty Space" or "Open Admissions") in *Double Image Theatre's Off-Off Broadway Festival Plays, Fourth Series* (New York: Samuel French, Inc., 1983) SF 16637, NSHS 27533, ISBN 0-573-60044-9

Lauro, Shirley, "Open Admissions," new revised edition of a one-act version of a full-length drama by Shirley Lauro, 1m1f, **analyzed in Part 4, p. 224,** (published with and can pair with "An Empty Space" or "Nothing Immediate") in Double Image Theatre's *Off-Off Broadway Festival Plays, Fourth Series* (New York: Samuel French, Inc., 1983), SF 17640, NSHS 27533, ISBN 0-573-60044-9 [Note: An excellent nationally televised version starred Jane Alexander.]

Lauro, Shirley, "Sunday Go to Meetin'," a ten-minute play (genre?), 4f, SF

Lazarus, John, "Babel Rap," a comedy, 2m, in *Six Canadian Plays* (Toronto, Ontario, Canada: Playwrights Canada Press, 1992), ISBN 0-88754-469-X, PCP

Lazarus, John, "Curtains for a Crazy Old Lady," a play with music, 1m2f, in *Homework & Curtains* (Toronto, Ontario, Canada: Playwrights Canada Press, 1991), ISBN 0-88754-500-9, PCP

Lazarus, John, "Homework for Men," a drama, 2m, in *Homework & Curtains* (Toronto, Ontario, Canada: Playwrights Canada Press, 1992), ISBN 0-88754-500-9, PCP

Leary, Denis, "No Cure for Cancer," a satire, 1m, (New York: Anchor Books, 1992) ISBN 0-385-45581-3

Lee, Jim, "Will Someone Please Tell Me What's Going on Here?" a comedy, 2m2f, SF, NSHS pb8110, NSHS pb8153

Lee, Maryat, "Four Men and a Monster," a drama, 3m, SF 8642, NSHS pb7898

LeFevre, Adam, "Americansaint," a ten-minute play (genre?), 3m1f, (published with and can pair with "Après Opéra," "'The Asshole Murder Case,'" "Bread," "Cold Water," "Cover," "Downtown," "The Drummer," "The

Luft, Carrie, "Erasure," a drama, 1m2f, in *Cool Guys Don't Go out with Smart Girls and Other Revelations*, BP

Luft, Carrie, "Free the Frogs," a drama, 1m2f, in *Cool Guys Don't Go out with Smart Girls and Other Revelations*, BP

Luft, Carrie, "Purpose of the Moon," a drama, 2f, BP

Luna, José (Mexican playwright), *"El hacha"* ["The Axe"?], a *farsa* [farce], 2m1f, OEN, NSHS pb8189

Lynch, Peg, "To Open, Pry Cover," a comedy, 2m1f, (published with and can pair with "Dutch Treat," "Fishing Hat," "Just a Little Something for Christmas," or "What's That Tune") in *Ethel and Albert Comedies*, SF 7645 (anthology), SF 22718 (single play), NSHS pb7825 (anthology)

Lynch, Peg, "What's That Tune," a comedy, 2m1f, (published with and can pair with "Dutch Treat," "Fishing Hat," "Just a Little Something for Christmas," or "To Open, Pry Cover") in *Ethel and Albert Comedies*, SF 7645 (anthology), SF 25659 (single play), NSHS pb7825 (anthology)

M

Maar, Paul (German source playwright), "Noodle Doodle Box," a comedy for children translated from the German by Anita and Alex Page, 3m or 3f, BP

Macaulay, Pauline, "Monica," a drama, 3m, SF, NSHS 16674

MacIvor, Daniel, "See Bob Run," a drama, 1m, (published with and can pair with "Wild Abandon: The Study of Steve") in Daniel MacIvor's *See Bob Run & Wild Abandon* (Toronto, Ontario, Canada: Playwrights Canada Press, 1990), ISBN 0-88754-486-X

MacIvor, Daniel, "Wild Abandon: The Study of Steve," a drama, 1m, (published with and can pair with "See Bob Run") in Daniel MacIvor's *See Bob Run & Wild Abandon* (Toronto, Ontario, Canada: Playwrights Canada Press, 1990), ISBN 0-88754-486-X

Mack, Carol K., "a.k.a. Marleen," a comedy, 3f, (published with and can pair with "Postcards") in *Postcards and Other Short Plays*, SF 3912, NSHS pb7905

Mack, Carol K., "Postcards," a comedy, 3f, (published with and can pair with "a.k.a. Marleen") in *Postcards and Other Short Plays*, SF 18939, NSHS pb7905

Mack, Carol K., "Unprogrammed," a play (genre?), 2m1f, in *The Best American Short Plays, 1990*, edited by Howard Stein and Glenn Young (New York: Applause Theatre Book Publishers, 1992), ISSN 1062-7561

Mackay, Constance D'Arcy, "The Beau of Bath," a verse drama, 2m1f, BP, NSHS 19990

Mackay, Constance D'Arcy, "Counsel Retained," a verse comedy, 1m2f, BP, NSHS 19990

Mackay, Constance D'Arcy, "Gretna Green," a verse drama, 1m2f, BP, NSHS 19990

Mackay, Constance D'Arcy, "Prince of Court Painters," a verse drama, 1m2f, BP, NSHS 19990

Mackay, Constance D'Arcy, "The Silver Lining," a verse comedy, 2m1f, BP, NSHS 19990

MacLaughlin, Wendy, "Watermelon Boats," a ten-minute drama, 2f, (published with and can pair with "Americansaint," "Après Opéra," "'The Asshole Murder Case,'" "Bread," "Cold Water," "Cover," "Downtown," "The Drummer," "The Duck Pond," "Eating Out," "Electric Roses," "The Field," "4 A.M. (open all night)," "Looking Good," "Love and Piece," "Loyalties," "Marred Bliss," "Perfect," "The Road to Ruin," "Spades," "Watermelon Boats") in *25 10-Minute Plays from Actors Theatre of Louisville,* edited by Actors Theatre of Louisville (New York: Samuel French, Inc., 1989), ISBN 0-573-62558-1, SF 6716, NSHS pb2977; (also published with and can pair with "Advice to a New Actor," "The Affidavit," "The American Way," "Anniversary," "Auld Lang Syne, or I'll Bet You Think This Play Is About You," "Bug Swatter," "Checkers," "Coming for a Visit," "Dalmation," "Dog Eat Dog," "Drowned Out," "Fireworks," "Interview," "Jumping," "Money," "One Beer Too Many," "Phonecall from Sunkist," "Potato Girl," "Property of the Dallas Cowboys," "The Split Decision," "Valley Forgery," or "Widows") in Norman A. Bert's *Norman A. One-Act Plays for Acting Students*, MPL, ISBN 0-916260-47-X, pb7929

MacLeod, Wendy, "The Lost Colony," a comedy, 2m2f, (published with and can pair with "The Shallow End") in Wendy MacLeod's *The Shallow End and The Lost Colony* (New York: Dramatists Play Service, Inc., 1993), DPS 4064, NSHS pb8148

MacLeod, Wendy, "The Shallow End," a comedy, 4f, (published with and can pair with "The Lost Colony") in Wendy MacLeod's *The Shallow End and The Lost Colony* (New York: Dramatists Play Service, Inc., 1993) DPS 4064, NSHS pb8148

MacMillan, Mary, "A Fan and Two Candlesticks," a verse comedy, 1m2f, SKC, NSHS 27002

Magnuson, James, "No Snakes in the Grass," a drama, 2m1f, SF 771

Maloney, Peter, "Last Chance Texaco," a drama, 3f, (published with "Pastoral") SF 13887, NSHS pb7893

Malta, Demetrio Aguilera, *"El tigre"* ["The Tiger"], an Ecuadorian drama (*en español*/in Spanish), 4m, FCE, NSHS 29520

Mamet, David, "All Men Are Whores: An Inquiry," a sketch, 2m1f, (part of "The Blue Hour: City Sketches") in *Short Plays and Monologues*, DPS 3025

Mamet, David, "Businessmen," a sketch, 2m, (part of "The Blue Hour: City Sketches") in *Short Plays and Monologues*, DPS 3025

Mamet, David, "Bobby Gould in Hell," a comedy, 3m1f, (published with and can pair with "The Devil and Billy Markham," by Shel Silverstein) in *Oh, Hell! Two One-*

ther and Son," or "Forbidden Fruit") in *The Necklace and Other Stories*, SF 15990, DPC N10, NSHS 27500, NSHS pb7919

Mauro, Robert, "The Audition," a drama for youth, 2m, (published with and can pair with "The Cabbie from Calcutta," "A Death in the Family," "Going Down!" "The Day Mother Left Home," "The Golden Door," "Joan," "The Man in the Box," "My Baby," "My Friend Never Said Goodbye," "The No-Fault Driving School," "The Park Bench," "The Proposal," "Sherlock Holmes: 10 Minutes to Doom," or "Uptown/Downtown") in Robert Mauro's *Two-Character Plays for Student Actors: A Collection of 15 One-Act Plays* (Colorado Springs, Colorado: Meriwether Publishing, Ltd., 1988), MPL

Mauro, Robert, "The Day Mother Left Home," a drama, 2f, (published with and can pair with "The Audition," "The Cabbie from Calcutta," "A Death in the Family," "Going Down!" "The Golden Door," "Joan," "The Man in the Box," "My Baby," "My Friend Never Said Goodbye," "The No-Fault Driving School," "The Park Bench," "The Proposal," "Sherlock Holmes: 10 Minutes to Doom," or "Uptown/Downtown") in Robert Mauro's *Two-Character Plays for Student Actors: A Collection of 15 One-Act Plays* (Colorado Springs, Colorado: Meriwether Publishing, Ltd., 1988), MPL

Mauro, Robert, "A Death in the Family," a drama for youth, 2m, (published with and can pair with "The Audition," "The Cabbie from Calcutta," "The Day Mother Left Home," "Going Down!" "The Golden Door," "Joan," "The Man in the Box," "My Baby," "My Friend Never Said Goodbye," "The No-Fault Driving School," "The Park Bench," "The Proposal," "Sherlock Holmes: 10 Minutes to Doom," or "Uptown/Downtown") in Robert Mauro's *Two-Character Plays for Student Actors: A Collection of 15 One-Act Plays* (Colorado Springs, Colorado: Meriwether Publishing, Ltd., 1988), MPL

Mauro, Robert, "The Golden Door," a drama for youth, 2f, (published with and can pair with "The Audition," "The Cabbie from Calcutta," "A Death in the Family," "Going Down!" "The Day Mother Left Home," "Joan," "The Man in the Box," "My Baby," "My Friend Never Said Goodbye," "The No-Fault Driving School," "The Park Bench," "The Proposal," "Sherlock Holmes: 10 Minutes to Doom," or "Uptown/Downtown") in Robert Mauro's *Two-Character Plays for Student Actors: A Collection of 15 One-Act Plays* (Colorado Springs, Colorado: Meriwether Publishing, Ltd., 1988), MPL

Mauro, Robert, "My Baby," a drama for youth, 2f, (published with and can pair with "The Audition," "The Cabbie from Calcutta," "The Day Mother Left Home," "A Death in the Family," "Going Down!" "The Golden Door," "Joan," "The Man in the Box," "My Friend Never Said Goodbye," "The No-Fault Driving School," "The Park Bench," "The Proposal," "Sherlock Holmes: 10 Minutes

to Doom," or "Uptown/Downtown") in Robert Mauro's *Two-Character Plays for Student Actors: A Collection of 15 One-Act Plays* (Colorado Springs, Colorado: Meriwether Publishing, Ltd., 1988), MPL

Mauro, Robert, "Sherlock Holmes: 10 Minutes to Doom," a drama for youth, 2m, (published with and can pair with "The Audition," "The Cabbie from Calcutta," "The Day Mother Left Home," "A Death in the Family," "Going Down!" "The Golden Door," "Joan," "The Man in the Box," "My Baby," "My Friend Never Said Goodbye," "The No-Fault Driving School," "The Park Bench," "The Proposal," or "Uptown/Downtown") in Robert Mauro's *Two-Character Plays for Student Actors: A Collection of 15 One-Act Plays* (Colorado Springs, Colorado: Meriwether Publishing, Ltd., 1988), MPL

Mauro, Robert, "Uptown/Downtown," a drama for youth, 1m1f, (published with and can pair with "The Audition," "The Cabbie from Calcutta," "The Day Mother Left Home," "A Death in the Family," "Going Down!" "Joan," "The Golden Door," "The Man in the Box," "My Friend Never Said Goodbye," "My Baby," "The No-Fault Driving School," "The Park Bench," "The Proposal," or "Sherlock Holmes: 10 Minutes to Doom") in Robert Mauro's *Two-Character Plays for Student Actors: A Collection of 15 One-Act Plays* (Colorado Springs, Colorado: Meriwether Publishing, Ltd., 1988), MPL

May, Elaine, "Adaptation," a comedy, 3m1f, DPS 630, NSHS pb8031

May, Elaine, "Not Enough Rope," a farce, 1m2f, **analyzed in Part 4, p. 221**, BP, SF 85, NSHS pb5466, NSHS pb7751

Mayer, Paul Avila, "The Frying Pan," a drama, 2m1f, in *Three Hand Reel*, DPS 4510

McBride, Vaughn, "Go Back to Your Precious Wife and Son," a comedy from Kurt Vonnegut, Jr., 3m1f (1 male is a boy), (can pair with "The Lie") DPC G50, NSHS pb7968

McBride, Vaughn, "The Lie," a drama from Kurt Vonnegut, Jr., 3m1f, (can pair with "Go Back to Your Precious Wife and Son") DPC L75

McBride, Vaughn, "The New Girl," a comedy, 2f, SF 16047, NSHS 27502

McBrien, Richard, "Period," a farce, 2m1f, in *Off-Off Broadway Festival Plays, Series 6*, SF 18139

McCormack, Tom, "American Roulette," a drama, 2m1f, DPS 745, NSHS pb7800

McDonough, Jerome, "The Betrothed," a drama, 1m2f, (can pair with "Filiation," "Juvie," or "The Old Oak Encounter") ISBN 0-573-62040-3, SF 265, NSHS 7510

McDonough, Jerome, "Filiation," a drama, 3m1f, (can pair with "The Betrothed," "Juvie," or "The Old Oak Encounter") IEC, NSHS

McDonough, Jerome, "Juvie," a drama, 3m or 4m, (can pair with "The Betrothed," "Filiation," or "The Old Oak Encounter") HDS

McDonough, Jerome, "The Old Oak Encounter," a comedy, 2m2f, (can pair with "The Betrothed," "Filiation," or "Juvie") IEC, NSHS pb108

McFadden, E. A., "Why the Chimes Rang," a Christmas drama, 3m1f, BPF

McGaughan, Geraldine, "Afterwards," a drama, 3m1f, SF 210, NSHS pb8019

McKeaney, Grace, "Chicks," a comedy, 1m3f, (published with and can pair with "The Coming of Mr. Pine" or "Fits and Starts") **analyzed in Part 4, p. 192**, in *Chicks and Other Short Plays*, SF 5210, NSHS pb7949, NSHS pb8091, NSHS pb7949

McKeaney, Grace, "The Coming of Mr. Pine," a comedy, 1m3f, (published with and can pair with "Chicks" or "Fits and Starts") in *Chicks and Other Short Plays*, SF 5210, NSHS pb7949, NSHS pb8091, NSHS pb7949

McKeaney, Grace, "Fits and Starts," a comedy, 2m2f, (published with and can pair with "Chicks" or "The Coming of Mr. Pine") in *Chicks and Other Short Plays*, SF 8138, NSHS pb7949, NSHS pb8091, NSHS pb7949

McKinney, Gene, "The People in the Glass Paperweight," a tragicomedy, 2m1f, (can pair with "When You're by Yourself, You're Alone") BP, SF 18627, NSHS pb5461

McKinney, Gene, "When You're by Yourself, You're Alone," a satirical comedy, 4m, (can pair with "The People in the Glass Paperweight") SF 25668, NSHS pb8080

McLellan, C. M. S., "The Shirkers," a thriller, 2m1f, SF 21690

McLure, James, "Laundry and Bourbon," a comedy, 3f, (published with and can pair with "Lone Star"; also, can pair with "Pvt. Wars") in *Texas Plays*, edited by William B. Martin (Dallas, Texas: Southern Methodist University Press, 1990), ISBN 0-87074-300-7, ISBN 0-87074-301-5, DPS 2790, NSHS pb7920

McLure, James, "Lone Star," a comedy, 3m, (published with and can pair with "Laundry and Bourbon"; also, can pair with "Pvt. Wars") in *Texas Plays*, edited by William B. Martin (Dallas, Texas: Southern Methodist University Press, 1990), ISBN 0-87074-300-7, ISBN 0-87074-301-5, DPS 2910, NSHS pb7920

McLure, James, "Pvt. Wars," a comedy, 3m, (can pair with "Lone Star" or "Laundry and Bourbon") DPS 3745

McNally, Terrence, "Botticelli," a drama, 3m (1m is a bit), (published with and can pair with "Tour" or "Next" [revised version]) in Terrence McNally's *Apple Pie* (New York: Dramatists Play Service, Inc., 1969), DPS 825, NSHS pb8164

McNally, Terrence, *"¡Cuba Si!"* an open stage fantasy, 1m3f, DPS 1490, NSHS pb8036

McNalley, Terrence, "Sweet Eros," a comedy, 1m1f, (published with and can pair with "Witness") DPS 4385, NSHS pb8043

McNally, Terrence, "Tour," a drama, 3m1f (+ 1m bit) [de-

scribed in DPS catalog as for 2m +2 bits], (published with and can pair with "Next" [revised version] or "Botticelli") in Terrence McNally's *Apple Pie* (New York: Dramatists Play Service, Inc., 1969), DPS 825, NSHS pb8164

McNalley, Terrence, "Witness," a black comedy, 3m1f, (published with and can pair with "Sweet Eros") DPS 4385, NSHS pb8043

McNeal, Claude, "The Courting of Kevin and Roxanne," a drama, 2m1f, SF 5717

McPherson, Nancy, "Camouflage," a Scottish play (genre?), 2m2f, in *Triad 73*, NPN

Mearns, Robert, "Now Departing," a comedy, 2m, in *Off-Off Broadway Festival Plays, Series 9*, SF 16059, NSHS 27532

Mearns, Robert, "Senior Prom," a comedy, 1m1f, **analyzed in Part 4, p. 240**, (published with and can pair with "Dispatches from Hell," "Molly and James," or "12:21 P.M.") in Double Image Theatre's *Off-Off Broadway Festival Plays, Tenth Series* (New York: Samuel French, Inc., 1985), SF 21652, NSHS 27488, ISBN 0-573-68904-0

Medcraft, Russell, "The First Dress Suit," a comedy, 2m2f, SF 8624, NSHS pb8069

Medoff, Mark, "Doing a Good One for the Red Man," a farce, 2m1f, (published with and can pair with "The Froegle Dictum" or "The Ultimate Grammar of Life") in Mark Medoff's *Four Short Plays* (New York: Dramatists Play Service, Inc., 1974) DPS 3107, NSHS pb8211, NSHS 26932

Medoff, Mark, "The Froegle Dictum," an absurdist comedy, 2m2f, (published with and can pair with "Doing a Good One for the Red Man" or "The Ultimate Grammar of Life") in Mark Medoff's *Four Short Plays* (New York: Dramatists Play Service, Inc., 1974), DPS 3107, NSHS pb8211, NSHS 26932

Medoff, Mark, "Ultimate Grammar of Life," a black comedy, 2m1f, (published with and can pair with "Doing a Good One for the Red Man" or "The Froegle Dictum") in Mark Medoff's *Four Short Plays* (New York: Dramatists Play Service, Inc., 1974) DPS 3107, NSHS pb8211, NSHS 26932

Melfi, Leonard, "Mr. Tucker's Taxi," a play (genre?), 2m2f, (published with and can pair with "Lena and Louie," "Rusty and Rico," "The Teaser's Taxi," "Toddy's Taxi," or "Tripper's Taxi") in Leonard Melfi's *Later Encounters: Seven One-Act Plays* (New York: Samuel French, Inc., 1980), SF 15705, ISBN 0-573-60050-3, NSHS

Melfi, Leonard, "The Shirt," a drama, 2m1f, (published with and can pair with "Birdbath," "Ferryboat," "Halloween," or "Lunchtime") in *Encounters: Six One-Act Plays*, SF 21608

Melfi, Leonard, "The Teaser's Taxi," a play (genre?), 2m2f, (published with and can pair with "Lena and Louie," "Mr. Tucker's Taxi," "Rusty and Rico," "Toddy's Taxi," or

"Tripper's Taxi") in Leonard Melfi's *Later Encounters: Seven One-Act Plays* (New York: Samuel French, Inc., 1980), SF 22620, ISBN 0-573-60050-3, NSHS

Melfi, Leonard, "Toddy's Taxi," a play (genre?), 2m2f, (published with and can pair with "Lena and Louie," "Mr. Tucker's Taxi," "Rusty and Rico," "The Teaser's Taxi," or "Tripper's Taxi") in Leonard Melfi's *Later Encounters: Seven One-Act Plays* (New York: Samuel French, Inc., 1980), SF 22723, ISBN 0-573-60050-3, NSHS

Melfi, Leonard, "Tripper's Taxi," a drama, 2m2f, (published with and can pair with "Lena and Louie," "Mr. Tucker's Taxi," "Rusty and Rico," "The Teaser's Taxi," or "Toddy's Taxi") in Leonard Melfi's *Later Encounters: Seven One-Act Plays* (New York: Samuel French, Inc., 1980), SF 22764, ISBN 0-573-60050-3, NSHS

Meltzer, Daniel, "Movie of the Month," a comedy, 2m, SF 17621

Meltzer, Daniel, "Waiting for to Go," a comedy, 1m1f, in *The Square Root of Love*, SF 21314

Merriam, Eve, "At Her Age," a drama, 1m3f, SF 3674

Merriam, Eve, Jack Hofsiss and Paula Wagner, "Out of Our Father's House," a play (genre?) with music based on Eve Merriam's *Growing up Female in America*, 3f (in six roles), SF 811, BP

Merzer, Glen, "Going Nowhere Apace," a ten-minute play (genre?), 1m3f, SF

Metcalfe, Stephen, "Sorrows and Sons," a drama, 3m, (published with and can pair with "Spittin' Image") in *Sorrows and Sons*, SF 21741, NSHS pb7896

Metcalfe, Stephen, "Spittin' Image," a drama, 2m, **analyzed in Part 4, p. 246**, (published with and can pair with "Sorrows and Sons") in *Sorrows and Sons*, SF 21742, NSHS pb7896

Meyer, Michael (translator from Swedish), Strindberg, August, "Miss Julie," a drama, translated by Elizabeth Sprigge, 1m2f (+extras), (can pair with "The Stronger") in *Eight Plays for Theatre*, edited by Robert Cohen (Mountain View, California: Mayfield Publishing Company, 1988), SF 15116; (translated by E. M. Sprinchorn, in *Seeds of Modern Drama*), SF 15674; (translated by Harry G. Carlson, in *Strindberg: Five Plays*), DPS 273; (translated by Michael Meyer) WKW, CPC, NSHS 29262, NSHS 19878, NSHS 19883, NSHS 29323, NSHS 29252, NSHS 5211, NSHS 27003, NSHS 16361, NSHS 20545

Meyer, Michael (translator from Swedish), "The Stronger," a drama by August Strindberg, 2f (+extra), (can pair with "Miss Julie") in *Plays by August Strindberg*, DPS 252, NSHS 29262

Michael, Lambe, "The Private Lives of Sherlock Holmes," a parody, 2m2f, in *Triad 65*, NPN

Miles, Keith, "Chekhov," a drama, 1m1f, **analyzed in Part 4, p. 191**, ISBN 0-573-60049-X, (published with "Dostoevsky") in *Russian Masters*, SF 20091, NSHS

p2511

Milgrim, Sally-Anne, "And None for the Road," a drama for youth, 3m1f (+ extras), in Sally-Anne Milgrim's *Plays to Play with Everywhere*, drawings by Anthony Vercesi (New York: Samuel French, Inc., 1991), ISBN 0-573-65225-0

Millar, Thomas P. (Canadian playwright), "Graduation Suite: The Contract," a comedy, 1m3f, (published with and can pair with "Graduation Suite: Shifting Gears") in Thomas P. Millar's *Graduation Suite* (West Vancouver, British Columbia, Canada: Palmer Press, 1987), ISBN 0-9693271-0-2, PAL

Millar, Thomas P. (Canadian playwright), "Graduation Suite: Shifting Gears," a drama, 1m2f, (published with and can pair with "Graduation Suite: The Contract") in Thomas P. Millar's *Graduation Suite* (West Vancouver, British Columbia, Canada: Palmer Press, 1987), ISBN 0-9693271-0-2, PAL

Miller, Arthur (1915-), "Clara," a drama, 3m1f, (published with and can pair with "I Can't Remember Anything"; also, can pair with "The Last Yankee") in Arthur Miller's *Danger: Memory!: Two Plays* (New York: Dramatists Play Service, Inc., 1987), DPS 1526, NSHS pb7869

Miller, Arthur (1915-), "I Can't Remember Anything," a drama, 1m1f, (published with and can pair with "Clara"; also, can pair with "The Last Yankee") in Arthur Miller's *Danger: Memory!: Two Plays* (New York: Dramatists Play Service, Inc., 1987), DPS 1526, NSHS pb7869

Miller, Arthur (1915-), "The Last Yankee," a drama, 2m, (can pair with "Clara" or "I Can't Remember Anything") DPS 2783

Miller, Ev, "The Leather Belt," a drama, 2m2f, DPC, NSHS pb163

Miller, Jason, "Lou Gehrig Did Not Die of Cancer," a comedy, 1m2f, (published with and can pair with "It's a Sin to Tell a Lie") DPS 3162

Milligan, Jason, "The Best Warm Beer in Brooklyn," a comedy, 3m, (published with and can pair with "John's Ring," "Next Tuesday," "Nights in Hohokus," or "Shoes") in *New York Stories: Five Plays About Life in New York*, SF 3953

Milligan, Jason, "Can't Buy Me Love," a comedy 3f, (published with and can pair with "Instincts," or "Lullaby") in *Southern Exposures: Five Plays About Life in the South*, SF 5779

Milligan, Jason, "Instincts," a drama, 2m, (published with and can pair with "Can't Buy Me Love," or "Lullaby") in *Southern Exposures: Five Plays About Life in the South*, SF 11656

Milligan, Jason, "John's Ring," a comedy, 3f, (published with and can pair with "The Best Warm Beer in Brooklyn," "Next Tuesday," "Nights in Hohokus," or "Shoes") in *New York Stories: Five Plays About Life in New York*,

SF 12635

Milligan, Jason, "Life After Elvis," a comedy, 3m1f, (published with and can pair with "Money Talks," "Road Trip," or "Shore Leave") in *Cross Country: Seven More One-Act Plays*, SF 14194

Milligan, Jason, "Lullaby," a drama, 2f, (published with and can pair with "Can't Buy Me Love," or "Instincts") in *Southern Exposures: Five Plays About Life in the South*, SF 14681

Milligan, Jason, "Money Talks," a comedy, 2m1f, (published with and can pair with "Life After Elvis," "Road Trip," or "Shore Leave") in *Cross Country: Seven More One-Act Plays*, SF 15265

Milligan, Jason, "Next Tuesday," a comedy, 1m1f, (published with and can pair with "The Best Warm Beer in Brooklyn," "John's Ring," "Nights in Hohokus," or "Shoes") in *New York Stories: Five Plays About Life in New York*, SF 15984

Milligan, Jason, "Nights in Hohokus," a comedy, 2m, (published with and can pair with "The Best Warm Beer in Brooklyn," "John's Ring," "Next Tuesday," or "Shoes") in *New York Stories: Five Plays About Life in New York*, SF 16649

Milligan, Jason, "Road Trip," a drama, 2m1f, (published with and can pair with "Life After Elvis," "Money Talks," or "Shore Leave") in *Cross Country: Seven More One-Act Plays*, SF 20136

Milligan, Jason, "Shoes," a drama, 3m, (published with and can pair with "The Best Warm Beer in Brooklyn," "John's Ring," "Next Tuesday," or "Nights in Hohokus") in *New York Stories: Five Plays About Life in New York*, SF 21135

Milligan, Jason, "Shore Leave," a drama, 4m, (published with and can pair with "Life After Elvis," "Money Talks," or "Road Trip") in *Cross Country: Seven More One-Act Plays*, SF 21117

Milne, Barbara, "The Wall Hanging," a drama, 1m2f, DPC W52, NSHS pb181

Milton, David Scott, "Duet," a drama-comedy, 1m, formerly available from SF

Mitchell, Ken (Canadian playwright), "Heroes," a black comedy, 3m1f, (published with and can pair with "Babel Rap") in *Six Canadian Plays* (Toronto, Ontario, Canada: Playwrights Canada Press, 1992), ISBN 0-88754-469-X, PCP

Mizer, Jean, "Golden Slippers," a drama, 1m3f, HPC

Moffatt, Margaret, "All Risks," a drama, 4f, in *Triad 78*, NPN

Montley, Patricia, "Valley Forgery," a brief satire, 3f, (published with and can pair with "Advice to a New Actor," "The Affidavit," "The American Way," "Anniversary," "Auld Lang Syne, or I'll Bet You Think This Play Is About You," "Bug Swatter," "Checkers," "Coming for a Visit," "Dalmation," "Dog Eat Dog," "Drowned Out,"

"Fireworks," "Interview," "Jumping," "Money," "One Beer Too Many," "Potato Girl," "Property of the Dallas Cowboys," "The Split Decision," "Watermelon Boats," or "Widows") in Norman A. Bert's *Norman A.One-Act Plays for Acting Students*, MPL, ISBN 0-916260-47-X, pb7929

Mori, Brian Richard, "Dreams of Flight," a tragicomedy, 2m, DPS 1721

Morris, Peter, "The Heartbreak Tour," a comedy, 2m2f, in *Off-Off Broadway Festival Plays, 15th Series*, SF 10687, NSHS pb8079

Morrison, Katherin E., "Lost in the Shuffle," a comedy, 4f, (Franklin, Ohio: Eldridge Publishing Company, 1987) EPC

Morse, Jack, "The Uncertain Samaritan," a comedy, 2m1f, DPC, NSHS pb192

Morse, Jack, "Violets, Gladiolas and Arthur's Breakfast," a drama, 1m1f, DPC, NSHS pb6085

Mortimer, John (English playwright and barrister), "Bermondsey," a drama, 2m2f, in *Come as You Are*, SF 4626, NSHS pb8037

Mortimer, John (English playwright and barrister), "The Dock Brief," a comedy, 2m, **analyzed in Part 4, p. 198**, (can pair with "What Shall We Tell Caroline?"), SF 6649, NSHS

Mortimer, John (English playwright and barrister), "Gloucester Road," a drama, 2m2f, SF, NSHS pb8037

Mortimer, John (English playwright and barrister), "Lunch Hour," a drama, 1m2f, SF 14662

Mortimer, John (English playwright and barrister), "Marble Arch," a comedy, 2m2f, SF, NSHS pb8037

Mortimer, John (English playwright and barrister), "Mill Hill," a comedy, 2m2f, in *Come as You Are*, SF 15665

Mortimer, John (English playwright and barrister), "What Shall We Tell Caroline?" a comedy, 2m2f, (can pair with "The Dock Brief"), SF 25658

Morton, John Maddison, "Box and Cox," an English farce, 2m1f, **analyzed in Part 4, p. 189**, BP (no royalty with purchase of three copies), SF 4672 (no royalty), HDS, GCB, NSHS 5345

Mosel, Tad, "Impromptu," a drama, 2m2f, **analyzed in Part 4, p. 208**, DPS 2495, HDS, NSHS 21387

Mrozek, Slawomir [Polish playwright, 1930-   ), "Striptease" [1961], a drama, 2m, SF, NSHS 29300

Mueller, Lavonne, "Advice to a New Actor," a brief monologue, 1m or 1f, (published with and can pair with "The Affidavit," "The American Way," "Anniversary," "Auld Lang Syne, or I'll Bet You Think This Play Is About You," "Bug Swatter," "Checkers," "Coming for a Visit," "Dalmation," "Dog Eat Dog," "Drowned Out," "Fireworks," "Interview," "Jumping," "Money," "One Beer Too Many," "Phonecall from Sunkist," "Potato Girl," "Property of the Dallas Cowboys," "The Split Decision," "Valley Forgery," "Watermelon Boats," or "Widows") in Norman A. Bert's *Norman A.One-Act Plays for Acting Students*, MPL, ISBN 0-916260-47-X, pb7929

Mueller, Lavonne, "The American Way," a brief comedy, 1m2f, (published with and can pair with "Advice to a New Actor," "The Affidavit," "Anniversary," "Auld Lang Syne, or I'll Bet You Think This Play Is About You," "Bug Swatter," "Checkers," "Coming for a Visit," "Dalmation," "Dog Eat Dog," "Drowned Out," "Fireworks," "Interview," "Jumping," "Money," "One Beer Too Many," "Phonecall from Sunkist," "Potato Girl," "Property of the Dallas Cowboys," "The Split Decision," "Valley Forgery," "Watermelon Boats," or "Widows") in Norman A. Bert's *Norman A.One-Act Plays for Acting Students*, MPL, ISBN 0-916260-47-X, pb7929

Munro, H. H. (Hector Hugh, a.k.a. Saki , source Scottish short story writer, 1870-1916), "Dusk," a comedy adapted by Jules Tasca from Saki (H. H. Munro), 3m, (published with and can pair with "The Background," "Blind Spot," "The Hen," "The Reticence of Lady Anne," "Secret Sin" "The Tiger," or "The Unrest Cure") in Jules Tasca's *Tales by Saki: Adapted for Stage by Jules Tasca* (New York: Samuel French, Inc., 1989), ISBN 0-573-62560-3, SF 22133, NSHS pb7798

Munro, H. H. (Hector Hugh, a.k.a. Saki , source Scottish short story writer, 1870-1916), "The Open Window," a comedy, adapted by James Fuller from the short story by Saki (H. H. Munro), 1m3f (+ extras), (can pair with "Vicky") DPC O17, HDS, NSHS

Munro, H. H. (Hector Hugh, a.k.a. Saki , source Scottish short story writer, 1870-1916), "The Reticence of Lady Anne," a comedy adapted by Jules Tasca from the short story by Saki (H. H. Munro), 1m, (published with and can pair with "The Background," "Blind Spot," Dusk," "The Hen," "Secret Sin," "The Tiger," "The Unrest Cure") in Jules Tasca's *Tales by Saki: Adapted for Stage by Jules Tasca* (New York: Samuel French, Inc.), ISBN 0-573-62560-3, SF 22133, NSHS pb7798, NSHS pb8113

Munro, H. H. (Hector Hugh, a.k.a. Saki , source Scottish short story writer, 1870-1916), "Secret Sin," a comedy adapted for the stage by Jules Tasca from the short story by Saki (H. H. Munro), 2m1f, (published with and can pair with "The Background," "Blind Spot," Dusk," "The Hen," "The Reticence of Lady Anne," "The Tiger," "The Unrest Cure") in Jules Tasca's *Tales by Saki: Adapted for Stage by Jules Tasca* (New York: Samuel French, Inc.), ISBN 0-573-62560-3, SF 22133, NSHS pb7798, NSHS pb8113

Munro, H. H. (Hector Hugh, a.k.a. Saki , source Scottish short story writer, 1870-1916), "The Unrest Cure," a comedy adapted for the stage by Jules Tasca from the short story by Saki (H. H. Munro), 2m1f, (published with and can pair with "The Background," "Blind Spot," "Dusk," "The Hen," "The Reticence of Lady Anne," "Secret Sin," or "The Tiger") in Jules Tasca's *Tales by Saki: Adapted*

for Stage by Jules Tasca (New York: Samuel French, Inc.), ISBN 0-573-62560-3, SF 22133, NSHS pb7798, NSHS pb8113

Munro, H. H. (Hector Hugh, a.k.a. Saki , source Scottish short story writer, 1870-1916), "Vicky," a comedy by Phyllis Vernick from Saki (H. H. Munro), 2m2f, (can pair with "The Open Window") DPC V13

Murch, Edward, "The Revival," a comedy, 1m2f, BP

Murphree, Dorothy R., "The Mask," a drama, 2m2f, DPC M22, HDS, NSHS pb180, NSHS pb7743, NSHS pb7745

Murray, William (translator from Italian), "I'm Dreaming, but Am I?" [*"Sogno (ma forse no),"* 1931] a drama by Luigi Pirandello, 2m1f, (published with and can pair with "At the Exit," "Chee-Chee," "The Man with the Flower in His Mouth," or "The Vise") in Pirandello's *One-Act Plays*, translated into English from the original Italian by William Murray (New York: Samuel French, Inc., 1970), SF 11601, NSHS, ISBN 0-573-60039-2

Murray, William (translator from Italian), "The Vise" [*"La Morsa,"* 1910], a drama by Luigi Pirandello, 2m2f, (published with and can pair with "At the Exit," "Chee-Chee," "The Man with the Flower in His Mouth," or "I'm Dreaming, but Am I?") in Pirandello's *One-Act Plays*, translated into English from the original Italian by William Murray (New York: Samuel French, Inc., 1970), SF 24601, NSHS

N

Nash, N. Richard, "Rouge Atomique," a fantasy-drama, 2f, DPS 3895

Nass, Elyse, "Admit One," a comedy, 1m1f, (published with and can pair with "The Cat Connection" or "Second Chance"; also, can pair with "Avenue of Dream") in Elyse Nass' *Three One-Act Plays About the Elderly* (New York: Samuel French, Inc., 1990), ISBN 0-573-69205-X, SF 5785, NSHS pb8161

Nass, Elyse, "Avenue of Dream," a drama, 2f, (can pair with "Admit One," "The Cat Connection" or "Second Chance") DPS 875

Nass, Elyse, "The Cat Connection," a comedy, 2f, (published with and can pair with "Admit One" or "Second Chance"; also, can pair with "Avenue of Dream") in Elyse Nass' *Three One-Act Plays About the Elderly* (New York: Samuel French, Inc., 1990), ISBN 0-573-69205-X, SF 5785, NSHS pb8161

Nass, Elyse, "Second Chance," a comedy, 2f, (published with and can pair with "Admit One" or "The Cat Connection"; also, can pair with "Avenue of Dream") in Elyse Nass' *Three One-Act Plays About the Elderly* (New York: Samuel French, Inc., 1990), ISBN 0-573-69205-X, SF 21661, NSHS pb8161

National Christian Education Council (?), "The Flame," a biblical parable, 2m2f, in National Christian Education Council's *The Flame* (Redhill, Surrey, England: National Christian Education Council, 1990), ISBN 0-7197-0709-9, NCE

Nelson, Eileen, "Baby Talk," a drama, 4f, in *Triad 69*, NPN

Neuman, Colleen, "Admissions," a drama, 3f, PDS

Niggli, Josephine (a.k.a. Josefina, Mexican-born American playwright), "Tooth or Shave," a comedy, 2m2f, SF 22730, NSHS pb8088 [Note: Niggli's "Sunday Costs Five Pesos," 1m4f, SF 1010, despite its cast size being beyond the scope of this index, merits passing mention as a hilarious ethnic comedy that could pair with "Tooth or Shave."]

Nigro, Don, "Animal Salvation," a bare-stage dramatic monologue, 1m, (published with and can pair with "Boneyard," "The Dark," or "Diogenes the Dog") in *Genesis and Other Plays*, SF 3704, NSHS

Nigro, Don, "Autumn Leaves," a bare-stage (+ four wooden chairs) comedic monologue, 1f, (published with and can pair with "Border Minstrelsy," "Golgotha," "The King of the Cats," "Madeline Nude in the Rain Perhaps," "Mink Ties," "Picasso," "Sudden Acceleration," or "Winchelsea Dround") in *Winchelsea Dround and Other Plays: Nine Monologue Plays* (New York: Samuel French, Inc., 1992), ISBN 0-573-62598-0, SF 25226

Nigro, Don, "Bible," a bare-stage dark comedy, 1m2f, (published with and can pair with "Scarecrow"; also, can pair with "Crossing the Bar" or "God's Spies") in *Something in the Basement and Other Plays*, SF 4699, NSHS

Nigro, Don, "Binnorie," a drama, 2f, in *The Gypsy Woman and Other Plays*, SF 4201

Nigro, Don, "Boneyard," a bare-stage comedy, 1m2f, (published with and can pair with "Animal Salvation," "The Dark," or "Diogenes the Dog") in *Genesis and Other Plays*, SF 4210, NSHS

Nigro, Don, "Border Minstrelsy," a bare-stage comedic monologue, 1m, (published with and can pair with "Autumn Leaves," "Golgotha," "The King of the Cats," "Madeline Nude in the Rain Perhaps," "Mink Ties," "Picasso," "Sudden Acceleration," or "Winchelsea Dround") in *Winchelsea Dround and Other Plays: Nine Monologue Plays* (New York: Samuel French, Inc., 1992), ISBN 0-573-62598-0, SF 4220

Nigro, Don, "Crossing the Bar," a comedy, 1m2f, (published with and can pair with "God's Spies"; also, can pair with "Bible") ISBN 0-573-60050-3, SF 5935, NSHS 27501

Nigro, Don, "The Dark," a bare-stage dramatic monologue, 1m, (published with and can pair with "Animal Salvation," "Boneyard," or "Diogenes the Dog") in *Genesis and Other Plays*, SF 5938

Nigro, Don, "The Daughters of Edward D. Boit," a dark comedy, 4f, **analyzed in Part 4, p. 196**, (published with and can pair with "Specter" or "The Woodman and the Goblins") in *Green Man and Other Plays*, SF, NSHS pb7916,

ISBN 0-573-62207-8

Nigro, Don, "Diogenes the Dog," a bare-stage comedic monologue, 1m, (published with and can pair with "Animal Salvation." "Boneyard," or "The Dark") in *Genesis and Other Plays*, SF 6737

Nigro, Don, "God's Spies," a comedy, 1m2f, (published with and can pair with "Crossing the Bar") ISBN 0-573-60050-3, SF 9643, NSHS 27501

Nigro, Don, "Golgotha," a bare-stage dramatic monologue, 1m, (published with and can pair with "Autumn Leaves," "Border Minstrelsy," "The King of the Cats," "Madeline Nude in the Rain Perhaps," "Mink Ties," "Picasso," "Sudden Acceleration," or "Winchelsea Dround") in *Winchelsea Dround and Other Plays: Nine Monologue Plays* (New York: Samuel French, Inc., 1992), ISBN 0-573-62598-0, SF 9942

Nigro, Don, "The King of the Cats," a bare-stage dramatic monologue, 1m, (published with and can pair with "Autumn Leaves," "Border Minstrelsy," "Golgotha," "Madeline Nude in the Rain Perhaps," "Mink Ties," "Picasso," "Sudden Acceleration," or "Winchelsea Dround") in *Winchelsea Dround and Other Plays: Nine Monologue Plays* (New York: Samuel French, Inc., 1992), ISBN 0-573-62598-0, SF 13037

Nigro, Don, "Madeline Nude in the Rain Perhaps," a bare-stage dramatic monologue, 1m, (published with and can pair with "Autumn Leaves," "Border Minstrelsy," "Golgotha," "The King of the Cats," "Mink Ties," "Picasso," "Sudden Acceleration," or "Winchelsea Dround") in *Winchelsea Dround and Other Plays: Nine Monologue Plays* (New York: Samuel French, Inc., 1992), ISBN 0-573-62598-0, SF 14942

Nigro, Don, "Mink Ties," a bare-stage comedic monologue, 1m, (published with and can pair with "Autumn Leaves," "Border Minstrelsy," "Golgotha," "The King of the Cats," "Madeline Nude in the Rain Perhaps," "Picasso," "Sudden Acceleration," or "Winchelsea Dround") in *Winchelsea Dround and Other Plays: Nine Monologue Plays* (New York: Samuel French, Inc., 1992), ISBN 0-573-62598-0, SF 15600

Nigro, Don, "Picasso," a bare-stage comedic monologue, 1m, (published with and can pair with "Autumn Leaves," "Border Minstrelsy," "Golgotha," "The King of the Cats," "Madeline Nude in the Rain Perhaps," "Mink Ties," "Sudden Acceleration," or "Winchelsea Dround") in *Winchelsea Dround and Other Plays: Nine Monologue Plays*, SF 15600

Nigro, Don, "Scarecrow," a bare-stage drama, 1m2f, (published and can pair with "Bible"; also, can pair with "Crossing the Bar" or "God's Spies") in *Something in the Basement and Other Plays*, SF 21619

Nigro, Don, "Sudden Acceleration," a bare-stage comedic monologue, 1m, (published with and can pair with "Autumn Leaves," "Border Minstrelsy," "Golgotha," "The

King of the Cats," "Madeline Nude in the Rain Perhaps," "Mink Ties," "Picasso," or "Winchelsea Dround") in *Winchelsea Dround and Other Plays: Nine Monologue Plays*, SF 21414

Nigro, Don, "Winchelsea Dround," a bare-stage dramatic monologue, 1f, (published with and can pair with "Autumn Leaves," "Border Minstrelsy," "Golgotha," "The King of the Cats," "Madeline Nude in the Rain Perhaps," "Mink Ties," "Picasso," or "Sudden Acceleration") in Don Nigro's *Winchelsea Dround and Other Plays: Nine Monologue Plays* (New York: Samuel French, Inc., 1992), ISBN 0-573-62598-0, SF 25226

Nigro, Don, "The Woodman and the Goblins," a bare-stage dark comedy, 1m3f, (published with and can pair with "Specter" or "The Daughters of Edward D. Boit") in *Green Man and Other Plays*, SF 25731, NSHS 7916

Noble, Dennis, "A Game," a drama, 4m or 4f, (can pair with "The Puppet Master") SF, IEC 062-5

Noble, Dennis, "The Puppet Master," a bare-stage fantasy, 2m1f, (can pair with "A Game") BP

Nolte, Charles M., "Do Not Pass Go," a drama, 2m, UM

Noojin, Randy, "Boaz," a drama, 2m, (can pair with "Unbeatable Harold" or "You Can't Trust the Male") DPC B57, NSHS pb184

Noojin, Randy, "Unbeatable Harold," a comedy, 1m1f, (can pair with "Boaz" or "You Can't Trust the Male") DPC U19, NSHS pb171

Noojin, Randy, "You Can't Trust the Male," a comedy, 1m1f, (can pair with "Boaz" or "Unbeatable Harold") DPC Y18

Norman, Marsha, "Third and Oak: The Laundromat," a comedy, 2f, (can pair with "Third and Oak: The Pool Hall") DPS 4485

Norman, Marsha, "Third and Oak: The Pool Hall," a comedy-drama, 2m1f, (can pair with "Third and Oak: The Laundromat") DPS 4486

Norman, Victoria, "The Pledge," a drama, 2f, in *Off-Off Broadway Festival Plays, 15th Series*, SF 18953, NSHS pb8079

Nottonson, Ira N., "Will You Join Me for Dinner," a comedy, 2m2f, BP, NSHS pb8155

O

O T'ae-sok (Korean playwright), "The Drug Peddler," a comedy, 1m, PIR

O'Brien, John, "Memory," a drama, 3m1f, DPC M52

O'Casey, Sean (Irish playwright, 1880-1964), "The End of the Beginning," a comedy, 2m1f, LD, NSHS 28268

O'Casey, Sean (Irish playwright, 1880-1964), "A Pound on Demand," a brief sketch, 3m1f, LD, NSHS 28268

O'Donnell, Mark, "The Goblins Plot to Murder God," a ten-minute play (genre?), 1m2f or 3f or 3m or 2m1f or 4m or 4f or 1m3f or 2m2f or 3m1f, (can pair with "Marred Bliss") formerly available from SF

O'Donnell, Mark, "Marred Bliss," a ten-minute play (genre?), 2m2f, (published with and can pair with "Americansaint," "Après Opéra," "'The Asshole Murder Case,'" "Bread," "Cold Water," "Cover," "Downtown," "The Drummer," "The Duck Pond," "Eating Out," "Electric Roses," "The Field," "4 A.M. (open all night)," "Looking Good," "Love and Peace, Mary Jo," "Loyalties," "Perfect," "The Road to Ruin," "Spades," or "Watermelon Boats"; also, can pair with "The Goblins Plot to Murder God") in *25 10-Minute Plays from Actors Theatre of Louisville*, edited by Actors Theatre of Louisville (New York: Samuel French, Inc., 1989), ISBN 0-573-62558-1, SF 6716

O'Hara, Frank, "Try! Try!" a verse comedy, 2m1f, GP, NSHS 16607

O'Neill, Eugene Gladstone (American playwright, 1888-1953)**, "Before Breakfast," a drama, 1f, analyzed in Part 4, p. 185**, DPS 405, (published with and can pair with "The Dreamy Kid," "Fog," "Shell Shock," "Thirst," or "A Wife for a Life") in *Eugene O'Neill's Complete Plays, 1913-1920,* Vol. 1, ed. by Travis Bogard (New York: Random House, Inc., 1988), ISBN 0-940450-48-8, NSHS pb8121

O'Neill, Eugene Gladstone (American playwright, 1888-1953), "The Dreamy Kid," a drama, 1m3f, (published with and can pair with "Before Breakfast," "Fog," "Shell Shock," "The Sniper," "Thirst," or "A Wife for a Life") in *Eugene O'Neill's Complete Plays, 1913-1920,* Vol. 1, ed. by Travis Bogard (New York: Random House, Inc., 1988), ISBN 0-940450-48-8, DPS 405, NSHS pb8121

O'Neill, Eugene Gladstone (American playwright, 1888-1953), "Fog," a drama, 2m1f or 3m1f, not to be confused with the one-act play of the same name by Robert Patrick (published with and can pair with "Before Breakfast," "The Dreamy Kid," "Shell Shock," "The Sniper," "Thirst," or "A Wife for a Life") in *Eugene O'Neill's Complete Plays, 1913-1920,* Vol. 1, ed. by Travis Bogard (New York: Random House, Inc., 1988), ISBN 0-940450-48-8, NSHS pb8121

O'Neill, Eugene Gladstone (American playwright, 1888-1953), "Hughie," a drama, 2m, (can pair with "Before Breakfast," "The Dreamy Kid," "Fog," "Shell Shock," "The Sniper," "Thirst," or "A Wife for a Life") in *Eugene O'Neill's Complete Plays, 1932-1943* (New York: Library of America, 1988), ISBN 0-940450-48-8, DPS, NSHS 11910, NSHS 28438, NSHS 27069

O'Neill, Eugene Gladstone (American playwright, 1888-1953), "Recklessness," a drama, 2m2f (can pair with "Before Breakfast," "The Dreamy Kid," "Fog," "Shell Shock," "Thirst," or "A Wife for a Life") in *Eugene O'Neill's Complete Plays, Vol. 1, 1913-1920,* ed. by Travis Bogard (New York: Random House, Inc., 1988), ISBN 0-940450-48-8, SF 20655

O'Neill, Eugene Gladstone (American playwright, 1888-

1953), "Shell Shock," a drama, 4m or 3m (+ extra m), in Eugene O'Neill, *Complete Plays,* Vol. 1, SF 21616; also DPS 405, (published with and can pair with "Before Breakfast," "The Dreamy Kid," "The Sniper," "Thirst," or "A Wife for a Life") in *Eugene O'Neill's Complete Plays, 1913-1920,* Vol. 1, edited by Travis Bogard (New York: Random House, Inc., 1988), ISBN 0-940450-48-8, NSHS

O'Neill, Eugene Gladstone (American playwright, 1888-1953), "The Sniper," a drama, 4m (+ 4m extras), (published with and can pair with "Before Breakfast," "The Dreamy Kid," "Shell Shock," "Thirst," or "A Wife for a Life") in *Eugene O'Neill's Complete Plays, 1913-1920,* Vol. 1, ed. by Travis Bogard (New York: Random House, Inc., 1988), ISBN 0-940450-48-8, probably DPS (?), NSHS

O'Neill, Eugene Gladstone (American playwright, 1888-1953), "Thirst," a drama, 2m1f, *Eugene O'Neill's Complete Plays, 1913-1920,* Vol. 1, SF 22627; also (published with and can pair with "Before Breakfast," "The Dreamy Kid," "Fog," "Shell Shock," "The Sniper," or "A Wife for a Life") in *Eugene O'Neill's Complete Plays, 1913-1920,* Vol. 1, ed. by Travis Bogard (New York: Random House, Inc., 1988), ISBN 0-940450-48-8, NSHS pb8121

O'Neill, Eugene Gladstone (American playwright, 1888-1953), "The Web," a drama, 2m1f, in *Eugene O'Neill's Complete Plays, 1913-1920,* Vol. 1, ed. by Travis Bogard (New York: Random House, Inc., 1988), ISBN 0-940450-48-8, NSHS pb8121, SF 25613

O'Neill, Eugene Gladstone (American playwright, 1888-1953), "A Wife for a Life," a drama, 3m, (published with and can pair with "Before Breakfast," "Fog," "The Dreamy Kid," "Shell Shock," "The Sniper," or "Thirst") in *Eugene O'Neill's Complete Plays,* Vol. 1, *1913-1920,* ed. by Travis Bogard (New York: Random House, Inc., 1988), ISBN 0-940450-48-8, SF 25615, NSHS pb8121, probably DPS

Oates, Joyce Carol, "The Ballad of Love Canal," a drama, 3m1f, in Joyce Carol Oates' *The Ballad of Love Canal* (New York: Plume [New American Library], 1991), ISBN 0-452-26701-3, NAL

Oates, Joyce Carol, "The Eclipse," a drama, 1m3f, (published with and can pair with "Toneclusters") in *In Darkest America,* SF 7633, NSHS pb8092

Oates, Joyce Carol, "Procedure," a ten-minute play (genre?), 2f, (can pair with "The Ballad of Love Canal," "The Eclipse," or "Toneclusters") formerly available from SF

Oates, Joyce Carol, "Toneclusters," a bare-stage drama, 1m1f, (published with and can pair with "The Eclipse") in *In Darkest America,* SF 22727, NSHS pb8092

Ogden, Alan, "Better Halves," a play (genre?), 4f, in *Triad 68,* NPN

Okimoto, Jean Davies, "Hum It Again, Jeremy," a drama for youth, 3m1f, in *Center Stage: One-Act Plays for Teen-*

age Readers and Actors, edited by Donald R. Gallo (New York: Harper & Row, 1990), ISBN 0-06-022170-4, ISBN 0-06-022171-2, HR

Olfson, Lewy, "Great Caesar's Ghost," a farce for youth, 4m, in Sylvia E. Kamerman's *The Big Book of Comedies: 25 One-Act Plays, Skits, Curtain Raisers, and Adaptations for Young Actors* (Boston: Plays, Inc., 1989), ISBN 0-8238-0289-2, PI

Oliver, William I., "The Stallion," a drama, 3m1f (+ extras), MM, NSHS 2401

Olsson, Ninnie (source writer), "Stomach-Ache," a musical for children translated and adapted by Anita Page and Lisa Tate from Ninnie Olsson, 1m2f, BP

Orr, Mary, "Roommates," a bare-stage comedy, 2f, in Mary Orr's *Roommates* (New York: Dramatists Play Service, Inc., 1989), DPS 3871

Orton, Joe (English playwright, 1939-1967), "The Ruffian on the Stair," a drama, 2m1f, in *The Complete Plays of Joe Orton,* SF 20638

Owens, Daniel W., "The Box," a symbolic allegory in seven scenes, 3m1f (+ extra), (published with and can pair with "Birth of a Blues!" "Gettin' It Together," "Hospice," or "The Past Is the Past") in *New Plays for the Black Theatre,* edited by Woodie King, Jr. (Chicago: Third World Press, 1989), ISBN 0-88378-124-7, TWP

Owens, Rochelle, "Chucky's Hunch," a comedy-drama, 1m, SF

Owens, Rosemary, "The Haunted Auditorium," a mystery, 2m2f, DPC H12

P

Page, Alex, and Anita Page (translators from German), "Noodle Doodle Box," a comedy for children by Paul Maar translated from the German by Anita and Alex Page, 3m or 3f, BP

Page, Anita, and Alex Page (translators from German), "Noodle Doodle Box," a comedy for children by Paul Maar translated from the German by Anita and Alex Page, 3m or 3f, (can pair with "Stomach-Ache") BP

Page, Anita, and Lisa Tate (adaptors), "Stomach-Ache," a musical for children translated and adapted from Ninnie Olsson, 1m2f, (can pair with "Noodle Doodle Box") BP

Pape, Ralph, "Girls We Have Known," a comedy, 2m, (published with and can pair with "Soap Opera" or "Warm and Tender Love") in *Girls We Have Known and Other One Act Plays,* DPS 2137

Pape, Ralph, "Soap Opera," a comedy, 1m2f, (published with and can pair with "Girls We Have Known" or "Warm and Tender Love") in *Girls We Have Known and Other One Act Plays,* DPS 2137

Pape, Ralph, "Warm and Tender Love," a comedy, 1m1f, (published with and can pair with "Girls We Have

Known" or "Soap Opera") in *Girls We Have Known and Other One Act Plays*, DPS 2137

Parente, Paul, "Two and Twenty," a bare-stage comic-drama, 1m1f, in *Off-Off Broadway Festival Plays, 12th Series*, SF 22244

Parker, Dorothy, "Here We Are," a comedy from the short story of the same name, 1m1f, **analyzed in Part 4, p. 206**, variously published in Modern Library, possibly SF (?), which controls Dorothy Parker's *Ladies of the Corridor*, NSHS pb4019, NSHS 14824, NSHS 20483, NSHS 21389, NSHS 21514, NSHS 21776

Parker, Louis N., "A Minuet," a drama, 2m1f, in *One Act Plays for Stage and Study: A Collection of Twenty-five Plays by Well-known* [sic] *Dramatists, American, English and Irish, First Series*, preface by Augustus Thomas (New York: Samuel French, Inc., 1925), SF 15675, NSHS pb5469

Parkhirst, Douglas, "This Way to Heaven," a fantasy-comedy, 2m2f, , HDS, SF 1073, NSHS pb8081

Parnell, Peter, "Scooter Thomas Makes It to the Top of the World," a drama, 2m, HDS, DPS 3982

Patrick, John (1905-), "Ambiguity," a comedy, 2m1f, in *Sex on the Sixth Floor*, SF 3630

Patrick, John (1905-), "Aptitude," a comedy, 2m1f, in *People!* SF 18041

Patrick, John (1905-), "Boredom," a comedy, 2m1f, in *People!* SF 18041

Patrick, John (1905-), "The Chiropodist," a comedy, 2m2f, (published with and can pair with "The Psychiatrist," "The Gynecologist," or "The Physician") in John Patrick's *The Doctor Will See You Now* (New York: Dramatists Play Service, 1991, DPS 1677

Patrick, John (1905-), "Christmas Spirit," a comedy, 2m1f, in *People!* SF 18041

Patrick, John (1905-), "Co-Incidence," a comedy, 2m1f, in *It's a Dog's Life*, SF 11087

Patrick, John (1905-), "Compulsion," a comedy, 2m1f, (published with and can pair with "Integrity" or "Habit") in *Divorce—Anyone?* DPS 1675

Patrick, John (1905-), "Confession," a comedy, 2m1f, (published with and can pair with "Loyalty" or "Empathy") in *Suicide—Anyone?* DPS 4340

Patrick, John (1905-), "Decisions," a comedy, 2m1f, in *Love Nest for Three*, SF 6635

Patrick, John (1905-), "The Divorce," a comedy, 2m1f, in *It's a Dog's Life* SF 11087

Patrick, John (1905-), "Empathy," a comedy, 2m1f, (published with and can pair with "Loyalty" or "Confession") in *Suicide—Anyone?* DPS 4340

Patrick, John (1905-), "Fettucine," a comedy, 2m1f, in *That's Not My Father!* SF 8166

Patrick, John (1905-), "Frustration," a comedy, 2m1f, in *Sex on the Sixth Floor*, SF 8077

Patrick, John (1905-), "The Gift," a comedy, 2m1f, in *It's*

a Dog's Life, SF 11087

Patrick, John (1905-), "The Gynecologist," a comedy, 2m2f, (published with and can pair with "The Psychiatrist," "The Chiropodist," or "The Physician") in John Patrick's *The Doctor Will See You Now* (New York: Dramatists Play Service, 1991, DPS 1677

Patrick, John (1905-), "Habit," a comedy, 2m1f, (published with and can pair with "Compulsion" or "Integrity") in *Divorce—Anyone?* DPS 1675

Patrick, John (1905-), "Integrity," a comedy, 2m1f, (published with and can pair with "Compulsion" or "Habit") in *Divorce—Anyone?* DPS 1675

Patrick, John (1905-), "Loyalty," a comedy, 2m1f, (published with and can pair with "Empathy" or "Confession") in *Suicide—Anyone?* DPS 4340, SF 11087

Patrick, John (1905-), "Masquerade," a comedy, 2m1f, in *That's Not My Father!* SF 15583

Patrick, John (1905-), "Optimism," a comedy, 1m2f, in *That's Not My Mother!* SF 17954

Patrick, John (1905-), "The Physician," a comedy, 2m1f, (published with and can pair with "The Chiropodist," "The Gynecologist," or "The Psychiatrist") in John Patrick's *The Doctor Will See You Now* (New York: Dramatists Play Service, 1991), DPS 1677

Patrick, John (1905-), "Progression," a comedy, 2m1f, in *Love Nest for Three*, SF 18602

Patrick, John (1905-), "The Psychiatrist," a comedy, 2m1f, (published with and can pair with "The Chiropodist," "The Gynecologist," or "The Physician") in John Patrick's *The Doctor Will See You Now* (New York: Dramatists Play Service, 1991, DPS 1677

Patrick, John (1905-), "Raconteur," a comedy, 2m1f, in *That's Not My Father!* SF 19974

Patrick, John (1905-), "Redemption," a comedy, 2m1f, in *That's Not My Mother!* SF 20924

Patrick, John (1905-), "Seniority," a comedy, 2m1f, in *That's Not My Mother!* SF 20970

Patrick, John (1905-), "Strategy," a comedy, 2m1f, in *Love Nest for Three*, SF 21603

Patrick, John (1905-), "Tenacity," a comedy, 2m1f, in *Sex on the Sixth Floor*, SF 22602

Patrick, Robert, "Action," a comedy, 2m2f, part of the comedy suite *Lights, Camera, Action*, in Robert Patrick's *Cheep Theatricks*, SF 3008

Patrick, Robert, "The Arnold Bliss Show," a farce, 3m1f, in Robert Patrick's *Cheep Theatricks*, SF 3655

Patrick, Robert, "Bill Batchelor Road," a drama, 3m, (published with and can pair with "Fairy Tale," "Fog," "Odd Number," "One of Those People," "Pouf Positive," or "The River Jordan") in Robert Patrick's *Untold Decades* (New York: St. Martin's Press, Inc., 1988), ISBN 0-312-02307-3

Patrick, Robert, "Camera," a comedy, 2m2f, part of the comedy suite *Lights, Camera, Action,* in Robert Patrick's

Cheep Theatricks, SF 302

Patrick, Robert, "Fairy Tale," a drama, 2m (+ extras), (published with and can pair with "Bill Batchelor Road," "Fog," "Odd Number," "One of Those People," "Pouf Positive," or "The River Jordan") in Robert Patrick's *Untold Decades* (New York: St. Martin's Press, Inc., 1988), ISBN 0-312-02307-3

Patrick, Robert, "Fog," a drama, 2m (+ extras), not to be confused with the one-oct play of the same name by Eugene O'Neill (published with and can pair with "Bill Batchelor Road," "Fairy Tale," "Odd Number," "One of Those People," "Pouf Positive," or "The River Jordan") in Robert Patrick's *Untold Decades* (New York: St. Martin's Press, Inc., 1988), ISBN 0-312-02307-3

Patrick, Robert, "Help, I Am," a monologue (drama), 1m, in Robert Patrick's *Cheep Theatricks*, SF 10629

Patrick, Robert, "Lights," a comedy, 2m2f, part of the comedy suite *Lights, Camera, Action* in Robert Patrick's *Cheep Theatricks*, SF 14604

Patrick, Robert, "My Cup Ranneth Over," a comedy, 2f, DPS 3300

Patrick, Robert, "Odd Number," a drama, 3m, (published with and can pair with "Fairy Tale," "Fog," "Bill Batchelor Road," "One of Those People," "Pouf Positive," or "The River Jordan") in Robert Patrick's *Untold Decades* (New York: St. Martin's Press, Inc., 1988), ISBN 0-312-02307-3

Patrick, Robert, "One of Those People," a drama, 2m, (published with and can pair with "Odd Number," "Fairy Tale," "Bill Batchelor Road," "Fog," "Pouf Positive," or "The River Jordan") in Robert Patrick's *Untold Decades* (New York: St. Martin's Press, Inc., 1988), ISBN 0-312-02307-3

Patrick, Robert, "One Person," a bare-stage monodrama, 1m, in Robert Patrick's *Cheep Theatricks*, SF 17602

Patrick, Robert, "Pouf Positive," a drama, 1m, (about AIDS, can pair with Harvey Fierstein's "Safe Sex," Alan Bowne's "Beirut," Patricia Loughrey's "The Inner Circle," or Lanford Wilson's "A Poster of the Cosmos") (published with and can pair with "Fairy Tale," "Fog," "Bill Batchelor Road," "One of Those People," "Odd Number," or "The River Jordan") in Robert Patrick's *Untold Decades* (New York: St. Martin's Press, Inc., 1988), ISBN 0-312-02307-3

Patrick, Robert, "Preggin and Liss," a tragicomedy, 2m, in Robert Patrick's *Cheep Theatricks*, SF 18605

Patrick, Robert, "The Richest Girl in the World Finds Happiness," a bare-stage farce, 1m3f, in Robert Patrick's *Cheep Theatricks*, SF 20602

Patrick, Robert, "The River Jordan," a drama, 4m, (published with and can pair with "Bill Batchelor Road," "Fairy Tale," "Fog," "Odd Number," "One of Those People," or "Pouf Positive") in Robert Patrick's *Untold Decades* (New York: St. Martin's Press, 1988), ISBN 0-312-02307-3

Paxson, Omar, "Letty," a drama, 3m1f, AR, NSHS pb5724

Payne, Lucile Vaughan, "The Boy Upstairs," a comedy, 2m2f, SF 4663, NSHS pb8072

Peditto, Paul, "Of All the Wide Torsos in All the Wild Glen," a comedy, 2m2f, DPC O47

Peluso, Emanuel, "Good Day," a drama, 2m1f (1m silent), DPS 2170

Peluso, Emanuel, "Hurricane of the Eye," a drama, 2m1f, DPS 2450, NSHS pb7724

Peluso, Emanuel, "Little Fears," an *avant-garde* comic drama, 2m2f, DPS 2880, NSHS pb7742, NSHS pb7752

Peple, Edward, "The Girl," a drama, 3m, in *One Act Plays for Stage and Study: A Collection of Twenty-five Plays by Well-known* [sic] *Dramatists, American, English and Irish, First Series*, preface by Augustus Thomas (New York: Samuel French, Inc., 1925), SF, NSHS

Peregrina, Sergio (Mexican playwright), *"Volver a decir el mar,"* ["I Speak Again of the Sea"], a drama *en español* [in Spanish], 1m, **analyzed in Part 4, p. 258**, OEN, NSHS pb8189

Perkins, David, "Pals," a drama, 2m2f, BP

Perry, Marjean, "A Trap Is a Small Place," a drama, 1m3f, **analyzed in Part 4, p. 254**, MMP, NSHS 2401

Petrushevskaya, Lyudmila (source Russian playwright), "The Visit," a ten-minute play (genre?), translated by Steve Jones, 1m1f, not to be confused with the full-length play of the same name by Friedrich Dürrenmatt, SF

Pfeffer, Susan Beth, "World Affairs," a drama, 1m3f, in *Center Stage: One-Act Plays for Teenage Readers and Actors*, edited by Donald R. Gallo (New York: Harper & Row, 1990), ISBN 0-06-122170-4, ISBN 0-06-022171-2, HR

Phillips, Louis, "The Singer in the White Pajamas," a drama, 3m1f, DPC S97

Phillips, Marguerite Kreger, "Grandma and Mistletoe," a Christmas comedy, 1m3f, TSD, NSHS 10922

Pielmeier, John, "A Ghost Story," a drama, 2m1f, (published with and can pair with "A Gothic Tale" or "A Witch's Brew"; can pair with "Pillow Talk") in *Haunted Lives*, DPS 2297

Pielmeier, John, "A Gothic Tale," a drama, 2m1f, (published with and can pair with "A Ghost Story" or "A Witch's Brew"; can pair with "Pillow Talk") in *Haunted Lives*, DPS 2297

Pielmeier, John, "Pillow Talk," a ten-minute play (genre?), 2m2f (can pair with "A Ghost Story, " "A Gothic Tale," or "A Witch's Brew"), not to be confused by the play of the same name by Peter Tolan, SF

Pielmeier, John, "A Witch's Brew," a drama, 2m1f, (published with and can pair with "A Ghost Story" or "A Gothic Tale"; can pair with "Pillow Talk") in *Haunted Lives*, DPS 2297

Pierce, Carl Webster, "The Laziest Man in the World," a comedy, 4m, SF 14915 (no royalty), HDS, NSHS pb8157

Pilch, Michael (translator from French), "Night Errant" [*"Feu la Mère de Madame,"*], a comedy by Georges Feydeau, translated from the original French by Michael Pilch, 2m2f, SF 16056, NSHS pb8071

Pintauro, Joseph, "Charlie and Vito," a drama, 2m, (published with and can pair with "Flywheel and Anna" or "Uncle Zepp") in *Cacciatore*, DPS 1210

Pintauro, Joseph, "Uncle Zepp," a drama, 1m, (published with and can pair with "Charlie and Vito" or "Flywheel and Anna") in *Cacciatore*, DPS 1210

Pinter, Harold (English playwright, 1930-   ), "The Basement," a drama, 2m1f, DPS 935, NSHS pb7967

Pinter, Harold (English playwright, 1930-   ), "The Black and White," a revue sketch, 2f, (published with and can pair with "The Black and White," "The Collection," "The Dwarfs" "The Lover," "Special Offer," or "Trouble in the Works") in Harold Pinter's *Plays: Two* (London and Boston: Faber & Faber, 1991), ISBN 0-571-16075-1; and (published with and can pair with "Applicant," "Interview," "Last to Go," "That's All," "That's Your Trouble,"or "Trouble in the Works") in *Revue Sketches* DPS 1765, NSHS 27487, NSHS pb7737, NSHS pb8102

Pinter, Harold (English playwright, 1930-   ), "The Collection," a drama, 3m1f, (can pair with "The Dumb Waiter") in *The Pinter Plays* DPS 270; and (published with and can pair with "The Black and White," "The Dwarfs," "Last to Go," "The Lover," "Special Offer," or "Trouble in the Works") in Harold Pinter's *Plays: Two* (London and Boston: Faber & Faber, 1991), NSHS pb8102, ISBN 0-571-16075-1, DPS 2980, NSHS 27487

Pinter, Harold (English playwright, 1930-   ), "Dialog for Three," a revue sketch, 2m1f, SF, NSHS 27487

Pinter, Harold (English playwright, 1930-   ), "The Dumb Waiter," a drama, 2m, (can pair with "The Collection") in *The Pinter Plays*, DPS 270

Pinter, Harold (English playwright, 1930-   ), "The Dwarfs," a drama, 3m, (published with and can pair with "The Black and White," "The Collection," "Last to Go," "The Lover," "Special Offer," or "Trouble in the Works") in Harold Pinter's *Plays: Two* (London and Boston: Faber & Faber, 1991), ISBN 0-571-16075-1; and in *Revue Sketches*; DPS 1765, NSHS pb7737, NSHS pb8102

Pinter, Harold (English playwright, 1930-   ), "Family Voices," a drama, 2m1f, (published with and can pair with "A Kind of Alaska," "One for the Road," or "Victoria Station") in Harold Pinter's *Other Places*, DPS 3548, NSHS pb8041

Pinter, Harold (English playwright, 1930-   ), "Interview," a revue sketch, 2m, (published with and can pair with "Applicant," "The Black and White," "Last to Go," "That's All," "That's Your Trouble," or "Trouble in the Works") in *Revue Sketches*, DPS 1765, NSHS 27487

Pinter, Harold (English playwright, 1930-   ), "A Kind of Alaska," a drama, 1m2f, (published with and can pair with "Family Voices," "One for the Road," or "Victoria Station") in Harold Pinter's *Other Places: Four Plays*, DPS, NSHS pb8041 [Note: The catalog says, "If produced separately, 'A Kind of Alaska' may be presented only with another play written by Harold Pinter or with a companion piece approved by Mr. Pinter. In the latter instance all requests must be approved in writing by the Play Service."]

Pinter, Harold (English playwright, 1930-   ), "Last to Go" a drama, 2m or 3m, (published with and can pair with "The Black and White," "The Collection," "The Dwarfs," "The Lover," "Special Offer," or "Trouble in the Works") in Harold Pinter's *Plays: Two* (London and Boston: Faber & Faber, 1991), ISBN 0-571-16075-1; and (published with and can pair with "Applicant," "The Black and White," "Interview," "That's All," "That's Your Trouble," or "Trouble in the Works") in *Revue Sketches*; DPS 1765, NSHS pb7737, NSHS pb8102, NSHS 27487

Pinter, Harold (English playwright, 1930-   ), "The Lover," a bizarre comedy revue sketch, 2m1f, (published with and can pair with "The Black and White," "The Collection," "The Dwarfs," "Special Offer," "Trouble in the Works") in Harold Pinter's *Plays: Two* (London and Boston: Faber & Faber, 1991), NSHS pb8102, ISBN 0-571-16075-1; and (published with and can pair with "Applicant," "Interview," "Last to Go," "That's All," or "That's Your Trouble") in *Revue Sketches*, HDS DPS 1765, DPS 2980, NSHS 27487, NSHS pb7737,

Pinter, Harold (English playwright, 1930-   ), "The New World Order," a sketch, 3m, DPS 3368

Pinter, Harold (English playwright, 1930-   ), "One for the Road," a drama, 3m1f, (published with and can pair with "Family Voices," "A Kind of Alaska," or "Victoria Station") in *Other Places*, DPS 3548

Pinter, Harold (English playwright, 1930-   ), "Silence," a comedy, 2m1f, SF, NSHS 27487

Pinter, Harold (English playwright, 1930-   ), "A Slight Ache," a drama, 2m1f (1m silent), DPS 375

Pinter, Harold (English playwright, 1930-   ), "Special Offer" a drama, 3m, (published with and can pair with "The Black and White," "The Collection," "The Dwarfs," "Last to Go," "The Lover," or "Trouble in the Works") in Harold Pinter's *Plays: Two* (London and Boston: Faber & Faber, 1991), ISBN 0-571-16075-1; and in *Revue Sketches*; DPS 1765, NSHS pb7737, NSHS pb8102

Pinter, Harold (English playwright, 1930-   ), "That's All," a revue sketch, 2f, **analyzed in Part 4, p. 250**, (published with and can pair with "Applicant," "The Black and White," "Interview," "Last to Go," "That's Your Trouble," or "Trouble in the Works") in *Revue Sketches*, DPS 1765, NSHS 27487

Pinter, Harold (English playwright, 1930-   ), "That's Your Trouble," a revue sketch, 2m, (published with and can pair with "Applicant," "The Black and White," "Interview," "Last to Go," "That's All," or "Trouble in the Works") in *Revue Sketches*, DPS 1765, NSHS 27487

Pinter, Harold (English playwright, 1930-), "Trouble in the Works," a revue sketch, 2m, (published with and can pair with "The Black and White," "The Collection," "The Dwarfs," "The Lover," or "Special Offer") in Harold Pinter's *Plays: Two* (London and Boston: Faber & Faber, 1991), ISBN 0-571-16075-1; and (published with and can pair with "Applicant," "Interview," "Last to Go," "That's All," or "That's Your Trouble") in *Revue Sketches*, DPS 1765, NSHS 27487, NSHS pb7737, NSHS pb8102

Pinter, Harold (English playwright, 1930-), "Victoria Station," a comedy, 2m, (published with and can pair with "Family Voices," "A Kind of Alaska," or "One for the Road") in *Other Places*, DPS 3548, NSHS pb8041

Pirandello, Luigi (Italian playwright, 1867-1936), "At the Exit," [*"All' uscita,"* 1922] a drama, 3m1f (+ extras), (published with and can pair with "Chee-Chee," "I'm Dreaming, but Am I?" "The Man with the Flower in His Mouth," or "The Vise") in *Pirandello's One-Act Plays*, translated into English from the original Italian by William Murray (New York: Samuel French, Inc., 1970), SF 15602, NSHS, ISBN 0-573-60039-2

Pirandello, Luigi (Italian playwright, 1867-1936), "Chee Chee," [*"Cecè,"* 1920] a drama, 2m1f, (published with and can pair with "At the Exit," "I'm Dreaming, but Am I?" "The Man with the Flower in His Mouth," or "The Vise") in *Pirandello's One-Act Plays*, translated into English from the original Italian by William Murray (New York: Samuel French, Inc., 1970), SF 5630, NSHS

Pirandello, Luigi (Italian playwright, 1867-1936), "I'm Dreaming, but Am I?" [*"Sogno (ma forse no),"* 1931], a drama, 2m1f, (published with and can pair with "At the Exit," "Chee-Chee," "The Man with the Flower in His Mouth," or "The Vise") in *Pirandello's One-Act Plays*, translated into English from the original Italian by William Murray (New York: Samuel French, Inc., 1970), SF 11601, NSHS, ISBN 0-573-60039-2

Pirandello, Luigi (Italian playwright, 1867-1936), "The Imbecile," a comedy translated by William Murray, 3m1f, in *Pirandello's One-Act Plays*, SF 11602

Pirandello, Luigi (Italian playwright, 1867-1936), "The Man with the Flower in His Mouth," [*"L'uomo dal fiore in bocca,"* 1923] a drama, 2m1f, **analyzed in Part 4, p. 216**, (published with and can pair with "At the Exit," "Chee-Chee," "I'm Dreaming, but Am I?" or "The Vise") in *Pirandello's One-Act Plays*, translated into English from the original Italian by William Murray (New York: Samuel French, Inc., 1970), SF 15602 (state translator when ordering), NSHS, ISBN 0-573-60039-2

Pirandello, Luigi (Italian playwright, 1867-1936), "The Vise" [*"La Morsa,"* 1910] a drama, 2m2f, (published with and can pair with "At the Exit," "Chee-Chee," "I'm Dream-

ing, but Am I?" or "The Man with the Flower in His Mouth") in *Pirandello's One-Act Plays*, translated into English from the original Italian by William Murray (New York: Samuel French, Inc., 1970), SF 24601, NSHS

Plowman, Gillian, "Cecily," a drama, 3f, DPC C83

Plowman, Gillian, "The Primrose Path," a comedy, 1m2f, in *Triad 73*, NPN, DPC P70

Plowman, Gillian, "The Wooden Pear," a drama, 1m1f, in *Triad 74*, NPN, DPC W71

Plunkett, Edward John Moreton Drax, (Lord Dunsany, 18th Baron, Irish poet and dramatist, 1878-1957), "The Jest of Hahalaba," a drama, 4m, SF, NSHS 27039

Plunkett, Edward John Moreton Drax, (Lord Dunsany, 18th Baron, Irish poet and dramatist, 1878-1957), "Two Bottles of Relish," a mystery by Edward Darby from Lord Dunsany, 2m2f, HDS, DPC T45, NSHS pb139

Poliakoff, Stephen, "Hitting Town," a play (genre?), 1m2f, SF 10648, NSHS pb7806

Porter, Robert Neil, "Christmas Tea," a Christmas fantasy, 1m2f (+voice), DPS

Porter, William Sydney (O. Henry, source American short story writer, 1862-1910), "The Last Leaf," a drama by Thomas Hischak from O. Henry, 2m2f, PDS

Potocki, Waclaw (Polish playwright and poet, 1625-1696), "Cassander, Man of Letters," a comedy, translated by Daniel Gerould, 3m1f, (published with and can pair with "The Blind One-Armed Deaf-Mute," "Cassander Supports the Revolution," "Cassander's Trip to the Indies," "Giles in Love," "The Shit Merchant," or "The Two Doubles") in *Gallant and Libertine, Divertissements and Parades of 18th Century France*, SF5756, NSHS pb7927, ISBN 0-933826-49-4

Potocki, Waclaw (Polish playwright and poet, 1625-1696), "Cassander Supports the Revolution," a comedy, translated by Daniel Gerould, 3m1f, (published with and can pair with "The Blind One-Armed Deaf-Mute," "Cassander Supports the Revolution," "Cassander, Man of Letters," "Cassander's Trip to the Indies," "The Shit Merchant," or "The Two Doubles") in *Gallant and Libertine, Divertissements and Parades of 18th Century France*, SF 5757, NSHS pb7927, ISBN 0-933826-49-4

Potocki, Waclaw (Polish playwright and poet, 1625-1696), "Cassander's Trip to the Indies," a comedy, translated by Daniel Gerould, 3m1f, (published with and can pair with "The Blind One-Armed Deaf-Mute," "Cassander Supports the Revolution," "Cassander, Man of Letters," "Giles in Love," "The Shit Merchant," or "The Two Doubles") in *Gallant and Libertine, Divertissements and Parades of 18th Century France*, SF 5758, NSHS pb7927, ISBN 0-933826-49-4

Povod, Reinaldo, "Nijinsky Choked His Chicken," a drama, 2m (that is, adult male + 12-year-old boy), in *La Puta Vida*, SF 14673

Povod, Reinaldo, "South of Tomorrow," a drama, 3m, in *La*

Puta Vida, SF 14673

Powers, Tom, "Dark Glasses," a monodrama, 1m, SF, NSHS 6066

Powers, Tom, "Emergency, Stand By," a drama, 1m, SF (probably out of print), NSHS 2189

Prida, Dolores, "To Be Very Easy" [*"Coser y Cantar"*], a bilingual drama in English and Spanish, 2f, in Dolores Prida's *Beautiful Señoritas & Other Plays*, edited and introduced by Judith Weiss (Arte Público Press, 1991), ISBN 1-55885-026-0, APP

Prideaux, James, " An American Sunset," a comedy, 1m2f, (published with and can pair with "Stuffings") DPS 750

Prideaux, James, "The Autograph Hound," a comedy, 1m2f, (published with and can pair with "Lemonade") DPS 865

Prideaux, James, "Lemonade," a bare-stage comedy-drama, 2f, (published with and can pair with "The Autograph Hound") DPS 865

Prideaux, James, "Stuffings," a comedy, 2m1f, (published with and can pair with "An American Sunset") DPS 750

Pryor, Deborah, "The Love Talker," a drama, 1m3f, DPS 2977, NSHS pb7962, NSHS pb8023, NSHS pb7962

Purdy, James, "Cracks," a drama, 2m2f, cited in *The Best Plays of 1963-1964*, edited by Henry Hewes

Purdy, James (source writer), "Sermon," a drama by Ellen Violett (not to be confused with David Mamet's "A Sermon"), 1m, cited in *The Best Plays of 1963-1964*, edited by Henry Hewes

Purkey, Ruth Angell, "The Leprechaun," a fantasy, 3m1f, BP, NSHS 19998

Purkey, Ruth Angell, "Pink Lemonade for Tomorrow," a drama, 2m2f (+ optional chorus), BP

Q

Quinn, Susan, "The Luck of the Draw," a play (genre?), 1m2f, in *Triad 75*, NPN

Quintero, Joaquín and Serafín Álvarez (Spanish playwrights, brothers, Serafín 1871-1938 and Joaquín 1873-1944), "A Sunny Morning" [*"Mañana de sol,"* 1905], a comedy by brothers Serafín and Joaquín Álvarez Quintero, 2m2f; [1] translated from the Spanish by Robert Lima, in *La Voz*, Vol. VII, no. 4, New York, January, 1963, agent is Continental, address unknown; [2] translated by Lucretia Xavier Floyd, in *Thirty Famous One-Act Plays*, ed. by Bennett Cerf and Van H. Cartmell (New York: Random House, Inc./Modern Library, 1943); and [3] in *One-Act Plays for Secondary Schools* (New York: French, n.d.), edited by James Weber and Anson Weber (Boston: Houghton Mifflin, 1923); [4] in *Drama of the East and West*, edited by Jean Edades and Carolyn E. Fosdick (Manila: Bookman, 1956); [5] in *Fifty Contemporary One-Act Plays*, edited by Frank Shay and Pierre Loving (Cincinnati: Steward Kidd, 1921), SF; [6] "A Bright Morning," translated by Carlos C. Castillo and E. L. Overman, in *Continental Plays,* Vol. 1, edited by Thomas H. Dickenson (Boston: Houghton Mifflin, 1935); [7] in *Poet Lore*, XXVII, Boston, 1916; and [8] "A Sunny Morning," translated by Isaac Goldberg, in *Stratford Journal*, Vol. I, Boston, 1916; BP, SF 1012, NSHS 2189, NSHS 19878, NSHS 19883

R

Raine, David S., "Passage," a drama, 2m, DPC P65, NSHS pb172

Rame, Franca, and Dario Fo (Italian source playwrights), "A Woman Alone" a monologue, 1f, (published with and can pair with "An Arab Woman Speaks," "Alice in Wonderless Land," "The Bawd—the Christian Democrat Party in Chile," "Bless Me Father for I Have Sinned," "Coming Home," "The Dancing Mistress: On the Assembly Line," "The Eel-Woman," "Fascism 1922," "I'm Ulrike—Screaming," "It Happened Tomorrow," "Mamma Togni," "Medea," "Michele Lu Lanzone," "A Mother," "Nada Pasini," "The Rape," "Rise and Shine," "The Same Old Story," or "The Whore in the Madhouse") in Franca Rame and Dario Fo's *A Woman Alone & Other Plays* (London: Methuen, 1991), ISBN 0-413-64030-2

Rame, Franca, and Dario Fo (Italian source playwrights), "An Ordinary Day," a comedy translated from the original Italian by Joe Farrell, 1m2f (voices), (published with "The Open Couple") SF 17940

Rame, Franca, and Dario Fo, "The Whore in the Madhouse," a monologue, 1f, (published with and can pair with "An Arab Woman Speaks," "Alice in Wonderless Land," "The Bawd—the Christian Democrat Party in Chile," "Bless Me Father for I Have Sinned," "Coming Home," "The Dancing Mistress: On the Assembly Line," "The Eel-Woman," "Fascism 1922," "I'm Ulrike—Screaming," "It Happened Tomorrow," "Mamma Togni," "Medea," "Michele Lu Lanzone," "A Mother," "Nada Pasini," "The Rape," "Rise and Shine," "The Same Old Story," or "A Woman Alone") in Franca Rame and Dario Fo's *A Woman Alone & Other Plays* (London: Methuen, 1991), ISBN 0-413-64030-2

Ramsey, Patricia, "A-Killin'," a drama, 2m1f, DPC K22

Randolph, Larry, "Crosspatch," a comedy from Anton Chekhov, 1m2f, HDS, DPC C36

Randolph, Larry, "Tomato on Tuesday," a comedy, 1m2f, DPC, NSHS pb6100

Raspanti, Celeste, "I Never Saw Another Butterfly," a one-act cutting, 2m2f, DPC I33

Rayfield, James, "I Hate Mothers," a comedy, 1m2f, BP

Reale, Willie, "Fast Women," a comedy, 2m1f, (published with "Many Happy Returns") DPS 3052

Rebeck, Theresa, "Does This Woman Have a Name?" a comedy, 1m2f, in *Off-Off Broadway Festival Plays, 15th Se-*

ries, SF 6732, NSHS pb8079

Reddin, Keith, "After School Special," a drama, 3m1f, in Keith Reddin's *Big Time: Scenes from a Service Economy and After School Special* (New York: Broadway Play Publishing, Inc., 1988), ISBN 0-88145-063-4, BPP

Reddin, Keith, "Desperadoes," a drama, 2m1f, in *"Desperadoes": "Throwing Smoke": "Keyhole Lover,"* DPS 1622

Reddin, Keith, "Keyhole Lover," a drama, 2m1f, in *"Desperadoes": "Throwing Smoke": "Keyhole Lover,"* DPS 1622

Reingold, Jacquelyn, "Freeze Tag," a comedy, 2f, SF 8678

Ribman, Ronald, "The Burial of Esposito," a drama, 3m1f, (published with and can pair with "The Son Who Hunted Tigers in Jakarta" or "Sun-Stroke") in *Passing Through from Exotic Places*, DPS 3585

Ribman, Ronald, "The Son Who Hunted Tigers in Jakarta," a drama, 2m1f, (published with and can pair with "Sun-Stroke" or "The Burial of Esposito") in *Passing Through from Exotic Places*, DPS 3585

Ribman, Ronald, "Sun-Stroke," a fantasy, 3m1f, (published with and can pair with "The Son Who Hunted Tigers in Jakarta" or "The Burial of Esposito") in *Passing Through from Exotic Places*, DPS 3585

Rice, Howard, "Tradition 1A," a dramatic monologue, 1m, in *Off-Off Broadway Festival Plays, 14th Series* (New York: Samuel French, Inc., 1989), ISBN 0-573-62363-5, SF 22753

Richardson, Alan (Scottish playwright), "The Broken Band," a Scottish drama, 2m2f (+ extra), (can pair with "Perfect Partners" or "Telltale") in Alan Richardson's *The Broken Band* (Glasgow, Scotland: Brown, Son & Ferguson, Ltd., 1990), ISBN 0-85174-588-1

Richardson, Alan (Scottish playwright), "Perfect Partners," a Scottish drama, 2m2f (+ extra), (can pair with "The Broken Band" or "Telltale") in Alan Richardson's *The Broken Band* (Glasgow, Scotland: Brown, Son & Ferguson, Ltd., 1990), ISBN 0-85174-588-1

Richardson, Alan (Scottish playwright), "Telltale," a Scottish drama, 2m2f (+ extra), (can pair with "The Broken Band" or "Perfect Partners") in Alan Richardson's *The Broken Band* (Glasgow, Scotland: Brown, Son & Ferguson, Ltd., 1990), ISBN 0-85174-588-1

Rifkin, Don, "Two Eggs Scrambled Soft," a comedy, 1m2f, (published with and can pair with "A Brief Period of Time") in Don Rifkin's *A Brief Period of Time and Two Eggs Scrambled Soft: Two One-Act Plays* (New York: Dramatists Play Service, Inc., 1989), DPS 1127

Ringwood, Gwen Pharis, "Still Stands the House," a drama, 2m2f, SF 21338, NSHS pb8050

Rivera, José, "Tape," a drama, 1m1f or 2m or 2f, in *Dramatics*, 65 (May 1944): 24-26, ICM

Robertson, Joe, "The Promise," a drama, 2m2f, ELD

Rock, Andrew, "Answers on a Postcard," a play (genre?), 1m3f, in *Triad 75*, NPN

Rodriguez, Dailyn, "College Letters," a comedy-drama, 2f, in *Throwing Off the Covers: A Collection of Four One Act Plays*, BP

Rodriguez, Dailyn, "Gunshot Love," a comedy-drama, 2m2f, in *Throwing Off the Covers: A Collection of Four One Act Plays*, BP

Rogers, J. W., Jr., "Judge Lynch," a drama, 2m2f, in *One Act Plays for Stage and Study: A Collection of Twenty-five Plays by Well-known* [sic] *Dramatists, American, English and Irish, First Series*, preface by Augustus Thomas (New York: Samuel French, Inc., 1925), SF, NSHS

Rogerson, Fred, "Weird Is the Night," a long one-act comedy, 4f, DPC W14

Roome, D., "Faith, Hope, and Cyanide," a comedy, 2m2f (+voice), DPC F10, NSHS pb134

Rosenberg, James L. (translator from German), "The Curve," a drama by Tankred Dorst (Swiss playwright), 3m, NTK, 16622

Rosenblatt, Arthur S., "Please Hang Up," a comedy, 1m2f, DPC P58, NSHS

Rostand, Edmond (French source playwright, 1868-1918), "The Romancers," a comedy, Aurand Harris from Edmond Rostand's first act of *Les Romanesques*, the basis for the musical *The Fantasticks*, 3m1f, BP

Rusch, Christine, "Potato Girl," a brief drama, 1m2f, (published with and can pair with "Advice to a New Actor," "The Affidavit," "The American Way," "Anniversary," "Auld Lang Syne, or I'll Bet You Think This Play Is About You," "Bug Swatter," "Checkers," "Coming for a Visit," "Dalmation," "Dog Eat Dog," "Drowned Out," "Fireworks," "Interview," "Jumping," "Money," "One Beer Too Many," "Phonecall from Sunkist," "Property of the Dallas Cowboys," "The Split Decision," "Valley Forgery," "Watermelon Boats," or "Widows") in Norman A. Bert's *One-Act Plays for Acting Students*, MPL, ISBN 0-916260-47-X, pb7929

Rush, David, "Life Is Only Seven Points," a drama, 2m1f, DPC L53, NSHS pb158

Rustan, John, and Frank Semerano, "Stray Cats," a comedy, 2m1f, AR, NSHS pb6842

Ruthenberg, Grace Dorcas, "The Gooseberry Mandarin," a fantasy, 2m2f, GBC, NSHS 6066

Ryerson, Florence, and Colin Clements, "Angels Don't Marry," a comedy, 1m2f, SF

Ryerson, Florence, and Colin Clements, "Ladies Alone," a comedy, 3f, SF 14608, NSHS pb7906

Ryerson, Florence, and Colin Clements, "Movie Mother," a comedy, 1f, **analyzed in Part 4, p. 218**, possibly SF (?), NSHS pb6066

S

Sabath, Bernard, "A Barbarian in Love," a comedy about Mark Twain, 2m1f, (published with and can pair with

"The Loneliest Wayfarer" "Summer Morning Visitor," or "The Trouble Begins at 8,") in *Twain Plus Twain* (New York: Dramatists Play Service, Inc., 1984), DPS 4635, NSHS pb8024

Sabath, Bernard, "The Loneliest Wayfarer," a comedy about Mark Twain, 2m1f, (published with and can pair with "A Barbarian in Love," "Summer Morning Visitor," or "The Trouble Begins at 8") in Bernard Sabath's *Twain Plus Twain* (New York: Dramatists Play Service, Inc., 1984), DPS 4635, NSHS pb8024

Sabath, Bernard, "Summer Morning Visitor," a comedy-drama about Mark Twain, 1m2f, (published with and can pair with "A Barbarian in Love," "The Loneliest Wayfarer" or "The Trouble Begins at 8") in Bernard Sabath's *Twain Plus Twain* (New York: Dramatists Play Service, Inc., 1984), DPS 4635, NSHS pb8024

Sabath, Bernard, "The Trouble Begins at 8," a comedy-drama about Mark Twain, 3m1f, (published with and can pair with "A Barbarian in Love," "The Loneliest Wayfarer," or "Summer Morning Visitor") in Bernard Sabath's *Twain Plus Twain* (New York: Dramatists Play Service, Inc., 1984), DPS 4635, NSHS pb8024

Sachs, Hans, (German playwright and meistersinger, 1494-1576), *"Das heiss Eysen"* ["The Hot Iron"], a farce, 1m2f, (published with and can pair with *"Der farendt Schuler im Paradeis"* ["The Wandering Scholar in Paradise"] or *"Der Doctor mit der grosen Nasen"* ["The Doctor with the Big Nose"]) in Hans Sachs' *Meistergesänge Fastnachtsspiele Schwänke*, compiled by Eugen Geiger (Stuttgart: Phillip Reclam jun., 1981), ISBN 3-15-007627-7, NSHS

Sachs, Hans, (German playwright and meistersinger, 1494-1576), *"Das Kalberbruten"* ["The Brooding of the Calf"], a German-language fastnachtsspiel, 2m1f, HDB, NSHS

Sachs, Hans, (German playwright and meistersinger, 1494-1576), *"Der Doctor mit der grosen Nasen"* ["The Doctor with the Big Nose"], a farce, 2m1f, (published with and can pair with *"Dass heiss Eysen"* ["The Hot Iron"], *"Der Rossdieb zu Funsing mit den tollen diebischen Bauern"* ["The Horsethief at Funsing with the Fantastic Thief-like Farmers"], or *"Der farendt Schuler im Paradeiss"* ["The Wandering Scholar in Paradise"]) in Hans Sachs' *Meistergesänge Fastnachtsspiele Schwänke*, compiled by Eugen Geiger (Stuttgart: Phillip Reclam jun., 1981), ISBN 3-15-007627-7, NSHS

Sachs, Hans, (German playwright and meistersinger, 1494-1576), *"Der fahrende Schuler im Paradies,"* a German-language *fastnachtsspiel*, 2m1f, HDB, NSHS pb7746

Sachs, Hans, (German playwright and meistersinger, 1494-1576), *"Der farendt Schuler im Paradeiss"* ["The Wandering Scholar from Paradise"], a farce, 2m1f, (published with and can pair with *"Dass heiss Eysen"* ["The Hot Iron"] or *"Der Doctor mit der grosen Nasen"* ["The Doctor with the Big Nose"]) in Hans Sachs' *Meistergesänge*

Fastnachtsspiele Schwänke, compiled by Eugen Geiger (Stuttgart: Phillip Reclam jun., 1981), ISBN 3-15-007627-7, NSHS

Sachs, Hans, (German playwright and meistersinger, 1494-1576), *"Der ins Paradies fahrende Schuler,"* a German-language farce, 2m1f, HDB

Sachs, Hans, (German playwright and meistersinger, 1494-1576), *"Der Rossdieb zu Funsing"* ["The Horsethief at Funsing"], a German-language *fastnachtsspiel*, adapted by Horst Ulrich Wendler, 4m, MVH, NSHS pb95

Sachs, Hans, (German playwright and meistersinger, 1494-1576), *"Der Rossdieb zu Funsing mit den tollen diebischen Bauern"* ["The Horsethief at Funsing with the Fantastic Thief-like Farmers"], a *fastnachtsspiel*, 4m, HDB, NSHS pb7746

Sachs, Hans, (German playwright and meistersinger, 1494-1576), *"Der Rossdieb zw* [sic] *Fünssing mit den dollen diebischen Pauern"* / *"Der Rossdieb zu Funsing mit den tollen diebischen Bauern"* ["The Horsethief at Funsing with the Fantastic Thief-like Farmers"], a *fastnachtsspiel*, 4m, (published with and can pair with *"Dass heiss Eysen"* ["The Hot Iron"], *"Der Doctor mit der grosen Nasen"* ["The Doctor with the Big Nose"], or *"Der farendt Schuler im Paradeiss"* ["The Wandering Scholar in Paradise"]) in Hans Sachs' *Meistergesänge Fastnachtsspiele Schwänke*, compiled by Eugen Geiger (Stuttgart: Phillip Reclam jun., 1981), ISBN 3-15-007627-7, NSHS

Sachs, Hans, (German playwright and meistersinger, 1494-1576), *"Der Teufel im Haus"* (or, *"Der fahrende Schuler mit dem Teufelsbannen"*) ["The Devil in the House"], a *fastnachtsspiel*, adapted by Horst Ulrich Wendler, 3m1f, MVH, NSHS pb95

Sachs, Hans, (German playwright and meistersinger, 1494-1576), *"Disputation zw* [sic]*ischen einem Chorherren und Schuhmacher darin das Wort . . ."* / *"Disputation zw* [sic]*ischen einem Chorherren und Schuchmacher darinn das wort gottes vnd ein recht Christlich wesen verfochten würdt"* ["Disputation between a Choir Director and a Shoemaker during Which the Word of God and a True Christian Being Was Argued About"], a *fastnachtsspiel*, 3m1f, in Hans Sach's *Die Wittenbergisch Nachtigall: Spruchgedicht, Vier Reformationsdialoge und das Meisterlied das Walt Got*, compiled by Gerald H. Seufert (Stuttgart: Philipp Reclam jun., 1974), Universal-Bibliothek Nr. 9737/38/38a, ISBN 3-15-009737-1, NSHS

Sachs, Hans, (German playwright and meistersinger, 1494-1576), *"Ein Dialog, dessen Inhalt ein Argument der Römer gegen das christliche Häuflein, Geitz und andere öffentliche Laster betreffend, diskutiert"* / *"Ein Dialogus des inhalt ein argumennt der Römischen wider das Christlich heüflein den Geytz auch ander offenlich laster etc. betreffend"* ["A Dialogue the Content of Which Is an Argument between the Romans and a Small Band of

Christians Pertaining to Extreme Stinginess and Other Public Vices"], a *fastnachtsspiel*, 2m, in Hans Sach's *Die Wittenbergisch Nachtigall: Spruchgedicht, Vier Reformationsdialoge und das Meisterlied das Walt Got*, compiled by Gerald H. Seufert (Stuttgart: Philipp Reclam jun., 1974), Universal-Bibliothek Nr. 9737/38/38a, ISBN 3-15-009737-1, NSHS

Sachs, Hans, (German playwright and meistersinger, 1494-1576), *"Ein Gespräch eines evangelischen Christen mit einem Lutherischen . . ." / "Ein Gespräch von den Scheinwerken der Gaystlichen vun jren gelübdten damit sy zuuerlesterung des bluts Christi vermaynen selig zu werden"* ["A Conversation of an Evangelistic Christian with a Lutheran in Which the Angry Charge of Those Who Call Themselves Lutheran Is Pointed out and Is Being Stressed in Brotherly Fashion"], a *fastnachtsspiel*, 3m, in Hans Sach's *Die Wittenbergisch Nachtigall: Spruchgedicht, Vier Reformationsdialoge und das Meisterlied das Walt Got*, compiled by Gerald H. Seufert (Stuttgart: Philipp Reclam jun., 1974), Universal-Bibliothek Nr. 9737/38/38a, ISBN 3-15-009737-1, NSHS

Sachs, Hans, (German playwright and meistersinger, 1494-1576), *"Ein Gespräch von den Scheinwerken der Geistlichen" / "Ein Gespräch von den Scheinwerken der Gaystlichen vun jren gelübdten damit sy zuuerlesterung des bluts Christi vermaynen selig zu werden"* ["A Conversation about Pretended Good Deeds of the Clergy"], a *fastnachtsspiel*, 3m, in Hans Sach's *Die Wittenbergisch Nachtigall: Spruchgedicht, Vier Reformationsdialoge und das Meisterlied das Walt Got*, compiled by Gerald H. Seufert (Stuttgart: Philipp Reclam jun., 1974), Universal-Bibliothek Nr. 9737/38/38a, ISBN 3-15-009737-1, NSHS

Sachs, Hans, (German playwright and meistersinger, 1494-1576), *"Frau Wahrheit will niemand beherbergen"* [Mrs. Truth Will Not Take in Anybody Overnight"] a *fastnachtsspiel*, 1m2f, HDB, NSHS

Sachs, Hans, (German playwright and meistersinger, 1494-1576), "The *Narrenschneiden*, or The Fool-Ectomy," a *fastnachtsspiel*, translated by I. E. Clark, 3m or 3f, IEC, NSHS pb94

Sachs, Hans, (German playwright and meistersinger, 1494-1576), *"Sankt Peter vergnugt sich mit seinen Freunden unten auf Erden,"* a *fastnachtsspiel*, translated from the original German into modern German by Heinrich Detjen, 4m, HDB, NSHS pb63

Sachs, Hans, (German playwright and meistersinger, 1494-1576), (source German playwright), "The Shoemaker's Wife," a farce by David Thompson from Hans Sach's *"Der Todte Mann,"* 2m1f, (no royalty with purchase of three copies) BP 4663, NSHS 19998, NSHS pb7799

Safirstein, E. J., "Waterworks," a comic-drama, 1m3f (+ 1m voice), in *Award-Winning Plays: Waterworks/E. J. Safirstein/When Esther Saw the Light/Michael Sargent*

(New York: Samuel French, Inc., 1989), ISBN 0-573-62613-8, SF 25616, NSHS pb7947, NSHS pb8014

Saki (**H. H. Munro**, source Scottish short story writer, 1870-1916), "Dusk," a comedy adapted by Jules Tasca from the short story by Saki (H. H. Munro), 3m, (published with and can pair with "The Background," "Blind Spot," "The Hen," "The Reticence of Lady Anne," "Secret Sin," "The Tiger," or "The Unrest Cure") in Jules Tasca's *Tales by Saki: Adapted for Stage by Jules Tasca* (New York: Samuel French, Inc., 1989), SF 22133, NSHS pb7798

Saki (H. H. Munro, source Scottish short story writer), "The Open Window," a comedy, James Fuller from H. H. (Saki) Munro, 1m3f (+ extras), DPC O17, HDS, NSHS

Saki (H. H. Munro, source Scottish short story writer), "The Reticence of Lady Anne," a comedy, Jules Tasca adapted from the short story by Saki (H. H. Munro), 1m, (published with and can pair with "The Background," "Blind Spot," "Dusk," "The Hen," "Secret Sin," "The Tiger," or "The Unrest Cure") in Jules Tasca's *Tales by Saki: Adapted for Stage by Jules Tasca* (New York: Samuel French, Inc., 1989), ISBN 0-573-62560-3, SF 22133

Saki (H. H. Munro, source Scottish short story writer, 1870-1916), "Secret Sin," a comedy adapted for the stage by Jules Tasca from the short story by Saki (H. H. Munro), 2m1f, (published with and can pair with "The Background," "Blind Spot," "Dusk," "The Hen," "The Reticence of Lady Anne," "The Tiger," or "The Unrest Cure") in Jules Tasca's *Tales by Saki: Adapted for Stage by Jules Tasca* (New York: Samuel French, Inc., 1989), ISBN 0-573-62560-3, SF 22133, NSHS pb7798, NSHS pb8113

Saki (H. H. Munro, source Scottish short story writer), "The Unrest Cure," a comedy adapted for the stage by Jules Tasca from the short story by Saki (H. H. Munro), 2m1f, (published with and can pair with "The Background," "Blind Spot," "Dusk," "The Hen," "The Reticence of Lady Anne," "Secret Sin," or "The Tiger") in Jules Tasca's *Tales by Saki: Adapted for Stage by Jules Tasca* (New York: Samuel French, Inc., 1989), ISBN 0-573-62560-3, SF 22133, NSHS pb7798, NSHS pb8113

Saki (Hector Hugh Munro, source Scottish short story writer), "Vicky," a comedy, Phyllis Vernick from Saki (H. H. Munro), 2m2f, DPC V13

Sanders, Dudley W., "Maggie and the Bird Go Fishing," a comedy, 2m1f, BP

Saroyan, William (American playwright, 1908-1981), "Once Around the Block," a comedy, 3m1f, SF 17622, NSHS pb8039

Sartre, Jean-Paul (French philosopher, novelist and playwright, 1905-1980), "No Exit," a lengthy one-act existentialist fantasy-drama, 2m2f, SF 765

Savage, George, "Make-Up," a comedy, 2f, (published with and can pair with "The Dormant Heritage," "Enterprising Oswald," "Girls Will Be Girls," "Grandma Fought the Indians," "Paris Sets the Styles," "'Rosemary—That's for Remembrance,'" "She Goes the Rounds," or "Truant Husbands") in *Two by Two* BP, NSHS pb6044, NSHS 29326

Schenkkan, Robert, "Intermission," a drama, 4m, (published with and can pair with "Lunch Break" or "The Survivalist") in *Four One-Act Plays by Robert Schenkkan: Conversations with the Spanish Lady/Lunch Break/Intermission/The Survivalist,* DPS 3972, NSHS pb8022

Schenkkan, Robert, "Lunch Break," a drama, 2m, (published with and can pair with "Intermission" or "The Survivalist") in *Four One-Act Plays by Robert Schenkkan: Conversations with the Spanish Lady/Lunch Break/Intermission/The Survivalist,* DPS 3972, NSHS pb8022

Schenkkan, Robert, "The Survivalist," a drama, 1m, (published with and can pair with "Intermission" or "Lunch Break") in *Four One-Act Plays by Robert Schenkkan: Conversations with the Spanish Lady/Lunch Break/Intermission/The Survivalist,* DPS 3972, NSHS pb8022

Schisgal, Murray, "The Basement," a drama, 2m1f, (published with and can pair with "Fragments," "Memorial Day," or "The Old Jew") in *Five One Act Plays*, DPS 3975, NSHS pb6057

Schisgal, Murray, "Closet Madness," a comedy, 2m, in *Closet Madness & Other Plays*, SF 5678, NSHS 27490

Schisgal, Murray, "Dr. Fish," a comedy, 2m2f, DPS 1330, NSHS pb8044

Schisgal, Murray, "The Flatulist," a black comedy, 2m, (published with and can pair with "Little Johnny" "The Pushcart Peddlers," or "Walter") in *The Pushcart Peddler, The Flatulist and Other Plays*, DPS 3740

Schisgal, Murray, "Fragments," a drama, 2m2f, (published with and can pair with "The Basement," "Memorial Day," or "The Old Jew") in *Five One Act Plays*, DPS 3975, NSHS pb6057

Schisgal, Murray, "Jealousy," a comedy, 2m1f, (published with and can pair with "There Are No Sacher Tortes in Our Society"; also can pair with "The Pushcart Peddlers") DPS 2598

Schisgal, Murray, "Little Johnny," a drama, 2m1f, (published with and can pair with "The Flatulist," "The Pushcart Peddlers," or "Walter") in *The Pushcart Peddler, The Flatulist and Other Plays*, DPS 3740

Schisgal, Murray, "The Old Jew," a drama, 1m, **analyzed in Part 4, p. 222**, (published with and can pair with "The Basement," "Fragments," or "Memorial Day") in *Five One Act Plays*, DPS 3975, NSHS pb6057

Schisgal, Murray, "The Pushcart Peddlers," a comedy, 2m1f, (published with and can pair with "The Flatulist," "Little Johnny," or "Walter") in *The Pushcart Peddler, The Flatulist and Other Plays*, DPS 3740

Schisgal, Murray, "The Rabbi and the Toyota Dealer," a comedy, 2m, in *Closet Madness & Other Plays*, SF 19990,

NSHS 27490

Schisgal, Murray, "74 Georgia Avenue," a drama, 2m, (published with and can pair with "The Consequences of Goosing" or "How We Reached an Impasse on Nuclear Energy") in *Man Dangling*, DPS 3032

Schisgal, Murray, "Summer Romance," a comedy, 1m3f, in *Closet Madness & Other Plays*, SF 221397, NSHS 27490

Schisgal, Murray, "There Are No Sacher Tortes in Our Society," a comedy, 2m1f, (can pair with "The Pushcart Peddlers"; published with and can pair with "Jealousy") DPS 2598

Schisgal, Murray, "The Tiger," a drama (not to be confused with the play of the same name by Jules Tasca from Sali, a.k.a. H. H. Munro and, furthermore, not to be confused with the play of the same name by Demetrio Aguilera Malta), 1m1f, (published with and can pair with "The Typists") DPS 4545

Schisgal, Murray, "The Typists," a drama, 1m1f, (published with and can pair with "The Tiger") DPS 4545

Schisgal, Murray, "Walter," a comedy, 1m1f, (published with and can pair with "The Flatulist," "Little Johnny," or "The Pushcart Peddlers") in *The Pushcart Peddler, The Flatulist and Other Plays*, DPS 3740

Schneider, Barbara, "Crossings," a drama, 1m2f, (published with and can pair with "Flight Lines") DPS 2012

Schneider, Barbara, "Flight Lines," a drama, 1m2f, (published with and can pair with "Crossings") DPS 2012

Sears, Joe, "Eddie Lee, Eddie Lee," a comedy, 1m2f, SF 6991

Seiler, Conrad, "Good Night, Caroline," a farce, 2m2f, DPS 2175, NSHS pb8030

Seligman, Marjorie, "'Rosemary—That's for Remembrance,'" a comedy, 2f, (published with and can pair with "The Dormant Heritage," "Enterprising Oswald," "Girls Will Be Girls," "Grandma Fought the Indians," "Make-Up," "Paris Sets the Styles," "She Goes the Rounds" or "Truant Husbands") in *Two by Two*, BP, NSHS pb6044, NSHS 29326

Semerano, Frank, and John Rustan, "Stray Cats," a comedy, 2m1f, AR, NSHS pb6842

Serpas, Stephen, "Waning Crescent Moon," a drama, 2m1f, BP

Severson, William, "The Path of the Ancient Chinaman," a drama, 2m1f, AR

Shachnovitz, Sura, "A Blind Date with Mary," a comedy, 1m2f, in *Off-Off Broadway Festival Plays, 14th Series*, SF 4703

Shaffer, Peter (English playwright, 1926-   ), "The Private Ear," a comedy, 2m1f, BP, HDS, (can pair with "The Public Eye") SF 855, NSHS pb5485, NSHS 29198

Shaffer, Peter (English playwright, 1926-   ), "The Public Eye," a comedy, 2m1f, BP, (can pair with "The Private Ear") SF 856, NSHS pb5474, NSHS pb8168

Shaffer, Peter (English playwright, 1926-   ), "White Liars,"

0-14-045031-9, ISBN 0-14-045024-6, SF 10670, NSHS

Shaw, George Bernard, (Irish-born English playwright and author, 1856-1950), "The Music-Cure," a comedy, 2m1f, (published with and can pair with "Annajanska, the Bolshevik Empress," "Augustus Does His Bit," "The Dark Lady of the Sonnets," "The Glimpse of Reality," "How He Lied to Her Husband," "O'Flaherty V. C.," "Overruled," or "Village Wooing") in [George] Bernard Shaw's *Selected Short Plays*, definitive text under editorial supervision of Dan H. Laurence (London: Penguin Books, Ltd., 1988), ISBN 0-14-045031-9, ISBN 0-14-045024-6, SF 15711, NSHS

Shaw, George Bernard, (Irish-born English playwright and author, 1856-1950), "O'Flaherty V. C.," a comedy, 2m2f, (published with and can pair with "Annajanska, the Bolshevik Empress," "Augustus Does His Bit," "The Dark Lady of the Sonnets," "The Glimpse of Reality," "How He Lied to Her Husband," "The Music-Cure," "Overruled," or "Village Wooing") in [George] Bernard Shaw's *Selected Short Plays*, definitive text under editorial supervision of Dan H. Laurence (London: Penguin Books, Ltd., 1988), ISBN 0-14-045031-9, ISBN 0-14-045024-6, SF 17607, NSHS

Shaw, George Bernard, (Irish-born English playwright and author, 1856-1950), "Overruled," a comedy, 2m2f, (published with and can pair with "Annajanska, the Bolshevik Empress," "Augustus Does His Bit," "The Dark Lady of the Sonnets," "The Glimpse of Reality," "How He Lied to Her Husband," "The Music-Cure," "O'Flaherty V. C.," or "Village Wooing") in [George] Bernard Shaw's *Selected Short Plays*, definitive text under editorial supervision of Dan H. Laurence (London: Penguin Books, Ltd., 1988), ISBN 0-14-045031-9, ISBN 0-14-045024-6, SF 17651, NSHS

Shaw, George Bernard, (Irish-born English playwright and author, 1856-1950), "Village Wooing," a comedy, 1m1f, (published with and can pair with "Annajanska, the Bolshevik Empress," "Augustus Does His Bit," "The Dark Lady of the Sonnets," "The Glimpse of Reality," "How He Lied to Her Husband," "The Music-Cure," "O'Flaherty V. C.," or "Overruled") in [George] Bernard Shaw's *Selected Short Plays*, definitive text under the editorial supervision of Dan H. Laurence (London: Penguin Books, Ltd., 1988), ISBN 0-14-045031-9, SF 24604

Shawn, Wallace, "The Fever," a drama, 1m, in Wallace Shawn's *The Fever* (New York: Noonday Press, 1991), ISBN 0-374-52270-7; also in *The Fever* (New York: Dramatists Play Service, 1992), DPS

Shem, Samuel, "Napoleon's Dinner," a comedy, 3m, (published with and can pair with "Room for One Woman") in *Napoleon's Dinner and Room for One Woman*, SF 16602, NSHS pb7921, ISBN 0-573-60052-1

Shem, Samuel, "Room for One Woman," a drama, 3f, (published with and can pair with "Napoleon's Dinner") in *Napoleon's Dinner and Room for One Woman*, SF 20636, NSHS pb7921, ISBN 0-573-60052-1

Shengold, Nina, "Women and Shoes," a sketch, 2m, JAT

Shepard, Sam, "Action," a drama, 2m2f, in *Fool for Love & Other Plays*, SF 3603, NSHS pb8099

Shepard, Sam, "Cowboy Mouth," a lengthy one-act drama, 2m1f, in *Fool for Love & Other Plays*, SF 5158, NSHS pb8099

Shepard, Sam, "Cowboys #2," a drama, 4m, (published with and can pair with "4-H Club," "Killer's Head," "Red Cross" or "The Rock Garden") in *Unseen Hand & Other Plays*, SF 5721, NSHS pb7928, ISBN 0-553-34263-0

Shepard, Sam, "Fool for Love," a lengthy one-act drama, 3m1f, HDS, NSHS pb8099

Shepard, Sam, "The 4-H Club," a drama, 3m, (published with and can pair with "Cowboys #2," "Killer's Head," "Red Cross" or "The Rock Garden") in *The Unseen Hand and Other Plays*, SF 8641, NSHS pb7928, ISBN 0-553-34263-0

Shepard, Sam, "The Holy Ghostly," a drama, 3m1f, in *The Unseen Hand and Other Plays*, SF 10655

Shepard, Sam, "Killer's Head," a drama, 1m, (published with and can pair with "Cowboys #2," "The 4-H Club," "Red Cross" or "The Rock Garden") in *The Unseen Hand & Other Plays*, SF 13610, NSHS pb7928, ISBN 0-553-34263-0

Shepard, Sam, "Red Cross," a drama, 1m2f, in "Chicago and Other Plays," and (published with and can pair with "Cowboys #2," "The 4-H Club," "Killer's Head" or "The Rock Garden") in *The Unseen Hand & Other Plays*, SF 20611, NSHS pb7928, ISBN 0-553-34263-0

Shepard, Sam, "The Rock Garden," a drama, 2m1f, (published with and can pair with "Cowboys #2," "The 4-H Club," "Killer's Head" or "Red Cross") in *The Unseen Hand & Other Plays*, SF 20625, NSHS pb7928, ISBN 0-553-34263-0

Shepard, Sam, "Shaved Splits," a drama, 3m1f, in *The Unseen Hand and Other Plays*, SF 21674

Shepard, Sam, and Joseph Chaikin, "Savage/Love," a monodrama, a bill of theatre poems, 1m, in *Sam Shepard: Seven Plays*, SF 21637

Shepard, Sam, and Joseph Chaikin, "Tongues," a monodrama, a piece for voice and percussion, 1m, **analyzed in Part 4, p. 253**, in *Sam Shepard: Seven Plays*, SF 22733, NSHS 28227

Shine, Ted, "Contribution," a comedy, 1m2f, DPS 1425

Shirley, J. Michael, "The Doctor Is In," a comedy, 2m2f (6 flexible roles), ELD

Shurtz, Raymond King, "Cowboys, Indians and Waitresses," a comic-drama, 2m1f, in *Off-Off Broadway Festival Plays, 17th Series*, SF 349

Silverman, Judd, "Correct Address," a drama, 2m, in *Off-Off Broadway Festival Plays, 17th Series*, SF 342

Silverstein, Shel, "The Devil and Billy Markham," a bare-stage comedy, 1m, (published with and can pair with "Bobby Gould in Hell," by David Mamet) in *Oh, Hell! Two One-Act Plays* (New York: Samuel French), ISBN 0-573-69254-8, SF 6728, NSHS pb8115

Simms, Willard, "The Acting Lesson," a drama, 3m1f, (part of the trilogy *Variations on an Untitled Theme* and can pair with "Miss Farnsworth") DPS 620, NSHS pb8082

Simms, Willard, "Miss Farnsworth," a comedy-drama, 3m1f, (part of the trilogy *Variations on an Untitled Theme* and can pair with "The Acting Lesson") DPS 620

Simms, Willard, "Now [or Soft Discs Don't Drive Hard Enough]," a comedy, 3m1f, in *Then and Now*, DPS 4482, NSHS pb8026

Simms, Willard, "The Passing of an Actor," a comedy-drama, 3m1f, (part of the trilogy *Variations on an Untitled Theme*) DPS 3575

Simms, Willard, "Then [or I Love Lucy Who?]," a comedy, 3m1f, in *Then and Now*, DPS 4482, NSHS pb8026

Simms, Willard, "Two's a Crowd," a comedy, 1m1f, DPS 4670

Simpson, N. F., "The Form," a comedy, 2m2f, SF 8639, NSHS pb8066

Simpson, N. F., "A Resounding Tinkle," a comedy, 1m2f, ISBN 0-573-02229-1, SF 20, NSHS pb5477

Skinner, Cornelia Otis, "American Ancestor Worship," a pick-and-choose bill of satirical skits, **analyzed in Part 4, p. 181**, 1f, DPC, NSHS

Slaight, Brad, "Sightings," a comedy, 2m1f, (can pair with "Senior Prom") in *High Tide*, BP

Slocum, Richard (adaptor from Japanese), "The Gemshield Sleeper," a Kabuki and puppet drama for children based on a Japanese version of a classic fairy tale, 3m1f, (published with and can pair with "The Fisherman and the Flounder" or "The Love Song of A. Nellie Goodrock") in Richard Slocum's *The Gemshield Sleeper and Other Plays for Children* (New York: Samuel French, Inc., 1988), ISBN 0-573-65223-6, SF

Slocum, Richard, "The Love Song of A. Nellie Goodrock," a melodrama for children, 2m2f (+ extras), (published with and can pair with "The Fisherman and the Flounder" or "The Gemshield Sleeper") in Richard Slocum's *The Gemshield Sleeper and Other Plays for Children* (New York: Samuel French, Inc., 1988), ISBN 0-573-65223-6, SF

Slocum, Richard, "Proposin'," a comedy western from Anton Chekhov, 1m2f, BP

Smiley, Sam, "Date," a comedy, 1m3f, SF 6605, NSHS pb7727

Smiley, Sam, "Property of the Dallas Cowboys," a brief comedy, 1m2f, (published with and can pair with "Advice to a New Actor," "The Affidavit," "The American Way," "Anniversary," "Auld Lang Syne, or I'll Bet You Think This Play Is About You," "Bug Swatter," "Checkers," "Coming for a Visit," "Dalmation," "Dog Eat Dog,"

"Drowned Out," "Fireworks," "Interview," "Jumping," "Money," "One Beer Too Many," "Phonecall from Sunkist," "Potato Girl," "The Split Decision," "Valley Forgery," "Watermelon Boats," or "Widows") in Norman A. Bert's *One-Act Plays for Acting Students*, MPL, ISBN 0-916260-47-X, pb7929

Smith, Beatrice S., "The Mice That Ate the Money," a dramatization of a folktale from India, 4m, in *The Big Book of Folktale Plays*, edited by Syliva E. Kamerman (Boston: Plays, Inc., 1991), ISBN 0-8238-0294-9

Smith, Betty, and Chase Webb, "Mañana Bandits: A Legend of the Rio Grande," a drama, 4m, GCB, NSHS 5345

Smith, Leo, "Whence," a drama, 1m1f, SF 25661

Smith, Steven, and Tom Dudzick, "Me Too, Then!" a comedy, 2m1f, **analyzed in Part 4, p. 217**, in *Off-Off Broadway Festival Plays,* Vol. 5, SF 15651, NSHS 27534

Smith, Valerie, and Michael Bigelow Dixon, "The Pick-Up," a comedy, 2m2f (+ optional extras), (published with and can pair with "Blind Alleys" or "Clean") in *Big Trouble: Six 10-Minute Plays from Actors Theatre of Louisville*, IEC 324-1

Snodgrass, Katherine, "Haiku," a drama, 3f, in *The Best Short Plays, 1988-1989*, edited by Ramon Delgado (New York: Applause Theatre Book Publishers, 1989); also in Katherine Snodgrass' *Haiku* (New York: Samuel French, Inc., 1989), ISBN 0-573-63254-5, SF 10650

Sodaro, Craig, "Cradle Camp," a drama, 1m3f, ACP

Sorkin, Aaron, "Hidden in This Picture," a satire that subsequently became the second act of *Making Movies*, 4m, (published with *Making Movies*) also in *The Best American Short Plays, 1990*, edited by Howard Stein and Glenn Young (New York: Applause Theatre Book Publishers, 1991), ISSN 1062-7561, SF 10687

Souchuk, Perry, "The Pleasure of Detachment," a play (genre?), 2m2f (+ extras), in *Antaeus: Plays in One Act*, No. 66, edited by Daniel Halpern (Spring 1991), ISBN 0-88001-268-4, ANT

Soyinka, Wole, "The Golden Accord," a ten-minute play (genre?), 2m1f, SF

Spalter, Max (translator), *Last Days of Mankind*, Act V, Scene 54, a monologue excerpt from the original German full-length play by Karl Kraus, 1m, KV, NSHS 29408

Spera, Robert, "The Field," a ten-minute play (genre?), 2m, (published with and can pair with "Advice to a New Actor," "The Affidavit," "The American Way," "Anniversary," "Auld Lang Syne, or I'll Bet You Think This Play Is About You," "Bug Swatter," "Checkers," "Coming for a Visit," "Dalmation," "Dog Eat Dog," "Drowned Out," "Fireworks," "Interview," "Jumping," "Looking Good," "Money," "One Beer Too Many," "Phonecall from Sunkist," "Potato Girl," "Property of the Dallas Cowboys," "The Split Decision," "Valley Forgery," "Watermelon Boats," or "Widows") in *25 10-Minute Plays* *from Actors Theatre of Louisville,* edited by Actors Theatre of Louisville (New York: Samuel French, Inc., 1989), ISBN 0-573-62558-1, SF 6716

Sprigge, Elizabeth (translator from Swedish), Strindberg, August, "Miss Julie," a drama, translated by Elizabeth Sprigge, 1m2f (+extras), (can pair with "The Stronger") in *Eight Plays for Theatre,* edited by Robert Cohen (Mountain View, California: Mayfield Publishing Company, 1988), SF 15116; (translated by E. M. Sprinchorn, in *Seeds of Modern Drama*), SF 15674; (translated by Harry G. Carlson, in *Strindberg: Five Plays*), DPS 273; (translated by Michael Meyer) WKW, CPC, NSHS 29262, NSHS 19878, NSHS 19883, NSHS 29323, NSHS 29252, NSHS 5211, NSHS 27003, NSHS 16361, NSHS 20545

Sprinchorn, E. M. (translator from Swedish), Strindberg, August, "Miss Julie," a drama, translated by E. M. Sprinchorn, 1m2f (+extras), (can pair with "The Stronger") in *Seeds of Modern Drama*), SF 15674; in *Eight Plays for Theatre,* edited by Robert Cohen (Mountain View, California: Mayfield Publishing Company, 1988), SF 15116; (translated by Harry G. Carlson, in *Strindberg: Five Plays*), DPS 273; (translated by Michael Meyer) WKW, CPC, NSHS 29262, NSHS 19878, NSHS 19883, NSHS 29323, NSHS 29252, NSHS 5211, NSHS 27003, NSHS 16361, NSHS 20545

Ssu Fan, "Longing for Worldly Pleasures," a Chinese traditional K'unshan play, 1m or 1f, **analyzed in Part 4, p. 214,** in Adolphe C. Scott's translation of *Traditional Chinese Plays,* Volume 2 (Madison, Wisconsin: The University of Wisconsin Press, 1969), ISBN 0-299-05370-9, ISBN 0-299-05734-1

Stein, Mark, "The Groves of Academe," a comedy drama, 2m, (published with and can pair with "The Plumber's Apprentice"), DPS 2245

Stetson, Jeff, "The Meeting," a drama, 3m, DPS 3108

Stevenson, Robert Louis (source Scottish short story writer and novelist, 1850-1894), "The Sire deMaletroit's Door," a drama by Jules Tasca, 2m1f, DPC S75, NSHS pb161

Stevenson, Robert Louis (source Scottish short story writer and novelist, 1850-1894), "Will," a drama by Jules Tasca from Robert Louis Stevenson, 2m2f, BP

Stewart, Luke, "Daft Danny," a comedy, 3m1f (+voice), SF 6602, NSHS pb7744

Stone, Trude, "Hello, Ma!" a comedy, 2f, **analyzed in Part 4, p. 205,** in *Off-Off Broadway Festival Plays,* Vol. 5, SF 10630, NSHS 27534

Strand, Richard, "Harry and Sylvia," a comedy-drama, 3m1f, AR, NSHS pb5723

Strindberg, August (Swedish playwright, 1849-1912), "Miss Julie," a drama, translated by Elizabeth Sprigge, 1m2f (+extras), (can pair with "The Stronger") in *Eight Plays for Theatre,* edited by Robert Cohen (Mountain View, California: Mayfield Publishing Company, 1988), SF

15116; (translated by E. M. Sprinchorn, in *Seeds of Modern Drama*), SF 15674; (translated by Harry G. Carlson, in *Strindberg: Five Plays*), DPS 273; (translated by Michael Meyer) WKW, CPC, NSHS 29262, NSHS 19878, NSHS 19883, NSHS 29323, NSHS 29252, NSHS 5211, NSHS 27003, NSHS 16361, NSHS 20545

Strindberg, August (source Swedish playwright, 1849-1912), "Outlanders," a drama by Amlin Gray from August Strindberg, 3m1f, (published with and can pair with "Wormwood") in *Zones of the Spirit,* DPS 5043, NSHS pb7915

Strindberg, August (Swedish playwright, 1849-1912), "The Stronger," a drama, translated by Michael Meyer, 2f (+extra), **analyzed in Part 4, p. 247,** (can pair with "Miss Julie") in *Plays by August Strindberg,* DPS 252, NSHS 29262

Strindberg, August (source Swedish playwright, 1849-1912), "Wormwood," a drama by Amlin Gray from August Strindberg, 3m1f, (published with and can pair with "Outlanders") in *Zones of the Spirit,* DPS 5043, NSHS pb7915

Stroppel, Frederick, "A Chance Meeting," a comedy, 2m1f, in *Off-Off Broadway Festival Plays, 15th Series,* SF 5787, NSHS pb8079

Stroppel, Frederick, "Mamet Women," a comedy, 2f, (published and can pair with "Domestic Violence," "Morning Coffee," "Package Deal," or "Single and Proud") in Frederick Stroppel's *Single and Proud and Other Plays* (New York: Samuel French, Inc.), ISBN 0-573-69411-7, SF 15585, NSHS pb8090

Stroppel, Frederick, "Package Deal," a comedy, 2f, (published and can pair with "Domestic Violence," "Mamet Women," "Morning Coffee," or "Single and Proud") in Frederick Stroppel's *Single and Proud and Other Plays* (New York: Samuel French, Inc.), ISBN 0-573-69411-7, SF 17955, NSHS pb8090

Stroppel, Frederick, "Single and Proud," a comedy, 1m3f, (published and can pair with "Domestic Violence," "Mamet Women," "Morning Coffee," or "Package Deal") in Frederick Stroppel's *Single and Proud and Other Plays* (New York: Samuel French, Inc.), ISBN 0-573-69411-7, SF 21158, NSHS pb8090

Swanson, Maura, "Gotta Dance," a comedy, 1m2f, in *Dramatics,* 64, no. 9 (May 1992): 22-25. Inquiries regarding performance rights and royalties should be directed to the playwright at 339 Skyline Drive, Cold Spring, Kentucky 41076.

Sweet, Jeffrey, "After the Fact," a comedy-drama, **analyzed in Part 4, p. 179,** 1m1f (can pair with "Cover" and "Last Day of Camp), ISBN 0-573-62028-8, SF 3608, NSHS 27521, PSP

Sweet, Jeffrey, "Last Day of Camp," a ten-minute play (genre?), 2m1f, (can pair with "After the Fact" and "Cover") SF 13852

Sweet, Jeffrey, with Stephen Johnson and Sandra Hastie,

"Cover," a ten-minute play (genre?), 2m1f, (published with and can pair with "Advice to a New Actor," "The Affidavit," "The American Way," "Anniversary," "Auld Lang Syne, or I'll Bet You Think This Play Is About You," "Bug Swatter," "Checkers," "Coming for a Visit," "Dalmation," "Dog Eat Dog," "Drowned Out," "Fireworks," "Interview," "Jumping," "Looking Good," "Money," "One Beer Too Many," "Phonecall from Sunkist," "Potato Girl," "Property of the Dallas Cowboys," "The Split Decision," "Valley Forgery," "Watermelon Boats," or "Widows") in *25 10-Minute Plays from Actors Theatre of Louisville,* edited by Actors Theatre of Louisville (New York: Samuel French, Inc., 1989), ISBN 0-573-62558-1, SF 6716

Swet, Peter, "The Interview," a drama, 2m, DPS 2560

Swicord, Robin, "Criminal Minds," a comic drama, 2m1f, SF, NSHS pb7512

Synge, John Millington (Irish poet and playwright, 1920- , 1871-1909), "In the Shadow of the Glen," a comedy, 3m1f, in *Complete Plays of Synge,* SF 11646, NSHS 27039, NSHS pb4019 NSHS 14824, NSHS 20483, NSHS 21389, NSHS 21514, NSHS 21776

Synge, John Millington (Irish poet and playwright, 1920- , 1871-1909), "Riders to the Sea," a drama, 1m3f, **analyzed in Part 4, p. 235,** BP, HDS, SF 920, NSHS 2212, NSHS 7095, NSHS 8162, NSHS 16020, NSHS 16370, NSHS 16374, NSHS 19878, NSHS 19883, NSHS 21405, NSHS 26428, NSHS 29310 [Note: Some critics call this "the greatest one-act play ever written."]

T

Taggart, Tom, "She Goes the Rounds," a comedy, 2f, (published with and can pair with "The Dormant Heritage," "Enterprising Oswald," "Grandma Fought the Indians," "Make-Up," "Paris Sets the Styles," "'Rosemary—That's for Remembrance,'" or "Truant Husbands") in *Two by Two,* BP, NSHS pb6044, NSHS 29326

Taikeff, Stanley, "Ah, Eurydice!" a lyrical fantasy, 2m1f, DPS 645

Tally, Ted, "Silver Linings," bare-stage revue sketches, 2m1f, DPS 4088

Tasca, Jules, "The Background," a comedy adapted for the stage from the short story by Saki (H. H. Munro), 3m1f, (published with and can pair with "Blind Spot," "Dusk," "The Hen," "The Reticence of Lady Anne," "Secret Sin," "The Tiger," or "The Unrest Cure") in Jules Tasca's *Tales by Saki: Adapted for Stage by Jules Tasca* (New York: Samuel French, Inc., 1989), ISBN 0-573-62560-3, SF 22133, NSHS pb7798, NSHS pb8113

Tasca, Jules, "The Baker's Neighbor," a comedy, 4m or 4f, BP

Tasca, Jules, "The Best Souvenirs," a comedy [set in Venice], 2m1f, (published with and can pair with [Athens:] "Passion Comedy," [Engelberg:] "Swiss Miss," [London:] "A

Day in the Night of Rose Arden," [Munich:] "A Side Trip to Dachau," [Paris:] "Escape," [Rome:] "Going to the Catacombs," or [Vienna:] "The Stop at the Palace") in Jules Tasca's *Tour di Europa* [Tour of Europe] (New York: Samuel French, Inc.), ISBN 0-573-69222-X, SF 4708, NSHS pb8105

Tasca, Jules, "Between the Lines," a comedy, 1m2f, in *The God's Honest, An Evening of Lies,* SF 3983, NSHS

Tasca, Jules, "Blind Spot," a comedy adapted for the stage from the short story by Saki (H. H. Munro), 3m, (published with and can pair with "The Background," "Dusk," "The Hen," "The Reticence of Lady Anne," "Secret Sin," "The Tiger," or "The Unrest Cure") in Jules Tasca's *Tales by Saki: Adapted for Stage by Jules Tasca* (New York: Samuel French, Inc., 1989), ISBN 0-573-62560-3, SF 22133, NSHS pb7798, NSHS pb8113

Tasca, Jules, "Brothers," a drama by, 3m1f, in *The God's Honest, An Evening of Lies,* SF 4162

Tasca, Jules, "The Devil," a farce from Guy de Maupassant, 2m2f, in (published with and can pair with "Father and Son," "Forbidden Fruit," or "The Necklace") *The Necklace and Other Stories,* SF 15990, NSHS 27500, NSHS pb7919

Tasca, Jules, "Dusk," a comedy from Saki (H. H. Munro), 3m, (published with and can pair with "The Background," "Blind Spot," "The Hen," "The Reticence of Lady Anne," "Secret Sin," "The Tiger," or "The Unrest Cure") in Jules Tasca's *Tales by Saki: Adapted for Stage by Jules Tasca* (New York: Samuel French, Inc., 1989), ISBN 0-573-62560-3, SF 22133, NSHS pb7798, NSHS pb8113

Tasca, Jules, "Escape," a comedy [set in Paris], 2m2f, (published with and can pair with [Athens:] "Passion Comedy," [Engelberg:] "Swiss Miss," [London:] "A Day in the Night of Rose Arden," [Munich:] "A Side Trip to Dachau," [Rome:] "Going to the Catacombs," [Venice] "The Best Souvenirs," or [Vienna:] "The Stop at the Palace") in Jules Tasca's *Tour di Europa* [Tour of Europe] (New York: Samuel French, Inc.), ISBN 0-573-69222-X, SF 7635, NSHS pb8105

Tasca, Jules, "Going to the Catacombs," a drama [set in Rome], 3f, (published with and can pair with [Athens:] "Passion Comedy," [Engelberg:] "Swiss Miss," [London:] "A Day in the Night of Rose Arden," [Munich:] "A Side Trip to Dachau," [Paris:] "Escape," [Venice] "The Best Souvenirs," or [Vienna:] "The Stop at the Palace") in Jules Tasca's *Tour di Europa* [Tour of Europe] (New York: Samuel French, Inc.), ISBN 0-573-69222-X, SF 9701, NSHS pb8105

Tasca, Jules, "Hardstuff," a drama, 2m, in *The God's Honest, An Evening of Lies,* SF 10608

Tasca, Jules, "The Hen," a comedy adapted for the stage from the short story by Saki (H. H. Munro), 2m2f, (published with and can pair with "The Background," "Dusk," "The Reticence of Lady Anne," "Secret Sin," "The Tiger," or

"The Unrest Cure") in Jules Tasca's *Tales by Saki: Adapted for Stage by Jules Tasca* (New York: Samuel French, Inc., 1989), ISBN 0-573-62560-3, SF 22133, NSHS pb7798, NSHS pb8113

Tasca, Jules (adaptor), "Mrs. McWilliams and the Lighting," a comedy from Mark Twain, 2m1f, in *Five One-Act Plays by Mark Twain*, SF 15613

Tasca, Jules (translator from French and adaptor), "The Necklace," a drama from Guy de Maupassant, 1m2f, **analyzed in Part 4, p. 219**, (published with and can pair with "The Devil," "Father and Son," or "Forbidden Fruit") in *The Necklace and Other Stories*, SF 15990, DPC N10, NSHS 27500, NSHS pb7919

Tasca, Jules, "Opening Act," a comedy, 2m1f, in *The God's Honest, An Evening of Lies*, SF 17663

Tasca, Jules (adaptor), "The Reticence of Lady Anne," a comedy adapted from the short story by Saki (H. H. Munro), 1m, in Jules Tasca's *Tales by Saki: Adapted for Stage by Jules Tasca* (New York: Samuel French, Inc., 1989), ISBN 0-573-62560-3

Tasca, Jules, "Romance Ranch: The Fantasy Bond," a drama, 1m1f, (published with "The Dark," "The Fantasy Bond," "Inflatable You," "The Man in Blue," "Penance," or "Snocky") in *Jules Tasca's Romance Ranch,* a suite of eight one-act plays set in Romance Ranch Hotel, in Los Angeles (New York: Samuel French, Inc., 1991), ISBN 0-573-62434-8, SF 8162

Tasca, Jules, "Romance Ranch: Finding the Love of Your Life", a drama, 2m1f, (published with "The Dark," "The Fantasy Bond," "Inflatable You," "The Man in Blue," "Penance," or "Snocky") in *Jules Tasca's Romance Ranch*, a suite of eight one-act plays set in Romance Ranch Hotel, in Los Angeles (New York: Samuel French, Inc., 1991), ISBN 0-573-62434-8, SF 7997

Tasca, Jules, "Romance Ranch: Inflatable You," a comedy, 2m, (published with "The Dark," "Data Entry," "The Fantasy Bond," "Finding the Love of Your Life," "The Man in Blue," "Penance," or "Snocky") in Jules Tasca's *Romance Ranch*, a suite of eight one-act plays set in Romance Ranch Hotel, in Los Angeles (New York: Samuel French, Inc., 1991), ISBN 0-573-62434-8, SF 11112

Tasca, Jules, "Romance Ranch: Penance," a drama, 2m, (published with "The Dark," "Data Entry," "The Fantasy Bond," "Finding the Love of Your Life," "Inflatable You," "The Man in Blue," or "Snocky") in *Jules Tasca's Romance Ranch*, a suite of eight one-act plays set in Romance Ranch Hotel, in Los Angeles (New York: Samuel French, Inc., 1991), ISBN 0-573-62434-8, SF 17974

Tasca, Jules, "Second Vows," a comedy, 2m1f, in *The God's Honest, An Evening of Lies*, SF 21653

Tasca, Jules, "Secret Sin," a comedy adapted for the stage from the short story by Saki (H. H. Munro), 2m1f, (published with and can pair with "The Background," "Blind Spot," "Dusk," "The Hen," "The Reticence of Lady

Anne," "The Tiger," or "The Unrest Cure") in Jules Tasca's *Tales by Saki: Adapted for Stage by Jules Tasca* (New York: Samuel French, Inc., 1989), ISBN 0-573-62560-3, SF 22133, NSHS pb7798, NSHS pb8113

Tasca, Jules, "A Side Trip to Dachau," a drama [set in Munich], 2m1f, (published with and can pair with [Athens:] "Passion Comedy," [Engelberg:] "Swiss Miss," [London:] "A Day in the Night of Rose Arden," [Paris:] "Escape," [Rome:] "Going to the Catacombs," [Venice] "The Best Souvenirs," or [Vienna:] "The Stop at the Palace") in Jules Tasca's *Tour di Europa* [Tour of Europe] (New York: Samuel French, Inc.), ISBN 0-573-69222-X, SF 21667, NSHS pb8105

Tasca, Jules (adaptor), "The Sire deMaletroit's Door," a drama from Robert Louis Stevenson, 2m1f, DPC S75, NSHS pb161

Tasca, Jules, "The Stop at the Palace," a drama [set in Vienna], 1m2f, (published with and can pair with [Athens:] "Passion Comedy," [Engelberg:] "Swiss Miss," [London:] "A Day in the Night of Rose Arden," [Munich] "A Side Trip to Dachau," [Paris:] "Escape," [Rome:] "Going to the Catacombs," or [Venice] "The Best Souvenirs") in Jules Tasca's *Tour di Europa* [Tour of Europe] (New York: Samuel French, Inc.), ISBN 0-573-69222-X, SF 21806, NSHS pb8105

Tasca, Jules (adaptor), "Support Your Local Police," a satire from Mark Twain (a.k.a. Samuel Langhorne Clemens), 3m, in *Five One-Act Plays by Mark Twain*, SF 21606

Tasca, Jules (adaptor), "That Pig, Morin," a drama by Jules Tasca from Guy de Maupassant, 2m2f (+ 2m extras), (published with and can pair with "The Devil," "Father and Son," or "Forbidden Fruit") in *The Necklace and Other Stories*, SF 15990, DPC N10, NSHS 27500, NSHS pb7919

Tasca, Jules, "The Tiger," a comedy adapted for stage from the short story by Saki, a.k.a. H. H. Munro (not to be confused with the play of the same name by Murray Schisgal and, furthermore, not to be confused with the play of the same name by Demetrio Aguilera Malta), 2f, (published with and can pair with "The Background," "Blind Spot," "Dusk," "The Hen," "The Unrest Cure," "The Reticence of Lady Anne," or "Secret Sin") in Jules Tasca's *Tales by Saki: Adapted for Stage by Jules Tasca* (New York: Samuel French, Inc., 1989), ISBN 0-573-62560-3, SF 22133, NSHS pb7798, NSHS pb8113

Tasca, Jules, "The Twin Mendaccios," a farce, 1m1f, in *The God's Honest, An Evening of Lies*, SF 22243

Tasca, Jules, "The Unrest Cure," a comedy adapted for the stage from the short story by Saki (H. H. Munro), 2m1f, (published with and can pair with "The Background," "Blind Spot," "Dusk," "The Hen," "The Reticence of Lady Anne," "Secret Sin," or "The Tiger") in Jules Tasca's *Tales by Saki: Adapted for Stage by Jules Tasca* (New York: Samuel French, Inc.), ISBN 0-573-62560-

3, SF 22133, NSHS pb7798, NSHS pb8113

Tasca, Jules (adaptor), "Will," a drama from Robert Louis Stevenson, 2m2f, BP

Tate, Lisa, and Anita Page (adaptors), "Stomach-Ache," a musical for children translated and adapted by Anita Page and Lisa Tate from Ninnie Olsson, 1m2f, BP

Taylor, Alec (English playwright), "Candy-Floss Man," a drama, 2m2f, (can pair with "The Green-Eyed Monster Comic Strip") in Alec Taylor's *Candy-Floss Man* (Macclesfield, Cheshire, England: New Playwrights Network, 1991), ISBN 0-86319-274-2, NPN

Taylor, Alec (English playwright), "The Green-Eyed Monster Comic Strip," a drama, 2m2f, (can pair with "Candy-Floss Man") in Alec Taylor's *Candy-Floss Man* (Macclesfield, Cheshire, England: New Playwrights Network, 1991), ISBN 0-86319-273-4, NPN

Taylor, Drew Hayden (Canadian playwright), "Toronto at Dreamer's Rock," a Canadian Indian drama, 3m, in Drew Hayden Taylor's *Toronto at Dreamer's Rock and Education Is Our Right: Two One-Act Plays* (Saskatoon, Saskatchewan, Canada: Fifth House, 1990), ISBN 0-920079-64-4, FH

Taylor, Glenhall, "The Perfect Tribute," a drama, 3m (+ extras), in *The Big Book of Holiday Plays: 21 Modern and Traditional One-Act Plays for the Celebration of Christmas*, edited by Sylvia E. Kamerman (Boston: Plays, Inc., 1988), ISBN 0-8238-0288-4

Taylor, Renée, and Joseph Bologna, "Alan, Betty and Riva," a comedy, 1m2f, in *Bedrooms*, SF 244

Taylor, Renée, and Joseph Bologna, "Nick and Wendy," a comedy, 2m1f, in *Bedrooms*, SF 244

Tellez, Leticia (Mexican playwright), "The Third Law of Newton" ["La tercera ley de Newton,"] a *farsa*/farce in Spanish/*en español*, 2m1f, OEN, NSHS pb8189

Terefenko, Thomas, "Emil's Leap," a comedy, 2m2f, PPC, NSHS pb54

Terry, Megan, "Calm Down Mother," a bare-stage drama, 3f, SF 301, NSHS pb7961

Terry, Megan, "Ex-Miss Copper Queen on a Set of Pills," a drama, 3f, (published with "People vs. Ranchman") SF 7650, NSHS pb7895

Terry, Megan, "Keep Tightly Closed in a Cool Dry Place," a drama 3m, SF 13605, NSHS pb7899

Terry, Megan, "The Pioneer," a drama, 2f or 2m, IEC

Terry, Megan, "Pro Game," a drama, 3m1f or 1m3f, EIC 217-2

Thompson, David (adaptor from German), "The Shoemaker's Wife," a farce from Hans Sachs' *"Der Todte Mann,"* 2m1f, (no royalty with purchase of three copies) BP 4663, NSHS 19998, NSHS pb7799

Thompson, Ernest, "The Constituent," a comedy, 2m, (published with and can pair with "A Good Time" or "Twinkle, Twinkle") in *Answers*, DPS 810

Thompson, Ernest, "Twinkle, Twinkle," a comedy, 2m1f,

(published with and can pair with "The Constituent" or "A Good Time") in *Answers*, DPS 810

Tobin, Scott, "Cotton Girls," a comedy, 3f, BP

Toddie, Jean Lennox, "A Bag of Green Apples," a drama, 1m3f (1 male child, 2 females, 1 female child), (can pair with "Lookin' for a Better Berry Bush") in Jean Lennox Toddie's *A Bag of Green Apples* (New York: Samuel French, Inc., 1990), ISBN 0-573-62032-6, SF 4705, NSHS pb8109

Toddie, Jean Lennox, "Lookin' for a Better Berry Bush," a comic drama, 2f, (can pair with "A Bag of Green Apples") in Jean Lennox Toddie's *Lookin' for a Better Berry Bush*, (New York, Samuel French, Inc., 1991), ISBN 0-573-63301-0, SF 14927

Toddie, Jean Lennox, "A Scent of Honeysuckle," a bare-stage comedy-drama, 3f, **analyzed in Part 4, p. 239**, (published with "A Little Something for the Ducks") ISBN 0-573-60059-7, SF 21041, NSHS 27492

Toddie, Jean Lennox, "Tell Me Another Story, Sing Me Another Song," a bare-stage drama, 2f, SF 22033, NSHS 27504, NSHS 27504

Tolan, Peter, "Best Half-Foot Forward," a sexual comedy, 4m, (published with and can pair with "Pillow Talk") in Peter Tolan's *Stay Carl Stay, Best Half-Foot Forward, and Pillow Talk: Three One-Act Plays* (New York: Dramatists Play Service, Inc., 1991) DPS 4266, NSHS pb7887 [Note: For adult audiences.]

Tolan, Peter, "Pillow Talk," a comedy, 2m, not to be confused by the play of the same name by John Pielmeier, (published with and can pair with "Best Half-Foot Forward") in *Stay Carl Stay, Best Half-Foot Forward, and Pillow Talk: Three One-Act Plays* (New York: Dramatists Play Service, Inc., 1991), DPS 4266, NSHS pb7887

Tompkins, Frank G., "Sham," a satire, 3m1f, BP

Topor, Tom, "Answers," a drama, **analyzed in Part 4, p. 183**, 3m, DPS 811, NSHS 29209, NSHS pb8208

Topor, Tom, "But Not for Me," a comedy, 2m1f, (published with "Here to Stay") in *Romance*, SF 20085

Topor, Tom, "Here to Stay," a comedy, 2m1f, (published with "But Not for Me") in *Romance*, SF 20084

Tovatt, Patrick, "Bartok as a Dog," a drama, 2m2f, DPS 932, NSHS pb7966, NSHS pb8034, NSHS pb7966

Tovatt, Patrick, "Husbandry," a drama, 2m2f, SF, NSHS pb7509

Tremblay, Brian, "Mandy and the Magus," a children's musical (singing) in three scenes, 2m2f, (one male is boy, one female is girl) in *Class Acts: Six Plays for Children*, edited by Tony Hamill (Toronto, Ontario, Canada: Playwrights Canada Press, 1992), ISBN 0-88754-487-8, PCP

Truex, James, "She Walks in Beauty," a television sketch appropriate for stage, 2m2f, NSHS 8266

Twain, Mark (subject here, a.k.a. Samuel Langhorne Clemens, 1835-1910), "The Loneliest Wayfarer," a comedy by Bernard Sabath about Mark Twain, 2m1f, (published with and can pair with "A Barbarian in Love," "Summer Morning Visitor," or "The Trouble Begins at 8") in Bernard Sabath's *Twain Plus Twain* (New York: Dramatists Play Service, Inc., 1984) DPS 4635, NSHS pb8024

Twain, Mark (source American short story writer), "Mrs. McWilliams and the Lighting," a comedy by Jules Tasca from Mark Twain, 2m1f, in *Five One-Act Plays by Mark Twain*, SF 15613

Twain, Mark (source American short story writer, a.k.a. Samuel Langhorne Clemens, 1835-1910), "Summer Morning Visitor," a comedy-drama by Bernard Sabath about Mark Twain, 1m2f, (published with and can pair with "A Barbarian in Love," "The Loneliest Wayfarer," or "The Trouble Begins at 8") in Bernard Sabath's *Twain Plus Twain* (New York: Dramatists Play Service, Inc., 1984), DPS 4635, NSHS pb8024

Twain, Mark (source American short story writer, a.k.a. Samuel Langhorne Clemens, 1835-1910), "Support Your Local Police," a satire by Jules Tasca from Mark Twain, 3m, in *Five One-Act Plays by Mark Twain*, SF 21606

Twain, Mark (source American short story writer, a.k.a. Samuel Langhorne Clemens, 1835-1910), "The Trouble Begins at 8," a comedy-drama by Bernard Sabath about Mark Twain a.ka. Samuel Langhorne Clemens, 3m1f, (published with and can pair with "A Barbarian in Love," "The Loneliest Wayfarer," or "Summer Morning Visitor") in Bernard Sabath's *Twain Plus Twain* (New York: Dramatists Play Service, Inc., 1984), DPS 4635, NSHS pb8024

Twedt, Jerry, "The Dropout," a drama, 2m2f (+voice), PPC, NSHS pb7726

U

Urdahl, Richard, "My Son's the One in the Flowered Apron," a comedy, 2m2f, BP

Urdahl, Richard, "This Isn't Scarsdale, Gus," a comedy, 2m1f, in *Don't Listen to Us Lord We're Only Praying*, BP

V

Vachss, Andrew, "Placebo," a drama, 1m, in *Antæus: Plays in One Act*, no. 66 (Spring 1991), Antæus [Ecco Press], ISBN 0-88001-268-4

Valdez, Luis, *"Las Dos Caras del Patroncito"* ["The Two Faces of the Dear Boss"], an agitprop (political satire), 3m, **analyzed in Part 4, page 215**, (published with and can pair with "The Militants") in Luis Valdez' *Luis Valdez—Early Works: Bernabé and Pensamiento Serpentino* (Houston, Texas: Arte Público Press, 1990), ISBN 1-55885-003-1, APP, NSHS

Valdez, Luis, "The Militants," an agitprop (political satire), 3m, (published with and can pair with *"Las Dos Caras del Patroncito"* ["The Two Faces of the Dear Boss"]) in Luis Valdez' *Luis Valdez—Early Works: Bernabé and Pensamiento Serpentino* (Houston, Texas: Arte Público Press, 1990), ISBN 1-55885-003-1, APP, NSH

Van Horne, Janice, "Fine Line," a comedy, 2f, SF 8130

van Itallie, Jean-Claude, "Final Orders," a satire, 2m, (published with and can pair with "Sunset Freeway" or "Bag Lady") in *Early Warnings*, DPS 1767

van Itallie, Jean-Claude, "Harold," a satire, 2m1f, (published with and can pair with "Eat Cake," "The Girl and the Soldier," "Photographs: Mary and Howard," "Rosary," or "Thoughts on the Instant of Greeting a Friend on the Street") in *Seven Short and Very Short Plays*, DPS 4726, NSHS pb65

van Itallie, Jean-Claude, "Motel," a masque for three dolls from "America Hurrah," 3m or 3f, (in doll masks and bodies + offstage voice) in *America Hurrah*, DPS 705

van Itallie, Jean-Claude, "Rosary," a comedy by Jean-Claude Van Itallie, 1f, **analyzed in Part 4, p. 237**, (published with and can pair with "Eat Cake," "Girl and the Soldier," "Harold," "Photographs: Mary and Howard," or "Thoughts on the Instant of Greeting a Friend on the Street") in *Seven Short and Very Short Plays* DPS 4726, NSHS pb65

van Itallie, Jean-Claude, "Take a Deep Breath," 2m1f, DPS, NSHS pb65

van Itallie, Jean-Claude, "War," a drama, 2m1f, (published with and can pair with "The Hunter and the Bird" or "I'm Really Here") in *Five Short Plays*, DPS 4725, NSHS pb7878

van Itallie, Jean-Claude, and Joseph Chaikin, "Struck Dumb," a drama, 1m, in *The Best American Short Plays, 1990/ 1991-1992*, 2 vols., edited by Howard Stein and Glenn Young, Applause, ISSN 1062-7561

Vaughan, Sylvia (English playwright), "Bella, Bella," a comedy, 4f, (can pair with "Lifestyles") in Sylvia Vaughan's *Bella, Bella* (Macclesfield, Cheshire, England: New Playwrights Network, 1989), ISBN 0-86319-221-1

Vaughan, Sylvia (English playwright), "Lifestyles," a drama, 2f, (can pair with "Bella, Bella") in Sylvia Vaughan's *Lifestyles* (Burton Joyce, Nottingham, England: Playwrights Publishing Company, 1991), ISBN 0-873130-03-1

Vernick, Phyllis, "Don't Wake Henry," a drama, 2m2f, PPC, NSHS pb7796

Vernick, Phyllis, "Vicky," a comedy from Saki (H. H. Munro), 2m2f, DPC V13

Villane, Ron, "An Empty Space," a drama, 1m1f, **analyzed in Part 4, p. 200**, (published with and can pair with "Open Admissions" or "Nothing Immediate") in Double Image Theatre's *Off-Off Broadway Festival Plays, Fourth Series* (New York: Samuel French, Inc., 1983), Samuel

French, Inc., 1983), SF 7613, NSHS 27533, ISBN 0-573-60044-9

Violett, Ellen, "Encore," a drama from James Purdy, 2m1f, cited in *The Best Plays of 1963-1964*, edited by Henry Hewes

Violett, Ellen, "Everything Under the Sun," a drama from James Purdy, 2m, cited in *The Best Plays of 1963-1964*, edited by Henry Hewes

Violett, Ellen (adaptor), "Sermon," a drama from James Purdy (not to be confused with David Mamet's "A Sermon" or James Purdy's "Sermon,"), 1m, cited in *The Best Plays of 1963-1964*, edited by Henry Hewes

Vonnegut, Kurt, Jr. (source short story writer), "The Lie," a drama by Vaughn McBride from Kurt Vonnegut, Jr., 3m1f, DPC L75

W

Wagner, Paula, Jack Hofsiss, and Eve Merriam, "Out of Our Father's House," a play (genre?) with music based on Eve Merriam's *Growing up Female in America*, 3f (in six roles), SF 811, BP

Walker, Peter, "Hey Neighbor!" a comedy, 1m3f, BP

Wallace, Joseph (adaptor from Russian), "A Wild Boor," a farce by Joseph Wallace from Anton Chekhov, 2m2f, (Boston: Baker's Plays, 1991) BP. [See also "A Bear with a Sore Head," an adaptation by Brian J. Burton and translations of "The Bear," by Michael Frayn and Ronald Hingley.]

Warburton, N. J., "Don't Blame It on the Boots," a comedy, 1m3f, SF 6713, NSHS pb7910

Ward, Douglas Turner, "Brotherhood," a black comedy, 2m2f, (can pair with "Happy Ending") DPS 1155, NSHS pb7965, NSHS pb8151

Ward, Douglas Turner, "Happy Ending," a satiric comedy, 2m2f, (can pair with "Brotherhood") DPS 1560, NSHS 8148

Waterhouse, Keith, "The Sponge Room," a play (genre?), 2m1f, cited in *The Best Plays of 1963-1964*, edited by Henry Hewes

Waterhouse, Keith, "Squat Betty," a play (genre?), 2m1f, cited in T*he Best Plays of 1963-1964*, edited by Henry Hewes

Watson, Ara, "Bite the Hand," a comedy, 1m2f, (published with and can pair with "Mooncastle") DPS 1033

Watson, Ara, "The Duck Pond," a ten-minute drama, 1m2f, (published with and can pair with "Americansaint," "Après Opéra," "'The Asshole Murder Case,'" "Bread," "Cold Water," "Cover," "Downtown," "The Drummer," "The Duck Pond," "Eating Out," "Electric Roses," "The Field," "4 A.M. (open all night)," "Looking Good," "Love and Peace, Mary Jo," "Loyalties," "Marred Bliss," "The Road to Ruin," "Spades," or "Watermelon Boats") in *25 10-Minute Plays from Actors Theatre of Louisville*, edited by Actors Theatre of Louisville (New York: Sam-

uel French, Inc., 1989), ISBN 0-573-62558-1, SF 6716

Watson, Ara, "Mooncastle," a comedy, 2m1f, (published with and can pair with "Bite the Hand") DPS 1033

Watson, Donald (translator from French), "The New Tenant," a farce by Eugene Ionesco, 3m1f, in Eugene Ionesco's *Three Plays by Ionesco* and in Eugene Ionesco's *Amédée/The New Tenant/Victims of Duty*, translated by Donald Watson (New York: Grove Press, 1958), ISBN 0-8021-3101-8, SF 16617, NSHS pb8118

Watson, John (Scottish playwright), "The Night Out," a comedy, 2m2f, in John Watson's *The Night Out* (Glasgow, Scotland: Brown, Son & Ferguson, 1992), ISBN 0-85174-612-8

Watson, William, "The Breaking of Bread," a drama, 2m, BP (no royalty with purchase of three copies)

Waxman, Rena, and Stanley Waxman, "Welcome Home," a comedy, 1m1f, SF, NSHS pb6046

Waxman, Stanley, and Rena Waxman, "Welcome Home," a comedy, 1m1f, SF, NSHS pb6046

Way, Brian, "Adventure Faces," a play (genre?) for children, 2m2f, BP

Way, Brian, "Balloon Faces," a play (genre?) for children, 2m2f, BP

Way, Brian, "The Bell," a play (genre?) for children, 2m2f, BP

Way, Brian, "The Clown," a play (genre?) for children, 2m2f, BP

Way, Brian, "The Decision," a play (genre?) for children, 2m2f, BP

Way, Brian, "The Hat," a play (genre?) for children, 2m2f, BP

Way, Brian, "The Key," a play (genre?) for children, 2m2f, BP

Way, Brian, "The Ladder," a play (genre?) for children, 2m2f, BP

Way, Brian, "The Lantern," a play (genre?) for children, 2m2f, BP

Way, Brian, "Magical Faces," a play (genre?) for children, 2m2f, BP

Way, Brian, "The Mirrorman," a play (genre?) for children, 2m2f, BP

Way, Brian, "Mr. Grump and the Clown," a play (genre?) for children, 2m2f, BP

Way, Brian, "On Trial," a play (genre?) for children, 2m2f, BP

Way, Brian, "The Valley of Echoes," a play (genre?) for children, 2m2f, BP

Way, Brian, "The Wheel," a play (genre?) for children, 2m2f, BP

Wayne, Edna Zola, "Girls Will Be Girls," a comedy, 2f, (published with and can pair with "The Dormant Heritage," "Enterprising Oswald," "Grandma Fought the Indians," "Make-Up," "Paris Sets the Styles," "'Rosemary—That's for Remembrance,'" "She Goes the

Rounds," or "Truant Husbands") in *Two by Two*, BP, NSHS pb6044, NSHS 29326

Weaver, Richard, "And Jack Fell Down," a drama, 2m1f, IEC 023-4

Weaver, Richard, "The Chastening," a drama, 3m, IEC 023-4

Webb, Chase, and Betty Smith, "Mañana Bandits: A Legend of the Rio Grande," a drama, 4m, GCB, NSHS 5345

Weik, Mary Hays, "Moonlight," a comedy, 3m1f, MAC, NSHS 15088.

Weinstock, David, "Dawn Will Come," a morality play, 3m, SF 6608, NSHS pb7900

Welch, Peggy, "I Know This for Sure," a Christmas drama, 4f, ELD

Weller, Michael, "The Bodybuilders," a comedy, 3m1f, (published with and can pair with "Tira Tells Everything There Is to Know About Herself") DPS 1065, NSHS pb8046

Weller, Michael, "Tira Tells Everything There Is to Know About Herself," a black comedy, 1m1f, (published with and can pair with "The Bodybuilders") DPS 1065, NSHS pb8046

Wells, Mike (English playwright), "Prisoners," a drama, 2f, in Mike Wells' *Prisoners* (Macclesfield, Cheshire, England: New Playwrights Network, 1991), ISBN 0-86319-262-9, NPN

Wellwarth, George E. (translator from German), "Freedom for Clemens," a dark comedy by Tankred Dorst, translated from the German *"Freiheit für Clemens,"* 2m1f, (published with and can pair with "Let's Eat Hair!" [*Essen Wir Haare!*] or "Nightpiece [*Nachtsstück*]) in *Postwar German Theatre*, GB, NSHS pb7857

Wellwarth, George E. (translator from German), "Let's Eat Hair!" an absurdity by Carl Laszlo, translated by George E. Wellwarth from the German *"Essen Wir Haare!"* 2m1f, (published with and can pair with "Freedom for Clemens" [*"Freiheit für Clemens"*] or "Nightpiece" [*"Nachtsstück"*]) in *Postwar German Theatre*, GB, NSHS pb7857

Wesley, Richard, "The Past Is the Past," a drama with background music, 2m, (published with and can pair with "Birth of a Blues!" "The Box," or "Gettin' It Together") in *New Plays for the Black Theatre*, edited by Woodie King, Jr. (Chicago: Third World Press, 1989), ISBN 0-88378-124-7, DPS 3595

West, Don, "Vacant Possession," a drama, 2m2f, SF 24608 NSHS pb8065

Whithill, Faith, "Beast of a Different Burden," a comedy, 2m1f, SF 4620

Whitlow, Roseanna Beth, "Thistle Blossoms," a drama, 2f, PDS

Wiese, Anne Pierson, "Coleman, S. D.," a drama, 1m2f, FDG, NSHS

Wilde, Oscar Fingal O'Flahertie Wills (Irish playwright, 1854-1900), "A Florentine Tragedy," a drama, 2m1f, in

24 Favorite One-Act Plays, edited by Bennett Cerf and Van H. Cartmell (New York: Doubleday & Company, Inc., 1958), NSHS pb4019 NSHS 14824, NSHS 20483, NSHS 21389, NSHS 21514, NSHS 21776

Wilde, Percival, "The Finger of God," a drama, 2m1f, BP, NSHS pb5489, NSHS 27108

Wilde, Percival (adaptor from French), "Nanny," a comedy by Henri Duvernois, adapted by Percival Wilde from the original French, 2m1f, BP, NSHS 19987

Wilde, Percival, "The Noble Lord," a comedy, 2m1f, BP, NSHS pb5468

Wilder, Thornton (1897-1975), "The Drunken Sisters," a comedy, 1m3f, published with *The Alcestiad*, SF 6682, NSHS pb7942

Wilder, Thornton (1897-1975), "Love and How to Cure It," a comedy, 2m2f, in *The Long Christmas Dinner & Other One-Act Plays*, SF 14657

Wilder, Thornton (1897-1975), "Queens of France," a satiric comedy, 1m3f, **analyzed in Part 4, p. 233**, SF 886, NSHS pb7963

Wilder, Thornton (1897-1975), "Someone from Assisi," a symbolical play (genre?), 1m3f, SF 21735

Wildman, Paul G., "A Personal Thing," a comedy, 4m, SF 18634, NSHS pb8040

Wilhelm, Le, "The Road to Nineveh," a Christmas comedy, 2m1f, in *Off-Off Broadway Festival Plays, 17 Series*, SF 19979

Wilhelm, Le, "Strawberry Preserves," a comedy-drama, 3m1f, in *Off-Off Broadway Festival Plays, 13th Series*, ISBN 0-573-62364-3, SF 21770, NSHS pb8083

Williams, John W., "Looking Good," a ten-minute play (genre?), 2m, (published with and can pair with "Advice to a New Actor," "The Affidavit," "The American Way," "Anniversary," "Auld Lang Syne, or I'll Bet You Think This Play Is About You," "Bug Swatter," "Checkers," "Coming for a Visit," "Dalmation," "Dog Eat Dog," "Drowned Out," "Fireworks," "Interview," "Jumping," "Money," "One Beer Too Many," "Phonecall from Sunkist," "Potato Girl," "Property of the Dallas Cowboys," "The Split Decision," "Valley Forgery," "Watermelon Boats," or "Widows") in *25 10-Minute Plays from Actors Theatre of Louisville*, edited by Actors Theatre of Louisville (New York: Samuel French, Inc., 1989), ISBN 0-573-62558-1, SF 6716

Williams, Norman, "Protest," a play (genre ?), 1m3f, publisher unknown (?), NSHS

Williams, Tennessee (a.k.a. Thomas Lanier Williams, American playwright, 1911-1983), "Auto-da-fe," a drama, 1m3f, in *27 Wagons Full of Cotton*, DPS 485

Williams, Tennessee (a.k.a. Thomas Lanier Williams, American playwright, 1911-1983), "The Case of the Crushed Petunias," a lyrical fantasy, 2m2f, in *American Blues*, DPS 710, NSHS pb6064

Williams, Tennessee (a.k.a. Thomas Lanier Williams, American playwright, 1911-1983), "The Chalky White Substance," a drama, 2m, in *Antæus: Plays in One Act*, edited by Daniel Halpern, no. 66 (Spring 1991), ISBN 0-88001-268-4, ANT

Williams, Tennessee (a.k.a. Thomas Lanier Williams, American playwright, 1911-1983), "The Dark Room," a drama, 1m2f, in *American Blues*, DPS 710, NSHS pb6064

Williams, Tennessee (a.k.a. Thomas Lanier Williams, American playwright, 1911-1983), "Hello from Bertha," a drama, 4f, in *27 Wagons Full of Cotton*, DPS 485

Williams, Tennessee (a.k.a. Thomas Lanier Williams, American playwright, 1911-1983), "I Rise in Flame, Cried the Phoenix," a drama about D. H. Lawrence, 1m2f, DPS 2475

Williams, Tennessee (a.k.a. Thomas Lanier Williams, American playwright, 1911-1983), "The Lady of Larkspur Lotion," a dramatic sketch, 1m2f, in *27 Wagons Full of Cotton*, DPS 485

Williams, Tennessee (a.k.a. Thomas Lanier Williams, American playwright, 1911-1983), "The Last of My Solid Gold Watches," a drama, 3m, in *27 Wagons Full of Cotton*, DPS 485

Williams, Tennessee (a.k.a. Thomas Lanier Williams, American playwright, 1911-1983), "The Long Goodbye," a drama, 2m2f, in *27 Wagons Full of Cotton*, DPS 485

Williams, Tennessee (a.k.a. Thomas Lanier Williams, American playwright, 1911-1983), "The Long Stay Cut Short, or The Unsatisfactory Supper," a drama, 1m2f, in *American Blues*, DPS 710, NSHS pb6064

Williams, Tennessee (a.k.a. Thomas Lanier Williams, American playwright, 1911-1983), "Lord Byron's Love Letter," a drama, 1m3f, in *27 Wagons Full of Cotton*, DPS 485

Williams, Tennessee (a.k.a. Thomas Lanier Williams, American playwright, 1911-1983), "A Lovely Sunday for Creve Coeur," a drama, 4f (+ extras), (can pair with "The Case of the Crushed Petunias" or "The Chalky White Substance") in Tennessee Williams' *The Theatre of Tennessee Williams*, Vol. 8 (New York: New Directions Publishing Corporation, 1992), ISBN 0-8112-1201-7, NDP

Williams, Tennessee (a.k.a. Thomas Lanier Williams, American playwright, 1911-1983), "Something Unspoken," a drama, 2f, **analyzed in Part 4, p. 243**, in *27 Wagons Full of Cotton*, DPS 485

Williams, Tennessee (a.k.a. Thomas Lanier Williams, American playwright, 1911-1983), "The Strangest Kind of Romance," a dramatic sketch, 3m1f, in *27 Wagons Full of Cotton*, DPS 485

Willinger, David, "Andrea's Got Two Boyfriends," a comedy-drama, 3m1f, DPS 787, NSHS pb8122

Willis, Jane, "Men Without Dates," a comedy, 3m, (published with and can pair with "Slam!") DPS 3117

Willis, Jane, "Slam!" a comedy-drama, 2m, (published with and can pair with "Men Without Dates") DPS 3117

Wilson, August, "Testimonies," a series of four monologues, 1m, in *Antæus: Plays in One Act*, no. 66 (Spring 1991), Antæus [Ecco Press], ISBN 0-88001-268-4

Wilson, Dorothy Clarke, "This Night Shall Pass," a religious drama, 2m1f, BP, NSHS pb5442

Wilson, Lanford, "Brontosaurus," a comedy-drama, 1m2f, (can pair with "Cabin 12") DPS 1150

Wilson, Lanford, "Days Ahead," a play (genre?), 1m, DPS, NSHS 29301

Wilson, Lanford, "Eukiah," a ten-minute drama, 2m, in *Dramatics*, 63, no. 3 (November 1991): 16-19, SF

Wilson, Lanford, "The Great Nebula in Orion," a drama, 2f, (published with and can pair with "Ikke, Ikke, Nye, Nye, Nye") DPS 1905

Wilson, Lanford, "Ludlow Fair," a drama, 2f, DPS 205, NSHS pb7789

Wilson, Lanford, "The Madness of Lady Bright," a drama, 2m1f, DPS 355, NSHS 29301, NSHS pb7760

Wilson, Lanford, "A Poster of the Cosmos," a drama, 1m, (about AIDS, can pair with Harvey Fierstein's "Safe Sex," Alan Bowne's "Beirut," Patricia Loughrey's "The Inner Circle," or Robert Patrick's "Pouf Positive") (published with and can pair with "The Moonshot Tape"); also in *The Best Short Plays* (New York: Applause, 1989) and in *The Way We Live Now: American Plays & the AIDS Crisis*, edited by M. Elizabeth Osborn (New York: Theatre Communications Group, 1990), ISBN 1-55936-006-2, ISBN 1-55936-005-4, DPS 3696

Wilson, Lanford, "Say De Kooning," a play (genre?), 1m2f, available only in manuscript from DPS

Wilson, Lanford, "Stoop," a bare-stage turn, 3f, (published with and can pair with "Wandering") DPS 3930, NSHS 29301, NSHS pb7732

Wilson, Lanford, "Thymus Vulgaris," a comedy drama, 1m2f, DPS 4535

Wilson, Lanford, "Wandering," a bare-stage turn, 2m1f, (published with and can pair with "Stoop") DPS 3930, NSHS 29301, NSHS pb7760

Winters, Marian, "All Saint's Day," a drama, 2m, DPS, NSHS 29200

Winther, Barbara, "Anansi, the African Spider: How Anansi Brought the Stories Down," a children's comedy, 1m3f, 2m2f, 3m1f, 4m, or 4f (+ extras), (published with and can pair with "Anansi, the African Spider: Tall-Tale Man," "Ijapa, the Tortoise: The Bush Spirits," or "Two Dilemma Tales: The Snore or the Song") in Barbara Winther's *Plays from African Tales: One-Act, Royalty-Free Dramatizations for Young People, from Stories and Folktales of Africa* (Boston: Plays, Inc., 1992), ISBN 0-8238-0296-5, PI

Winther, Barbara, "Anansi, the African Spider: Tall-Tale Man," a children's comedy, 1m3f, 2m2f, 3m1f, 4m, or 4f (+ extras), (published with and can pair with "Anansi, the African Spider: How Anansi Brought the Stories

Down," "Ijapa, the Tortoise: The Bush Spirits," or "Two Dilemma Tales: The Snore or the Song") in Barbara Winther's *Plays from African Tales: One-Act, Royalty-Free Dramatizations for Young People, from Stories and Folktales of Africa* (Boston: Plays, Inc., 1992), ISBN 0-8238-0296-5, PI

Winther, Barbara, "Ijapa, the Tortoise: The Bush Spirits," a children's comedy based on a Nigerian folktale, 1m1f, 2m, or 2f, (published with and can pair with "Anansi, the African Spider: How Anansi Brought the Stories Down," "Anansi, the African Spider: Tall-Tale Man," or "Two Dilemma Tales: The Snore or the Song") in Barbara Winther's *Plays from African Tales: One-Act, Royalty-Free Dramatizations for Young People, from Stories and Folktales of Africa* (Boston: Plays, Inc., 1992), ISBN 0-8238-0296-5, PI

Winther, Barbara, "Two Dilemma Tales: The Snore or the Song," a children's comedy based on a West African Story, 3m1f (+ extras), (published with and can pair with "Anansi, the African Spider: How Anansi Brought the Stories Down," "Anansi, the African Spider: Tall-Tale Man," or "Ijapa, the Tortoise: The Bush Spirits") in Barbara Winther's *Plays from African Tales: One-Act, Royalty-Free Dramatizations for Young People, from Stories and Folktales of Africa* (Boston: Plays, Inc., 1992), ISBN 0-8238-0296-5, PI

Wise, William, "Traveler's Rest," a drama, 1m1f, IEC 194-X

Witten, Matthew, "The Ties That Bind," a drama, 1m2f, in *Off-Off Broadway Festival Plays, 11th Series*, SF 22679, NSHS 27508, NSHS pb749

Wood, Margaret, "Day of Atonement," a melodrama, 3m1f, SF 6611, NSHS pb8097

Woodward, Laurie, "Night Voice," a suspense drama, 4f, BP

Wright, Denise Anton, "Back-to-School Blues," a puppet play for children in five scenes, 1 puppeteer presenting 4 characters, (published with and can pair with "The Boy Who Cried Wolf," "The Case of the Disappearing Books," "Dragon Draws a Picture," "The Easter Egg Hunt," "Easter Rabbit's Basket," "Elephant's Sneeze," "Fox Learns a Lesson," "The Halloween Costume," "The Leprechaun's Gold," "The Lion and the Mouse," "Little Red Riding Hood," "The Monkey and the Crocodile," "The Mysterious Egg," "The Pumpkin Thief," "Santa Cures a Cold," "Take Me to Your Library," "The Three Billy Goats Gruff," "The Town Mouse and the Country Mouse," "Turkey's Thanksgiving Adventure," "Witch Gets Ready," "Witch's Valentine," or "Witch's Winter Kitchen") in Denise Anton Wright's *One-Person Puppet Plays*, illustrated by John Wright (Teacher Idea Press, 1990), ISBN 0-87287-742-6, TIP

Wright, Denise Anton, "The Boy Who Cried Wolf," a puppet play for children, 1 puppeteer presenting 4 characters, (published with and can pair with "The Back-to-School Blues," "The Case of the Disappearing Books,"

"Dragon Draws a Picture," "The Easter Egg Hunt," "Easter Rabbit's Basket," "Elephant's Sneeze," "Fox Learns a Lesson," "The Halloween Costume," "The Leprechaun's Gold," "The Lion and the Mouse," "Little Red Riding Hood," "The Monkey and the Crocodile," "The Mysterious Egg," "The Pumpkin Thief," "Santa Cures a Cold," "Take Me to Your Library," "The Three Billy Goats Gruff," "The Town Mouse and the Country Mouse," "Turkey's Thanksgiving Adventure," "Witch Gets Ready," "Witch's Valentine," or "Witch's Winter Kitchen") in Denise Anton Wright's *One-Person Puppet Plays*, illustrated by John Wright (Teacher Idea Press, 1990), ISBN 0-87287-742-6, TIP

Wright, Denise Anton, "The Case of the Disappearing Books," a puppet play in 2 scenes for children, 1 puppeteer presenting 3 characters, (published with and can pair with "The Boy Who Cried Wolf," "The Back-to-School Blues," "Dragon Draws a Picture," "The Easter Egg Hunt," "Easter Rabbit's Basket," "Elephant's Sneeze," "Fox Learns a Lesson," "The Halloween Costume," "The Leprechaun's Gold," "The Lion and the Mouse," "Little Red Riding Hood," "The Monkey and the Crocodile," "The Mysterious Egg," "The Pumpkin Thief," "Santa Cures a Cold," "Take Me to Your Library," "The Three Billy Goats Gruff," "The Town Mouse and the Country Mouse," "Turkey's Thanksgiving Adventure," "Witch Gets Ready," "Witch's Valentine," or "Witch's Winter Kitchen") in Denise Anton Wright's *One-Person Puppet Plays*, illustrated by John Wright (Teacher Idea Press, 1990), ISBN 0-87287-742-6, TIP

Wright, Denise Anton, "Dragon Draws a Picture," a puppet play for children, 1 puppeteer presenting 2 characters, in Denise Anton Wright's *One-Person Puppet Plays*, illustrated by John Wright (Teacher Idea Press, 1990), ISBN 0-87287-742-6, TIP

Wright, Denise Anton, "The Easter Egg Hunt," a puppet play in 3 scenes for children, 1 puppeteer presenting 4 characters, in Denise Anton Wright's *One-Person Puppet Plays*, illustrated by John Wright (Teacher Idea Press, 1990), ISBN 0-87287-742-6, TIP

Wright, Denise Anton, "Easter Rabbit's Basket," a puppet play in 3 scenes for children, 1 puppeteer presenting 3 characters, in Denise Anton Wright's *One-Person Puppet Plays*, illustrated by John Wright (Teacher Idea Press, 1990), ISBN 0-87287-742-6, TIP

Wright, Denise Anton, "Fox Learns a Lesson," a puppet play for children, 1 puppeteer presenting 3 characters, in Denise Anton Wright's *One-Person Puppet Plays*, illustrated by John Wright (Teacher Idea Press, 1990), ISBN 0-87287-742-6, TIP

Wright, Denise Anton, "The Halloween Costume," a puppet play in 4 scenes for children, 1 puppeteer presenting 4 characters, in Denise Anton Wright's *One-Person Puppet Plays*, illustrated by John Wright (Teacher Idea Press,

1990), ISBN 0-87287-742-6, TIP

Wright, Denise Anton, "The Leprechaun's Gold," a puppet play for children, 1 puppeteer presenting 2 characters, in Denise Anton Wright's *One-Person Puppet Plays*, illustrated by John Wright (Teacher Idea Press, 1990), ISBN 0-87287-742-6, TIP

Wright, Denise Anton, "The Lion and the Mouse," a puppet play for children, 1 puppeteer presenting 2 characters, in Denise Anton Wright's *One-Person Puppet Plays*, illustrated by John Wright (Teacher Idea Press, 1990), ISBN 0-87287-742-6, TIP

Wright, Denise Anton, "Little Red Riding Hood," a puppet play in 2 scenes for children, 1 puppeteer presenting 3 characters, in Denise Anton Wright's *One-Person Puppet Plays*, illustrated by John Wright (Teacher Idea Press, 1990), ISBN 0-87287-742-6, TIP

Wright, Denise Anton, "The Monkey and the Crocodile," a puppet play for children, 1 puppeteer presenting 2 characters, in Denise Anton Wright's *One-Person Puppet Plays*, illustrated by John Wright (Teacher Idea Press, 1990), ISBN 0-87287-742-6, TIP

Wright, Denise Anton, "The Mysterious Egg," a puppet play in 5 scenes for children, 1 puppeteer presenting 4 characters, in Denise Anton Wright's *One-Person Puppet Plays*, illustrated by John Wright (Teacher Idea Press, 1990), ISBN 0-87287-742-6, TIP

Wright, Denise Anton, "The Pumpkin Thief," a puppet play for children, 1 puppeteer presenting 2 characters, in Denise Anton Wright's *One-Person Puppet Plays*, illustrated by John Wright (Teacher Idea Press, 1990), ISBN 0-87287-742-6, TIP

Wright, Denise Anton, "Santa Cures a Cold," a puppet play in 3 scenes for children, 1 puppeteer presenting 4 characters, in Denise Anton Wright's *One-Person Puppet Plays*, illustrated by John Wright (Teacher Idea Press, 1990), ISBN 0-87287-742-6, TIP

Wright, Denise Anton, "Take Me to Your Library," a puppet play for children, 1 puppeteer presenting 2 characters, in Denise Anton Wright's *One-Person Puppet Plays*, illustrated by John Wright (Teacher Idea Press, 1990), ISBN 0-87287-742-6, TIP

Wright, Denise Anton, "The Three Billy Goats Gruff," a puppet play for children, 1 puppeteer presenting 4 characters, in Denise Anton Wright's *One-Person Puppet Plays*, illustrated by John Wright (Teacher Idea Press, 1990), ISBN 0-87287-742-6, TIP

Wright, Denise Anton, "The Town Mouse and the Country Mouse," a puppet play in 2 scenes for children, 1 puppeteer presenting 4 characters, in Denise Anton Wright's *One-Person Puppet Plays*, illustrated by John Wright (Teacher Idea Press, 1990), ISBN 0-87287-742-6, TIP

Wright, Denise Anton, "Turkey's Thanksgiving Adventure," a puppet play for children, 1 puppeteer presenting 2 characters, in Denise Anton Wright's *One-Person Puppet*

Plays, illustrated by John Wright (Teacher Idea Press, 1990), ISBN 0-87287-742-6, TIP

Wright, Denise Anton, "Witch Gets Ready," a puppet play for children, 1 puppeteer presenting 4 characters, in Denise Anton Wright's *One-Person Puppet Plays*, illustrated by John Wright (Teacher Idea Press, 1990), ISBN 0-87287-742-6, TIP

Wright, Denise Anton, "Witch's Valentine," a puppet play in 2 scenes for children, 1 puppeteer presenting 4 characters, in Denise Anton Wright's *One-Person Puppet Plays*, illustrated by John Wright (Teacher Idea Press, 1990), ISBN 0-87287-742-6, TIP

Wright, Denise Anton, "Witch's Winter Kitchen" a puppet play for children, 1 puppeteer presenting 2 characters, in Denise Anton Wright's *One-Person Puppet Plays*, illustrated by John Wright (Teacher Idea Press, 1990), ISBN 0-87287-742-6, TIP

Y

Yeats, William Butler (Irish poet and playwright, 1920- , 1865-1939), "A Full Moon in March," a drama, 2m2f, MAC, NSHS 16618

Yeats, William Butler (Irish poet and playwright, 1920- , 1865-1939), "Purgatory," a melodrama, 3m1f, **analyzed in Part 4, p. 231**, in *Eleven Plays by W. B. Yeats* and in *The Modern Theatre*, Vol. 2, SF 18674, NSHS 16369

Yeats, William Butler (Irish poet and playwright, 1920- , 1865-1939), "The Resurrection," a drama, 4m (+3 musicians), MAC, NSHS 16618

Yerby, Lorees, "Save Me a Place at Forest Lawn," a comedy-drama, 2f, **analyzed in Part 4, p. 238**, HDS, DPS 3955, NSHS pb7914

Z

Ziegenhagen, Eric, "Seniority," a play (genre?), 1m2f, in *Sparks in the Park, and Other Prize-Winning Plays: From the 1987 and 1988 Young Playwrights Festivals: Produced by the Foundation of the Dramatists Guild*, edited by Wendy Lamb (New York: Dell Publishing Company, 1989), ISBN 0-440-20415-1

Part 3   *GLOSSARY OF GENRES*

A Small Dictionary of Dramaturgical Terms

> This small dictionary of dramaturgical terms explains genre identifications used in this guide. The definitions may help the reader to know enough about a given play to decide whether to pursue investigation. Many identifying terms supplied by authors or catalogers are idiosyncratic rather than common jargon in theatre, still they contribute to the investigator's search.
>
> *Genre* is a synonym for type or kind. It groups various literary works by form, technique, or subject matter into types or categories. The term, often loosely used, reflects numerous principles and kinds of literature.
>
> Traditionally, genres include the tragic, comedic, epic, lyric, pastoral. Currently, genre divisions might also include novel, short story, essay, perhaps television play or motion picture scenario—or one-act play.
>
> Genre classification infers formal or technical characteristics among similar works regardless or time or place of composition, author, or subject matter; it also infers that characteristics defining a particular group of works are basic in discussions of literary art. Critics frequently regard genre distinctions as useful descriptive devices albeit arbitrary ones. A good explanation of genre appears in *A Handbook to Literature*, fourth edition, by C. Hugh Holman (Indianapolis, Indiana: Bobbs-Merrill Educational Publishing, 1980), pp. 119-20.
>
> Here, each definition carries an example from the Title Index.

abridgment/adaptation: a shortening/rearrangement of another work. Example: "Villainous Company," an abridgment/adaptation by Amlin Gray of Shakespeare's *Henry IV, Parts I and II*, 3m.

abstraction: a play that is wholly or partly not representational. Example: "Ohio Impromptu," an abstraction by Samuel Beckett, 2m or 2f.

absurd comedy: a play that is clearly untrue or unreasonable, therefore laughable. Example: "What Did You Say 'What' For?" an absurd comedy by James Paul Dey, 1m1f.

absurdist comedy: a play that is clearly untrue or unreasonable, therefore laughable. Example: "The Froegle Dictum," an absurdist comedy by Mark Medoff, 2m2f.

absurdity: a theatre-of-the-absurd play, often using comedic elements in a nihilistic vein, that is, denying the existence of any basis for knowledge or truth. Example: "Let's Eat Hair!" an absurdity by Carl Laszlo, translated from the German by George E. Wellwarth, 2m1f.

adult comedy: a humorous treatment of the battle of the sexes, sometimes risqué. Example: "The Slot," an adult comedy by Tom Gillespie, 1m1f.

allegory: a play in which people, things, and happenings have another meaning. Example: "Dansen," an allegory by Bertolt Brecht, translated by Rose and Martin Kastner, 2m.

avant-garde: a play pushing the limits of convention. Example: "Little Fears," an avant-garde comic drama by Emanuel Peluso, 2m2f

167

bare-stage: a play requiring no scenery and no properties or minimum properties, sometimes called *open-stage*. Example: "Slow Memories," a bare-stage drama by Barry Litvack, 1m3f.

bizarre comedy: a play strikingly out of the ordinary treating trivial material superficially or amusingly or showing serious and profound material in a light, familiar, or satirical manner. Example: "The Lover," a bizarre comedy by Harold Pinter, 2m1f.

black comedy: a play essentially a comedy but emphasizing outrageous, serious elements. Example: "Play for Germs," a black comedy by Israel Horovitz, 2m.

brief sketch: a skit; a short, light, informal play. Example: "Night," a brief sketch by Harold Pinter, 1m1f.

chamber opera: an opera for intimate theatre. Example: "Agnes," a chamber opera by Michael John LaChiusa, 1m2f.

chamber play: a theatrical work for intimate staging. Example: "Listening," a chamber play by Edward Albee, 1m2f.

choreopoem: a play in dance-accompanied verse form. Example: "From Okra to Greens: A Different Kind of Love Story," a choreopoem by Ntozake Shange, 1m1f (+ dancers).

comedic monologue: a solo playlet with more or less humorous treatment of characters and situation, with a nontragic ending. Example: "Axis Sally," a comedic monologue by Don Nigro, 1f.

comedy: the genre of dramatic literature treating trivial material superficially or amusingly or showing serious and profound material in a light, familiar, or satirical manner. Example: "The Devil and Billy Marshall," a comedy by Shel Silverstein, 1m.

comedy drama/comedy-drama: a play blending light and serious elements. Example: "Brothers in Arms," a comedy drama by Merrill Denison, 3m1f. Example: "After the Fact," a comedy-drama by Jeffrey Sweet, 1m1f.

comedy in rhyme and rhythm: a funny play in music and doggerel. Example: "Ladies of the Mop," a comedy in rhyme and rhythm by Aurand Harris, 4f.

comedy-satire: a play in which abuses, follies, stupidities, and vices are ridiculed. Example: "Suppressed Desires," a comedy-satire by Susan Glaspell, 1m2f.

comedy western: a play blending humorous elements in an Old West context. Example: "Proposin'," a comedy western by Richard Slocum from Anton Chekhov, 1m2f.

comic drama/comic-drama: a play blending light and serious elements. Example: "Inflatable You," a comic drama by Jules Tasca, 2m. Example: "Two and Twenty," a comic-drama by Paul Parente, 1m1f.

comic sketch: a skit, or a short, light, informal play focusing on incongruities. Example: "Mr. Foot," a comic sketch by Michael Frayn, 1m1f.

comic skit: a sketch, or a short, light, informal play. Example: "Man on the Ledge," a comic skit by Randy Galvin, 1m1f.

craft cycle drama: a medieval Bible-history play produced by the Trade Guilds of England and Scotland. Example: "The Fall of Lucifer," a craft cycle drama from "N. towne Plays," 4m.

curtain-raiser comedy: a play designed to precede on the program a more significant presentation. Example: "Mr. Happiness," a curtain-raiser comedy by David Mamet, 1m.

dark comedy: a play essentially a comedy but emphasizing profound elements. Example: "The Reticence of Lady Anne," a dark comedy by Jules Tasca, 1m1f.

drama: a serious play. Example: "Kaspar," a drama by Peter Handke, 1m.

drama-comedy: a hybridized play employing both drama and comedy, a play essentially a drama but with suddenly incongruous elements. Example: "Chucky's Hunch," a drama-comedy by Rochelle Owens, 1m.

dramatic monologue: a serious solo piece, usually but not necessarily short. Example: "Nightmare with Clocks," a dramatic monologue by Don Nigro, 1m.

dramatic reading: a staged reading of material other than a playscript. Example: "Great Moments in American Oratory," a dramatic reading by Val Cheatham, 4 narrators (male or female).

duologue: a play for two actors. Example: "Pepper and Sand," a duologue by Emlyn Williams, 1m1f.

fantasy-comedy: a play characterized by comic elements amid unrestrained fancy, extravagance, caprice, eccentricity. Example: "This Way to Heaven," a fantasy-comedy by Douglas Parkhirst, 2m2f.

fantasy-drama: a play characterized by dramatic elements amid unrestrained fancy, extravagance, caprice, eccentricity. Example: "Conversations with the Spanish Lady," a fantasy drama by Robert Schenkkan, 1m1f.

farce: a funny play in which plot and broad action dominate. Example: "The Adjustment," a farce by Albert Bermel, 1m1f.

farce melodrama: a funny play in which plot and broad action dominate, with extravagant theatricality, superficial characterization, and predominance of plot and physical action. Example: "The Banker's Dilemma," a farce melodrama by Cleve Haubold, 2m2f.

fastnachtsspiel: a carnival or Shrovetide secular play from 15th-century Germany, usually a broad farce and abbreviated morality play; a Mardi Gras play. Example: *"The Narrenschneiden,"* a *fastnachtsspiel* by Hans Sachs, 3m or 3f.

half-hour monologue: a solo performance of approximately a half-hour's duration. Example: "A Chip in the Sugar," a half-hour monologue by Alan Bennett, 1m.

K'unshan **play:** a highly stylized one-act play from the Ming Dynasty, 1368-1644. Example: "Longing for Worldly Pleasures," a traditional *K'unshan* play by Ssu Fan, 1f.

light and dark show: a play blending comedic and tragic elements. Example: "Recensio," a light and dark show, a drama by Eddie de Santis, 1m1f.

masque: a short allegorical stage entertainment, popular in the 16th and 17th centuries but still used, that features masked actors. Example: "Motel," a masque for three dolls from *America Hurrah*, by Jean-Claude Van Itallie, 3m or 3f.

melodrama: a play with extravagant theatricality, superficial characterization, and predominance of plot and physical action. Example: "The Pedestrian," a melodrama by Ray Bradbury, 2m.

mime: a play without words. Example: "Act Without Words (1)," a mime by Samuel Beckett, 1m.

mono-drama/monodrama: a play for one actor. Example: "One Person," a mono-drama by Robert Patrick, 1m.

monologue: a play for one actor; sometimes, a portion of a play. Example: "Help, I Am," a monologue (drama) by Robert Patrick, 1m.

morality play: a play employing allegorical characters, that is, personifications of abstractions, popular in the 15th and 16th centuries but sometimes useful in modern communication from playwright to audience. Example: "Dawn Will Come," a morality play by David Weinstock, 3m.

musical comedy: a funny play with integrated music. Example: "The Hunting of the Snark," a musical comedy by R. Eugene Jackson, 4m or 4f.

mystery: used in two different ways in dramatic literature, it can be a medieval play about any of the fifteen events in the lives of Jesus and Mary, or it can be a play focusing on the unexplained, secret, or unknown, usually with a revelation in the final resolution. Modern example: "Two Bottles of Relish," a mystery by Lord Dunsany, 2m2f.

mystery melodrama: a play focusing on the unexplained, secret, or unknown, usually with a revelation in the final resolution; it uses extravagant theatricality, superficial characterization, and a predominance of plot and physical action. Example: "The Rats," a mystery melodrama by Agatha Christie, 2m2f.

mystery play: a drama from the European Middle Ages portraying an event in the life of Jesus. Example: "The York Play of the Crucifixion," a mystery play, 3m.

nonliteral exercise: a practice of acting virtuosity and technique. Example: "Comings and Goings," a nonliteral exercise by Megan Terry, 1m1f.

passion play: a stage presentation of the life and crucifixion of Christ. Example: "Crisscross," a bare-stage five-minute passion play, 2m.

piece for voice and percussion: a theatrical program relying only on the spoken voice and sharp striking sounds. Example: "Tongues," a piece for voice and percussion by Sam Shepard and Joseph Chaikin, 1m.

play: a script of unidentified genre by the author, catalog, or agent. Sometimes this is intentional; sometimes it is carelessness. Example: "Mr. Tucker's Taxi," a play by Leonard Melfi, 2m2f.

play with music: a play thoroughly integrated with music. Example: "Out of Our Father's House," a feminist drama with music by Paula Wagner, Jack Hofsiss, and Eve Merriam, 3f.

playlet: a short play. Example: "Colette in Love," a playlet by Lavonne Mueller, 1m1f.

radio play: a script for the mind's eye via radio (and sometimes stage). Example: "Sanibel and Captiva," a radio play (drama) by Megan Terry, 1m1f.

revue sketch: a short dramatic/comedic situation presented as a separate unit in a program; sometimes called a *blackout*. Example: "Applicant," a revue sketch by Harold Pinter, 1m1f.

romance: a play in which the emphasis is on love and/or adventure. Example: "Still-Love," a romance by Robert Patrick, 1m1f.

romantic comedy: a comedy centering on love between the sexes. Example: "The New Quixote," a romantic comedy by Michael Frayn, 1m1f.

romantic farce: a broad comedy blending incongruous situations with lightly treated love. Example: "Pastiche," a romantic farce by Nick Hall, 2m2f.

satire: a play in which abuses, follies, stupidities, vices are ridiculed. Example: "If Men Played Cards as Women Do," a satire by George S. Kaufman, 4m.

satiric comedy: a play in which abuses, follies, stupidities, vices are ridiculed. Example: "Queens of France," a satiric comedy by Thornton Wilder, 1m3f.

satiric fantasy: an unreal play in which abuses, follies, stupidities, vices are ridiculed. Example: "Motel," a satiric fantasy by Jean-Claude van Itallie, 3m or 3f (in doll masks and bodies + offstage voice).

science-fiction play: a play extrapolating man's use of science between the currently possible and the ultimately possible. Example: "Camera Obscura," a science-fiction play by Robert Patrick, 1m1f.

sentimental comedy: a humorous, emotional play. Example: "The 75th," a sentimental comedy by Israel Horovitz, 1m1f.

short audio and visual piece for the stage: here, an experiment in minimalism. Example: "Breath," a short audio and visual piece for the stage by Samuel Beckett, 1 voice.

sing-along musical mellerdrammer: a parody of a melodrama welcoming audience participation through singing. Example: "Bloodline," a sing-along musical mellerdrammer by Richard S. Dunlop, 2m2f.

***Sprechstuck*:** a speaking, an autonomous prologue to an old play, not to revolutionize but to sensitize. Example: "Self-Accusation," a *Sprechstuck* by Peter Handke, 1m1f.

suspense drama: a play focusing on the unexplained, secret, unknown, usually with a revelation in the final resolution. "Diary," a suspense drama by Marcia Ann Shenk, 1m1f.

symbolical play: a play emphasizing allusions and allegory. Example: "Someone from Assisi," a symbolical play by Thornton Wilder, 1m3f.

ten-minute drama: a serious play under ten minutes in playing time. Jon Jory has exploited and published this format and even has established an annual festival for it in Actors Theatre of Louisville. Jory writes, commissions, and solicits plays in this format. Example: "Blind Alleys," a ten-minute drama by Michael Bigelow Dixon and Valerie Smith, 2m2f.

theatre poems: separate poetic selections woven into a program. Example: "Savage/Love," a bill of theatre poems by Sam Shepard and Joseph Chaikin, 1m.

thriller: a play hugely dependent on plot surprises and twists. Example: "The Shirkers," a thriller by C. M. S. McLellan, 2m1f.

traditional *K'unshan* play: a highly stylized one-act play from the Ming Dynasty, 1368-1644. Example: "Longing for Worldly Pleasures," a traditional *K'unshan* play by Ssu Fan, 1f.

tragedietta: a little tragedy. A Shavian term born of his beginnings as a musical critic. Example: "The Glimpse of Reality," a tragedietta by George Bernard Shaw, 4m.

tragicomedy: a play combining elements of tragedy and comedy. Example: "The White Whore and the Bit Player," a tragicomedy by Tom Eyen, 2f.

turn: a short play with an odd twist or a starring focus. Example: "Wandering," a turn by Lanford Wilson, 2m1f.

whimsical comedy: a humorous play with oddly abnormal elements. Example: "Three on a Bench," a whimsical comedy by Doris Estrada, 2m2f.

white version: a play originally written for white actors portraying Negroes, here given in a version for white actors portraying whites. Example: "The No 'Count Boy," a white version by Paul Green, 2m2f.

Part 4 | *PLAYBILLS WITH SCRIPT ANALYSES*

*A Menu of Twenty-five Suggested Theme Programs
with Eighty Play Analyses, Alphabetical by Title*

> Part 4 addresses active theatre needs. Anyone staging bills of one-act plays might consider any of these twenty-five suggested theme programs. Following the program suggestions are eighty play analyses to aid choice.
>
> A common theme through the several plays of a bill melds the components into an organic whole. The suggested programs presented here list scripts in playable sequence. If the bill proves too long, a given play might be dropped.
>
> Intermissions are a subjective element and may occur as needed—but the fewer and shorter the better. Breaks of a minute or two between plays and a single intermission of seven minutes work well.

Actors

"**Old Jew, The,**" a drama by Murray Schisgal, 1m, (published with and can pair with "Memorial Day," "The Basement," or "Fragments") in *Five One Act Plays,* DPS 3975, NSHS pb6057

"**Purple Door Knob, The,**" a comedy by Walter Prichard Eaton, 3f, SF 863, NSHS pb7959

"**Senior Prom,**" a comedy by Robert Mearns, 1m1f, in *Off-Off Broadway Festival Plays, Tenth Series*, SF 21652, NSHS 27488

"**Impromptu,**" a drama by Tad Mosel, 2m2f, DPS 2495, HDS, NSHS pb2572

Ambition

"**Comanche Café,**" new revised version of a drama by William Hauptman, 2f, ISBN 0-573-62131-4, in *Domino Courts/Comanche Café*, SF 5686, NSHS pb91

"**Queens of France,**" a satiric comedy by Thornton Wilder, 1m3f, SF 886, NSHS pb7963

"**Lip Service,**" a drama by Howard Korder, 2m, in *"The*

Middle Kingdom" and "Lip Service": Two Short Plays, SF 14166, NSHS 27513

"**Twelve Pound Look, The,**" a comedy by J. M. Barrie, 2m2f, BP, SF 1095, NSHS 19878, NSHS 19883

Anglo Lite

"**Dock Brief, The,**" a comedy by John Mortimer, 2m, (billed with "What Shall We Tell Caroline?") SF 6649, NSHS facsimile

"**Box and Cox,**" an English farce by John Maddison Morton, 2m1f, BP (no royalty with purchase of three copies), SF 4672 (no royalty), HDS, GCB, NSHS 5345

"**How He Lied to Her Husband,**" a farce by George Bernard Shaw, 2m1f, in *Selected Short Plays*, SF 10670, NSHS pb7424, NSHS pb2819

Dance

"**Longing for Worldly Pleasures,**" a traditional *K'unshan* play by Ssu Fan, 1f, UWP

"**Dance and the Railroad, The,**" a drama by David Henry Hwang, 2m, in *The Dance and the Railroad and Family Devotions*, DPS 1523, NSHS pb7918

"archy and mehitabel," a musical comedy by Joe Darion and Mel Brooks, with music by George Kleinsinger and lyrics by Joe Darion, 3m1f (+singers/dancers), MTI

Death

"Death of the Hired Man, The," a drama by Jay Reid Gould from Robert Frost, 2m2f, DPC D13, HDS, NSHS 6071

"Man with the Flower in His Mouth, The," a drama by Luigi Pirandello translated from the original Italian by William Murray, 2m1f, in *Pirandello's One-Act Plays*, SF 15602

"Other Player, The," a drama by Owen G. Arno, 3m or 3f, DPS 3550, NSHS pb7344

"Phoenix Too Frequent, A," a comedy by Christopher Fry, 1m2f, DPS, HDS

Dominance

"Stronger, The," a drama by August Strindberg, translated by Michael Meyer, 2f (+extra), (can pair with "Miss Julie") in *Plays by August Strindberg* DPS 252, NSHS 29262

"Sing to Me Through Open Windows," a drama by Arthur Kopit, 3m, (published with and can pair with "The Questioning of Nick," "The Hero," or "The Conquest of Everest") in *The Day the Whores Came out to Play Tennis and Other Plays* SF 21705, NSHS pb7930, ISBN 0-374-52233-2

"Something Unspoken," a drama by Tennessee Williams, 2f, in *27 Wagons Full of Cotton*, DPS 485

"Hello, Ma!" a comedy by Trude Stone, 2f, in *Off-Off Broadway Festival Plays,* Vol. 5, SF 10630, NSHS 27534

Ethnic

"Los Dos Caras del Patroncito/The Two Faces of the Boss," an agitprop by Luis Valdez, 3m, APP, NSHS facsimile

"Dance and the Railroad, The," a drama by David Henry Hwang, 2m, in *The Dance and the Railroad and Family Devotions*, DPS 1523, NSHS pb7918

"Open Admissions," new revised edition of a one-act version of a full-length drama by Shirley Lauro, 1m1f, ISBN 0-573-60044-9, in *Off-Off Broadway Festival Plays,* Fourth Series, SF 17640, NSHS 27533

"Soul Gone Home," a comedy by Langston Hughes, 3m1f, HOA, NSHS 16174

Family

"American Ancestor Worship," a pick-and-choose bill of

satirical skits by Cornelia Otis Skinner, 1f, in *One Woman Show: Monologues as Originally Written and Performed by Cornelia Otis Skinner*, DPC, NSHS pb147

"Fumed Oak," a comedy by Noel Coward, one of the *Tonight At 8:30* series, 1m3f, BP, SF 450, HDS, NSHS 19878, NSHS 19883

"Harmfulness of Tobacco, The," a farce monologue by Anton Chekhov, 1m, SF

"Riders to the Sea," a drama by John Millington Synge, 1m3f, BP, HDS, SF 920, NSHS 19878, NSHS 19883, NSHS 7095, NSHS 2212, NSHS 16020, NSHS 21405, NSHS 26428, NSHS 16370, NSHS 16374, NSHS 29310

Far Out

"Ping," an abstraction by Samuel Beckett, 1m or 1f, DPS, NSHS facsimile

"Sing to Me Through Open Windows," a drama by Arthur Kopit, 3m, (published with and can pair with "The Questioning of Nick," "The Hero," or "The Conquest of Everest") in *The Day the Whores Came out to Play Tennis and Other Plays* SF 21705, NSHS pb7930, ISBN 0-374-52233-2

"Tongues," a monodrama, a piece for voice and percussion by Sam Shepard and Joseph Chaikin, 1m, in *Sam Shepard: Seven Plays* SF 22733, NSHS 28227

"Shrew You, or Who Hath Need of Men? As Goode Accounte As Anye Knowne Describing How Sweet Shagsper Shuffles Off His Mortal Coil," a comedy by Lewis W. Heniford, 2m2f, WO, NSHS

Feminism

"That's All," a revue sketch by Harold Pinter, 2f, (published with and can pair with "Trouble in the Works," "The Black and White," "Last to Go," "Applicant," "Interview," or "That's Your Trouble") in *Revue Sketches*, DPS 1765, NSHS 27487

"American Ancestor Worship," a pick-and-choose bill of satirical skits by Cornelia Otis Skinner, 1f, DPC, NSHS

"Amelia Lives," a drama by Laura Annawyn Shamas, 1f, DPC, NSHS pb141

"Twelve Pound Look, The," a comedy by J. M. Barrie, 2m2f, BP, SF 1095, NSHS 19878, NSHS 19883

Friendships

"Save Me a Place at Forest Lawn," a comedy-drama by Lorees Yerby, 2f, HDS, DPS 3955, NSHS pb7914

"Spittin' Image," a drama by Stephen Metcalfe, 2m, (published with and can play with "Sorrows and Sons") in *Sorrows and Sons*, SF 21742, NSHS pb7896

"**Dance and the Railroad, The,**" a drama by David Henry Hwang, 2m, in *The Dance and the Railroad and Family Devotions*, DPS 1523, NSHS pb7918

"**12:21 P.M.,**" a comedy by F. J. Hartland, 2m1f, in *Off-Off Broadway Festival Plays, Tenth Series*, SF 22772, NSHS 27488

The Great Mistake

"**Man with the Flower in His Mouth, The,**" a drama by Luigi Pirandello translated from the original Italian by William Murray, 2m1f, in *Pirandello's One-Act Plays*, SF 15602

"*Vanities [Act I],*" the first act of a comedy by Jack Heifner, 3f, in *Vanities*, SF 120, NSHS PB92

"**Necklace, The,**" a drama by Jules Tasca from Guy de Maupassant, 1m2f, (published with and can pair with "Father and Son," "The Devil," or "Forbidden Fruit") in *The Necklace and Other Stories*, SF 15990, DPC N10, NSHS 27500, NSHS pb7919

"**Box and Cox,**" a English farce by John Maddison Morton, 2m1f, BP (no royalty with purchase of three copies), SF 4672 (no royalty), HDS, GCB, NSHS 5345

Greed

"**Olives, The**" ["*Las Aceitunas*"], a *paso* by Lope de Rueda, 2m2f, CML.

"**Queens of France,**" a satiric comedy by Thornton Wilder, 1m3f, SF 886, NSHS pb7963

"**Frog Prince, The,**" a comic fantasy by David Mamet, 2m2f, ISBN 0-573-65220-1, SF 472, NSHS 27529

"**Box and Cox,**" an English farce by John Maddison Morton, 2m1f, BP (no royalty with purchase of three copies), SF 4672 (no royalty), HDS, GCB, NSHS 5345

Guilt

"**Answers,**" a drama by Tom Topor, 3m, DPS 811, NSHS 29209

"**Nightingale, A,**" a drama by Horton Foote, 3m1f, DPS 3845, NSHS

"**Last Days of Mankind,**" an excerpt (Act V, Scene 54) by Karl Kraus, translated by Max Spalter from the original German, 1m, KV, NSHS 29408

"**Purgatory,**" a melodrama by William Butler Yeats, 3m1f, in *Eleven Plays by W. B. Yeats* and in *The Modern Theatre, Vol. 2*, SF 18674, NSHS 16369

Homosexuality

"**Box Office,**" a comedy by Elinor Jones, 1m, (can pair with "What Would Jeanne Moreau Do") published with "What Would Jeanne Moreau Do," SF 4670, NSHS pb7960

"**Rosary,**" a comedy by Jean-Claude Van Itallie, 1f, (published with and can pair with "Eat Cake," "Harold," "Photographs: Mary and Howard," "Thoughts on the Instant of Greeting a Friend on the Street," or "Girl and the Soldier") in *Seven Short and Very Short Plays*, DPS 4726, NSHS pb65

"**Something Unspoken,**" a drama by Tennessee Williams, 2f, in *27 Wagons Full of Cotton*, DPS 485

"**Trap Is a Small Place, A,**" a drama by Marjean Perry, 1m3f, MMP, NSHS 2401

Identity

"**Phoenix Too Frequent, A,**" a comedy by Christopher Fry, 1m2f, DPS, HDS

"**After the Fact,**" a comedy-drama by Jeffrey Sweet, 1m1f, ISBN 0-573-62028-8, SF 3608, NSHS 27521

"**Bespoke Overcoat, The,**" a tragedy by Wolf Mankowitz, 4m, SF 4627, NSHS 19991

"**Suppressed Desires,**" a comedy by Susan Glaspell, 1m2f, BP, HDS, NSHS pb5483, NSHS 19878, NSHS 19883

Jewishness

"**Jewish Wife, The,**" a drama by Bertolt Brecht translated into English by Eric Bentley, 1m1f, BP, in *The Jewish Wife and Other Short Plays*, SF 604, NSHS 29533

"**Suburban Tragedy,**" a drama by Jerome Kass, 1m1f, (published with and can pair with "Make Like a Dog" or "Young Marrieds at Play") DPS 2662, NSHS

"**Bespoke Overcoat, The,**" a tragedy by Wolf Mankowitz, 4m, SF 4627, NSHS 19991

"**Hello, Ma!**" a comedy by Trude Stone, 2f, in *Off-Off Broadway Festival Plays, Vol. 5*, SF 10630, NSHS 27534

Loneliness

Villane, Ron, "An Empty Space," a drama, 1m1f (published with and can pair with "Open Admissions" or "Nothing Immediate") in Double Image Theatre's *Off-Off Broadway Festival Plays, Fourth Series* (New York: Samuel French, Inc., 1983), Samuel French, Inc., 1983), SF 7613, NSHS 27533, ISBN 0-573-60044-9

"**Suburban Tragedy,**" a drama by Jerome Kass, 1m1f, (published with and can pair with "Make Like a Dog" or "Young Marrieds at Play") DPS 2662, NSHS

"**Not Enough Rope,**" a farce by Elaine May, 1m2f, BP, SF 85, NSHS pb5466, NSHS pb7751

Marriage

"**Birthday Present, The,**" a drama by Peter Brook, 1m2f, DPC B21, NSHS pb6070

"*Volver a decir el mar,*" a drama by Sergio Peregrina, 1m, OEN, NSHS

"**Here We Are,**" a comedy by Dorothy Parker, 1m1f, NSHS pb4019, NSHS 7094, NSHS 13286, NSHS 14824, NSHS 20483, NSHS 21389, NSHS 21514, NSHS 21776, NSHS 28435

"**Laughs, Etc.,**" a comedy by James Leo Herlihy, 1f, (published with and can pair with "Terrible Jim Fitch" or "Bad Bad Jo-Jo") in *Stop, You're Killing Me*, DPS 4290, NSHS pb7924

"**Bespoke Overcoat, The,**" a tragedy by Wolf Mankowitz, 4m, SF 4627, NSHS 19991

Mom

"**Movie Mother,**" a comedy by Colin Clements and Florence Ryerson, 1f, SF, NSHS 6066

"**Animal,**" a bare-stage comedy by Oliver Hailey, 1f, (published with and can pair with "Picture" or "Crisscross") in *Picture Animal Crisscross: Three Short Plays*, DPS 3655, NSHS pb7922

"**Scent of Honeysuckle, A,**" a bare-stage comedy-drama by Jean Lenox Toddie, 3f, ISBN 0-573-60059-7, (published with and can pair with "A Little Something for the Ducks") SF 21041, NSHS 27492

"**Hello, Ma!**" a comedy by Trude Stone, 2f, in *Off-Off Broadway Festival Plays,* Vol. 5, SF 10630, NSHS 27534

Once Upon a Time

"**Frog Prince, The,**" a comic fantasy by David Mamet, 2m2f, ISBN 0-573-65220-1, SF 472, NSHS 27529

"**Playe Called the Foure PP, The: A Newe and a Very Mery Enterlude of a Palmer, a Pardoner, a Potycary, and a Pedler,**" a medieval comedy by John Heywood, 4m, ATB, HMC, NSHS 29216

"**archy and mehitabel,**" a musical comedy by Joe Darion and Mel Brooks, with music by George Kleinsinger and lyrics by Joe Darion, 3m1f (+singers/dancers), MTI

Politics

"**To Burn a Witch,**" a drama by James L. Bray, 4f, DPC T32, HDS, NSHS pb160

"**Rising of the Moon, The,**" a comedy by Lady Isabella Augusta Gregory, 4m, SF 20040 (no royalty in U.S.A., royalty in Canada), NSHS 19878, NSHS 19883, NSHS 16020, NSHS 21405, NSHS 26581, NSHS 20718

"**Conversation at Night with a Despised Character: A Curriculum for Our Times,**" a drama by Friedrich Dürrenmatt translated by Robert David Macdonald from the original German, 2m, DPC C32, NSHS pb177

Sexual Control

"*Estoy enamorado de tu hermana,*" a *farsa* by Jesús Assaf, 1m2f, OEN, NSHS

"**Stronger, The,**" a drama by August Strindberg, translated by Michael Meyer, 2f (+ extra), (can pair with "Miss Julie") in *Plays by August Strindberg*, DPS 252, NSHS 29262

"**Birthday Present, The,**" a drama by Peter Brook, 1m2f, DPC B21, NSHS pb6070

"**Rapes,**" a play by Mario Fratti, 2m1f, in *Races*, SF

Suicide

"**Before Breakfast,**" a drama by Eugene O'Neill, 1f, DPS 405

"**Spared,**" a bare-stage drama by Israel Horovitz, 1m (recorded voices), (published with and can pair with "Stage Directions"; also, can pair with "Hopscotch" or "The 75th") in *The Quannapowitt Quartet*, DPS 4235, SF 990, NSHS pb6068

"**Passport,**" a drama by James Elward, 1m, (published with and can pair with "Mary Agnes Is Thirty-five") in *Friday Night*, DPS 2045, NSHS 29204

"**Ledge, Ledger, and the Legend,**" a comedy by Paul Elliott, 3m or 3f, DPC L15, HDS, NSHS pb142, NSHS pb7941

Surreality

"**Thursday Is My Day for Cleaning,**" a comedy by Jordan Crittenden, 1f, SF 22692, NSHS

"**Chicks,**" a comedy by Grace McKeaney, 1f, in *Chicks and Other Short Plays*, SF 5747, NSHS pb7949

"**Overtones,**" a drama by Alice Gerstenberg, 4f, BP, SF 17912, NSHS 19878, NSHS 19883

"**Daughters of Edward D. Boit, The,**" a dark comedy by Don Nigro, 4f, (published with and can play with "Specter" or "The Woodman and the Goblins") in *Green Man and Other Plays*, SF, NSHS pb7916, ISBN 0-573-62207-8

Visitors

"**Call, The,**" a drama by William Inge, 2m, DPS manuscript, NSHS pb86

"**Me Too, Then!**" a comedy by Tom Dudzick and Steven Smith, 2m1f, in *Off-Off Broadway Festival Plays, Vol. 5*, SF 15651, NSHS 27534

"**Chekhov,**" a drama by Keith Miles, 1m1f, ISBN 0-573-60049-X, (published with "Dostoevsky") in *Russian Masters*, SF 20091, NSHS p2511

War

"**Spittin' Image,**" a drama by Stephen Metcalfe, 2m, (published with and can play with "Sorrows and Sons") in *Sorrows and Sons*, SF 21742, NSHS pb7896

"**Rising of the Moon, The,**" a comedy by Lady Isabella Augusta Gregory, 4m, SF 20040 (no royalty in

U.S.A., royalty in Canada), NSHS 19878, NSHS 19883, NSHS 16020, NSHS 21405, NSHS 26581, NSHS 20718

"Last Days of Mankind," an excerpt (Act V, Scene 54) by Karl Kraus, translated by Max Spalter from the original German, 1m, KV, NSHS 29408

"Jewish Wife, The," a drama by Bertolt Brecht translated into English by Eric Bentley, 1m1f, BP, in *The Jewish Wife and Other Short Plays*, SF 604, NSHS 29533

Eighty script analyses follow. ➲

List of Plot Analyses and Comments, with Page Numbers

To facilitate choice, eighty play analyses with comments appear in the following pages. The format presents (a) information as it might appear on the printed program for the production and (b) the plot with an evaluation to assist selection.

After the Fact

by Jeffrey Sweet

Dramatis Personae

Tentative Cast

Mrs. Lorraine Spaulding, 24 actually [f], _____

Mr. Ernest Justin Herbert, 63 possibly [m], _____

Place: A newspaper office in Taylor Ridge, an American town.
Time: The present. [Note: Copyright 1981.]

Available from Samuel French, Inc. [#22; ISBN 0-573-62028-8]

Plot

Herbert enters Lorraine's office at the town newspaper and presents the obituary she has written on his friend. Amid realistic conversational digressions on both sides that thwart their communication, he persists in specifying errors in the newspaper item. They disagree on the significance of the errors. He regards her as insensitive; she regards him as unfair. Each lands telling blows. He drives her to pleading for her job. She rebuts by handing him his own obituary file to edit. Herbert, here only on an impulse while he happened to be in the neighborhood, unexpectedly has to confront his own mortality. Lorraine, an aspiring journalist, has to confront her inability to communicate.

Comment

Two neatly balanced characterizations as well as staging with "a minimum of fuss" [p. 20] make this play an appealing production possibility. The protagonist is Herbert. The play studies societal values of longtime resident versus newcomer as well as generational biases.

Started in the "New Play Readings" series at the Long Wharf Theatre, formally premiered at the Victory Gardens Theatre, Chicago, this play can share a double bill with "Porch," also by Jeffrey Sweet. The script originally appeared in *Dramatics* magazine.

1m1f, comedy drama   *Themes:* xenophobia and ageism

Amelia Lives

by Laura Annawyn Shamas

Dramatis Persona

Tentative Cast

Amelia Earhart, daring aviatrix, mid-thirties; a striking woman,
clad in flying togs; intelligent; with a dry sense of humor;
angelic but ghostly; at home in the sky [f], _____

Place: An airplane in flight over the Pacific Ocean.
Time: July, 1937.

Available from The Dramatic Publishing Company.

Plot

Amelia, sitting in the plane, tries after three hours of no contact to reach cutter *Itasca*. Almost out of fuel, she reminisces about her first free flight, at age six, off her Granny's barn roof, to impress her friend Frankie. Shifting to another memory, she and her little sister Pidge plot to free an abused horse; their action leads to the horse's death. Next memory: she tries to reason her father out of his alcoholism. Memory: she tries to petition for a better English teacher, but no one responds. Additional scenes tumble into her mind. Pidge in Toronto studies to become a teacher; Amelia studies first aid and works in a military hospital, where she meets aviators. She sees her first air show and decides to fly, but pneumonia delays this start. She recovers, moves to Los Angeles, gets a job as a telephone operator to finance flight lessons. Sam be-comes her first boyfriend; unfortunately, he guides her family into bad investments. Amelia solos. Her parents divorce. She breaks up with Sam. Family events form a background to her real love, flying. Inspired by Lindbergh's famous flight, she becomes at twenty-seven the first woman passenger to cross the Atlantic. This brings her celebrity and a husband who manages her career. She flies the Atlantic alone. She wins honors, meets famous world leaders, becomes a role model for women, sets flying records. She suffers the death of her father and pays his debts. With Lindbergh capturing so many firsts, Amelia aspires to achieve the first air circum-navigation close to the equator. On this fateful flight, she is trying radio contact to cutter *Itasca*. She struggles against the final descent of her plane.

Comment

This highly challenging script won the Edinburgh Fringe First Award for Outstanding New Drama. The one-act script cites a playing time of seventy-five minutes. Exact-ing technical demands raise many problems that are integral to a successful production. The show should not be attempted without serious commitment by the company. Its literary merit is ragged, its insights few; but enthusiastic audience enjoy-ment of a skilled production would be likely in many venues.

1f, drama

Themes: feminism, aviation, and celebrity

American Ancestor Worship

by Cornelia Otis Skinner

Dramatis Persona

Tentative Cast

The Western Descendant, A California Socialite;
and The Western Ancestress, A Spanish Prostitute [f], _____

Place: At a dressing table in a bedroom and at the upstairs window of a bedroom.
Time: 1984 and 1834.

Available from The Dramatic Publishing Company.

Plot

(1984) The California Socialite happily prepares her granddaughter for a fancy dress ball in the finery of her own great grandmother. This is the social event of the year, with the very best people from Pasadena, Santa Barbara, and Pebble Beach and with pointed exclusion of the Hollywood set. She finishes by adding the great-grandmother's high comb and shawl. She wants the girl to know how special it is to have valid ancestry, pure Castilian blood from Doña Consuelo Rosario de los Juntos y Perez Jesús Maria y Smith. The husband Smith seems to have been a seafaring gentleman. How

nice it would have been to have a portrait of the ancestress in her comb and mantilla, such a grande dame!

(1834) The Spanish Prostitute calls from her window down to the newly arrived sailor, whose name is Smith like every other Norte Americano. An earlier Smith had given her a comb and a mantilla and a baby. From this Smith, she accepts silver *reales* and throws down the key. He must not wake the baby, Consuelo Rosario de los Juntos y Perez Jesús Maria y Smith.

Comment

This "one-sided dialogue" is from a collection, *One Woman Show: Monologues as Originally Written and Performed by Cornelia Otis Skinner*. The Preface directs how to stage any of the collection. With more than two dozen sketches

from which to choose, an actress can easily find one appropriate to occasion. They are short, trenchant, and always astute.

1f, comedy

Themes: heritage and women

Animal

by Oliver Hailey

Dramatis Persona

Tentative Cast

The Woman [f], _____

Place: At the foot of a tree, near a vacation place.
Time: Summer.

Available from Dramatists Play Service.

Plot

The Woman, dressed in summer black, calls up into imaginary trees on the rented summer place. She spots Claire Marie hiding in one. She cannot understand how a twelve-year-old would risk soiling her matching dress, slip, and panties. Above all, The Woman does not want Claire Marie to sulk the way the girl's father did; he died in the top of a cottonwood, sulking. The father had had a heart condition brought on by climbing trees. He had taught the little girl to climb, probably to elude her mother as he was doing. The Woman spots "that damn doll," which she had tried to leave behind. She knows this is a result of the father's insane teaching—a doll called "Mother" in lieu of recognizing the real mother. The Woman hears the guest children arriving for the party that has been planned to introduce Claire Marie to people her own age. She threatens to have the children come out there and tease Claire Marie. She again demands the doll. It comes hurtling down against her face. The Woman promises the first game for the children will be to find Claire Marie and the prize will be the doll. She goes to get the guests to start the game. After a brief pause, piece by piece, Claire Marie's clothing falls to the ground.

Comment

This playlet has much surface comedy, but the subtext reveals a biting condemnation of misguided parenting. Almost all of the burden for the show falls on the actress, who can use it as a handy, brief showcase for her talent; it is a good audition piece. Aside from arranging to have the clothes descend, technical problems are few and simple.

1f, comedy

Themes: parenting and grief

Answers

by Tom Topor

Dramatis Personae

Tentative Cast

Ed [m], _____

Frank [m], _____

Suspect [m], _____

Place: Interrogation room, Homicide South, Manhattan.
Time: The present. [Note: Copyright 1973.]

Available from Dramatists Play Service, Inc.

Plot

Ed and Frank assail the Suspect in an interrogation room. These detectives impose an identity on him that he rejects and that he would correct if his wallet had not been lifted. They say he murdered a woman. He claims to have been asleep in his room at the time. They tempt him to a drink of whiskey, then knock it from his hand, blaming him for making a mess. In a staccato barrage of accusative details and questions, the detectives psychologically abuse the Suspect. He lengthily claims innocence and demands to see their notes on the interrogation. They tease him with the notebook but ultimately allow him to read their conclusion: "Suspect wrong man." He responds with weary hope and accepts whiskey-laced coffee. They follow their brief kindnesses with another fast, long inquisition and record on tape his disjointed answers as incriminating misstatements. They claim he has assaulted them and the law. Reduced to babbling incoherence and left by himself with a confession to sign, the Suspect picks up the pen.

Comment

In this strong indictment of misguided police tactics, both of the detectives, both of them unrelenting antiheroes, personify evil. Only the Suspect suffers emotional change, being driven to submission. The street language and allusion to prison rape pose problems for some theatre companies. Production needs are undemanding.

3m, drama

Themes: police brutality and suspect's rights

archy and mehitabel

by Joe Darion and Mel Brooks
Music by George Kleinsinger, Lyrics by Joe Darion

Dramatis Personae

Tentative Cast

Mehitabel, a cat [f], _____

Archy, a cockroach [m], _____

Narrator, a newspaper reporter [m], _____

Big Bill [m], _____

The Cronies [trio and chorus, m and f], _____

Place: The Big City.
Time: The present. [Note: *Shinbone Alley* opened on Broadway on April 13, 1957.]

Available from Music Theatre International.

Plot

The Narrator, a newspaper reporter, tells how Archy, a poetic cockroach, came to be a reporter. Every morning the Narrator rushes eagerly to his office typewriter where Archy has jumped from key to key through the night, writing about the inhabitants of Shinbone Alley, particularly about the vicissitudes in the life of the joyous cat Mehitabel. Archy sings about her. Mehitabel has a soul too gay and a conscious too frail, he thinks. She and her cronies sing and yowl and dance in the moonlight, until the cops come. She grudgingly allows Archy to give unsought—and ignored—blue-nosed advice: he tries to get her to accept a job as a house cat. She sings about his maddening interference and her fondness for him, nevertheless. Archy sings of his philosophy, about politics, ethics, nature study. He cannot get his mind off Mehitabel. He is dismayed when she introduces him to her latest romance, Big Bill, "the biggest, ugliest, meanest Tom cat in the whole wide world." Bill routs Archy and romances Mehitabel in song and dance. Having found her true romance, she runs off with Bill. Archy, trying to concentrate on other characters in Shinbone Alley, sings of Broadway, "The Lightning Bug." The Narrator knows this is false cheer. Then suddenly, Archy sings of Mehitabel's return. She has been deserted by Bill but has three kittens by which to remember him. She and a trio of the cronies sing of her ambivalence toward motherhood. Mehitabel sees them as hampering her life-style, but when a rainstorm comes, Archy get her to rescue the little dears. She thanks him with a scolding. However, Mehitabel does take his advice to accept a job as a house cat. As weeks pass, Archy misses and sings of the old Mehitabel he used to know. He regrets having robbed her of her joyous life-style. At that darkest moment, though, he hears her approaching, singing, dancing, celebrating her abandonment of being a house cat. She and the cronies sing and dance together, as of old. Archy has learned that he must accept her for what she is—"just plain wonderful." He proudly calls her his friend.

Comment

The full-length version was produced on Broadway as *Shinbone Alley*, and the music was recorded on the Columbia Masterworks album, featuring Carol Channing, Eddie Bracken, David Wayne, Percival Dove, and The Heathertones. The one-act version runs twenty-plus minutes. Singing and dancing demands are light, but good talent would enhance any production. The mood is upbeat. The script offers an excellent chance to try musical comedy without mounting a full-blown, full-length production. Royalties are higher than for a nonmusical, of course.

3m1f (+singers/dancers), musical comedy

Themes: friendship and choice of life-style

Before Breakfast

by Eugene O'Neill

Dramatis Persona

Tentative Cast

Mrs. Rowland [f], _____

Place: A small kitchen-dining room in a flat on Christopher Street,
New York City.
Time: Eight-thirty in the morning, early fall, 1916.

Available from Dramatists Play Service.

Plot

Before breakfast on a sunshiny day in early fall, Mrs. Rowland comes from the bedroom, still pulling herself together in a slovenly fashion. In her early twenties but appearing older, she wearily prepares coffee. Suddenly remembering something, she calls Alfred, her husband. Covertly taking a large drink of gin, she hides the bottle and calls again. She searches his clothes, finding a letter that she reads and replaces. She commences a litany of nagging. He is at fault for pawning his watch; now they do not know the time. He is at fault for the place's being a mess. She must go out to sew for money. Now the rent is due and he is jobless, absorbed in his silly poetry. Irritated at his delay and silence, she checks to see that he is up. Satisfied that he is, she resumes nagging. He came in drunk last night. She has only stale bread and butter to serve with the coffee. Peering off at him, she considers his tramp-like appearance disgust-ing. He reaches a trembling hand into the room to obtain hot water. She sweeps the floor viciously, hearing the sound of his razor stropping. She ridicules his once-wealthy parents, his Harvard education, even his having married her because she was pregnant with a child that was born dead. She challenges him about Helen, whom she sees as one of many women fawning on him. His cry of pain lets her know he has cut himself shaving. She looks out at him with a shudder, unable to take his staring at her. Urging him to hurry, she eats and sips coffee. The tirade continues, about Helen whoever-she-is, and climaxes in a promise that he will never get a divorce. Another groan of pain from him satisfies her. But she detects dripping water. Yelling at him and getting no answer, she looks through the doorway then "shrieks wildly and runs to the other door, unlocks it and frenziedly pulls it open, and runs shrieking madly into the outer hallway."

Comment

A challenge for an aspiring actress, this short play by the foremost American dramatist is nearly the kind of melodrama O'Neill hated and rebelled against, but the layers of character give it integrity. Some of his vicious but complex later women, such as the grand Electra, flow from this tiny fountainhead. Production demands are few. The situation is timeless, so period staging is less important.

1f, drama

Themes: suicide and marriage

The Bespoke Overcoat

by Wolf Mankowitz

Dramatis Personae

Tentative Cast

Morry, a tailor [m], _____

Fender, a warehouse clerk [m], _____

Ranting, his employer [m], _____

A Clerk, also a weight-lifter [m], _____

Places: [A] Ranting's warehouse, [B] limbo, [C] Morry's room.
Time: That in the heart of a drunken tailor. [Note: Copyright 1956.]

Available from Samuel French, Inc.

Plot

Sixteen scenes in three areas tell the story. [Scene **1**, Area B] Morry explains how Fender, before he recently died, wanted him to repair a twenty-year-old coat. [**2**, C] Fender's ghost has come to Morry for a favor. [**3**, A] Ranting, Fender's employer, refuses to help him finance a new coat and suggests he go to Morry to mend the old one. [**4**, C, B] Fender arranges with Morry a bespoke (commissioned) overcoat. [**5**, C] Morry, taking a sewing break to eat black bread and herring, brags about the coat's quality. [**6**, B] Ranting, forking chopped liver to his mouth, considers automation but settles for having a good clerk. [**7**, A] Fender, dining on a bagel, enjoys rehearsing a story he will share with Morry. Ranting admonishes him for leaving crumbs that might draw mice. [**8**, C] Fender checks the progress on the coat and pays forty shillings down. Morry promises himself a brandy that night. [**9**, B] On the subway, Ranting shows off his new American coat and advises knocking off the booze to be able afford such quality. [**10**, C] Morry arrives home drunkenly to find Fender, who has lost his job. Morry promises to finish the coat although Fender cannot pay for it. [**11**, B] Fender, near death, wishes he had told off Ranting; instead, his pride has made him play down his dire straits. [**12**, A] Morry arrives at Ranting's warehouse to deliver the coat. A new Clerk is performing Fender's accounting. Ranting gives uncertain directions about finding Fender. [**13**, C] Fender has been given leave from the afterlife Jewish hotel to which he has been assigned. His ghost assuages Morry's guilt about not having finished the coat sooner. Fender tactfully declines the coat, saying that Ranting owes him a sheepskin coat for forty-three years' service. Morry suggests they go to the warehouse and take the coat. [**14**, A] The Clerk, having deciphered Fender's accounting system, describes his off-hours preoccupation with bodybuilding to become Mr. Universe. [**15**, B] Morry cautions Fender about drinking so much. Fender is unable to walk through the wall but fortunately still has the key. [**16**, A] Inside the warehouse, Fender selects the coat he wants, bids Morry good-bye with "A long life to you, Morry. Pray for me." Fender fades. Morry, putting on his hat, renders the Hebrew Prayer for the Dead until barrel-organ music takes over.

Comment

Director and actors must research Yiddish consciousness. Morry, the protagonist, twice solves problems for his friend Fender, first, how to live, and second, how to die. The "Author's Note" explains Mankowitz' indebtedness to Alec Clunes, whose original production avoided having Fender be a ghost and, instead, had him be the center of a "sustained typically overlong Jewish joke—than which there is no sadder and no funnier story." Simultaneous staging keeps production needs simple and the pacing easy.

4m, comedy

Themes: Jewishness and survivability

The Birthday Present

by Peter Brook

Dramatis Personae

Tentative Cast

Celia, a young woman [f], _____

Older Woman [f], _____

Michael, a year or two older than Celia [m], _____

Place: [A small room without much furniture,] London.
Time: The present. [Note: Copyright 1969.]

Available from The Dramatic Publishing Company.

Plot

The Older Woman relaxes Celia until the doorbell rings then goes into another room as Celia admits Michael. Celia serves drinks for them both; they are obviously a divorced couple. He notes that her decorations are familiarly placed in her new flat. They strain for civil conversation. She has surprised him with a birthday present after seven years. They reminisce about their erstwhile happiness in Venice and other bonds. He reveals that he has remarried, unhappily, and wants to know her motive for luring him here. He senses in her a lingering love. He gives her a kiss. She asks for another. The Older Woman enters to interrupt their fervent kissing. She sends Celia unsatisfied to another room, then reveals that Celia, her patient, merely is undergoing unorthodox treatment. The Older Woman dismisses Michael's protests. "It will not be necessary for you to see her again." She intimidates him into leaving unsatisfied.

Comment

A flaw is the melodramatic protagonist: the Older Woman, least onstage and psychologically two-dimensional, shows no growth. The sufficiently universal situation allows altering the British locale, if expedient. Production needs are undemanding.

1m2f, drama   *Themes:* psychiatry and marriage

Box Office

by Elinor Jones

Dramatis Persona

Tentative Cast

Jerry Jennings, 32 [m], _____

Place: Box office of a small off-Broadway theatre that looks onto the street.
Time: The present. [Note: First produced May, 1980.]

Available from Samuel French, Inc.

Plot

Jerry, on telephone duty, answers in somewhat robotic fashion queries about performances and seats for the current show *Jellybeans*. He avoids any personal interaction with callers. His patience somewhat thin, he calls Cathy, a friend, to share his troubles. Yesterday was his birthday, he has been seven years in this box of an office, and a passing dog has wet his geraniums out front. When he objected about the dog, its owner called him a fag. Even Miss Fairchild and her Girl Scouts who sell cookies and win tickets to the show are irritating him. He describes to Cathy the wall between him and his parents, their unaccountable blind eye to his being gay. He tells her he left Philip last night and fears receiving a phone call from him. Even newspaper headlines are conspiring against him, loading him with too much about which to feel guilty. Cathy suggests he quit the job. He tells her of a Japanese coming-of-age ritual which involves gazing into a basin of water for an omen of a happy future, that is, seeing the moon reflected clearly. He goes into his need to leave Philip. Anyhow, Philip was appalled at Jerry's pretending to Lauren Bacall that he was a publisher and promising to leave her a copy of a book. Business calls about tickets interrupt his personal chat with Cathy, and he grows increasingly terse with callers, even lying to them. Philip telephones; Jerry pleads business and says he will call him later. Having gathered his thoughts, Jerry dials Philip. He says he needs time and space on his own and impulsively declares he is going to Japan and quickly says good-bye. His commitment is now real. He tends to the geraniums, quits his job, promises Cathy that he will tell her everything at supper.

Comment

First produced in a one-act festival at Circle Repertory Theatre in New York City, May, 1980, the script is clever, current, character driven, a delightful turn for a good actor. The balance is to keep Jerry sympathetic despite his anger and rudeness. Production problems are few, but a telephone is a vital property, and city sounds would help.

1m, comedy

Themes: homosexuality and friendship

Box and Cox

by John Maddison Morton
Revised by Margaret Mayorga for use by American players

Dramatis Personae

Tentative Cast

John Box, a printer [m], _____

James Cox, a hatter [m], _____

Mrs. Bouncer, the landlady [f], _____

Place: A room in a lodging house in a congested district.
Time: The present. [Note: First produced November, 1847.]

Available from Baker's Plays and Samuel French, Inc.

Plot

Cox ponders his haircut when Mrs. Bouncer, his landlady, arrives to tidy his room. He complains about the depletion or disappearance of his candles, wood, sugar, and matches. Also, there is the lingering smell of smoke. She supposes that the lodger in the attic may be a smoker. Cox has passed a man on the stairs as he goes and returns home. Promising to return at nine o'clock, he leaves. The landlady soliloquizes about her scheme: she has let the one room to both Mr. Cox and Mr. Box because the work hours of one complement those of the other. Mr. Box arrives, ready for rest but curious about the man he always passes on the stairs. Mrs. Bouncer mentions the gentleman in the attic. She asks Box to cease smoking as a favor to him, but Box refuses. When she goes, he sets to preparing his meal of bacon. While Box rests on the bed with curtains drawn, Cox returns, having just been given a holiday by his employer. He suspects that the landlady is using his fire and his pan to cook bacon. He removes it and puts his chop on the gridiron. When he goes out for a moment, slamming the door, the noise alerts Box, who suspects the landlady is using his cookware because of the chop.

He removes the chop, throws it out the window and puts on his bacon. Cox returns, finding the bacon instead of his chop and encountering Box. They have just confirmed that both are being rented the same quarters, when Mrs. Bouncer returns. She admits her scheme and suggests that one of the men move to the attic. With her gone to prepare the attic room, they quarrel. They discover both are involved with the same Penelope Ann Wiggins, and both want to get out of the entanglement. They consider dueling but settle for throwing dice. This fails, as each has loaded dice, set to come up sixes. Tossing coins fails, too, as each has a coin with two heads. A letter arrives with news that their rich widow has met a fatal accident, bequeathing her wealth to her intended husband. Now they quarrel over the inheritance. Just as they agree to share fifty-fifty, a letter arrives with news that the rich widow survived her accident. They are arguing over who must marry the widow, when word comes that she has eloped with a Mr. Knox. Delighted, Box and Cox declare themselves brothers and agree to continue Mrs. Bouncer's arrangement of their sharing quarters.

Comment

One of the most famous short plays from the mid-1800s, the comedy holds up a century and a half later. It is pure farce using stock characters. Originally produced and set in London, the play is easily Americanized. Bed curtains, slammable doors, a practical (workable) griddle, and such offer some production problems. Costumes and props, essential to the milieu, might cause problems, too. Director and actors could have a romp with this show.

2m1f, farce

Themes: mistaken identity and greed

The Call

by William Inge

Dramatis Personae

Tentative Cast

Terry, middle-aged [m], _____

Joe, forty-some [m], _____

Place: Terry's apartment on a high floor, on New York's East Side.
Time: The present. [Note: Copyright 1968.]

Available from Dramatists Play Service, Inc.

Plot

Joe, in a silk-and-brocade Oriental uniform, tardily arrives at his brother-in-law's apartment, having climbed the twenty-two flights of stairs because he does not like elevators. He criticizes the decor of the apartment, particularly the paintings. While his sister Thelma is out at a rehearsal, Terry attempts to help him settle in as a guest. Joe pointedly retains his suitcases of "private things" and disparages the view, opting for a hotel. He recounts that his plane trip was made awful by wild teenagers. Refusing any refreshment except a glass of water, he explains that he is to represent his lodge back in Billings and lead a parade at a convention. Terry wants Joe to see Thelma's opening night replacing Mary Martin in a Broadway hit. Joe accepts only if he can stand at the back of the theatre, all alone. He recounts caring for his mother in her decline; while on the contrary, his four siblings "got away" to lead successful lives. Terry offers to find a hotel for him; Joe prefers to wander and find a place on his own. He details his other sister's unhappy marriage and his estrangement with her. Also, he does not like "those people" in magazines and in Thelma's life. When Terry goes to dress, Joe frantically tries to telephone a number the operator says does not exist. He blames the operator for not completing the connection, for cutting him off from everything he has ever believed in. He recovers from his tears just as Terry returns, ready to walk with him to find a hotel. Joe firmly rejects help in carrying the heavy suitcase and proudly groans under the weight of his keepsakes as he follows Terry out the door.

Comment

Joe, isolated except when leading the convention's parade, filled with despair and hate, conditions his visit to foster guilt in his hosts. The suitcase metaphor, nearly too blatant, says one chooses and cherishes one's burdens. Terry, caring, open, kind, self-aware, refuses to be drawn into Joe's value system and becomes largely reactive. The author avoids an almost obligatory confrontation, focusing like Chekhov on character over plot.

In production, decor and properties must suggest wealth and taste. Joe's colorful uniform is essential.

2m, drama

Themes: guilt, self-sacrifice, provincialism, and family

Chekhov

by Keith Miles

Dramatis Personae

Tentative Cast

Anton Pavlovich Chekhov, 41 [m], _____

Olga Leonardovna Knipper, 31 [f], _____

Place: Garden, Chekhov's house, Yalta.
Time: April, 1901.

Available from Samuel French, Inc. [#20091; ISBN 0-573-60049-X]

Plot

Olga plans to corner Anton into a proposal of marriage. He arrives late, distracted by domestic sanitation problems. They argue about his awkward compliments on her clothing and acting. She broaches the subject of her departure from his house. When he does not object, she calls him "evasive." He does digress at every chance and disparages himself. Even when she declares her love, he diverts the conversation and teases her. They reminisce about productions of his plays. She volunteers, "You are all that I want in a man," and he talks of champagne and Tolstoy, medicine and religion. He enacts to her delight his abridgment of his *play Ivanov*.

Then he finally responds to her overtures by declaring his love. Immediately, again he digresses and comes back to the issue only when she insists. He describes lengthily his unreadiness for marriage. But, little by little, he edges into an oblique proposal.

She accepts.

Comment

This script involves two historical personalities, about whom much reference material is available to support authenticity. Any production company would benefit substantially from knowledge gained about Chekhov's and Knipper's connection to the Moscow Art Theatre, which informed 20th-century drama and acting. Costumes suggesting Russia in 1901 are necessary. Setting and props do not present much of a challenge. The real challenge is to the actors and director.

1m1f, comedy

Themes: feminism, Moscow Art Theatre, playwriting

• •

Chicks

by Grace McKeaney

Dramatis Persona

Tentative Cast

Miss Phallon, kindergarten teacher, 38 or 45 [f], _____

Place: A kindergarten classroom in a Midwestern public school.

Time: Four school days.

Available from Samuel French, Inc.

• •

Plot

[Public Life, Day One] Speaking to her twenty-five kindergarten children (i.e., the audience), Miss Phallon calls for order. Today wraps up the first week of kindergarten here. She is ready for the musical portion of the afternoon. "Life is short," she says. "Let's get it right!" While the children sing, she rests her head on the desk. [American History, Day Two] In a Colonial wig and hat to celebrate Thanksgiving, she retrieves a gun from a child. Changing to a cheap Indian headdress and donning war paint, she acts out a unique version of Indians spotting the first white men. She weaves her causes into the history lesson. Despite a headache and after a little lie-down on her desk, she recoups enough to tickle some students. [Biology Etc., Day Three] Class starts with a display of sex education dolls, Bill and Jill. Miss Phallon cuts short a revealing private story, remembering the savage note from the principal about the last such episode. Nevertheless, she rambles on about wombs and lack of love. [Freedom, Day Four] Just before the Christmas break, she explains Lincoln's freeing the slaves, relating it to her freedom after her dependent father goes to the nursing home. She announces a replacement teacher will take her place with them in January. She says farewell. "Anything you owed has been paid in full because your skin is soft, and your eyes are clear and your smiles are ready. None of you owe anything. You're a gift all by yourselves. Goodbye, Chicks."

Comment

The author suggests brief blackouts, to gain continuous action. The actress should be adept at the piano, "able to pick-out snatches of songs when needed for emphasis or fun." With utmost intensity and zest, the character yearns for perfection in an imperfect world. Black changes of costume and set pieces are a challenge. The language is raunchy, integral to the author's intent and appropriate to college/university or adult production companies and audiences.

1f, comedy

Themes: kindergarten, mental health, and teaching

Comanche Café

by William Hauptman

Dramatis Personae

Tentative Cast

Ronnie, 25 [f], _____

Mattie, 45 [f], _____

Place: Behind the Comanche Café, in southern Oklahoma.
Time: Sunday, the late 1930s.

Available from Samuel French, Inc. [ISBN 0-573-62131-4]

Plot

Ronnie dislikes much about the first day on her job as waitress at the Comanche Café: having to work on Sundays, the fresh tourists, the smallness of the town. Mattie, overweight, a fourteen-year veteran here, describes how she likes serving truck drivers, salesmen, farmers. Ronnie claims premonitions from ghosts. As everybody else seems to be leaving Oklahoma, she wants to go, too, maybe to California in order to break into movies. She has seen postcards of California. She is on the lookout for the right man so she can stop work. Mattie recalls running away with a man. Ronnie, inexperienced, wants Mattie to describe making love. Mattie recounts the beauty of the night with that man, her being photographed standing in front of his car next morning, and her decision to return here to work. Ronnie urges Mattie not to give up. Mattie knows that postcards and photographs do not show real life; she needs only her work—and "a bed, and a sink, and a chair, and a window." Ronnie wants never to be that way. She plans as soon as possible to see the big cities up North or California. She might even go South, to Florida or Georgia. She builds to a cry of need and determination, "Wonderful things all over America! And I'm going to see them all. Just let me go anyplace but here—in Oklahoma."

Comment

This very short play depicts a generational gap about approaching life. The characterizations are beautiful. Ronnie becomes the central character because she has a problem to solve and the drive to attempt solving it. Mattie, a kind of Chorus, knows life within the confines of her world and gives her wisdom to Ronnie on how to accept and adjust. Selective realism presents the stage as nearly empty. Many small for-sale plaster statures help set the tone. Specified costumes are waitress uniforms. The sound of wind pervades throughout. This show was first produced professionally at the American Place Theatre in November, 1976.

2f, drama   *Themes:* ambition and 1930s Great Depression

Conversation at Night with a Despised Character
(a curriculum for our times)

by Friedrich Dürrenmatt, translated by Robert David Macdonald

Dramatis Personae

Tentative Cast

A Man [m], _____

Other [m], _____

Place: A room.
Time: Night, sometime in the future. [Note: Copyright 1957.]

Available from The Dramatic Publishing Company.

Plot

An intruder breaks into the waiting Man's darkened study. The Man turns on the light and welcomes him. The Other apologizes about breaking a valuable amphora, then determines no one else is in the flat to impede his killing the Man. He is fulfilling his fifty-year role of the country's public executioner. He defers an offered drink until after the job. The Man, at odds with the country's totalitarian power structure, wants, at least, to have his avid murderer understand his political resistance. The Man despises being killed by a mere civil servant, although he likes the murderer's expertise. Granted respite to smoke, the Man hears about the Other's life as a prisoner let out from time to time to kill simple criminals and enemies of the state. The Other explains his view on the Art of Dying: whereas public trials and executions achieved a dignity, hidden trials and assassinations bring "a wretched death." Asked for advice on dying, the Other responds, "With humility, sir." The Man counters with a promise to fight and calls at the window for help. He sees that no help is coming, resists a bit more, then accepts defeat. The Other discourses on the incomprehensibility of killing humble innocents; their revenge is that they remain unforgettable. He has learned that he can kill men but not ideas, that "this world must break in fragments" that God's Kingdom may come. The Man deprecates such platitudes, but he comfortably and confidently accepts death as an humble innocent in God's plan, saying, "The fight will be taken up again and again, somewhere, sometime, by somebody, and at any moment."

Comment

The Man's existential dramatic want is to control his own death: he has lost everything, and anything he does—even manipulating his own death—can only bring improvement. The role requires complex characterization: there is much subtext in the lines. The role of the Other matches it. Directions specify, "Some may see this play as being very realistic; others may want to do it completely differently. Therefore stage directions for the play are left to the discretion of the director, as are stage design and the use of properties." A cover illustration from the BBC production starring Sir John Gielgud and Sir Alec Guiness shows realism in design and properties.

2m, drama

Themes: artistic freedom, bravery, murder, police brutality, and totalitarianism

The Dance and the Railroad

by David Henry Hwang

Dramatis Personae

Tentative Cast

Lone, 20, ChinaMan railroad worker [m], _____

Ma, 18, ChinaMan railroad worker [m], _____

Place: A mountaintop near the transcontinental railroad.
Time: June, 1867.

Available from Dramatists Play Service.

Plot

[*Afternoon.*] Lone, practicing opera steps on a mountaintop, suffers an interruption by Ma, who introduces himself and advises Lone that the striking railroad laborers in the camp below despise him for his aloofness. He dismisses the advice and Ma, as well. [*Afternoon, a day later.*] Ma again interrupts Lone's practice, this time asking to be taught opera, so he can return to China and perform and possess wealth and women. Lone mocks his credulity. They roll dice; Lone always wins. When Lone throws the dice into the bushes, Ma finds them and receives them as a gift. Lone offers to teach Ma opera if he will say the other laborers are "dead men," whose muscles only work for the white man. Although Ma cannot say that, Lone accepts him as a student while the strike lasts. [*Late afternoon, four days later.*] Lone and Ma do physical exercise. Ma wants to play the role of Gwan Gung, the god of fighters and adventurers. Lone responds that Ma can perhaps be the Second Clown and recounts his own long ap-

prenticeship. Lone induces Ma to enact a duck, deserts him, returns as a tiger, then becomes a locust; they fight in character. When Ma falters, Lone dares him to be a locust till morning and goes. [*Late that night.*] Alone and suffering, Ma stays in locust character and recalls Second Uncle, who tortured grasshoppers. His pride in his endurance grows. [*Just before the following dawn.*] Lone approaches Ma, singing. Lone has not slept, either, his mind on the strikers. He will let Ma play Gwan Gung and has brought him rice and duck to celebrate. The ChinaMen have won their strike. Ma wants to do an opera about himself and induces Lone into an enactment and dance. In their battle with sticks, Ma is injured slightly. Lone attends the wound and consoles Ma's fears of not returning home. He admits his own error about the strikers' having no chance to win. Ma abandons his study of acting study, enjoys his new friendship, and goes. Lone dances for no reason at all. The sun begins to rise.

Comment

The New Federal Theatre, under a grant from the U.S. Department of Education, commissioned this play. First at the Henry Street Settlement's New Federal Theatre, March 25, 1981, then at the Anspacher Theatre of the New York Shakespeare Festival Public Theatre, July 16, 1981, the play had an auspicious start. Prerequisites to the roles are Chinese

cultural awareness and technical acting skills. Historical accuracy in costuming requires research. Scenery is outdoors. The tapestry of the play is complex; to the themes listed below in the margin, one could add several others: dance, railroads, Old West, Chinese opera, slave-like labor, and strikes.

2m, drama

Themes: Chinese-Americans, dance, and friendship

The Daughters of Edward D. Boit

by Don Nigro

Dramatis Personae

Tentative Cast

Mary Louisa (in red) [f], _____

Julia (on the floor with her doll Ppaul) [f], _____

Florence (against the urn) [f], _____

Jane (looking out from the darkness) [f], _____

Place: Exactly as depicted in the painting by John Singer Sargent.
Time: Sargent painted the girls in 1882.

Available from Samuel French, Inc.

Plot

Mary Louisa and Julia converse about each other and their sisters, Florence and Jane. They talk about an ocean voyage, when Julia had gotten sick all over the waiter. Mary Louisa philosophizes that the four girls are concepts trapped in the art of John Singer Sargent, their real selves already dead. Florence, more unto herself, recognizes no other existence than the painting. Julia, driven always by a need to go to the bathroom, considers her sisters weird. Mary Louisa brings Jane into the discussion by trying to draw a secret from her. Jane discloses a liaison with the ship's Italian steward. Mary Louisa discounts the truth of the episode. Florence wants details of it, and Julia accuses her of being interested in the steward. Mary Louisa ventures that the cen-tury of being frozen in the painting has given Julia time to fantasize. The sisters discuss what sex is like, alluding to what did or did not happen to Florence and Jane regarding the steward. Jane claims a stronger bond with the lover because she teased him whereas Florence gave in. Mary Louisa extols to Florence the supreme advantage of their all being art, not people: "You are loved in another, more wonderful way than any flesh and blood experience could grant you. . . . It only takes the possibility of a mere audience of one to justify our existence." Florence claims a sexual adventure with Henry James, but she declines to tell the details: "not in a million, million years." Julia responds, "That's okay. We can wait," as the scene fades.

Comment

The daughters, posed to match the painting by Sargent, can move hands, exchange looks, relate to one another with body language. The differences in age allow subtle differences in angles of perception. Using less-is-more physical techniques, actresses can focus on vocal characterizations. The sophistication of concepts does not cancel any of the ample comedic moments. Requisite study of Singer's painting offers interdisciplinary opportunities, giving school productions a chance to involve both the art and drama departments.

4f, dark comedy

Themes: reality versus art; and time

The Death of the Hired Man

by Jay Reid Gould from Robert Frost

Dramatis Personae

Tentative Cast

Warren [m], _____

Mary [f], _____

Edna [f], _____

Silas [m], _____

Place: On or near the porch of a New England farmhouse.
Time: Evening gloaming, early 1900s.

Available from The Dramatic Publishing Company.

Plot

Warren, repairing a bridle, calls Mary. She and Edna come from the house. He teases them about gossiping and Edna's readiness to remarry. They broach the subject of Silas, the hired man; he has returned to the area and will be coming here. Warren recounts Silas' faults as a farmworker. Right after Warren leaves on an errand, Silas arrives. Mary gets tea for the old man. He reminisces about working the farm with a college lad, particularly on the hayrack. He rejects Mary's suggestion that he contact his well-to-do brother. When he claims this as his home, she welcomes him to stay and takes him inside to warm by the stove. Warren returns. Mary says, "Silas is back. . . . Be kind to him." She almost overcomes her husband's reservations about the old man's return. Warren goes into the kitchen to discuss the matter with Silas. She watches the moon and a passing cloud. Warren returns to tell her the old man has died.

Comment

Despite a few moot extrapolations, the famous poem by Robert Frost receives in this script a nearly literal translation to the stage, with much of the phrasing intact. The invocation of both naturalism and poetry poses for the director an interesting challenge. Subtle lighting changes enhance the naturalistic/romantic milieu. An evening of poetry could use this short play as a separate segment on the bill.

2m2f, drama   *Themes:* death and family

```
• • • • • • • • • • • • • • • • • • • • • • • • • • • • • • • • • • • • • • • • • •
```

The Dock Brief

by John Mortimer

Dramatis Personae

Tentative Cast

Morgenhall, an unsuccessful barrister [m], _____

Fowle, an unsuccessful criminal [m], _____

Place: A prison cell.
Time: The present.

Available from Samuel French, Inc.

```
• • • • • • • • • • • • • • • • • • • • • • • • • • • • • • • • • • • • • • • • • •
```

Plot

At rise, Morgenhall rescues Fowle from an apparent suicide attempt, but Fowle has been trying only to see from the barred window the end of a race at nearby Epping Forest. Morgenhall, introducing himself as the assigned barrister and savoring his first Dock Brief, banters with his client Fowle to establish rapport. The barrister cites his qualifications for the assignment and refuses to accept Fowle's confession of spousal murder. Fowle admits to having picked Morgenhall by just shutting his eyes and pointing to the group of available barristers. Morgenhall rises above the slight and starts the interview. Fowle's wife had been a compulsive prankster, driving him to distraction. He began to hope that she would run off with Bateson, the lodger, a partner in many practical jokes. Fowle would not leave his wife; he asks, "Who'd have fed the birds?" Morgenhall sees that the jury would regard Fowle as an unsympathetic figure. He pictures bringing in a surprise witness. They enact the scene, then realize it was a false hope, as there is no such witness. They try a scene interrogating the lodger, but Fowle notes a vital flaw: the lodger was in jail when the murder occurred. They try a scene interrogating a doctor, but it does not work. Morgenhall practices his rousing summation to the jury and puts both of them in good spirits. They are called to court. Later, Morgenhall comes to the cell to console Fowle for their defeat. However, Fowle consoles him, even congratulates him on tactics. The barrister is ready to appeal the case, but Fowle says no. Morgenhall describes the bond between them, which Fowle admits, but he still does not want the case appealed, as he has been freed. The judge has dismissed the case because the defense was so inept, and Fowle appreciates the shrewd "dumb tactics." He promises to contact Morgenhall if he ever crosses the law again. They depart, whistling together. Morgenhall even executes "a small, delighted dance" on the way out.

Comment

The playwright, best known in the United States for authoring the BBC's *Rumpole of the Bailey* series, has expressed amazement at the worldwide popularity of this one-act. The secret might well be the complex, offbeat characterizations, which obscure the seriousness of the admitted murder and build sympathy for both criminal and barrister. The murder seems past, almost irrelevant, remembered humorously in a style favored by the British. Catching the Britishness of this play is the paramount challenge to producing it. Technical problems are slight.

2m, comedy

Themes: friendship and judicial system

```
• • • • • • • • • • • • • • • • • • • • • • • • • • • • • • • • • • • • • • • • • • •
•                                                                                    •
•                          The Drummer                                              •
•                                                                                    •
•                          by Athol Fugard                                          •
•                                                                                    •
•                          Dramatis Persona                                         •
•                                                              Tentative Cast        •
•   The Man [m], _____                  •
•                                                                                    •
•                      Place: A city pavement.                                       •
•          Time: Morning. [Note: First produced February 27, 1980.]                  •
•                                                                                    •
•                  Available from Samuel French, Inc.                                •
•                                                                                    •
• • • • • • • • • • • • • • • • • • • • • • • • • • • • • • • • • • • • • • • • • • •
```

Plot

The Man, a bum, still sleepy, encounters a pile of rubbish, waiting to be cleared away. He seeks whatever helps the day's survival. A discarded chair makes his search more comfortable. He finds a drumstick, discards it. When he finds a second drumstick, he retrieves the first, for a set. After savoring the sounds of an ambulance siren and then of a fire engine, he taps idly with a drumstick on the lid of a trash can. Intrigued, he starts a little tattoo on the lid. He empties the trash can and upends it to find a better sound. City noises increase; so does his drumming. He finds a cape amid the trash. Dressed and armed with his sticks, he "sets off to take on the city." It is full of drums, "and he has got drumsticks."

Comment

Commissioned and first produced by Actors Theatre of Louisville for instructional and performance use by its Apprentice Company, this sketch affirms how little discoveries can resurrect and reorient the human spirit. For staging, trash should be easy to come by, and city sounds are available from recorded sound effects or recorded from life. Because of the distinction of this South African author, the content takes on special meaning: it is part of his dialogue with the world about race in South Africa and humanity in general. It could serve as an attention-catcher for any convocation addressing race.

1m, drama

Themes: hope and poverty

```
• • • • • • • • • • • • • • • • • • • • • • • • • • • • • • • • • • • • • • • • • • • •
```

An Empty Space

by Ron Villane

Dramatis Personae

Tentative Cast

Rich, 35 [m] , _____

Judy, 35 [f], _____

Place: An empty space.
Time: The present. [Note: Copyright 1980.]

Available from Samuel French, Inc. [#5; ISBN 0-573-60044-9]

```
• • • • • • • • • • • • • • • • • • • • • • • • • • • • • • • • • • • • • • • • • • • • •
```

Plot

Rich, divorced for four years, is packing to move to less expensive quarters when his ex-wife enters their former home. Judy has come to collect possessions and memorabilia he has set aside for her. They reminisce over photographic slides while he prepares tea. She disturbs him by discarding much he has saved for her. She does accept her grandmother's radio. They talk about relationships since their divorce. She has a date and must hurry away. He compliments her appearance and laments her having become a stranger. When Judy warms enough to laugh with him, he asks her to break the date and have dinner with him. She refuses: "We would both regret it." Rich explains that he is just trying to save their six years together from fading, from becoming an empty space. She kisses him on the cheek and explains that she loved him, but that love does not guarantee compatibility. They kiss gently; it does not cause her to stay. After an exchange of compliments, she leaves. Starting to discard what Judy deemed as garbage, Rich retrieves the slides and studies them.

Comment

Neither role is particularly challenging, but each rings of truth and deserves honest acting. The protagonist, Rich, has found divorce not the solution in his life; he cannot resolve his failed six-year marriage and move on, even four years later. Judy more realistically remembers the past and seeks a better future. Their conflict exemplifies a problem rampant in American society. Space staging makes the production extremely simple. As a brief prologue, three women in black symbolically place three boxes on stage; the bit could be cut at the director's discretion. This play was performed at Double Image Theatre under the aegis of Iona College.

1m1f, drama

Themes: divorce, family, and loneliness

Estoy enamorado de tu hermana/
I Am in Love with Your Sister

by Jesús Assaf

Dramatis Personae

Tentative Cast

Martha, *un año menor que Aurora/*
    a year younger than Aurora [f], _____

Gilberto, *joven trabajador y estudioso/*
    young worker and student [m], _____

Aurora, *hermana mayor/*
    older sister [f], _____

*Lugar/*Place: San Andrés Tuxtla, Veracruz, México.
*Época/*Time: *Actual/*The present.

Available from Organización Editorial Novaro, S.A.
Calle 5, No. 12, Naucalpán de Juarez, México, D.F.

Plot

The actors introduce the play and its characters. Gilberto and Martha encounter each other on her way from the market. He walks her home and asks to see Aurora. With irritation and some hesitation, Martha fetches her older sister. When it is apparent the others need privacy, Martha disgustedly leaves. Gilberto wants Aurora to have her mother permit them to walk together tomorrow. They settle on ten minutes before eleven o'clock. Gilberto leaves and Aurora tells her sister how happy she is. Each girl says that Gilberto loves the other. At the appointed time, Gilberto and Aurora walk. He says he has loved her since childhood. When Aurora tells him how much Martha cares for him, he says he cares for Martha as a friend, no more. Gilberto tells the audience in an aside how, during his courtship of Aurora, Mar-

tha avoided him. He rushes off to school. In an aside, Gilberto tells how Aurora presses him to spend more time with her, away from his school and work. When they next meet, she does demand that he choose between her and all these other commitments. He does not meet her terms, so she breaks their engagement. He loses himself in his work and studies. Sometime later, he encounters Martha. He drifts into a relationship with her. She senses that he still loves Aurora and leaves him. When he and Aurora happen to meet, immediately they know they still love each other. Aurora explains how she broke from him because Martha planted seeds of doubt about his love. Martha, knowing she has lost Gilberto, leaves home. Aurora and Gilberto hope that she will find the happiness they have found.

Comment

This script by a youthful playwright about a love triangle was chosen by the anthologist, a leading Mexican dramatist, as representative of modern theatre in Mexico. It is not

a polished work, but it captures the intensity of sibling rivalry and some of the personal choices young students and workers face. It moves well onstage.

1m2f, *farsa*

Themes: courtship and sibling rivalry

The Frog Prince

by David Mamet

Dramatis Personae

Tentative Cast

The Prince [m], _____

A Servingman [m], _____

The Witch [f], _____

A Milkmaid [f], _____

Place: A Wood.
Time: Once upon a.

Available from Samuel French, Inc.

Plot

[*Summer*] The Prince has his Servingman gather flowers in the Wood. The Prince tries to comprehend Nature's plan about flowers. He notices An Old Peasant Woman walking nearby but expiates on the bouquet in his hand, for his sweet Patricia. So caught up, he even participates in the flower gathering, once the daffodils have been identified to him. The Servingman reassures him that the *People* love The Fair Patricia, too. The Old Peasant Woman draws nearer. She ignores the Prince's conversational niceties and demands he give her the gathered flowers. She disdains proffered bribery and the rightness of his picking flowers here for his Betrothed, The Fair Patricia. She changes the Prince into a frog, in which state he must remain "until a pure and honest woman of her own free will shall plant a selfless kiss upon your lips." The catch is that he must not tell of his former state. [*Fall.*] The Prince has taken up with a Milkmaid. When he suggests a kiss, she is distracted by distant death knells for a bridegroom, actually the Prince who has been missing for two months. Protocol demands he be mourned today, so The Fair Patricia can wed his cousin tomorrow. The Prince again suggests a kiss. When she demurs, saying she could kiss only her betrothed, he offers marriage. She reveals that she loves another, but they lack twenty-five Gold Coins to buy her fiancé out of his apprenticeship. She goes, and he tells the Servingman to got to the palace and get some money hidden in a Big Blue Book. Tonight, when he gives the Milkmaid the money, he thinks she will kiss him. [*Winter*] The Prince and the Servingman huddle by a campfire. In the newspaper, the Prince reads of hard times. Also, the locks on the palace have been changed and The Fair Patricia has issued a warrant for anyone even looking like the former ruler. The Milkmaid enters, unhappy, as the Bailiff, hearing a remark against The Fair Patricia, has taken away her fiancé, his farm, and her cow. The Servingman produces a golden sword; he leaves to take it to town in order to gain money to buy the Milkmaid food and a cow. [*Spring*] The Prince is writing a poem until the Milkmaid breaks his concentration. She has been preparing a farm for planting. The Prince has been low, but he feels better now. He has been picking flowers for the Servingman's grave. The Milkmaid has brought him her shawl before her departure south to join her fiancé. She invites the Prince to come along. He declines, wishes her well. She kisses him farewell and leaves. He changes from Frog to Prince. The Old Peasant Woman appears. He tells her of his spiritual growth. She asks him for the flowers he has been gathering. After thinking about the situation, he hands them to her. She thanks him. He puts the Milkmaid's shawl over his uniform and starts out of the Wood.

Comment

The playwright is among the most important of the 1980s in the United States. About this short play, Mamet states, "*Generally*, the production should look as if it had come out of an eighty-year storage." Less specifically, he says, "The transition of the Prince into a Frog and, later, back again is left to the discretion and theatrical imagination of the interested parties." This script has wide age appeal.

2m2f, comedy

Themes: dysfunctional family and survivability

Fumed Oak

by Noël Coward

Dramatis Personae

Tentative Cast

Elsie Gow, daughter of Doris and Henry [f], _____

Doris Gow, wife of Henry [f], _____

Mrs. Rockett, mother of Doris [f], _____

Henry Gow, husband, father, son-in-law [m], _____

Place: The Gows' sitting-room [possibly 1935].
Time: (1) Eight-thirty on a spring morning and (2) seven-thirty that evening.

Available from Baker's Plays and Samuel French, Inc.

Plot

At breakfast, Henry eats silently while the three females in his life quarrel and carp. His daughter, Elsie, argues with his wife, Doris, about the girl's putting her hair up. Doris and Henry's mother-in-law, Mrs. Rockett, argue about how to treat physical complaints of Elsie and Mrs. Rockett. Doris even suggests that her mother move in with another relative. The argument shifts back to views about raising Elsie. The girl leaves for school with money from her grandmother given despite her mother's objections. When his wife takes his cup and saucer from his hand, Henry quietly leaves the room. The two women interrupt their attacks on each other to focus on him. Upon his return, they are galvanized for an attack. He comes in, dressed for departure. Their attack becomes sidetracked, and he leaves the two of them quarreling. At seven-thirty that evening, Elsie, Doris, and Mrs. Rockett are preparing to leave for the cinema when Henry arrives. Doris, in her parting shots at him, discovers something amiss: Henry is different. He has been celebrating the sixteenth anniversary of their initial intimacy, which put Doris in the family way and produced Elsie, oddly enough, over three years later. Doris tries to regain control, but Henry cannot be stopped. He demands that they sit while he has his say. In turn, he clarifies just how awful each of the three is. When he threatens to strike Mrs. Rockett, she obediently sits. He recounts to Doris how he has been putting aside money for this break. She will have a roof and enough money on which to survive without him. He is off to unannounced lands. He gives parting advice to his spoiled daughter, who can go to work in a year or so. He takes his last look at the three generations, wishing them well. Their wails sound as he jauntily departs, slamming the door behind him.

Comment

Coward deftly uses his stock characters—harridan wife, harpy mother-in-law, hateful daughter, turning-worm husband, making each an actor's dream. This extremely funny show is nearly actor-proof, even without proper dialect; it is an excellent piece for beginners, although rather long, about forty minutes.

Coward's self-defined "small talent to amuse" is belied by the really full measure of comedy in this play. The more of the "fumed oak" atmosphere, the English middle-class monotony, that can be captured, the better. Technical support, therefore, is critical.

1m3f, comedy

Themes: dysfunctional family and mid-life crisis

The Harmfulness of Tobacco

by Anton Chekhov

Dramatis Persona

Tentative Cast

Marcellus Nyuehin, a henpecked husband [m], _____

Place: The platform in the hall of a provincial club.
Time: 1889.

Available from Samuel French, Inc.

Plot

Nyuehin, the speaker for the evening, enters majestically, bows, adjusts his waistcoat and begins to lecture. Present at his wife's behest to speak for charity and admittedly not a professor with university degrees, he explains that nonetheless he has worked for thirty years on academic problems, most recently having submitted for publication a large article, "The Ill Effects of Coffee-itis and Tea-mania on the Organism." His topic today: the harm of smoking and taking snuff. He advises those present who may be scared by the idea of a "dry, strictly scientific speech" to go. Asking doctors in the audience to pay particular attention, he identifies tobacco not only as harmful but also useful as a medicine: indeed, his wife used it as an enema some eighteen years ago. An attack of asthma interrupts his volley of details identifying tobacco. This leads to digressions about his family. He refocuses on the topic by seeking the cause of the choking fit. A pancake menu earlier in the day seems significant. He recounts his duties at his wife's boarding school to bolster the point. Anyway, the students ate pancakes, while he ate a veal roast to keep it from spoiling. Then he had to eat five pancakes denied the students for disciplinary reasons; this, too, required a preliminary glass of vodka. A look at his watch brings him back to the lecture subject. Before he can cite a chemical formula, though, he feels compelled to advertise the school. He returns to the formula while taking snuff; he suspects the girls have substituted face powder or whatever. Blame rests on the audience for such behavior. He resumes the diatribe against nicotine only to detect smiles in the audience. This brings to mind his nine daughters and the problem of dowries. He weeps at the goodness of his wife and his own weakness. He recommends marriage to young men and confides that his daughters are "on view on high days and holidays in their Aunt Natalya's house," where snacks are served. Another look at his watch brings him to cut short the lecture. Straightening his waistcoat, he departs as majestically as he entered.

Comment

Scripting this sort of brief vaudeville turn helped Chekhov earn his way through medical school and gave him practice in comedy that later would prove so valuable. Ample stage directions aid the performer in phrasing and visualization. Lighting requires only that necessary for public speaking. There are no sound effects. The set is simply a platform before the audience. End-of-the-century (1889) costuming and personal props would be an asset.

1m, comedy

Themes: family relationships and lecturing

Hello, Ma!

by Trude Stone

Dramatis Personae

Tentative Cast

Ma, early 50s [f], _____

Dee, daughter, about 27 [f], _____

Place: Ma's and Dee's apartments.
Time: Morning. [Note: First produced February 27, 1980.]

Available from Samuel French, Inc.

Plot

Ma prepares party favors for oldsters. With Mrs. Dawson on the telephone, she reviews her list for the Friday party. Then Dee calls with news that Andy has proposed. Ma recalls Harry as a recent interest. Dee thinks Andy a better catch, but wants Ma's advice. Ma gives none, and Dee calls her reluctance cowardly. When Ma predicts Dee's subsequent dissatisfaction with either suitor, Dee hangs up in a fury. Ma gets a call from Sol, who makes a date for lunch and cheesecake tomorrow noon. Dee calls Sandy with news that she has married Andy and is calling Ma to tell her. Ma receives Dee's call, notes that she has not heard from her in two weeks. Dee hastily apologizes, says she was off on a two-week honeymoon, and asks Ma to mail her wedding check right away. Ma calls Sol to have some company for dinner. Dee, back from a broken marriage after one week, telephones Sandy with the news. Then she calls Ma, who reassures her that the wedding money does not have to be repaid. Dee telephones again, to say she and Harry have made up. Ma calls Sol for consolation. Dee calls Sandy to make a just-us-girls date. She calls Ma about her breakup with Harry, rejects well-meant advice, and hangs up angrily. Ma calls Sol to make a date. Dee, to Sandy, explains getting furniture deposit money back; she will tell her more at lunch tomorrow. Ma, to Dee, notes the passage of weeks since they spoke. As Dee is in a hurry, Ma quickly mentions her own getting married and going away for two weeks, then hangs up. Dee, to Ma, furiously wants to know about the wedding and why she was not told. Ma mentions that Dee never has time to listen. Dee worries about Ma's losing the money Dee stands to inherit. Ma tells her not to worry, that she and Sol will give leftover money to a nursing home to keep their offspring from fighting over it. In haste, Ma mentions Sol's "unmarried son, about thirty-seven," and wonders what might come of his and Dee's meeting someday. Dee, to the abandoned telephone, asks, "Ma? Hello, Ma?"

Comment

All of the twenty-some items on the property list are easily available. All of the set pieces are common. Necessarily quick clothing changes need ample rehearsal. The lighting cues are critical, as are the sound cues for the telephones. The mother-daughter relationship is stereotypical and trite, but it remains an audience favorite. Ma has many clever lines.

2f, comedy

Themes: dominance and parenting

Here We Are

by Dorothy Parker

Dramatis Personae

Tentative Cast

He [m], _____

She [f], _____

Place: A Pullman compartment on a train to New York City.
Time: Slightly past 6:30 p.m., in the late 1930s.

Available from *The Collected Stories of Dorothy Parker*
(New York: Random House, 1942)
and from Samuel French, Inc.

Plot

The groom settles the luggage in the train com-partment and undertakes awkward conversation with his new bride. They have been married about two hours and twenty-six minutes and are en route to their honeymoon destination. They can think of nothing other than the forthcoming embarrassing consummation, but they are too embarrassed to talk of it and dwell on anything else. They discuss the wedding, everyone's dress and demeanor there. She rattles on about the bridesmaids. He responds a bit too approvingly on one of them, which makes his bride jealous. He tries to explain that the bridesmaids will be no part of his life, which makes his bride upset that he does not care for her friends. She worries, too, that he will not get along with her family. They mend that misun-derstanding only to fall into another about his appreciation of her hat. They drift into accusations about former personal relationships with other people. The jealousy calms down. They discuss trivial ways to spend the evening in the hotel. She has letters to write. She objects to his objections about this activity. They agree not to quarrel about letters and slip into the old quarrel over her hat. Agreeing not to differ on the hat, they concentrate again on not talking about the obvious focus of their thinking.

Comment

The format is short story, but the dialogue provides a viable playscript. Also, the short story has many descriptions tantamount to stage directions. Samuel French, Inc., provides a stage adaptation. The gentle comedy depends on the couple's naïveté; therefore, evocation of the late 1930s is important. Actors must convincingly portray embarrassment about sex. The play's Pullman compartment need only be suggested. Costuming and props should reflect the late 1930s; otherwise, the show is extremely simple to stage.

1m1f, comedy

Themes: marriage and young love

How He Lied to Her Husband

by George Bernard Shaw

Dramatis Personae

Tentative Cast

He [m], _____

She [f], _____

Her Husband [m], _____

Place: Her flat on Cromwell Road, London.
Time: Eight o'clock in the evening.

Plot

He arrives in evening dress with flowers for her. Alone for a moment, he relishes every hint of her and prepares for her entrance. She enters resplendent in dress and diamonds, ready for the theatre. She announces that she has lost his poems and fears her husband will find them and know they are about her. He promises to write her better poems, missing her point. Moreover, Her Husband's female relatives will have a field day with the poems; indeed, one sister may have them in her hands now. He proposes they two leave this house for a life together, continuing to do all they do now. He is ready to tell her husband of their love, borrow his carriage, and leave to see *Lohengrin*, either that or *Candida*. She cannot abide *Candida*, which has caused so much mischief. She curtly critiques that play's flaws. He stands willing to challenge her husband to fisticuffs. In his ardor, he breaks her fan, a par-ticular favorite. She has not had time to read all of the poems and asks him to recall names in them. She wants him to say her name in the poems is a literary allusion, not a specifica-tion of her. Her Husband comes in with a message his sister wants him to call upon her. She announces a change of plans: no theatre this evening. Her Husband displays the poems. He attempts the planned lie, but Her Husband sees through it. Her Husband resents the suggestion that his wife is not suit-able for these poems. He, ready to fight, falls backward over a stool, earning a bump on his head and chagrin. She de-mands that Her Husband, who is a prizefighter, not fight now. When He angrily admits the poems were for the wife, Her Husband delightedly apologizes and asks to have the poems printed, to allow showing them around a bit. He suggests a title: *How He Lied to Her Husband.*

Comment

First produced at Berkeley Lyceum Theatre, New York City, September 26, 1904, then at Royal Court Theatre, Lon-don, February 28, 1905, Shaw's playlet is arguably Ameri-can rather than Irish or British, having opened on Broadway and survived in American vaudeville. The Shavian anti-romanticism found in so many of his long scripts works to good effect here, echoing *Candida* in particular. Actors can enjoy the badinage and comedy-of-manners ironies. The act-ing style must be early twentieth century. The period staging requires considerable effort.

2m1f, high comedy

Themes: deception and wordplay

Plot

Two actors and two actresses, called just an hour earlier to the theatre, have been told by the stage manager to go directly onto a dark stage, to face an audience, and to improvise a play. They argue about trusting the stage manager and fumble their way forward to meet the challenge. The lights come on. Tony brags about his professional credits while trying to explain the situation to the audience. When Winifred ridicules Tony, Ernest takes over. Lora lends encouragement, but Winifred taunts him, too, causing him to yield. Winifred, hating the theatre and her own cloudy career, characterizes herself as always playing "the leading lady's best friend." Lora, following her, suffers doubts about being an actress. Ernest lists the three conditions of their situation: (1) the play will not end until the stage manager likes the performance, (2) no one is permitted to leave the stage until the play has ended, and (3) the play must imitate life. Tony disagrees, saying instead, "It's supposed to be life." Winifred defends Tony against Ernest, surprising herself. Lora and Ernest, in shadow and speaking as from a great distance, play Greek chorus, coming back into the scene when Winifred and Tony confuse reality and acting. Tony wants Winifred to leave with him. She has unfinished business—she wants to make Ernest face himself as living only for applause. Lora hesitates to résumé the play, not wanting to be disappointed again. Winifred and Ernest jointly cajole her to continue with them. As they enthusiastically weigh plot twists, the lights begin to dim, marking the end of the play. They are in darkness as they were at the beginning, literally and figuratively. Ernest worries about the audience. Winifred advises that actors should not worry about the audience: actors learn to improvise in the theatre; audiences learn to improvise in life.

Comment

Tad Mosel, a product of Amherst College, Yale Drama School, and Columbia University, wrote this play at Yale before his successful scripting career in television. Inspired by Pirandello, Mosel asks here: "How much truth and how much illusion does a person need to live a balanced life?" The set, with slight alterations, can be bare stage. Props are few. The characters are varied and grow somewhat. To an audience unaware of Pirandello, this is a facile introduction to probing levels of reality on stage.

2m2f, drama

Themes: acting and levels of reality

The Jewish Wife

by Bertoldt [or Bertolt] Brecht

Dramatis Personae

Tentative Cast

The Wife [f], _____

The Husband [m], _____

Place: An apartment home in Frankfurt, Nazi Germany.
Time: Evening, 1935.

Available from Samuel French, Inc.

Plot

The Wife is packing, choosing items to take or leave. Tiring for the moment, she uses the telephone to contact friends. She calls bridge and moviegoing partners, a Herr Doktor and his Frau Thekla, to say she is going away for a time. Looking after her husband, Fritz, she calls another friend, Lotte Shoeck, to arrange continuation of a regular bridge session next Tuesday. She calls Gertrude, asking her to handle chores for Fritz. She calls Anna, wanting her to be good to Fritz a little at first, insisting that Anna not come to see her off at the station. She burns her book of personal telephone numbers. She rehearses a little speech to her husband. In little ways, he has accommodated to Nazi political correctness. She, herself, has even slipped into ranking the value of people. Her departure is her gesture to help him keep his position as chief surgeon at the clinic, where he has already taken cuts and slurs for his connection to her. Her ire grows at his complicity, so her tirade admits that she plans to find another man elsewhere, one who will be allowed to keep her. She pictures Fritz letting her leave, with faint protest. At that moment, The Husband comes home. He acts exactly as she has foreseen.

Comment

Brecht's short play has appeared as part of various versions of the full-length play chiefly known as *The Private Life of the Master Race*. It bitterly indicts the "good German," who passively enabled Hitler to embark on his "final solution" to the Jewish presence in Nazi Germany. Production needs are simple although elements suggesting time and place would help greatly. A German accent is optional but contributive.

1m1f, drama

Themes: feminism, Holocaust, Jewishness, marriage

Last Days of Mankind (Act V, Scene 54)

by Karl Kraus, translated from the original German by Max Spalter

Dramatis Persona

Tentative Cast

The Carper [m], _____

Place: A desk in an office.
Time: Five o'clock.

Available from Kosel-Verlag.

Plot

At his desk, The Carper reads about a time-motion study of turning a tree into a newspaper. He sees himself writing a tragedy on the demise of mankind. He calls out for individuality. He wonders why mankind obeys blindly its duplicitous leadership. He addresses a young artistic self, one who was led into four years of filth and wetness. The recollection of danger and discomfort flows forth as a deluge: old Serbs killed because they were Serbs, technology used in hysteria for greater killing, the role of the press with its enabling propaganda, the similarity of generals to whores, murdered ones lingering to incite revenge, horrible details not remembered in peacetime. The Carper has archived enough wartime reality to remind the world afterward. His is a manifesto for mankind to hear—if not mankind, then God: " . . . even if He has renounced for all time any connection with the human ear. May He receive the keynote of this time, the echo of my bloody madness, whereby I, too, share in the guilt for these noises. May He let it count as a redemption!" From outside comes the far-distant call of a newspaper vendor.

Comment

This biting indictment of war signals the angst in the German soul about its role in European history during the twentieth century. Of course, one should read the source play for external evidence of The Carper's mental state, but this excerpt stands well alone. In the vast theatre literature of antiwar calls, this compares well with the more famous works of Euripides, Ernst Toller, Irvin Shaw, and others. Staging problems are few. Good lighting and sound would help. Costuming is not difficult. The producer should find a proper showcase for this, as it is too brief on its own.

1m (+ voice), drama

Themes: redemption and war

Laughs, Etc.

by James L. Herlihy

Dramatis Persona

Tentative Cast

Gloria, in her thirties [f],_____

Place: A bare stage.
Time: Happy hour.

Available from Dramatists Play Service.

Plot

Gloria sits in a modernistic easy chair, by a small table with cigarettes, ashtray, and her highball. She disregards her husband's objections to tell Ceil and Harry about Friday night. Three Boys from the apartment upstairs (one wants to bed her) accepted her invitation for drinks. They brought Jo-Anne, "a dreadful little stump of a thing," who became the evening's star, the "unappetizing little bitch!" Gloria then invited the entire cast of an integrated revue. The Africans attracted Tom, so Gloria telephoned more friends to come for "laughs, etc., at Gloria's. And Tom's." One of the Boys backs Gloria into the bedroom—to ask her for money to save the sick Jo-Anne, her sickness being drugs. The party went all night. At dawn, one guest, an Italian, sang on the balcony, and a distant voice sang back, "Follow, Follow, Follow," bringing everyone to tears. Prompted by Harry to get to the punch line of the story about Jo-Anne, Gloria adds, "Forgive me then, I thought I said: the poor little thing did indeed die." It made her and Tom feel wretched, of course. Gloria learned about the death from the bedroom Boy, whom she still adores.

Comment

With a prop list of five items, no set, and an easily obtainable costume, this show poses no staging problems. It is almost entirely up to the actress, who must comprehend irony, the tide upon which this show sails. Some of the material calls for an adult company and audience. It would be a good introduction to a program about drugs or dysfunctional marriage.

1f, comedy

Themes: introspection and marriage

Ledge, Ledger, and the Legend

by Paul Elliott

Dramatis Personae

Tentative Cast

Pete, 25 [m], _____

J.M. [m], _____

P.J. [m], _____

Place: Outside ledge of a tall building.
Time: The present. [Note: Copyright 1972.]

Available from Dramatic Publishing Company.

Plot

Pete edges his way along a ledge of an old tall building. J.M. interrupts Pete's suicide preparation by joining him on the ledge. J.M. presents his business card as a suicide guide; he taunts Pete about being an amateur and reduces Pete to tears. Pete puts himself under J.M.'s guidance to achieve a stylish end. They bargain over the rates. J.M. starts coaching by analyzing environment. In response to J.M.'s first point, "getting attention," Pete impetuously drops a shoe, but it lands on a fire escape. Chastised by J.M. that there are right ways and wrong ways, Pete then follows explicit directions about dropping the other shoe. It hits a windshield below and draws a crowd. Pete, ready to proceed, is slowed by J.M.'s warning to wait for better coverage—police, firemen, TV. J.M.

prompts Pete to yell and build the crowd's interest. Pete's efforts spark disgust from J.M., who threatens to resign the coaching job. Pete bribes him with watch and wallet to stay on the job. J.M., encouraged by Pete's renewed efforts, explains how to embellish the leap with body language. The two agree that the moment is right. As Pete starts to jump, another suicide guide, P.J., interrupts and joins them. The two guides argue over turf, and P.J. disparages J.M. as a failure and a fraud. Pete, however, decides to honor his commitment to J.M. and dismisses P.J., only to find J.M., feeling disgraced, ready to jump. Pete talks J.M. out of jumping. The two, now exhilarated and revitalized, leave to enjoy a steak together and get on with living.

Comment

Clever and well paced, this script offers an acting romp with broad characterizations. Gender is irrelevant in casting. The show plays well with any or all of the roles countercast to gender. Production needs are undemanding for props and costumes. Environmental sound effects would be helpful. The set is extremely simple: "The ledge makes a corner about

half way across the stage and disappears from view." Placing the action on the edge of the apron is an easy, practical option; that has the advantage of allowing another show to be set up behind the main curtain and ready to go immediately afterward.

3m, farce

Themes: self-esteem and suicide

Lip Service

by Howard Korder

Dramatis Personae

Tentative Cast

Len Burdette, a man in his early thirties [m], _____
Gilbert Hutchinson, a man in his sixties [m], _____

Place: A morning talk show, Roberson City, New England.
Time: Over the course of several months, 1985.

Available from Samuel French, Inc. [#14166]

Plot

Nineteen short scenes show Len, an ambitious young television talent, climb to local stardom. (*scene 1*) He panders to Gil, veteran host of a show Len has joined. (*2*) Len wangles an opening monologue, (*3*) discloses a lust for fame, (*4*) abandons his marriage. (*5*) Students at a high school assembly about career broadcasting see Gil as Len's on-air partner. (*6*) Len, shallow, piqued, seeks reassurance about technique from Gil. (*7*) Len, playing the clown, foils Gil's on-air seriousness. (*8*) Seeking Gil's sympathy, Len reveals infidelity to his third wife. (*9*) Len ridicules Gil on the air, then glibly apologizes. (*10*) He practices personae to a mirror. (*11*) Len reveals eagerness to reshape the show and misses Gil's resentment. (*12*) Len attempts to seduce and ridicule a woman in a bar. (*13*) Len downplays having assumed Gil's lead on the show. (*14*) Len slathers clichés on a guest. (*15*) In the Green Room, Gil and Len cannot talk to each other. (*16*) Gil learns that he is off the show. (*17*) Len announces on-air Gil's departure to the Caribbean. (*18*) Len, meeting Gil in a bar, tries a hail-fellow routine that Gil does not buy. Len miscomprehends, dismisses Gil's denunciation, and suggests Gil write about famous people or something. (*19*) Gil, now an author, appears on Len's show. Len, ever the same, fails to grasp Gil's growth and self-esteem.

Comment

This trenchant commentary on venal ambition features choice characterizations. A production note suggests selective realism, "a simple matter of a few well-placed chairs, with perhaps the set for the talk show having some elaboration as a point of focus." A few carry-on props and minimal costume changes suffice. Three offstage or recorded voices underpin the crisp pace. Language adjustments are necessary for most high school productions.

2m, drama

Themes: ambition and broadcasting

Longing for Worldly Pleasures

by Ssu Fan

Dramatis Persona

Tentative Cast

Chao Se K'ung, a young Buddhist nun [f or m], _____

Place: Sacred Peach Nunnery, China.
Time: Probably Ming Dynasty (A.D. 1368-1644).

Available from University of Wisconsin Press.

Plot

Se K'ung sings plaintively of a monk who left his monastery to retrieve his mother from the gates of Hell. She describes her own circumstances as a devotee in the Sacred Peach Nunnery from early youth. She detests her shaved head and looks at young men sporting by the temple gate. She longs for love. Her family had placed her here; she had not chosen to come. The rituals do not assuage her longing, although she reads diligently and attends to duties. Even the statues around her disturb her thoughts. At every turn, she cries, "My heart burns as though on fire." With the abbess and other nuns away, she renounces her commitment to Buddha and escapes down the mountain. On her final words, "I only want to have a child. I shall die of happiness," she "takes three steps towards the entry corner, claps her hands three times with a smile for the audience, and makes her exit."

Comment

The script does not attempt historical accuracy, being primarily a theatrical entertainment. The demanding role keeps the performer onstage throughout in a progression of moods: indignation, mental conflict, renunciation of her way of living, return to world pleasures. Script notes say the role requires "a mastery of that utter precision and form that only the mature Chinese artist can bring to a part." But other performers might aspire to learn enough precision and form to carry the role—with the help of a culturally knowledgeable choreographer. The bulk of the script is stage directions, in such detail as to enable the aspiring performer. Musical accompaniment is "a seven-holed bamboo flute (*ti-tzu*), the principal instrument; a small gong (*hsiao-lo*); the small single-skin (*tan-p'i ku*); and wooden clappers, or time beaters (*pan*)." Elaborate costuming and exotic props are vital. Carpets, curtains, and a small wooden table and two chairs furnish the stage.

1f or 1m, Chinese traditional *K'unshan* play

Themes: Chinese theatre and social protest

Los Dos Caras del Patroncito/The Two Faces of the Boss

by Luis Valdez

Dramatis Personae

Tentative Cast

Esquirol/Farmworker [m], _____

Patroncito [m],_____

Charlie: Armed Guard [m], _____

Place: The grape fields of Delano, California.
Time: September, 1965.

Available in *Luis Valdez—Early Works: Actos, Bernabé and Pensamiento Serpentino*
(Houston: Arte Público Press, 1971).

Plot

The Farmworker greets the audience and explains how he has been brought from Mexico to scab in the grape fields. His Patroncito (dear boss), wearing a yellow pig mask, drives up in an imaginary limousine. Patroncito wants the Farmworker to work harder and shows him how. Patroncito describes his love for his Mexican workers, and the Farmworker keeps trying to shine his boss' shoes. Charlie (*la jura* or "rent-a-fuzz"), apelike, starts to attack the Farmworker, but Patroncito sends him back to the road to watch for union organizers. The Farmworker agrees to ev- erything said against the strikers and to the treatment he is receiving. The Patroncito laments his own riches as a bur- den, revealing that sometimes he would like to be a Mexican, without worries. As a game, he exchanges roles with the Farmworker, who rapidly assumes the dominant position. Charlie returns, unaware of the game that has become seri- ous, and drags the Patroncito off to whip him. Doffing the pig mask, the Farmworker addresses the audience. He will give back the house, land, car to the boss—but he will keep the cigar.

Comment

The Preface to the play explains the social context in which El Teatro Campesino improvised the play now in written form. It reveals anger and hope. The strike that pro- voked this playlet sparked the Chicano rise to political strength in the American Southwest. The stereotypical characters suit broad farce. The humor and slapstick work even for an audi- ence unaware of the initial social lampoon. Probably, this script should not stand alone, though; it should be part of a larger statement. Production needs amount to little more than masks, placards, and simple hand props.

3m, agitprop   *Themes:* Chicano heritage and social injustice

The Man with the Flower in His Mouth

by Luigi Pirandello

Dramatis Personae

Tentative Cast

The Man with the Flower in His Mouth [m], _____

An Easygoing Commuter [m], _____

A Woman in Black [f], _____

Place: The sidewalk in front of an all-night café in some large city.
Time: A few minutes past midnight.

Available from Samuel French, Inc.

Plot

The Man sits at a table, watching the Commuter at the table next to him sip a mint frappe through a straw. The Man surmises the Commuter has missed his train. The Commuter blames the near-miss on being loaded with packages for his wife and daughters. Women must buy fripperies! he maintains. He even imitates their mannerisms. He now must wait for the next train three hours hence and has left his wrapped packages in the checkroom. The Man extols how exquisitely clerks wrap sold goods. He has taken to observing the details of life now. The details spark his imagination and keep his mind busy. When the Commuter says how much fun such speculation could be, the Man irritatedly challenges him about visits to doctors. The Man berates the furnishings and anthropomorphizes the chairs on which people sit and wait for medical verdicts. Building a sullen rage, the Man rails at the thirst for life. He spots a Woman in Black wearing an old hat with drooping feathers. He identifies her as one who tracks him. He leads the Commuter to a street lamp and discloses a violet nodule under his mustache, an epithelioma, which will bring his death in an unspecified time, maybe eight or ten months. Regardless of the Woman's wanting him to stay at home, he must roam, finding stimuli to occupy his mind and keep his thoughts off death. His mood shifts. He jauntily asks the Commuter to find a tuft of grass at his country home and count the blades. "As many blades as you can count, that's the number of days I still have to live. . . . Be sure you pick me a nice fat one." He laughs. "Good night, my dear sir." The Man starts to strolls off, but remembering his wife is probably lurking around the corner, quickly turns and scurries in the opposite direction.

Comment

Pirandello is famous for his questioning reality and plumbing levels of perception. His body of work won the Nobel Prize for Literature in 1934. Here, in small, is an exquisite presentation of his preoccupations. Characterizations offer interesting challenges. Clever designing could simplify the requested elaborate set, but the special ambience is vital to the play. The street lighting, the sound of a mandolin, the café and night noises must receive attention in the production. Sophisticated companies would do well to revive this short play.

2m1f, drama

Themes: addressing strangers, cancer, death, and madness

Me Too, Then

by Tom Dudzick and Steven Smith

Dramatis Personae

Tentative Cast

Vera [f], _____

Slats [m], _____

Leonard [m], _____

Place: The living room of Vera's apartment
on West 72nd Street, New York City.
Time: The present. [Note: First produced March 4, 1980.]

Available from Samuel French, Inc.

Plot

Vera rushes into her apartment to answer the telephone. It is her mother. Vera explains that she and Leonard were at a pharmaceutical movie. Harpo, her parrot, keeps interrupting, and Vera tries to teach it Leonard's name. The bird combines the name with "I'm gonna puke!" and will not stop repeating it. While feeding the bird, she tells it of again seeing Slats the clown perform at a local theatre. She would love to meet him. Leonard calls, and she reassures him that she has typed his speech for the pharmaceutical conclave tonight. Slats arrives in costume. He has tracked her down between performances to thank her for her regular attendance at his shows and to ask a favor. A booking agent will be at his show tonight, and Slats thinks Vera's laughter in the audience would bring him luck. She has forty-five minutes to think it over. He hides in the kitchen as Leonard arrives. Leonard's happiness about the potential of his speech tonight fades when Slats enters and draws Vera into comic routines. The men are oil and water. Vera must choose whose evening performance she will attend. Peering out the window, Slats describes a robbery in progress at Leonard's pharmacy across the street. Leonard reports it to the police and goes to check matters. Slats admits to Vera the story was a hoax to let him plead his case. Leonard returns and furiously berates the clown. Leonard says he will pick up Vera for the taping of his speech and leaves. Slats repeats his request that she be at his show, suddenly kisses her and leaves. Leonard returns for Vera and has compromised enough to offer to take her to a Woody Allen movie after the taping. Vera, however, is off to laugh at Slats' performance for the agent. Promising to meet Leonard for the movie, she rushes out, leaving him with the bird.

Comment

This farce has wonderful pace, many extremely funny gags—both visual and spoken. The Slats role requires expert clowning. All roles need sharp timing. Of course, the voice of the parrot should come from Harpo, whether the bird be real or *faux*. Otherwise, the props, set, lighting, and sound are not difficult. The subject and script have wide appeal.

2m1f, farce

Themes: clowning and offbeat romance

Movie Mother

by Colin Clements and Florence Ryerson

Dramatis Persona

Tentative Cast

Mother [f], _____

Place: Casting office of a motion picture studio, southern California.
Time: Morning. [Note: Copyright 1937.]

Available from Samuel French, Inc.
Published in *One-Act Plays for Today*,
edited by Francis J. Griffith and Joseph Mersand (New York: Globe, 1945).

Plot

Gwendolyn's mother enters armed with a bag, a determined hat, and her small daughter, ready for the casting fray. She addresses the imaginary receptionist. When the little girl protests that her name is not Gwendolyn Dawn but Gwendolyn Smith, the mother suppresses the objection. Gwendolyn's résumé is brief—no experience in pictures. However, her skills in toe, tap, and acrobatics will be enough to carry her to the top, her mother feels. Mrs. Smith cautions her little dear against saying horrid things to competitors also waiting for interviews. Gwendolyn must not even stick out her tongue at them. It would be better, too, if Gwendolyn sat still and kept her hands in proper places. She should not play with the Venetian blinds, nor the typewriter, and should stop pulling out the typewriter ribbon. When mother and daughter gain access to Mr. Harris, the casting director, the mother continues to rein in Gwendolyn, who has a clear penchant for saying the wrong thing. Considerable tension ensues from Mr. Harris' having a boil on his nose, on which Gwendolyn unfortunately focuses. During the audition, Gwendolyn recites awkwardly and manages to break the director's glasses. To pay for the broken glasses, Gwendolyn gets a part—in a scene with a "hundred and fifty other hoodlums." The mother reckons every great artist must start somewhere and accepts the job.

Comment

This comedic monologue, called here a monodrama, typifies solo comedy character routines. The effect is spoiled if anyone but the mother is visible. The stock type of pushy stage mother persists, and the piece can be updated; however, playing it in 1937 costume gains a nice effect. The mother does not have to be eccentric, just a sufferer of tunnel vision about her daughter. Even beginning actresses can handle this monologue. Coauthor Ryerson, with noteworthy screenwriting credits, had opportunity to observe this character type firsthand.

1f, comedy   *Themes:* cinema and motherhood

The Necklace

adapted by Jules Tasca from Guy de Maupassant

Dramatis Personae

Tentative Cast

Henri Loisel, in his 30s [m], _____

Mathilde Loisel, in her 30 [f], _____

Jeanne Forestier, in her 30s [f], _____

Place: A small impoverished apartment in a run-down section of Paris.
Time: Before 1900.

Available from Samuel French, Inc.

Plot

As Henri arrives at his humble home, his wife, Mathilde, says a visitor is expected: Jeanne Forestier, Mathilde's closest friend long ago. Mathilde wants Jeanne to know of the 36,000 francs they have repaid through ten years of deprivation. That money replaced a lost necklace that Mathilde had borrowed from Jeanne for a ball. Jeanne arrives, confused about the long separation from her friend and about her friend's present low estate. When reminded of the party ten years ago, she recalls details only slowly at first. Then she remembers more. Mathilde had been a sensation in an elegant gown set off by the borrowed necklace. A week later, she had returned the necklace, and then Mathilde and Henri

gave up their apartment and disappeared. Jeanne had tried to find her friend. Mathilde discloses having lost the necklace while running for a cab after the party. She describes bitterly how she and Henri slaved ten years because of the replacement's cost. She explains that, after all this, she has no material possessions: only pride is left to her.

Jeanne, horrified, reveals that the necklace was a fake, worth 500 francs at most; her husband would not let her lend the real one, even to a best friend. Jeanne cries, "Oh my God! Oh, my Lord! Mathilde, why couldn't you come to me? Why?"

Comment

Guy de Maupassant, one of the major 19th-century short story writers, speaks to modern concerns about human dilemmas and foibles. The source of this play is one of his most famous stories. The brief script by Jules Tasca tightly focuses on the short story's obligatory scene: the prideful protago-

nist faces the horrible irony of her fate. Staging requires period costuming, scenery, and props. All three roles are multi-layered. This outstanding adaptation fits many schools' curricula.

1m2f, drama

Themes: false pride, Paris, and poverty

A Nightingale

by Horton Foote

Dramatis Personae

Tentative Cast

Vonnie Hayhurst, 40 [f], _____

Mabel Votaugh, 42 [f], _____

Annie Gayle Long, a young woman [f], _____

Mr. Long, 35 [m], _____

Place : The kitchen of Mabel and Jack Votaugh, Houston, Texas.
Time: Around 7:00 a.m., early April, 1924.

Available from Dramatists Play Service, Inc.

Plot

Vonnie, just back from a trip, has come over to visit Mabel, who is expecting a young woman, Annie. Mabel recounts at length the tragic background of the young woman. As a girl, Annie saw her banker father shot to death by a farmer on whom the father had foreclosed. Annie and her mother went away, but in time Annie married and now lives within streetcar distance. She has taken to visiting Vonnie, a habit which Vonnie's husband, Mr. Long, disapproves. When Annie arrives, her behavior is unbalanced, and her speech rambles, even into memories of the shooting. She fails to follow Vonnie's explanations of local events and confuses the names of her own children. Annie asks to be taught how to pray, then does not pay attention. The older women discuss local church intrigues despite Annie's interruptions. Mr. Long arrives to retrieve his wandering young wife. She voices fears of being killed like her father. To return to work, the husband must put Annie on one streetcar home while he takes another. They leave. After Mabel and Vonnie gossip for a time, Annie returns, alone, looking for the children she remembers having brought with her this morning. Mabel sends her off to the streetcar again, this time with a prayer on a piece of paper to focus her mind. Annie leaves, but she returns almost immediately to announce she has decided to go to a matinee at the picture show. She then sings for the ladies.

Comment

This play can stand alone or serve as the first of three acts in *The Roads to Home.* (The second act is "The Dearest of Friends," with two males and two females; the third act is "Spring Dance," with three males and one female. The three acts are, of course, interrelated.) The pace is definitely Southern, in the style of this author's many other noteworthy scripts. Except for capturing subtleties of era and ambience, the production problems are simple and few.

1m3f, drama

Themes: insanity, marriage, and religion

Not Enough Rope

by Elaine May

Dramatis Personae

Tentative Cast

Miss Edith Friedlander, 30 [f], _____

Claude, 30 [m], _____

Mrs. Pierce, 80 [f], _____

Place: One floor of a rooming house.
Time: The present. [Note: Copyright 1964.]

Available from Samuel French, Inc.

Plot

Edith, lonely, is fussing around her room in a boardinghouse. Claude arrives with cartons and a suitcase and enters his room opposite. No sooner does he start to settle than Edith comes over to borrow rope to hang herself. He has only twine, that around his cartons. While coaxing the twine from him, she describes some of her idiosyncrasies—to his great disinterest. Claude takes twine from his cartons to lend to her. Back in her locked room, Edith, to the accompaniment of a recording of Judy Garland's "I'm Biding My Time," climbs a chair, nails the twine into the wall, and kicks the chair out. Falling to the floor, she restrings the twine across a ceiling pipe then around her neck, leaving no slack. Coincidentally, the song ends, so she calls Claude to restart it. Wanting only to practice his drums, he reluctantly agrees to help but lacks a key to her room. His key does not fit, so he awaits her suggestions. Still balanced precariously, she considers options. Suddenly, Edith apprehends the difference between twine and rope—and that her sign to commit suicide specifically involved rope. She begs Claude to save her. Irritated, he returns to his room to practice. Mrs. Pierce, hailing from a room down the hall, furious at the noise, wheels her chair to Claude's door. The three quarrel loudly. Mrs. Pierce returns to her room. Claude, repacking his gear to leave, discovers that he needs his twine back. He breaks into Edith's room to retrieve it. Grateful at having been saved, she wants to leave with him. He rejects the suggestion. She then struggles to reclaim the twine. He punches her to liberate his twine and extricate himself, then he departs. Again lonely, Edith goes down the hall and climbs into bed beside an unresponsive Mrs. Pierce.

Comment

The three quirky characters are absurd and farcical. Strictly two-dimensional, showing no growth, they illustrate hilarious self-absorbed interaction. A design style of selective realism could allow using three freestanding doors and invisible walls. Suspending the twine on wall and pipe is the only technical problem.

1m2f, comedy

Themes: self-absorption and loneliness

The Old Jew

by Murray Schisgal

Dramatis Persona

Tentative Cast

The Old Jew [m], _____

Place: A poorly furnished room in a tenement building, New York City.
Time: Afternoon.

Available from Dramatists Play Service.

Plot

The Old Jew studies his own physical appearance, adding touches. He telephones the Operator for assistance on completing a telephone call. When he rambles, the Operator cuts him off. He incompetently sings a Hebrew prayer or song and draws protests from neighbors. He goes to the door and admits three imaginary neighbors, a delegation asking him to leave the premises. His one-sided conversation reveals his relationships with them. He tries to be a good host. His concern about being a good Jew emerges, as he has not gone to the Synagogue in two decades yet he must pray. He wants them to understand his dilemma. He reminisces about the young lady friend to whom he was once engaged. Days when he had a chance for a happy life are past, too many chances missed. He now counts the members of the delegation as his only friends. He tries to dissuade them from leaving, but they do. Answering the telephone, the Old Jew transforms into a thirty-year-old actor. Off come the wig and the makeup. He explains to his caller, Jerry, that he wants to move in with him for a couple of weeks until he gets an acting job. He alludes to his girlfriend, who wants him to give up acting for a normal lifestyle and hints that he may break up with her (echoing the wrecked romance of the Old Jew). He recommits himself to his acting career regardless of what other people want of him. Having handled the immediate career crisis, he ends the telephone call and meditates.

Comment

Any aspiring actor must face the costs of choosing that profession. To that actor, the pressure sometimes is great. This tour de force, first performed at the Berkshire Theatre Festival, in Stockbridge, Massachusetts, on August 16, 1966, with Dustin Hoffman as the Old Jew, offers any strong actor a rewarding interpretive challenge as well as an opportunity for introspection about a stage career. The undemanding set, costume, and props make it easy to stage, and the burden is on the actor. Some research into Judaic ritual is necessary.

1m, drama

Themes: acting and religion

The Olives/*Las Aceitunas*

by Lope de Rueda, translated from the original Spanish by Angel Flores

Dramatis Personae

Tentative Casting

Toribio, an old man [m], _____

Menciguela, his daughter [f], _____

Agueda de Toruegano, his wife [f], _____

Aloja, a neighbor [m], _____

Place: A peasant hut in Spain.
Time: A stormy afternoon, around 1535.

Available in *Spanish Drama*, edited by Angel Flores (New York: Bantam, 1962).

Plot

Toribio rushes into his poor house, seeking haven from the storm, finds only his daughter Menciguela. He seeks his wife, but she has gone to help at a house nearby. Agueda returns just then and the two quarrel about supper. He unloads his cargo of wet firewood. Drenched and hungry, he is in no mood for his wife's sharp remarks. Agueda sends the daughter out to make the father's bed and questions Toribio about planting their olive-shoot. Wife and husband commence dreaming of good fortune from the olive trees. She insists that he charge at least two Castilian *reales* for a half

peck, but he fears that is too much. The daughter, now back, finds herself caught between their demands that she agree with a given price: Toribio threatens to beat her, and Agueda strikes her for disobedience. Aloja, a neighbor, enters and protects the daughter. Aloja asks Agueda to leave for a moment while he straightens matters. He asks to see the olives over which they are quarreling. Upon learning that Toribio has just planted one shoot, Aloja berates the family. As they happily prepare for supper, still dreaming of riches, the neighbor leaves in disgust.

Comment

This play is quite brief, making it a good curtain raiser. Several English translations exist; however, a Spanish-language production is not out of reach because of the script's brevity. The stock characters in this *paso* derive from Spanish folklore and the commedia dell'arte. They are the stuff

of farce and great fun to portray, posing no problems of subtlety. Period costuming and scenery would help greatly. Area staging could allow a comic exterior storm effect on the apron at the beginning and give a coziness to the interior action.

2m2f, comedy

Themes: family relationships, greed, and Spain

Open Admissions

by Shirley Lauro

Dramatis Personae

Tentative Cast

Alice Stockwell [f], _____
Calvin Jefferson [m], _____

Place: A cubicle Speech Office at a city college in New York.
Time: The present. Late fall. 6:00 p.m. [Note: Original copyright 1979.]

Available from Samuel French, Inc. [#5; ISBN 0-573-60044-9]

Plot

Alice telephones her daughter that she has kept a class late and has to attend a meeting, so she will not be home for dinner. Calvin, trying to contain his rage and frustration, looms in the doorway and frightens her. He insists on discussing his grades now, despite her rush. Seeing his intensity, she grants him a few minutes. Why does he always get a B grade on each project, he asks. She reminds him of his substandard-urban-speech problem and defensively coaches him on *ass-king* versus *ax-ing*. He demands being taught how to organize his ideas instead of just getting B's. What does a B stand for! Alice describes her overload after twelve years here on an academic treadmill. He rejects her bid for sympathy, backs her over a desk, screams, "You gotta give me my education!" and tears up the textbook. In anguish and despair, he cries. When his sobs subside, Alice admits wanting to help him. But he has been passed through the educational system for social reasons, not for academic achievement; in spite of his intelligence, his educational level now is too low for a speech teacher in sixteen weeks to help him as he wants. He says, "Then I'm finished, man." Alice asks for his trust, that she will teach him what she can. She coaches him on *asking*. He progresses from his pronunciation to hers as the lights fade.

Comment

Both roles provide excellent challenges. "The play begins on a very high level of tension and intensity and builds from there," the author says. The roles are so evenly balanced that the play almost could be staged with either as the protagonist, but it is Alice who finally moves to solve the dramatic impasse and brings them both toward hope. Depiction of shortcomings in the open-admissions policy arouses thought about an important socioeducational problem. The role of Calvin can be adjusted from deprived black to that of another ethnic underclass. Production demands are slight.

First performed at the Double Image Theatre, this story later became a full-length play as well as a feature-length teleplay. The excellent expanded versions do not overshadow this short script.

The Other Player

by Owen G. Arno

Dramatis Personae

Tentative Cast

Dr. Becker, headmistress, 48 [f], _____

Mrs. Corlin, a parent, 49 [f], _____

Petra Cross, a student, 15 [f], _____

Place: A dormitory room, Grey-Matthews School for Girls, New England.
Time: 11:20 a.m. in late June. [Note: Copyright 1964].

Available from Dramatists Play Service, Inc.

Plot

Corlin, wealthy and successful in business but now burdened with grief, has come to her daughter Jennifer's exclusive school to gather the girl's belongings. Jennifer has drowned in a pool accident. The mother wants to understand more of the girl she perhaps has neglected emotionally. Dr. Becker, the headmistress, tries to ease the situation, then leaves the distraught mother alone, promising to be available in the front office. Petra, a quite shy student, enters; after awkwardly extending condolences, she asks to search for her tennis racquet. Petra's aggressive rummaging impacts brutally on Corlin. When the racquet is found, the woman presses for proof of ownership. The girl, driven to assert herself, claims that the racquet, once her father's and the only one with which she can properly play, was stolen to disadvantage her in the tournament Jennifer won. Corlin threatens to go to Dr. Becker with this story unless Petra details the whole incident. Once Petra does talk, she recounts Jennifer's deeds of bullying, blackmail, and assault. The shocked mother, in tears, makes Petra accept the racquet. The girl leaves. Corlin sits, confused and devastated. However, Petra reenters, extends the racquet, and says enigmatically, "I'm sorry. I made it all up, ma'm. I just wanted Jennifer's tennis racquet."

Comment

Advertised as a script for three males or three females, this play offers three strong roles. Indeed, the cast need not be exclusively male or female; each gender combination supplies subtle differences in the overall impact. To solve name problems, *Peter* could be *Petra*, and the remembered *Jeffrey* could be *Jennifer*. As the central character, Mrs. Corlin is the mother who drives the action. The O. Henry-like ending is a shock. Stage directions specify a realistic setting with numerous props that contribute greatly to the ambience and storyline.

3f or 3m or mixed, drama

Themes: death, deceit, grief, and parenting

Overtones

by Alice Gerstenberg

Dramatis Personae

Tentative Cast

Harriet [f], _____

Hetty [f], _____

Margaret [f], _____

Maggie [f], _____

Place: Harriet's fashionable living room.
Time: Mid-afternoon, mid-1920s.

Available from Baker's Plays and Samuel French, Inc.

Plot

Harriet, in a light, jealous-green gown, and Hetty, her other self in a similar but darker gown, argue over who better controls Harriet's wealthy husband, Charles. Hetty hates Charles Goodrich, but Harriet covers up that hatred. They await the arrival of a guest, the wife of John Caldwell, an artist Hetty once loved and Harriet had rejected as too poor. Hetty wants to make the guest jealous. Harriet and Hetty quarrel so severely that Harriet regains her supremacy only with difficulty. She welcomes Margaret, in a lavender chiffon gown, and fails to see Maggie, the other self, in a similar but purple gown; Hetty and Maggie do see each other. As the surface selves politely discourse, the inner selves snipe at each other, speaking the hidden truth of the relationship. The tea ritual allows Harriet and Margaret to compliment one another. Margaret seeks a commission for her husband to paint Harriet (they need the money). Harriet says she will ask her husband about the commission (she wants to see the artist again). A cymbal crashes; lights go out. When the lights return, only Harriet and Margaret are visible, exchanging fond good-byes.

Comment

This warhorse script serves all-female-cast needs well. Theatre companies composed entirely or primarily of females are always looking for such scripts. Obviously, the costumes are paramount in staging this show, as the author so carefully describes them and their symbolism. A judicious use of sound, aside from the cymbal crash, could fit well here. The four characterizations are clearly written. The plot is simple. An interesting directing approach would be to rehearse only Harriet's and Margaret's lines as a scene. Their civility established, the addition of Hetty and Maggie as clashing alter egos then would make clear the dramatic counterpoint intended by the playwright.

4f, comedy

Themes: envy and Freudian psychology

```
• • • • • • • • • • • • • • • • • • • • • • • • • • • • • • • • • • • • •
```

Passport

by James Elward

Dramatis Persona

Tentative Cast

Charlie Meseger, 41 [m], _____

Place: The living room of Charlie's apartment, in the West 80s, New York City.
Time: Midnight. The present. [Note: Premiered February 8, 1965.]

Available from Dramatists Play Service, Inc.

```
• • • • • • • • • • • • • • • • • • • • • • • • • • • • • • • • • • • • •
```

Plot

Charlie, a little drunk from celebrating the start of the weekend, returns home to find mail inside his door. He sorts through and reads some of the mail, satirizing its impersonality. Somewhat maudlin, he considers telephoning Emily, his ex-wife, whose lawyer cleaned him out. What about his father, who would only compare him adversely to his brother, Len? Charlie mulls over some sort of temporary visa from life. What about telephoning the "Redhead in the Village," the poet? She is missing from his address book. What about his psychiatrist, Dr. Cerdek? Or Fatso, really John M. Treshler, advertising editor and his boss? Charlie recognizes that he will call nobody nor use the passport. He thinks about working on "After This, Our Exile," his unfinished novel; he fantasizes about success. Dissatisfied after reading a few passages, he browses his college yearbook. Then a rumpled wedding picture calls to mind his failed marriage. Self-loathing grows. Returning his attention to the telephone, he fumbles onto a recorded voice giving the time. He cries out in frustration his fears to the voice. He takes a bottle of pills from his pocket and counts out an overdose. However, drunkenness lulls him into unconsciousness, and "the pills dribble down from his relaxed hand onto the floor."

Comment

Charlie is a drunk, a failure with family, friends, and employer. Nonetheless, audience sympathy for the character is imperative, so the performer should be capable of winsome humor. Charlie, in struggling against the odds, shows dignity; that striving redeems him to the audience. By accident, he survives; perhaps tomorrow he will win his struggle. The role can be played by either gender; race and ethnicity are irrelevant. For example, an African-American actress could give interesting dimensions to the character. Technical problems are slight.

1m, drama

Themes: self-esteem and suicide

A Phoenix Too Frequent

by Christopher Fry

Dramatis Personae

Tentative Cast

Dynamene, a young widow [f], _____

Doto, servant to Dynamene [f], _____

Tegeus-Chromis, a guard [m], _____

Place: The underground tomb of Virilius, near Ephesus, in western Asia Minor.
Time: Two in the morning.

Available from Dramatists Play Service and Hansen Drama Shop.

Plot

Doto watches over her mistress, Dynamene, who sleeps beside the body of her recently buried husband Virilius. An owl's cry wakens the mistress, who resumes her mourning; she is in her second day of vigil here. She praises her husband and allows the slave to mourn him, too. Tegeus, posted to guard six hanged bodies through the night, arrives to check the light he has detected. As Dynamene is either preoccupied with mourning or is asleep, Doto welcomes the company of the soldier. He opens his packet of food and wine, and she joins him, quickly refreshing her spirits. She even suggests a kiss "to go moistly to Hades." The mistress awakens and wants to know who the soldier is. Her beauty immediately conquers him, and he happily shares his wine with her, too. Doto is now quite drunk. The wine begins to affect Dynamene and Tegeus. Their conversation ripens into infatuation as Doto sleeps. The intimacy deepens when they discover having shared a childhood vacation area without having met then. She tries to remind herself of her present duty to mourn, but his ardor draws her toward him. Suddenly, he recalls his duty and leaves to check on the six hanging corpses. While he is gone, Dynamene tries to convince Doto to abandon the tomb and go away. When the servant realizes that her mistress wants privacy with Tegeus, she agrees to leave, passing on the steps the returning soldier. He is ready to die: he might as well kill himself because one of the bodies is missing. The idea comes to Dynamene to substitute Virilius for the missing body. Before getting into action, the new lovers turn again to the bottle and toast Virilius. Doto, eavesdropping on the steps, toasts both masters.

Comment

Despite the tomb setting, this script is a comedy of manners. As in all of Fry's plays, the language is stellar. Here, the comedy and characterizations also are superb. High school companies would find in this script a chance to stretch, and adult companies with a degree of sophistication would do well to consider it. Any group liking the script might also consider Fry's full-length *The Lady's Not for Burning*. Proper costuming, props, and lighting are essential.

1m2f, comedy

Themes: death, love, and duty

Ping

by Samuel Beckett

Dramatis Persona

Tentative Cast

Ping [m], _____

Place: The mind.
Time: The perception.

Available from Dramatists Play Service, Inc.

Plot

The playwright uses only free associations, stream of consciousness, and interior monologue without context. No plot, as such, exists; beyond logic, characterization becomes the plot.

Comment

The author poses a tour de force for a male or female actor. The monologue voices mental chaos struggling for self-understanding through unity, coherence, and emphasis. Beckett, inclined here as elsewhere to distill language to its essence and ultimately to silence, weaves mind fragments into a tapestry of sound. A close study of his most experimental play, *Breath,* would illumine this piece. One feasible interpretation is that the entire monologue can be an answer to a devised question. To explain the puzzle Beckett offers, one can variously weight repetitions and ideas. For example, close study shows patterns uniting sensory elements, such as colors trying to escape whiteness. Body parts strive for color, identity, purpose, and success. Poetic devices, like alliteration and assonance, give conflicting crosswinds to the sails of Beckett's thoughts. Words familiar and invented (such as *unover* and *haught*) follow one another predictably and unpredictably (such as in the phrase "the same same time"). *Ping* interrupts, disjoins, allowing the mind to digress. In closing, Beckett says, "Head haught eyes white fixed front old ping last murmur one second perhaps not alone eye unlustrous black and white half closed long lashes imploring ping silence ping over."

This a script for the adventurous, for the lover of language and silence, for male or female actor. In the total absence of written directions, even to the identification of the speaker, the director can stage the production any way the imagination leads, as long as one is true to the cause of Beckett. Lighting and sound could be used to great effect, even becoming participants in the poetry. Scenery and properties give similar possibilities. One production of this script ran about seven minutes.

1m, drama

Themes: meaning of life and self-understanding

The Playe Called the Foure PP: A Newe and a Very Mery Enterlude of a Palmer, a Pardoner, a Potycary, and a Pedler

by John Heywood

Dramatis Personae

                                                                    Tentative Cast

A Palmer [m],   _____

A Pardoner [m],   _____

A Potycary [m],   _____

A Pedler [m],   _____

Place: A crossroad rest stop, England.
Time: Midday, in good weather, 1521-25.

Available in *Chief Pre-Shakespearean Dramas*, edited by Joseph Quincy Adams
(New York: Houghton Mifflin Company, 1924).

Plot

The Palmer introduces himself and tells of his travels to holy places. While he speaks, the Pardoner enters with his packet of pardons and relics. First disparaging the Palmer's travels then denying any disparagement, the Pardoner disputes with the Palmer over who can better save souls. During this, the Potycary enters with his packet of medicines. He claims to have sent more souls to heaven than either of the other two, as, indeed, no one goes there until death. The Pedler with his pack on his back enters and seeks an activity to pass the time of resting. After a short truce in which the Palmer, Pardoner, Potycary, and Pedler sing an unspecified song, they lapse into accusing one another of fraud, of lying. All agree to pass the time with a lying contest, the Pedler being judge. They start by kissing a relic of the Pardoner, which chokes them. They also reject other relics and tokens the Pardoner offers, but they accept his flask. The Potycary offers various of his wares, which they also reject. Then he goes first in the contest. He recounts treating a woman with a potion and an anal bung; the gases built to such a force that the explosion sent the bung against a castle and knocked it down. The woman is now in good health. Next the Pardoner recounts the situation of a woman who died. To save her, he went first to Purgatory and then to Hell; there he found the woman ruining the food in the kitchen and the devils glad to be rid of her. The woman is now at home, alive and well. The Palmer briefly explains that, despite what the other two have said against women, he has never seen one out of patience. Not only the Pedler but also the Pardoner and Potycary agree that this is the biggest lie possible and award the Palmer the prize. The penalty is that the losers must bow to the winner. The Palmer addresses an epilogue to the audience, commending it to God and asking approval of the playwright's pastime just presented here.

Comment

This script is rather long and presents transliteration problems. On the other hand, it offers rich satire about pretenders. Each of the four roles is strong and individual. The costuming from the early 1500s should be easy to achieve, and the props are simple. Some research for the song would allow the staging not to fall back on "Greensleeves," although that would serve; a round is appropriate, too. The simplest of scenery would fit.

4m, comedy

Themes: contest, medieval society, and Catholicism

Purgatory

by William Butler Yeats

Dramatis Personae

Tentative Cast

A Boy [m], _____

An Old Man [m], _____

Man in the Window [non-speaking m], _____

Woman in the Window [non-speaking f], _____

Place: A ruined house and a bare tree in the background.
Time: Night. [Note: Premiered 1938.]

Available from Samuel French, Inc.

Plot

An Old Man, who is a pedlar, and his son arrive at a ruined house in the country, once the home of the Old Man's mother. He wants his bastard son to study the house and tree. The boy, unconcerned that nobody is present at the house, hears from the Old Man that souls come from Purgatory to places such as this. The Old Man insists that the lad know what happened here. Into this house, the Old Man's newly married parents had come, unblessed by their families. His father had dissipated the family funds, had ignored his wife and son, and, when the son was sixteen, drunkenly had burned the family home. At that time, the son had stabbed his drunken father and had thrown the body into the flames; then he had fled and become a pedlar on the roads. Now, on this anniversary of his parents' orgiastic wedding night, the returning pedlar hears hoofbeats of his drunken father's arrival home. He knows his own begetting is occurring in the sexual revelry behind the window above. The light in the window fades. The pedlar accuses his son of trying to steal from him, and the Boy threatens patricide. The two struggle over the money, spilling it. The pedlar again and again stabs, killing his son with the knife that had killed his own father a generation earlier. He cleans the knife and picks up the scattered money. But ending the misbegotten family line has not ended the dilemma. The pedlar's drunken father rides again to the recurring debased union. The Old Man pleads to God to release his mother's soul from the Purgatory in which she eternally repeats her sin.

Comment

Here is a grand chance for the production company to stretch its abilities. The strong conflicts in this short play and the soaring poetry let the actors veer from naturalism toward operatic heights. Devices and themes are reminiscent of Sophocles' *Oedipus Rex* and Strindberg's *The Ghost Sonata*. Lighting and music are crucial to the desired poetic effect.

3m1f, drama   *Themes:* idealism, materialism, family murder, sin, and guilt

The Purple Door Knob

by Walter Prichard Eaton

Dramatis Personae

Tentative Cast

Mrs. Bartholomew, an old lady [f], _____

Mrs. Amanda Dunbar, her servant [f], _____

Viola Cole, a preeminent young actress [f], _____

Place: The bedroom of Mrs. Bartholomew, a second-story chamber
in a little Massachusetts village.
Time: Afternoon, late 1920s.

Available from Samuel French, Inc.

Plot

Mrs. Bartholomew, invalid and bedridden and bored, asks her nurse-companion, Mrs. Dunbar, for entertainment but rejects every suggestion. She yearns for "something new, somebody new." Into these doldrums arrives Viola Cole, who wants to buy the front-door knob. The hostess and visitor vie for conversational dominance, the old lady playing on being an invalid, the actress on being deeply concerned. When Mrs. Bartholomew challenges Viola's knowing about and wanting the doorknob, the actress identifies herself and her fame. It happens that the old lady used to love the theatre; she asks about and praises long-departed famous actors. She offers the doorknob in exchange for a well-acted scene. Viola agrees—if Mrs. Bartholomew will portray a queen for the duologue. The actress supplies improvised crown and scepter, and the old lady transforms into a queen with Cleopatra qualities. Viola prepares herself, becomes a suppliant, and begs for the rescue of a kidnapped sister, for which the ransom is "the great jewel of Egypt—it is the royal amethyst!!" Viola's intensity and acting skill win the old lady's admiration and the doorknob. They summon Mrs. Dunbar to have Viola's chauffeur remove the doorknob. The actress seeks Mrs. Bartholomew's friendship and with a kiss promises to return. After she leaves, the nurse-companion agrees to call a handyman to secure the front door, then settles the happy old lady into a satisfied rest.

Comment

The author, a well-known American theatre scholar in the 1930s and 1940s, here gives a good example of sentimental comedy. From an earlier era, this script merits current presentation. It has slight literary quality and shows self-indulgence for theatre folk (because of its focus on their concerns); still it offers valid entertainment for the general public.

Queens of France

by Thornton Wilder

Dramatis Personae

Tentative Cast

Marie-Sidonie Cressaux, an attractive young woman [f], _____

M'su Cahusac, a lawyer [m], _____

Madame Pugeot, a plump little bourgeoise [f], _____

Mamselle Pointevin, a spinster schoolmistress [f], _____

Boy, an extra, [m], _____

Old Woman, an extra [f], _____

Place: A lawyer's office in New Orleans.
Time: 1869.

Available from Samuel French, Inc.

Plot

M'su Cahusac, having summoned Marie-Sidonie Cressaux to his office for a strictly confidential interview, warns she is in danger. He has found her to be the true and long-lost heir to the throne of France. Overawed by the prospect of such rank, she suspects a mistake and moves to go. He tells how the New Orleans *Times-Picayune* will publish her name, how the bishop and the mayor will call upon her, and more. When he offers her money, she declines, but she seems less unconvinced and will return Thursday morning. Her exit coincides with the entrance of Madame Pugeot. The lawyer explains to his new arrival that the previous lady wants to purchase a house and garden. Madame Pugeot snipes at the previous lady's reputation then accepts solicitations about her own royal family. She dotes on all of her family except her husband, who has scoffed at her regal claim, so she now willingly hides such matters from him. M'su Cahusac explains that the Historical Society, in France, needs money to research proofs of her claim. She promises that she will bring tomorrow at three papers for the sale of her house. The bell rings and Mamselle Pointevin starts to enter; the lawyer asks her to wait in the park a few minutes. Madame Pugeot, accepting the lawyer's explanation that the waiting woman wants to make a will, dismisses her as a poor schoolteacher. She, herself, off to the Cathedral, wonders where she as Queen of France will eventually rest. He declares that her tomb will be in the church of St. Denis. She goes. M'su Cahusac immediately welcomes Mamselle Pointevin, who haughtily objects to having been kept waiting. She finds her role as schoolmistress humiliating and the wait for recognition as Queen of France annoying. The lawyer reads a letter from the Historical Society citing need of a final verifying document. He insists that her home, perhaps even the burial clothing of her father, must hold this last bit of needed evidence. She faces a lengthy search. To allay misgivings about her claim, he gives her the letter from the Historical Society and promises never to mention to anyone this whole affair. She goes. A bell announces a female centenarian, her wheelchair pushed in by a boy. M'su Cahusac kisses the ancient extended hand, murmuring, "Your Royal Highness."

Comment

Wilder, Pulitzer-Prize-winning novelist and dramatist, emphasizes plot and character here. Indeed, both require much analysis. The ending is ambiguous; M'su Cahusac may be villain or patriot. The Louisiana dialect helps to establish place. Set and dress are not easy challenges. This is a show for sophisticates.

1m3f (+ 1m and 1f extras), comedy   *Themes:* greed and self-delusion

Rapes

by Mario Fratti

Dramatis Personae

Tentative Cast

Deborah, 19, naive, vulnerable, sensitive, and attractive [f], _____

Tony, 30, tall, blond, handsome, and intelligent [m], _____

Vic, short and dark [m], _____

Place: A kitchen in a village apartment, in New York City.
Time: 2:00 a.m.

Available from Samuel French, Inc.

Plot

Deborah enters the apartment, followed by Tony. He challenges her wisdom about coming to his apartment while knowing so little about him. She calmly makes tea for them. She seeks conversation. The talk settles on rape. She tells him about having been raped by a cop and about a teenage consensual experience. But she wants to talk about him. He says her attitude invites rape: "She who gets raped wants to get raped." She defies his analysis even while telling him of being raped ten times. He calls her sick; she says she seeks communication, human warmth, love. He calls to another room, "I did my best," and tells Deborah the man entering is his brother Vic, the policeman who assaulted her. Vic has suffered nightmares, remorse; he wanted to marry Deborah. But what he has overheard makes Vic regard her as a slut. He offers her to Tony, telling him to kick her out when he's through with her. Deborah smiles and offers herself to Tony. They smile at each other with understanding.

Comment

The author is a ranking Italian dramatist now living in New York City, who says, "My fundamental concern is human distress, . . . the grotesque of human behavior in contemporary society." The characterizations are valid, complex, and haunting. The subject matter is challenging but not universally appealing. Production problems are slight.

2m1f, drama

Themes: sexual abuse and grotesquerie

Riders to the Sea

by John Millington Synge

Dramatis Personae

Tentative Cast

Nora, a young girl [f], _____

Cathleen, about 20 [f], _____

Maurya, their mother [f], _____

Bartley, their brother [m], _____

Place: Cottage kitchen, on an island off the west of Ireland.
Time: 1904.

Available from Baker's Plays and Samuel French, Inc.

Plot

Nora and Cathleen have settled their mother to rest for a time. Out of her presence, they must check a shirt and stocking of a man drowned off Donegal to see if they belong to their brother Michael. They worry about their brother Bartley, now maybe the last of the line, who wants to travel to Connemara. If anything happen to him, their mother will have lost a husband, a father-in-law, and six sons to the sea. Maurya, though, interrupts them; she cannot rest and comes in to sit by the fire. Bartley comes in, needing rope to fashion a halter for the mare he is taking to the horse fair. Maurya keeps referring to burying Michael and does not want to risk Bartley on this journey he is planning. He promises that he will be gone at most four days and leaves. Maurya mourns at his departure, as if he will never return. Discovering that Bartley has not taken food, the sisters send their mother out with bread to give him. They retrieve the shirt and stocking from hiding and determine that they are Michael's. Hearing their mother, they put the clothing into a hole in the chimney corner. Maurya enters still holding the bread. She saw Bartley riding the red mare but also saw Michael on the gray pony. Maurya tells of seeing mourners arriving. Just then, mourners do arrive. Cathleen hands her mother the clothes that belonged to Michael. Men bring in the body of Bartley on a plank with a bit of sail over it and lay it on the table. One of the women says that the gray pony knocked him into the sea. Maurya speaks of being free of fear of the sea, which can take no more from her. Cathleen gives the men who will make the coffin the bread intended for Bartley. Released from her nine days of crying and keening, Maurya transcends grief and summarizes her loss, saying that people must be satisfied with proper burials and expect no more.

Comment

Many critics hold this play to be the best one-act ever written. Its depiction of fate and then Maurya's insight and transcendence suit high tragedy. The tension of waiting for tragic news marks Synge's highest artistry in any of his six plays. This is almost drama without plot, that is, stasis after earlier catastrophe, an unwinding of the inevitable. Serious production companies would do well sooner or later to undertake this play. A necessary production prelude is a study of Irish drama.

1m3f, tragedy

Themes: fate and grief

The Rising of the Moon

by Lady Isabella Augusta Gregory

Dramatis Personae

Tentative Cast

Sergeant, oldest of the policemen [m], _____

Policeman X [m], _____

Policeman B [m], _____

A Ragged Man [m], _____

Place: Side of a quay in a seaport town, Ireland.
Time: A moonlit night, 1907.

Available from Samuel French, Inc.

Plot

A Sergeant and two policemen are pasting placards. At this dock, they post a notice of one hundred pounds' reward for a wanted man who has escaped from gaol (jail). The Sergeant elects to mind this place where a refuge might meet a boat, while the others continue elsewhere with the brushes, paste, placards, and lantern. The wanted criminal is popular with the public, making apprehension more difficult. A Ragged Man tries in the dim moonlight to slip past the Sergeant. When challenged, the Man identifies himself as Jimmy Walsh, a poor ballad-singer and ballad-peddler. The Sergeant refuses to let him pass, so the Man lingers, on the chance that some passing sailor will buy his wares. The Sergeant at first orders the Man to return to town but relents when the Man claims to know the criminal's appearance and lets the Man join the watch. They talk of the hard times.

Now and again, the Man sings—for courage, he says. The two upon discovering they both know a certain tune begin to share philosophical outlooks. They ponder the odd idea that, had life chanced differently, the Sergeant and the criminal might each have had the other's fate. A boat arrives in the darkness, and the Man sings loudly to signal to it. The Sergeant sees the Man is the sought criminal, a person fighting for Irish freedom. Just then, the other policemen return. The Man hides and the Sergeant protects him by lying to the other two. The Sergeant sends the other policemen away. The Man emerges from hiding, promising to do as much for the Sergeant "when the small rise up and the big fall down . . . when we all change places at the Rising of the Moon." The Sergeant wonders about being a great fool for having lost the reward.

Comment

Lady Gregory (1852-1932) looms as a giantess in the late-nineteenth-century Irish literary renascence. As director of the Abbey Theatre and playwright, she supplied nearly forty plays. Although her fervent patriotism permeates this significant short play, the content rises above propaganda into universal truths. Producers must study political and physical details of the historical environment to capture the full Irish spirit. Here, though, the particular situation posits the general condition of political underdogs, so this play can serve as agitprop (agitational propaganda) or as hopeful observation.

4m, comedy   *Themes:* Ireland, police, and war

```
• • • • • • • • • • • • • • • • • • • • • • • • • • • • • • • • • • • • • • •
•                                                                           •
•                            Rosary                                        •
•                                                                           •
•                     by Jean-Claude Van Itallie                           •
•                                                                           •
•                          Dramatis Persona                                •
•                                                    Tentative Cast         •
• A Young Nun [f] _____          •
•                                                                           •
•                Place: A seat on a subway train, New York City.            •
•                Time: After the morning. [Note: Copyright 1973.]           •
•                                                                           •
•                 Available from Dramatists Play Service, Inc.              •
•                                                                           •
• • • • • • • • • • • • • • • • • • • • • • • • • • • • • • • • • • • • • • •
```

Plot

A Young Nun sits on the subway, returning to her convent after an event at a home where she had gone to solicit alms. Subway vibrations shake her hands and body. She is alone on the stage. Behind her, in a film projection, her nude image is "playing beautifully and freely amidst patterns of light on the debris of a destroyed building or old lot." The Young Nun vacillates between fervent prayer and obsessive stream-of-consciousness recall. She greatly needs help after "an encounter with a woman." She had gone to the woman's house for alms, accepted the invitation to enter, sat "on the edge of velvet," and felt the caress on her arm. She had heard taffeta rustle, seen the gold bracelet, smelled perfume of temptation and forgetfulness, felt the hand on her arm. Amid patterns of falling light, amid sounds through closed French doors of street children shouting and playing, she had felt the woman's hand, soft like roses, insinuate itself. Her habit had fallen like black blood onto the velvet. The Young Nun recalls kissing a skirt's hem; she confuses the woman and Mother Mary, interchanging their attributes. She cries, "What is love? Oh, Mary? What is love? I no longer know anything." She begs both Mary's protection and punishment for having sinned. Confusing the ambience of the woman's parlor with that of the church, the Young Nun pleads, ". . . My redeemer cometh, he will lead me into forgetfulness."

Comment

This extremely brief script fits agitational theatre in that it can easily offend religious sensibilities in many audiences. The subject matter and multimedia production techniques are old hat, yet the terse, tense writing provides a considerable artistic challenge to the director and actress. They need familiarity with the life-style and psychology of this American Catholic nun. The record is that van Itallie wrote this script to complement Phill Niblock's film using actress Marcia Jean Kurtz on Welfare Island, New York. However, stage directions state, "The piece may be spoken with other available visual material projected on the background, as the director sees fit."

1f, drama   *Themes:* homosexuality and religious guilt

```
• • • • • • • • • • • • • • • • • • • • • • • • • • • • • • • • • • • • • • •
•                                                                           •
•                    Save Me a Place at Forest Lawn                         •
•                                                                           •
•                           by Lorees Yerby                                 •
•                                                                           •
•                          Dramatis Personae                                •
•                                                        Tentative Cast     •
•   Clara, octogenarian [f], _____      •
•   Gertrude, her contemporary [f], _____      •
•                                                                           •
•                   Place: The interior of a cafeteria.                     •
•      Time: Lunch hour, the present. [Note: Premiered May 8, 1963.]         •
•                                                                           •
•                  Available from Dramatists Play Service.                  •
•                                                                           •
• • • • • • • • • • • • • • • • • • • • • • • • • • • • • • • • • • • • • • •
```

Plot

Clara and Gertrude shuffle into the cafeteria's seating area, each with a tray loaded with food. They quibble about choosing the best table. Gertrude excuses herself, and Clara promises to hold her seat. Alone, she switches desserts. They worry about disposing of the trays properly, wipe the silverware with a napkin, and begin to eat. Gertrude notices her gravy running right into her string beans, but she refuses to challenge the restaurant after the last time. She is so upset that Clara reminds her others might be watching and think them senile. At an impasse, they try a few moments of silence, which causes Clara to refer to permanent silence. That, too, upsets Gertrude. She fears outliving everyone she knows. She even has religious doubts now. She sees life as a race she has lost, her features crumble. Gertrude admits to being unready for death. They talk of death as best being a surprise present. Clara announces having arranged for a place at Forest Lawn. They differ excitedly about cremation. Gertrude demands Clara's opinion on whether Gertrude is wishy-washy. Clara invites Gertrude along today at the arrangement for a crypt in her own mausoleum. When Gertrude grows feisty, Clara scowls and urges to her friend to eat so they can leave. They get onto name preferences and into song; nostalgia brings them to tears. Again, Clara fears making a spectacle, having people judge them. Clara wonders about the gender of people in heaven. They spot Albert Hoagbarth in line; he has given them both attention. Clara rages when Gertrude resorts to a magnifying glass to see better. Gertrude sulks. She brings up her husband's spiritual infidelity with Clara and says she did not leave Harry because it would have meant an end to her friendship with Clara. Clara wants to atone somehow. Gertrude says, "Take me with you," meaning she wants to be buried beside Clara. Gertrude must excuse herself again as they prepare to leave for the funereal appointment. She leans down to Clara and warmly exclaims to her, "Oh, Clara . . . it means so much . . . to have a friend waiting."

Comment

First produced at the Pocket Theatre, New York City, on May 8, 1963, this script offers two splendid roles, especially regarding age portrayal. The setting needs but four or five tables with chairs. Extras at these tables are optional. Sound effects could contribute greatly. The structure of the plot is tight, with excellent segments and plausible transitions. The script beautifully delineates preoccupations, personal values, and friendship in old age.

2f, comedy-drama   *Themes:* friendship and optimism

Scent of Honeysuckle

by Jean Lenox Toddie

Dramatis Personae

Tentative Cast

Jessie, 77 [f], _____

Susan, her mother (as remembered) [f], _____

Kate, her daughter, 45 [f], _____

Place: The sitting room in Jessie's home.
Time: Tea.

Available from Samuel French, Inc. [ISBN 0-573-6059-7]

Plot

Kate, on a cold December day, has come to move her mother from the family home to Kate's home twenty-five miles away. Jessie has packed a suitcase but now announces that she is not moving. Kate tries to placate the old lady with a cup of tea before they leave and reminisces with her. Susan, the mother Jessie remembers, materializes and talks to Jessie. Kate, never seeing Susan and only hearing Jessie, repeatedly misunderstands, taking this as more evidence to support the move. Jessie knows that in old age "memories have texture and take up space." She recalls how through Susan's prompting she met and married Kate's father. Kate rejects Jessie's reliving the past as hallucinations, and they argue over the family doctor's diagnoses and advice. Susan intervenes by humming and dancing, focusing Jessie's attention on the scent of honeysuckle outside. Kate reminds Jessie that this is not the season for honeysuckle. Jessie fails in an attempt to rise and tells Kate, "I'll go quietly. . . . I'll be in safe hands." Kate goes to get gas for the car and to give her mother a few minutes to say good-byes to the house. Susan gently assists Jessie's transit from life.

Comment

This sentimental drama calls attention to a growing social problem—caring for the aged. Its three strong roles illuminate how different the members of the same family can be. Jessie in consulting her past and following her premonition to resolve this crisis of old age centers the story. Kate, through slight adjustments in the script, could be a male role. Stage directions specify space staging and minimal props.

3f, drama

Themes: family and old age

```
•••••••••••••••••••••••••••••••••••••••••••••••
•                                               •
•                  Senior Prom                  •
•                                               •
•                by Robert Mearns               •
•                                               •
•               Dramatis Personae               •
•                                  Tentative Cast •
•   Steven [m], _____ •
•   Sherri [f], _____ •
•                                               •
•   Place: A secluded park in a small town on the coast of North Carolina. •
•      Time: The present [1984], late May, a Saturday close to midnight. •
•                                               •
•            Available from Samuel French, Inc.  •
•                                               •
•••••••••••••••••••••••••••••••••••••••••••••••
```

Plot

Sherri tries to reassure Steven that the bruise near his left eye and the torn sleeve of his shirt are not so bad. When Steven learns that Sherri had known her regular boyfriend had threatened to attack him, he grows angry, worried about his looks for an audition two days from now. He starts to leave, but she refuses to go. She has looked forward too long to this night and wants a romantic interlude. Angrily he kisses her, and she slaps him, hitting his wound. He tries to dispel her awe of his being a sometime professional actor. He, too, had wanted the night to fulfill a dream and apologizes for what has happened. She has thought his seven letters and a small gift were great, but it is his considering her closer to his image of Juliet than any girl he had ever met that matters most. He recalls that she had responded to his acting as standing for "all the beauty in the world." In this moment of confession, she asks him to kiss her. He does, then remembers being over seven years her senior. She says she is ready for her first affair, with him. He talks her out of taking that step now, but they both admit love for the other.

Comment

This sentimental story of dreams about first love should have wide appeal. A bare or nearly-bare stage suffices. Costumes pose few problems: prom outfits are called for. Music and lighting are vital production elements. Aside from a few expletives, the script suits most high school guidelines. The content suits college level, also, because the male is in his mid-twenties.

1m1f, comedy

Themes: young love and acting

Shrew You; or, Who Hath Need of Men? As Goode Accounte As Anye Knowne Describing How Sweet Shagsper Shuffles Off His Mortal Coil

by Lewis W. Heniford

Dramatis Personae

Tentative Cast

Madame Mnemosyne, a lively female, 2500-plus years old,
mother of nine muses [f], _____

Wm(ina) Shagsper, 52 years old, a near-female dead author [m or f], _____

Petruchio, 21 and 45 years old, a suitor then a husband [m], _____

Katharine, 17 and 41 years old, a shrew then a wife [f], _____

Place: An anteroom to afterlife.
Time: April 23, 1616 anno Domini

Available from Wordsss.

Plot

Newly dead, Shagsper arrives at the wrong spiritual processing room. He learns from Madame Mnemosyne, the attendant, that in this experimental afterlife Zeus has all beings remain or become female. Shagsper abhors losing his manhood, even in death. The attendant refers him to Zeus but warns that he must have a good case for any request. To frame a solid case, Shagsper calls up his lovers from *The Taming of the Shrew*. Petruchio embodies manhood, and certainly Katharine needs him, as the play goes. The two, though somewhat older now, reenact their famous meeting scene. Madame Mnemosyne records it with a crystal ball, and Shagsper is armed with evidence that men are necessary. He thanks the audience for its attention and departs to plead his case.

Comment

This script, using the style of James M. Barrie's stage directions, talks as much to the actors as to the audience; much of the fun is in the stage directions. Shakespeariana, especially apocryphal tales of his death, and Greek ideas of afterlife here require comic perspective. The scenery is minimal, suggestive of both an ancient scriptorium suitable for a personnel processing room and a room in Baptista's house, Padua, 1592, from Act II, Scene i, *The Taming of the Shrew*, by William Shakespeare. Many props are vital to the comedy. Mnemosyne must have minimal tap-dancing skills. Actors must speak comfortably the frequent iambic pentameter.

2m2f, fantasy-comedy

Themes: Greek afterlife and Shakespeare

Sing to Me Through Open Windows

by Arthur Kopit

Dramatis Personae

Tentative Cast

Andrew, The Boy [m], _____
Ottoman, The Man [m], _____
The Clown [m], _____

Place: A bare stage, surrounded by drapes.
Time: Morning or afternoon, spring or winter.

Available from Samuel French, Inc.

Plot

Andrew, The Boy, recalls five years ago, when he met The Man and The Clown. The Man, Ottoman, was arising from bed, and The Clown, Loveless, was arranging the room. The Man and The Clown differ over having the windows open. The Clown announces that Andrew has arrived. The Man at first does not register the name; but, when he does, he reacts with alarm and confusion. The Man asks The Clown to find some other costume for tomorrow and narcissistically studies himself in the mirror. The Boy arrives. Andrew and Ottoman talk casually about weather, The Boy's growth; then they remark on five years ago, when Andrew first arrived, lost and frightened. Andrew, ready for high school, attempts to tell Ottoman something, calling him Mr. Jud, but their ritual of magic sidetracks him. Ottoman stages a show with a dead rabbit. The Clown, returning uninvited, joins the show for Andrew, who ignores the sometime-brutal tension between the adults in their performance. Andrew waylays the memory, talks of his younger self in third person. He knows that these men meant something special to him long ago—when his parents were a disappointment to him. Now he is ready to part, saying, "I love you, Mr. Jud, I love you." Andrew leaves. The men argue over whether Andrew has left forever. Ottoman, saying all is over for him, slumps, his eyes closing. The Clown places the body in the magic trunk. The Boy steps from the shadows, watches this event and its fading. He leaves unhurriedly.

Comment

Kopit's plays, dramatic and musical, have appeared on Broadway. A characteristic is mystery: some matters are unclear, some clear matters are not what they seem. Here is a memory play, from Andrew's perspective. The five-year anniversary alluded to may be a key, as it brought Andrew into the lives of the other men and their relationship to each other shifted at that time. The tension and mutual need between the men must be inferred from character analysis; the script has many obscure directions touching this. Companies must have considerable talent and production capacity to stage this show.

3m, drama

Themes: coming-of-age, magic, and dominance

Something Unspoken

by Tennessee Williams

Dramatis Personae

Tentative Cast

Miss Cornelia Scott, 60, imperious [f], _____

Miss Grace Lancaster, 40-45, dependent [f], _____

Place: Miss Scott's breakfast area in her ornate home, Meridian, Mississippi.
Time: Morning, November sixth.

Available from Dramatists Play Service.

Plot

Cornelia is on the phone, pretending to be her own secretary, trying to contact Esmeralda Hawkins at the annual election meeting of the Confederate Daughters. Grace, having overslept, enters in her dressing gown. A "mysterious tension, an atmosphere of something unspoken" marks their relationship. Cornelia, having already opened the mail, one of Grace's tasks, and having already checked items to order from the Gramophone Shoppe in Atlanta, usually a shared activity, focuses on telephoning Esmeralda, her contact at the meeting where Cornelia, though absent, wants to be chosen Regent of the Confederate Daughters by acclamation. Cornelia directs Esmeralda's political maneuvers and asks for regular progress reports. Between calls, she celebrates the fifteenth anniversary of Grace's arrival. After Grace's husband had

died, Cornelia invited her to move in as secretary-companion. After all this time, Cornelia wants to remove the persistent, impenetrable wall that separates them. Grace eludes her directness and maintains the wall between them, the separation by something unspoken. Cornelia learns by telephone that the best offer Esmeralda can arrange is the Vice-Regency. Cornelia adamantly rejects that inferior office, explaining that she has other commitments for her time and must resign from the local chapter of the Confederate Daughters. She directs Grace to start the letter of resignation. Grace displays a momentary "slight, equivocal smile," one that is "not quite malicious but not really sympathetic." Then she exclaims over a gift from Cornelia, "What lovely roses! One for every year!"

Comment

Williams, throughout his career, used one-act plays to sketch prototypes of subsequently-famous characters in his full-lengths. Adumbrations of Blanche (*A Streetcar Named Desire*) and Sebastian's mother (*Suddenly Last Summer*) are evident here. He treats homosexuality here to the extent that his time and place allowed; the tentative approach in this treat-

ment has been outdistanced by him and other playwrights, but the play presents a tension pitting sexual forthrightness against indirection that is yet viable. Productions needs are extremely simple except for the few suggestions of era. The script adapts to television easily and offers a good choice for actors and crew to try television production.

2f, drama

Theme: homosexuality and dominance

Soul Gone Home

by Langston Hughes

Dramatis Personae

Tentative Cast

The Mother, middle-aged [f], _____

The Son, Ronnie Bailey, 16 [m], _____

First Man in White Coa [m], _____

Second Man in White Coat [m], _____

Place: A tenement room, third floor, apartment five.
Time: Night.

Available from Harold Ober Associates.

Plot

In the middle of a bare, ugly, dirty tenement room lies the body of a Negro youth, hands folded across his chest, pennies on his eyes—"a soul gone home." His mother kneels beside the cot weeping and loudly simulating grief. He speaks, casts the coins across the room, sits up in bed, and challenges her. He says that she has been a bad mother. He lacked proper food, grew up in the street, and had to sell newspapers as soon as he could walk. She claims that she often lacked money for food, that he was sickly, unable to earn his way. She says his unwanted birth and burdensome childhood have been a big worry; now that he has grown to an age to be of some use to her, he has died, and not properly died, either. She persuades him to die again, this time properly. As two men in the white coats of city health employees come to claim the body, the mother weeps hysterically. After they take her son, the mother dresses for a night of whoring, promising to buy some flowers for her no-good son.

Comment

Langston Hughes, a major American black poet, offers an achingly funny, brief satirical allegory. Aspiring directors have a wide range of possible interpretations. Helpful stage directions give many hints of the author's intent.

3m1f, comedy

Themes: dysfunctional family and survivability

Spared

by Israel Horovitz

Dramatis Persona

Tentative Cast

Man, ancient [m], _____

Voices_____

Place: Outdoors; near Lake Quannapowitt; Wakefield, Massachusetts.
Time: The present. [Note: Premiered March, 1974.]

Available from Dramatists Play Service, Inc.

Plot

The Man, having failed in over sixty suicide attempts, chronologically recounts his life. Remembered aspects, presented as separate selves of the Man, laugh, scream, and comment, "Poor child." The Man explains life, focusing on ages five, fifteen, nineteen, twenty-two, thirty-two, thirty-three, thirty-four, thirty-six, forty, forty-three, fifty-six, sixty-one, sixty-two, sixty-four, and now sixty-eight. His other selves comment antiphonally; they "work as warring contraries." Unable to recall securely his own life's events, he does know that he asked his mother to kiss him and hold him gently. Her smiling response, "Poor child," has characterized his whole life and suicidal adventures. Still, the Man must live because he has always been spared.

Comment

This challenging script evolved from performances during 1973-1976 in several locales. An appended note details the author's desires about vocal interpretation, lighting, sound, and set. Four distinct voices, spoken and recorded, must be achieved by the actor. Lighting requires only two spotlights. Sound requires six loudspeakers, used alone or together. The set requires a chair on a high platform, with escape stairs at rear. The author specifies that the play be performed without intermission.

1m (+voices), drama

Themes: meaning of life and guilt

Spittin' Image

by Stephen Metcalfe

Dramatis Personae

Tentative Cast

Bucky, a youth of college age [m], _____

Megs, about ten years older [m], _____

Place: A university dormitory room.
Time: November, 1974.

Available from Samuel French, Inc.

Plot

Bucky wakens at his desk to Megs' loud knocking on the door. He has been cramming for exams, and Megs poses a decided interruption. Bucky tries to end the visit quickly, but Megs will have none of that. With his truck, Bertha, parked outside, Megs wants to stretch a bit and catch up on his buddy's life. Bucky briefly gives in to the onslaught. Then he insists that he needs to study. Megs offers him a pill to stay awake. In pleading for conversation, Megs accidentally calls Bucky *Bobby*, shocking him. He crumples pages on Bucky's desk then apologizes. Bucky cannot get his unwanted guest to leave, and the guest starts acting more and more erratic. Bucky discloses that he is failing, needs to study; still Megs lingers, once nearly falling asleep. Megs ignores the increasingly strong demand that he leave. He notes the clear likeness of Bucky to the youth's older brother, Bobby. But Bucky relates how hard it is to live up to expectations that he be another Bobby. Bobby wrote a letter to his younger brother from Vietnam and let Megs copy it. Megs talks Bucky into reading it aloud. Bucky asks if Megs has any friends, and Megs sidesteps the question by recounting his flashbacks to the war. Bucky agrees that he and Megs will do "buddy things" sometime, that he will try to take over some of Bobby's role in Megs' life. Bobby finally gets Megs to leave but relents, asks Megs to stay, drops his effort to study, and asks Megs to take him for a ride in Bertha.

Comment

The audience for this heart-wrenching study must accept barracks language. The foul language suits so totally Megs' character that euphemisms cannot be substituted without loss of dramatic impact. Both roles challenge. Even in the 1990s, the agony of Vietnam comes through. The tightly written script poses few other production problems.

2m, comedy

Themes: war and friendship

The Stronger

by August Strindberg

Dramatis Personae

Tentative Cast

Miss Y. [Amelia/Millie], an actress, unmarried [f] _____

Mrs. X., an actress, married [f] _____

Place: A corner of a ladies' restaurant, Sweden.
Time: Christmas Eve, 1889.

Available from Samuel French, Inc. [#14166]

Plot

Miss Y. sits at her table with a partly emptied bottle of beer and reads illustrated weeklies. Mrs. X. arrives in hat and winter coat with a Japanese basket. In monologue, she targets Miss Y. Mrs. X. feels sorry for anyone reading in a restaurant on Christmas Eve. She has been shopping and shows a doll for her Lisa and a cork pistol for her Carl. Her shooting the pistol at Miss Y. occasions mention of their rivalry at the Royal Theatre, which Miss Y. had to leave. Mrs. X. displays tulip-embroidered slippers for her husband, Bob. She is confused when Miss Y. laughs at her bragging about having such a fine, faithful husband, although, she says, ". . . All women seem to be crazy after my husband." Mrs. X. even toys with jealousy against Miss Y. but, instead, invites her to spend the evening with her and Bob, to end the unpleasantness among the three, particularly end the unfriendliness between the other two. Then she realizes the unfriendliness has been masking intimacy between Miss Y. and Bob. Mrs. X. moves in disgust to an adjoining table but cannot resist continuing the attack. She reveals what a dominance Miss Y. has had in her marriage and declares her hatred of her. She regards Miss Y. as a failed actress and person. She brags, "Perhaps, after all, I am the stronger now," and cites the silence of Miss Y. as evidence. She thanks Miss Y. for having taught her how to dominate and leaves for home—and her husband.

Comment

The paradox of this famous playlet is that Miss Y., the silent woman, is the titular character: the stronger. A theatre axiom is that one can determine the quality of the acting by watching an actor silently reacting; this one-act is a wonderful test for a performer. The Waitress rarely receives mention in *dramatis personae* for this play, so Strindberg must have disregarded the role as psychologically non-functionary. Staging needs, except for period costumes and props, are few.

2f, drama

Themes: Christmas and dominance

Suburban Tragedy

by Jerome Kass

Dramatis Personae

Tentative Cast

Mr. Stein [m], _____

Mrs. Goldman [f], _____

Place: A college classroom outside New York City.
Time: Evening, the present. [Note: Copyright 1966.]

Available from Dramatists Play Service.

Plot

Mr. Stein, a young teacher, reminds Mrs. Goldman, an attractive middle-aged lady, that the time allotted for the exam is over. She is counting words to be sure she has written the five hundred assigned for the essay. He explains the word count was merely a guideline and tells her that having had her as a student has been a pleasure. When she asks, he confirms he is leaving to teach at another college. She recounts how having him as a teacher has eased her attempting classes at this point in her life. He reassures her that she contributed well to his class and should continue to do well. She brings up Jewishness as a shared experience. They both miss New York City. She describes the marriageable qualities of her twenty-four-year-old daughter and shows a photograph. She is taken aback when he reveals that he married at nineteen and more so when he mentions an older wife and three children. She pries into his life, wondering if he is happily married. He admits having rushed into marriage to appease his dying mother and starts to leave. She stops him with an invitation to her house for "just" an hour. She really wants him to accept her proposition, has even dreamed about him. She is planning to leave her husband after marrying off her daughter and to return to New York City. He gently rejects her offer. "Oh, that's too bad. That's too bad," she says, shakes her head and leaves sadly.

Comment

The situation of two disparate, frustrated people finding brief common ground resonates fairly universally. In a beautiful interlude, the housewife who wants more out of life reaches out in desperation to an improbable lover and has to accept his gentle rejection. Estelle Parsons originated the role at Stage 73, in New York City, March 5, 1966; John Karlen played the teacher. This show has simple requirements for set, props, lights, and sound.

1m1f, drama

Themes: infidelity, Jewishness, loneliness, and May-December romance

Suppressed Desires

by Susan Glaspell

Dramatis Personae

Tentative Cast

Henrietta Brewster [f], _____

Stephen Brewster [m], _____

Mabel [f], _____

Place: An upstairs studio apartment, Washington Square South,
with a view of Washington Arch.
Time: The present. [Note: Copyright 1951.]

Available from Baker's Plays.

Plot

Stephen reacts poorly to the coffee Henrietta has served him. She asserts that his dejection has a deeper cause than coffee: he will not accept psychoanalysis. She figures he is suffering from suppressed desire. Mabel, happy and normal, beginning a stay with them, joins the table. Henrietta frets over her sister's not eating breakfast. Then Henrietta insists on interpreting Mabel's dream about being a hen, declaring it as a call for Mabel to get a divorce. Mabel, resisting the idea, arguing against it, accidentally breaks a plate and confuses names. Henrietta urgently wants to take her sister to a famous psychiatrist. Stephen slips out to see that doctor without telling his wife. Henrietta leaves a recommended book on psychoanalysis for Mabel to read. When Mabel carelessly drops the book, she begins to wonder if all of her acts do suggest an underlying unhappiness. Two weeks later, Henrietta reports to Stephen her delight about having Mabel in the care of the famous doctor. Stephen reveals his own visit to the psychiatrist, who has proclaimed that Stephen must get free of marriage to find real happiness. When Mabel reports that the psychiatrist has exposed Mabel's suppressed desire for Stephen, Henrietta deserts her own blind faith in the famous doctor as well as in psychiatry and insists that her sister and husband do the same.

Comment

This play lampoons the growing influence of psychiatry in America in the early 1920s. In two scenes, it runs rather long, but the tightness of the plot keeps the comedic aspects afloat. The apartment requires a breakfast area for Scene 1 and an office area with drafting equipment for Scene 2. Period costume would easily establish era. However, placing the show in the present still works in the 1990s, as the comedy holds up well.

1m2f, comedy

Themes: psychiatry and marriage

That's All

by Harold Pinter

Dramatis Personae

Tentative Cast

Mrs. A. [f], _____
Mrs. B. [f], _____

Place: A conversational site.
Time: A conversational moment.

Available from Samuel French, Inc. [#14166]

Plot

Mrs. A. entertains Mrs. B. She explains that she always puts the kettle on at a certain time. Then, regularly on Thursdays, a mutual acquaintance comes around. The tea used to be on Wednesdays, but the acquaintance, after she moved away from around the corner, changed the meeting time to Thursdays: she could not find a butcher in her new neighborhood. The acquaintance had decided to stick to her own butcher and come down on Thursdays. On one of those trips, Mrs. A. met her at the butcher's. Mrs. A., who always shops at the butcher's on Fridays, had just happened in there for a bit of meat, just by chance, on that Thursday. At that time, Mrs. A. learned of the acquaintance's weekly returns to the neighborhood. The acquaintance had explained that she came in that day to get meat for the weekend; it would last her until Monday. She could serve fish Monday through Thursday; she could always serve cold meat if a change were needed. So, there and then, Mrs. A. invited her to come in after the visit to the butcher. The acquaintance had done just that. Mrs. A. thinks the Thursday visits a bit odd, because it changed the Wednesday tradition of their teatime. The acquaintance still comes in from time to time. She does not come in so much. That's all.

Comment

This brief sketch reflects Pinter's fascination with conversational language. He specifies no time or place. He specifies fifteen pauses and one long pause—no other stage directions. The challenge in Pinter's plays is finding the subtext, so actors not interested in character analysis for subtext should not attempt this sketch. The stagers have free rein; less is more might be a useful guideline.

Thursday Is My Day for Cleaning

by Jordan Crittenden

Dramatis Persona

Tentative Cast

Mrs. Louise McFadden, 33 [f] _____

Place: An empty living room, 6181 Glen Hollow Drive.
Time: Thursday morning.

Available from Samuel French, Inc.

Plot

Following the sound of a gunshot, Louise enters the living room carrying a pistol. She controls herself enough to telephone the police. The desk clerk insists on a long list of personal details in establishing her identification. A knock at the door and a note through the brass mail slot draw her from the telephone. She tries to return to the telephone conversation, but more knocking interrupts. She drifts into an exchange of notes through the slot until an origami-swan note comes through. The correspondent cannot speak, but she regales him with details of her childhood through the slot. She goes into her adult relationships (particularly Douglas) and their drawbacks. Then she married John but never told him of Douglas. Another note hurts her feelings, and she tries to return the swan. It goes out, it goes in, through the slot several times until she points the gun through the slot and fires. With no trace of the distraught state just moments ago, she recounts to "hon" on the other end of the line the troublesome vacuum cleaner's being given to nightmares. Even as she is talking, the telephone rings, again and again. She rips the receiver cord from the base of the telephone to stop the ringing and continues her conversation into the mouthpiece, looking forlorn and defeated.

Comment

Production problems are few. The door and slot are critical. The origami swan must be reproduced for each performance, as the violent shoving destroys it. Audiences react variously to gunshots, so a notice in the program or an announcement before the show would be a wise gesture. A sound track elaborating Louise's mental state might be highly contributive. This show easily wins audience interest and approval. It could serve production groups as early as junior high school. There is no pretense to literary quality, but it is a great romp for an actress.

1f, comedy   *Themes:* communication and surrealism

To Burn a Witch

by James L. Bray

Dramatis Personae

Tentative Cast

Ruth Hanna Smith, a pretty, zestful young girl [f], _____

Mary Abigail Gentry, an attractive, serene young girl [f], _____

Dame Stanley, older woman [f], _____

Place: A cell-like room, Salem, Massachusetts.
Time: May 14, 1683.

Available from The Dramatic Publishing Company.

Plot

Mary has been confined for nine days, Ruth one week, to make them confess to witchcraft. As Ruth nears the breaking point, Mary remains steadfast to her claim of innocence and her faith in God's protection. Mary tries to comfort her longtime friend. Ruth lacks such faith and rejects counsel that life is but a preparation for afterlife. At this moment, Dame Stanley, accompanied by Widow Jones, comes to read a proclamation from the community. It charges the two with Satanic events. A fire is being readied for them unless they confess and repent. Ruth accedes to the demand; Mary cannot confess. Dame Stanley challenges Ruth to prove repentance by persuading Mary to confess. The older women leave to give Ruth time. Her pleadings to Mary fail, so Ruth resorts to threats. She will pretend a seizure and convince the women that Mary alone is a witch. Mary resists, placing no blame. Ruth calls the women and tells them Satanic events have occurred that prove Mary to be a witch. When they hesitate to believe her, Ruth feigns a seizure and convinces them, saving herself and condemning Mary to the fire. Mary, not even allowed time to pray, will yet pray as they walk forth. Dame Stanley says, "You see, witch, today you lose everything." Mary answers, "No, Dame Stanley, today I gain everything."

Comment

A sensitive psychological portrayal of the falsely accused, this play sounds cries from early American history that have echoed in modern times, specifically in the early 1950s. Many high schools study *The Crucible,* by Arthur Miller; this popular short script presents in brief some of the conflict in Miller's famous full-length play. Staging is simple, with emphasis on costumes and lighting.

4f, drama

Themes: witchcraft and martyrdom

Tongues

by Sam Shepard and Joseph Chaikin

Dramatis Personae

Tentative Cast

Speaker [m], _____

Percussionist [non-speaking m], _____

Place: A bare stage.
Time: Real time.

Available from Samuel French, Inc.

Plot

The performer describes someone of varied human dimensions, a person who is part of other people and of nature. Tonight, the person hears a new voice. It tells him he is isolated. He mourns his state, dies, and leaves his body. He considers the mundane aspects of his human existence, and varied voices speak through him of their lives. Voices come singly then in a duologue about hunger. Hunger grows into an amorphous foe. Voices cry the preciousness of now. But the moment speeds past. The person wonders about his state of death. To music from the Glenn Miller era, the person sings about "from this moment on." Then he turns to correspondence, studying complimentary closes of letters. In other voices, he tries to communicate. In a concluding litany, he explains "when you die." This shifts into an upbeat extolling of nature and people. The person can hear, feel, and learn: "Tonight I'm learning its language."

Comment

The plot description focuses on the speaker. Of equal importance is the percussionist. The playwright says, "Actors wishing to perform this piece would necessarily have to develop their own means and experiment according to their given situation. The various voices are not so much intended to be caricatures as they are attitudes or impulses . . . ." He adds, "The choices of instrumentation can be very open, but I feel they should stay within the realm of percussion." The production company must find the right audience for this piece; it is not for everyone. Still, the challenges are intriguing. Dauntless artists can delight in this piece.

1m (+percussionist), piece for voice and percussion

Theme: voices and perception

```
• • • • • • • • • • • • • • • • • • • • • • • • • • • • • • • • • • • • • • • •
•                                                                            •
•                    A Trap Is a Small Place                                •
•                                                                            •
•                          by Marjean Perry                                 •
•                                                                            •
•                          Dramatis Personae                                •
•                                                               Tentative Cast
•   Stella, about 30 [f], _____       •
•   Mrs. Asher, about 25 [f], _____       •
•   Jessica, about 29 [f], _____       •
•   Andrew Middleton, 36 [m], _____      •
•                                                                            •
•              Place: A small apartment in New York City.                    •
•           Time: About two o'clock on a rainy day in November.             •
•                                                                            •
•                 Available from Margaret Mayorga Play.                      •
•                                                                            •
• • • • • • • • • • • • • • • • • • • • • • • • • • • • • • • • • • • • • • • •
```

Plot

In a fastidiously neat, cramped living room and dinette apartment, Stella prepares a festive dining table then hides it behind a screen. A young housewife neighbor, nosy and obtuse, comes to recruit a baby-sitter. Stella says that Jess cannot oblige as they are having a tenth anniversary celebration of meeting—a surprise for Jess. Jess arrives home and urges Mrs. Asher to stay and chat. Stella urges her departure. Jess is tired, and Stella pampers her. At Stella's prompting, they reminisce about their first meeting. Stella wants more of Jess' time and attention, resenting Andrew, Jess' beau. Stella presents roses, wine, and cake, forging ahead with the celebration, trying to break through Jess' lassitude. Jess, having recently received her third annual proposal from Andrew, bemoans her pointless existence and wishes he would give her the attention he gives his mother. Stella wants them to declare a new mutual commitment by leaving now to shop for a better place to live outside the city. As they are getting ready to go, Stella's pressure causes Jess to rebel, to assert her independence. Just then, Andy arrives and Jess tries to get him to take her out. However, he has news to tell her that will not wait. Although his boss has finally given him the needed promotion that would allow him to marry, it entails a move to another state. He and his mother are moving, and he says he will write Jess. She presents him with a now-or-never choice for their relationship. He explains that he has promised this as a special trip to his mother, that Jess would be out of place. He evades Jess' ultimatum, promises to write, and leaves. Jess retreats to the bathroom. Stella dons a dressing gown, refills the glasses with wine. When Jess returns, Stella resumes their party by offering a glass. Jess, still dumbstruck, takes the glass.

Comment

Despite the exposition's being uninspired, the supporting characters' being strictly two-dimensional, and the themes' being almost cliché, the playwright manages to imbue the conflict with shading, subtlety, and laudable verisimilitude. Stella, an interesting antiheroine, adroitly manipulates Jessica, who easily gains audience sympathy. The well-knit script skillfully uses adumbration, irony, symbolism, and understatement. The roles of Stella and Jess are challenges worth meeting.

1m3f, drama

Themes: homosexuality, personal disorientation

The Twelve-Pound Look

by James M. Barrie

Dramatis Personae

Tentative Cast

Sir Harry, on the verge of knighthood [m], _____

Lady Sims, his wife [f], _____

Butler [m], _____

Kate, a typist [f], _____

Place: A drawing room in London.
Time: Late morning. [Note: First production date, 1910.]

Available from Baker's Plays and Samuel French, Inc.

Plot

Harry Sims has enlisted his wife to practice his being knighted, which is scheduled to occur come Thursday. She timidly strives to accommodate his vanity. Into this satisfying scene comes the butler to announce the arrival of Kate, a typist, who will handle the flood of forthcoming congratulations with tactful notes of appreciation. The women get along well. Sir Harry, though, reacts strongly to the typist and dismisses his wife. Left to themselves, Sir Harry and Kate allude to their past as man and wife and their surprise at this first meeting since she deserted him. He wants her to envy his present wife and two sons as symbols of all she forfeited. Kate's self-confidence increases his discomfort. They agree to trade confidences, however. He will recount finding her farewell letter, and she will disclose the name of the man who enticed her away. He tells of the humiliating moment he and his friends found her letter; he even lets her retrieve as a keepsake her letter. Hesitant, she keeps her bargain: she reveals that there was no other man. She had implied another man only to salve his injury. She recalls the emptiness of their life together. She determined to find a way to support herself and break free. She bought a typewriter, taught herself to use it, and started earning money with it. When she had earned a sum equivalent to the cost of the typewriter, twelve pounds, she had the confidence to go. Having had her say, she urges him to be kind to his present wife, to watch out for any twelve-pound look in her eyes. Just then, his wife brings his sword to give him a chance to show it off. Again the women get along well, to his displeasure. Kate leaves with a possibly impertinent curtsy. Lady Sims speaks of her almost with envy and asks if typewriters are very expensive.

Comment

The twelve-pound look symbolizes emancipation of women. Barrie's famous short play espouses a feminism ahead of its time. The stage directions reflect his style as a novelist and supply some of the script's chief delights, reflecting a penchant for and skill with insightful, clever details. Plentiful character nuances allow actors to build really three-dimensional portrayals. The stage directions greatly entertain the production company, but, alas, the audience lacks access to them and remains unaware of their existence. For proper effect, the production's style needs period acting, costumes, properties, and set.

2m2f, comedy

Themes: feminism and dysfunctional family

12:21 P.M.

by F. J. Hartland

Dramatis Personae

Tentative Cast

Kevin, Joel's best friend [m], _____

Joel, the bridegroom [m], _____

Janet, Joel's sister [f], _____

Place: Kevin's very sloppy studio apartment.
Time: Early afternoon. [May, 1985]

Available from Samuel French, Inc.

Plot

Kevin, in jeans and a grubby sweatshirt, sleeps at the kitchen table, surrounded by empty liquor bottles. Joel arrives at 12:21 to collect his best man for a 12:30 wedding. While Joel gathers the right clothing, Kevin sneaks drinks. As Joel attempts to dress him, Kevin wants to reminisce about how they met and became best friends. Janet, sister of the bridegroom, comes by to hurry everything; two hundred and thirty-three guests are waiting at St. Agnes Cathedral. Janet raves about Kevin's irresponsibility and incompetency, claiming to have given fair warning, to which no one listened. Joel negotiates twenty minutes from her, and she leaves to wait outside. Kevin suffers remorse and has a crying jag. He again reminisces, about a week's vacation at the shore. He brings out a photograph of them both he wants to share. Kevin fears that their relationship will be different after the wedding.

He brings up the company softball tournament they won— through Kevin's incompetence and Joel's skill. Joel gets sucked into a reenactment of the winning run. When Joel again focuses on getting his best man ready, going to bring some coffee, Kevin removes all his clothes for the wedding and resumes drinking. He cries and attempts an apology, overcome at losing his best friend. Janet's return interrupts their uncomfortable embrace. Joel stalls for time and makes a last effort to persuade Kevin to come along, despite Janet's haranguing. When Janet says she is leaving and taking Joel's transportation to the wedding, Joel demands the rings from Kevin, saying he can never forgive this disappointment. Joel storms out, followed by his sister. Kevin looks in the mirror, tries to drink, and cannot. He collapses into tears, crying, "I'm sorry, Joel. I'm really sorry."

Comment

This show opened at the Quaigh Theatre and later appeared in the tenth Annual Off-Off-Broadway Original Short Play Festival, sponsored by Double Image Theatre, New York City, in May, 1985. It has drive, energy, and currency, with elements of farce, character comedy, and serious drama. Audience appeal is strong. Production requirements are fairly simple. School and community theatre groups would do well to consider it.

2m1f, farce

Themes: alcoholism, friendship, and marriage

Vanities, Act 1

by Jack Heifner

Dramatis Personae

Tentative Cast

Joanne [f], _____

Kathy [f], _____

Mary [f], _____

Place: A high school gymnasium.
Time: Fall, 1963.

Available from Samuel French, Inc.

Plot

Three cheerleaders are practicing their yells. They argue over their failure in a particular routine. Perhaps the band is to blame, they think. The crowd, too, is at fault for not supporting them. They consider banning anyone who doesn't cheer properly. Arguing over getting someone to do the invocation, they drift back into blaming the crowd and the band, particularly its girl members and majorettes. One of the majorettes, Sarah, has an especially dubious reputation. They consider how to react when a boyfriend's hands wander. When Mary discloses that Kathy's Gary has been dating Sarah, Kathy has to confess she (not Sarah!) and Gary were the couple showing so much passion at the drive-in. They refocus on another job, deciding the theme for the football dance. When they decide and assign themselves the best tasks, they plot how to get one of the three elected Football Queen by the team. They vow to go to college together and protect each other socially. They may even become cheerleaders there; they agree on that even if they cannot decide on their subject majors. On this Friday, November twenty-second, their rally preparations are interrupted by the intercom's announcement that the president has been shot. The dismissal of classes for the rest of the day will spoil the pep rally; however, the three rejoice that the football game will take place as planned in the evening.

Comment

This first scene of *Vanities* works well as a one-act play, which justifies its inclusion here; perhaps, too, the cast will be inspired to go ahead and stage the full three scenes. Only the first scene, though, suits most high school theatre groups; the other two are adult in subject matter. To the point here, there is enough satire in this scene to impart a sharp message. The first scene needs only a bare stage, cheerleading costumes from 1963, few props.

3f, comedy

Themes: assassination and popularity

Volver a decir el mar / I Speak Again of the Sea

por/by Sergio Peregrina

Dramatis Persona

Tentative Cast

Muchacho/Youth, *como de 16 o 17 años*
/about 17 or 17 years old [m] _____

Escenario/Place: *Una pequeña capilla*/A small chapel.
Epoca/Time: *A las nueve de la noche*/9:00 p.m.
[Note: First performed in March, 1974.]

Available from Organización Editorial Novaro, S.A.

Trama/Plot

Organ music, slow and low, fills a small chapel that has a Virgin, flowers, and an occupied confessional, near which sits the Muchacho. He speaks as if to Juanita, his beloved. He berates her for her grief and guilt. He cries, as he knows she is crying, but he tries to stop his and her tears. Times past were better, he remembers. Neither he nor she is to blame for the present. He considers how their friends react to their problem. Perhaps with his thirty pesos, they can survive. Above all, he seeks calm. A beach would give him that. He focuses on the Virgin for a time, then says they must leave on their journey.

Comentario/Comment

The actor undertaking this role must play a range of emotions, as the essence of the piece is quick crosscurrents of emotions. He verges on heartbreak, seeing the contrast of his and Juanita's unspecified dilemma with the honeymoon-like situation he recalls. The mood is quintessentially Mexican: "*Volver a decir lo que no puedo cantar sin el corazón partir*/I speak again of what I am unable to sing without the heart breaking." The ambience must reveal that.

1m, drama

Themes: meaning of life and programmed guilt

Part 5 | *SOURCE DIRECTORY FOR SCRIPTS*

This section clarifies the source abbreviations used throughout this guide to identify publishers as well as other agencies from which scripts and production rights might be obtained.

The information appears in (a) a list of keys for plays cited in the guide and in (b) a list of addresses with annotations.

Most sources cited can lead the reader to scripts and/or production rights. As the publishing industry is in constant flux, some companies and catalogs are ephemeral. This guide cannot always name the current source of scripts and current production rights for a given work; however, it strives to furnish substantive leads in the search, even listing alternate addresses.

A. Source Keys for Plays Cited in This Guide

ACP	=	Art Craft Publishing Company
AFA	=	Ashley-Famous Agency, Inc.
ANC	=	Anchor Books
AND	=	Andre Deutsch, Ltd.
ANT	=	Antæus [Ecco Press]
APP	=	Arte Público Press
AR	=	At Rise
ATB	=	Applause Theatre Book Publishers
BMC	=	Bobbs-Merrill Company, Inc.
BNA	=	Bohan-Neuwald Agency, Inc.
BP	=	Baker's Plays
BPP	=	Broadway Play Publishing, Inc.
BSF	=	Brown, Son & Ferguson, Ltd.
CBC	=	Chilton Book Company
CC	=	The Century Company
CPP	=	The Currency Press Pty., Ltd.
CSS	=	Charles Scribner's Sons
DAC	=	D. Appleton-Century Company
DC	=	Doubleday & Company, Inc.
DP	=	Dover Publications Inc.
DPC	=	The Dramatic Publishing Company
DPS	=	Dramatists Play Service
EPC	=	Eldridge Publishing Company
FCE	=	Fondo de Cultura Económica
FDG	=	The Foundation of the Dramatists Guild, Inc.
FF	=	Faber & Faber, Ltd.
FH	=	Fifth House
FSG	=	Farrar, Straus and Giroux
GAU	=	George Allen & Unwin, Ltd.
GB	=	Georges Borchardt
GBC	=	Globe Book Company
GCB	=	Garden City Books
GP	=	Grove Press
GPC	=	Greenberg Publishing Company
HDB	=	Hillgers Deutsche Bucherei
HDS	=	Hansen Drama Shop
HMC	=	Harold Matson Co., Inc.
HOA	=	Harold Ober Associates
HP	=	Hanbury Plays
HPC	=	Heuer Publishing Company
HR	=	Harper & Row
HW	=	Hill and Wang
ICM	=	International Creative Management
IEC	=	I. E. Clark, Inc.
IPC	=	International Play Co., Inc.
ISA	=	Incorporated Society of Authors
IUP	=	Indiana University Press
JAT	=	Judith Anderson Theatre
KV	=	Kosel-Verlag
LD	=	League of Dramatists
LLA	=	Lantz-Donadio Literary Agency
MAC	=	Macmillan Publishing Co., Inc.

MMP = Margaret Mayorga Play
MPL = Meriwether Publishing Ltd.
MR   = Margaret Ramsay, Ltd.
MVH = Mitteldeutscher Verlag Halle
NAL = New American Library
NCE = National Christian Education Council
NDP = New Directions Publishing Corporation
NPN = New Playwrights Network
NSHS = North Salinas High School
NTK = Ninon Tallon Karlweis
OB   = Orchard Books
OEN = Organización Editorial Novaro, S.A.
PAL = Palmer Press
PCP = Playwrights Canada Press
PDS = Pioneer Drama Service, Inc.
PI   = Plays, Incorporated
PIR = Pace International Research
PLP = Playwrights Publishing Company
PPC = Performance Publishing Company
PPI = Players Press, Inc.
PPR = Playlab Press
PSP = Playwrights Press
PT   = Playbox Theatre
RP   = Riverrun Press
SF   = Samuel French, Inc.
SFC = Scott, Foresman, and Company
SKC = Stewart Kidd Company
SLA = Sterling Lord Agency
TCG = Theatre Communications Group
TIP = Teacher Ideas Press
TL   = Talonbooks, Ltd.
TPH = The Play House
TSD = T. S. Denison & Company, Inc.
TSP = Third Side Press
TWP = Third World Press
UM   = University of Minnesota Press
UWP = University of Wisconsin Press
WMA = William Morris Agency, Inc.
WO   = Wordsss
WW   = WordWorkers

B. Source Addresses

ACP: Art Craft Publishing Company, Box 1058, Cedar Rapids, IA 52406; telephone (319) 364-6311.

A catalog of nearly 150 scripts, only four of which use casts of four or fewer actors: "The Half Hour," a drama by Don Helland, 1m2f (also available from HPC); "Cradle Camp," a drama by Craig Sodaro, 1m3f; "Sidetracked," a drama by Carl Albert, 2m2f (also available from HPC); "Just Us Girls," a comedy by Gordon

Mauermann, 4f.

AFA: Ashley-Famous Agency, Inc., (no street address available) New York, NY; no telephone listed as of March, 1994.

ANC: Anchor Books, 666 5th Avenue, New York, NY 10103.

AND: Andre Deutsch, Ltd., 7-9 Pratt Street, London NW1 0AE, England.

ANT: Antæus [Ecco Press], 100 West Broad Street, Hopewell, NJ 08525.

APP: Arte Público Press, University of Houston, 4800 Calhoun, Houston, TX 77004; telephone (713) 749-4768.

AR: *At Rise [: A Magazine in Four Acts]*, 9838 Jersey Avenue, Santa Fe Springs, CA 90670; no telephone listed as of March, 1994.

Quarterly publication containing scripts available for production, such as "After a Thousand Victories," a drama by Arnold Powell, 1m1f, AR, NSHS.

ATB: Applause Theatre Book Publishers, 211 West 71st Street, New York, NY 10023; telephone (212) 595-4735; fax (212) 721-2856.

BMC: Bobbs-Merrill Company, Inc., now part of Macmillan Publishing Co., Inc., 866 Third Avenue, New York, NY 10022; telephone (212) 702-2000, (800) 257-5755.

BNA: Bohan-Neuwald Agency, Inc., 27 West 96th Street, New York, NY 10025; no telephone listed as of March, 1994.

BP: Baker's Plays, Walter H. Baker Company, 100 Chauncy Street, Boston, MA 02111; telephone (617) 482-1280; fax (617) 482-7613; Western Representative Samuel French, Inc.

A major source for scripts, its business focus is the East Coast of the United States. Its catalog duplicates many items with Samuel French, Inc. Recommended for reference collections.

BPP: Broadway Play Publishing, Inc., 357 West 20th Street, New York, NY 10011.

BSF: Brown, Son & Ferguson, Ltd., 4-10 Darnley Street, Glasgow G41 2SD, Scotland.

CBC: Chilton Book Company, 401 Walnut Street, Philadelphia, PA 19106; telephone (215) 964-4000, (800) 695-1214.

Yaakov and Greenfieldt's *Play Index 1988-1992* (see Bibliography hereinafter, p. 267) in its Directory of Publishers and Distributors puts the address as 1 Chilton Way, Radnor, PA, 19089-0230.

CC: The Century Company is not listed in *Books in Print 1990-91: Publishers*.

CPP: The Currency Press Pty., Ltd., 330 Oxford Street, P.O. Box 452, Paddington, New South Wales 2021, Australia.

CSS: Charles Scribner's Sons, under Macmillan Publishing Co., Inc., 866 Third Avenue, New York, NY 10022; telephone (212) 702-2000 or (800) 257-5755.

DAC: D. Appleton-Century Company, now under Prentice Hall, a Division of Simon & Schuster, Inc., 15 Columbus Circle, New York, NY 10023; telephone (212) 373-8500.

DC: Doubleday & Company, Inc., 666 5th Avenue, New York, NY 10103; telephone (212) 765-6500; (800) 223-6834.

DP: Dover Publications Inc., 180 Varick Street, New York, NY 10014; telephone (212) 255-3755, (800) 223-3130.

DPC: The Dramatic Publishing Company, 311 Washington Street, P.O. Box 129, Woodstock, IL 60098; telephone (815) 338-7170; fax (815) 338-8981.

> A major source for scripts of distinction. The play publishing house with the largest holdings. All libraries and producers of one-act plays should obtain and use this catalog.

DPS: Dramatists Play Service, 440 Park Avenue, South, New York, NY 10016; telephone (212) 683-8960; fax (212) 213-1539.

> A major source for scripts. All libraries and producers of one-act plays should obtain and use this catalog.

EPC: Eldridge Publishing Company, P.O. Box 1595, Venice, FL 34284; telephone (800) HI-STAGE; fax (800) 453-5179.

FCE: Fondo de Cultura Económica, Avenida de la Universidad, 975, México 12, D.F., México.

FDG: The Foundation of the Dramatists Guild, Inc., 234 West 44th Street, New York, NY 10036; telephone (212) 398-9366.

> *Young Playwrights Festival* contains scripts by playwrights between the ages of eight and eighteen. Any interested producer should address the playwright in care of The Foundation of the Dramatists Guild, Inc.

FF: Faber & Faber, Ltd., 3 Queen Square, London WC1N 3AU, England; also, 50 Cross Street, Winchester, MA 01890.

FH: Fifth House, 620 Duchess Street, Saskatoon, Saskatchewan, Canada, S7K 0R1.

FSG: Farrar, Straus and Giroux, Inc., 19 Union Square West, New York, NY 10003.

GAU: George Allen & Unwin, Ltd., 40 Museum Street, London W.C.1, England; no telephone listed in New York as of March, 1994.

GB: Georges Borchardt, 12 West 55th Street, New York, NY (no ZIP code available); telephone (212) 753-5785.

GBC: Globe Book Company, New York, NY (no ZIP code available); telephone (201) 592-2640. Company is not listed in *Books in Print 1992-93*.

GCB: Garden City Books, 201 East 57th Street, New York, NY (no ZIP code available); no telephone listed as of March, 1994.

GP: Grove Press, 841 Broadway, New York, NY 10103-4793; telephone (212) 614-7850.

GPC: Greenberg Publishing Company, 7566 Main Street, Sykesville, MD 21784; telephone (410) 795-7447.

> This agency may have formerly been in New York City.

HDB: Hillgers Deutsche Bucherei, Berlin-Grunewald and Leipzig, Germany.

HDS: Hansen Drama Shop, 718 East 3900 South, Salt Lake City, UT 84107; telephone (801) 268-8753.

> This broker reports cast orders to the publisher, from whom the information comes. Royalty fee should be remitted directly to the publisher.

HMC: Harold Matson Co., Inc., 276 5th Avenue, New York, NY 10019; telephone (212) 679-4490.

HOA: Harold Ober Associates, 40 East 49th Street, New York, NY 10017; telephone (212) 759-8600.

HP: Hanbury Plays, Keeper's Lodge, Broughton Green, Droitwich, Worcestershire WR9 7EE, England.

HPC: Heuer Publishing Company, Drawer 248, Cedar Rapids, IA 52406; telephone (319) 364-6311, (800) 950-7529; fax (319) 364-1771.

> The 1991-92 catalog lists three scripts using casts of four or fewer actors.

HR: Harper & Row [HarperCollins Publishers] 10 East 53rd Street, New York, NY 10022-5299.

HW: Hill and Wang, Division of Farrar, Straus & Giroux, 19 Union Square West, New York, NY 10003; telephone (212) 741-6900; (800) 242-7737, (800) 638-3030.

ICM: International Creative Management, Attention Brad Kalos, 40 West 57th Street, New York, NY 10019.

IEC: I. E. Clark, Inc. Saint John's Road, Schulenburg, TX 78956-0246; telephone (409) 743-3232.

IPC: International Play Co., Inc., 489 Fifth Avenue, New York, NY (no ZIP code available); no telephone listed as of March, 1994.

ISA: Incorporated Society of Authors, 1 Central Buildings, Westminster, London, SW 1, England.

> Applications regarding amateur acting rights should be made to the Secretary of Rights, ISA. These plays may now be in public domain.

IUP: Indiana University Press, 601 North Morton Street, Bloomington, IN 47404-3797.

JAT: Judith Anderson Theatre, 422 West 42nd Street, New York, NY (no ZIP code available); telephone (212) 564-7853.

KV: Kosel-Verlag, Kaiser-Ludwigs-Platz 5, Munchen 15, Germany.

LD: League of Dramatists, 84, Drayton Gardens, London, SW10 95B, England.

LLA: Lantz-Donadio Literary Agency, 111 West 57th Street, New York, NY 10019; no telephone listed as of March, 1994.

MAC: Macmillan Publishing Co., Inc., 866 Third Avenue, 7th Floor, New York, NY 10022; telephone (212) 702-

2000, (800) 257-5755.

MMP: Margaret Mayorga Play, attention Eric Howlett, 16 Berwick Street, Newton Centre, MA 02159; no telephone listed as of March, 1994.

MPL: Meriwether Publishing Ltd., P.O. Box 7710, Colorado Springs, CO 80933; telephone (719) 594-4422, (800) 937-5297.

> Alternate address is 885 Elkton Drive, Colorado Springs, CO 80907; (719) 594-4422.

MR: Margaret Ramsay, Ltd., 14a Goodwin's Court, St. Martin's Lane, London, W.C.2, England.

MVH: Mitteldeutscher Verlag Halle (Saale). Druck: VEB Peter-Presse, Leipzig, Germany.

NAL: New American Library, 1633 Broadway, New York, NY 10019; telephone (212) 392-8000.

> Yaakov and Greenfieldt's *Play Index 1988-1992* (see Bibliography hereinafter, p. 267) in its Directory of Publishers and Distributors puts the address as 375 Hudson Street, New York, NY 10014.

NCE: National Christian Education Council, Robert Denholm House, Nutfield, Redhill, Surrey RH1 4HW, England.

NDP: New Directions Publishing Corporation, 80 8th Avenue, New York, NY 10011; telephone (212) 255-0230.

NPN: New Playwrights Network, 35 Sandringham Road, Macclesfield, Cheshire SK10 1QB, England.

> Publisher of Triad series of plays, sixteen volumes.

NSHS: Library Drama Collection, North Salinas High School, 55 Kip Drive, Salinas, CA 93906; telephone (408) 753-4230, extension 207; fax (408) 449-9414.

> This public secondary school library has the largest drama holdings in its Central Coast geographical area, with emphasis on small-cast scripts, many of them out-of-print and some of them unpublished originals. Contact is the librarian.

NTK: Ninon Tallon Karlweis, 250 East 65th Street, New York, NY 10021; no telephone listed as of March, 1994.

OB: Orchard Books, 95 Madison Avenue, New York, NY 10016.

OEN: Organización Editorial Novaro, S.A., Calle 5, No. 12, Naucalpan de Juarez, Mexico, D.F., Mexico

> Anyone wanting to stage plays published by OEN should address Dr. Luis Guillermo Piazza at this address. [*Las autorizaciones pueden solicitarse pro medio este Editorial, a/c Dr. Luis Guillermo Piazza*] The fifteen scripts in *Teatro joven de Mexico* are compiled and introduced by Emilio Carballido, one of Mexico's leading playwrights.

PAL: Palmer Press, 659 Clyde Avenue, No. 23, West Vancouver, British Columbia V7T 1C8, Canada.

PCP: Playwrights Canada Press, 54 Wolseley Street, 2nd Floor, Toronto, Ontario M5T 1A5, Canada.

PDS: Pioneer Drama Service, Inc., P.O. Box 22555, Den-

ver, CO 80222-0555; telephone (303) 759-4297 or (800) 333-7262; fax (303) 759-0475.

> Four new small-cast one-act plays appear in the spring 1994 catalog.

> Albert Groff's "Not My Cup of Tea" (3f) is in the spring 1992 catalog of nearly 150 scripts; only this one of the nine one-act plays offered calls for four or fewer actors.

PI: Plays. Inc., 8 Arlington Street, Boston, MA 02116.

PIR: Pace International Research, P.O. Box 51 Arch Cape, OR 97102; no telephone listed as of March, 1994.

PLP: Playwrights Publishing Company, 70 Nottingham Road, Burton Joyce, Nottingham NG14 5AL, England.

PPC: Performance Publishing Company, Elgin, IL 60120; no telephone listed as of March, 1994.

PPI: Players Press, Inc., P.O. Box 1132, Studio City, CA 91614-0132.

> Publisher of theatre books by Samuel Elkind, the author of the Foreword in *1/2/3/4 for the Show* (see p. ix).

PPR: Playlab Press, P.O. Box 185, Ashgrove, Queensland 4060, Australia.

PSP: Playwrights Press, P.O. Box 1076, Amherst, MA 01004.

PT: Playbox Theatre, in association with Currency Press Pty., Ltd, 330 Oxford Street, P.O. Box 452, Paddington, New South Wales 2021, Australia.

RP: Riverrun Press, 1170 Broadway, Room 807, New York, NY 10001.

SF: Samuel French, Inc., 7623 Sunset Boulevard, Hollywood, CA 90046-2795; telephone (213) 876-0570; fax (213) 876-6822 Hollywood, (212) 206-1429 New York, (416) 363-1108 Canada.

> Yaakov and Greenfieldt's *Play Index 1988-1992* (see Bibliography hereinafter, p. 267) in its Directory of Publishers and Distributors puts the address as Samuel French, Inc., 45 West 25th Street, New York, NY 10036, and the London address as Samuel French, Ltd., 52 Fitzroy Street, London W1P 6JR, England.

> The play publishing house with the largest holdings. All libraries and producers of one-act plays should obtain a current catalog.

SFC: Scott, Foresman, and Company, 1900 East Lake Avenue, Glenview, IL 60025. Now a subsidiary of Time, Inc.; telephone (708) 729-3000.

SKC: Stewart Kidd Company (no street address available), Cincinnati, OH; no telephone listed as of March, 1994.

> This company may be defunct.

SLA: Sterling Lord Agency, address undetermined; telephone (212) 696-2800.

TCG: Theatre Communications Group, 63 Perry Street, #12, New York, NY 10014; telephone (212) 697-5230.

TIP: Teacher Ideas Press, P.O. Box 3988, Englewood, CO 80155-3988.

TL: Talonbooks, Ltd., 201/1019 East Cordova, Vancouver, British Columbia V6A 1M8, Canada.

TPH: The Play House, 525 East 54th, Kansas City, MO 64110; no telephone listed as of March, 1994.

TSD: T. S. Denison & Company, Inc., 9601 Newton Avenue, South, Minneapolis, MN 55431; telephone (612) 888-1460, (800) 328-3831.

      Do not confuse this company with Dennison Publications, says *Books in Print 1992-1993*.

TSP: Third Side Press, 2250 West Farragut, Chicago, IL 60625-1802.

TWP: Third World Press, 7822 South Dobson Street, Chicago, IL 60619.

UM: University of Minnesota Press, 2307 University Avenue SE, Minneapolis, MN 55414; telephone (612) 624-2516, (800) 388-3863.

      Yaakov and Greenfieldt's *Play Index 1988-1992* (see Bibliography hereinafter, p. 267) in its Directory of Publishers and Distributors puts the zip code as 55455-3092.

UWP: University of Wisconsin Press, 114 North Murray Street, Madison, WI 53715-1199; telephone (608) 262-8782.

WMA: William Morris Agency, Inc., 1350 Avenue of the Americas, New York, NY 10019

WO: Wordsss, P.O. Box 111, Carmel-by-the-Sea, CA 93921-0111; telephone (408) 624-6960; voice or fax (408) 624-1164; e-mail heniford@ix.netcom.com.

      Alternate address is P.O. Box 299, Carmel-by-the-Sea, CA 93921-0299.

      Lewis W. Heniford's "Love's Light Wings" (2m2f), "An Odious Damned Lie" (1m1f), and "Shrew You; or, Who Hath Need of Men? As Goode Accounte As Anye Knowne Describing How Sweet Shagsper Shuffles Off His Mortal Coil" (2m2f) are available through Wordsss. Also, available in North Salinas High School library collection.

WW: WordWorkers, 115 Arch Street, Philadelphia, PA 19106; no telephone listed as of March, 1994.

BIBLIOGRAPHY

The data in this guide come primarily from these sources, which supply the best available data on small-cast one-act plays. They contain information beyond the focus of this index that might be useful to researchers. Annotations amplify the citations with commentary and supplementary data, sometimes giving play examples from the Title Index to clarify the pertinence of the citation.

Following the primary source citations are supplementary sources that help the researcher to go beyond the scope of this guide.

Primary Data Sources

[ACP] Art Craft Publishing Company, ed. *1989-90 Catalog of Select Plays and Musicals.* Cedar Rapids, Iowa: Art Craft Publishing Company, 1989.

A catalog of nearly 150 scripts by journeymen authors; four of the scripts use casts of four or fewer actors.

[BP] *Baker's Plays and Theatre Resource Directory,* 1993/ 94. Boston: Walter H. Baker, 1993/94.

Since 1845, Baker's Plays has supplied playscripts and performance rights, adding through the years theatre books, stage makeup, sound effect and dialect tapes. BP shares some of its annual catalog with Samuel French, Inc., and other publishers. BP enjoys recognition as a preeminent source for scripts and can help production companies staging small-cast plays. Cited in Hunter's drama bibliography.

Cerf, Bennett. *At Random: The Reminiscences of Bennett Cerf.* New York: Random House, 1977.
ISBN 0-394-47877-0.

DIALOG Database Catalog. Palo Alto, California: Dialog Information Services, Inc., 1993.

The DIALOG Information Retrieval Service of Dialog Information Services, Inc., has been active since 1972. Its over 400 databases, broad in scope, include some sources relevant to theatre research. Even without special focus on theatre and drama, DIALOG offers references beyond those normally accessible in print.

Many other on-line services are available. Significantly, on-line searches of databanks can find items much more quickly than manual searches. Electronic information retrieval is the wave of the future, and use of it is often worth the effort.

[DPC] *Catalog of Plays and Musicals 1994.* New York: Dramatic Publishing Company, 1993.

Script offerings through 1993. Founded in 1885 by Charles Sergel, DPC has grown into one of the best publishing houses, listing many authors of renown. Supersedes *Complete New Catalog of Plays and Musicals 1992.*

[DPS] *Complete Catalog of Plays 1991-1992.* New York: Dramatists Play Service, Inc., 1992.

Script offerings through 1992. Founded in 1936 by prominent playwrights and theatre agents, DPS has become a major play licensing agency. The catalogue includes most of the major American plays since its founding. In 1983, the house expanded beyond handling only nonprofessional leasing rights to include professional leasing rights. Its Obie Award for commitment to the publication of new work signals a laudable bias.

[EPC] Eldridge Publishing Company, ed. *Eldridge Plays and Musicals 1993-94.* Venice, FL: Eldridge Publishing Company, 1993.

265

Agent for "I Know This for Sure," a drama by Peggy Welch Marshon (4f); "The Last of Captain Bedford," a drama by Pat Cook (2m2f); and "The Promise," a drama by Joe Robertson (2m2f). No other four-or-fewer casts in plays listed. The address of Eldridge Publishing Company is P.O. Box 1595, Venice, FL 34284; telephone (800) HI-STAGE; fax (800) 453-5179.

Hall, Donald, ed. *The Oxford Book of American Literary Anecdotes*. New York: Oxford University Press, 1981.

A handy source for anecdotes, presented by themes. Cited by Introduction, p. xvii.

[HDS] Hansen Drama Shop/Costume Closet. ed. *1989-90 Hansen Drama Shop Catalogue*. Salt Lake City, UT: Hansen Drama Shop/Costume Closet, 1989.

The address of Hansen Drama Shop/Costume Closet is 718 East 3900 South, Salt Lake City, UT 84107; telephone (801) 268-8753.

[HPC] Heuer Publishing Company, ed. *1993-94 Catalog of Select Plays and Musicals.* Cedar Rapids, Iowa: Heuer Publishing Company, 1993.

The 1993-94 catalog offers thirty-seven one-act plays, two for four or fewer actors. Information regarding entries has been improved.

The 1991-92 catalog offered around forty one-act plays, three for four or fewer actors. The information regarding any entry is sparse.

Hitchcock, L. A. "The Play's the Thing . . . If You Can Find It! An Assessment of Play Indexes." *RQ* 29:248, Winter 1989.

An intensive analysis that is well worth the attention of frequent users of play indexes.

Logasa, Hannah, and Wilfred Ver Nooy, compilers. *An Index to One-Act Plays*. Boston: F. W. Faxon, 1924.

Bibliography of one-act plays written in English or translated into English, published since 1900. The information regarding any entry is sparse. In Clark Library, San Jose State University, reference center, call #Z5781.L83. The 2nd (1932-1940), 4th (1948-1957), and 5th (1956-1964) supplements are also in Clark Library. Cited in Hunter's drama bibliography, listed here.

Losey, Jessie Louise. *A Selected, Annotated List of One-Act Plays for Festival Use*. Emporia, Kansas: Graduate Division, Kansas State Teachers College, 1955.

Originated as a master's thesis at KSTC, Emporia, Kansas, 1955. In Clark Library, San Jose State University, reference center, call #Z5781.L85. Annotations are sparse.

[MPL] Meriwether Publishing Ltd., P.O. Box 7710, Colorado Springs, CO 80933; telephone (719) 594-4422, (800) 937-5297.

Alternate address is 885 Elkton Drive, Colorado Springs, CO 80907; (719) 594-4422.

National Council of Teachers of English. Committee on Playlist. *Guide to Play Selection*, 2nd ed. New York: Appleton-Century-Crofts, 1958.

The information regarding any entry is sparse. First edition by Milton Myers Smith, 1934. In Clark Library, San Jose State University, reference center, call #Z578.N265 1958.

[IEC] *1993-1994 Catalog of Plays & Musicals*. Schulenburg, Texas: I. E. Clark, Inc., 1993.

An offering of over a hundred short plays, including a few by well-known authors.

The earlier *1991 Catalog of Plays* is an offering of around fifty-six short plays. In addition to children's theatre, there are twenty-seven one-act plays.

Founded in 1956, I. E. Clark, Inc., is a family operation self-described as happy where it is.

[PDS] Pioneer Drama Service, Inc., ed. *Plays & Musicals: Spring 1994*. Denver, CO: Pioneer Drama Service, Inc., 1992.

The spring 1994 catalog lists but four small-cast one-act plays.

The 1993-94 catalog lists those four above as well as "The Wall," by Richard Lauchman.

The spring 1992 catalog of nearly 150 scripts includes only nine one-act plays; one calls for four or fewer actors. Information in entries is not really helpful, as overselling is characteristic.

[SF] Samuel French, Inc., ed. *The 1992 Supplement to the Basic Catalog of Plays*. Hollywood, California: Samuel French, Inc., 1992.

This supplement to the *Basic Catalog* (**see next two items**) lists recently acquired as well as other selected titles. The reader seeking more must refer to the basic catalog published July, 1991, or to the latest annual or supplement.

_____. *Samuel French's Basic Catalogue of Plays*. Hollywood, California: Samuel French, Inc., 1991.

This complete catalog lists all titles published and controlled by Samuel French, Inc., up to and including July, 1991. This is the major source for acting versions of scripts. Founded in 1830, incorporated in 1899, the oldest and largest of drama specialty houses has seven central offices—New York, Hollywood, Toronto, London, Manchester, Nairobi, and Sydney. Of note to playwrights is that this company considers any play submitted for publication. Cited in Hunter's drama bibliography, listed here. See items above and below.

_____. *Basic Catalogue of Plays and Musicals.* 1994 edition. Hollywood, California: Samuel French, Inc., 1993.

311 pp. See two items above. Supplements to this *Basic Catalogue* featuring new acquisitions and some popular plays are scheduled for 1995 and 1996.

Scott, Adolphe C., translator. *Traditional Chinese Plays*, Volume 2. Madison, Wisconsin: The University of Wisconsin Press, 1969.

ISBN 0-299-05370-9/0-299-05374-1. Source for "Ssu Fan/Longing for Worldly Pleasures," a traditional *K'unshan* one-act play from the Ming Dynasty, 1368-1644. In *Books in Print 1990-91* but not in *Books in Print 1992-1993*, which cites two other books by Adolphe C. Scott on Chinese drama.

Yaakov, Juliette, and John Greenfieldt, ed. *Play Index, 1988-1992; An Index to 4,397 Plays.* New York: H. W. Wilson, 1988.

ISSN 0554-3037. Valuable series. Prior volumes cover 1949-1952, 1953-1960, 1961-1967, 1968-1972, 1973-1977, 1978-1982, 1983-1987. The List of Collections Indexed cites anthologies and individual plays in written in or translated into English. The Directory of Publishers and Distributors, pp. 537-42, in *Play Index* complements the Source Directory for Scripts found here in *1/2/3/4 for the Show*, p. 259.

Young, Glenn, ed. *Applause Theatre Book Review and Catalog.* New York: Applause Theatre Book Publishers, 1989.

Founded in 1980 as a drama book purveyor, ATB now publishes theatrical literature, too. The attitude is "theatre biz, albeit theatre with a spine." Titles distributed by Grove Press. Notably, it publishes playwrights Beckett, Mamet, Pinter, Rabe, and Stoppard.

Other Data Sources for Ensuing Research

Researchers should consider these additional leads to find small-cast one-act plays, many of which were unavailable to present research.

American Library Association, ed. *Subject Index to Children's*

Plays Chicago: American Library Association, 1940.

Supplements the Playbills section (Part 4) as a logical second, though limited, source for plays on given themes. Worth remembering is that it is a half-century older than the theme index herein. Cited in Hunter's drama bibliography, listed here.

Antæus: Plays in One Act, edited by Daniel Halpern. *Antæus*, 66 (Spring 1991).

ISBN 0-88001-268-4. Published by Ecco Press, 100 West Broad Street, Hopewell, NJ 08525.

Austin, Ian. *For Ladies Only: Five One-Act Plays with All Women Casts.* Ashgrove, Queensland, Australia: Playlab Press, 1988.

ISBN 0-908156-31-6. Foreword by Babette Stephens. The address of Playlab Press is P.O. Box 185, Ashgrove, Queensland, 4060, Australia.

Barnes, Peter. *The Spirit of Man and More Barnes' People: Seven Monologues.* New York: Methuen & Company, Ltd., 1990.

ISBN 0-413-63130-3. Addresses are 7/8 Kendrick Mews, London SW7 3HG, England, and 29 West 35th Street, New York, NY 10001.

Benson, E. "The Brock Bibliography of Published Canadian Plays in English, 1766-1978; Wagner, A." *Modern Drama* 24:116-19, No. 1, 1981, and *WLWE-World Literature Written in English* 21:127-29, No. 1, 1982.

Unavailable to present research, the bibliography reviewed in these issues of *Modern Drama* 24:116-19, No. 1, 1981, and *WLWE-World Literature Written in English* 21:127-29, No. 1, 1982. Opens an unfamiliar door for theatre groups in the United States. From over two hundred years of dramatic achievement in Canada come numerous short, small-cast plays. Production companies should pursue this lead. Dialog on-line citation 00236955 in File 439, Genuine Article #NQ445: Arts & Humanities Search. Corporate Source: University of Guelph, Guelph, Ontario N1G 2W1, Canada.

Berquist, G. William. *Three Centuries of English and American Plays: A Check List.* New York: Hafner, 1963.

Because of the scope, the information regarding any entry is sparse. It is chiefly useful here to verify the canon of a playwright. Cited in Hunter's drama bibliography, listed here.

Best Plays, The, 1894 to date. New York: Dodd, Mead, 1920 to date.

The series set of forty-four volumes to 1976, ISBN 0-405-07637-1, listed in March, 1994, at $1270 from Ayer

Company Publications, Inc., P.O. Box 958, Salem, NH 03079; telephone (603) 669-5933.

The series, of course, has changed editors and titles over the past century. The merit of each annual in this series varies according to the wisdom of its editor. Volumes are not anthologies, as the current title might suggest, nor are they compilations of synopses. The series features play abridgments, allowing the reader to catch much of the essence of a play. Supplementary sections of each volume document then-current theatre. Emphasis is on popular, commercial theatre; hence, coverage of one-act plays is peripheral. Nevertheless, close study of one-act bills can prove useful to theatres seeking scripts for small casts. Not all of the cited titles reach publication, but knowledge of where they were produced can help one to search for scripts and staging rights. Cited in Hunter's drama bibliography, listed here.

Bollow, Ludmilla. *One-Acts and Monologues for Women*. New York: Broadway Play Publishers, 1983.

Address of Broadway Play Publishers is 249 West 29th Street, New York, NY 10001.

Carpenter, C. A. "10 Modern Irish Playwrights—A Comprehensive Annotated Bibliography; King, K.," *Modern Drama* 24:116-19, No. 1, 1981.

Unavailable to present research, the book reviewed in this issue of *Modern Drama* shows great promise of containing most helpful annotations. There is a strong legacy of meritorious small-cast plays in Irish theatre, many of which audiences in the United States have found accessible. Dialog on-line citation 00113287 in File 439, Genuine Article #LK208: Arts & Humanities Search. Corporate Source: State University of New York, Binghamton, NY 13901.

_____. "20 Modern British Playwrights—A Bibliography, 1956 to 1976; King, K." *Modern Drama* 24:116-19, No. 1, 1981.

Unavailable to present research, this bibliography reviewed in *Modern Drama* shows great promise of containing most helpful annotations and probable inclusion of one-act British plays. Dialog on-line citation 00113286 in File 439: Arts & Humanities Search 1980-199111W1. Corporate Source: State University of New York, Binghamton, NY 13901.

Chicorel, Marietta, ed. *Chicorel Theatre Index to Plays in Anthologies, Periodicals, Discs and Tapes*, Vol. 1. New York: Chicorel Library Publishing Company, 1970.

SBN [sic] 87729-001-6. LC 71-106198. This 1970 Chicorel index lists possible sources, but clear designa-

tions of one-act small-cast plays are few.

See also Marietta Chicorel's *Chicorel Theatre Index to Plays in Anthologies & Collections, 1970-1976*, Volume 25. American Library Publishing Company, 1976. Text edition, $125.00. ISBN 0-934598-68-1. The American Library Publishing Company is listed in *Books in Print: Publishers 1992-1993*.

Corrigan, Beatrice. *Catalogue of Italian Plays, 1500-1700*. Toronto: University of Toronto Press, 1961.

The two dominant Italian styles of the sixteenth and seventeenth centuries, *commedia erudita* and *commedia dell'arte*, emphasized plot over complexity of character and of motive and emotion. *Commedia dell'arte* companies often had few actors and staged shows of four-or-fewer roles. The number of plays is great. The difficulty is finding acting scripts, which makes Corrigan's catalogue worth investigating. Giovanni Rucellai (1475-1525), Pietro Aretino (1492-1556), Giambattista Giraldi (1504-73), and Giacinto Andrea Cicognini (1606-60) are playwrights to note in that outpouring of Italian drama. Much of the product from that time does not achieve literary status, but revivals have historic value and can often find an appreciative modern audience, particularly for farce. Cited in Hunter's drama bibliography, listed here. In the Library of the University of Toronto.

Davies, R. "The Brock Bibliography of Published Canadian Plays in English, 1766-1978; Wagner, A.," *Canadian Theatre Review* 31:144-45, Summer, 1981.

Unavailable to present research, the bibliography reviewed in this issue of *Canadian Theatre Review* opens an unfamiliar door for theatre groups in the United States. From over two hundred years of dramatic achievement in Canada come numerous short, small-cast plays. Production companies should pursue this lead. Dialog on-line citation 00324170 in File 439: Arts & Humanities Search. Genuine Article#: QF885. Corporate Source: Queens University, Kingston, Ontario K7L 3N6, Canada.

Erdmenger, M., H. Priessnitz, and D. Rowlands. "Additions to Bibliography of English Radio Plays." *Anglia-Zeitschrift fur Englische Philologie* 101:117-40, Nos. 1-2, 1983.

This Italian-language book review and bibliography focuses on English scripts for radio. As imaginative stage direction can easily and economically transfer radio plays to the theatre, this listing of one hundred and ninety-two such scripts is a potential gold mine for a production company. Four or fewer actors certainly can handle multiple roles in production. Dialog on-line citation 00338050 in File 439: Arts & Humanities Search. Genuine Article#: QL585.

Firkins, Ina Ten Eyck, compiler. *Index to Plays 1800-1926.* New York: H. W. Wilson, 1935.

   Unavailable to present research, this index spanning one hundred and twenty-six years of plays might include one-acts. One should note the 1935 publication date as a major limitation for suiting the needs of most production companies for more-current scripts. Cited in Hunter's drama bibliography, listed here.

Foster, D. W. "A Bibliography of Contemporary Hispano-American Plays—Spanish; Neglia, E., Ordas, L." *Chasqui-Revista de Literatura Latinoamericana* 10:92, No. 1, 1980.

   This English-language review in the Spanish-language journal *Chasqui-Revista de Literatura Latinoamericana* describes a bibliography directly touching the distinct need for contemporary Hispano-American one-act scripts. With the growing Hispanic/Latino demographics in the United States, such sources as this are increasingly useful. Dialog on-line citation 00220966 in File 439: Arts & Humanities Search. Genuine Article#: NE744.

Garvor, Juliet. *One-Act Dramas.* Franklin, Ohio: Eldridge Publishing Company, 1986.

   The address of Eldridge Publishing Company is P.O. Drawer 216, Franklin, OH 45005.

Gosher, Sydney Paul. *A Historical and Critical Survey of the South African One-Act Play Written in English.* Pretoria: University of South Africa, 1988.

   Unavailable to present research and not available from University Microfilms International. Gosher's abstract follows here as a lead for dramas treating ethnic issues in a strife-torn society, with resonances for American audiences. A paucity of such plays might be supplemented by citations in Gosher's work. There is no clue about cast size/gender, but chances are favorable that some short plays for four or fewer characters can be found through this lead.

   The aim of this thesis is to trace the history of the South African one-act play in English and detail its progress to the present day. In order to do this, it was first necessary in Chapter One to chart the somewhat nebulous history of the one-acter in Western Europe, from its earliest beginnings in classical Greece to its use as an after-piece and finally as a curtain-raiser. Chapter One also deals with the history of the one-act play in the twentieth century, [sic] and concludes with a discussion of its characteristics and criteria.

   Chapter Two surveys the early history of the South African one-acter (up to 1930). The contribution of Boniface, who wrote the first recorded South African one-act play in English, is assessed and plays by Black and Goudvis are deemed to have considerable merit.

   The first part of Chapter Three (1931-1949) deals with the contribution, among others, of H. I. E. Dhlomo, Baneshik, Masson, and Sowden, while the second part presents an account of the establishment of FATSSA and the substantial influence it exerted on the growth of the one-act play. Chapters Four and Five, which contain the main body of the thesis, attempt to locate plays within socio-historic contexts and focus upon fundamental political changes affecting the framework of South African society.

   The effect of censorship is scrutinized in Chapter Four and important dramatists of the 1950s and 1960s—Laite, Fugard, Krige and Rive—are examined.

   In the fifth chapter, five issues are investigated: one-act plays are assessed not only as literary texts but also as they appear in performance; the problem of the evaluation of the protest play receives attention; the operation of dominant political and social themes is demonstrated; the contribution of the amateur stage to the development of the one-act play is considered; and, finally, the conclusion is drawn that the state of the one-act play is sound and its strength shown by the social and cultural heterogeneity of theme displayed.

   Appendices giving details of playwrights and play collections, a bibliography, and an index are included at the end of the thesis.
   Promoter: E. Pereira. Source: Dissertation Abstracts International, Vol. 50/09-A, p. 2707. Item (0596).

Hart, C. "The Brock Bibliography of Published Canadian Plays in English, 1766-1978; Wagner, A." *Theatre Research International* 6:228, No. 3, 1981.

   Unavailable to present research, the bibliography reviewed in this issue of *Theatre Research International* opens an unfamiliar door for theatre groups in the United States. From over two hundred years of dramatic achievement in Canada come numerous short, small-cast plays. Production companies should pursue this lead. English-language book review. Dialog on-line citation 00171164 in File 439: Arts & Humanities Search. Genuine Article#: MK979.

Hecht, L. "Polish Plays in Translation—An Annotated Bibliography; Gerould, D., Taborski, B., Hart, S., Kobialka, M.," *Slavic and East European Journal* 29:99-100, No. 1, 1985.

English-language book review. Dialog on-line citation 00595204 in File 439: Arts & Humanities Search. Genuine Article#: ALF95.

_____. "Soviet Plays in Translation—An Annotated Bibliography; Law, A. H., Goslett, P." *Slavic and East European Journal* 29:99-100, No. 1, 1985.

English-language book review. Dialog on-line citation 00595203 in File 439: Arts & Humanities Search. Genuine Article#: ALF95. Corporate Source: George Mason University, Fairfax, VA 22030.

Hill, Frank Pierce, compiler. *American Plays Printed, 1714-1830; A Bibliographical Record.* Stanford, California: Stanford University, 1934.

This listing of American plays from pre-Revolutionary and post-Revolutionary half-centuries might be a valuable lode for mining by production companies. Plays from the era deserve more attention than they have gotten. American theatre by 1714 had active theatre as far-flung as Charles-Town, South Carolina, Williamsburg, Virginia, and New York. By 1750, more towns had become cities and enjoyed theatre. In the sixty years after the Revolution, splendid theatre buildings arose to house burgeoning attendance, and playwriting kept pace in varied genres. One-act scripts for small casts are there for the finding. Cited in Hunter's drama bibliography, listed here.

Hunter, Frederick J., compiler. *Drama Bibliography: A Short-Title Guide to Extended Reading in Dramatic Art for the English-Speaking Audience and Students of Theatre.* Boston: G. K. Hall & Company, 1971.

Although two decades older than the present guide, Hunter's bibliography has many promising leads. It is the source for several items listed here to aid ensuing research. The lack of annotations limits its helpfulness.

Katrak, K. H. "Soyinka, Wole—Bibliography, Biography, Playography; Page, M." *Research in African Literatures* 12:553-63, No. 4, 1981.

English-language book review. Dialog on-line citation 00186385 in File 439: Arts & Humanities Search. Genuine Article#: MT885. Corporate Source: Columbia University, Barnard College, New York, NY 10027.

Kennedy, Adrienne. *Adrienne Kennedy in One Act.* Minneapolis, Minnesota: University of Minnesota Press, 1988. ISBN 0-8166-1691-4; 0-8166-1692-2. Address is 2037 University Avenue, S.E., Minneapolis, MN 55455-3092.

Lamb, Ruth S. *Bibliografía del Teatro Mexicano del Siglo XX*/Bibliography of Twentieth-Century Mexican Theatre.

México, D.F.: Ediciones de Andrea, 1962.

This Spanish-language annotated bibliography includes works written by Mexicans and by some foreigners supporting the modern theatre movement in Mexico. Each citation begins with the name of the author or pseudonym, if any. The titles of the dramas are unedited; appearances in reviews, periodicals, and anthologies until 1961 are noted. This work complements the compiler's *Breve historia del teatro mexicano*/Brief History of the Mexican Theatre (México: Studium, 1958). The scope is 20th-century drama in Mexico. This bibliography is an obligatory source for anyone studying modern Mexican theatre. The contact is Librería Studium, Apartado Postal 20979—Admn. 32, México 1, D.F., México. Available in the North Salinas High School library, NSHS 16399.

Litto, Frederic M. *American Dissertations on the Drama and the Theatre: A Bibliography.* Kent, Ohio: Kent State University Press, 1969.

This dissertation illustrates the major gap in scholarship regarding the one-act play form. *American One-Act Plays* or a synonym is missing as a search term in the key-word-in-context index. The search term *monologue-drama* shows but a single work, one by Cornelia Otis Skinner.

Macmillan, Dougald, compiler. *Catalogue of the Larpent Plays in the Huntington Library.* San Marino, California: The Huntington Library, 1919.

Recommended only for the adventurous. As the Huntington Library is a treasure trove of obscure scripts, there is an outside possibility this catalogue reveals short scripts for small casts. Cited in Hunter's drama bibliography, listed here.

Marino, J. A. G. "An Annotated Bibliography of Play and Literature," *Canadian Review of Comparative Literature/Revue Canadienne de Littérature Comparée.* 12:306-58, No. 2, 1985.

English-language book review. Dialog on-line citation 00693232 in File 439: Arts & Humanities Search.

Nicoll, Allardyce. *History of English Drama,* 6 Vols. London: Cambridge University Press, 1962.

Nicoll, as the preeminent theatre scholar of his generation, alludes to many significant short plays, giving their dramaturgical and historical context. Cited in Hunter's drama bibliography, listed here.

Ottemiller, John Henry. *Index to Plays in Collections; An Author and Title Index to Plays Appearing in Collections Published Between 1900-1962,* 4th ed. New York: Scarecrow Press, 1964.

The first six decades of the twentieth century provided a vast number of short plays. Having appeared in collections, these plays more often than not were not separately published or issued by play-publication houses in their catalogs. Therefore, research in such collections should serendipitously disclose usable scripts for small casts. Cited in Hunter's drama bibliography, listed here.

Padovano, Anthony T. *Conscience and Conflict; A Trilogy of One-Actor Plays: Thomas Merton, Pope John XXIII [and] Martin Luther*. Mahwah, NJ: Paulist Press, 1988.

ISBN 0-8091-3001-7. The address of Paulist Press is 997 MacArthur Boulevard, Mahwah, NJ 07430.

Pape, Ralph. *Girls We Have Known, and Other One Act Plays*. New York: Dramatists Play Service, 1984.

Not cited in *Books in Print 1992-1993*. International Standard Book Number unavailable. Library of Congress number is 84-223003.

Patitucci, Karen. *Three-Minute Dramas for Worship*. San Jose, California: Resource Publications, Inc., 1989.

ISBN 0-89390-143-1. The address of Resource Publications, Inc., is 160 East Virginia Street, Suite 290, San Jose, CA 95112.

Peacock, G. "The Brock Bibliography of Published Canadian Plays in English 1766 to 1978; Wagner, A.," *Theatre History in Canada/Histoire du théâtre au Canada* 5:96-97, No. 1, 1984.

Unavailable to present research, the bibliography reviewed in this issue of *Theatre History in Canada/Histoire du théâtre au Canada* opens an unfamiliar door for theatre groups in the United States. From over two hundred years of dramatic achievement in Canada come numerous short, small-cast plays. Production companies should pursue this lead. Dialog on-line citation 00489275 in File 439: Arts & Humanities Search. Corporate Source: University of Alberta, Edmonton, Alberta T6G 2E1, Canada.

Pence, James H. *The Magazine and the Drama; An Index*. New York: The Dunlap Society, 1896.

This index could offer obscure scripts, because short plays frequently reach print in magazines rather than through publication houses. Consequently, these scripts regularly are missed by bibliographers. Cited in Hunter's drama bibliography, listed here.

Pfanner, H. F. "Expressionism in Switzerland; Volume 1, Narrative Prose, Mixed Genres, Poetry; Volume 2, Plays, Essays—Editorial Report, Bio-Bibliography; Epilogue—German; Stern, M." *Literature Music Fine Arts* 17:48-49, No. 1, 1984.

This English-language book review in *Literature Music Fine Arts* cites Swiss expressionistic plays. Playwrights of short plays frequently have employed that genre, so the possibility of finding such scripts is good. Dialog on-line citation 00461647 in File 439: Arts & Humanities Search. Genuine Article#: SS450.

The Players Library, *The Catalogue of the Library of the British Drama League with Supplements*. London: Faber & Faber, 1950-1953.

The British Drama League speaks for playwrights in the United Kingdom and controls rights to many of their long and short plays. Cited in Hunter's drama bibliography, listed here.

"Polish Plays in Translation—An Annotated Bibliography; Gerould, D.; Taborski, B.; Hart, S.; Kobialka, M." *Théâtre en Pologne/Theatre in Poland* 26:24, No. 5, 1984.

Unavailable to present research, the English-language book review in *Théâtre en Pologne/Theatre in Poland* describes a bibliography that offers intriguing potential in the search for short, small-cast scripts. Jerzy Grotowsky and other Polish directors have forged exciting theatre before and since liberation in 1990. They have been on the cutting edge of international theatre. Much of their work has been in one-act format. Dialog on-line citation 00508150 in File 439: Arts & Humanities Search. Genuine Article#: TM270.

Roden, Robert F. *Later American Plays, 1831-1900; Being a Compilation of the Titles of Plays by American Authors Published and Performed in America Since 1831*. New York: The Dunlap Society, 1900.

Seventy years of nineteenth-century American plays must contain a substantial number of short plays, some at least with small casts. This is a good bet for ensuing research. Cited in Hunter's drama bibliography, listed here.

Salem, James M., ed. *Drury's Guide to Best Plays*, 4th ed., Metuchen, NJ: Scarecrow Press, 1987.

ISBN 0-8108-1980-5. Unavailable to this writer, the title appears a likely source, perhaps with references to one-act plays. It should aid ensuing research. The 1969 second edition is cited in Hunter's drama bibliography, listed here. Cited in *Books in Print 1992-1993*.

Vincent, T. "Fugard, Athol—Bibliography, Biography, Playography; Vanderbroucke, R." *Research in African Literatures* 15:458-61, No. 3, 1984.

Unavailable to the present writer, the playography in this English-language book review of this South African's work has possibilities for further research regarding short scripts. His recurring theme of apartheid continues to resonate with audiences even after radical changes in the political structure of the Union of South Africa. Dialog on-line citation 00491039 in File 439: Arts & Humanities Search. Genuine Article#: TD177. Corporate Source: University of Lagos, Department of English, Lagos, Nigeria.

Wertheim, A. "10 Modern American Playwrights, an Annotated Bibliography; King, K." *Literary Research Newsletter* 8:21-22, No. 1, 1983.

This English-language book review in the *Literary Research Newsletter* covers modern American playwrights who characteristically have experimented with the short format. Often, these playwrights' later famous works echo their one-act probings; study of the one-act headwaters contributes to understanding the wider flow of their full-length works. Edward Albee, William Inge, Tennessee Williams, and Arthur Miller all have written of their high regard for short plays. Hence, this source has good potential for ensuing research, particularly with the help of the annotations. Dialog on-line citation 00398961 in File 439: Arts & Humanities Search. Genuine Article#: RP304 Corporate Source: Indiana University, Bloomington, IN 47401.

Wright, D. A. *One-Person Puppet Plays*. Englewood, CO: Teacher Ideas Press, 1990.

ISBN 0-87287-742-6. Illustrations by John Wright. The address of Teacher Ideas Press is P.O. Box 3988, Englewood, CO 80155-3988.

About the Author

Lewis W. Heniford, drama teacher, actor, librarian, videographer, and writer, trained in the postgraduate theatre program at the University of North Carolina/Chapel Hill with the Carolina Playmakers. He holds an A.B. degree in English from U.N.C., a Master of Library and Information Science degree from San Jose State University, and a Ph.D. degree in Speech and Drama from Stanford University. He has taught drama and directed plays in North Carolina, Montana, California, Germany, and Mexico—in high schools, community colleges, universities, and community theatres.

The Carolina Playmakers' legendary high regard for the one-act play format conditioned Dr. Heniford's entire career in theatre. Since 1947, he has directed or produced more than a thousand short plays. Some of these have won statewide awards in North Carolina and Montana. Some have appeared on the programs of California statewide theatre and library conventions.

He received a U.S. Office of Education grant to found PACTO (Pan-American Community Theatre Organization) and has directed and produced one-act and full-length Spanish-language plays.

His students present short plays throughout the academic year, averaging one each week and taking shows off campus to appropriate venues in their community.

He established a major collection of one-act plays, many of them rare; these scripts are available to the public (see *NSHS*, in Part 5, p. 262). Currently, he is developing a CD-ROM database of one-act plays.

Dr. Heniford's own writing includes short and long plays, a novel, computer guides, and interactive multimedia software.